Like People in History

Like People

in
History

FELICE PICANO

VIKING

VIKING
Published by the Penguin Group
Penguin Books USA Inc., 375 Hudson Street, New York, New York 10014, U.S.A.
Penguin Books Ltd, 27 Wrights Lane, London W8 5TZ, England
Penguin Books Australia Ltd, Ringwood, Victoria, Australia
Penguin Books Canada Ltd, 10 Alcorn Avenue, Toronto, Ontario, Canada M4V 3B2
Penguin Books (N.Z.) Ltd, 182–190 Wairau Road, Auckland 10, New Zealand

Penguin Books Ltd, Registered Offices: Harmondsworth, Middlesex, England

First published in 1995 by Viking Penguin, a division of Penguin Books USA Inc.

5   7   9   10   8   6   4

PUBLISHER'S NOTE
This is a work of fiction. Names, characters, places, and incidents either are
the product of the author's imagination or are used fictitiously.

Portions of this novel first appeared in *Art & Understanding, Global City Review, Sodomite
Invasion Review*, and *The Violet Quill Reader*, edited by David Bergman, St. Martin's Press.

Grateful acknowledgment is made for permission to reprint excerpts
from the following copyrighted works: "Blowin' in the Wind" by Bob Dylan. Copyright ©
1962 by Warner Bros. Music; © renewed 1990 by Special Rider Music. All rights reserved.
International copyright secured. Reprinted by permission. "The Wanderer" from *Collected
Shorter Poems 1927–1957* by W. H. Auden. Copyright © 1934 and renewed 1962 by
W. H. Auden. Reprinted by permission of Random House, Inc.

"solstice," "nightcall," and "beach north truro, 1985" by Paul Grady, Jr., appearing on pages
377, 470, and 508, are published by arrangement with Paul Grady, Sr.

LIBRARY OF CONGRESS CATALOGING-IN-PUBLICATION DATA
Picano, Felice [date]
Like people in history / Felice Picano.
p.   cm.
ISBN 0-670-86047-6
I. Title.
PS3566.I25L5   1995
813'.54—dc20   94-38159

This book is printed on acid-free paper.

Printed in the United States of America
Set in Janson Text
Designed by James Sinclair

To Bob Lowe, 1948–1991

Aimable lecteur,—mon semblable,—mon frère . . .

Acknowledgments

Several people were helpful to me in getting this book this far and I'd like to thank them: Malaga Baldi for her calmness and her faith and for making me finish it, hard as that was at the time. Ed Iwanicki for his vision and the largeness of his grasp and for his good sense and smart editorial comments. Will Meyerhofer, David Drene, Jenifer Levin, Michelle Karlsberg, and David Ankers, who read early portions of the manuscript or heard me read from it and who responded instantly. Linsey Abrams, David Bergman, and Don Larventz, who asked to publish excerpts. The many people "on the road" in the past two years who listened to me read from the novel and who commented favorably. Paul Grady, Sr., for letting me use some of the wonderful poems his son wrote. And Edmund White, who let me use his title, from an unpublished novel.

Contents

How many roads must a man walk down
before you call him a man . . . ?
—Bob Dylan

Book
One

Gold Dust
Twins

1991 AND 1954

"Are you sure?"

"What?"

"Are you sure about this?" Wally asked.

I must have looked dumbstruck, because he went on.

"Going up there!" He prodded. "Now? Tonight?"

That at least was a question I could answer.

"We've *got* to go up there," I said. "It's his birthday!"

We were standing in the lobby of Alistair's building, the last shafts of a cerise sunset reflecting off the Hudson and somehow managing to obliquely strike this one marble wall. It's not the grandest building Alistair has ever lived in, nor was the man in uniform behind the desk the most pretentious I'd ever dealt with for Alistair's sake, but he was tall, with skin the color of whole nutmeg, and he was quite stately in that Russian green serge uniform, and he was definitely at any minute about to either sneer at us or call some janitorial person to sweep us out.

"We're going up!" I said, with tons of pseudo-decision in my voice.

"Name?" the man in uniform asked, although he'd had me tell it a dozen times earlier that month.

"Sansarc," I replied. "Roger."

3

He picked up the desk phone—a *faux*-marble affair with scores of buttons matching his epaulets—and without looking at it impressively struck the correct number.

I moved Wally away from the desk far enough to say, "If we didn't appear at his forty-fifth birthday, Alistair would hunt us down through the streets of the city, through the alleyways and sewers and . . ."

Behind me I heard the man in uniform mispronounce my name. This was evidently something that whoever answered—doubtless the White Woman—was used to, as the man in uniform hung up and said, as if I didn't already very well know, "Sixteen-J."

"If *you* didn't appear," Wally corrected me.

We walked to the elevators through about a quarter mile of post-modernist interior decor, pretty well disguised as fake ecru adobe. At the far end was a wall-sized mirror, enough for me to glance at what the building staff had seen and snorted at—two homosexuals in black denims with black leather Patrick sneakers and worn army jackets of slightly differing cut and shades of brown. Wally, of course, had his Miss Porter's School posture and his shock of auburn hair to set him apart. And his youth. And his good looks. Whereas I . . .

The elevator door opened and a mixed-gender couple in matching black skintight Lycra bicycie outfits—hers striped hot pink, his aqua— shoved their eighty-speed mobelium sprocketed-to-death machines at us until we were pinned against the far wall. They pointedly ignored us in their perfectly coordinated twenty-four-year-old blindness.

"Fucking breeders!" Wally shouted after them.

" 'Scuse me?" The male member of the duo turned around. Completely oblivious.

I pushed Wally into the elevator, and mercifully the door shut on us.

Wally checked his widow's peak in the fish-eye corner mirror, then slid me against one wall and began to tongue-kiss me as though he were trying to ingest both of my tonsils simultaneously. This, of course, was intended to shut me up and to incite any purple-haired woman with a Lhasa apso unfortunate enough to have rung for the elevator.

None rang, however, so I enjoyed having my epiglottis ravaged before Wally pulled away to the far wall and began to sulk.

"Getting het up for the action at Gracie Mansion?" I asked.

"Are you going to give it to him?" Wally asked back.

Neither of us was prepared to answer the other's questions. So we smiled stonily at each other.

"You did bring it, didn't you?" Wally nudged.

"*Them!* Not *it. Them.* Sixty of *them!* Yes, I brought them."

"Wrapped in what? Some cutesy little malachite box in the shape of Minnie Mouse's vulva?"

The door opened at the sixteenth floor.

"It's none of your business."

Wally stood in front of the door, trapping me, keeping it from closing.

"You've made it my business over the past two weeks of breast-beating, moaning, sighing, outbursts, tears, and pacing the damned living/dining/den area floor!"

"You're right, Wals. I've been a complete turd about it."

That admission so surprised him he let me slip out. I skipped down the hallway to the noise at 16J and rang the bell.

"I'm not staying," Wally whispered Hecate-like into my ear as the door was opened by Alistair's latest in a series of what he affectionately called his "amahs," one James Orkney Downes, a pale fattish man somewhere between thirty and Alzheimer's whom Wally called "Dorky" to his face and whom at home we referred to by Alistair's initial description of him as "The Last Truly White Woman in America."

"Oh, it's you," the White Woman intoned, moving aside to let us in. Somewhere within we heard what sounded like Ustad Akbar Khan playing the "Final Sunrise Raga." "He's over there, with the crowd." The White Woman lifted a snub nose to point politely.

Then, blessed by that muse of wit that sometimes descends even to the gutter, the White Woman looked at Wally's T-shirt—white block letters on a pure black background reading "DIE YUPPIE SCUM!"—and uttered, "That's cute."

I dragged Wally away before mayhem erupted, toward the group I assumed to be surrounding our host.

One hand searched like a living creature through a phalanx of backs ranged before us until fingertips touched my chin. The various backs between us were divided, and Alistair's face popped out, mostly eyes and cheekbones.

"Welcome to Mother Gin Sling's!" he shouted. Then glancing seductively as he could at Wally: "Mother Gin Sling's never closes!"

The others were swept away and the two of us engulfed in Alistair's
army, leggy ambience. He gestured at a large fake Louis Quinze *fau-
teuil*, onto which he dropped.

"Dearest Cuz." Alistair smiled benevolently upon me, at the same
time gesturing in the direction of two stools he wanted us to pull up and
sit upon so as to be closer to him. "And you, Wallace, you shockingly
handsome child stolen by my *cousin au second degré* out of your happy
bassinet," gesturing for Wally to do the same. "How sweet of you to
come celebrate with me. How beyond sweet!"

I was always surprised how Wally—who dishes Alistair to filth behind
his back—simply basked almost openmouthed in his presence. Hypnosis, Wally always insisted, and it was true that he usually snapped out of
it, if not completely, within five or ten minutes.

"How especially sweet of you," Alistair went on, "since I know you
have Serious Business to attend to tonight—the demonstration," he
said. "I know you especially, Wallace dear, must be itching to get out of
this lumber room of deadwood and get over there with all your young
and angry little friends."

I was checking Alistair over. He looked no worse tonight than
he had recently—indeed, somewhat better. I decided he was wearing
cosmetics.

"We can't stay long," I said for the two of us.

"Naturally," Alistair allowed. Then he took Wally's hand in his and
put on what I've come to know as Sincere Personality Number Three.
"Joshing aside. I think it's terribly important what you ACT OUT people are doing."

"ACT UP," I corrected. Wally was too transfixed by Sincere Number Three to notice the libel. Or to notice that those streaks of gray in
Alistair's hair were gone, erased no doubt by the White Woman's lib-
eral application of Loving Care Mousse, Ash Blond . . . Not that I don't
myself sometimes "touch up."

"We do appreciate it. Really we do," Alistair said. "We depend upon
it at times to get through the day."

I thought, Now really, you've gone too far.

Wally, evidently still stupefied by whatever mesmeric pheromones Alistair was emitting, said, "We're doing it for ourselves too."

"I'm doing it for the B.V.M.," I said. "I'm dedicating this entire action to her, you know. I'm wearing a blue shift under this, and at the crucial moment I'll strip and reveal it."

This was what I called "cutting through the shit with garden shears."

"Isn't Cuz a pill?" Alistair said, laying a hand upon my knee. I couldn't help but feel it flutter there. And suddenly I realized what was different about him. The tic was gone, the bunched-up Guillain-Barré tic that had disfigured the left half of Alistair's face for weeks. Replaced, I supposed, by this unceasing subtle shaking. A form of Parkinson's, I assumed.

I was about to ask Alistair about it, and to find out the clever little name he and the White Woman had given it, when we were all saved by the bell. Someone from Show Biz had just been admitted, and Alistair's sixth sense about The Rich and Glamorous went onto full Red Alert. He removed his hand from my knee to pat his over-perfectly coiffed hair in preparation for the Meeting.

I got up and grabbed Wally.

"Let's get a drink."

"Can't have any liquor on our breath," Wally insisted. "Marshals insist on that."

"Cream soda," I protested, "Cel-Ray!" Neither of which I was certain he'd ever heard of, growing up as he had somewhere in Montana.

"Tonic water and lime," Wally said to the bartender standing behind the cloth-draped table set up between the kitchen and living room. "Who the hell is Mother Gin Sling?"

"You had to be there," I said.

"Another one of your Alistair stories?" Wally asked with a hint of scorn. I wondered if he knew he had a blackhead. Probably not. He'd scream if he did, drag me into the john and insist I help get it out. *Pop!*

"A minute ago Alistair could have fed you a live baby and you would have gobbled it down without salt," I said haughtily. "It's not another Alistair story. It's from a Josef von Sternberg movie, *The Shanghai Gesture*."

"Dietrich?" Wally asked, and in that second I knew why I loved him: he tried, he actually tried, to know something that interested me, even though to someone his age it must have seemed chronologically about equal to the Parting of the Red Sea.

"Actually it was someone named Ona Munson no one ever heard of before or since," I explained. "She was probably sucking Sternberg's boot tips at the time. But she made a terrific Mother Gin Sling. Victor Mature was Dr. Omar. Very handsome with oiled hair and a fez. Very decadent. He seduces Gene Tierney into gambling."

"Tierney ended up in a nut hatch, didn't she?"

I beamed with pleasure. I could take Wally anywhere. Chip on the shoulder or not.

"Not until after *Laura*. In this film she was unbelievably beautiful," I said, remembering the clean new print on videotape I'd recently seen.

Wally had meanwhile become aware that he was being eyed by the bartender, a model-actor-waitress of no discernible attractions. To be nice to me and nasty to the flirter, Wally grabbed and kissed me, perfectly in profile to the bar.

"So when are you going to give him your gift?" Wally asked.

"I thought . . . as we leave?"

"You're still not sure whether you should give it to him, are you?"

"Of course I'm not sure. They're not Sen-Sen!"

"You got them. You spent two weeks among some of the scrungiest faggots I ever laid eyes on, in dives even I wouldn't go near, for two weeks, collecting enough of them. And you're not giving them to him?"

"Look, Wally, I know you don't approve."

"I told you before . . ."

"Some smidgen of religion or something your grandmother once said or an item in *Senior Scholastic* or . . ."

"Whatever you do, just fucking do it, okay!"

". . . so I can't blame you, for not approving," I continued, unfazed. "But he came to me. He asked me. I couldn't refuse him. Could I?"

"You've never refused him before."

"That's not true."

"When?" Wally demanded.

"I have."

"When?"

"Sometime I'll tell you when."

But of course he was ninety-nine percent right.

"Well, I'm tired of the suspense," Wally said. "I'm not hanging around here for you to do it. I'm leaving now. I'll be downstairs at Hunan Hell eating Hummingbird Scrota in Oyster Sauce."

I could have stopped him, but the truth was I was conflicted enough without having Wally's presence and disapproval to add to it.

And there was Alistair, still enthroned, surrounded by admirers new and old, common and semi-regal, and I didn't know when I could, or if I could, or even if I *should*, give him the sixty electric-blue-and-red Tuinals with which he fully intended to end his life tonight.

"So how do you think he looks?"

I smelled the White Woman before I heard his words: an odor close to that of brand-new Naugahyde in a late-sixties-model Ford. Actually I felt him before I smelled him. He's like one of those Black Holes in Space: he absorbs everything around him for about a yard circular. Molecules shed their magnetic and electrical charge when he approaches: it's depressing and draining, like the few minutes immediately preceding a spectacular thunderstorm. Except, in his case, the storm never arrives.

"He looks tarted up," I said.

"That's what he wanted."

"At least the tic's gone."

"Did you notice his hands? He can hardly use them. I have to cut up his food. Sometimes even feed him. He's got medicine for it, but he says it makes him so sleepy he calls himself Parko the Narko."

This was the cutesy name I'd been waiting for.

"You're a saint, Dorky. You'll go to heaven with your shoes on. Bally oxblood wingtips," I specified.

"I don't mind. I'm . . ."

". . . nothing. Alistair's everything," I finished the sentence.

"You're in a bad mood," the White Woman concluded without rancor, and swept his electron-removal unit to another section of the party.

Well, we'd talked and I'd been rude to him. As usual.

"Someone told me that absolute hunk is your lover."

The speaker was the bartender, mercifully silent until then.

"I don't get it," he continued, fatuous as predicted. "You're nothing special."

"I have a huge dick. Size of a small child's arm."

"You're kidding," he said, checking my crotch.

"Left it at home tonight. Actually," I intimated, crooking a finger for him to lean over the bottles and glasses and lemon wedges, "I do have a secret weapon."

"You do?"

"I do. It seems that Socrates was right: Virtue does attract Beauty."

"Huh?"

I breezed away into a corner where I could sip my vodka-less tonic and mope. I'd expected that "Huh" and that crack. In fact, everything so far tonight had been so as usual I felt in my pocket to make sure the two wrapped plastic vials of Tueys that alone made this night Significant and Different were still there.

Then, to make it even more as usual, someone located the record collection and put on Gloria Gaynor's first LP.

As usual. All of it as usual.

Except that I hadn't lied to Wally. I *had* refused Alistair something he'd asked for, something he'd wanted badly. Refused him more than once. Once at the very beginning.

That early October day in 1954 seemed no different from any other as I left school for the day. It was still too early for leaf change and recent rains had swept away the summer dust that collected in the gutters of our ordinarily spotless Long Island neighborhood. Three o'clock in the afternoon gave us fourth-graders plenty of time for games and mischief before sunset led to homework, dinner, and if we were good, "Captain Video" followed by "Your Show of Shows" on TV.

As we fled the school building, Augie turned to me and yelled, "My house! Half an hour! Magnets!" He charged off right, toward home, the overstuffed, aged leather satchel he used as a schoolbag bumping against his leg where it had already rubbed smooth a notch in each of his corduroy trousers.

August Herschel was my class friend, a heavyset boy with curly coffee-with-cream hair and cloudy blue eyes set deep in what was already a grown-up's face. Not the brightest boy in the world, he was good-natured and loyal, always curious and eager to follow my more arcane suggestions for amusements. Also a terrific pitcher in our Saturday after-noon baseball games up at the lots on Vanderveer Street. Augie liked me, and had sworn undying friendship to me since the second grade, when, at a Thanksgiving pageant given by our class in the school audi-torium, I—dressed as an Iroquois—had only half inadvertently dumped most of the contents of a papier-mâché cornucopia filled with colorful but hard little gourds on top of May Salonen, Augie's least favorite classmate, knocking her down just as she was about to make her big speech, causing her to forget her lines, burst into tears, and resist any at-tempts at comforting by our teacher. This had forced down the curtain on the stupid play, and given us the rest of the afternoon off.

More important these days, Augie was a solid and accepted member of the rest of the fourth-grade boys. Not that I thought much of that undistinguished ragtag bunch. But after a year-long infatuation with Grace Del Verdi, which had kept me in her and other females' com-pany, what I needed more than anything else in the world now, for my sanity as well as for my reputation at school, was the company—and the acceptance—of boys my age.

I turned left and desultorily fell in with Ronny Taskin and his friends, who walked home the same way I did. Ronny was a tall, skinny boy who worked out with Indian clubs, a holdover from his father's days as a cir-cus stuntman. That remnant of carnival glamour was all I could see in Ronny to give him precedence among us.

"Magnets? What's magnets?" Ronny turned all the way around to ask me.

"Those things that make iron stick to them," I explained. "Augie and I are fooling around with them. Trying to make things move. We broke a light bulb last time."

That last detail seemed to satisfy him that ours was an acceptable activity.

"You should be practicing batting for Saturday," Tony Duyckman said.

"I'll always be a lousy batter. My left eye's too bum," I added, refer-ring to an infant accident which had left me astigmatic and, while dramatic enough in the telling, unfortunately hadn't left a scar, except inside my eyeball, where no one but an ophthalmologist could see it.

The boys broke off in twos and threes, leaving me to dawdle the rest of the way home with Kerry White, a small, thin boy with excessive blond hair, himself a hanger-on of the group. We were silent until I reached the path to our door, where I left him with a curt "Bye," to which he responded with a sunny smile and overeager farewell.

Too bad for Kerry, I thought, even lower than me with the other guys. I opened the screen door, hoping I'd never fall so low as to walk home with five other kids without being spoken to and then be satisfied with someone saying good-bye. I grabbed the kitchen door handle and it didn't open. It was stuck or—locked!

Café curtains misted the kitchen-side windows. Even so, peering through I didn't see my mother anywhere in the room. So I knocked on the door. Then on the kitchen window. When that didn't work, I dragged my schoolbag to the front of the house and tried that door. Also locked. I rang the bell, knocked, shouted, and walked all over the grass down the slope to the garage door, located under the living room windows. No car in the garage. And the door was also locked.

I sat down in despair awhile, reading into these locked doors, that empty garage, the worst: my mother had left. Or, some terrible accident had befallen my father and sister and she'd rushed out to the hospital. I'd not been very nice to anyone in my family of late, and I was feeling guilty. Finally I got up and slogged over to our neighbor's house.

Mrs. Furst didn't know anything. Or said she didn't. She was busily entertaining a bevy of women in their mid-sixties, all of them sipping coffee out of narrow porcelain cups as they eyed an orange-frosted angel food cake. No, Mrs. Furst assured me, she had not seen my mother leave, and she had no message for me. In fact, she seemed to have but one thing on her mind: how long she could keep those biddies from attacking her culinary masterpiece.

Which reminded me that I was hungry too. My pockets contained only nine cents, not even enough for a Mars bar, but I knew that my mother kept a charge account open at a local grocery. I brazenly charged a Yoo-Hoo chocolate soda, a rectangular single-serving pineapple pie, and just to make it look legit, a box of Gold Dust cleanser.

I moped, eating in front of the grocery until several local women passed by and one of them asked me why I wasn't at home. I noticed the time on the "Moderne" 7-Up advertising clock in the window. I was late for Augie.

He was changed into his dungarees, in his backyard, playing with his metal dump trucks when I arrived, and he immediately asked why I was still in my school clothing. When I explained that my mother wasn't home and my house was locked up, he said I could borrow a pair of his overalls. I did, and they were so large I could wear them easily over my school pants and shirt.

The next hour was misery. I was too depressed to think about all the neat things I'd previously planned to do with the large magnet we'd found in his father's toolshed. Every once in a while I would sigh, and when Augie asked what was wrong, I'd reply, "Oh, nothing!" Then I mysteriously asked if he thought his folks would let me move in until I could find a job.

"Sure!" Augie said. But Augie would have replied the same if I'd asked him for all the blood in his body. Worse, he seemed to take my plight altogether too lightly, continuing to fill up, move along, and empty his toy metal trucks with exasperating imperturbability. In Augie's world my anxieties were unthinkable: "You're nuts to worry, your mother probably went out to get her hair done." I suddenly saw myself as Augie must see me: exotic and neurasthenic. And I suddenly saw Augie clearly: too unimaginative, too plain stupid to recognize that a future existed; possibly a not very pretty one.

This led to new guilt at my failure even to be a good friend, and I began talking about Ronny Taskin's pals and the upcoming game. Finally I let Augie pitch balls to me and tried batting them. We were in the middle of that when he was called inside to do his homework and I was sent home.

I didn't run all the way; I loitered on street corners staring at caterpillars fallen to the sidewalk. I counted bicycles dropped willy-nilly on front lawns or parked in tiers upon kickstands in driveways. I dreaded reaching our block. I turned into it reluctantly, so afraid to see the kitchen door still shut against me I wouldn't look up until I was directly in front of it.

It was still locked. I collapsed onto my schoolbag and contemplated suicide.

"His shirt was out of his pants. His shoes were caked with dirt. His mouth was a mélange of pineapple and some brown goo. His hair hadn't been combed all day. He looked like an urchin photographed outside some shanty in Appalachia"—that's how Alistair later on described me at our first meeting.

Alistair, on the other hand, was superb in a brand-new complete Hopalong Cassidy outfit, midnight-black with silver trim, including the arabesque-studded leather holster and silver-plated six-shooter, the authentic black-and-white pony Western boots, and the cream-colored felt ten-gallon hat with black embroidery.

He stepped out of the front seat of my mother's old Roadmaster, dropped a suitcase on the flagstones, and waited until my mother—carrying a larger suitcase—joined him before he said, "We used to have tramps in our neighborhood too. My mother usually gives them a five and tells them to get a haircut."

Astonished by this effrontery, as well as by the apparition that had uttered the words, I jumped up ready to punch him to the ground.

"You poor thing!" My mother suddenly dropped the suitcase and swept me up in a hug. "You must have been here an hour!" she said into my hair. "And I forgot to tell you I was going to the airport."

The airport? I pulled away from my mother. "What airport?"

"Idlewild," replied the monstrosity in my favorite cowboy star's outfit.

"It all happened so quickly," my mother said, trying to defend herself. "I knew he was coming in sometime today, but not exactly when. Then his mother called and I wasn't sure I knew the way and I got lost twice going there . . ."

"You flew in a plane?" I asked, writhing with envy.

"Four hours," he replied smugly.

My mother unlocked the kitchen door, reached back for his suitcase, and half lifted, half dragged it over the threshold. She gestured us in.

"By the way, this is your cousin, Alistair Dodge."

"Second cousin, actually," Alistair corrected.

My mother couldn't resist being demonstrative to me again. She half hugged me, then sat me down at the Formica table in the breakfast nook, signaling Alistair to join us. "You must be starving," she said to me. "He's used to a little snack after school," she explained to Alistair, which irritated me even further. He seemed indifferent as he removed his cream felt hat and sat down directly across from me. "In fact, you must be starving too."

"Dodge is a car," was all I could say.

"We're not *those* Dodges," Alistair replied. "My grandmother says *we're* tons older than those Dodges. She calls them upstarts."

My mother was hustling behind us, getting food together.

I stared at Alistair, and if I'd hated him on sight, I now knew at least three reasons why. Four: he looked like me. Oh, not exactly. He was taller, and narrower waisted. His hair was a paler blond than mine, and unlike mine, it wasn't darkening—and wouldn't darken—to brown. But even as unformed, unsettled-faced nine-year-olds, we had the same features. It was more than uncanny to me. I'd just really become aware of my face, my features, my self as it were, during those past months among Grace and Dawn and Lois with their attachment to and growing obsession with mirrors and their own physical uniqueness. Now I felt as though this stranger had just appeared and stolen what I'd thought was mine.

My mother set down tall glasses of milk and an assortment of snacks between us: Oreos, Fig Newtons, what appeared to be a homemade marble-swirl bundt cake.

"Well look at you two!" she said, sitting down on a third side to us. "You could be brothers rather than cousins once removed."

The phone rang, and she answered it and moved into the dining room to talk to Augie's mother.

"How long you planning to stay?" I asked: no subtlety at all.

"As long as the divorce takes."

"Divorce" was a word I'd never heard before from a child. "What divorce?"

"My father and mother's divorce," he said, delicately biting around the edge of a Fig Newton. "They're having a custody battle to see which one gets me."

Custody battle? What was that? I pictured two adults facing each other with guns in their holsters, about to draw like they did on TV.

"My dad thinks he'll win because he found my mother with a . . . a corespondent!" He whispered the last word.

"Isn't that someone you write to?"

"God, you're naive!"

"Where's this battle happening?"

"Grosse Pointe. Actually, the court is in Detroit. But we're from Grosse Pointe."

I tried picturing Detroit, Michigan. On our school map it was pink and broken into two pieces by one of the Great Lakes.

"Chief Pontiac," I said. "The Indian."

"They make Pontiacs up in Flint," he corrected. He got off his chair and carried his half-finished glass of milk over to the Pyrex coffeemaker, then he adroitly poured some of the dark liquid into his glass. "Flint is a dreary place."

My mother turned back into the kitchen, wrapped in pink telephone-wire spirals.

Now he's going to get it, I thought.

"Oh, I'm sorry, Alistair. I didn't know you . . ."

"That's okay, Cousin Eleanor, I can help myself." He showed her the glass. "I'm used to taking mine *au lait*!" he said.

She left the room, and I watched as he actually dipped his Oreos—whole, without separating them and licking off the cream—into the cof-feed milk, sitting in my kitchen and eating my snack, calling my mother "Eleanor," which was reserved for adults only, speaking French, having flown in a plane, with his parents divorced and battling for him, and I knew a fate had befallen me far worse than the abandonment I'd earlier feared.

When my mother came back into the kitchen to sit, she bumped against my schoolbag and it opened up.

"What's this?" she asked, pulling out the box of Gold Dust cleanser I'd bought before.

"I picked up a box at Wallford's," I said, embarrassed. "I know how you're always running out."

"I've stopped using this. I'm using Ajax now. Gold dust at my feet," she added, musingly.

"Huh?"

"That's what you two are," my mother said, holding the box on the table in front of us, "my Gold Dust Twins!"

I envisioned the next few days as pure torture. I was wrong. Well, it was torture, but of a different kind than I had supposed.

To begin with, Alistair wasn't under my feet day and night as I'd at first feared. In fact, I hardly saw him. I continued my life as usual, going to school, playing with Augie, undergoing the humiliation of batting one early evening, and striking out in several ways with Ronny Taskin's gang.

And my second cousin was nowhere in sight. He acted more like an invalid than a pest. He was still asleep in the guest bedroom each morning I woke up, breakfasted, and went to school. He was up by the time I came home after three, but sometimes in his room, reading a hardcover novel in bed, or out in the backyard, on a chaise longue, wearing my dad's oversized sunglasses, with one of my mother's movie magazines and a glass of milky coffee on the side table. Alistair stayed up long after I went to bed—sometimes talking to my parents; at other times watching "Studio One" and other post–10 P.M. programs alongside them in the living room.

One day I flashed into the house to change into my roller skates and Alistair was talking on the phone, taking notes with my mother's ballpoint pen, asking questions of whoever was on the other line. Another afternoon I found him in my sister Jennifer's bedroom, perched on the edge of her pink chenille bedspread, which was strewn with copies of *Seventeen* and makeup color charts, saying to her, "No. I'd go with the peach halter top. The beige holds down the color of your hair." He glanced at me, and my sister looked out at me in the hallway and soundly slammed the door in my face. That night I woke up past midnight and had to use the bathroom. I was surprised to see a light on, then thought it must have been so he wouldn't lose his way in the dark. But when I emerged from the john, I heard what were clearly the sounds from our TV, low but on. I peeped a look and spotted Alistair, all alone, looking small on the sofa, the night wind from a slightly open window behind him lightly furling his hair, as he puffed on one of my mother's Tareyton filter cigarettes. The film on the Motorola—it had to be "The Late Show"—had men in suits talking quickly and a woman in a slinky black dress. I could make no sense out of what they were saying.

He'd arrived on a Monday, and now it was Saturday. Not a particularly clement Saturday either. I was eating breakfast, watching Farmer Gray cartoons on TV, when Alistair emerged from his bedroom at 10:30 A.M. and drifted into the kitchen where he bussed my mother's cheek, murmuring "Good morning, Cousin Eleanor," grasped his glass of café au lait, wandered out to the front garden, where my dad in huge stained gardening gloves was pruning back the recalcitrant roses, greeted him, then roamed back into the "family room."

My mother said the words I'd been dreading all week. "Why don't you two *do* something together today?"

"Like what?" I asked, then quickly added, "It looks like rain."

"Take Alistair to the movies."

This was an all-afternoon affair, beginning with cartoons and *News of the Globe*, moving on through Coming Attractions, into endless serials, and climaxing in a feature film. Seven hundred boys and a few intrepid girls; noise and chaos—fine with me. Except I had no intention of having Augie or Ronny Taskin or in fact anyone I knew catch sight of Alistair, let alone with me.

Before I could think up a lie, Alistair said, "I did notice a new Joan Crawford at the Bedlington when we were shopping yesterday."

I'd seen the soppy display cards for the weeper too and would endure Chinese water torture first.

"*Bwana Devil*'s at the Community," I replied. "It's Three-D. Lions jump out at you and spears are thrown at your face."

"Charming!" was Alistair's reply. But my parents were planning to shop in a garden supply place miles away, then visit my reputedly ill Great Aunt June (no relation to Alistair). They'd be out all afternoon, and it was clear I was to be saddled with him for the day.

I wondered how to disguise myself so my friends wouldn't know me. But we were thrust out of the house with a dollar apiece so suddenly I found myself walking more or less next to him down Spring Boulevard, headed toward the movie theaters. "More or less" since I moved us to the next, far less frequented street and kept my distance from him once we got there, circling trees, walking on lawns and even in the street, as though there were infinite spots of compelling curiosity for me, while he kept to the center of the sidewalk. Should any kid approach, I could stop to tie my Keds and let Alistair walk on.

As it turned out, no one did meet us. And at the corner of Maxwell Avenue, when I stopped and was about to lay down the law to Alistair about sitting somewhere else, he simply said, "I'm going to *Torch Song*. See you later."

"Wait!" I caught up with him. "If we don't get back home together, they'll know."

"Don't worry. I'll think of something," he said and aimed for the Bedlington Theater.

Kerry White was waiting under the vast expanse of the Community Theater's marquee. Evidently for someone he knew to go inside with, because the minute I arrived, he bought his ticket, waited for me, and walked in with me. Inside the huge, ornate movie house, I spotted Augie and Ronny holding their fingers sideways over the water fountain, spurting it hard at three nearby girls. We pooled our cash and raided the refreshments counter for jujubes, popcorn, and Pez. We entered the auditorium just as the lights went down—a group of six, with Kerry trailing along—forced out a row of seven-year-olds who'd had the nerve to take our usual spot, and sat down. For a blissful three hours I completely forgot about Alistair Dodge.

I was reminded of him suddenly, in a most ghastly fashion, sometime during the icky love scene—in disgusting 3-D—of the feature film, when the fat woman who passed for a Saturday matinee usherette flashed her beam all over us, to our complaints of "Hey, watch that!"

"Are these your friends?" she asked.

Teary voiced, Alistair said yes and thanked her. He sat down right next to me! I saw the entire four months' past work on my reputation swept away in an instant.

Even in the dark, even with those ridiculous cardboard 3-D glasses on, I could tell I—we—were being watched by a dozen eyes. I didn't know what to do. Ignore him? Tell him to get out?

Before I could figure out what to do, Alistair put on his glasses and spoke up in a voice free of any tears.

"Anyone here got a cigarette?"

"I do," Kerry White, of all people, piped up and withdrew from his top pocket a crumpled but entire Camel. Alistair took it and to our astonishment lighted up and began to puff on it.

"I didn't know you were coming in here," I whispered furiously.

"Don't worry," Alistair said in a loud voice. "I didn't pay. I never pay in movies. That was just an act. You go up to some stupid-looking adult and tell her you can't find your seat."

On top of his smoking, this statement was startlingly neat. Ronny Taskin whistled.

"Never?" Tony asked.

"Never! Ooh oh, here comes the Hag." He put out the cigarette just as the matron thundered past us down the aisle, looking for the perpetrator.

Once the movie was over and we had all excitedly left the theater, the others could get a good look at Alistair. This, I thought for sure, would be the test. But if they noticed anything odd about his clothing, it was lost in their amazement at how alike he and I looked, something I'd tried to forget.

I was forced to admit we were related and that Alistair was staying with us. We drifted out of the crowd of kids emerging from the movie house, and Alistair pointed to a side alley, where we ducked in, and where, amid torrents of filthy water dripping off the roof from the downpour we'd missed, he leaned against a dryish wall, calmly completed his cigarette, and released tantalizing hints about himself to what even I had to admit soon became an impressed group of what I had previously thought were half-intelligent boys.

No wonder they were taken in. If, at our house, Alistair acted like my mother's slightly younger buddy, here, among Ronny Taskin and Guy Blauveldt, he was a perfect facsimile of a suburban lad. I could see them, especially Kerry White, hanging on Alistair's every word and checking it against the unspoken code of our age group.

Only Augie didn't appear taken in. He asked the key question. "Rog bringing you to our ball game tomorrow?"

Now, from what I'd seen, Alistair had about as much interest in baseball as he did in caterpillars. Imagine my surprise when he said, "Sure, what time?"

"You any good at batting?" Tony Duyckman asked.

"Three-forty last year," Alistair shocked me by saying.

"What position you play?" Ronny asked, suspicion rising in him.

"I like to pitch," Alistair said, "but ever since I met Whitey Ford, I really like playing catcher."

Two spectacular shocks. None of us actually *liked* to catch. And he'd actually met Whitey Ford, who had explained to Alistair the importance of good catching to effective pitching.

We drifted in a tight, admiring crowd all the way up Spring Boulevard, where the others all but hoisted Alistair to their shoulders when we arrived.

As they left, I said to him, "You'd sure better know how to bat. And to catch."

"I learned all that crap when I was six. I had a sports tutor."

"I hope you know what you're doing, Alistair. Because it'll be my butt on the line tomorrow."

"Calm down, Cuz. They're only kids. When you've been wheeling and dealing with adults as long as I have, kids are a cinch!"

The next morning was Sunday: a big breakfast then church. My sister, Jennifer, had refused to join us for the past year, "out of principle." Alistair joined her, saying "No offense. I'm used to my own parish."

When we got home, Jennifer had gone off to some friend's house, "to help paint scenery," her note said. Alistair was just getting off the phone when I came in to change out of my good clothes. My parents remained outside talking to Mrs. Furst and her grumpy husband.

"Don't you ever get off the phone?" I asked.

"Don't worry! They're collect calls," Alistair said, and sat down dispiritedly.

"Who are you calling all the time?"

"Lawyers. My mother's lawyer and my father's lawyer. The custody battle," he explained, then added, "I think I'll take her lawyer's offer."

It must have been clear that I hadn't a clue to what he was talking about.

"You see, they both want me. For different reasons, of course. And since they know I'll influence the judge if it comes to a bench decision, they're trying to settle out of court."

"What are they offering you?"

"The expected junk," he said airily. "Private school and college tu-ition. An Alfa Romeo when I'm sixteen. Of course, my dad has far more money than my mom does. But that could change depending upon whom she goes out with."

It all sounded so strange, I asked the next, natural question. "Which of them do you like better?"

"My mom's a tramp. But my dad's a hypocrite. He'd probably raise me better, but he once threatened me with military school. She'll prob-ably screw up her finances until she lets me take over, but she'd never do anything to hurt me."

I was so astonished by his assessment I didn't know what to say.

"What's most important," Alistair concluded, as the phone began to ring again, "is that she'll interfere less in my life."

He picked up the phone and said, "Tom? . . . Uh-huh? Fine! Tell him I'll make no claims on him beyond my grandmother's trust. . . . He will? Then that's it. Oh, and Tom, once this is settled, why don't you connect my mother up to your investment person? She's a complete dip when it comes to money."

They spoke a few minutes more before I went off to change my clothing.

When I arrived back in the living room, my parents were on the sofa, sitting on either side of Alistair, my mother holding his hand.

"You'll be able to see him if you want, won't you?" my mother was asking.

"Twice a year, Fourth of July week and the week after Christmas."

"When do they expect the paperwork to be done?" my father asked.

"A week, week-and-a-half. Can I impose on your hospitality a little longer?" Alistair asked in a small, pleading, sad voice.

"Of course you can," my mother said, and hugged him to her breast. Both she and my father looked solemn and sad, the way grown-ups looked at funerals and whenever the accountant came by.

"Don't forget we have a ball game at two," I shouted.

"Are you up to going today?" my mother asked Alistair.

"He promised to catch," I reminded him.

"It'll help me forget," Alistair said in that same fake, melancholy tone of voice.

I could have puked right there.

The ball game was not the disaster I'd feared. Despite having had a sports tutor, Alistair's batting was nothing like the .340 average he claimed. He did get off a couple of exciting pop flies and batted two men home. His catching was better—quiet, almost professional, unextravagant. Until, that is, Augie got up to pitch.

We had a roster of pitchers: Augie, Ronny, and Bob Cuffy were the top. If one of them couldn't make a game, Tony Duyckman, Randy McGregor, I, and even Kerry White were listed. I was a fair pitcher. At least my astigmatism didn't get in the way, as I could compensate for it by control of the ball. But we were seldom given the chance in a real game, and that was okay by most of us. Of the three best, Augie was the ace. There was something about that oversized, unkempt boy turning from hippo to gazelle on the pitcher's mound that staggered strangers we played and continually amazed his friends.

Imagine, then, my surprise when in the middle of the eighth inning, Alistair called time, stood up, and went to the mound to talk to Augie. Though the diamond was hardly regulation size, I was still far enough away from them in the backfield to not hear a word they said. What I saw was Augie's initial acceptance of criticism, his subsequent surprise, and the way he angled out his chin slightly to the left as Alistair went on talking. I'd learned that that jaw angle meant "No! Absolutely not! Not on your life."

Evidently Alistair didn't read the silent protest. He went on jawing a while longer then returned to home plate. I could see his fingers working signals behind the mitt so intensely the batter had to have seen too. Alistair was asking for a curve down. Augie threw a straight ball. The batter missed. Alistair asked again for a curve down. Augie threw a side curve. The batter struck out again. Alistair almost poked holes in the dirt under his fingers demanding a curve down. I could see Augie shift his stance as he did whenever he felt overpowered by someone. He threw a curveball down, and the batter smacked it dead on. The ball flew fast enough and tantalizingly low enough for Augie, the short-stop, and me, running at top speed, to grab at and miss it. It hit the streetlight pole on the corner of Vanderveer Street so hard it shattered the glass—yards from where it hit—and left the pole strumming like a tuning fork.

Augie moaned, then turned over the mound to Ronny. Ronny pitched well, but we had only an inning to make up for the three runs Augie had allowed on that homer, and we just couldn't do it.

Still, the game had been exciting, and nearly twenty of us sauntered up the street into the local White Castle for soda and burgers in pretty high spirits. Augie and I hung back so I could try to comfort him silently. This almost worked until Alistair dropped back from the others just as we reached the parking lot of the White Castle, to say, "You should have pitched the curve down when I asked for it."

To which Kerry and Tony replied loudly, "Yeah!" before going inside and helping the others send the middle-aged counterman and his teen-queen-daughter waitress into total confusion with a score of conflicting orders.

Augie didn't want to go inside.

"I know he's your cousin, Rog, but . . . ," he stammered, "he shouldn't just go around, you know . . . telling people . . . what to . . . do!"

"Ignore him, Augie. He'll be gone soon."

"What if he was right?"

"He wasn't."

"He was taught by Whitey Ford!"

"He *met* Whitey Ford!" I corrected.

"I don't know, Rog."

"Let's go inside. Or there won't be anything left for us to eat."

That motivated Augie. Even so, it was clear that Alistair had been bad-mouthing him to the others. Augie and I sat alone, and only Bob Cuffy came to talk to us, the others remaining among themselves.

At home, later, I caught Alistair leaving his room to go take a bath. He had enough towels for five people and was carrying a small leather bag which I knew from my father held toiletries.

"That was a rotten thing to do today!" I said.

"What are you talking about? Oh, that game! They're all just kids, you know."

I was about to ask what he thought I was, or for that matter, he was.

"All you need to do to control kids like that is learn a little psychology," Alistair concluded shrewdly. "Believe me, it will make your life a lot easier."

The split among us fourth-grade boys only seemed to widen in the next few days at school. I didn't much mind, but Augie was feeling ostracized for the first time in his life, and for something he hadn't even done. To make him feel better I decided to try to bring him and Alistair together. I hoped this would accomplish two things: let Alistair see how hurt and confused Augie was by what he'd done and thus bring out whatever good qualities might still lurk in my second cousin's breast; and show Augie that Alistair hadn't meant to hurt him specifically, that he pretty much did it naturally, running roughshod over everyone, moving from one scene of destruction to the next without much thought and little care for his effect. Maybe, just maybe, I was foolish enough to think, they'd even come to like each other, befriend each other, thus healing the wider social rift among us.

I chose Thursday afternoon to do that. "Thor's-day," Alistair explained. "He was the thunder god of the ancient Teutons. Always causing a storm. You wouldn't happen to know any Wagner? No, I thought not."

"Why won't you come over to Augie's?" I argued. "His garage is full of all sorts of neat things. Augie's dad's an inventor for Bell Labs."

"No, thanks," Alistair said, plumping himself down on the family room sofa. "There's a movie on TV I want to see. *Shall We Dance*," he confided.

I didn't know it.

"It's terrif," Alistair assured me. "Astaire, Rogers, Gershwin."

I'd never heard of any of them.

"It never ceases to amaze me! Here you are, living not thirty miles from the Chrysler Building, and for all you care you might as well be in . . . Paducah!"

The film on "Million Dollar Movie" began, and I could see in its first ten minutes that it would be just like all the other movies Alistair had watched since he arrived: well-tailored people in over-smart settings saying clever things and occasionally breaking into song and dance.

I waited for a commercial before saying, "That's not what it's like, you know!"

"What?"

"Manhattan."

"How would you know?" Alistair asked.

"Because I've been to Manhattan. To Radio City Music Hall and the Roxy Theater and to the circus at Madison Square Garden and to Broadway to see *South Pacific* and to Central Park and to the Plaza Hotel and to the Empire State Building. And it's not like in those movies."

"You still wouldn't know," he said, unfazed, "since the Manhattan in those movies takes place after you've gone to bed. At nine," he added, rubbing it in.

"I've been up late in Manhattan," I said. "I even went to dinner at '21.' "

"When?" He clearly disbelieved me.

"For Jennifer's birthday. My parents took us."

Now, it was true that they'd taken my sister; I'd just slept over at Augie's that night. Still, she'd come back with so many details of the event and brought them up so often over the following days that I felt I actually had gone with them. Details, I might add, I now began to enumerate.

"We had snails for appetizers. They looked burnt, but they tasted okay."

"*Escargots au beurre noir,*" Alistair said.

"There was a waiter whose only job was getting us wine."

"The *sommelier.*"

"There were waiters everywhere, coming and going all during the meal, emptying ashtrays, filling our glasses of water. A special one brought us dessert. I had cold ice cream inside a cooked crust," I added, thinking surely this impossibility would get him.

"Baked Alaska," Alistair murmured.

"So I know! And it's not like it is in those movies."

"It sounds exactly like those movies!"

"But that's not the way people live," I argued.

"That's the way *I'm* going to live. In a penthouse in Manhattan with a chauffeur and servants and wonderful, talented Social Register friends and beautiful things all around me. Quiet now, the commercial's over."

Not five minutes later, Ronny Taskin and his gang pulled up outside the house on their bikes. There must have been ten of them, yet Kerry White was delegated to come inside and ask if Alistair wanted to go biking with them.

To ask Alistair—not me.

"I don't have a bike here," he said apologetically, clearly torn between watching his movie and joining an outing in which he would have a starring, or at least costarring, role.

"What about Rog's bike?" the only recently insignificant Kerry had the temerity to ask.

"I'm using it!" I said.

"Well, you could borrow one of mine," Kerry told Alistair.

Who'd ever paid enough attention to the pipsqueak to notice he had more than one bike?

"At home," Alistair said, "I have a Schwinn Black Phantom, with three speeds."

"Me too," Kerry said. Then, lest Alistair consider him forward, he explained, "What I mean is, you can ride that one. I'll take the other."

Outside the others were shouting for Kerry to shake a leg.

Alistair waffled. "Well, if you really want me to."

"I do! We all do!"

Alistair hopped on Kerry's Black Phantom, while its owner jumped onto Tony Duyckman's handlebars and they all took off. Ten minutes later, as I was coasting down the hill of Spring onto Watkins Avenue, headed toward Augie's, I saw the group several blocks away. Kerry was on his older bike, riding between Ronny Taskin and Alistair in the vanguard of a flock of other boys.

That spelled an end to my peacemaking efforts.

I kept telling myself that Alistair wouldn't be around much longer. But somehow that didn't seem to work. He'd usurped my place—or a place I'd been looking forward to filling—among my classmates without even going to school with them. Except for Augie Herschel, virtually none of them spoke more than a word or two to me anymore.

At home it was just as bad. My mother would come into the family room late in the afternoon. I'd be struggling with math homework on the carpet in front of the TV. Jennifer would be on the sofa painting her toenails different colors to see which one she liked best. Alistair would be propped up on pillows in front of the coffee table, playing solitaire and humming along with my sister and her small pink plastic portable radio, to the sounds of the hit songs of the day—"Hernando's Hide-away," "Steam Heat," "They Call the Wind Maria." Mom would say, "I'm about to start dinner. You like veal cutlets, don't you?"

I'd look up to say, sure, veal was all right. And I'd see that my mother was looking at and asking Alistair.

Who would reply, "Are you going to try that lightly peppered sauce we were looking at in *Redbook*?"

To which she would gush some vaguely affirmative reply and vanish back into the kitchen to try the recipe.

She used to ask *me*.

Or, it would be after dinner. I'd be in the living room, playing with my Lincoln Logs, building not one of the dumb, expected log cabins illustrated on the outside and inside of the box, but instead my version of a Bronze Age fortress, using other logs snapped together to more or less form ships with battering rams, like the bulky triremes I'd recently seen in some movie about Roman times, and my dad, reading the paper nearby, would say, "What do you think? The Dodgers going to take the pennant this year?"

Before I could formulate an answer, I'd hear Alistair—in the opposite chair, checking his stocks in another section of my father's paper—say, "They're overrated. They have little real batting strength and their pitching is almost nil. The Giants will show them up for how second-rate they are. And I pick the Indians to sneak by the Yankees to clinch the American League pennant."

I could have been invisible for the rest of their detailed conversation, replete with batting averages and ERA and RBI statistics.

And the truly awful thing was, Alistair was right. Not ten months later I'd be in Ebbets Field with my dad, watching the third and final

play-off game—much more exciting than any World Series game to follow that season—and I'd watch the Giants fulfill Alistair's predictions
and blow away any hopes the Brooklyn Bums had for a Series title.

But . . . my dad used to ask *me*.

What Alistair thought about sports, finance, world politics, favorite
TV personalities, the latest movie, the newest hairstyle, the up-and-
coming pop singer filled our house, my ears, and my mind day in and
day out, unceasingly. Jennifer would mention that her friend Sue's family had just gotten a golden retriever puppy, and Alistair would expatiate
upon how to train the breed, what not to feed them, and what illnesses
they were prone to. My dad would mention that a friend of his had just
landed a position at a large advertising agency, and Alistair would know
not only the company's top executives, but several of its most successful
ad campaigns—and the year's past billing.

Because the clothing he'd brought with him, despite being two suitcases full, proved to be inadequate to Alistair's needs once he'd joined
the fourth-grade crowd's afterschool activities, my mother loaned him
mine. When I found them going through my closet and drawers and began to complain, my mother quickly said, "Don't be so selfish. These
are just old things anyway." The "old things" included my favorite, perfectly worn dungarees, which naturally fit Alistair to perfection; my
green felt and white-leather-sleeved stadium jacket, in which he looked
like a young honor student; even my extra-comfortable pullover cable-
knit sweater.

It was just that outfit that Alistair was wearing one evening, a few
minutes before dinner, when he sped up to the front of our house and
skidded to a stop on my bicycle—which he hadn't even bothered to ask
to borrow. I'd gone outside to wait for him by the garage, so we could
have it out, over his taking the bike, without disturbing the others. But
my dad had decided that was exactly the right time to spray his over-
pampered and underachieving roses. And my mother had come out to
tell my father he had a phone call. And my sister had that second
stepped out, to tell my mother that the water for the noodles was boil-
ing on the stove.

I watched from a slightly hidden spot not four yards away as Alistair
wheeled up, got off the bike and smiled at the massed and admiring

group. I couldn't help but see them all stop as though frozen as he approached. Couldn't help but see him—on my bike, dressed in my clothing, resembling me—completely fulfill for each member of my family
what I had never been able even to approach. It was a profoundly disturbing few moments, as he pulled the bike up the steps and parked it,
then kissed my mother's cheek, and my father dropped his spray can and
put an arm around Alistair's shoulder, and they all went inside, talking
together, a unity.

It was only as my sister reopened the front door to let out her pet cat
that I was noticed. From the surprised, slightly puzzled look on her face,
I could tell that for the briefest of moments she hadn't recognized me.

Then she said, "When you're done skulking about, *we're* having dinner in five minutes."

As it turned out, Alistair didn't have dinner with us that night, but
cleaned up, changed into some of his own clothing, and allowed my father to drive him the few blocks up to Kerry White's house on Hill
Crest Lane. This was supposedly a big deal, as Mr. White was a stockbroker with a large old firm on Wall Street, the Whites' house and
three-acre property were the largest and best kept in the area, and the
Whites themselves were considered the social cream of the neighborhood, until now completely out of reach of us mere Sansarcs. So I was
hardly surprised but I was thoroughly disgusted when my mother didn't
a bit mind this delay of our meal so Alistair could hobnob with the
Whites. Instead she hummed merrily all the while she served us, and
once we were all eating, she said to my dad, "Dinner at the Whites'
house. Maybe . . ."

Maybe what? Probably that she, they, possibly all of us, might be invited
to the Whites' for dinner someday, simply because we were Alistair's
cousins.

If that turned out to be the case, I'd never go.

Saturday afternoon, Augie and I were practicing up in the Vanderveer
lots, away from the junior high school boys who were having a real
game, when Guy Blauveldt and Carmine DeRosa biked up.

I'd been batting better that day than ever before. And Augie was trying out his new curveball, both of us attempting to gain confidence for
the game the following afternoon, when Guy shouted, "Not bad. But
you're wasting your time."

"I know I'll never be as good as you, Guy, but how about shutting up
and letting me practice?"

"I didn't mean you, Rog. I meant Augie was wasting his time," Guy
said. "He's been knocked down the roster for tomorrow's game."

"By who?" both of us demanded to know.

"I don't know."

"When?"

"This morning. We just passed Tony Duyckman coming out of the
Superette with his mom, and he told us."

"Who else was there?" Augie wanted to know.

"Why weren't we told about this meeting?" I persisted.

"Hey! I don't know. I wasn't there!"

Augie and I surrounded him. I shoved my bat handle into Guy's front
spokes so he couldn't move.

"Don't give me that crap!" I said. "Tell us!"

"Ask Tony. Or better still, ask your cousin. He's the one who called a
meeting."

"Let him go!" Augie said.

"Who else was there?" I demanded.

"Tony. Ronny. Coupla other guys."

"The shrimp?" I asked, meaning Kerry White.

"I guess so. The meeting was at his house."

"He'll die like a dog!" I pulled the bat out of the spokes, and Guy was
smart enough to leap onto his bike before I could smash it to smither-
eens. "They'll all die like dogs." I kept swinging the bat, but by now
Guy and Carmine had biked out of range and were looking back. I noted
that they were headed toward Ronny's house.

Despite Augie's protests to "forget about it, will ya," I got him on his
bike and we also headed for Ronny Taskin's house.

"You're on the top of that pitching roster, or someone dies!" I
shouted at Augie enough times to get him annoyed and angry too.

As I'd suspected, we found Guy and Carmine's bikes thrown down on the lawn by Ronny's back porch. We dropped ours on top of them, then fought our way through the brambles surrounding the supposedly padlocked and unused side door of the Taskins' big, old freestanding garage.

They were all there waiting for us: Ronny, Tony, Kerry, Bob, and my second cousin, with the messengers announcing our arrival still breathless from their ride.

I had my bat in my hand and was swinging it. "Okay, Alistair, outside."

"Wait a sec, Cuz. What's all the commotion about?"

"You know damned well. The pitching roster."

Kerry had the nerve to speak up. "We voted on it. Fair and square."

"Who voted for it? You, yourself, and you? This is a team, remember?"

"Doesn't make any difference," Alistair said. "You two would have been outvoted anyway."

"Who suddenly made you manager of this team?" I asked. "You don't even live here!" I spat out the words.

"I'm manager of the team," Ronny said.

"Since when? Another phony vote this morning? We don't have a manager. And there's no reason to move Augie down because one guy hit a home run off him last week."

"There's a perfectly good reason," Alistair said. "He can't follow the catcher's suggestions." The catcher, of course, being himself. "Whereas everyone on the roster now can."

"There's no rule I ever read that says the pitcher's got to do what the catcher says!" Augie finally spoke up on his own behalf.

"Al's the best pitcher we ever had," Ronny said. "He tagged two guys coming home last night."

Thus revealing that they'd played a game and hadn't even told us.

"Look, Cuz." Alistair had pulled out the roster they'd schemed on all morning. "Augie's on it."

I looked. "Fifth. After Ronny and Tony and Bob Cuffy—and Kerry?" I looked at the little squirt with disdain. "This one couldn't pitch horseshit into a barn with a shovel."

"That's the roster we agreed on," Ronny said.

"You're shortstop," Alistair said, attempting a final placation.

"Forget it! I'm not playing shortstop or any other position with cheaters. Not tomorrow and not ever again!"

"Me either," Augie said.

"Me either," Bob Cuffy unexpectedly piped up, followed by Carmine.

"We'll put together our own team," I said.

Now, this was clearly an unexpected move, and compelling in its potential for disaster to their plans.

"I've got an idea," Alistair said, suddenly conciliatory. "Since you won't accept the democratic way, how about we flip a coin for it?"

"Whose leaded coin?" I asked. We all had one.

It was Guy who came up with the brilliant idea that we shoot marbles for the winning roster: it required skill as well as chance and would take time, not a few seconds, thus allowing us all to feel that something competitive—and thus real—was taking place.

We agreed to meet back at the spot in an hour to shoot for the roster. Whoever won would then gracefully concede defeat and accept the winners' roster. At least for tomorrow's game.

Augie was the best marble player among the four of us, so we all rode over to his house and spent a half hour picking through his collection of marbles to find five other ones to complement his winner, a big, almost pure ebony, completely unfaceted onyx. On the way over I stopped at my house, dashed into my bedroom, and grabbed my own bag of playing marbles.

We arrived back at Ronny's garage. He'd cleared a space in the dirt in back of it and drawn a circle with a stick. The rules were agreed upon: six marbles each until all the marbles were gone but the winning one.

I shouldn't have been surprised that Alistair had gotten himself selected as their side's champion. But there he was, already hunkered down, six carefully selected marbles from the others' collection at his side. I recognized Guy's tortoiseshell and Tony's blue-and-white sailboat, so named because that's what the facet looked like when you held it up to the light.

Ronny and Bob Cuffy did fingers for choosing, three out of four, and Ronny won. Augie placed his least valuable agate into the circle, and

Alistair shot it far out past the lines with a big, badly colored cat's-eye. That became Alistair's and went into the center. Augie sliced it right to the other side of the circle line. Alistair chose a pinkstone agate as man, and Augie shot that out too. But he could only side-slice the tortoise-shell, and he lost two stones to Alistair before he had another go at it. By then the tortoiseshell had been retired (to Guy's relief) and replaced by the sailboat. Augie took that easily with his big onyx blaster. But Alistair won it back. On and on they went, until Augie hit lucky and the onyx al-most cracked the sailboat in half knocking it out of the ring. Alistair now had one stone left.

He stood up and began to powwow with the others.

"Don't worry," I said to Augie. "You'll take him out and you'll pitch first tomorrow."

They returned to the ring, and Alistair said, "It's obvious that I can't win unless I have a stone as good as Augie's onyx."

"Does that mean you're giving up?" I asked.

"No. It means that I need a stone as good as the onyx. I'm told there's only one other stone in this neighborhood that good. Your tourmaline."

"My tourmaline?" I gasped.

Now this was indeed a true fact. For the past two years, my tourma-line had terrorized the marble rings of our suburb, so dominating the game it effectively ended all play. However, my tourmaline wasn't merely a big, dense, beautiful multicolored stone. It was a gift from my uncle Ted, a Navy captain, who'd bought the large, expensive stone in Ceylon when he was on duty, and had it turned into special gifts for us—earrings for my mom, a charm for my sister's bracelet, and a play-ing marble for me. The thought of letting another person, never mind Alistair, use it was so unthinkable to me it literally nauseated me.

"You've got it," Ronny said. "That means you guys intended to use it."

"Did not!"

"Then why'd you bring it?"

"No one's using my tourmaline but me," I declared.

"In that case you'll have to shoot against Augie," Alistair said, effec-tively trapping me.

"Use the tortoiseshell," I said. "That's still left."

"Everyone knows it's not as good," Kerry said.

"Then use your head," I told him. "It's about the right size."

We were gridlocked.

Alistair stood up and said, "Well, guys, I've done everything I know to make this a fair match."

The logical next assumption was that I was the one being unfair.

"I'm not playing against Augie. Period."

"Then give me the tourmaline," Alistair said.

I didn't know what to do. Looking at Augie was no help. Despite his terrific shooting, he now wore that hangdog look that showed that he was already defeated—not by a marble shooter, but by the complications my second cousin had introduced into the game, into our friendship, into poor Augie's until-then Edenically innocent life.

"We're waiting!" Kerry sang out.

I promised myself that the minute Alistair had gone back to Michigan, I'd waylay the little creep and beat him to the consistency of tapioca.

I snuck a look at Alistair. He was enjoying this, really and truly enjoying the predicament he'd gotten me into, watching and waiting what I'd do to get out of it. That infuriated and decided me.

"Fine! I'll shoot against Augie!" I declared.

Before any of them could respond, I went to the circle, dropped to one knee, pulled out the tourmaline, and shot it hard, directly into the blank, glazed surface of the onyx lying in the middle of the ring.

It gave the onyx a good smash and sent it whirling and gyrating out of the circle, then sent it whirling and gyrating back in again, where the onyx stopped, inert.

"No fair!" Alistair shouted behind me.

"It was a good shot!" the others shouted.

It had been a good shot, an honest shot with a freak result. Any marble player worth his oats could see I'd really given it everything.

The next shot was Augie's, and he took my tourmaline easily. A few days later, he actually tried to let me win it back. I said no, he should keep it.

As for Alistair, he was livid. Truly livid, in that I'd done the honorable thing the honorable way and had honorably lost a valuable—even a legendary—marble, even if to my friend, and not one among them could say I'd in any way balked or complained about it.

He waited until we got home before shoving me into the wall behind my bedroom door. Holding my own bat horizontally against my neck until I began to feel faint from lack of blood and oxygen, he spoke in the quietest and nastiest voice I'd ever heard out of a human.

"I really thought I'd taught you a lesson back there, Cuz. But you just won't learn, will you?"

His face was mine, but distorted dreadfully.

I got a grip on the bat and tried to push it away.

"You think just because you stuck up for that poor, stupid, fat boy that you're some sort of hero, don't you?"

I'd gotten a grip on each of his hands, but he had the angle and leverage on me.

"Well, just remember this, Cuz. Schmucks like that will come and go in your life. They don't mean a thing. I'm the one who counts. I'm the one you're going to have to face and deal with. Because I'm the one who's going to be around for a long, long time.

"You got that?" he emphasized with another burst of pressure, as I began to see spots in front of my face and black out.

"Good!" he said. "Don't ever forget it!"

"Missing him already?"

I snapped to attention. Alistair was leaning into the little cul-de-sac behind the enormous fake columns he'd had installed and painted *faux* marble a year ago by a former trick, now part of some rehab program funded by Afghan or Moroccan millionaires to "Aid the Arts" and help some of their best former customers recover from decades of drug abuse.

"Him who?" I asked.

"Who else? Wallace the Red. I saw him vanish into the crowd and out the door like a sword through hot butter."

"He was hungry for Szechuan food."

"Bless his metabolism," Alistair said, with less irony than usual. "Indeed. Bless anyone for still having a metabolism! I was thinking of installing paramecia or something prevertebrate like that into my intestine so I might once again recognize what used to be called an appetite."

"You don't look that bad," I lied.

"You mean I don't look like 'Gee, guys, I've been in Auschwitz and I managed to get out' yet?" Alistair asked. "The Duchess of Windsor was wrong: You *can* be too thin. Give me a hand," he added, literally dropping a nearly fleshless and thus lightweight and fragile arm onto my shoulder.

"Where we going?"

"The loo."

"What happened to what's-his-name?" I asked as I steered Alistair into the hallway. "The star?"

"He left."

"How was he?"

"Flawless. He didn't once mention *It*," Alistair said.

"Is that good or bad?" I asked; these days one could never be certain whether one should or shouldn't. The epidemic seems to have developed an ever-metamorphosing construct of etiquette. I sometimes think there should be an Illness Manners Crisis Hotline you can phone to get the latest subtle twist.

"Good for him," Alistair explained. "He'd only say the wrong thing."

We'd gotten to the john, and I knocked hard enough to awaken anyone catnapping within.

"It's all yours," I declared, opening the door.

"Come in with me."

"It hasn't come to that, has it?"

"No, silly. I want you to fix my face."

Alistair's bathroom was large, but when he'd redone the apartment a year ago during a burst of unexpected energy, he'd enlarged it further by absorbing two closets, then he'd followed through the postmodern architectural theme of the building to what I considered illegal lengths. If the large living-dining area was post-Pompeii, the bathroom was late Dark Ages. The stall shower—big enough to hold a medium-sized dyers' guild—was in the color of, and with that puddinglike texture of, alabaster you see only at the Cloisters. The floorboards had come from a

twelfth-century Norman mill. The sliding doors were artfully mo-
saicked chunks of stained glass of the same period, but from a Silesian
monastery. The rest of the large room followed the motif: the fixtures
looked like baptismal fonts, the walls were scattered with sour-faced
Madonnas holding goggle-eyed infants against fields of ancient gold
leaf, each set within its own little house—a frame resembling nothing
more than a cowshed, behind which lurked a cabinet for toiletries. Next
to the Madonnas floated several antique mirrors of varying sizes, the
bluish glass much impinged upon by thick frames filled with hordes of
pouting, rather bony cherubim. It was into one of these that Alistair
thrust his face.

"Hit those pin spots," he commanded. "The controls are inside that
little baldachin right by your hand."

After some hit-and-miss, I found the correct button and Alistair's
head was thrown into strong, white illumination.

He'd opened one of the cabinets and withdrawn two vials of ecru liquid.

"Where would we be without Cover-Up?" Alistair sighed, handing
the two little bottles to me. "You'll have to do it for me. The way my
hands shake I'll end up looking like Clarabelle."

"You don't need it," I said. But of course in this light I could very clearly
see he did. The White Woman had been far too stinting earlier, and I
could see three KS lesions already showing through his ministrations.

"Use the darker color in front, the lighter on my neck," Alistair
said, as I chose and began applying. "Old trade secret of the stars, that!"
Alistair went on. "Keeps the wrinkles from showing under key lights."

His skin looked papery as a wasp's nest wherever a bone was prominent—on the bridge of his nose, at either eyebrow ridge, under his im-
perfectly shaven chin.

"Garbo teach you this?" I asked.

"Actually it was Bette Midler. Before she got it fixed, her nose bone
bent like that road sign in Monterey spelling out 'Hills and Curves Next
74 Miles'! I watched her paint a line straight down and shade in both
sides. Not that it was ever a petite button, but she made herself look like
Esther the Queen redivivus."

"When was that?'

"Continental Baths. Seventy-two? Seventy-four?" Alistair slowly shifted the planes of his face in the mirror. "You're in love with that little schmuck, aren't you?"

"Hold still."

"I can tell. All the signs are there," Alistair said.

"Nefertiti, gone four thousand years, could tell," I said. "I mean Wally's only been living with me over a year."

"Have you awakened in the middle of the night and wanted to strangle him in his sleep? That's the only way I've ever been certain I loved someone."

"There are less homicidal ways."

"None as certain," Alistair argued. "You're not bad at this. I guess it was all your zits that made you master of the makeup jar."

"I never had zits," I said. "You taught me how to do this."

"I did?" Alistair seemed amazed. "When?"

"When we were adolescents. We practiced on that pretty girl with all those beauty marks she hated. Judy something. In California."

"She married a maharaja," Alistair said, musing. "Or became a maharishi. I don't remember which. So are you and the little beast going to exchange rings in the Sheep Meadow and all that homo-tripe?" Alistair asked.

"Wally would rather blow up the Sheep Meadow," I said.

"He sort of reminds me of myself at that age."

"Come off it. At Wally's age all you wanted was your name etched on double glass doors on Fifty-seventh and Fifth."

"That's enough," Alistair said. "I don't want to look like Dietrich."

I pulled back a second. Then I placed my own face next to Alistair's in the mirror. Difficult to believe we'd once looked so alike. Oh, the structure was there all right: the identical wide brows, the little dents at each temple, the long, somewhat aristocratic nose. But the lower part of my face was round—though not yet jowly—whereas his was pointed. And his lips were fleshier; even the gauntness of his illness hadn't affected them.

"You do!" I said louder than necessary. "You look like Dietrich in the early seventies in Paris. When she was wearing those silver sequined gowns they had to break several ribs to stuff her into and singing 'Lili

Marlene' for the eleven thousandth time during yet another of her innu-
merable farewell performances at the Paris Opera House."

"Shameless flattery," Alistair sniffed, but he preened too.

He was busy making big lips at himself in the mirror and saying
"Daw-a-ling" when he suddenly asked, "You did bring my gift?"

I turned away and began deliberately shoving the little brush inside
each vial of Cover-Up and carefully screwing closed each cap.

"Remember when my mother called us the Gold Dust Twins?" I asked.

"Your mother was a doll, but she saw things no one else did."

"Must run in the family. Remember Great Aunt Lillian? How she
used you in her séances?"

"Did you bring my gift?" He repeated his question quietly but firmly.

"I brought it, but I still don't think . . ."

"What you think is inconsequential at this late date, Cuz."

"It's not that late."

"Be real for once. Nothing is working anymore."

"Nothing?"

"Oh, Dr. Jekyll says he recently discovered a T cell, and my Billy
Reuben is about the same as that of an Arctic sardine." He turned to me.
"But do let's face facts. I spike a fever to a hundred and four every other
day. And it's already passed the brain-blood barrier and damaged my
cerebral cortex. I can't remember anything anymore. Orkney's taken to
using little yellow glue-on notes on things like salad forks and needle
cases so we won't be too embarrassed."

"It's age, my own memory is—"

"Shut up and listen, Rog. My boats are burned," he said, carefully
enunciating. "And I'm a big enough girl to realize it's time for a final
Viking do. Shields inverted! Flames to the top of the mast! Floating out
in Long Island Sound!"

I half sat, half collapsed on the toilet.

"Oh, come on! Don't be like that!" Alistair said brightly. "We've
planned this for weeks. Don't spoil it."

"I can't believe it's . . . over."

"Look on the bright side, Cuz. You'll soon be the last queen left in New
York who necked at Le Jardin with the son of a President in Office."

"I never did that."

"You did too! Stephen Ford. Was it Jack Ford? *One* of the Ford boys."

"Not me," I declared.

"It was. A big beefy blond. Remember? Fran Lebowitz was at the next table, and as we entered, you said, 'Don't let her see me,' even though she wouldn't have known you from King Kong. Ultraviolet came over to her table with Jack or Steve or Whomever Ford in tow, and he sat down next to you while she joined Fran, and next thing I knew you two were gone. I later found you in the men's room lounge pressed into the wallpaper doing the heaviest fully clothed petting act I've seen outside of Tijuana."

I remembered the incident, and the boy, but I still disbelieved him about it being one of President Ford's sons.

"If it is true," and I stopped him from interjecting, "who'll be around to remind me?"

"You'll remind yourself. You'll sit yourself down with magnums of Dom Pérignon and write your memoirs."

"I never did anything, and what I did I'll need you to remember."

"It would be fun if I remained as a tiny voice. Who was that pretty boy in Ovid? Tithonus? He became Aurora's lover, and she managed to get him eternal life, but she forgot to ask for eternal youth too and he shriveled away to the size of a cricket."

"Tennyson," I said. " 'The woods decay, the woods decay and fall.' Don't take them, Alistair!"

"Of course I'm going to take them. And you know what? I found these clever little things." He pulled out a little plastic packet of flesh-colored patches the size of a nickel. "Anti–Lupe Velez Syndrome patches," he said. "I place one on each pulse point on the back of my neck, and these'll keep me from getting nauseated and looking like shit when they find the body."

"Does the White— Does Orkney know about this?"

"He'll go to sleep in his usual sublime ignorance and awaken to what I trust will be only a tiny iota less ignorance tomorrow morning."

"What if something goes wrong? Shouldn't he know?"

"Be real, Cuz. He's one of those Vermont WASPs who cut open their bellies to keep their babies warm in winter. He'd never approve of me escaping from one second of earthly suffering."

"Wally too. We've argued over this all week."

"Really! I'd think he'd want to see me out of the way!"

"He's conflicted," I temporized.

"Neither of them have suffered as you and I have, Cuz. Physically or ethically."

"And neither of them ever had as much fun."

"Or fought as bitterly."

"Or loved as hopelessly."

"Or . . ."

I hung on Alistair's breath.

"—Saw as many bad movies!" he exploded.

We both laughed till I said, "Or screwed as many pretty boys."

"Or been as badly screwed by as many pretty boys," Alistair completed the list with a chortle. "One of whom was considerate enough to have led us to this very moment."

My high spirits sank.

"Which is about to end as planned. You will give me my forty-fifth birthday present. Then kiss my well-cosmetized cheek, and leave me. Forever."

He was serious now. Exhausted too.

I stood up, dug into my deep pocket, and handed over the little package. It was wrapped in black paper with a narrow black ribbon.

"Happy forty-five," I said. And as he collapsed onto the toilet seat I'd just vacated, I kissed one of the cheeks I'd just made up.

"Thank you, Cuz. These wrappings! Couldn't you find anything with a skull-and-crossbones motif?" He ripped off the paper and held the palm-sized ebony-colored metal Sobranie cigarette box in one skeletal hand, then lifted its lid and said in a voice I'd never before heard out of him, "Ah, my hot-pink-and-electric-blue darlings!"

Alistair looked up at me as though surprised I was still there. "What are you waiting for? Go."

"I'm waiting for you to say something final to me."

"Make sure they play Ravel's *Ma Mère l'oye* at my memorial service. The four-hand piano version."

"Oh, Alistair! That's not what I mean!"

He smiled an odd, crooked smile, doubtless twisted by the same

Parkinson's that had affected his hands. "What's left to say? No, really, Cuz. What haven't we said? What haven't we *done* to each other?"

I left the bathroom. Left the apartment. Got into the elevator and descended.

When it arrived at the third floor, for the blue-haired old woman with the beribboned dachshund to get in, she was treated to the possibly not too daily sight of a grown man soundly and methodically banging his head against the cleverly pre-aged wood paneling.

Book
Two

Silhouettes
on the Shade

1991 AND 1961

Wally was in the Chinese restaurant, at the table closest to the kitchen and farthest from the expanse of windows fronting Broadway. It never ceased to amaze me how the lad had a sixth sense for placing himself less than a yard away from wherever the help ate. Since it was nearly nine o'clock, and the restaurant nearly empty of customers, three young waiters and an older man, whom I guessed to be a chef from his food-spattered full apron, were already attacking an enormous bowl of rice noodles with assorted vegetables.

Less surprising than Wally's instinct for getting nitty-gritty with the laboring class was the fact that he wasn't alone. I recognized one companion from the back as I entered—Junior Obregon—the other I didn't know.

I sat down in front of a giant porcelain teapot surrounded by plates of what had recently been General Ts'o's Chicken and Three Mountain Prawn.

The strange overhead illumination in the restaurant made everyone look slightly green, including Wally, who, being supernaturally hand-some, instead of looking seasick like the rest of us, now resembled some superb wild woodland creature just flitting out into light from a deep forested glade.

As he always does in public—whether we're speaking that day or not—Wally made sure to lean over and kiss me full on the lips.

It had its usual effect: the two waiters said something and giggled, allowing Wally to be superior and indifferent.

"You know my Sig Oth," Wally said to Junior Obregon, who grunted out, "How's it hanging, man."

I turned to the third diner. He was slim and pale, with bittersweet-chocolate straight hair. Nice face, even handsome, save for the eyebrows that connected without pause over his nose and shadowed his surprisingly dark blue-black eyes. Oddly, instead of making him look like a Neanderthal, they gave him a sad, even a somewhat tragic cast. I decided with no proof at all that he and Junior were doing it.

"James Niebuhr," he introduced himself, with a strong, large hand thrust out for me to shake across the ravages of noodles in cold sesame sauce. I noticed paper cuts in the thumb and index finger and guessed he worked in design or art directing. "And yes, I'm distantly related to *the* Niebuhr."

"I gotta piss!" was Junior Obregon's loud announcement. He continued to sit there, chewing on a chopstick while glowering at me.

Now Junior and me, we have history. About two years ago, I was walking home from watching a third-rate foreign film at a local cinema when he accosted me at Seventh Avenue and Twelfth Street. Junior is lanky, and handsome in that strange blond-Latin way—you know, hair a little too thick, eyes a little too brown, face a little too pitted. His leather jacket is always open, and a work shirt is open to his navel even when it's so cold out sleeping sparrows are falling like stones out of trees. So I looked, immediately thought, Trouble, and moved on.

Junior Obregon is no fool, and he caught on to what I was thinking. So he followed me all the way home, sometimes behind me, sometimes on the side, a couple of times even in the gutter, all the time talking dirty to me, but in reality challenging me.

When we got to my place, he stopped my hand at the front door and said, "I need it *bad*!"

"If you're looking for money, forget it," I said, hard as ice.

"No, man!" with that accent. "Just a little action."

I still thought he was trouble, but I've been gay long enough to know even the worst men can be quite amenable when they're suffering from a case of blue balls and you're the one designated to help them.

As I let him in, I continued calculating: I was big enough to take him without a weapon if he got itsy. But if he were armed . . . Before he could think, I spun Junior around, pushed him against the corridor wall, and frisked him. He didn't complain. He did not breathe a word. I didn't find a weapon, and all the while I was saying to myself, "Honey! You are one hard queen!" thinking what a great story this would make when I told Alistair the next day on the phone.

Inside the apartment he stripped off his pants and dropped onto my sofa, working up his dick. I blew him and he left. The entire encounter took at most ten minutes. I never asked his name and he never offered it.

He appeared a year later, stepping out of Tisch Hall in company with Wally and some of his cohorts. At which point it became clear he wasn't the Puerto Rican ex-con with the hots he'd pretended to be, but merely another NYU film school student, son of successful and well-off parents who lived in semirural New Jersey.

I didn't care. But evidently Norberto Juan Maria Obregon the Third— that was Junior's full name—did care, especially because he'd been found out playing a most unenlightened role of Latino trade. He'd silently resented me for it ever since, even though I never told Wally or anyone else.

"So Wally said you do . . . What is it?" Niebuhr asked.

"Drug pushing!" Wally said.

"I'm an axe murderer," I readily agreed and poked through their dishes searching for something edible.

"No," James said. "You're like a writer or something."

I turned to Wally. "To answer your question: yes, I gave Alistair the pills. All sixty-four."

"You'll burn in Hell," Wally said with no emotion. He'd located a prawn and fed it to me with his chopsticks.

Junior Obregon got up to piss.

"You wrote a book, didn't you?" Niebuhr asked. "*The Sexual Underclass.* Junior's Soc professor has it on his reading list."

"He's losing his memory," I said to Wally, referring to Alistair. "The virus has already reached his brain. I've seen what it's like when they become demented. You haven't."

"Why not just wait outside his building and knife him?" Wally asked.

"He barely gets out anymore. Too exhausted to walk."

Niebuhr continued to ignore our conversation. "Junior said that his prof said it was the best study of the rise of the gay political minority after Stonewall."

Wally was bored by the conversation. He stood up and began distributing "Silence=Death" leaflets onto the restaurant tables.

"You joining us at Gracie Mansion, James?" I suddenly asked.

The caterpillar across his brow lifted up twice, registering surprise.

"You mean you're comin' too?"

"Think I'm too old?"

He shrugged.

"I was demonstrating before you were born," I said, regretting it the minute I said it. "I'm an old hand at this shit."

"Oh, yeah?" he asked.

"Chicago. '68. D.C. against the war in Vietnam in '64. On the SNCC busses down south a few years earlier." Even I was getting tired of hearing myself recall it, like some old anarchist giving a liturgy of the assassinations he'd flubbed, the riots he'd almost provoked.

"No wonder . . . ," James said. Then he explained, "I could never figure out why a great-looking guy like Wally would get involved in a transgen thing."

Read trans-generational. Read I'm old enough to be his father but neither look it nor act like it. Read eternal Peter Pan. Read refusing to grow up and accept that life stinks and people are worthless. Read I'll be ninety and in a wheelchair and still picketing the White House. Read . . .

"You ready, Bluebeard?" Wally was at my shoulder, all his leaflets having been distributed.

"Aren't we waiting for Junior?"

Wally pointed. Junior was outside on the street already. With him were four other guys I recognized from the two chaotic Monday night sessions I'd attended at the group's new headquarters.

When we got out, Junior counted off bodies for taxis, Gracie Mansion being unattainable from here by public transport except with bus transfers and other old-lady stuff like that. Wally and I were left alone for a cab.

"You lose," I said, as he pushed me into the taxi.

Our cabby was a fat-faced, young but very nervous Indian Muslim, who seemed visibly relieved when Wally told him to head east toward Gracie Mansion instead of to a Hundred and Thirty-eighth Street or the abandoned wharves at Jersey City. Wally and I settled into the backseat and sat with our knees close together. I was looking out the window, trying not to think about Alistair staring at those Tuinals and stroking them like a lover's scrotum when we reached Central Park West and Wally tapped my knee.

"Look at him staring at us in the mirror every few seconds. Bet he's scared shitless to have two genuine perverts in the car."

Wally's love of provoking straights should by now be apparent.

"Let's get there without incident, okay?"

Wally's response was to put an arm around my shoulder and hug me. This didn't in the least bit reassure me that I could count on his good behavior. I could see the driver's large brown eyes widen in the rearview mirror.

"What cross street you taking?" Wally asked loudly.

"Excuse, please?" the driver asked.

"Because if you're thinking of taking Eighty-sixth Street, you're going to run into heavy traffic. I suggest Eighty-fourth or Eighty-eighth."

Wally was rewarded by the expected response: "I am driving this car."

"In fact," Wally said, not about to stop now that he'd begun, "I happen to *know* you're going to run into traffic by Second Avenue at the latest."

The large, unstable brown eyes shifted in and out of the rearview mirror. "You think I haven't driven to this place before?" he asked. "I know this place and on Tuesday night at ten-thirty P.M. is quite vacant."

"Tonight is not going to be vacant," Wally shouted. Then, to me, "Is it, Sugar?"

"Is always vacant on Tuesday night at ten-thirty P.M.," the cabby insisted.

We'd pulled out of the park and onto Eighty-sixth Street at Fifth. Traffic ahead looked sparse.

"You're seeing?" the driver asked.

Wally turned to me and began to nibble my ear. The large eyes in the rearview mirror looked away.

The cabby almost ran the light at Lex. Ahead, I could see traffic thickening on Eighty-sixth. Wally was now French-kissing me. The cabby couldn't stop looking at us in the mirror. At Third Avenue, two turning busses were stopped in the middle of the intersection. The brown eyes continued to look back and forth at us then at the road ahead.

By Second Avenue, I could see dozens more taxis here than one would have expected. Ahead of us, I saw the cab with Junior Obregon and Reinhold's distant relation in the backseat.

At First Avenue, we stopped dead in traffic.

Wally dropped his head into my lap and began nuzzling my crotch.

In the rearview mirror, the eyes were searching for and not finding Wally: they were startlingly large.

Horns were blaring all around us. Ahead, the traffic jam was solid all the way to FDR Drive. Wally lifted his head, and though I couldn't see his face, I was sure he was doing something amazingly lewd with his mouth. He dropped his head again. I thought the cabby's large brown eyes would pop out of their orbits.

The horns blowing in and out of chorus were suddenly punctuated by the electronic wail of an EMS van. Which occasioned even more horn blowing, and heads out the window shouting. Evidently the emergency unit was coming up First, right at us.

We'd been moving a few feet at a time, and the preoccupied cabby suddenly found himself sticking out about three quarters into the avenue, any further progress blocked by cross cars inching past, any possible backward move stopped by cars who'd pulled up close behind. The blare from the horns and the shouting from nearby drivers and pedestrians waiting to cross was both fierce and ugly. Our cabby was trapped, and if he'd been nervous before, now he was a complete wreck. He shouted back, he swore, he tried moving the car ahead—right into the side fender of a sedan—prompting its driver to stop dead, get out of his car, and begin thumping on our cab's hood. Our driver rolled up his window and backed away, lightly tapping the front bumper of the car behind.

His head in my lap, Wally was laughing.

Finally, the EMS van pulled through, and in a matter of seconds traffic began to move again. Drivers got back in their cars, and everyone moved. Our cabby charged ahead, swerved to a sudden stop with a screech of all four tires at the line of parked cars. He turned around and began shouting:

"You cannot do this! You cannot! You have almost made me a accident!"

When I continued to ignore him, he got out of the car and opened the back door. Wally had turned around, still leaning across my knees, and he put a casual hand up to the side of his head.

"Well? What's holding us up now?" Wally asked.

"You must get out," the driver was shouting. He made the error of reaching forward in an attempt to touch Wally, who kicked out violently. The driver drew back. "You cannot do this. You cannot!"

"Do what?" Wally asked, totally blasé.

"You know very well what. Filths! Terrible filths!"

"All the filth is in your mind!" Wally said. "Now, get back in and drive us to where we want to go."

"Never! Never! With all this filths!" the driver insisted. "You must get out!"

"Not until you've driven us to where we're going," Wally insisted, quietly, rationally, implacably.

"This I will not do! You must get out!"

"Not on your life!"

"Then I will call a gop." That's how he pronounced it.

The driver spun around in the street, looking for a policeman. Naturally none was present, several precincts full having been drained and with their hands full a few blocks away at Gracie Mansion. He reached into the front seat, pulled out the change maker, flagged shut the meter, and removed the keys from the ignition. We weren't going anywhere. This was serious. The cabby now began making wider forays from the taxi, still looking for a cop. Whenever he returned to the cab, he'd repeat that we had to get out or stop "making filths." And Wally would say something irritatingly casual like "Sue me!"

This ridiculous standoff might have gone on all night, but as I sat there listening to them, I suddenly had this image of Alistair's locked bathroom door, with the White Woman on the other side, pounding, pounding and shouting Alistair's name, and behind the door, Alistair on the floor, his head on the floorboards haloed by a score of Tuinals.

I knew it wouldn't happen precisely that way. And I knew there was nothing I could do now—could I tell him not to take the pills I myself had given? But the awful vision on top of the annoyance of Wally pulling exactly what I had feared he would try to pull with this cabby was too much for me.

I extricated myself from under Wally's body and began to open the door on the other side of the taxi.

"Where are you going?" Wally almost shouted.

"Got to find a phone," I said.

"Rog!" He grabbed me by the collar of my Sauvage leather jacket, sounding betrayed. "This is important!"

"You've been provoking him since we got into the cab."

"But . . ." Wally's eyes opened huge whenever he had something crucial to say, as though Nature, realizing what it had produced in Wally, further aided him in a fix by increasing the hypnotic qualities of those orbs. ". . . He's discriminating against us."

I awkwardly half stood, half rested one bent knee upon the seat.

How could I make him see reason? "We're two blocks from a massive demonstration. Can't you wait to be political until we get there?"

"Rog, we've got to take a stand whenever and wherever we are," he insisted. To me, this was the instant-gratification argument, and what we had was the gay generation gap in a nutshell.

"Fine." I opened the taxi door, interrupting what I suspected was going to be a well-rehearsed speech. "You take *this* stand. I'm going to the demonstration and take *that* one."

Wally had released his grip on my jacket. He now grabbed my knee. "Wait!"

I could see the cabby three-quarters of the way down the block, trying to shake coins back from a public telephone that had no function except to gobble money. One could hardly expect his mood to show much improvement when he did return.

Abruptly Wally said, "Why is it suddenly that I don't know for certain what's right!"

I was astonished by this cry of anguish torn from his otherwise Apollonian chilled soul.

"I know I'm right about this," he went on. "And yet I want like crazy to get out of here and already be at Gracie Mansion!"

I could see the cabby kicking the telephone: a substantial athletic feat given his weight and rotundity.

"Ro-ger! Help me!"

"How can I help you, Wals? I'm part of your problem!"

As Wally couldn't help me about Alistair's probable suicide either, being he opposed it so totally.

"And this poor schmuck of a cabby," I went on, beginning to see it all link up, "he's probably convinced that he's taking a stand, because you and I are some kind of crypto-racists, discriminating against him because his skin is brown."

Wally's mouth dropped open.

"As those cooks in the Hunan Hell before probably thought we were discriminating against them or at least offending them by kissing in public."

I could see that Wally saw it all come together. But I could also see the cabby, in a complete state of fuming ire after his run-in with NYNEX-on-a-stick, was now trudging back toward the taxi.

"But, Rog . . . ," Wally asked, "if that's all true, then . . . where does it . . . stop?"

What was I supposed to say? What the humanists for centuries have said? That only brotherhood stops it? Love? He'd laugh me around the corner if I even hinted at it.

I began to say "I don't know, Wals," then changed it to "It stops with you and me. In bed together."

This was something Wally not only understood but wouldn't mock. At least I hoped for the sake of us he wouldn't.

He looked unpersuaded, so I got out of the taxi. The cabby was approaching fast; his hatred seemed to have intensified on his scowling face. He'd grasped his metal change maker through its back handle in one fat hand and now held it out as though it were brass knuckles. He trudged toward me like doom.

This was it. He'd slug me. Wally would slug him. We'd never get to the demonstration, but would instead be arrested for brawling in the gutter.

Then Wally was out of the taxi, blocking me. It looked as though he were holding out something in his hand. Yes, he was holding out a ten-dollar bill, thrusting it at the cabby. I knew Wally had already spent his money tonight, so this had to be his only-in-a-dire-emergency cash kept in his Levi's tiny hip pocket. A real sacrifice.

"Keep the change!" Wally said brightly to the suddenly befuddled taxi driver. All I could do was shrug. I slowly stumbled after Wally, who'd already strode off, headed up Eighty-sixth Street.

As I passed the cabby, I saw him fingering something in his other hand, the one *not* holding the change maker; it looked like some kind of beads. Yes, that's exactly what it was—prayer beads! I was so surprised not to see a knife or blackjack that it didn't strike me for a minute why he'd been fingering the beads: he'd been praying there wouldn't be a fight—even in his great anger and sense of righteousness. The opening lines of *The Dhammapada* flew into my mind: "All living creatures fear death."

Two blocks farther up, I spotted Wally. He was across the street, holding a phone, waving the receiver at me.

When I managed to get through the traffic to where he stood, Wally said, "You were going to call Alistair?"

I took the receiver and hung it up. "You never stop! You're incorrigible!"

Wally wasn't in the least upset. He took my hand and pulled me along.

"C'mon, slowpoke. The demonstration will be over!"

"But I've got to stop him from taking the pills!" I said. "I've got to reach Orkney and tell him."

"No," Wally said. Grabbing me by one shoulder, Wally began to lead me away, up the sloping walkway to the promenade, repeating, "No. You've already done what you had to."

"But . . . If Orkney knew . . ."

Wally walked me over to the steel pipes running horizontally along the river side of the promenade. Across the churning water was Long Island, Queens, Sunnyside. I found myself thinking, Sunny side of the street. Gold dust at my feet. Clouds had begun to thicken the night sky. I could make out the pearled necklaces of lights from three bridges.

"If I call now, I can stop him!" I explained.

"You have to let whatever happens happen," Wally said. "It's out of your hands now, Rog."

He wasn't kidding, nor was he setting me up for some judgmental shit. This was Wally being Wally. The real Wally. The Wally I could trust, could rely on. The Wally who sometimes—not often but sometimes—saw with total clarity and let me know it.

"Then he'll die," I said.

"He'll die," Wally confirmed.

I pulled away. This was too much. "He doesn't deserve this!"

"Doesn't he?" Wally asked. "He's done awful things to you."

I stared at his unyielding face, then I let Wally take my arm and move me toward Gracie Mansion. He was right, of course, Alistair had done terrible things to me. Terrible things to several people.

I'd never met my mother's cousin Diana, so when the plane finally landed at Burbank Airport just before sunset that late June day, I had no idea whom or what to expect. Given what little I'd overheard between my parents and my sister of Cousin Diana's history—divorces, remarriages, travels to strange places—I expected someone totally glamorous: a combination of Barbara Rush and Dagmar.

What I got instead was a slightly spiffier version of my mother. True, Cousin Diana wore dark glasses and a silk kerchief tied around the middle of her long, thick, unnaturally blond-streaked hair, not covering it so much as dividing it and lifting it off the back of her neck. Also true, she wore a silk blouse unbuttoned in front much farther down than I would have expected to see on a woman her age, close-fitting tan slacks that revealed more of her than if she'd been nude, and high-heeled sandals through which her bright carmine big-toe nails glimmered. She was waiting for me at Arrivals, and she recognized me instantly—from photos my mother had sent, I assumed—gathered me up into her musky, rather large bosom (unhindered by any bra, I couldn't help but note), and welcomed me with a hug and a light kiss.

"It wasn't too awful a flight?" she asked in a voice suggestive of the onset of laryngitis.

This had been my first airplane flight, filled with wonder upon wonder. I replied, "It was okay."

She'd already corralled a redcap, who located my two suitcases and brought them out to the parking lot. As I stepped out of the hangarlike building, I felt I was stepping into a place truly different from any I'd known before: dry, warm weather, yet balmy, with breezes, an astonishingly cloudless blue sky, a bright disk of sun slowly descending toward a horizon defined by a distant mountain range. Palm trees were the tallest nearby objects. Rows and rows of them patrolled everywhere I looked, guarding the low, wide airport buildings, the immense parking lots. But what impressed me most was the enormous amount of sheer wasted space everywhere I happened to glance.

Cousin Diana's car was a six-year-old Chrysler station wagon, a stodgy high-bodied vehicle with wood paneling except for its forest-green metal hood and roof. Drearily suburban, I thought, until I jumped into the front passenger seat and noted that the speedometer went up to 120 mph, and when I started to roll down the windows, she asked, "Wouldn't you rather have the air-conditioning?"

Wouldn't I?

The late fifties and early sixties were the years of great construction of the L.A. freeway system. As we drove south out of Burbank Airport, along Vineland Avenue toward the mountains ahead, I was constantly amazed to see enormous sections of crisscrossing cloverleaf ramps just sitting there in midair every few miles, unconnected to any likely road. For Cousin Diana they were merely a nuisance, obstacles to be gotten around, objects worthy of passing interest—"This is where the Ventura and Hollywood freeways will meet. Eventually. Up ahead is Ventura Boulevard. But that's different."

In fact, Cousin Diana had a constant patter of conversation filled with names and Spanish-sounding places, few of which I understood. Her nonstop conversation was more or less as follows:

"I told Dario this car wasn't taken care of properly the week in the shop. I should have taken the Bentley, even though he just washed and polished it!"—To me, the Chrysler ran fine. But a Bentley? They had a Bentley? I'd never seen one outside the auto show at the Coliseum. Who was Dario?

And:

"I hoped your cousin would come with me to meet you. But he's been gone all day. I know he had a dance class earlier, and he probably went to Topanga to surf. Or over to Judith's. Even so, I wish he'd check in once in a while."—What cousin? Alistair? A *dance* class? Where was Topanga? Who was Judith? Did mother and son *ever* see each other?

And:

"Now you tell Inez if there's anything special you eat. And, of course, anything you won't or can't eat. Are you allergic to anything? Alfred's allergic to almost everything. Your cousin's a vegetarian. Lacto-ovo type, of course. Almost all of us are, except Dario, of course, which drives Inez crazy. She's off Sundays, so we generally eat out. Or fix it ourselves. Do you cook? Dario's wonderful with the barbecue. Do you like barbecue?"—Lacto what? Inez, I guessed, was their cook. But who was Alfred? And *who* was Dario?

And:

"We're not going directly to our place, you understand. If we were to do that, you'd have to take Ventura almost to Stone Canyon then . . . What am I saying? You wouldn't know Beverly Glen from Mulholland, would you? We really should stop up at the project. Alfred should be there. And your cousin might be too, although that's unlikely. I'll call the house from there. Dario might know where he is."—What project? What kind of project? Who was this Alfred? And, above all, who was the omniscient Dario?

We'd already driven into the mountains upon a road that began to swerve and curve and rise ever more narrowly, so that while on one side we hugged flower- and vine-covered retaining walls with steep little stairways leading up to front and side entrances, on the other side we overlooked little more than the roofs of other houses, or an occasional carport, sometimes a group of trees, beyond which I caught sudden glimpses of abysslike drops, and beyond them an immense sweep which Cousin Diana assured me at various points was "the valley," then confused me by calling "the city," although the two views looked alike and in the second one I could make out nothing from this distance even vaguely like an *urbs*—no skyscrapers, no public buildings, nothing but miles upon miles of evenly ranged rectangular blocks of single-story houses, surrounded by greenness and outlined by the omnipresent palms.

The Chrysler arrived at a longer though not straighter road—Laurel

Canyon Boulevard—and after driving a few miles, we turned off again and commenced to wind around the city and valley until we reached a second wide road, which she assured me was Coldwater Canyon, though it looked the same to me. A dozen turns later, we were on a long dirt road ascending deep into dry chaparral.

"I hate this part," Cousin Diana said as we approached and bumped hard over a rough apex of dirt road. Ahead I saw that our route suddenly dropped onto a wide apron of peninsula high above its surroundings, stripped bare of foliage, upon which a dozen long irregular foundations and three halfway completed houses perched, arranged more or less around a splayed semicircle of dirt lane evidently later to be paved. Tractors, steam shovels, dump trucks, flatbeds, and pickups littered the area. At least twenty workmen were in sight, busy at various tasks. I assumed this was the "project" she'd mentioned as we'd left the airport, but I was most struck by how very high and isolated it all was, overlooking the surrounding land the way a medieval castle lorded it over its demesne.

I was drawn to the spectacular view. While Cousin Diana parked and strode about looking for someone—Alfred? Dario?—I walked as close to the edge of the butte as I could, bypassing a gigantic hole which I supposed had been dug for a future swimming pool. From where I stood on the cliff, it must have been close to six hundred feet down. Far below, a double-lane road unfurled aimlessly through more dry, wooded hills, which seemed to go on and on in gnarled humps to the horizon in every direction.

"I wager you don't have anything like this back east," a man's voice said in a British accent.

Astonishing really that Oxonian voice, given that the person containing it looked like another of the laborers on the property, by now finishing work for the day and beginning to drive off. Tall, shambling, wearing filthy overalls and no shirt to hide his dirt-streaked, potbellied, straggly-haired torso, but a crushed and tar-stained, overwashed powderblue baseball cap that shadowed his shaggy eyebrows and deep-set eyes, the man smiled crookedly through an unkempt mustache and beard, and when I didn't answer, he asked, "I'm not mistaken? You are the cousin?"

I stood up to say yes and introduce myself and to shake his hand, but it was so dirty he wouldn't and I couldn't.

"Alfred Descoyne at your service, sir!" He gestured what might have been a bow at me. "Named after the old Poet Laureate. Or the West Saxon king who let the old lady's corn cakes burn to a crisp. Never quite sure which. Al to my friends and the men here. But Alfred at the house, what with Alfred and Alistair and too many Al's altogether, if you get my drift."

Behind us we heard Cousin Diana's throaty shout.

"Her Grace," Alfred said, indifferently nodding back to where Cousin Diana was picking her way toward us through various pieces of equipment. Looking me up and down, Alfred said, "You look fit enough. If ever you want to get your hands blackened, you're welcome to give a hand here. We're behind schedule and always short of help and we pay a good wage." He pronounced schedule as though it had no c, which surprised me. "But as you're on holiday," he went on, "I suspect you'll prefer laying about and all that other la-di-da His Nibs has made into an art."

"There you are, Alfred." Cousin Diana reached us. "Stop!" she commanded uselessly as he grabbed her with one muscular begrimed arm and pulled her over for a rough kiss. "You two have met, I see," she said, pulling herself away from him and continuing to slap at his exploring hands.

"What is this?" I asked.

"Our development," she replied. "Fourteen homes with pools and views."

I wondered who the "our" referred to.

"Creosote Crescent," Alfred said, smiling crookedly at his own joke.

"It's called Chaparral Point!" she corrected.

"Alistair bought the land and hired the architect, and they worked up the plans," Cousin Diana explained. "But, as usual, once it got going, he left me with all the hard work."

"She's a regular devil behind that earth mover!" Alfred joked.

"Don't listen to him!" she said to me. To Alfred: "I couldn't reach him on the phone. Has he been here today?"

"Rang up once. Didn't have the honor myself."

They moved away to have a more private conversation, from which I gathered problems existed. Still, I was impressed. My cousin, the troublemaker, was a land development entrepreneur!

Within minutes of our arrival, the place was emptied of workers. We left too, Diana and I in the station wagon, Alfred—with a torn T-shirt on—following in a pickup. Off the mesa, the setting sun was more apparent. For another fifteen minutes, we drove through patches of low-angled, almost woundingly intense orange sunlight alternating with deep, chilled shadow. It was dark when at length we drove in through a gateway and parked. The sky had turned that electrical blue it sometimes does, which only served to throw into greater relief the thick slabs of front walls draped with unknown blooms, which was all I could make out of the house.

I was shown to my room—a suite really—off one long corridor, with glass doors opening onto a balcony overlooking the huge backyard, terrace, and pool. I showered, changed, and after wandering about the oddly split-level house, found my way to the large space-age kitchen, where a rotund ink-haired woman—Inez, I gathered—was holding court, simultaneously talking quickly in a thick accent, cooking four or five dishes, and mixing drinks for Cousin Diana, Alfred (somewhat cleaned up if no less scruffy), and to my surprise, me. The three of us dined about an hour later, with candles on the table, in the glass-enclosed dining room overlooking the by now bluely lighted pool, and I was so overexcited and exhausted I began to fall asleep sometime during "Gunsmoke" and allowed myself to be led to bed.

All in all, I thought in the few seconds before I conked out completely, my visit had begun auspiciously. I liked Cousin Diana, Alfred, Inez, and above all I liked California. But then, I hadn't seen Alistair yet. Nor had I met Dario.

My eyes flashed open. Russian-green shades allowed slashes of morning sun to slide in. Redwood beams crossed the ceiling. I was in a strange room. Then I remembered: California.

Outside my window—all sounds seemed mere inches away—I heard a sudden and very loud splash of water.

I jumped out of bed and leapt to the window—in time to see a slender figure slide underwater through the pool to the other side. It bunched up, then slid underwater in the opposite direction. At that end a head rose out of the water briefly then dunked back in as the youth continued his below-surface laps back and forth, again and again, coming up for air sometimes after one lap, more often after two. I was so enthralled by the rhythm I almost missed seeing the other figure, kneeling among the wide shelf of plants under the dining room, where sneering birds of paradise jostled one another. From my angle all I could make out of the second person was strong, tanned knees in beige shorts, a wide-brimmed sunhat, and large, dirty brown-gloved hands working trowels and shears. I suppose what made me look at the second figure was the fact that instead of working, he was looking so much at the first figure. I decided that the man in the hat and shorts was Dario, the delphinid-boy in the pool my second cousin Alistair.

Downstairs, Inez waved a big earthenware mug at me.

"Coffee!" she said. "But stay off my floor. I just washed."

I was sent out to the terrace, where she handed me the coffee through a little window then leaned on the sill and took my break-fast order as though she were a waitress working one of the new take-out burger stands Cousin Diana and I had passed the day before. I settled myself at the outside table and sipped my coffee, trying to get my bearings.

Not the easiest task. Like the rest of the house, the terrace was on several not completely distinctive levels, set amid a lush growth of the oddest assortment of flowers and trees: candleflower bushes dwarfed by cypress trees, next to screw cacti, next to stands of tall nearly black iris, next to what looked like giant powder puffs on long stems. Their cam-ouflage, as well as my difficulty in telling one long, almost identical glass-and-cedar-walled wing from another, or in guessing what each sudden outcropping of granitic wall contained, kept me from ever really discovering the complete plan of the house, even when it was later shown to me.

I'd been sitting with my coffee for maybe five minutes when the swimmer came up the steps, shaking his wet head like a great dog.

"Hey! Watch it!" I jumped out of my chair.

"Sorry!"

He didn't sound or look sorry. What he looked was tall and tan and confused.

"Hand me that terry robe, will you."

It was clear he had no idea who I was. This, strangely enough, pleased me. I sat down. He pulled a pack of Tareytons out and lit one. After exhaling, he was about to say something, then thought better of it and instead inhaled again, looking away.

I followed his glance down to the nearest level beyond the pool, where the man in shorts and gloves and sunhat was now working in a bed of tubular orange flowers. As his head was down, I couldn't see his face.

Inez came out of the house with my breakfast on a tray, and with it a second, prescient, mug of coffee for him.

"Oh!" He suddenly seemed to understand. "I thought you were here to see Mother."

"This is your cousin from Nueva York," Inez said. "Eat all!" she commanded. "Him!" referring to Alistair, with a Latin shrug, "he eats who knows what? The air, I think."

When she'd gone, I ate. Alistair smoked and looked away.

"I remember you differently," he mused. "Smaller or . . . different!" he concluded vaguely.

I said we'd both changed, physically at least, and while we could no longer be taken for twins, sitting next to each other, we still shared some features. "Of course, you're taller," I assured him. I noticed a half-moon scar over one eyebrow. "How did you get that?"

"This?" touching it gently, as though it were still fresh. "Diving off a cliff in Acapulco. Mexico." He added, "Twelve stitches. I needed something anyway. You know, to put on my passport where it says any scars or distinguishing features. A rather high cliff at that," he mused again, puffing distractedly. "You're here for how long?"

"Don't have a clue."

"I see. Well, it's a pretty drab scene, as you can tell, what with the Mexican Mama and Alfred Engels and Mother Courage all rushing about trying to be busier and more virtuous than Saint Agatha. Still, I suppose," he said, looking at me directly for the first time, "you're presentable enough to take around. You don't surf, do you?"

I'd surfed some at Gilgo Beach and told him.

"Well, that's a point in your favor," he said and was once more distracted, looking at the gardener. Who, surprisingly, in those few minutes of our chat, had managed somehow to move much closer to us, perhaps by leaping the way frogs do, as I hadn't seen him rise once. "Don't pay any attention to Dario. He's sort of brain-damaged. Not to mention fixated upon me!"

Alistair stubbed out his cigarette determinedly, grabbed a bottle of tanning lotion from the pocket of his robe, and walked down to the lower level of the terrace, a scant few feet away from the gardener. There, he dropped himself facedown onto the warm flagstones and held the bottle out, directly into a stand of gigantic cannas where the gardener had last been seen. He had to shake it and gesture a few more times before a gloved hand reached out through the stalks for the bottle.

"Pronto, pronto," I heard Alistair mumble.

The gloves came off, and now two bare, tanned, strong hands emerged from the cannas and began to slather the greasy liquid over Alistair's shoulders and back.

"Anche le gambe," Alistair said, and the hands moved slightly to smear the backs of Alistair's long legs.

"Anche cui," Alistair said, pulling down his trunks to expose his buttocks, pinkly white against the otherwise tan back. The hands pulled back as though burnt. I saw the sunhat bob away into the deepest part of the garden.

"You jerk!" Alistair sang out after him.

At that instant, the glass doors slid open and a pretty, petite dark-haired girl my age stepped onto the terrace and shouted, "You lose!" She was wearing Ray-Bans, a pale blue sunsuit, and white ankle socks under ivory-colored high-heeled espadrilles.

Alistair's head popped up. "Park your twat, Judy. I'm busy," he said in a bored tone of voice.

She seemed unoffended, even amused. She lifted her Ray-Bans to gaze seductively at me, made kissy-mouth, then slinked over and sat so close our legs touched.

"You must be Mr. Gorgeous Cousin," she cooed, revealing startlingly gray eyes. "I hope you're not a complete pervert like Stairs."

"That's Judas," Alistair said. "Ignore it and it goes away."

"Not today, Pooch," she said. "We've got serious slumming to do. Do pull up your bloomers. Everyone's seen that tired old moon!"

"What slumming?" Alistair asked.

"You promised to buy me something expensive today."

"Not an engagement ring, however," he said, standing up and joining us on the terrace. To me he said in a tone of complete incredulity, "She refuses to perform fellatio. She'll die an old maid!"

"I thought taunting the Dim Sicilian put you in a good mood," she mused. She suddenly screamed at me—I'd stood up with the tray— "Drop it!" I did. "Look at yourself!" I did, expecting to see my fly opened or half the *huevos rancheros* in my lap. Nothing.

"Stairs!" she cried in alarm. "Look at the apparel!"

"The shirt offends the eyes," he agreed darkly. "The trousers cry out betrayal! Don't you have shorts? And those sneakers! Complete pigs! Cannot be destroyed quickly enough!"

"Cousin-kins," she said and cuddled up to me, "you'll never attract an anilinguist dressed like an aging concierge. Stairs, we simply can't let him out in public like this!"

They each grabbed an arm and dragged me up to my room where, over my protests, Alistair stripped me down to my BVDs while they hunted though my clothing for something suitable. Only one T-shirt— "White and honest," Alistair declared—and a pair of close-fitting swim trunks were deemed "at all usable"; the rest were dropped in a corner.

"Put on the suit," Judy said. "Oh, don't be gauche, darling. I've seen more dick than you've got ingrown hair. Nice butt," she concluded. "Must be genetic. Stairs swears great and binding oaths on his buttocks."

I was dragged to Alistair's suite and into his dressing room, where they rummaged through his castaways—most of the clothing looking unworn to me—until an outfit was put together for me that wouldn't too much offend their sensibilities. Alistair then dressed, and in minutes we were outside, headed for her sky-blue Corvette, when I remembered my wallet in my room.

Coming downstairs, I saw Inez talking on the phone and wondered whether I should tell her I was going out. She seemed busy, so I headed for the front door. I opened it directly into the approaching figure of the mysterious gardener. He stopped. I stopped.

I'd seen so little of him before that I must have gaped openmouthed a long time. I was amazed that he wasn't the gargoyle I'd expected from all of Alistair's talk about him, but instead strikingly handsome, with a face as perfect as though it had been sculpted, with an unblemished tan, long, almond-shaped gray eyes, the entire astonishment framed by exquisite ringlets of jet-black curls.

"*Signore,*" he finally said, bowing slightly.

Confounded by the unexpected sight of him, moved and stirred in some way I didn't at all understand, simultaneously frightened by my confusion, completely unable to reply, I managed to edge my way around him and stumble out to the gravel driveway, where Alistair gestured for me to hop on the back.

"Ciao, Dario," he yelled blithely as we tore off through a squall of flying gravel.

Alistair never did buy Judy anything expensive that day. As we charged onto Beverly Drive, headed toward Sunset, she spotted two convertibles filled with teenagers, parked side by side blocking traffic. Their occupants confabbed excitedly with Judy and Alistair, and it was decided that we should all go to the beach. Judy turned right and began a long chase through Westwood and Bel Air, across the San Diego Freeway—still not yet fully planted—to where Sunset Boulevard became higher and ever more twisting, through a section named Pacific Palisades, from which I could finally see the surf, then down to the ocean itself and along the shore, through towns with odd names like Malibu, until we'd lost the other cars, then found them together, parked at a decrepit open-window restaurant hangout that looked more like a gas station.

"We're this close," Alistair shouted at Judy. "Might as well!"

Without asking what he meant, Judy gunned the Vette past the restaurant, despite shouts from the others who'd seen us. Five minutes later, we were coasting around the immense curve of beach hugging the exposed yellow flank of mountain cliff, passing little but an occasional fishing-tackle-and-bait shop. The omnipresent mountain cliffs gave way suddenly, and I could see a dry valley widen diagonally to the road and sand. A few shops and several cottages were scattered throughout the dale; more cluttered the beach. Tiny road signs successively announced that rock slides, mud slides, and another twenty miles of curving road lay ahead.

"Topanga," Alistair shouted over the rush of wind.

Driving past the cottages, Judy slowed down unaccountably and stopped.

"Last stop! All out!" she shouted. "No transfers!"

I followed as they slogged through the sand toward a distant edifice, a barely standing shack nearest the tide line of all the houses on the beach, its unevenly formed roof shaded by trellises that looked as though they supported not only surprisingly large blooms of purple morning glory but the house itself. As we came closer, Alistair and Judy veered toward the ocean side, where we were greeted by an almost solid fence composed of a score of used surfboards roughly roped together, with an occasional rubber raft stuffed between. A large, sand- and wind-whittled sign had been hung across two boards, hand-painted to read "Keep Out!—Danger!—Mad Woman Within!"

As though in instant confirmation, as we reached the only open side of the place, we heard a female voice shouting—or was it singing?—over loud pop music inside.

They went right in, but I stayed out among the strew of bleached, barnacle-crusted anchors and odd flowerpots—an old motorcycle helmet, an ancient table lamp hollowed out—scarcely containing the copious white, carmine, and fuchsia geraniums. Six unmatched pieces of old den furniture completed the informal veranda's decor.

I'd halted because I'd noticed boys surfing, maybe six of them, each more accomplished than the other. I'd also recognized how good the boys had to be. Those waves were a surfer's dream—or nightmare: huge, so high you could have driven a Volkswagen through the tunnels they formed; regular as a bank clerk's hours yet so powerful that even that far from shore they exposed vast tracts of sand beneath each drawing-in of the tide.

"You ready to ride the Thundering Appaloosa?" I heard a raspy yet young voice ask.

I looked around and spotted its source: sitting astride the open sill of the bow window was a slender youth wearing the most bleached and tattered denims I'd ever seen. He was barefoot, with long, almost prehensile toes and the flat, apparently muscleless torso and all-tendons arms of a surfer since infancy. His face was small, deeply tanned, and highlighted by albino tufts of eyebrow and eyelashes and a trainer mustache, mostly hidden by an all-encompassing sweep of sun-streaked blond hair, cut as though with a bowl over the top, but allowed to grow out to weird proportions.

"Is that what it's called?" I asked.

"Nah!" he rasped, then tumbled out the window onto a persimmon leather chair, using it as a springboard to somersault onto his feet. "See ya," he rasped again, then raced away, around the surfboards and out of sight.

"Where is that little son of a bitch?" a woman shouted, flying out the door after him.

I pointed to where he'd fled. She ran past the flowerpots and anchors and stood in the sand calling after him, "Next time, I'll rip your nuts off!"

She turned toward me. What I'd thought at first to be a middle-aged hag, from her voice and her stance and her girth and her sacklike housedress, was in fact a young woman, quite fat, not pretty, with a large mass of uncombed reddish hair. "Who're you?" she demanded.

"Came with Alistair," I said.

"Oh," she replied. "I thought you were another Skeezix."

She lumbered past me into the dilapidated house. "What are you waiting for? The butler? Come on in."

The largest room contained less real furniture than the outside: a half dozen mattresses on the floor, alongside partly burnt candles in bizarre holders and a half-furled sleeping bag. One ajar door revealed a bathroom, another a bedroom with a real double bed, probably hers; a third room was bare except for more mattresses. The kitchen was old-fashioned, large, right out of "Ozzie and Harriet," nearly filled up by a round oak table and ten chairs. Judy, Alistair, and the woman were seated at the arc closest to the window, sipping coffee from mismatched mugs. As I sat down, the woman grunted her satisfaction and poured me a mugful from a battered old percolator, all the while continuing her tirade.

". . . think they can get away with murder, little bastards! Give them all the head and cunt and food and uppers and downers a boy could ask for, but ask one to do a measly little favor . . . little pricks!"

"Jewel is housemother here," Judy said. Then she pointed outside to, I supposed, the youths riding the waves.

"Last week I got this refrigerator from Harry Calpard . . . you know old Harry, horny old fucker! For nothing! Well, maybe not exactly for nothing, but almost nothing, and how long do you think it took me to round up enough of those peckerheads to help me move it? Three days! Three fucking days! While cheese went sour and OJ turned to motor oil in the heat. Wouldn't have gotten it even then if I hadn't put my foot down and said not a dick gets milked till I get that fuckin' fridge. What's your name, honey? You a homo like Stairs here? This fruit gets more action off my boys than I do, and what does he give them? A ride in an Alfa Romeo. Dumb peckerheads!"

Jewel continued her monologue, not allowing me a break to get in an answer, getting more foul-mouthed and expressing more annoyance than I thought possible in one so young. Alistair and Judy sat back and laughed and goaded her on. I remained silent, picking up more salacious idioms, facts, and opinions in twenty minutes than I'd heard in my entire life. Clearly, she had been the model for their slightly wittier use of bad language.

From what I pieced together, Jewel had been married to a Seabee— "You never met a more scum-faced liar and thief, but he was hung like a negro donkey and beautiful as a picture book!"—when she was sixteen, and when he vanished two years later, she got the house, now universally known along the beach as "Jewel's Box." Directly in front of it was the Topanga Pipeline, favored by surfing denizens for thirty miles up the coast. One or two of them began to stop by for a "glass of OJ" and since Jewel was lazy and lonely, they'd stay for a hop in the sack. More and more of the youths started visiting, hauling junk over, bringing in mattresses, hanging out, sleeping over when things got difficult at home, until little by little, inexorably, without her quite knowing how, Jewel had become in her own words "functioning provider, bedmate, and mother confessor" to a gang of them.

Despite her complaints, it was clear that Jewel had gone from being a fat and unattractive teenager and neglected wife to being a local character—"al-leged in my own time." Her newfound fame, all the attention she got, the constant boys underfoot, the abundant sex she got from them were far more than a girl from Covina with her looks had any reason to expect out of life.

"Not that one of them is any good except for riding the pipeline and slipping a dick into a wet place," she concluded acidly.

As though on cue, the surfers arrived, all of them looking like slight variations on the first boy I'd seen: yelling, shoving their boards deep into the sand, punching and pushing one another, falling over the veranda furniture, spilling into the house through doors and windows, filling the kitchen, demanding food and drink, kissing, pinching, and groping Jewel, slapping palms high in the air to Alistair and Judy— until they had pretty much disrupted everything and emptied the coffeepot and several shelves of the refrigerator, and Jewel had had enough and simply stood there shrieking, "Out, out, out!" And all of us were forced out onto the veranda—except for one youth, Sandy, who was peremptorily called back in by his hostess, and who sheepishly returned inside, to a chorus of hootings, moanings, and fake orgasms by the others.

Judy, her car, and Alistair's cash were requisitioned for a trip to Granny Pizza, down the road. I joined her and "Crash," a red-haired boy, to bring back the goodies. All the short distance to the take-out place and back, Crash sat behind us, backward on the Vette's ledge, so that his legs lay spread across the trunk and his head lay in my lap—Judy would grab his nose instead of the gearshift every once in a while and say, "Oops."

While we waited for the pizzas, Crash told us he was the best backward surfer in the country, probably the world, which I thought a dubious distinction at best.

"I do everything backward or upside down," Crash said in his slow, deliberate way, and he went on to expound his theory of upside down and backward to us—"Ya see, if everything were upside down, then no one could hassle ya, because no one would know what side was up, ya get it?"

To which Judy replied, "Does that mean Jewel has to smell your nasty old feet while you're boffing her?"

I was surprised to see Alistair stripped down to his bathing trunks, surfing the pipeline with the others when we got back. Surprised, I suppose, to see how well he fit in with the others, who joshed with him and seemed to accept him as one of their own.

After we'd all eaten and lain around on the sand complaining that we'd eaten too much, I was also lured into the water. One of the fence boards was pulled up for me to ride, and Sandy, returned to his friends—"Hey, Lamebrain! It's your turn to play slip the weenie," he shouted to another lad as he exited—rode out next to me beyond the breakers, and in between chewing a wedge of vegetarian whole-wheat pizza and constantly rearranging his penis in his jams, he tried to explain to me how to "take the ass end of a wave" without killing myself.

Following about a hundred spills and near drownings, I managed to keep my footing long enough to ride a minor tunnel all the way in, stepping off the board onto a half inch of water and dry sand just as they did—to assorted cheers and jeers.

That was the signal for us to leave. Judy was already at the car, and I was shocked to see that it was almost sunset. The boys were still on their boards out at the breakers as we drove away.

"Have fun?" Judy asked, as she dropped us off at the house.

I'd thought that she'd paid particular attention to me that afternoon, given all the boys she'd been surrounded by. She'd gotten up from her towel to urge me on when I was riding a wave; she'd praised my nerve and resolve when I'd finally suceeded in taking one in.

"Sure," I said. "What about you? You hardly got wet."

"I have my own kind of fun," she said enigmatically. "Tomorrow?"

"Sure," I replied.

Alistair put a comradely arm about my shoulder as we walked to the house. "Don't get carried away, okay?" he said, as the Vette sent up a sheet of gravel driving away.

Before I could ask him to explain, we were inside, and Cousin Diana was standing there, holding a hand over the phone receiver.

"Whenever you find the time, Mr. Dodge."

Alistair let go of me. "What is it now?" The change in his voice was evident.

"I want to talk to you about Dario," she said.

"What about him?"

"Don't you want to shower and change, honey?" Cousin Diana asked me.

I took that as a command. Despite the noise of the shower from my rooms at the end of the big house, I could hear them shouting at each other.

That first day seemed to set the pattern for the following weeks. We'd get up, breakfast around the pool, Judy would come by or would phone, and after Alistair had annoyed Inez and played whatever game it was he was playing with Dario, we'd spend the rest of the day away from the house: hanging around Westwood's shopping area—filled with students and teens—or stopping by the Malibu beach house of a once famous German émigré novelist, to visit his two adolescent children, or driving down to Hollywood and Vine and wasting time, or sunning and playing volleyball at Will Rogers State Park with Siggie and Marie-Claude and other friends of Judy's, under tall cliffs at the top of which perched an enormous glass and redwood-roofed structure. I was told Aly Khan had erected it for Rita Hayworth as a honeymoon cottage. To each side and beneath the edifice—now a restaurant— could be seen cannon-emplacement bunkers built high into the cliffs during the last war, now gunlessly guarding the shore from Japanese sneak attacks. More often, we'd end up at Jewel's Box, which I soon realized was the preferred spot because it was farthest from interfering parents.

Before I'd left, my mother had told me that Alistair was different from the snotty know-it-all little boy he'd been at nine. During my first weeks in Southern California, I had to agree with her assessment. Possibly because he wasn't a stranger, but in his own element, Alistair was far friendlier to me, far easier with me than I had any right to expect. He introduced me to strangers without a hint of that involuntary wince teenagers make and other teens instantly recognize as saying, "I don't like him either, but I have to!"

Alistair left me and Judy together with no compunction while he went off with the others. He never once put me down or sneered at me. He would quietly and in detail explain who people I'd just met or was about to meet were and what their relationships were. Whenever I did something to show that I too fit in—chugalugging a bottle of beer, taking a strong wave into shore—he'd make sure the others knew of it: "Hey! Did you see that!"

Which hardly constituted intimacy. Alistair never told me anything in the least bit private, certainly not his hopes and dreams—and he never asked mine, or even allowed such a topic to arise. I knew that Judy wanted to become a Broadway dancer—a gypsy, she called it. Or a pediatrician. She wavered day to day. I told her my own troubles with my family that summer, how I'd come to hate everything about my life, and had so managed to annoy and depress them all that finally I'd been shipped off to here, this paradise, to cheer me up and, they hoped, to change my attitude. I didn't think I'd yet managed to change my mind about the complete hopelessness of my condition come next fall, when I was slated to go to a state college to study who knew what for Lord knew what kind of eventual career—all of them stank so far as I was concerned.

No, Alistair never spoke of his future, of his mother, or of Alfred. He never mentioned his father either. They seemed to see each other less and less as Alistair got older. And the one time I brought up how great I thought his business project was, Alistair said, "Who wants to work all one's life? This development ought to net me a half million. I'll invest that, and when I get my trust fund at twenty-one, I should be able to do whatever I want." Although what this latter consisted of, he wouldn't even deign to hint to me.

At first I'd assumed that he and Judy were going steady. Wasn't that why he'd been about to warn me on that first day? But as the days passed, I became increasingly uncertain about their relationship. Although Alistair and Judy were together every day, they never held hands, or smooched, or vanished suddenly, to make out the way all the "steadies" I'd ever known did. Once we would arrive at a place, Alistair seemed to leave Judy pretty much on her own. She'd pull out a paperback book or a fashion magazine and read, or talk to Jewel or Marie-Claude or me. From the instant we'd met, I'd thought Judy both incredibly pretty and ultrasophisticated. The more time I spent with her, the more I realized how much of that was merely on the surface. Underneath, Judy was very like the girls I'd known in high school: a little anxious, a little confused, eager to be liked, maybe even loved. When I asked if she minded Alistair ignoring her so much, she said, with a bit of irritation, "He's not my keeper, you know!"

Another time, while slathering suntan lotion upon the creamiest skin of her upper back, I said, "When you and my cousin are married . . ."

She sat up. "Married? You're kidding?"

"I thought . . ."

"If I marry anyone, it'll be Tab Hunter. Or Troy Donahue." She laughed suddenly. "Well, *one* of us will marry Tab Hunter or Troy Donahue."

"One of you?"

"Stairs or me," she said, as though I should already have known that. "My upper thighs, Stodge, please," she added, using the name she and Alistair had invented for me and which constituted my acceptance.

I could have, I should have, asked right then what exactly Judy meant. I thought I knew, but I was both confused and fearful of the explanation. Partly because the signals around me were so confounding.

Back home, in school, among my friends, boys that were effeminate or wimpy or sometimes just ugly, poorly dressed, and pimple-faced were often called faggots and fairies: everyone agreed; no explanations were necessary. In junior high, we'd been more open, more free. We'd played a game in class and through the halls where we'd do something, anything, to draw attention to our crotch in some way, and when someone fell for it and looked, we'd shout with joy, "Gotcha!" And it had been commonplace to push someone and yell out, "Eat it raw! Through a flavor straw."

At first, it seemed the same among the Jewel's Box gang of youths. They were always calling each other "homos," and should one of them become too tender or solicitous, another would quickly bare his bottom and say, "Kiss this, queer!" Jewel and Alistair and Judy were constantly referring to various people—among them my cousin—as "pervs and perverts." Walking with Crash and Sandy along the boardwalk at Venice one afternoon, I'd been surprised to hear Sandy say of a man sitting on a bench, "That guy's a hummersexual."

"Homosexual," I corrected.

"We call 'em hummersexual, because whenever you pass one, he goes, hmmmmmmm!" Sandy illustrated.

Sure enough as we passed by, the man went "Hmmmmmmmmm!"

Yet sometimes when I'd go into the house at Topanga for an OJ or soda, I'd find two or more boys napping together on a mattress in the darkened smaller bedroom, their clothes off, their legs and arms entwined, their hands wrapped around each other's penis. And whenever Alistair went into the smaller bedroom with one or more boys, "to drink beer and fool around," as Crash explained it, the door was firmly closed and everyone else excluded, suggesting *something* more than beer drinking was going on. Then there was the discussion held around an impromptu beach fire one overcast afternoon after Sandy's older brother Cryder had spent a night in jail for "soliciting" on Santa Monica Boulevard.

"Soliciting what?" I'd asked.

"Money, stupid," Stevie said.

I'd seen Cryder riding the Topanga Pipeline, a lean, aggressive boy. He didn't look like the type to beg for money on a street corner.

"I don't get it," I admitted, already expecting their jeers.

Stevie took it upon himself to explain. "Let's say you need some cash, fast. Can't get a job at our age, right? So you go a block north of Hollywood Boulevard, where the steps stick out almost to the street, and you sit there and wait till some guy comes by in a car. When he stops, you talk a little and he asks if you want a ride. You say sure, and you get in and you tell him your ma didn't get her paycheck and you need twenty bucks and he says sure, okay."

"He gives you the money just like that?"

"Well, usually you have to put out." Stevie emphasized the last two words. "We've all done it one time or another."

"It's easy," Spencer agreed. "I never wait more than five minutes."

"I made fifty bucks once," Crash boasted, then was forced to explain that that had required two drivers stopping.

All of which left me even more confused. What had they put out? What had they or the drivers done? If it was what I thought it was—no! It couldn't be! I let the subject drop.

After all, I didn't need money; after all, I was interested in Judy, who seemed interested in me. But although she'd slap my hand away whenever I was oiling her body and tried going into her bathing suit, she never got up or walked away. And once, when she was on her stomach reading and I was watching her bathing suit's dropped straps threaten to bare one of her breasts, she suddenly turned to me and saw what I was staring at and, to my surprise, pulled the blue cotton cup right off it, revealing a pointed red tip.

"There! Happy?" she asked.

"Let me touch it."

"Oh, okay!"

This lasted about five minutes while she continued—or pretended to continue—to read *Seventeen*, before someone came along and she slapped my hand away and popped the breast neatly back into her bathing suit.

It was the very next morning, over huge slices of Crenshaw melon and cups of thick Dominican coffee on the pool terrace, that Alistair said, "Stodge, Judas, you're going to have to play without me this morning."

"Why?"

"I've got to put on a jacket and tie and crap and go with *them* [meaning Cousin Diana and Alfred] to meet with some ghastly bank guy. Should be done by noon. Tell me your shit-ule [parodying Alfred's accent]. I'll catch up with you later."

Alistair didn't catch up with us that afternoon. He was lying on a chaise longue near the pool talking on the telephone when I returned.

"Do you mind?" he asked when I settled next to him. Then he half explained: "Lawyers!"

This was the Alistair from before that I'd remembered. I left.

A few hours later, however, he came into my room and sat there watching me go through my clothing—he and Judy had forced me to buy more at stores they'd selected—and he semi-apologized and explained a bit more:

"It's the project. Either I underbudgeted or Mother and Alfred are overspending. Whichever it is, we have to refinance. The guy we met the other day was a complete shark! Still was picking his teeth from eating the last idiot he'd snookered. I turned him down flat. *They* bitched and moaned, but . . . So, we're going to have to keep looking for a better deal. What a pain in the ass! Bankers!"

As he talked, I recalled the sense I'd had as a nine-year-old whenever Alistair had talked about custody and divorce. It all seemed so grown-up, and I so very backward. Even with his complaints, or maybe because of them, I once again felt out of it, behind the times, a kid.

"I mean, you're pretty settled here now, aren't you?" Alistair asked. Then before I could answer, he said, "Because with all this bullshit, it may be a few days before I can return to my adolescence."

"Sure, whatever you say, Stairs," I replied, thinking maybe now Judy and I could plan to be together and away from the Jewel's Box gang or Siggie and Marie-Claude, and I could, well, who knew what, exactly.

"Look, why don't you take the Chrysler? I know it's a ratty old wagon, but it'll get you there, right?" Alistair said.

That night, when I went to bed, I found the registration and car keys on my bed table. I wanted to thank Alistair, but I woke up late that morning and Inez said that all of them had already left the house.

"Poor Stairs!" Judy said, as I removed the entire top of her bathing suit later that day. "Forced to be normal!"

We were in a sandy little spot in a hidden gully, north of Jewel's Box, where I'd driven us that day. I murmured some reply and continued to kiss and fondle her. In return she reached over and began to play with my erection.

"Oooh, that's nice! But Stodge . . . ?" she asked.

"Ummmm?" I answered, in a state of extreme distraction.

". . . You try to put that thing inside me," she said breathily, "and you're a dead man!"

The discovery that Judy was a virgin, and intended to remain so for some time longer, rattled me considerably. It wasn't merely that from her and Alistair's talk I'd naturally assumed she was already far more experienced than I was; I'd also hoped she'd be the one destined to help me obtain that crucial, that very necessary, experience.

Ungallantly, I didn't quite believe her. Which was why the minute I got back to the house that afternoon, I went in search of Alistair. Surely, I thought, he'd tell me if she was telling the truth. And if not, why not.

Oddly, he wasn't anywhere to be found. Oddly, because his Alfa Romeo was parked out front. Perhaps something was wrong with it and he'd driven somewhere with *them* (I was already half accepting that like all grown-ups they were the enemy) using the Bentley. I knew he wouldn't be caught dead in a pickup, even one right off the assembly line, never mind Alfred's ratty, rattling vehicle. Did Inez know?

She was in the kitchen, singing along to the radio a tune that sounded familiar but whose words made no sense at all—"Do zilwets on dee shayda"—when I asked. "Pleezze, don't bother me. I've got a headache," she said, and went on to sing, "Hmmm, hmmm, de daaay-da."

He's here somewhere, I told myself.

Which of course led to another one of my continuing explorations of the house and property that had so far eluded my grasp. Built by either a student or imitator of Frank Lloyd Wright (it depended upon whether Cousin Diana or Alistair told the story) some ten years before for a toilet manufacturer and his family, the place had been added to considerably since originally planned, although always by the original architect and in the appropriate style—which explained the different levels inside and out, as well as the sudden turnings required to reach certain annexes. So, while not large, the property remained somewhat mysterious: what I'd thought before to be a purely design-element fieldstone wall, for example, was one day revealed as containing the furnace; the pool-pumping equipment was hidden under slabs of gray rock which formed the steps leading down to the flower garden. And this particular afternoon's ramblings were to lead to two discoveries. First, that the free-standing wooden structure half-hidden by boxwood that I'd always thought of as a garden shed was, in fact, the Italian gardener's—Dario's—room. Second, Alistair already knew that fact.

He was inside the room when I knocked on the windowless door. Inside, in bed, wearing nothing, smoking a Tareyton, and reading a copy of the *Wall Street Journal*, when I knocked, heard *"Pronto,"* and thinking he was Dario, opened the door and stepped in.

"What are you doing here?" we asked each other.

Alistair spoke first. Pulling me over to sit on the bed next to him, he said, "Isn't it cute? Look at the way he's made it homier!"

At first I didn't see what he meant. Aside from the large, low bed, the only furnishings were a battered rattan chest of drawers and what I took to be its companion chair.

Alistair pointed to one bare wall, the substantial floor molding transformed into a narrow shelf, upon which leaned an overdecorated mandolin, a cheap vase filled with dusty cloth roses, and a yellowing chromolith in a baroque frame of some unknown metal, the photo of an old woman in a dark dress, her face barely visible within the shadow of a black shawl drawn over her head. Above the bed a large sepia tint of a gruesomely contorted Crucifixion had been thumb-tacked to the wall, adorned with a wreath of fresh laurel leaves, now dry and crumbling.

"I thought you were him," Alistair said. "I need your help, Stodge."

That was a new one, I thought. If anyone needed my help less it was he. "How? What for?"

"To seduce Dario! Well, actually, I have seduced him. Now all I have to do is get him in the sack long enough and often enough to tie him to me by bonds lighter than air and tighter than steel."

What the hell was he talking about?

"What I actually need you to do is be lookout for us," Alistair said.

Before I could ask any of the dozen questions I had, he went on.

"Like most Mediterranean men, he's very sensual. Also chicken. So, if you're on guard while we're in here, it'll free his mind to do what we want to do."

He explained it so rationally, half my questions vanished.

"And the beauty of it," Alistair said excitedly, "is that you don't have to do anything. Just hang around the pool or up in your room, and if you see one of *them* happen to be looking for Dario when we're in here, you simply come warn us."

"How?"

"Knock on the door. Three times fast. Or on the window. It's hidden in the cypresses. Not hard to find."

As though I were to be tested immediately, we heard the door open. Dario looked in.

"Go! Go!" Alistair said, pushing me out. *"Vieni, amorino,"* he said to Dario, who stood as though dumbfounded on the lintel. I managed to sidle along the gardener to try to get past him. But if he saw me, he didn't give any indication. His entire field of vision seemed completely taken up by Alistair, risen upon the bed to his knees, his arms out in invitation. Dario stood there a minute in his canvas shorts, exuding a not unpleasant odor composed of loam, dirt, lilies, and sweat. Alistair was saying something I couldn't understand in Italian—given his reassuring tone, probably that they'd be private now that I was on guard. Dario continued to ignore me as he moved toward the bed slowly, I thought like someone in a trance.

I got out of the little house and closed the door behind me.

"Where is he?" Cousin Diana moaned.

Inez was slapping T-bones on the kitchen counter so hard she could have tenderized the bone. She didn't look up.

"Why is it," Cousin Diana went on, "whenever I want him, he's not around?"

Alfred was half snoozing; a can of beer placed atop his firm potbelly rose and fell, rose and fell. He didn't even bother to pretend to hear her.

"I've looked everywhere and I'll be damned if I can find him. Does he just blend into the trees or what?" Cousin Diana continued.

I was attempting to read *The Possessed*, which Judy had foisted on me a few days before and which I was slogging through for the sake of our re-lationship, fully understanding it—I'd read *The Magic Mountain* already; this was light stuff—and, worse, pretending to appreciate it.

"Isn't someone going to answer me!" Cousin Diana slapped Al-fred's arm.

The beer can bobbled and threatened to fall over, but though he barely opened one eye, he managed to catch it and mutter "Sodding kid!" before burbling back into somnolence.

"Roger?" She turned on me.

"I assumed your question was rhetorical."

Her eyes narrowed quickly. "You're even beginning to sound like him."

Which meant that she realized that after five weeks in L.A. I now dressed like her son, spoke like him, and went to places Alistair went—with his friends. Which was only natural.

"Well, it's not rhetorical, it's . . . What is it, Alfred?"

"Interrogational," he mumbled.

"I am not interrogating him! I'm simply asking a question. It's . . . in-formational," she decided, smoothly.

"Steak on the grill. Dinner in ten minutes!" Inez announced.

Alfred more or less came to life at this. I merely shrugged at Cousin Diana. "Wasn't he at Creosote Canyon?" I asked, my use of his nick-name causing Alfred to wink at me behind his beer can.

"Much earlier!" she admitted. "Haven't you seen him? Where have you been all day?"

"At the Slumbergs'," I said, using the name we'd invented for the once-famous émigré writer. "With Judy."

This was cause for new alarm. "Does your cousin know that you're with Judy every day?" Before I could answer, she went on. "You're not getting serious with her, are you? Because if you are . . . And what am I supposed to tell your mother when . . ."

"Cool down," Alfred commanded gruffly. "Let 'em have some fun."

"I'm setting the table," Inez said, in a threatening tone of voice.

Of course I knew where Alistair was, and it was eating me alive. He was in Dario's room doing something godawful with the gardener, and he knew very well what time dinner was, and it increasingly seemed to me that he not only didn't care what he was doing, but was drawing me into it too.

Two days before, there had been a close call. Some neighbors had appeared with Cousin Diana in the garden, and suddenly, instantly, she required Dario to show them something or other. I'd been in my bedroom gabbing on the phone with Judy when I saw and heard the four women below. I hung up, slipped out the door to the little balcony, slinked down to the terrace barely eluding discovery, and cut and slashed my arms and legs sneaking through the boxwood into the cypresses, where I frantically knocked on the window of the gardener's room. Then I stood there—in nothing but my underpants—praying as the women's voices got closer and closer, until I thought I'd scream out of frustration. Just as they reached the cottage, Dario came out, complaining about having a little flu. I waited till they were all out of range, then dashed in myself. Alistair was naked—natch—languidly smoking a cigarette. When I began to chastise him, he merely looked at me and said, "What can I do? He's such an animal, he can't be stopped!"

I could have said no to Alistair, I should have said no. But look at it this way: in return for that one small thing I was to do for him, he'd given me his car, his house, his friends, his wonderful way of life, the beach, sports, and fun in the unstintingly glorious summer weather; he'd given me a new, much more adult way of behaving myself, of dressing myself, of regarding myself; above all, he'd given me his girlfriend, to do with whatever I could get away with. Not only had he given all that to me, but he'd shown me in the greatest detail how to appreciate and enjoy it.

Yes, it was bribery. I blushed thinking it. But where would I have been this summer without it?

"If you want," I said, "I'll go look. Maybe he's in the garage?"

"Doubtless," Alfred sniped, "changing the fuel lines on the Bentley."

I snickered at the ludicrous vision. But I went anyway.

Outside the dining room, dusk was falling, the low sun striking off glints of orange here and there as though in final emphasis, making the rest of the garden look even more shadowy and overgrown. In fact, earlier that day, while sitting at the pool, I'd noticed that the mixed foliage did seem strangely luxuriant, despite Dario's continuous presence and activity snipping and clipping and pruning, despite growing piles of cuttings barely contained in large burlap sacks out by the entry gates, despite the general lack of rain or moisture-laden mists in the past few weeks. As I sidled past the stands of succulents, the baby cholla and Christmas cactus seemed to send out spiky shoots to grab at my socks and nip my bare calves.

From the dining room, I could be seen knocking at the door of the garden room, so I used my hands to machete my way through the boxwood, then brushed away flocks of tendrils vaguely attached to the encroaching cypress trees, their trunks dressed in verdigris, to knock at the little curtained window. While I waited for a response, I had the sensation that although it was nearly night, everything in the least bit botanic was growing inches per second around me. I knocked again.

After what seemed the longest time, I noticed the window open. I reached under the sill, lifted it, and spread the curtains.

The planned exhortation died on my lips.

Before me in the room, outlined by undulations of orange light in the gloaming, Alistair appeared to kneel on the bed, dancing some sort of Polynesian fertility rite, his head thrown back and forward, his arms lifting and falling, his body rocking, moans erupting from deep in his sternum.

I saw that he was kneeling upon the prone body of Dario, who lay under him, his arms crossed behind his dark hair, his entire body slowly writhing upon the mattress in that same tranced rhythm.

I don't know how long I stood there watching them, baffled/ashamed/ entranced by the sight, my nostrils filled with the nightrise of humus and dead leaves from about my feet and, wafting out from inside the room, another musk, sharper, undeniably biological. Suddenly I heard voices on the terrace.

"Stairs!" I whispered fiercely, hoarsely.

He turned to me, his eyes open yet unseeing, and he waved me away with a boneless gesture not unlike that of a Balinese dancer.

"Stairs! They're coming!" I whispered. "Quick!"

He merely leaned forward into the dark curls of Dario's head, the two of them curving like serpents, their orangely defined bodies flattening together, slowly twisting until now Dario was on top, the little sparks of late light remaining in the room tinting as with a kiss the rhythmical apex of his surging buttocks.

"Stairs!" I called out. "You have to stop!"

"What is it!" Cousin Diana's voice, only feet away.

I closed the window and pushed my way out of the boxwood.

"Roger? What are you doing? What's going on?"

Behind her, Alfred loomed, growling that his steak would be burned.

"Nothing," I lied.

"What are you doing there? What's . . ." She seemed to realize something, then turned and rushed to the garden room door. Before I could stop her, she pulled it open, and teetered on the lintel, before almost falling back into Alfred, who'd come up behind her.

He looked inside and muttered, "Sodding kid!" Then Alfred pulled her away and, with a burst of strength, grabbed her up in his arms and carried her off across the garden and terrace to the house, from whence I heard her begin to scream in an unnaturally high-pitched voice.

I no longer hesitated, but went to the door and closed it upon Dario's unceasing buttocks.

The dining room was set for four. I sat down numbly, and Inez immediately served me steak and cottage fries and spinach soufflé, which I ate, surprised by my appetite, my attention bifurcated by the decreasing sounds up a half flight of stairs of Alfred's deep voice and Cousin Diana's whimpers, and by the even more disturbing silence of the distant garden room, now just another undefined shadow in the dimmed outdoors.

Alfred came downstairs, tumbled into his chair, and Inez jumped up and served him. He ate with gusto. A few minutes later, the glass door opened and Alistair stepped in casually, as though he'd been taking a nightly promenade. He sat down and Inez served him, and he also ate with great appetite, despite the almost dreamlike look upon his face.

No one spoke a word. Once, just after Inez served apple pie à la mode, Alfred snorted suddenly, loudly. I jumped in my chair, prepared for an outburst that never arrived. But Alistair didn't seem to notice anything. He wolfed down his pie, drank his glass of milk like a good little boy, excused himself, and went up to his room.

As he reached the landing, Alfred said in a low voice, "Happy now?"

Alistair turned, in that single fluid gesture we'd seen Loretta Young use to turn after entering a room on TV. He stared with a distracted smile.

Dario was arrested the next morning before we woke up. No one said anything about the incident at breakfast or later that day, or in fact until two mornings later, when Cousin Diana suddenly announced, "You'll both have to come down to the courthouse with us for the hearing. Wear your best clothing." I turned to Alistair, but all he said was "The blue-and-maroon tie?" To which his mother nodded assent.

Alistair and I sat alone in the backseat of the Bentley as we drove to downtown L.A., and I kept trying to get his attention to find out what he intended to do, to say. But he eluded me from this close as he'd evaded me ever since that fateful evening.

Two men in gray pin-striped suits, with rich leather briefcases, met us in an anteroom.

"He's got a smart dago lawyer who's claiming entrapment," I heard one of them say, "but he knows it won't work. It's just for honor back in the old country."

They continued to talk, moving away from us. When Alistair asked where the men's room was, I got up my nerve and followed him.

I found him combing his hair at the row of sinks; he was being careful, precise.

"You're not going to let them throw him in jail, are you?" I asked.

"He's not going to jail. He's going back to Sicily."

"But . . . but aren't you going to say anything?"

"If they ask for details, I'm going to say he fucked me in the ass."

"That's what you wanted!" I protested.

He looked at me, then simply said, "I'm a minor."

"But it was all your doing!"

"Don't be a sap, Stodge. I don't intend on having any blot on my name or record. And if you're thinking of saying anything . . . Well, no one will believe you. They'll think you're just doing it to keep Judy to yourself. You understand that, don't you?"

I understood all too well. What I'd merely thought bribery had turned out to be Alistair's insurance on my silence.

He left the bathroom and I stood looking at myself: fool!

What I hadn't understood earlier was that I was to be put on the witness stand. Oh, it wasn't a real trial, only a judge and the lawyers and us and poor Dario—addled-looking and in need of a shave—at the defense table. Even so I was frightened. When Cousin Diana's lawyer called me up and asked me to tell what, exactly, I'd seen looking in the garden room window that night, my shame over my role in Dario's downfall and disgrace filled me so intensely that I blushed and stammered, and after all sorts of dithering, I ended up only answering yes and no— mostly yes—to the lawyer's deadly aimed, totally distorted questions.

Alistair was far cooler, saying he'd been so upset he'd managed to block most of it out. When he stepped down, I was astonished to see Judy appear. She was also put into the witness box, and the prosecuting attorney told us that allegations about her friend had been made and asked her would she answer them, and she said in a voice bold as brass, "Alistair is a completely normal boy of his age. Even if he is," and here she glared at me, "more of a gentleman than some other boys."

That was what did it for me. Judy lying like that, all of us turning to protect Alistair, when we all knew it was his fault. Even Alfred was complicit in his silence. I wouldn't look at anyone when we were sent out to the corridor to await a finding.

Alistair was called in to clarify a point for the judge in camera, as was Judy. I assiduously studied the designs on the marble floor until I thought I'd go cross-eyed. All at once, the lawyers came out of the chamber and it was over, Dario doomed to deportation.

As we were walking up to the house later that afternoon, I fell back to where Alfred was dawdling.

"Is that offer still open?" I asked. "You know, to work at Creosote Canyon?"

"It is," he said. "Anytime you want, lad."

"Tomorrow?" I asked.

"Sure." He held me hard around the shoulders as we went inside.

Alfred woke me up early the next morning, and we drove off in his pickup, and for the next four weeks of my stay, I worked alongside dirty, swearing, uneducated, often quite stupid adolescents and men. I worked well and kept my mouth shut, and I earned enough money that when I returned east, I could move out of my parents' house on the sly and pay my share of rent in an apartment on the Lower East Side with two other guys.

I never drove the Alfa Romeo or even the station wagon again— although Alfred loaned me the pickup once or twice for solitary weekend drives. I never went to the Slumbergs' or to Jewel's Box again; I never phoned or saw Judy again and barely saw Alistair, which seemed to suit us both fine.

The day before I was to fly back to New York, I was in the shacklike office of Alfred's construction unit drinking bad coffee out of a paper cup when he got a phone call from Cousin Diana's lawyer. The deportation paperwork had gone through finally, and Dario was to leave the next day. He'd asked for some of the things still left at the house. Alfred reluctantly said, "Yeah, yeah, the poor blighter!" When he hung up, he told me.

The next day, after work at the construction site, I went with him into the little garden house and collected the few items Alistair had pointed out—the mandolin and photograph and litho Crucifixion. I drove with Alfred down to the L.A. County Jail, where he'd been held all that time.

"Christ! I don't want to see him," Alfred said, punching the steering wheel. So I said I'd take the stuff in.

I didn't know what to expect, something out of a Cagney movie, I suppose. But Dario met me in a large, bright visitors' room. We were alone, with a dilatory guard outside chatting with a secretary. Dario wasn't wearing stripes, wasn't even wearing a prison uniform; he was in his own clothes, and he looked well, healthy, clean, perhaps relaxed for the first time since I'd met him, maybe even at peace with himself.

He opened the cardboard box and took out each item, greeting each like an old friend. It did me good to see him like that—not angry or bitter. He'd picked up some English in jail and spoke a little, saying how he was looking forward to getting back to Enna in September for the harvest. I reached out to shake his hand and wish him luck, but he said, "Please!"

I couldn't tell what it was he wanted from me. He was angling my body around with his hands, and I had to look over my shoulder at him, to ask what he wanted.

"Please. Just once!" he begged. "The pants down. No touch. Just—look!" He said that last word so oddly.

"What?" I asked. But I knew what he wanted. Although I was dusty and filthy from work all day, I was clean underneath. I turned, unbuckled, and dropped my denims and then my underwear, and stood there.

After what seemed a long time, I looked over my shoulder. Dario remained sitting, staring as though he were trying to remember something for a long time to come.

"Okay?" I asked.

He snapped out of it. "Okay!"

As I left the room, he said, "You see, this way I always remember what it was like to fall into hands of *Pericoloso Eroë*."

"Who?"

"*Eroë!* He shoots the arrows into the heart." Dario illustrated on himself.

"Eros! he meant," I explained to Wally, who'd caught up with me and sat me down on a bench facing the East River. "As in Cupid. A few years later when I was working in the bookstore I looked up the phrase in this huge Italian-American Dictionary we had on sale. 'Dangerous Eros' had been glossed by the editor, who wrote, 'So called because the Greeks and Romans considered Eros the most ruthless, the most potent god in the entire pantheon.' Odd, no?"

"Why would Eros be the most potent, the most ruthless?" Wally asked.

"You know, Wals, I asked someone that, and he said, 'Because Eros has no goal, only intention, when he shoots. And because his arrows never miss.' "

"Who told you that?" Wally asked.

"I don't remember," I lied.

We were close enough now to Gracie Mansion to hear voices chanting and a sudden burst of applause and cheers. The clouds were breaking up over the river, and the moon was making a debut; it looked full to me.

"Let's go!" I said.

"Are you all right?" Wally asked.

"I don't know, Wals."

"Come. It'll get your mind off him," he reasoned.

He took my hand and began leading me away. Two joggers followed by a Great Dane shot past us. Otherwise the promenade looked empty. Through the trees of Carl Schurz Park, I could see lights moving about. The media had arrived. Just in time too: someone was testing a microphone. Wally led me down a ramp, telling me that I'd be able to put my anger and frustration to some use down there, among others equally frustrated and angry. Suddenly, he stopped.

"It was that poet, wasn't it?" Wally asked. Then, "You know, about Eros?"

Matt. He meant Matt Loguidice. I didn't remember ever talking to Wally about Matt. Who had? Alistair. It had to have been Alistair.

"I told you, Wals, I don't remember."

"I'm sure that's who it was," Wally said in a determined tone of voice.

We'd reached another telephone booth. I stopped, put a coin in, and began to dial.

"What are you doing?" he asked, but he didn't try to stop me.

It rang twice. Then: "You have to get off the line, whoever you are," Alistair's voice said firmly, bubbling over with laughter. "I'm calling out."

"Stairs?" I asked, amazed and a little offended hearing him be so cheerful. Almost immediately, I regretted using our old nicknames.

"Stodge?" he asked back. "What are you doing calling? You've got to get off the line. I'm calling out."

A moment of panic, despite his obviously unpanicky tone of voice.

"We've run out of liquor. Can you believe it? The hostess's doom. But we simply undercounted the number of people who decided to come see the old thing! Place is packed. Stop that, you animal!" he added to someone in the room. "Stodge? You forget something?"

"What?" I was dumbfounded taking this all in. It seemed so utterly apart from how I was perceiving Alistair.

"I asked, did you forget something?"

"No. No. I . . ."

Wally was now making faces at me of total tedium and watch-checking ennui.

"Never mind," I said with fake enthusiasm. "Happy a hundred and three."

"Thank you, Twat!" he answered and hung up.

"Sounds like the party won't be over for a while," Wally commented.

"It's the party of the night," I admitted. "A social triumph!"

"Exactly what Alistair would want."

"I'm still going to stop him from taking those pills," I said.

"Fine," Wally said. "Let's do this event first. Then we'll come back."

"Together? You'll come back with me?"

"Don't read too much into it," he said.

"*Will* you come back with me?"

"I said I would, didn't I? Now, move. We're missing all the action!"

Book
Three

What's Goin'
Down

1991 AND 1969

The demonstration turned out to be impressive.

By the time Wally and I had dropped down the ramp and around to the front of Gracie Mansion, it was in full swing. Camera trucks from three networks, two local stations, and a cable station with pretensions had taken up positions as close to the action as possible—it was some of their brights we'd seen from the promenade. Their sight and sound crews, their equipment, their endless coiling snakes of heavy wire filled the gutters, swathed fire hydrants, and threatened to trip up those senior police officers assigned to the first line. Behind them, across the street, several squads of riot police had been lined up, complete with helmets and shields and who-knew-what-else that constituted their fullest gear, but it appeared that—especially with all the media present and all the dignitaries inside with the mayor—no one had decided whether they'd be used; behind their Fascist-newsreel drag, the men seemed relaxed, talking among themselves, fallen out of phalanx. The street they'd commandeered—only after the demonstrators and TV stations had arrived—was closed, all traffic diverted, except, as it turned out, official cars from within the mansion's parking lot, which were allowed to come and go.

To our amazement, somehow or other, this demonstration had re-

mained a secret. Amazing really, given how many hundreds of us had
known about it for days. The first wave of demonstrators had arrived,
exactly as planned, at the front gates just after the sixteen Mayors of
World Capitals had gone in to have their never-to-be-forgotten dinner
with our own city's mayor.

Exactly as planned, seventy-nine of the demonstrators had then proceeded to disrobe until they were wearing only some sort of loincloths
(with matching top pieces for the women à la Raquel Welch in *One Million Years B.C.*), then allowed themselves to be chained by cohorts all
along the fence around the mansion, in positions meant to be reminis-
cent of the Crucifixion.

In the intense glare of the television lights, they looked pretty awful. I
later found out that more than two-thirds of these volunteer martyrs
were truly ill: the rest were the thinnest, scrawniest men and women to
be found, with body and face makeup liberally applied to make them
look really bad. All seventy-nine were covered with hundreds of KS
lesions on their faces, arms, legs, and chests, some of which as one got
closer appeared to have been painted on. Most of them had blood bags
hung from the fence and attached to their wrists—each plastic bag
marked "Contaminated!" And each of them wore a sign around his
or her neck reading "Infected—Dying." Every once in a while, by
some signal I never managed to catch, one of them would moan even
louder then usual, or shriek suddenly, and slump. Other demonstrators
patrolling the fence in full medical drag would then go up to them,
check their pulses, and turn the signs around their necks to read "Dead—
of Neglect!"

Several hundred more demonstrators had formed a human chain and
were marching with the usual Silence = Death and Ignorance = Fear
signs, being led in their chants by men and a few women who I knew
from their yellow armbands were the demonstration marshals, trained
in civil disobedience to keep order and to interact with police if necessary and media if so fortunate.

Another group had chained themselves together to the front gates—
which had been closed by the mansion's guards in a predicted panic
when the place was first invaded—and they were mostly sitting or kneeling around the gates, upon which a large cloth banner had been hung

reading "Release The Funds And Save Lives!" The microphone I'd heard being set up was located here, and scores of demonstrators waited in line to stand in front of it and say a name very solemnly—presumably of a relative or friend who'd died.

As Wally and I pushed through the wooden horses set up everywhere willy-nilly, someone in riot gear actually made an attempt to stop us. But another cop dressed in blues waved us through, saying to the other in true New York cynicism, "Two more! What's the difference?"

In my growing excitement, I felt Wally hug me. "Isn't this great?" he shouted into my ear so as to be heard over all the noise.

"Terrif! Where do we go?"

"We've got to find Junior and the others."

Someone laid a hand on me. I expected another cop. Instead it was a tall, balding gay man my age with nice tits prominently displayed in an ACT UP black T-shirt, four rings in his left ear, and a yellow armband— a marshal.

"Do you belong to an affinity group?" the marshal asked, and I knew from his tone of voice and self-important air that he was that type of homosexual Bob Herron had first and forever defined as A Very Efficient Queen.

"We're looking for them!" Wally shouted into the VEQ's ear.

I thought the VEQ looked familiar.

"You'd better stick with me. Lilly Law was taken quite by surprise by all this, and she's getting a little nervous," the marshal yelled. He turned to me. "Don't I know you?" he shouted in my ear.

I shrugged and thought just what I needed in all this tumult was to play what Alistair always used to call Fag Genealogy: comparing lovers, boyfriends, tricks, jobs held, neighborhoods lived in, college, high school, junior high, and other schools attended right back to kindergarten and sometimes earlier.

"You do look familiar," I admitted.

After all, how many gay men in their forties still remained in the city? Not a hell of a lot. Only a few weeks before, I'd been walking around the Upper West Side with a friend from my days as a textbook editor who'd gone off to northern Michigan to teach Chaucer and had remained there for the last several decades. He suddenly stopped at Seventy-second and Amsterdam and said, "I've been here for a week. Where are all the men of our generation?"

"Dead!" I said.

"Come on!"

"They're dead. It's a fact. There's about six of us left."

That being so, I ought to know who this one was.

"What's your name?" I shouted into the marshal's ear.

"Ron Taskin."

"Not Ronny Taskin from Vanderveer Street?" I asked.

"Now I know who you are," he said, and swept me up in a hug. "I told Coffee I used to know you when your book came out. Where is he? He'd love to meet you. Coffee's my lover. Thurston's his real name. You know that old joke: like my men—black and strong and very sweet!"

Ronny Taskin! I couldn't believe it.

"Are you still using Indian clubs?" I asked.

His mouth flew open in surprise at my memory. "Not after the last one had to be surgically removed from my behind in the emergency ward!" He wiggled his rear end in emphasis, and we both laughed at his joke. Then I grabbed Wally and introduced him to Ron and tried to explain who he was. But Wally was distracted, looking for Junior and the others.

"There's hundreds of people here," I told Wally. "We could join any affinity group."

"We've *got* to find Junior and the others! I promised!"

He moved away into the crowd, and Ron found a slightly quieter spot among the wires of a CBS truck for us to talk.

"They're *so* intense at that age," Ron said. "You carry Pampers?"

"I can't believe you're gay," I said.

"As the nineties. Or you! As a boy you were so butch it hurt. Bike racing champ, marble wizard. Solitary and brooding. I thought you'd end up becoming a serial killer."

That was an odd thing to say. I'd always assumed I'd lived and died for social acceptance. "Me? You're kidding."

"Well, maybe until that incident with your cousin."

A subject I didn't feel like talking about. I deftly turned the conversation: "Do you ever see any of the others? Guy? What was the little prick's name? Kerry White?"

"Died in 'Nam."

My spirits began to drop. "Kerry? You're kidding."

"Closed coffin. His mother freaked out at the funeral, demanding it be opened. When they did, all she found was dirt and a few charred bones. She went bonkers after that. I lost track of the rest. What about your cousin?" Ron asked. Evidently he was going to insist. "The Ineffable Alistair Dodge? If he wasn't a baby faggot in training, I don't know who was. He knew virtually all of Clifton Webb's lines from *The Razor's Edge* and *Laura*."

"He turned out gay," I said, but now my spirits were plummeting. "He's here in town." And since it was Ronny Taskin, I had to add, "He's sick."

Ron's face fell into that set pattern we all knew how to use by now to give and receive bad news. "How's he doing?"

"Not good," I said, using the current euphemism to mean he was about to die. "How about you?"

Ron aped someone taking pills. "Five times a day," he sang.

Meaning AZT. Meaning he was sick too. "Damn!"

"And you?" he asked, concerned.

"Don't tell anyone, but I'm negative."

"You needn't be ashamed," Ron said.

"I don't know how it happened. I did all the wrong things with all the wrong people in all the wrong places at all the wrong times."

"Someone's got to escape."

"I know. But it's, well, embarrassing at times. Not to mention highly uncomfortable in existential terms."

" 'Me only cruel immortality/Consumes,' " Ron said, sympathetically.

That was the second time the Tennyson poem had come up.

"Something like that," I admitted.

Another marshal came over looking for Ron. As they stood aside talking, I saw Ron's face darken just the way it used to when he got angry as a kid, and I heard him suddenly burst out with "Shit! I warned him but he insisted!" As the other marshal left, Ron said, "Someone really sick collapsed on the fence. They're giving oxygen, but . . ."

Two other marshals came up to him. I heard him say, "Tell them he'll *die* if we don't have an EMS unit *now*!"

"I'd better see you later," I said.

"Let's get together sometime," Ron said. "I'm in the book. Under Ron Coffee. Tom! Wait! Where *is* that precinct lieutenant? I'll give *her* a piece of my mind!"

I was certain Ron would.

"I found them!" Wally said into my ear, then added darkly, "I think someone's in real trouble healthwise."

Junior Obregon, James Niebuhr, and their buddies were on line with the others, waiting to say their special names into the microphone. Two of them were arguing over the name of a friend both had been planning to say. James was trying to calm them down. I saw a solution:

"You want names," I said, "I've got a coupla score."

"You're kidding," Junior said.

"Got a piece of paper? I'll write down the first dozen or so that come to mind."

That sobered them up a little.

The EMS truck arrived with a police escort, which of all places in the city tonight was least needed here. Removing the stricken demonstrator, however, wasn't so simple, since one tenet of chaining demonstrators was that no one would admit to having keys to the locks. As a result, while a beefy guy with a plastic mask was busily blowtorching the chain, the EMS people were attempting to get the ill man stretched out on a gurney and attached to lifesaving equipment. I could see Ron Taskin among the group of ACT UP legal observers, ACT UP doctors, and high-ranking police officers surrounding the poor guy. Leave it to Ronny to become a Mover and Shaker, even with four earrings and highly visible erect nipples.

I wondered again about what he'd said concerning me being brooding and solitary as a child. I thought I'd worked my ass off to be just one of the guys. Serial killer, my foot! Since I'd become a Buddhist, it was all I could do to kill a cockroach. And look at the tailspin Alistair's request for death drugs had thrown me into.

"Do you know what name you're going to say?" James asked.

Just then I was shocked to hear a woman I didn't know at the microphone say the name Cleve Atchinson. Cleve used to be a fuck-buddy of mine back in the seventies, a sweet boy from Kentucky I'd lost track of years before. I remembered Cleve telling me in those ten- or twenty-minute periods between sex and him getting dressed to leave that he was an artist and was trying to get accepted into the School of Visual Arts for more training. Since he hadn't asked, I arranged to have a graphic artist I knew write up a completely bogus recommendation for him. I'd never seen any of Cleve's paintings, and I never found out if he ever was accepted. Hell, I didn't even know if he had any talent—besides his spectacular cocksucking. I'd left the city for a year, then Cleve had gone away, and I never heard from him again. Naturally, I hadn't known Cleve was sick.

Another page in my life erased, I thought, a page, an entire relationship, I'd probably never told a soul about. Without the young Kentuckian around anymore, did that mean my relationship with Cleve was now, in some twisted Lockean manner, relegated to the purely empirical—just one man's experience, forever uncheckable, doomed to unreliability? And didn't that make it tantamount to it not ever having happened? What about all those paragraphs and chapters others had filled in my life—Alistair most notably—would all that soon cease to exist? Was that what had made the past decade's losses so increasingly horrendous: the knowledge that my life was being reduced before my eyes from the richly detailed Victorian triple-decker we all supposedly carry, to a mere chapbook, a pamphlet of few pages, with wider white margins, spelling out a single, unclear thesis, accompanied by a single sheet of footnotes?

I had to tell someone about Cleve—find something trenchant and important about him and tell someone. What about Cleve had stood out? What had made him special? And who could I tell? Wally? Would he understand what I meant? What I feared?

"Well, do you know what name you're saying?" Wally repeated James's question into my ear.

"Give me a break, will you?"

"You'd better. 'Cause you're up next!" Wally said.

He slid up to the microphone, took it in his hand, and with those large, sad brown eyes, said the name of a graduate student who'd tutored him, added a few words about the man, and added his year of birth and death.

I was next. Jostled from behind by Junior Obregon, I went to the mike, gave my suddenly downcast lover a discreet pat on his ass—and froze.

Well, I didn't freeze so much as not know what to say. In front of me, several of the chained-together kneelers and sitters had somehow or other recognized me. I heard my name being said by several to others, "Sssanssssarc!" I was wondering how in the hell they knew me—the book hadn't sold that many copies or been that widely reviewed—when Junior prodded me from behind, urgently whispering, "Say the name, will ya!"

So I said the first name that came into my mind, "Matt Loguidice. Poet. Nineteen fifty to nineteen eighty-five."

And then I allowed Junior to shove me aside.

The look on Wally's face told me what I'd just done. As it registered and I began to move toward him, Wally turned away and vanished into the crowd. In my efforts to get past the bunch of them to Wally, I almost knocked over Reinhold's distant relation, who'd just gotten to the microphone.

I spent the next fifteen minutes looking for Wally, thinking if I could just lay hands on him, stop him, I'd be able to explain that it was his own doing—he'd brought up Matt earlier—that I'd said Matt's name.

This was nonsense and I knew it. As I'd stood on line awaiting my turn and hearing all those names and dates, I'd begun to feel that this was in some weird way like the children's religious instruction legend about appearing before St. Peter at the Gates of Heaven and saying the one word, remembering the single good deed, that would force those pearly gates to swing open. The truth had to be told: if saying one name, remembering and honoring one person in my life, could bring me celestial peace never ending, Matt's was the name.

At last I gave up my search and wandered over to where Junior, Niebuhr, and someone new had taken a break from their own search.

"Did you find him?"

"He's not here anywhere!" James assured me.

"What did you do to him?" Junior Obregon asked.

"Nothing."

"You must have said or done something," he argued.

Evidently, Junior's was that type of personality, not uncommon among homosexuals, called "an injustice collector"; except that, altruistically, he seemed to collect injustices for others as well as for himself.

"It's none of your business," I said, the "fuck yourself" silent.

Ever-fickle Fate chose that moment of my desperation for a reporter from one of the networks to decide that I and only I could possibly be his on-air spokesman for the event.

"Excuse me, Dr. Sansarc." The newscaster pushed Junior and the others aside with blond aplomb and shoved a microphone at me.

"I'm not a doctor," I retorted, surprised by his sudden appearance with two cameramen, light meter people, and a sound woman, who asked me to repeat myself.

Now, I'd seen this character before. In fact, Wally and I used to speculate on the sexual proclivities of this young semi-Adonis while watching "The Eleven O'Clock News," making up outrageous perversions that only someone so straight-looking could get away with—bestial anilingus, forced infant fellatio, etc. From this close, he was smaller, better looking, blonder, and altogether so ineffably clean-cut I now doubted whether he'd ever touched himself while urinating, never mind done anything as gross and vulgar as masturbating.

Undaunted by my unfriendly tone of voice, he told someone on his staff, "We can erase that." He blocked me, faced the camera, and said in an announcerish voice, "We're at the huge AIDS demonstration which erupted at Gracie Mansion. We're speaking to the noted author and social historian Roger Sansarc, who's a participant." As I wondered where he'd gotten all that from (Ron? An uncharacteristically spiteful Wally?), the newscaster spun toward me, shoving the microphone under my chin. "Tell us, Professor Sansarc, what set off this extraordinary outburst on a night calculated to embarrass the mayor?"

With all these faggots, why me? I thought. Behind me I heard Junior Obregon whisper, "Go, man! You're empowered!" So I figured, why the hell not?

This is what I said: "Two million six hundred thousand dollars of money specifically earmarked this past year for nondenominational hospice and hostel care units for AIDS patients has not been used by the city. We're here demanding to know why not, where those funds have gone to, and if and when those funds will be released so our sick and dying can receive adequate care."

That was it. He thanked me, still calling me Professor, which was a Fig Newton of his imagination, and took off at a trot toward his truck, yelling orders and questions simultaneously to his sight and sound crew. I took it I'd been successful and would be used later on the news.

Where I got that particular money figure from I'll never know. I guess I'd heard it bandied about during the Monday night meeting at the Community Center, as well as the various rumors about it. Even then, at the moment I'd been saying it, I had the queasy feeling that— like naming Matt Loguidice—this would come back to haunt me.

Not immediately, however.

"You were abso-fucking-lutely great!" Junior was jumping up and down, hugging me. Reinhold's distant relation stood there agape, then seemed to come to and said, "You know, I thought you were bullshitting about having done all this before."

Even Ron Taskin arrived to pat my shoulder and thank me for the good job—he'd been outside the truck's open door when I'd suddenly appeared on their video monitors being taped.

Sure I was pleased. But this was light shit. I still had to find Wally and attempt to explain what I would never in a million years be able to explain. I still had to get to Alistair's and stop him from taking those sixty-four Tuinals. And somehow or other I had to tell someone about Cleve Atchinson. Why me? I was thinking as the group around me continued its congratulations.

I was vaguely aware that Junior was trying to persuade the others to do something. He must have succeeded, because I was suddenly pulled out of the crowd to a less populous section of the fence, where two chained martyrs were being spoon-fed what looked like shrimp ramen by a volunteer.

"I told them we don't need Wally. You'll help us do it," Junior said very soberly indeed. "Now don't say you won't."

"Do what?"

Junior moved aside to reveal what the third guy was also covering. It looked like another banner.

"This is Paul Sonderling," Junior introduced us.

"Sure, I'll help. Where do you want to hang it?"

"There." Junior pointed to Gracie Mansion. "On the roof, hanging down."

"Why not hang it from the mayor's dick?" I asked

"No, really!" Junior said. "We've got it all planned out. Except that Wally was supposed to help."

"Was he?" Funny, I'd heard nothing about it.

"Paul here knows someone who already set it up for us," Junior said.

"This guy I met at the Jacks," Paul said, naming a noted club for mutual masturbators that met once a week, "has been working for the company that's been redoing the roof here. When I told him what we wanted to do, he said he'd help."

"The Homintern," I mumbled.

"What?" Junior and Paul asked.

"Homintern!" I repeated. "International Conspiracy of Homos. That's what Auden called us because we are everywhere and anywhere and only reveal ourselves when we choose to."

"Right on!" Junior enthused.

"Well, anyway," Paul went on, "my buddy installed hooks up there. Eight of them for us to hang the banner from. See!" He showed me how metal rings had been sewn into the top of the cloth. "So all we have to do is get it up there."

"*All?*"

"He also left a rope coiled for us to climb."

"Ninja Faggot Activists," I said with a sneer.

They took that in a better way than I'd intended it. Junior and Paul slapped hands high in the air, saying, "*That's* what we'll call ourselves."

"'Did he tell you how we get in?" I asked.

"He left a company truck parked around the corner." Paul showed me the keys. "The security guards here are used to seeing company trucks come and go. Once we've hung the banner, we'll drive it out."

"If we're not shot first."

"I told you he wouldn't go for it," James said.

"Was Wally really supposed to do it?" I had to know.

"You kidding? He helped plan it. And we need four people!"

"Four dedicated, committed people who won't rat on each other," Junior said, but I dismissed that as claptrap. I was beginning to think something far more dangerous.

"We'll be off the roof by the time it's unfurled," Paul said. "We'll be back in the truck by the time anyone notices it."

What I was thinking was that by joining them, helping them, stepping in for Wally, I would be reaffirming his commitment—and our commitment to each other. I knew this was false reasoning, specious logic, yet I also knew I owed Wally for saying Matt's name. Maybe, just maybe, doing this semi-sophomoric deed would blast that away before it took hold in his mind and really imperiled what we had together.

As though reading my mind, Reinhold's distant relation said, "Wally'll be pissed off if this doesn't come off. He was the brains behind it."

The brains, huh?

But the idea of draping an entire side of Gracie Mansion with our banner, and having all these self-important politicians come out and see it, did have its attractions. It would certainly cheer up this crowd and give everyone something to talk about for the next week. And since I'd already usurped the position of spokesperson for the TV camera, why shouldn't that false position be solidified by action?

"I'm in," I said, and raised my hand for a high slap.

The truck was where Paul had said it would be. Even better, it had one of those double-seat cabs for James and Junior to hide down in. Naturally, we were halted as we turned into the closed street, but Paul handled it easily.

"Jeez! Look at all the fags!" he said cheekily to the cop on duty.

The policeman attempted a wan smile. But it was evident that something at the demonstration—maybe the guy being driven off in an EMS unit—had reached him. "Keep that talk to yourself, okay?" Then he added as though his statement required an explanation, "Captain don't want any trouble here."

"Okay! Okay," Paul defended himself. "We just gotta drop off this crap." He nodded back to the truck's partly laden flatbed. "Boss wants it before he arrives tomorrow. Otherwise I gotta get up at three A.M."

For a half a minute, it looked as though the cop on duty was going to have to go higher up for permission.

"We'll be in and out in ten minutes!" Paul tried. "Fifteen tops!"

"Okay! Go!" the harassed policeman said.

As Paul had said, the mayoral security knew the truck and waved us in. We swung around the parking lot filled with stretch Mercedes and Lincolns, the mostly Third World chauffeurs of the various mayors sleeping at the wheel or reading in dimly lighted front seats. Three were standing atop the roof of one limo, trying to get a better look at the demonstration.

"We're in!" Paul cried exultantly to Junior and James, huddled in back.

He parked as close to the building as he could get, then turned so as to keep one side blind to any observers among the chauffeurs. We all slid out of the car, Junior holding the banner, all of us trying to remain cool. I recalled something Goethe had written in *Dichtung und Wahrheit* about seeing three men talking hurriedly and moving furtively at night and how that always meant some mischief was about to be done. As usual Goethe was right.

No one stopped us as we approached the building. I was surprised by how large it was. I'd hoped to hear the multilingual sounds of the sixteen mayors chatting inside, but everything in the immediate area was silent. The names being read by demonstrators were clear enough from here, as was the more generalized mass chanting of various slogans. But I was sure no one inside could hear them, since every window appeared to be locked. Only when the mayors had finished dinner and begun to drive out would they know the size and extent of the demonstration.

"Here!" Paul whispered. He'd found the way up to the roof. A shaky structure of hastily nailed together two-by-fours had been wedged into a corner of the edifice, but as the roofing work had already been completed, this construction had been half-dismantled and no longer reached the top. Paul was first to ascend, and the boards shook under him as he gave Junior a hand up. I lifted the banner up to them and followed, with James behind.

They'd found the coiled rope, and I could barely make out their bodies as each shimmied to the eaves. Next to me on the scaffolding, James seemed to be shaking, or was it the two-by-fours shaking? It sure wasn't me. Having already thrown my destiny to the gods, I was completely calm. A minute later I began to thank my own sense of vanity for twenty years of upper body exercises: although older than any two of my co–mischief makers put together, I ascended as easily and half somer-saulted over the projecting eaves to find myself on the surprisingly wide lip of the roof.

"Where's James?" Junior whispered.

I looked down. He was still clutching at the scaffolding. I was about to urge him to move his ass, when two policeman sauntered by chatting not a yard from where Reinhold's distant relation was trying to make himself invisible. I could hear their conversation: a slightly older cop telling his junior what he should never say to pick up a woman officer.

Once they were out of sight, James clambered up to the roof, rather awkwardly I thought. But then I'd taken him for an athlete, which he wasn't. The hand I took to pull him over the edge was large, cold, and clammy.

Paul had already reached the far end of the roof. He'd gotten the banner unrolled lengthwise, but it was still folded, so just the top of the message was visible upon the slanted roof, readable only by literate in-somniac birds and passing helicopter pilots. We would have to turn it over, attach it to the roof edge by fitting its metal eyes into the hooks left there by Paul's masturbation buddy, then lower it—still folded—over the eaves and down the side. Only then could we ourselves drop to the ground and, using a pull-cord on each side, completely unfurl it.

Naturally the metal eyes didn't exactly fit the hooks, despite infinite previous calculations. Then Junior Obregon discovered or just decided to admit to us that he suffered from severe acrophobia. He became so dizzy he had to lie down on the roof while James tried to help us and at the same time comfort him, until Paul said, "You guys better go. We'll finish this."

He was fitting hooks into eyes from one end of the roof, I the same from the other end. This provided me with a phenomenal view of the surrounding area, including most notably the demonstration we'd just left across the lawns and trees and through the fence. Thanks to the media, that scene was now so brightly lighted it took me a minute to register slight differentiations in the illumination as photographers' flashbulbs went off. As Paul and I neared each other in our task, James was already helping Junior toward the edge of the roof we'd ascended, saying, "Now I'll go down first and make sure you don't fall. Keep your eyes up. Don't look down, whatever you do. Okay?"

It is to Junior's credit that he merely said, "Okay," though the stran-
gled way it came out of his fear-riven throat suggested how scared he
really was.

I looked away from them to Paul and moaned, "Some Ninja Faggot!"

"I read somewhere," Paul said, "that the guy who threw the bomb at
Sarajevo had a fear of loud noises!" We giggled as we struggled to fit the
final recalcitrant eye into the final unbending hook. Once we could no
longer see Junior's head past the eaves, we crawled up the roof's slant a
bit, then lifted the unwieldy banner. We were trying to be as quiet as
possible, but a sudden wind rose and buffeted the long sheet of material
like a spinnaker on an oceangoing schooner. Paul was almost swept off
the roof, but the wind calmed down for a few seconds, and we took advantage of the calm to manage the banner over the side.

We quietly slapped palms at our success. Then we threw down the
two pull-cords on either side, waited a minute or so, and headed down.
When we looked over the side, we couldn't see Junior or James on the
scaffolding.

I couldn't believe they'd moved so quickly. "Where are they?"

"Back at the truck?" Paul suggested.

We climbed down the rope, and had to work to retain our balance
once we arrived at the by now really shaky scaffolding. Where were
those policemen? Had they been doing rounds? Or just passing by?
We'd have to be careful, maybe hide in the bushes. Paul showed me the
shortest path to the truck, then said, "Crawl there if you have to." He
tossed the coiled rope we'd used to climb up onto the roof, saying, "Do
I break balls or what?"

Now for the pull-cords. The two had to be pulled simultaneously.
We might only have a minute or two after the banner was unfurled to
get the hell out of there, although, because of the metal hook attach-
ments, the cops would have to go up onto the roof to get the banner
back down, which could take an hour, long enough for people at the
demonstration to see the message—and for the media to film and comment upon it.

I held my breath as I slid along the brick lower wall of the building
over to the pull-cord. There it dangled. All clear. *Wally*, I said to myself,
I hope you appreciate what I'm doing for you. I took the cord, looked back

for Paul, saw his hand grab his cord and—felt something very cold, very metallic, and very circular nudge at the carotid artery in my neck.

"Hold it!" I heard a nervous voice inches behind my left ear. "Or I'll shoot."

I knew then where James and Junior were: caught. As I was. For some absurd reason, all I could think of at the moment was that sweet dance-like tune of those two interweaving oboes in the "Esurientes" section of Johann Sebastian Bach's *Magnificat*.

"Don't shoot. I give up," I said.

"What are you doing here?" he asked. "Go on. Up against the wall." Louder he shouted, "I've got another one, Dak."

I thought, Oh, hell! After all this, I'm not going to let this fail *now*! So as I moved toward the wall, I pulled the cord with me. Hard.

Something up top snapped, and my side of the banner fell with a loud, shuddering thud like a ton of canvas.

"What the hell!" the cop shouted, falling against me. He almost poked a hole in my neck with his gun. "Get down! Down on the ground! What the hell's going on? Down! Face in the dirt."

As I was shoved down, I saw my half of the banner unfurled and prayed that Paul would do the same. Seconds passed slowly, then I saw the other half come slamming down. Paul had done it. Once again, I felt the cop half astride my body suddenly jerk at the sudden noise.

Meanwhile I thought of all the humiliating moments in my life—being eighty-sixed from Keller's for punching out a leather queen who'd been leaning on me all night, being knocked down by three crackheads between parked cars as they tore off my sneakers and liter-ally ripped my pants in half getting at my wallet—but this, *this* was surely the absolute limit.

"It's a goddamn banner, Joe!" The other cop was coming over to us. "They were hanging a goddamn banner from the roof of Gracie Man-sion!" His voice was filled with wonder and admiration. "Why not hang it on the mayor's dick? Come on, Joe, pat him down and back off."

I no longer felt the pistol barrel in my back, but I did feel myself be-ing expertly frisked.

"He's clean," my cop, Joe, said in what I thought was a disappointed tone of voice.

"Like the other two. Just demonstrators. You can get up now."

I stood up and brushed myself off. Dak was the cop facing me. "Look, you're trespassing and all. So we've got to arrest you," he said. "You know the drill, right? You turn around for the bracelet. How the hell did you guys get up there?"

I shrugged.

"We'd better tell the captain," Joe, the nervous younger cop, said.

Dak laughed. "You think he can't see the damn thing from where he is? It's half the size of the building. It can be seen from a mile away! You guys are really something else!" He shook his head in reluctant admiration.

Ten minutes later, I was being shoved out of the parking lot entry and into the open doors of a police van. True to his word, Paul had managed to get to the truck without being caught, and he'd already driven it back out.

The banner we'd put up had exactly the effect we'd intended. The demonstration had become twice as loud and active as when we'd left. A bunch of senior-looking police officers were huddled together, obviously trying to figure out what to do about the new headache we'd just presented.

I should have known that the same blond newscaster who'd "interviewed" me before would be on the spot to videotape me being led, handcuffed in a plastic loop, into a police van and to ask, with perfect naïveté, "Professor Sansarc, why did you help hang that banner?"

"Don't point your camera at me," I yelled. "Point it there! That's the story tonight!" I nodded back at Gracie Mansion, its upper floor covered by a banner reading "RELEASE THE FUNDS!"

To my surprise, the newscaster actually turned away from me and had the camera point at the banner. He was saying some shit or other about it into the microphone when the nervous young cop who'd caught me saw his chance and rabbit-punched me into the van. Admittedly he did it without much conviction, but it was hard enough to send me sprawling on the floor.

"You okay, man?" Junior Obregon's voice asked from inside the van. "Pig fucker!" he yelled at the cop.

Even though they were also bound in plastic loops, Junior and James helped me to my feet.

"They got us climbing down." James confirmed what I had suspected.

"Paul got away," I told them.

"Well, that's one out of four," James said.

"It's all my fault, isn't it?" Junior asked.

"Come on, June, we all knew the risks involved," James said coolly, but he still managed to sound irritated with himself and with us.

I sat down on the van bench opposite them. "The banner's up, isn't it?" I asked, thinking how proud and surprised Wally would be. "Stop bitching."

We were silent for a minute. Then Junior said, "Man, is my daddy going to burn my ass for this!"

We all laughed and were silent again.

Then I began to sing, "Eh-Es-Sur-Eee-Eee-En-Tes!"

The van door opened up, and there was Ron Taskin, all four earrings glittering, and with him a cop and one of the ACT UP legal advisors, who kept saying, "No one told me there was going to be an action tonight other than the fence-victims. Why can't you people tell me in advance, so I can get the paperwork prepared and the facts straight? Is that so much to ask? Is it?"

Ron ignored him, looked at me, and whistled, "Far fucking out, Rog!"

I took a bow.

"I'm simply going to have to call this an Unauthorized Action," the legal advisor was going on, "and we'll have to deal with it on that basis."

"Honey, you can call it Jane Wyman, if you want," Ron said.

"It'll be easier if you've got a lawyer," the distraught legal advisor said, looking pointedly at me.

"Okay," I said. "Anatole Lamarr. He lives in K-Y Plaza. Kips Bay," I had to explain to the legal advisor who was either Bridge and Tunnel or truly dim. "I'm sure Anatole will be delighted to be roused from his aloe-and-oatmeal Jacuzzi soak while watching taped reruns of 'L.A. Law' to come see me in some piss-stained slammer."

The legal advisor continued to bitch and moan about how un-authorized it all was, as he took down Junior and James's names, addresses, and other seemingly relevant data. He told us we'd have a legal advisor waiting wherever we were booked who would counsel us on our plea.

"Not guilty!" we all shouted.

"He or she will discuss all that there!" the legal advisor said.

A few minutes later, he and Ron were pushed away from the door by a female cop and the van was slammed shut and locked.

"Where we going?" Junior called out at our legal advisor through the grating into the van's front seat.

"Don't know yet. But we'll find you," the nervous legal advisor shouted back at us. "Mind you," he told the two cops who got into the van's front seat—a youngish man and the woman who'd locked us in— "I've got your names and badge numbers."

"Don't mind him," I told the two cops through the grating. "AZT makes him just a little bit frazzled. Me, it doesn't bother a bit. How about you guys?" I asked James and Junior, who caught the joke and replied, "I don't know, man, makes me horny all the time."

The two cops looked at each other a second, and she looked as though she were about to say something when James added, "Don't worry, Officers. We don't bite."

"We're just going a few blocks to the precinct house," the driver finally said out his window, to where I assumed the legal advisor was still waiting. "Okay? That okay with you?" he yelled back to us.

"Thank you, Officer Krupke!" I said.

Despite his announcement, we sat there longer. I continued humming the "Esurientes" and watched James and Junior settle down and begin nibbling at each other. I suppose they were finding their hands tied behind their back to be both a turn-on and a test to be gotten around, until finally James was leaning back on the bench and Junior was hovering over his lower torso, trying to open the front of James's button-fly jeans with his teeth.

Now, here, I thought, is a scene Alistair would appreciate in all its details and ironies. Alistair who . . . Ah, but there was the rub!

I thought about Alistair sending home all the party-goers and tucking the White Woman into his chenille-covered bed with its yacht-helm-motif backboard, feeding him a glass of milk and a few soda crackers, and remaining to read a page or two of Anne Beattie until Dorky began to snore; Alistair blowing a final kiss and tiptoeing out, going into his own bedroom and locking the door behind him, and spreading out those Tueys, perhaps calling each of them by the name of a trick or boy he'd possessed, as he downed them one by one, all sixty-four.

Anatole *had* to come to the precinct house. *Had* to get me out of jail tonight! So Alistair wouldn't die.

Maria and Debbie were lip-synching and dancing and gesticulating from their position atop the low wall surrounding the reflecting pool. Naturally, they had the full attention of the lunchtime dawdlers in front of the forty-story building. It was mid-August 1969, a lovely, hot Manhattan afternoon quickly coming on to 2 P.M., and my two co-workers were acting out the words of the song that Mary, Flo, and Diana Ross sang, their sound pouring out of Carl DeHaven's speaker-equipped portable radio a few feet away, while I turned aside slightly to cup in my hands and inhale deeply from a roach of grass I'd cocktailed into the emptied top of a Salem Long. In a few minutes, we'd have to leave this small spot of Urban Fun 'n' Sun and return upstairs to the tiny, airless, thin-walled cubicles that were called our offices in the large impersonal publishing firm where all four of us had been hired as high school and college textbook editors. It was a grim prospect, one I wanted to avoid as long as possible, to alter as much as possible in advance by sense-modifying drugs.

"Mr. Sansarc!"

Recognizing the voice, I immediately moved out of the halo of the marijuana smoke. The voice belonged to Frank Kovacs, my immediate superior, a man whose very voice—never mind his presence—for no reason I could precisely fathom, managed to induce within me that instinctual, that completely primitive "fight or flight reflex" we all supposedly hide somewhere in the deepest recesses of our being.

"Sorry to bother you on your lunchtime," Kovacs said, not sounding in the least bit sorry. Naturally, he didn't notice that behind him Maria and Debbie were rubbing their hands suggestively up the short lengths of their miniskirts then simultaneously giving him the finger in perfect slow four-time to the music. "Ah, but it'll be over soon, won't it?"

Kovacs said, managing even to find enjoyment in the anticipation of fun ended. I found myself thinking how much I detested the man. "So, to save time a little," he went on, "why don't you just come to my office as soon as you return to the office after lunch, which should be in a few minutes, anyway," he added and waited for me to respond.

Huh? What's he asking? Those phrases had piled up one after the other, like tiles raked off a roof, with none emphasized more than any other by sense or accentuation. Could I be that stoned on such a little hit?

Behind Kovacs, Debbie was now dry-humping Maria while Dusty Springfield moaned out some ballad I wasn't all that familiar with. I smiled at their antics and immediately Kovacs's suspicions were roused. He spun around to catch the two of them suddenly turning in perfect synch and doing an Al Jolson—all palms and mouths. Suddenly I understood what he'd asked. It wasn't something double-edged and fearful at all, just a simple question.

"Sure!" I said. "I'll come to your office. When?"

Kovacs was embarrassed by his own paranoia as he turned back to me, his top lip stretched across his teeth in what I took to be a facsimile of a smile. "When you return," he said, and added with rare graciousness, "Whenever you have a chance." Then he was gone. Debbie immediately began to mimic the strangulation of Maria—whose entire body jerked repeatedly—until the song was over and Carl signaled "That's All, Folks!"—and shut off the portable radio, signaling doom—or was it merely the end of lunch?

"What did Scrotum-Face want?" Debbie asked with her usual tact and inventiveness once we were in the elevator going up.

"Rog's body," Maria said. "Naked, spread out on toast points."

"No, no!" I moaned. "Death before dishonor."

Everyone on the elevator laughed. Our floor finally arrived, and the four of us—Maria, Carl, Debbie, and I—trooped off, as in a chain gang or conga line, winding through the cubicles of the twenty-sixth floor and breaking off one by one. I was last, and collapsed into my chair.

Immediately I telephoned Carl. "What am I doing with my life?" I asked him. "Why am I here?"

"You are repaying the karmic debt of a great criminal of the thirteenth century," he said in a perfect parody of a high-pitched, lilting Central Indian voice, "Burt-an the Yurt-man, a mass murderer and chicken-farm burner. You have no existence but to suffer, suffer, suffer!"

"You're no help," I said, hanging up.

Why *was* I here, anyway? To begin with, I was in this office because five months earlier a college friend who'd originally had this job had left for the Peace Corps and somehow managed to talk both the company and me into my taking his place. "You're immensely overqualified," he'd said to me. "It'll be a cinch."

He'd pretty much been correct. So far my job had consisted of (1) endless editorial meetings which concerned other people's projects, (2) writing captions for two hundred photos, illustrations, and maps for a newly revised edition of a much used high school history book, and (3) reading the manuscript of a new book on American history and evaluating it against three other books on the subject already available—one of them put out by this very publisher.

I once calculated that I actually labored for the company less than three hours per diem! I passed the rest of the office day at the coffee machine or on the phone with Carl, Maria, and Debbie, or in the men's room reading and doing endless crossword puzzles. When he'd recommended the job to me, my friend had warned me that I'd have lots of time to myself. "Whatever you do," he added, "don't be quick, don't be nimble, above all don't be efficient! They're all such dunderheads they'll think you're merely being superficial."

As a result of his warning, I'd recently spent a full three weeks reading and evaluating the new manuscript and comparing it to its closest competition—it should have taken no more than a week. What was I doing wasting my time like this? What was I doing wasting my time in Kovacs's office, which was where I found myself a half hour later.

"I've been going over your report on the Rainey/Schachter manuscript," Kovacs said, carefully sharpening the twelfth of twelve brand-new pencils he'd just taken from an opened package on his desk. He was referring to my most recent evaluation. "In fact . . . " Kovacs stopped his sharpening to line up the other eleven pencils and check their length. "Chas and I were discussing your report," he continued with a hint of something in his voice that I suspected was supposed to represent awe or importance, since "Chas" was Charles Knoxworth, Kovacs's own boss, the head of this entire department, a man I'd met once and naturally enough despised on sight.

"Oh?" I said. I'd never before seen anyone measure his pencils after they'd been sharpened, and I was indulging myself in this rare treat.

"Chas thinks you're a good writer," Kovacs said. "Chas doesn't think you'll be content to remain an editor. Chas thinks you'll be a writer yourself."

"Oh?" I asked, wondering if using the term "Chas thinks" as often as Kovacs did could be considered verbal masturbation.

"In fact, Chas thinks you're repressing your creative spirit, and that might explain why Chas thinks you've rushed this evaluation on the Rainey/Schachter manuscript."

"Rushed it?" I asked, amazed. I'd taken three weeks!

One of Kovacs's pencils was evidently a sixteenth of an inch too long: in need of immediate correction.

"There are factors to consider," Kovacs said, chugging away at the sharpener. "Once in use, these textbooks have to stand the Test of Time," he added, using his favorite cliché, one of little value these days since everyone in the universe was changing their textbooks, which explained why I'd done the evaluation and in fact why I had this job.

"So I should have taken longer?" I asked. I could have told him he'd never get all twelve pencils the same length. Why even bother, since once they were used they'd all be different lengths anyway?

"It's not the time element," Kovacs said, "so much as the amount of consideration, of pondering, of sheer mulling over that should go into a decision of this nature."

He was looking at the uneven pencils—trying not to be too obviously upset over them.

Now, it was true that I'd ended the report by saying that while the manuscript was fine, it struck me that there was no particular need for it: the market was already full of books on the subject, including a better one of our own. Could this have been a major tactical error on my part? If my report were being declined, did that mean that for some reason, Chas—or someone else higher up in the company—wanted the manuscript published? I needed some data.

"Tell me something, Frank." I tried the "friendly act" on him. "Has the company already paid for the Rainey/Schachter book?"

"There was an advance," he said offhandedly. "Not a large one. And an agreement. But not an unbreakable one."

We both knew that unlike with so-called trade books, the real money in textbooks was not in large, up-front advances but in endless years of eventually accruing royalties. I decided to try another tack: I'd inherited the manuscript from my friend, but perhaps he'd not been the first to see it.

"This wouldn't have been one of Chas's pet projects when he was in your spot?" I tried.

Kovacs had given up on the pencils and slipped them back into the box. Wrong move—their unevenness was now far more apparent. He slid them out again.

"No, I don't believe so."

"Tell you what, Frank, since you and Chas agree on this, why not let me see that manuscript again," I said, reaching for my report. "Perhaps I have been a bit hasty."

As I thought, Kovacs seemed relieved. Evidently he didn't know what the problem was either. Or he did know and couldn't bring himself to tell me.

"I knew you'd understand," he said, standing up and casually brushing the unevenly sharpened pencils into a drawer.

Debbie told me what I should do next:

"Nothing. Or rather nothing right away," she explained, as we walked out of the building toward the subway stop we shared. "And definitely nothing new. Don't reread any of it. Don't bother rewriting any of it. Wait about a month, then retype this same report on different paper. You should maybe use different-size margins or change the length of line so they'll think it's brand-new."

"You're kidding."

"Don't underestimate their intelligence. And if they aren't committed to the manuscript, all they want is a good excuse not to do it. Two negative reports, say, over a longish period of time . . . They're scot-free."

"What do I do at the office in the meantime?"

"Don't ask me," Debbie said, "I'm reading all of Proust. In the original. Hell, I'm learning French to read it."

Debbie saw her uptown train and decided to make a run for it. I daw-dled down the other side of the platform for the downtown local. I had to admit I wasn't all that eager to get home.

When I'd phoned Carl and asked what was wrong with my life, I'd meant more than just the job. I'd meant—everything! Here I was, twenty-four years old with no direction, no goal, except a vague one to someday be a writer, although of what and how I hadn't a clue. Not only was I goalless, but looked at straight on, I had nothing of my own. I'd inherited the job, which wasn't much, from one college friend. I'd in-herited my apartment from another friend, who believed that rent-controlled apartments should fall into the hands of one's sworn enemy before a stranger ever moved in. In fact, I'd even sort of inherited the young woman I was living with from a friend.

Not a college friend, however: Little Jimmy. I'd first met Little Jimmy at some party or other six months before and had pretty consis-tently run into him thereafter. Possibly because he'd also taken to hang-ing out with the loose group of pals I knew who centered roughly around an urban commune in the West Village. Jimmy came from North Carolina, and while small and lean physically, he was something of a big man when it came to women. In fact, he always had one or an-other terrific-looking woman whenever I saw him, most of them blond, and usually very cool. The most recent one, Jennifer, was a Minnesota girl so blond she faded into invisibility in bright light, yet so down-home I was astonished when she began confiding in me her plans for a new "act," which somehow or other involved a giant spider's web, painted black chains, and eight-inch high heels. It took me a while to figure out that quiet little Jennifer was not a Smith coed but—of all things—a carnival stripper.

Anyway, Jimmy had phoned me a few weeks earlier out of nowhere and asked if I could do him a favor. Money, I figured. I figured wrong.

"I've got too many blondes on my hands," Jimmy said, clearly de-lighted to be saying it. "I just got rid of one. I'm living with Jennifer and her sister. Now my old girlfriend Michelle's back in town. You remem-ber Michelle?"

I didn't. But I figured once you met one of Jimmy's women . . .

"Michelle's great!" Little Jimmy enthused. "She's unique! Know what I mean? At any rate she needs a place to stay for a short while. And I can't keep her here. You've still got that extra room and extra bed, don't you? She won't stay long. She's not sure what she's doing really, whether she's staying or going."

All of which turned out to be true, once Michelle arrived later that day, with her two large, leather saddle bags.

Seeing Michelle, I did remember her—vaguely—from the first time I'd met Little Jimmy. But Michelle was different from his others, altogether more "hip," with her homespun yet glamorous outfits, her long, lemon-chiffon-colored hair, her sweet little face—sincere big blue eyes, perfect nose and mouth—not to mention her ample, her dynamite, body.

"I'll try not to get in your space too much," Michelle said, once we'd settled her bags in. "I'll do my sewing and my art while you're at work, and I'll be out of here when you get home."

"Well, gee," I wanted to say, "you can get in my space a *little*!"

Michelle took over the small room off the kitchen which had been my own first bedroom in the apartment when I'd shared it and would in future be either a dining room or study. That first night, she went to Little Jimmy's place for dinner, and having scoped out his situation for herself—i.e., that he was drenched in women—she never went back. Nor, to my surprise, did he come visit her at my place. But as Michelle remained out late every night, until long after I was asleep—just as she'd predicted in those first days—I hardly knew she was there.

The major indications of her presence were half-smoked joints left in the living room ashtrays and a copy of the *I Ching* left open on the bathroom hamper, turned to Hexagram #56, The Traveler. Once I peeked into her bedroom, and saw a quite substantial sewing kit within its own separate and rather complex-looking leather bag; and alongside it, a large pad and a forty-color set of *Caran d'Ache* crayons.

I remember thinking how odd it was that this room—so recently *not* thought of, or when thought of considered merely a part of the apartment—had suddenly become alien to me, its contents mysterious, its very premises suddenly untouchable except for some particular and good reason.

The second weekend Michelle lived with me, a weasely guy named Leighton came by to take her out. He possessed all the appurtenances and accoutrements of a hip guy of the time—clothing, language, you name it—but I don't know why, I read him as a phony.

None of my damn business who Michelle went out with as long as she paid her rent and kept her part of the place clean. That's what I told myself time and again. That's what I told her when, at the end of the month, Michelle and I sat down over tea and grass one summer morning to discuss her future.

"It's great that you feel that way," she said, responding to my statement in her low-keyed, restrained voice, seemingly incapable of enthusiasm. "Because I'd like to stay here a little while longer."

"You would?" I guess I was both pleased and surprised.

"Jimmy was right. You're good people. Easy to get along with. No hassles."

It turned out Michelle had been living in other people's places for the past year, ever since she'd left the city to go across country and check out various arts and crafts scenes she'd heard about. She wanted to remain here long enough to do some work to show around and sell when she went out on the road again. Meanwhile, she'd stay in my guest room, pay the share of rent we'd agreed on, and not get in my space.

"You've got your life. I've got mine," she concluded.

She was wrong: I'd had nothing even vaguely like a life and had she been around during the evenings and weekends, she would have found that out herself. As for her life, I guessed it must include Leighton, and I didn't much care about that.

Michelle let out a bit more information. Her family came from coastal Massachusetts, and she'd be visiting her grandmother up there soon, partly to see her, partly to learn from her some specific New England stitchings Michelle was interested in, and partly to get money.

The only other information I discovered about her family was that it was "weird yet somehow boring at the same time." During a later, somewhat briefer tea together, it came out that Michelle was on the outs with her parents, like so many of my coevals, and that, far more surprisingly, she was on the lookout for a specific male—get this!—to father a child on her.

"Not that I want to get married, or do any of that conventional trip, you understand. I don't even want to live with the guy. Just conceive with him. I'll bring up the kid myself. This psychic astrologer and I worked out the best times to conceive and the best signs of guys to do it with."

This idea struck me as just about the height of cool, and I was feeling that altogether Michelle was completely out of my league—not to mention Little Jimmy's—when she said, "What's your birthdate anyway?" and when I told her, she said, "Well, you seem to fit. But so does Leighton." The guy she was seeing. Which somewhat explained why she was sleeping with him—since nothing else could explain it to me.

The next few weeks were odd. If Michelle had been a guy, indeed if she had been almost anyone else other than who she was, I would have been content to be paid some rent for a room I wasn't using. As it was, whenever she was in the apartment, I was always very aware of her presence, no matter if she were alone, working, which was most common, or if she were on the phone or—much more rarely—there with someone else, a woman friend, sometimes Leighton before they went out for the night.

This was undoubtedly my own fault. Michelle's presence had brought into high relief my own problems. Which could be summed up as follows: it had been two years since I'd been in a relationship with a woman, and that one had been a mistake. Well, maybe not a mistake so much as a failure. After close to a full year of dates, most of which had ended with kisses at her apartment door, or at rare times necking on the sofa while her roommate was on the phone, we'd still not gotten down to the nitty-gritty. It wasn't that I was afraid, or even that I was inexperienced. I simply wasn't that interested in screwing Janet. I wanted a relationship that might come to include sex eventually but that wasn't totally wrapped around it. However, that was not what Janet wanted. Or rather, what she wanted was her own idea of how it was all mixed up.

This had all come to a head one evening when we were necking and petting heavily on her sofa, our clothing all a mess, and she finally pulled me up and panted, "The bedroom," and when I protested, "What about Helena?" she said, "Helena's not here." Well, I was horny and we more or less made love, but it was no surprise to Janet that my ardor had cooled somewhat from what it had been before, on the sofa.

Afterward, Janet said, between puffs on her mentholated Kent, "It must be me. You were hotter than a pistol before."

"It's not you," I admitted. "It's me. I'm not sure we should be doing this."

"Why shouldn't we? Everyone else is. Even . . . Helena is."

"I know. But I feel like it's . . . I don't know . . . some sort of commitment I'm not ready to make."

"I'm not asking for any commitment," Janet quickly said. Then, "Who am I kidding? I'd love one. But I know now it's not going to be with you."

That ended our conversation, and a pall fell on our relationship after that. I called once or twice more to make a date to go out. Janet put me off twice—enough so I got the hint and stopped phoning. I halfheartedly thought Janet wasn't right for me, that I needed someone else. But I also harbored other, darker, different thoughts. What if I really didn't like girls at all? Sure, I could get erect with her, but I was young, I got erect when a dog barked, when a train whistle blew, hell, when the wind blew with a certain force. What if I weren't heterosexual at all, like everyone around me, but instead . . .

I didn't go that far. Yet I knew that when I'd come back from visiting my cousins in California, I'd gone right to my encyclopedia, right to the dictionary, and then to the local library to look up the word "homosexual" and read everything I could find about it. It wasn't much, and it was consistently negative, and I knew this couldn't be me, simply couldn't. On the other hand, everything I read, every word, had excited me unlike anything I'd ever read about regular man-woman sex—short, that is, of descriptions of actual intercourse, which I found to be exciting no matter who did it or how it was presented.

No, the real problem was that I didn't believe any of these writers. At least not until I came to the introduction of the 1949 *Kinsey Report*, which I read in the reference section of the library, and which seemed to conclude more or less what I'd heard from Alistair's surfing buddies: that all sorts of guys had some sort of sexual contact with one another, and it didn't necessarily mean anything. Leastways not that you were queer yourself. None of Jewel's boys at the Topanga beach house had had as much contact with girls as they had with one another, according to Jewel herself, Judy, and Alistair, and none of them were . . . I couldn't even bring myself to say the word.

That was how one of my arguments went. Its exact opposite said that none of this meant anything at all; I'd simply not found a young woman I loved, and when I did find her, none of this would make any difference: I'd want to screw her day in and day out, and I'd never again think about those surfer boys, or about how much other young men attracted me.

Now, it seemed, Fate had sent just such a young woman directly into my life; indeed, directly into my apartment. All I had to do now was take advantage of the fact. Because if I didn't, well, who knew what awful future awaited me? The way it turned out, none of it was up to me after all. Fate was at work, and everyone around me had some part to play.

Including Debbie. The very night Debbie had given me advice about work, she phoned me later. I'd done food shopping and had barely gotten in the door, when Debbie asked if I'd been listening to the radio.

"No, why?" I asked, wondering what new disaster in these years of terrible political disasters had happened now.

"Well, they're talking about all these rock groups that are getting together somewhere upstate New York this weekend to play a big outdoor concert," she said. "It sounds like everyone's going to be there. Don't you know anything about it?"

I didn't. Phone calls to our friends from work elicited more or less the same response. Maria had heard somewhat more. "They're saying everyone's going to show up: the Mamas and the Papas, Janis Joplin. Even the Beatles!"

"It might be a cool place to go," Carl said. "They were selling tickets through the mail, but they couldn't have sold them all."

So the concert upstate became known to me. But once we tried to make plans for getting there, it seemed pretty impossible to manage, especially without a car.

That night, I attended a party given by a friend of a friend of a friend and had a bad and boring and weird time, and I ended up pretty stoned and drunk. I crashed hard, naturally in my own bed, naturally alone, and awoke twice during the night needing a drink of water. The third time I got up, the bathroom was locked. I heard the shower running. Michelle must have come home. Sure enough, it was six A.M.

The kitchen was lighter. I got my drink there but avoided the brighter living room windows. I was back in bed, asleep again in a minute.

At first I wasn't sure whether it was a dream or not; too many of my dreams began this same deceptive way: I'm in bed, in my own bedroom, then . . . But I was awake, or somewhat awake. No, I must have been. After all, I felt warm, though I was naked, the top sheet twisted barely across the middle of my body. And there was Michelle, standing in the bedroom doorway, leaning against one side of it, her arms raised above her head, drying her hair with a towel. One hip shifted her weight to that side, and suddenly every angle softly flowed into another. She was wearing a pair of the palest blue panties and nothing else.

"You home?" I asked stupidly, my voice slurred despite all the water.

"Been out late?" she asked back. Her voice also sounded furred.

I said something I didn't remember as I finished saying it, and she answered something else I failed to grasp, then she said something I didn't understand even after a few seconds of silence. "Well, that looks interesting," she said, looking at my erection barely contained in the sheet. I found myself looking at it too, somewhat objectively, asking myself what it was doing there, then she was standing closer, no longer toweling off her hair, then somehow I was handing my erection over to her, and she was touching it, saying something in a low voice. Suddenly she was on the bed, straddled across my body, my erection inside her, and her hair was all over my face and chest and we were rocking together and apart and acting like I don't know, those ponies in that animated Russian fairy tale I used to see on TV all the time when I was a kid, so white and elegant and untamed, romping together in perfect synchronicity through snow-whitened pastures and huge iced fields.

"I figured it was okay, since you were within my list of possible birth signs," Michelle explained after the trumpeting orgasm which confirmed for me that the incident, though dreamlike, wasn't a dream. Her explanation, in all its prosaicness, was further proof, if any were needed.

"I better get dressed," I said, hoping she'd try to stop me. "I've got to go to work."

"That's a bummer." Michelle sat up and turned half aside, holding one breast as though testing a change in its mass as a consequence of intercourse. "I thought maybe you'd want to go upstate to this weekend thing."

"The concert they've been talking about on the radio? Sure! How?"

She and I pooled our resources: not much—renting a car was out of the question. I could take the afternoon off from work as sick leave. This was officially frowned on—it being a sunny Friday afternoon in the summer—but not impossible.

More important than any mere logistics was the stunning fact that I'd just been laid for the first time in months. This alone would, I was certain, significantly alter anyone's thinking. It went without saying that I was now certain I was in love with Michelle and she with me. We simply had to be together from now on. So I thought, okay, we'll follow her plan, even though it does seem kind of naive and mostly unworkable.

She and I were to meet back at the apartment, pack overnight bags— a blanket, towel, thermos of water, snacks, change of underwear—and take the Seventh Avenue IRT subway uptown, switch there to the Jerome Avenue line and take that train to its penultimate stop at the northernmost end of the Bronx. Michelle had done this before; she knew it was close to a major highway headed upstate. From there all we had to do was hitch a ride. If this concert was as big as everyone said it was and if it was being attended by as many hip people as the FM broadcasters assured us it was, we should have no trouble hitching a ride.

I'd briefly thought to tell my friends at work about our plan. But the truth was I wanted to be with Michelle, to have her to myself, partly because I was now able to, and partly because I still didn't myself believe in this sudden new relationship—I wanted to check it out for myself. So I didn't tell Debbie and Maria I was going; I did mention to Carl that I might be picked up by some friends of friends later that night or next morning, but I worked to make even that sound as unsubstantial as the plans we'd all ended up making the night before on the phone. Most important, I told no one I was planning to leave work "ill" that afternoon. Their surprise would help make it look more legitimate, should Kovacs ask where I was.

Michelle was packed when I got home, and even more enthusiastic for us to take off right away: she'd been listening to FM station reports all morning, and she regaled me with these facts: people had already begun to gather at the concert grounds; Crosby, Stills, Nash & Young, Joan Baez, Joni Mitchell, Dr. John, Janis Joplin, and the Jefferson Airplane all had agreed to be part of the concert. Dylan might still appear at the last minute; still no word on the Fab Four, but it looked like just about everyone else in rock or folk music would be there.

I changed out of my work clothes and into my denims and T-shirt to get into the mood. By noon the temperature outdoors was already in the mid-eighties, but I knew what mountain nights could be like and I packed my big Bolivian wool sweater. As for Michelle, besides her enthusiasm for our journey, I couldn't for the life of me figure out what else she was feeling—say, for example, about me, about us. This was crucial: because of what had happened last night, I'd put my entire future into Michelle's hands.

The subway trip seemed endless, even on the express train. We were the last passengers in our or any other car we could see. Equally empty once we arrived was the amazingly clean, white-tiled station at Mosholu Parkway, smelling heavily of recently used disinfectant. We trudged up out of dim tunnel lighting into broad daylight.

It was 2 P.M., and we were in the middle of nowhere. The subway station stairway sat surreally within grass and trees upon a broad, flat area of the northern Bronx dominated by a virtually untrafficked avenue. Across the street was another subway station as Dadaistically set amid suburban grass and trees. In the distance, we could make out a neighborhood of cottages cloistered by tall trees, enclosed by thick bushes, all loosely wrapped in hurricane fencing. In the opposite direction, low brick buildings were barely visible along a strip of such magnificent green I swore it had to be a golf course.

"This is the Bronx?"

"I told you," Michelle gloated.

Despite the heat, the short walk to the highway wasn't unpleasant. We bypassed the entry to Van Cortlandt Park to walk along a short block of square-roofed buildings two stories high, with shops on their lower levels: a shoemaker, a grocery store, a stationers, and a garden supply. I was reminded of the neighborhood I'd grown up in.

"What street is this?" I asked.

The closest signs read "Van Brunt Blvd." and "212th Street."

"I grew up in a place just like this, only in eastern Queens," I told Michelle, pointing southeast. "Only that one was called Vanderveer Street and Two Hundred and Twentieth Street."

The side of the highway: cars slipping by, those in the closest lane slowing to get off onto a ramp. We'd dropped our bags when one stopped.

"That's quick," I said, wondering if in fact it wasn't too quick.

"Looks like a cool guy driving," Michelle said. "Let's go."

An older guy definitely. At least twenty-six. With a full auburn beard and a spatter-dyed T-shirt and—we saw once he opened the front door of the pickup—tight-fitting denims like those we wore, and great-looking old cowboy boots.

"You headed upstate?" he asked, looking us over coolly.

I was about to say yes, when Michelle said, "We're going to the concert up there near Woodstock. You know about it?"

"It's closer to Bethel," he said, ignoring me totally now. "Up at Yasgur's farm. And you are in luck, pretty lady. I'm headed right up there."

"It far?" I asked, unwilling to be left out. Truth is, I didn't like either the way he was looking at Michelle or the way she was looking back at him.

"Not far once we cross the Hudson at the Tappan Zee Bridge; it's only an hour or so. You traveling together?" He had to ask the obvious. "Well, then throw your bags in the backbed." He smiled, and I had to admit it was a killer smile. "That's what it's called," he said to Michelle. "Honest injun."

I was busily trying to think of something to keep us from getting in the truck. But I knew I'd fail because he was taking us right there. And there was room, so what in the hell could I say?

"By the way, I'm Edgar," he introduced himself, at the same time he reached down a well-muscled forearm to pull Michelle up next to him inside the truck's cabin. I was left to throw our bags in back, next to a hundred-pound bag of cement. The truck was already rolling back onto the highway before I'd managed to get myself in or the door closed.

Michelle was already lighting up a pipeful of grass. I thought she was sitting awfully close to Edgar, given the hand gear was right against her leg and he kept his hand on it whether he was shifting or not.

"You two planning to be together for the weekend?" he asked. Uncool question, I thought. So obvious.

Evidently Michelle didn't think so. "We've planned to go to this concert gig," she said, which sounded awfully ambiguous to me.

I watched with undulled pain as during the rest of the drive Michelle slowly, but I thought surely, turned all of her attention from me to Edgar. It was subtle, doubtless, made up of some of the tiniest of attentions, of motions. But it was clear, and it was inexorable. She let us both know she preferred him, though she'd come with me; this despite the fact that, as Edgar told us, he was already "hooked up with my old lady"—Sarah, who was at this moment in their house near the Ashokan Reservoir, toward which we were headed.

Michelle got that information out of him, even got his astro-data out of him (I wasn't sure whether or not he fit her paternal sign format), using a series of questions and turnaround revelations.

My future was beginning to look so bleak I became increasingly silent, stared out at the scenery along the Governor Dewey Thruway, sulked over Michelle's faithlessness, then wondered if that's really what it was or if I were merely being stupidly overpossessive about her. After all, we'd only screwed once. It made no sense at all. Michelle was simply being herself and thus independent, and I was being ridiculously jealous and thus not at all myself. What had happened between us last night had been a fluke, a mistake: it meant nothing. I couldn't rely on it as an answer to my future.

But if that was true, what would this weekend turn out to be like?

Since I couldn't pull anything even close to an answer out of my head, I sulked more. Once when Michelle turned to hand me the pipe—finally remembering I was there, I thought—she had to tap my shoulder twice before I bothered to take it.

Past Kingston the thruway traffic thinned out. At the next turnoff, it thickened again as cars from various other directions joined us, and then we were off the main road, driving on a two-lane highway through the Catskills—this was real country to a city- and suburbs-raised boy.

The town of Woodstock itself seemed small and sort of makeshift, but it was evident even to strangers like me and Michelle that it wasn't usually so filled with cars and people. Edgar got stuck in what he told us was an unprecedented Main Street traffic jam and had to find a shortcut through several alleys, all the while asking, "Jesus! Where'd they all come from?"

Once we hit the road out of town, a sign suddenly announced the concert. By then traffic was thick coming and going from all the roads we could see, and people were simply abandoning their cars on the side of the road and walking to the place. "I don't believe this," Edgar said. We did: we'd been listening to the DJ's updated reports on the concert grounds.

The four-wheel drive on Edgar's pickup came in handy now. He drove alongside the parked and stopped cars as long as he could, then when it was clear we couldn't go any farther, he tore away on bare ground up through bushes and over a hill, onto a dirt road he alone could see, headed away rather than toward the concert ground, I thought. He slowed down once we reached an apple orchard. As we drove through, apples shaken from their branches by the truck's vibrations rattled onto the hood and roof. Finally, he stopped. We walked through the trees, polishing and chomping apples, headed toward a bluff that faced what Edgar remembered from earlier drives here on a dirt bike as "the only more or less bowl-shaped place in the whole area."

He was right about it being bowl-shaped. But even Edgar was astounded by how it had been transformed. Although it was still only about four in the afternoon, a hundred thousand people must have already congregated. From where we stood, the land dropped suddenly then rose all around like a multicolored Pointillist tablecloth being shaken of its crumbs. At the very far end, it dipped smartly then rose again. Sound and light structures had been set up at a distant rise; even from this far away, their metal glittered brightly in the afternoon sun. The little depression seemed to have been the original space laid out for the concert, but the crowd had already grown far beyond the established limitations. From where we stood, Michelle pointed out what must have been the original fence laid out around the concert area. I located what must have been the original parking lot, now partly wedged into a side of the crowd. Edgar spotted where the ticket takers had been. By the time we arrived at that spot some fifteen minutes later, even these vestiges of the original organization had vanished, absorbed into the ever growing mass of young people arriving by the hundreds every minute.

"I don't believe it," Edgar kept saying.

"I do," Michelle said. We were within the crowd now, and it was far out—simply amazing.

"Who *are* all these people?" Edgar asked.

"Us," Michelle replied.

"Us," I confirmed, repeating Jerry Garcia's line, "We're the people your mother warned you about."

My annoyance with Michelle was gone. I no longer cared how she acted, what she said, what she thought, whom she preferred, or even what happened next. It was more than being high from all the marijuana smoke in the air around us. I simply knew that I was going to have a good time this weekend. I could sense the assurance of it in the kids, in their easy, fun behavior, in the solidity of the very vibrations around us.

We passed about a score of Portosan toilets, which seemed to be all that had been brought in. An enterprising hot dog vendor and an ice-cream truck just managed to pull up to one edge of the crowd, and proceeded to sell out their entire stock in minutes. We kept walking, passing beautiful, young, stoned, dancing-to-the-portable-radio men and women, boys and girls. They were long-haired, or wore Afros. They had granny glasses on, or pale blue-, pink-, or yellow-lensed sunglasses. They wore shorts and halters, T-shirts and jeans. They were blond and brunette and red-haired, wearing it long and straight or kinky and fuzzy. Pale-skinned, tanned, olive-skinned, Creole yellow, and Nigerian brown, they were dancing and kissing and smoking grass and just standing around grooving on the sheer growing mass of themselves.

Up ahead, speakers were being tested at the sound structures, and it looked as though we'd easily find ourselves a good spot anywhere around here, since nobody was crowding anybody, and everyone was leaving more than enough breathing space.

Edgar kept saying, "I don't believe this."

He had wondered out loud about going back to his place and getting his old lady and the other couple visiting them, when he bumped into some friends who told him they were there already—house guests and all!—up ahead, closer to the musicians.

Close enough, it turned out once we got there, for us to see the stage clearly and anyone who'd be standing on it. Trucks and vans and other vehicles belonging to entertainers and technicians had begun to gather in numbers off to one side of the structure, and the speaker system—originally only at the stage area—was now being widely extended to enclose a much greater space. Allegedly the concert promoters had flown this new equipment onto the farm in helicopters. No music yet—the first acts were due to start by sundown.

Michelle, Edgar, and I settled in with his old lady and their house guests on their blanket, as they explained why and how they'd come here—driving over to check it out and remaining when they heard who'd be playing and singing. They had a jug of wine with them and grass, and we were all pretty comfortable by the time we could hear—clearly, if off-mike—the sounds of an electrified guitar, as someone warmed up.

Someone onstage—an engineer or promoter, it wasn't clear—asked for lights. They were provided, though it was still daytime. He then tested microphones and speakers. Once those were working, he left the stage. Seconds later, we heard a voice over the microphones.

"Welcome to the Woodstock Music Festival. Our first performer of many in the following two days will be Richie Havens."

Applause rumbled and cascaded so far around and in back of us that it was clear that many more people had arrived since we had. Havens started with his own characteristic guitar lick and distinctive lisping bass voice—the concert was on.

It lasted until about two o'clock that night, with Janis Joplin wailing out "Ball and Chain" until we thought she'd drop dead right there onstage. Depressing as that might sound, it wasn't—it was completely exhilarating; it left the crowd in the highest possible mood, demanding more.

We left our spot, marking it with some blankets, and headed along the bulk of the people toward where Edgar had parked the truck. The crowd seemed to have expanded to the edge of that orchard bluff. They'd brought portable radios and reel-to-reel tape players, and dozens were dancing around each piece of electronics, unwilling for the concert to end. Others were settling in for the night. No one knew how long the overhead lights would be on, but they only threw illumination so far anyway.

I was glad for my big Bolivian sweater, once we got to the pickup. It was chilly on the bluff. I was even more appreciative that we'd been invited to stay at Edgar and Sarah's. We all piled into the cab and back of the pickup. After fifteen minutes of rough riding, we finally hit a macadam road not completely parked over with cars for the concert. A half hour later, we arrived at Edgar and Sarah's house.

I don't know what I'd expected: a log cabin, I suppose. Instead, it was a single-story ranch house with a guest room, and an attic space over the bedrooms open to the living and dining space. That's where we could sleep, Sarah told Michelle; a spare mattress was already up there, and she handed me some blankets.

I washed up and climbed the ladder to the attic. Edgar and Tom also went to bed. It was chilly in the house, and I didn't undress until I'd laid out the blanket and mattress to my satisfaction; then I tore off my clothes and dove in. I lay there awhile, shivering to get warm, listening to the voices of Sarah, Francine, and Michelle as they quietly talked in the kitchen.

Throughout the day, I'd looked at Michelle for some sign as to what my behavior toward her should be. So far, what I'd gotten had been completely contradictory. For example, and most recently, she'd not protested these sleeping arrangements—which clearly signified that she and I were together, as together as say Sarah and Edgar or Francine and Tom. Yet she sure seemed to be avoiding as long as possible coming up to be with me. During the concert itself, she'd been great, openly physical, hugging me, dancing alongside me with one arm over my shoulder. When Joni Mitchell sang, we sat together quietly, and Michelle held my hand in her lap. But how much of that, I wondered, was mood, being in with what the moment and the music seemed to dictate? I still couldn't forget how she'd been with Edgar during the trip up this afternoon: more than anything else, that seemed to say that Michelle was with me only insofar as she had a use for me.

Didn't that pretty much sum up my relationships with women?

From within the warmth of my makeshift bed, I tried to make words out of the female voices downstairs, thinking they might be speaking about Michelle and me and would thus provide some hint as to what I should do next, but suddenly, without any warning at all, I fell asleep.

For all I knew, Michelle might never have come to bed at all that night. She was awake before me the following morning, down in the kitchen along with Francine and Sarah, all three of them busily cooking breakfast.

Baking too, it turned out.

"We were wondering if you guys would ever wake up," Michelle said. She wore a large hand-stitched apron over her skirt. She'd done something to her hair: maybe washed it, definitely put it up on her head in a style I'd never seen on her before, perhaps for the cooking, possibly in imitation of the other women. Whichever, she was unquestionably in a good mood.

"Isn't this all great!" Michelle enthused, her statement encompassing the kitchen and the large rough-hewn table where she motioned me to sit, while she poured coffee out of a battered metal coffeepot into a large hand-thrown mug. "This is exactly where I wanted to be this weekend!"

"Lucky thing Edgar picked us up when he did," I offered between sips.

"Nothing like that ever happens by chance," Francine said and smiled enigmatically. Sarah, at the stove, turned around, and the three of them stood within inches of one another, The Three Graces in Homespun, looking at me with a combination of satisfaction and secretiveness.

"It was *meant* to be," Sarah said. "Michelle was *meant* to be here."

She said it, and the others ever so slightly bristled behind her, as though daring me to deny it. But it was far too early in the morning for me to discuss Fate, Chance, and other ontological matters, and what seemed to matter in what they were saying, while it was quite vague, nevertheless was its exclusionary aspects. Properly excluded, I sipped my coffee in silence.

A huge breakfast, complete with homemade bread and ham steaks, distracted me more happily for the next ten minutes.

The smell of the coffee and food awakened Tom and Edgar. We were finishing breakfast when Sarah announced: "All the food in town is sold out. All the food in the surrounding towns too."

"There's going to be a lot of hungry people." Michelle said the obvious.

"So we're baking bread—for the people at the concert," Francine said.

"We're going to feed them," the three women concluded.

"The radio broadcaster said there's already a quarter million there," Edgar said. "How much bread do you intend to bake?"

By ten that morning, they'd baked about three dozen fat, thick loaves, which were sliced and buttered, with honey smeared on. These were put into all sorts of various sized baskets and open containers, and we three males and two of the women were assigned to help hand them out at Yasgur's farm. We figured perhaps four hundred people would each get a thick slab of fresh bread this morning.

The early morning clarity had given way to clouds, although the sun seemed at times to burn hard through the mist, as though trying to clear it off. It was warm again, warm and muggy. So many apples had fallen into the back of Edgar's pickup from the previous afternoon's stay in the orchard that looking at them Sarah mused, "Wouldn't these go well with the bread?" Answering her own question, she began stuffing her dress and apron pockets with apples.

We did the same, adding apples to whatever containers held the bread, picking more once we'd reached the orchard, where Edgar again parked.

Only a few steps down from the bluff today and we were directly within the crowd. We advanced in a ragged line, trying to remain about ten feet apart. Despite the morning mugginess, people seemed in a terrifically good mood, laughing, dancing, making out under and half-out of blankets. We saw small children playing; either we'd missed them last night or they'd just arrived. There were long lines near the portable toilets, and some people had found wellheads at various spots on the property and were washing up and drinking from them. The food we'd brought might be all some kids ate today—it was vocally appreciated, and we were all in terrific high spirits as we returned to the pickup and headed back to the house for more food.

As we were stepping into the kitchen, Michelle stopped me and quietly said, "Edgar and Sarah asked me to stay after Tom and Francine leave."

She said it with such finality, also with such exclusivity—I wasn't to dream I was also invited to stay, not that I'd even thought about it— that, coming on top of all that business earlier in the morning about her having been *meant* to be there, it made me believe I was supposed to feel as though I'd been slapped, or at least hurt in some less spectacular fashion. But I didn't feel hurt at all. Instead, I felt calm, detached, glad to be separated from the action, even a little relieved despite the accompanying and distinctive sense that her decision would somehow prove to be crucial in my life.

I was also curious.

I wondered which of them—Edgar or Sarah—had approached Michelle and asked her to stay—Edgar first or Sarah first, and when during our quite brief visit they'd had the time to confer with each other and agree upon the ménage à trois, which couldn't, after all, have been an everyday matter. I wondered how Michelle planned on telling Leighton, who was ostensibly waiting for her back in Manhattan. Above all I wondered who would father her child: Leighton, whose astro-data was up to snuff, or Edgar, whose wasn't?

To her I merely said, "Want me to mail your things here or what?"

For the first time, I could actually see Michelle thinking something, literally see her face thinking, My God, all of this is so complex and *that's* all he can think of? Of course it wasn't all I was thinking, but I certainly wasn't about to be accused of sensitivity. She sighed. "I'll let you know."

An hour later, we were all back in the crowd distributing a second baking and a second shaking of the apple trees' bounty, when I suddenly heard a very loud, very British male voice peremptorily utter:

"Boy! I say, boy! Would you bring that here?"

I turned to locate the source of the voice. Uneven as the crowd was, my path had taken me close to an outer edge near the earliest assigned parking area. At first I couldn't tell who exactly had called me, then I made out a dark blond head and an arm gesticulating out of the sunroof of a large, midnight-blue limousine stopped at the crowd's edge.

"Over this way! That's it!" He continued to encourage me and to wave me over as though I were a waiter in some vast outdoor café.

As I came closer, I could see he was a Long Hair, which somewhat obviated the fact of his annoyingly commanding tone of voice and his general condescension, as well as the very large limousine he was in and his black-skinned chauffeur. . . . Somewhat obviated it all. It also helped that I was in a smashing mood today, a little high from all the grass in the air around me, and completely ready to be entertained.

"What exactly do you have?" he asked. He'd pulled himself out of the sunroof to sit upon the limo's roof so that his legs hung over the side windows. It was clear now what he was: a tall, rich hippie half a decade my senior. His clothing, like the car, was expensive: the moiré silk shirt open low, down his hairless sternum, looked to be one-of-a-kind, the sequined black trousers fit his long, well-muscled legs as only custom-made garb could, the chunky, handmade jewelry on his wrists and around his neck proclaimed him a patron of the arts.

"Bread," I said. "Homemade bread with honey and butter. And apples."

"Sounds perfectly marvelous," he exclaimed.

I held my basket aloft for him to reach into.

"May I have some for my friend inside the car?" he asked.

"Sure."

He handed it in through the sunroof.

"We've been on the road all morning," he explained while chewing. "Mmm. Lovely. Just got here a short while ago. Astonishing crowd, don't you think?"

Now that I was looking at him close up, his face was attractive in that peculiarly British manner—both ugly and pretty at the same time, with far too much character, too much exaggeration of feature to be really handsome. His dark blond hair fell heavily straight to his shoulders and in thick sideburns deeply scalloped onto each cheek, to partly cover the ravages of once acned skin. Most striking was his luxuriantly lashed, almond-shaped eyes, which weren't dark, as one would expect such eyes to be, but instead exotically light blue-gray. His slender, aquiline nose and large mouth added an aristocratic touch, especially when his elastic lower lip formed a wicked, enchanting smile.

"Ummmn," he moaned in ecstasy as he bit into the hunk of bread, and honey-butter slipped down his chin. "Don't go," he quickly added when I turned to move into the crowd.

"Have to. There are still hungry people."

"Are you some kind of angel?" he asked, and fixed me with those pale eyes the way a collector fixes a rare specimen onto a page of vellum.

"Of course not." I laughed, aware I was blushing at his extravagant flattery. "Thank those three women." I tried pointing out Sarah, Francine, and Michelle handing out food in the distance. "They baked."

"I don't care a fig about them," he said, testily. More softly, "But I would like to thank you."

"You're welcome," I said, and since I was suddenly feeling his interest far too intently upon me, upon my body, upon my face, for comfort, I left the stopped limo and sailed into the crowd, continuing to hand out bread and apples, aware all the time of his gaze on my back.

"I'd like to do something nice for you," he called out.

"You don't have to," I called back. "Here," to people, "apples too! Fresh off the trees in that orchard."

"I'd very much like to," he continued to insist.

I now realized that the limo was alongside me. He remained atop the roof as the driver slowly drove on, stopping whenever I did.

"Something very special," he added, and he said it so lubriciously I blushed again. I was definitely feeling uncomfortable. Yet for the life of me I didn't want him to stop insisting.

"No, thanks!"

"I know some folk in the bands here today," he said.

I wasn't in the least bit surprised by this fact. I'd already guessed from his accent and car and clothing that he was connected with one of them.

"Do you want to meet someone?" he asked.

"Lennon and McCartney!" I shot back.

"They're not coming. Someone else?"

How could he know with such certainty they weren't coming? "Grace Slick?" I asked.

"And Marty and Jorma? Certainly. Anyone else?"

He was putting me on. I continued through the crowd, stopping to let folks rummage around for whatever they could find in my increasingly empty basket. The limo was there whenever I looked, my pal in his expensive duds washing down breakfast with a fifth of unblended Scotch.

"How about, oh, Stephen Sills?" he tried.

"Okay," I said, thinking that would shut him up.

"And Graham Nash? Or Julian Gwynne?" he said, naming two of the best bass-guitar players in the business.

"Great! Fine!" I said, amused. That he knew *all* of them seemed more and more unlikely.

"Really? You'd like to meet them? Nash and Gwynne?"

"Sure would."

"You would? Well, come on then, isn't that basket empty yet?"

"Almost," I admitted.

"Then you'll come in the car here and meet Julian Gwynne?"

"I don't know. I have to join up with my friends. We have to get back to the house for more food."

"You'd rather do that than meet Julian Gwynne?"

"I can do both," I temporized. The basket was empty. Only one apple left. I held it out, offering it to the general public, and suddenly felt his hand close around mine holding the apple. He lifted it to his mouth and bit into it richly with great smacking noises, apple flesh cracking, apple juices flowing down the stubble of his chin. He offered the apple to me.

"You finish it," I said.

"How can I tempt you if you won't even take a bite?" he asked in a tone of voice so obviously seductive it was both amusing and quite serious.

I bit into the apple.

"Tell you what. Come into the car now, and I'll suck your prick."

I pulled away, but he'd foreseen I'd do that: his other arm lashed forward to hold me tight.

"Wouldn't you like having your prick sucked?" he asked.

I continued to pull away. His arms were really strong. No chance I'd get loose.

"Wouldn't you like to meet Julian Gwynne and let me suck your prick?" he repeated.

"Is he in there?" I asked, trying to get away and look into the limo.

"He will be."

"Well, I'd meet him. But not . . . you know, the other."

"Then how about letting Julian Gwynne suck your prick?" he asked.

Fat chance of that happening. But if he'd let go of me . . . "Sure. Okay!"

"You will?" he asked.

"I said so! Now, let go!"

"Did you hear?" he asked into the car's open sunroof. "He said yes."

Confused now, I asked, "Is Julian Gwynne really inside?"

"Better than that." He still hadn't let go of my hands.

"Who then? Who's there?"

"Come on up," he spoke into the sunroof. "I'll collect on my bet."

"Bet? What bet? Who's there?" I asked, trying to see who it was.

I was still trying to figure out what he was talking about, when, of all people, Alistair Dodge popped through the limo's roof.

"*I* bet him your cherry," my second cousin said. His hair was long and darker than I remembered it, and he was also expensively and hiply dressed, if otherwise unchanged from the last time I'd seen him in Beverly Hills.

"I lost my cherry years ago," I said.

"I meant your homo-sexual cherry," Alistair clarified. "Which it appears you've just now promised to Julian."

"That was a joke," I said. "Besides, he's not even here."

"Isn't he?" the rich hippie on the car roof asked.

"Dear Cuz, Roger Sansarc," Alistair swung his legs over the side of the car, "allow me to introduce you to my friend, the infamous Julian Gwynne."

"You?" I asked the hippie.

"Me!" he said. "Come give us a kiss."

"What are you doing here?" I asked, holding back.

"What do you think? Playing with the band." Julian continued trying to pull me onto the roof next to him.

"No, I meant you, Alistair?"

He'd now slipped off the roof and, getting behind me, was helping to lift me up alongside Julian, who let go of my hands long enough to grab me around the waist.

"I was down in D.C. with Julian when the other members of the band called and said they were coming here. So we came too."

I had all sorts of questions I wanted to ask Alistair. But he simply walked away, looking, he said, for a place to urinate—"I'll find some bushes; I'm not waiting on line," he commented. "See you down there."

As though on cue, the limo lurched forward, and it was all I could do to hold on as we descended bumpily toward where the stage had been set up.

Any doubts I might have had about the rich hippie being Julian Gwynne were blown away the second we reached the performers' area, which had remained successfully fenced off from the crowd. The show's producers and the guards who worked for them knew him. The rest of his band had arrived not an hour before in the big van, and they and their girlfriends had instantly become the center of a general party which we instantly joined. I was introduced all round by Julian. I must have looked as goggle-eyed, as starry-eyed as I felt. "This your new doll?" Jimi Hendrix asked Julian at one point, and though I vigorously denied it, just being among them all I felt as though I'd died and gone to heaven.

Alistair arrived at the party a short time later, and he too seemed to be known among the various performers. References were made by some to a lavish party he'd thrown in L.A. at which certain deeds far too perverted for mixed company had been performed by various participants, as well as another, more staidly public party, attended by seemingly everyone in the music "Biz" in London. When it became known among the hangers-on that I was Alistair's cousin, my own status rose instantly. "He's rolling in it," a girl with a pentagram painted silver over one eye assured me of Alistair. "Great-looking, money to burn, terrific connections, always has good drugs, shame he doesn't go with girls!" she concluded with a sigh.

From this I assumed that (1) my cousin's real estate development of a decade before had paid off as handsomely as he'd hoped, and (2) he'd moved on from assignations in garden rooms with the staff to become fully, openly homosexual, and now associated with other homosexuals— such as Julian Gwynne, who not only was a famous rock musician, but who also appeared to be very much interested in me, even though I wasn't altogether happy about the nature of that interest.

I was really flattered by his attentions. But I was at this party under what I felt were false pretenses, and the longer I remained here, the worse it would be.

"I've got to get back to the people I'm staying with," I told Julian as soon as I found him. We were at the van door, already mostly open, someone's Siamese cat stretched out on the top step. Outside it had begun to rain.

"Why?" Julian asked.

"I don't know," I said. "Because they're the people I'm with."

"*We're* the people you're with now. Your cousin and I," Julian argued.

"I know, but I came with—"

"Wouldn't you *rather* be here with us? With me?" he asked, sadly.

"Well, sure, but—"

"I know what it is: you're disturbed about that little bet I made with Alistair, aren't you? You think it was frivolous."

I tried to tell him that its frivolity was hardly the point.

"Alistair told me I'd want you the minute I laid eyes on you," Julian interrupted. "A few months ago, when he and I were discussing why we'd never become lovers."

"Why *didn't* you two become lovers?" I had to ask.

"Too much alike," Julian said, opening the van door all the way and pulling me down to sit on the step between him and the purring, unmovable Siamese. " 'What you need,' Alistair lectured me in that tone of voice of his," Julian went on, " 'is someone who *looks* like me but *isn't* me. My second cousin Roger would do perfectly. If it weren't for the fact that he's impossibly hetero and you'd have to bust his cherry.' "

"You're making this up," I said and pushed his arm away. He'd draped it over my shoulder as he spoke.

"Scout's honor." Julian put up three fingers in some arcane gesture. "I mean, why should I make it up? Just to explore the delights and manifold mysteries of your undergarments?" He began to illustrate by poking those same fingers beneath my belt, pulling at my B.V.D.s. "Well, perhaps I would. But I'm not."

Behind us, the party was in full swing. Next to me, the Siamese was pretending not to listen to a word of what we said.

"You're not, are you?"

"Not what?" I asked, knowing full well what he was asking.

"That would be *too* grotesque if you were." Julian had wrapped both arms around me, and I had to pick them off finger by finger and yet not push over the cat, who was now looking at us with that mixture of annoyance and contempt cats do so well.

"You know, of course, that no one *is* anymore? Or at least if they are, they pretend not to be."

"Don't you think you've got that mixed up?" I asked, laughing at the faces he was making, delighted to be entertained by him.

"No, luv, you're the one who's a bit mixed up. C'mon, admit it. You find me devastatingly attractive, and you know you'll do anything to have me rip your clothing off and lick your nubile young body from head to toe. Yet you're held back by some nineteenth-century ideas of sexuality. Am I right or am I right?"

"Both," I admitted.

"Well, *that's* a relief!" he said, and grabbed me again even though I'd just managed to pick his hands off me altogether. "I thought you might actually be foolishly unreasonable and not admit the truth. Believe me, luv, I'll respect you as much in the morning as I do now."

"Which isn't much," I said.

"*Isn't?* Why, go find that cousin of yours and ask him if the minute I laid eyes upon you I didn't completely melt like an old plum jam left in the sun? Go on. There you were, walking all bare-chested through the crowd in the noon mist, exuding obvious pleasure not to mention delicious pheromones, and being so charitable. You looked like some apostle distributing fishes and loaves. Honest, you did. That's actually what I told your cousin. I did! Where is he? Alistair! Didn't I tell you young Rog here looked like that litho of St. Philip torn out of my tattered old Bible and tacked upon the wall of my bedroom in Southwark that I used to gaze upon daily and wank off to?"

"God!" I said. "You're such a liar!"

"Am not. Also I was hungry and wanted the food you were giving out. Give us a kiss, luv."

I pulled back. "No way."

"C'mon, don't be like that! This sodding bunch don't care what you or I do. Just a little . . ."

He managed to smudge his face across mine before I could pull back.

"Well, that's not very professional. I suspect you need a bit of training in that area."

"I do not."

"Well, then show us a professional one."

"No."

"Maybe later on," he suggested. "When there's not so many other sods around?"

"Maybe," I allowed. "Look, I really do have to get back to the house and tell them I wasn't stolen away by aliens."

"The day is still young," Julian said naughtily, his hands all over my body.

"C'mon! Let go," I said.

"Tell you what," he temporized. "I'll let you go under one condition: that Alton, my driver, takes you wherever you want. So long as you promise to come back with him."

"I don't want to miss your set. When do you go on?"

"We were slated for fifth this afternoon. But at this rate, who knows?"

It was indeed raining much harder now, with occasional rumbles of thunder. While I'd been in the van—and so very distracted by Julian—I'd not given a thought to what the rain would be like for the enormous crowd stuck out in the open. As the chauffeur drove out of the performers' area and around the throng, I wasn't surprised to see people huddling under makeshift covers and blankets; nor, I guess, was I surprised to see others naked, holding hands, singing and dancing around in the rain and mud.

I was certain the others had returned to the house. Even so, I asked Alton to drive near the orchard where Edgar had twice before parked. No, the pickup wasn't there, although the trees were rather sodden and bare of fruit.

The roads were more clogged than earlier in the day. People were still arriving, remaining in their cars because of the lashing downpour and frequent bolts of lightning.

"It won't last," Alton decreed. "Be over in a hour. Jes' a summer storm."

He negotiated the difficult passage out to the main road and followed my so-so directions to Edgar and Sarah's house, all with good humor.

I expected them to be together when I arrived, sitting around the trestle table in the big kitchen. In fact, I'd been looking forward to having them see me arrive in the limo and me having to tell them that I was going back to be with my millionaire cousin and Julian Gwynne. I had been especially looking forward to watching Michelle's reaction to that news. She might have been invited to stay here with Edgar and Sarah, but I was being driven by Gwynne's driver and returning to his party, and who knew, I might remain all night with him, if I wanted—spending the night in a hotel in Rhinebeck with Julian and Alistair and the entire rock band and its entourage. I thought this constituted revenge of a fairly high order, thought it all out in advance.

When we drove up to the house, Alton shut off the motor. "Boss said not to come back without you," he explained.

"I could be a while," I argued, not liking having my freedom curtailed, since I'd not yet made up my mind what I planned on doing.

"He ain't goin' anywhere without me," Alton argued back. " 'Sides, I can catch me some Z's here as good as dere."

I was even more irritated when I got indoors and the house was empty. Or rather looked empty. Then I realized that both bedroom doors were closed. They hadn't been closed earlier. That meant . . . The tin pot of coffee was still warm, and I poured a cup. I'd been smoking grass with Julian for the past few hours and was starving. Lucikly, some bread had been kept, and I smothered chunks with honey and butter. It was one of the best meals of my life.

Maybe they weren't all asleep, but out. No, Edgar's pickup and Tom's mustard-colored Datsun were still parked outside.

Well, maybe they were sleeping. Just sleeping.

How many to a bed? How many to *which* bed?

Thinking of the combinations possible sent me into giggles. Then I thought about where Michelle was sleeping. And with whom. Whoever it was, it clearly wasn't me. As she'd planned for me to find out. Well, wasn't that too bad! I thought. Maybe I didn't need Michelle. After all, I *hadn't* needed her until she moved in. Hell, I hadn't even known she existed until a few weeks ago. And while she'd been interesting, she'd never been *that* interesting. I could easily live without her. Had for how many years already? But just so she didn't get the impression I couldn't, I decided to write a short note:

Hey you guys! No one was home. And I thought it would be uncool to keep Julian Gwynne's limo driver waiting for me. So I'm splitting. See you sometime. Don't know when I'll get back to Manhattan. Better mail the keys.

Then I couldn't resist adding one more touch, a postscript for Michelle:

P.S. I guess it was just *meant to be!*

Much later that night, following the performances, I told Julian what I had written. I didn't explain who Michelle was, only that we'd come up together. But when he heard about all the bedroom doors being closed against me, he couldn't help but protest. "It's a good thing I took you away from those people."

He'd finally located a room in the Rhinebeck Hotel that had a lockable door, and had at last managed to pull me out of the enormous, noisy, messy performers-and-hangers-on party the entire place had erupted into several hours before. He'd also managed to locate an empty bed, and we were in it together, I quite stoned but by no means as stoned as I was pretending to be. "Why?" I asked, all innocence.

"Why?" Julian asked. "Why? Just think of the ghastly debaucheries they might have subjected you to," savoring them in his mind if not on his lips. "Here, let's get these off you," he added, giving my denims a great pull. "My, you American lads just wear underwear no matter what the situation, don't you?"

"Stop!" I protested and weakly batted away his prying fingers, so he had to use his teeth to grasp the elastic band of my underwear, which meant his hair was tickling my tummy and so I was laughing and rolling around.

"Who *knows* what perversions I might have fallen prey to," I replied, feeling, if truth be told, like some character out of Congreve, or was it Richardson? "Stop, vile ravisher!" I attempted.

"Don't be daft," he replied, having gotten my underwear mostly off by dint of his teeth and fingers. "You known damn well how extremely tacky it *would* have been, whereas here . . . with me . . ." Julian continued stripping off my socks and then looked me over as though I were a very welcome late snack brought up by the hotel's so far mythical room service. "Here, the perversions are perfectly ordinary ones. As I shall proceed to illustrate."

"What do you mean 'How is it with Julian'?" I asked. "It's completely impossible. As you very well know."

Alistair sighed and handed me the bong for another deep hit of Michoacán grass.

We were sitting on the terrace of his penthouse in Chelsea, only a few blocks from my own West Village apartment, yet light-years away in rent, decor, glamour, not to mention the amounts of time and cash lavished on the place.

It was a warm mid-October night, two months since Woodstock. On either side of us stood two perfectly trimmed orange trees, their light citrus oils flavoring the still night air. From inside, we could hear on the stereo the electrified guitar and ghostly vocals of a group called H. P. Lovecraft: their current hit, "The White Ship." A glance into any window off the enormous, wraparound terrace would show a dozen people within, still at the dinner table or stretched out upon divans built into the living room. The refectory table still hadn't been cleared: remnants of Alistair's huge Indian feast lay scattered about, despite the presence nearby—necking heavily with a guest—of Kenny, Alistair's soi-disant houseboy.

I could see Julian, who'd cornered two people between the dining room and kitchen, talking to them with that rapid, staccato movement of lips and head which I'd by now come to recognize as Stage Two: "I've got them hooked; now what exactly do I *want* with them?"

"So does this mean . . . ?" Alistair didn't know how to ask it. "I must sound like Suzy or Cholly Knickerbocker. But are you two splitting up?"

"I'm awfully fond of Julian," I began. "Grateful too. For everything!" I tried to encompass in a single word how much of my life had altered since meeting the rock star.

How explain how *much* it had changed? Outwardly, the only real changes were in my hours and in my associates. I still officially resided in four tiny rooms on the first floor of a West Village tenement. I still officially worked for the same textbook publisher as before. True, I was seldom home anymore except to change clothing or to pick up my mail. My real residence seemed to be one hotel suite or another: the Sherry in New York, the Biltmore in L.A. since we'd been eighty-sixed from the cottage at the Beverly Hills. Sometimes I thought I really spent the greatest amount of my time in an airplane seat flying between places. As for work, when I did arrive at the twenty-sixth-floor office—which was no more than one or at most two days per week, between Julian and the band's gigs—I seldom remained more than a few hours. What was odder was that that was okay too. I still hadn't gotten over how Frank Kovacs—that jerk among jerks—had taken me aside one afternoon and asked, "Is it true about Julian Gwynne?"

He had this stricken look on his face: I was about to reveal his hero as a major queer.

"Is what true?" What had Maria and Debbie told everyone?

"You know, that you're with him whenever you're not here?"

I thought, okay, here goes, I'm about to be fired for being a fag. But the up side was that I didn't need money, and I'd probably be able to collect unemployment insurance.

"It's true. I travel with him and the band wherever they go," I said.

Kovacs all but gushed. "I think Gwynne's the best ever. Even better than Clapton," he said with the sober tone in which people announce deaths and circumcisions. "Don't worry. I'll cover for you. Just keep Gwynne happy and make sure he keeps playing."

It was those words that best explained the way in which my life had changed. I was surrounded by, covered with, drenched in, unable to free myself from the enormous attentions and totally demanding needs of Julian Gwynne's larger-than-life ego.

"I think I understand your problem," Alistair said. He'd known Julian longer than I: surely, he ought to understand. "But you know," Alistair added darkly, "maybe the problem isn't Julian. Maybe it's . . ."

"What?"

"You know, being gay."

"Imagine a little thing like that crossing your mind."

"Well, you *have* been sitting on the fence about your sexuality for years."

"Who? Me? Are you kidding? I've done everything I could to get a girl."

"Please! Girls are a dime a dozen. I have to fight them off and I'm as fly as Oscar Wilde."

"Maybe that's because you have something they want? A name. Money. Where I have jack shit."

"I'm sorry. I've seen far sorrier specimens than you, dear Cuz, have babes lined up." He paused. "The thing is, even the dumbest woman has good intuition. And if their radar reads you're not sure what you want, they generally keep away, in droves." He moderated that. "C'mon, it's not *that bad* being a homo. I've not found it's limited me very much.

And since you're so anti-establishment and all, I would think it adds another feather in your cap. Wear your hair long. Smoke dope. Be against the war. Sixty-nine with a guy. Could you possibly be *more* anti-American if you tried?"

"Maybe." I moped. "But this may only be a phase," I argued, and when the look on his face demanded a response, I added, "I mean, I haven't yet *decided* whether this is it or not. I might still want to go out with women. I might! There are plenty of bisexuals, you know. Guys who date women and men."

"Fine!" Alistair said. "Do your own thing, man! But let me just give you a tip. I'd save that kind of bullshit for your mom and dad. What? They know?"

"My sister was talking about Julian and Dad said, 'Sounds like some commie-fag to me.' He was half baiting her, of course, but he wanted to say exactly that. So I said, 'He *is* a commie-fag. And so am I!' "

This event had only gone down a few days before our penthouse terrace conversation, and I vividly related the scene to Alistair, setting him inside that Long Island dining room he recalled from his youth, with the same relatives—older if not wiser—he well remembered.

"What did he say to that?" Alistair asked.

"Well, after he was done choking on his lamb, my mom said something like 'Serves you right, Richard, for baiting your son like that.' "

"She didn't believe you!" Alistair said.

"Not then, she didn't. Not till I began complaining about the bed Julian and I shared in the Drake when we were in Frisco. She got sort of white-faced, then pulled herself together and changed the subject. My sister's husband kept his head down and went on eating and eating."

"Imagine if they knew *I'd* engineered the affair," Alistair mused.

"They wouldn't believe it. You're still a good little boy to them," I said. "Anyway, you overestimate your role." As usual, I thought.

"You'll admit I was crucial?"

"Once you saw me, sure! You're hardly why I was at Woodstock."

"I might have assumed you'd be there. Everyone of a certain age between Maine and Virginia was."

"Well, no matter who arranged it, or even what happens to Julian and me, I'll always thank him for bringing you and me together again."

I meant it. Because in fact Alistair Dodge now was the changed person my mother had promised he'd be at sixteen—when he hadn't been. I didn't fool myself into believing that it was Love and Peace and drugs that had done the trick. Maybe what had finally calmed Alistair and allowed him to be himself—charming, bright, and funny—was simply success, and that he needn't ever have to worry about money again. Whatever was responsible, I only discovered it with many hesitations and reluctances during late summer and early autumn, as Julian courted me, and only because Julian's ego required that anyone he love in turn love everything and everyone else Julian loved—which happened to include Alistair.

"He did bring us together," Alistair agreed. "Last time . . . I didn't think you'd . . . I sent Julian to do my dirty work. I knew he wouldn't take no for an answer."

The French doors onto the terrace opened, and someone peered at us.

"C'mon out!" Alistair said. "Plenty of room."

Three new guests had arrived. Alistair rose to greet them and show them around. I heard him call the houseboy. "Kenny? Are you alive?" Getting no response, he went indoors with one of the three young men.

As the door opened wider, I heard the Isley Brothers chanting "Time" again and again over a ragalike bass guitar drone. I smelled a new brand of grass at the same time the two newcomers drifted across the terrace and offered me a hit. I offered them a seat. There followed the usual chat about how spacious the terrace was and how stupendous the view: it encompassed the West Village, the lower Hudson River right to the Statue of Liberty. A graceful arc of the Verrazano Narrows Bridge glittered in the distance.

When we stood up for me to point out more specific views, I confirmed that the young man not doing the talking was by far the more interesting-looking of the two. Unlike most people I now associated with, his hair—so black that like Clark Kent's in the comics it was blue—wasn't halfway down his back, but straight, in a natural-looking Beatles bowl cut. In contrast—and when I saw him by electric light and later in daylight this was even more striking—his skin was quite pale, ivory-white, as though he'd managed to avoid the entire recent summer. His eyes were another contrast: coal-black, lavishly lashed, probing, and restless.

I thought his face almost too perfectly featured—small nose, fine lips, cleft chin, deep little dimples—and from what I could see of his body in his black corduroys and short-sleeved chambray shirt, it also seemed petitely if perfectly proportioned. He looked as though he'd been drawn to model for a children's book, stories by the Brothers Grimm, say— except for those eyes: they smoldered like banked fires.

"Cord Shay," he introduced himself. The other was Christopher something or other. Their friend, Alan, now joined us. He carried the bong, newly filled with strong, sweet Michoacán grass, which Cord lighted.

"Know who's inside!" Alan gushed.

"I saw!" Cord said, a hint of sourness in his voice.

"Julian Gwynne," Alan went on, "from———," naming the band.

"I saw!" Cord repeated. "And I chose to come out here."

"Don't you like Gwynne?" I asked. If not, it would be a novelty.

"Never met him. Never want to," Cord added.

His sentences were like that: short, declarative, final somehow. When he looked at you, it was off to one side—not far, an inch—a fast glance; instant assessments seemed to be his métier.

"You know Gwynne well?" Christopher asked.

"Not well. We fuck," I said in the most casual way I knew how and reached for the bong from Alan, who'd begun choking on what he'd inhaled—I hoped because of what I'd just said. Over the top of the water pipe's mouthpiece, I saw Cord Shay stare at me. Did he believe me?

"How do you know Alistair?" Alan asked. I think he was expecting me to say we fucked too.

He was amazed when I said we were related, had known each other since we were boys.

Alistair chose that moment to come onto the terrace, check the bong, add grass, take a hit, pass it around. Inside, the music was the Turtles.

"Uh-oh!" I said. "Who put *that* on?"

"Take it *off*!" Alistair rushed in as we heard the record loudly scraped off the turntable. It was replaced by Dr. John's *Gris-Gris*.

"Julian lets everyone know his taste in music," I explained.

"Another reason to . . . ," Cord mumbled. "All stars . . . selfish!"

"We are all selfish," I said. "Some of us merely have more reason to be."

Cord shrugged and to my surprise allowed himself to be led inside by his friends. I almost joined them, eager to see whether he would change his tune once he was face-to-face with an actual rock star. My guess was he wouldn't. Even though I hoped he would. I remained outside, alone with the night.

I was wondering how to break off with Julian. He'd begun to intuit that—to see he'd been the way in for me to begin to acknowledge my interest in men as sexual/romantic objects—and also to intuit that he was losing me, and to my annoyed surprise, he'd begun to hold onto me all the tighter. It was all ego, I knew. He'd be just as happy to move on to fresh pastures—if only he could dump me first. But it was his very ego that I wanted to get away from.

I'd hoped Alistair would help with my Julian problem, but his willingness to talk about everything *but* when I'd brought it up was so strong, I suspected he'd be useless. Why? Because he was in the middle, naturally. But was that really the only answer? Might he be romantically interested in Julian? He seemed to me to be quite the most eligible young gay bachelor in town, yet despite all the guys around him, Alistair still remained strangely unattached.

I tried patching together bits and pieces of what my second cousin had told me about his life since we'd last seen each other, hoping to discover some telling pattern in the mosaic. Alistair had graduated private school at seventeen, not brilliantly, but not badly either. He'd attended UCLA at Westwood—more or less in his neighborhood—for two years. When the real estate development sold, he'd moved up to Palo Alto and Stanford. He'd taken a variety of business and prelaw courses, and again he'd done well if not brilliantly. He'd connected up with kids from affluent families and managed to get involved in another real estate project, in Fairfax, a "burgeoning" Bay Area suburb, north of San Francisco.

Alistair made Russian Hill his home when he got out of college. By then Diana and Albert had married and divorced, then gone their own ways: Albert up to Anchorage, Diana with a new man to Hancock Park—old L.A. money! Alistair took up with a well-off gay group on the Hill. He had one boyfriend, Michael Someone or Other from that set, and they went into business together, again in real estate, down the coast at Santa Clara, where the growing university brought a need for professional housing. Even though Alistair and Michael broke up, they still spoke often, since the project was incomplete. Figuring backward, I calculated that must have been when Alistair first met Julian Gwynne. From what I knew, they'd had a brief affair and been friends the entire past year. Which of them had done the breaking up?

"He's asking for you." Alistair meant Julian.

"In a sec. Tell me about the dark intense one."

"Cord Shay? Completely edible, isn't he?"

"Just spit out the toes and fingernails! Is he a homo?"

"Who knows?" Alistair shrugged. "I know he and Alan are thick in the draft resistance movement. Not SDS but some initials like that."

"Sounds 'Very Serious Indeed!' They one of your charities?"

"I guess. Alan wanted me to go to a cell meeting. Could you picture me with all those lean, ultra-macho guys who wear *plastique* taped around their nuts?" Alistair asked. "All I could think was, Whatever will I *wear*? And then, What if one of them *calls* on me?"

We laughed.

"Cord is advocating the overthrow of the universe?" I asked.

"Just the Selective Service."

"I hope it happens soon."

Alistair caught something in my tone of voice: "You're not in danger of being drafted?"

"I'm not? Truth is, I've been 2-A forever, but they must have found out I finally graduated, because last week I received 'Greetings' in the mail, along with two tokens to the board downtown."

"Are you worried?"

"I'm just being reclassified."

"I've heard," Alistair tried not to sound alarmist, "the minute they re-classify you, it's off to Fort Dix for basic training."

"I'm twenty-four years old," I argued. "The tri-state area is filled with eighteen-year-olds. They won't bother with me!"

"From Fort Dix they're going straight to Southeast Asia, Cord said."

"They want guys who can't write their names!" I protested, getting more nervous. "Not someone who's been taught via the Socratic method. Can you picture me in a gyrene's haircut, asking, 'But, Sarge, *why* exactly should I scream "Kill, Kill, Kill"?' "

"I hope you're right," Alistair said, and despite my facetiousness I felt a sudden chill: even if I did manage to get out of going to Southeast Asia, I'd still be drafted, pulled out of my comfy life, forced to take orders from cretins, forced to sleep and shit and shower with a hundred creeps! Yecch! "And you?" I asked Alistair.

"I took the Queer-Clause so fast pearls rolled all over that draft office."

"I thought you didn't want it on your record."

"In case I decide to run for senator?"

"I'm just repeating what you told me a few years ago."

Alistair shrugged. "A girl's entitled to change . . ."

"Anyway I thought you did all that just to break up your mother's relationship with Albert," I said, my vague "all that" being, I thought, understood to include my cousin's ill-fated relationship with the gardener.

"Want to know the funny part? As long as I was making trouble, they stayed together. The minute I left, they split."

I found myself thinking that one way Alistair now differed from how he'd been was his near refusal to talk about his family—partly, I suppose, because he now found them boring, and partly because, like Julian and virtually everyone nowadays, Alistair wanted to be considered sui generis: a complete, distinct individual. The end result was to make him humble, even modest.

"Ex-cuse me!" Kenny the houseboy was in the doorway. "Our guests are asking for you."

Meaning Julian was demanding me.

"Tell him to keep his falsies on," I blared, which made silly, skinny, unpretty Kenny shiver in delicious anticipation of an incident.

"When do you go for your physical?" Alistair asked. When I told him the date a few weeks hence, he said, "Don't worry, we'll keep you so doped up the night before, they wouldn't dream of taking you."

Inside, Iron Butterfly was playing "In-A-Gadda-Da-Vida" on the stereo, turned low. People were at the table drinking wine, smoking from the bong. Besides playing messenger, Kenny was clearing the table of the picturesque remains of *masalla murgh*, lamb *korma*, dal, roti, and various chutneys. Candles in the wrought-iron Mexican candelabra had burned down into grotesqueries. Marijuana smoke filled the air.

Julian was seated at the center of one long side of the table, approximately where Christ is placed in Da Vinci's mural. When I chose my own seat across from him, he glared at me, while continuing to pick at the torn ends of what had been a quite tasty *chapati*. Then he relented and kissed his fingers at me. I searched for and found Cord—standing against a wall near the kitchen: as far from Julian as he could get.

The bong was returned to Julian, who began to refill it.

Having an audience, naturally he played to it. Even without a musical instrument.

"This Michoacán grass," he began in his whiskey-fuzzy South London accent, "grows in only one place in the world!"

"Michoacán Province!" someone sassed.

Unfazed, Julian went on. "But *where* in that huge and wild province? I'll tell you where! It grows in a valley hidden within a giant underground cavern, fed by mountain streams and illuminated by air vents dangerously eroding the cavern's limestone roof."

He checked for listeners: most of the group was hooked.

"Only a hundred people in the world know the location of this miraculous subterranean two acres of farm," Julian went on.

"They belong to two families: the Figueras and the Modestos. The Figueras and Modestos do everything themselves: plant the grass, harvest it, weigh and wrap and porter the stuff out of the hidden valley.

"They only sell it clean. Stems are fed to the burros or burned for heat when they're camped at night upon the frigid Mexican plateau, headed toward the U.S. border at Arizona. I've bought kilos of the stuff and never counted more than a dozen seeds. When I unwrapped my first kilo," he paused, "it was so powdery, so rich with buds and flowers, I found myself blinded by a haze of cannabis pollen. Absolutely stoned in seconds without having smoked!"

He sipped his wine. We all turned to watch the person with the bong. Was it our imagination, or were we getting higher than usual?

We waited with anticipation. Part and parcel of the experience of smoking grass and calling ourselves "dopers" were the stories of where a particularly good batch had grown, a sort of oral tradition.

"Eventually," Julian continued, "I persuaded my dealer to bring me to the source of this wondrous bounty! One night, I was taken there.

We traveled for hours by jeep, then by mule. When we arrived, the blindfold was removed and I was in a dark place surrounded by all these amazing people with faces right off Olmec stone carvings."

Julian went on to tell how he managed to charm the Figuera-Modesto families—not into giving away their grass or the secret location of the site—but into making him an honorary member of their clan.

"At first they wanted to cut open my scrotum and take one *teste* out," Julian said, "since single-balledness is common among male Modestos, but I persuaded them that simple bloodletting would do."

He showed us a scar on his left thumb that might have come from anything, an accident with a milk bottle.

"I'm now a co-owner. I plant and reap my own parcel."

Expressions of "Gee-whiz!" and its variants went around the table.

I got up to take a piss.

The story was typical of Julian: far beyond even the legendary stories potheads commonly fabricated or overembroidered, it aimed into the realm of the singularly fantastic. But then, everything in Julian's life was fantastic, one of a kind, unprecedented. Nothing was, or could possibly be, common, nothing ordinary.

Including the story of how he'd met me, which I'd overheard as: "There he was, virtually naked in the rain, handing out fruit and freshly baked bread to hundreds of starving children at Woodstock. And he was a virgin!"

Would Julian have bothered with me if we'd met in a more ordinary way?

I wondered.

"You really don't see it?" Cord asked when I walked out of the john and looked into the kitchen.

"See what?" I asked.

"In him! Oh, never mind!"

I stopped Cord. "What?"

"He's so . . ." Cord searched for the word.

"Phony?" I asked. "Nah. He's just a big kid. A big deprived kid, enjoying himself for the first time in his life."

Cord shrugged. "You're more forgiving."

"Peace. Love. LSD, brother!" I gave the vee sign.

"But I guess you can afford to be," Cord said.

"What's that supposed to mean?"

But he'd gone into the dining room, where the group around the table was breaking up, people getting up to dance to the Stones' "19th Nervous Breakdown," and now Cord also was dancing—or rather shaking himself in place—surrounded by his friends. The next thing I knew they were all leaving.

"You like that bit o' fluff, do you?" Julian said into my ear a second later, as I watched from the sidelines.

"He's cuter than you are!" I provoked back.

"Far too serious," Julian pontificated. "He'll get in big trouble being that serious. Especially since he has such a little prick."

I was getting real tired of Julian knowing everything. "Who says he has a little prick?"

"He has. This big." Julian crooked his little finger.

"He does not!"

"He does too. And it'll hurt when he uses it on you," Julian said, "because he doesn't know *how* to use it. That type never does."

"Want to make a bet?"

"You would! You'd let him fuck you just to disprove me!"

Seeing how irritated I'd gotten him, I said, "I'd let him fuck me to irritate you!"

"You wouldn't dare!" Julian's face said he was joking, but his voice had taken on a certain hysterical edge I now recognized.

Others recognized it too; they'd turned toward us as a group.

"Oh, wouldn't I? Watch me!"

"You fucking little slut!" Julian shouted, as I'd known he would, and grabbed me, as I'd known he would.

I could just make out Cord Shay's face among the chorus watching as I hauled off to throw the right uppercut punch which would connect terrifically to Julian's jaw, knock him out cold, incite reams of gossip column speculation for weeks to come, and effectively end our romance.

"You're coming over later, aren't you?" Alistair asked over the phone.

"I've been at your place all week," I protested.

"Cord Shay might come," he tempted.

Cord had been there almost every night since he'd first appeared.

"You really don't have to baby-sit me, Alistair. I'll survive."

The truth was I appreciated like hell what I'd just called Alistair's baby-sitting. It was thirteen days since I'd decked Julian Gwynne, almost a week since he and his band had gone on their European tour, a tour I was supposed to have been part of.

Instead, I was stuck in this pasteboard cubicle again, nine to five, five days a week, my desk covered by pads of yellow legal paper upon which I doodled endlessly; the single manuscript I was supposed to be evaluating was untouched, in truth unread by me save for its ho-hum preface. Naturally I was second-guessing myself, wondering if in shoving off from Julian I'd completely ruined my life. He'd taken it hard at first, then—as I'd intuited—gone on with his life as though I'd never even happened. That hurt. Even worse, with Julian gone, there was little to divert, amuse, or enlighten my otherwise colorless life. Nothing but— now—the wild improbability of maybe later tonight getting close enough to Cord Shay to lay a tentative hand upon one of his perfect thighs, tightly clothed though it would no doubt remain within the unbreakable armor of his steel-gray work pants.

Alistair said, "I know you'll survive. I just thought you liked Cord."

"Of course I *like* him! I only wonder if I'm, you know, barking up the wrong tree." Before Alistair could say anything, I asked, "What did Alan say when you asked about Cord? You did ask?"

"I asked, and like Christopher before him, Alan was vague."

I sighed. I groaned.

"But neither of them is as cute as you," Alistair quickly said, "and Cord likes you. The only reason he's coming tonight is that I said you'd be here."

"Saith Alistair Dodge. Matchmaker from Hell," I said.

What I wanted to say was *Why? Why match me up with Cord?* Could Alistair merely be trying to cheer me up? That did fit in with what I'd so far seen of the new, improved, post-success Alistair. Why couldn't I believe it? Because, unenlightened me, I still hadn't forgotten the old Alistair, capable of anything.

No, the real problem was Cord Shay himself. I had to admit to myself

I wanted him, physically wanted him, and I'd never admitted that about any man or boy before. Sure, I was interested in his mind. Whenever we were together, we'd talk for hours, mostly about politics, and in fact, to show him I wasn't with him merely for his body or in fact myself brain-dead, I'd actually begun to talk back to him, which meant I'd had to actually think about what he was saying, which in turn meant that I was beginning to *think* radical politics for myself—exactly what Cord wanted me to be doing.

"Suit yourself," Alistair said. "Don't come. But don't complain to me if after all your softening up of Cord, someone else wangles him between the sheets."

He'd hit my hope, and fear, with the precision of a Kentucky marksman.

Maria suddenly appeared in my doorway shaking a piece of paper.

"I've got to go," I said into the receiver. "Alistair, I'll be there!"

I hung up as Maria handed me an interoffice memo, and I was so noodled that after reading it twice I still hadn't a clue what it was about. Maria said I had to sign, confirming I'd read it. I was left to stew about Cord Shay.

For a second, I actually thought of dialing Carl DeHaven in his cubicle on the other side of the twenty-sixth floor and asking if *this* could possibly be my real life; and if so, what I'd done to deserve it.

Then I remembered how Carl was acting around me recently, and I was dissuaded. We'd briefly, if to me unsatisfactorily, talked about this alteration in his behavior: what it came down to was that Carl thought I'd been deceiving him all these years by not telling him I was gay.

It didn't matter to Carl that I myself hadn't been at all cognizant of the fact. Nor did it matter that Carl had always thought Debbie and I were an item, and as soon as he found out we weren't, he'd moved in on her so aggressively they were now living together. It didn't even help that Carl considered Julian's band one of the all-time greats. His sense of betrayal remained—"God, the things I must have said about queers! Oops!"—and could not be shaken. We'd never be close again. Nor would Debbie and I, since she'd sworn fealty to Carl.

Which left me with Maria, dizzier than ever, and Frank Kovacs, more despicable than ever now that he was both fawning and just beginning to suspect the truth: my to-him-magical connection with his rock idol was over.

Which left me with Alistair, who'd become willy-nilly the somewhat distracted ringmaster of his own nightly circus. There were moments when I suspected that anyone with long hair and a pair of bell-bottoms capable of saying "Groovy!" would be admitted to the place. Little by little, however, the mass in what had become known as "Penthouse Perdu" (named after either the breakfast or Proust's novel; it was never made clear) could be separated more or less into three groups:

First were the activists, people like Alan and Christopher who were out to do something specifically political by changing the system, and who used Alistair's apartment as a sometime hangout, free all-night restaurant, telephone answering service, recruitment center, planning room, and fund-raising salon. All this, despite the fact that they were probably the most low-key of all Penthouse Perdu's denizens.

Second were the music people. Or rather, those who did everything but make music. They'd begun to gather with Julian Gwynne's appearance and had never left. A less constant, less fixed, far less quiet, more colorful group, these included Alton, Julian's newly unemployed chauffeur, various record promoters and group agents, out-of-work A & R people, an occasional backup singer, and several well-known Dope-Dealers-to-the-Stars.

The third group was general enough to include myself, Alistair and Kenny the houseboy's tricks, professional connections, recent acquaintances, models of both genders (one—a giant blond Viking—had recently OD'd on acid and howled like a wolf from the terrace most of one night), and friends from the West Coast who happened to be passing through. A group with all sorts of potential, including, as it did, wealthy Third-World Trash such as Nelson Albertavo III, the drop-dead handsome, pistol-toting bisexual tennis-champion nephew of a dictator in Central America; and, even sweeter, Ricardo Melendez, son of the Dominican Republic's consul to the United Nations, a youth with a very long penis and an equally active diplomatic passport, who possessed a propensity for all-night sodomy and for experimenting with new and different drugs he'd smuggle in via his embasssy's confidential pouches—*yage*, psilocybin, you name it!—and which he was delighted to share with anyone present.

Then there was Cord Shay, who stood apart in Penthouse Perdu and who became, as Alistair or anyone with eyes could clearly see, more tantalizing to me every time I met him. It was as though, my sexuality finally declared, my newly released psyche were now free to desire without bounds or limitations.

Tonight, I promised myself, I wouldn't go. Or I'd go and I'd keep away from Cord. Anything to try to forget how much I ached for him.

I hadn't counted on the Dolomite Dentist being present with a new toy.

The dentist's name was—improbably—Arthur Dalmatian. Equally improbable, he claimed descent from Slovenian aristocracy, leading us to confer upon him the above-mentioned moniker. Arthur had gained his entrée to Penthouse Perdu some months previous by performing first oral surgery then oral sex upon Alistair's person during the same visit to his Gramercy Park office, offering unusual drug combinations for both experiences and no explanations afterward.

Arthur was rather taller and thinner than seemed absolutely necessary, with a profile closely resembling one of those overstruck coins from the most degenerate era of the Antonines: an enormous hawk nose, piercing, nearly yellow eyes set into overlarge, flared eye sockets, a low, wide brow, out of which grew, as though perpetually slicked back from infancy, oily, thick hair of a peculiarly repellent shade of brown. What there was of Arthur's lower face supported a vulpine mouth and the merest hint of a chin. Nor was his physique prepossessing: his shoulders appeared to have been dislocated in infancy and reset somewhat awry, so his arms couldn't hang quite flat; his sternum was too low and oddly angled; his spine too high and a bit curved. In motion, Arthur half glided, then suddenly broke into a lurch, before seemingly recovering his balance and gliding again; he appeared to be pulled by the specific gravity of his huge proboscis. At rest, Arthur was an aged peregrine constantly scanning local air currents for unwary prey.

Notwithstanding his appearance, I'd found Arthur to be sweet and funny from the moment I'd met him at Alistair's. Arthur was lovely and kind; Arthur was generous with his time, his laughter, and above all his money (at least one semi-cute catamite lindyed in attendance at all times) and his drugs. Among his drugs this night was a new discovery for us, though not for an orthodontist like Arthur: nitrous oxide, or laughing gas.

Most of us were already high on postprandial wine and grass when this began, and we did as told.

Chaos ensued.

Something like an hour later, I found myself in Alistair's guest bed along with Arthur's boy *du jour*, Kenny the houseboy, and Cord Shay. When the air more or less cleared, Cord and I were kissing. We parted and looked at the other two, who were wildly, almost violently, sixty-nining. Cord laughed, clearly embarrassed, if not too much so, and said, "We better give them room."

We didn't take our eyes off each other until we were out of that bedroom. The living room was dimmed; it seemed covered with writhing bodies. We gingerly stepped over them and went outside, where a light mist had encapsulated the terrace within a network of nebulous light.

I wanted to kiss Cord again. His breath was so sweet, his mouth so tender.

Instead he lit cigarettes for us à la Paul Henreid and said, "Alistair said you have an extra room at your place."

Surprised by this line, I admitted I did.

"Where I'm staying now has gotten a little chancy." Cord paused until I'd understood the tone of voice he was using. I didn't fully understand his words, but I thought . . . "Do you think I could use your place a few days?" That same pause, demanding I listen to what was beneath the words. "Alistair offered this, but we think it might already be under surveillance."

Under surveillance? By the FBI?

Cord didn't elaborate, and his matter-of-fact, almost perfunctory way made it seem uncool, if not downright dangerous I thought, for me to ask details. I have to admit, the memory of my last guest and of our brief sexual liaison was unavoidable: I told him sure, he could use my extra room. We made plans: he'd pick up the extra keys at my office the following afternoon. Oh, and Cord promised not to bring or store dangerous matériel—that was the very word—in my apartment.

Given the tone of our conversation and the weather, an entire nexus of unspoken intrigue suddenly surrounded me. I felt I was playing the Alida Valli role in some forties black-and-white movie I'd never read the script for and somehow or other missed at our local revival house. Especially when someone peeked out the French doors onto the terrace, instantly vanished, and as though by pre-agreed signal Cord said, "I'd better go. See you tomorrow."

He was gone when a few minutes later I went back inside. I did find Alistair, alone in his bedroom, speaking as deliberately as he could into the telephone receiver, from which I guessed he was talking transatlantic. He hung up when he spotted me in the doorway.

"Hamburg!" As I'd already supposed, he'd been talking to Julian.

I resisted the impulse to ask how often they spoke and if Julian had asked about me.

"The show went well," Alistair offered. "But he wasn't able to get to sleep tonight."

"Tossing and turning all night?" I demanded, all innocence.

"Now, don't be cruel," Alistair replied tartly.

I picked up on it: "Tears on his pillow?" I asked sarcastically.

"Nothing but heartaches," Alistair assured me.

"Ain't that a shame!"

"Only you!" he scoffed.

"Oh, yes," I sneered, "he's the great pretender!"

"He holds his own," Alistair defended.

"Ask any girl!" I shrugged. Smartly adding, "Crying in the chapel."

"Why *do* fools fall in love?" Alistair wanted to know.

"Smoke gets in your eyes?" I suggested.

"Love potion number nine?" he wondered. Then, "Green onions?"

"That'll be the day." Philosophically adding, "Heartaches don't always last." Capping it off with, "See you in September."

"Party doll!" Alistair accused.

We fell on each other's shoulders whooping with laughter.

"Seventeen," I finally said, when I could talk again.

"Time out! I don't get that," Alistair said.

"I was counting the song titles we'd used," I said. "Seventeen."

"You're kidding! That's *got* to be a world record!"

"Eighteen if you count 'Seventeen,' " I said. "Or, rather, 'She's seventeen, she's beautiful, and she's mine!' "

More laughter.

We found Arthur in the kitchen, seated on a three-legged stool, eating ice cream out of a pint container. He offered us a taste, and I took it off his spoon and jumped a foot when the frozen metal hit the back of my mouth.

"Trrrroubbbble with your bicuspids, my deaaah?" Arthur asked in a Bela Lugosi accent.

"Wisdom teeth," I tried to say. "Three have attempted to come in, and not one has made it so far."

"Oh, yes, Alistair did say something about that. Let's see!" Arthur handed the ice cream to Alistair and grabbed my chin to look into my mouth. "Open wider, darrrrling," he said, back in the Lugosi mode. "Prrrretend it's Moby's dick! That's better!"

"The last one gave Rog a terrible time," Alistair said, happily scooping away at the ice cream now barred to me. "Pain for weeks in advance."

"No room!" the Dolomite Dentist declared and shut my mouth firmly. "One of the least discussed aspects of continuing human evolution I've noted," he went on, "is that thirty percent of the generation of Americans born since around 1940 will, for one reason or another, end up not with thirty-two, but only thirty, perhaps only twenty-eight, teeth in their mouths. Jawbones are getting smaller. I'll bet by the year 2000 it's a hundred percent of the world population."

He explained with little diagrams drawn on paper towels, and concluded, "I suggest you come to my office and I'll dig out either that wisdom tooth or the adjoining molar before one or both of them become badly impacted."

"Arthur will drown you in nitrous oxide, affection, and painlessness," Alistair said. All of which I suspected was true.

"But, Doctor," I quoted from a recent British comic film, "I'd rather have a baby!"

"Make up your mind, miss," Arthur replied without dropping a beat, "before I arrange the chair."

"I trust you suffered no discomfort," the Dolomite Dentist oozed.

I was slowly coming back to reality from my nitrous trip; the mask was removed from my nose; the air molecules in front of me had stopped dancing the Mashed Potato and were beginning to settle down.

Most of the equipment that had been in my mouth moments before had now been placed upon the tiny mobile table he pushed aside, as he shooed out his assistant and sat down.

I tried moving my mouth parts into speech. "Is it over?"

"In fact, I haven't really begun."

I stared at the glittering little instruments—weren't some of them bloodstained? Perhaps not.

"The problem is a bit more serious than I thought," Arthur said. "Oh, don't worry. Nothing I can't handle."

He went on to explain that my lower left wisdom tooth was coming in not straight but at an angle, pushing the last molar down, right into the jawbone. Naturally one or the other would have to come out. But despite X rays and much probing about the area, he wasn't completely certain if an infection had formed between the two. Just to make sure, he was putting off surgery for a few days, and prescribing large amounts of penicillin.

"I don't want any unpleasant surprises when I finally cut," Arthur said, without explaining what he meant: could Godzilla be lurking in there? Herbert Hoover, Jr.? The ghost of Che Guevara?

He also prescribed a painkiller I'd never had before: codeine, trying me with a pill while I was still in the chair. It hit by the time I left his office, just off Gramercy Park. Walking home down Park and along Fourteenth Street, I felt the soles of my boots floating a good quarter inch off the sidewalk.

Cord Shay wasn't there when I got home. To my lack of surprise: he'd moved in three days before and I'd barely seen him since. He wasn't there when I got home from work, and he was usually dead asleep in my guest bedroom when I left to go to work. He'd not been to Alistair's once since he'd gotten the keys from me, and the one time I point-blank asked Alistair what was going on, Alistair replied, "Some operation in progress. At least that's what Alan intimated."

I'd wait until the "operation" was over with before making my move.

That night I ate tepid chicken soup and yogurt and a few more codeine pills while watching television. I was just carefully brushing my teeth preparatory to going to bed when Cord came in with Alan and three guys I'd never seen before. He didn't introduce me to them but led them directly into his room and came into the bathroom and asked if they could have a little "privacy." Cord was looking great: he smelled like freshly pressed clothes.

"Thing is," he explained, "I wouldn't want you knowing anything you needn't know."

"In case they torture me?" I asked.

"Something like that," he said with a little smile.

He asked how my appointment with Arthur had gone, and when I told him I'd have to wait for the wisdom tooth to be pulled, he responded, "Tough luck!"

It was then, as I was thinking—Rog honey, you are completely incorrect and furthermore out of your mind about this totally straight boy!—that Cord did something: he patted my behind through my underwear and mumbled "Mmmm." In the mirror I could see his eyes watching his hands. He looked up suddenly, his usually hard-as-anthracite eyes gone suddenly soft, then he bussed my nape. A second later he backed out of the bathroom, leaving behind what I thought was a sign of clear interest if not an outright promise of lechery to come.

I listened to their voices—low and conspiratorial—until I fell asleep.

The next day at work, Arthur called to ask how I was doing. Not bad, I told him, but I was only eating soft food, and when I'd awakened in the morning, I'd felt enough discomfort to continue using the codeine.

He said to use as much as I needed: he'd boost the script at my pharmacy if needed. Meanwhile I was to fight off infection.

That day at the office seemed to pass by in an even more dreamlike fashion than usual. Ditto, the evening. I'd by now doubled my codeine intake, and spread out on my sofa, smoking grass, I enjoyed as never before Mahler's *Resurrection* Symphony on my stereo. I'd just gotten up to change the mood by putting the Stones' *Beggar's Banquet* album on my turntable when Cord came in.

"Feelin' no pain," I assured him.

Amazingly, he had nowhere to go, nothing to do, no one to telephone, and could think of nothing more pleasant than joining me on the sofa smoking grass and listening to Jagger & Co.

Two cuts into the album, I thought, this is nuts: I was trembling with passion and unfulfilled lust. I sat up, turned over, and carefully began to unbutton the front of Cord's short-sleeved shirt.

He didn't resist. Nor did he help me. He didn't even open his eyes.

I began kissing his smooth-skinned, nearly hairless torso all over, nibbling lightly on his nipples, then sliding into his navel. His armpits were also nearly hairless, almost sweet with musk. I traveled down the single line of dark hair below his navel into his belt. When I looked up, his eyes were still closed, his lips moving in silent speech.

Without lifting my mouth off him, slowly, so inexorably he would hardly be aware of it, I undid his buckle, then so quietly he'd barely notice, I snapped open the top metal button of his corduroy jeans, moving my mouth lower and lower as I gingerly unzipped him. Cord wore pristine white Jockey-type shorts of a brand I didn't know. I thought he was about to say something, to stop me in what I was doing, so I quickly began kissing the bulge in his underwear until it hardened and thickened. Seconds later, he was sidling, helping me pull down his pants. I never lifted my mouth until he was completely undressed.

I covered his lower body with my own naked upper torso. Julian Gwynne had predicted a small cock, and he hadn't been far off. Cord's wasn't large, but like all of him it was smooth-skinned and very pretty, with its pale white shaft and sore-red tip; perfectly proportioned, appropriate, part of him. I sucked him off twice without stopping. Cord's only comment the entire time was during his first climax: he began to sit up, gently lifted my hair off my face so we could make eye contact, looked as if he were about to ask me something, then finally murmured "Oh!" somewhat surprised and fell flat back again.

Physically I was satisfied: I'd come without touching myself. Psychically I was thrilled: I'd possessed Cord. We went to sleep quickly and deeply.

That was a Friday night. As Saturday ensued, I began to discover that two codeine at a time wasn't enough. I needed three, then four—and more often than before. (Hadn't Grace Slick and Marty Balin warned they'd do nothing for me?) Eating anything, even yogurt, now seemed impossible. I kept checking the bathroom mirror every half hour or so, certain my face was swelling on one side. When I peered inside my mouth in the mirror, it looked raw, rubicund.

I'd phoned the Dolomite Dentist at his Gramercy Park office twice and been told by his answering service he wasn't in but that my emergency message would be conveyed as soon as he checked in.

That was noon. By six he hadn't checked in. I phoned Alistair.

"I thought you knew where Arthur goes on weekends?" I asked.

"I do! I do! If I can only find the information! . . . It's somewhere in New Jersey."

"New Jersey!" It sounded as far as Nepal, Kamchatka, the Ross Ice Shelf.

"Where Arthur is in New Jersey, it's very nice. The Montclair area. Quite horsey," Alistair said.

"I'm feeling pretty horsey myself. Especially several teeth!"

"Are you running a fever?" he asked.

"Of course I am, Mother dear," I replied.

"Well if the penicillin isn't doing the trick, Daughter dear, I suggest some sort of homemade poultice."

But when he heard that I couldn't even take down directions to make one, Alistair promised to send over Kenny to make it for me.

Cord had gone out sometime after breakfast. He hadn't returned by nightfall. That was okay by me since I very well knew by now that I was unfit company for anyone: my mood swung back and forth between total despair, the certainty I'd die of pain—now increasing geometrically—and a complete and, yes, a definitely homicidal rage at Arthur Dalmatian for not taking the tooth out last week and for going off and leaving me like this.

Kenny the houseboy arrived with the poultice makings, but one look at me convinced him it was useless. Instead he dosed me with Nembutals out of his own private stash, stayed with me until I passed out, and let himself out.

The following day was Sunday. I awoke in pain, still hung over from the Nembies, and from there I proceeded to stumble downhill. I did somehow manage, by sipping it very very slowly, nearly an eighth of a cup of tepid coffee made the previous day. I attempted to plump myself onto pillows on my sofa and to try to look at what I was certain was my last morning on earth. Two-and-a-half bars of birdsong outside my window made me itch to strangle the feathered villain, to obliterate the entire avian population. Someone idling his motor a block away toyed unknowingly with his own death at my hands. Music, light, speech, food—anything in the least bit resembling human activity or pleasure was naturally completely out of the question.

Around two in the afternoon, Alistair called.

"You sound terrible!"

"You ought to see me," I managed to joke.

"I found the address and the phone number and called. Arthur won't be into his office till Tuesday."

I already knew that. "I'll be a mortality statistic by Tuesday."

"Arthur has an office in Jersey. It's primitive, not as well equipped and . . ."

"I can't wait. I'm going!"

". . . he won't have anyone to help him in surgery and . . ."

"I'm going," I declared.

Alistair bit the bullet. "I'll rent a car and driver and go with you."

"You're a saint," I declared.

I'd canonized him a bit prematurely. It required multiple phone calls and several hours for Alistair to come up with a car. By then it was late afternoon: new, shooting pains had begun, and indeed had already defined themselves into two distinct types—I called them Fire Engine Siren and Bolt from the Blue; neither were very pretty to watch.

They'd begun to modulate and meld so adeptly—themes in some Satanic duet—as we reached the other side of the George Washington Bridge that Alistair had to let me lie down alone in the limo's backseat, while he moved up front next to the driver. In the back, according to Alistair, I loudly moaned and groaned all the way to semirural Montclair.

I was far beyond caring what effect I made. Every bump the size of an atom in the asphalt not completely absorbed by the DeVille's shocks stilettoed me close to death. Once, when the car suddenly stopped to avoid hitting a child on a bike, I was thrown forward, smashed into the back of the front seat, and the dull, hard, sudden pain was such a sweet relief to me from the other sharper and more constant pain that I smiled, even cooed a bit, Alistair later told me, which badly frightened him and the driver.

Soon after that I blacked out. I came to and was semiconscious, and quite delirious, by the time we reached Arthur's country place. I remember little of what happened next, except that they moved me into his office: a room almost entirely surrounded with little panes of windows, as though it were a converted back porch, and he sat me in what looked like an ancient barber's chair. I also recall Arthur filling what looked like the largest needle in the world with a milky white fluid. At the time it made little difference what it might be since I glided in and out of consciousness throughout the procedure.

It was semi-dark when I awakened. I was lying upon an enormous, high-backed, tufted leather chesterfield in what looked to be Arthur's study or den. As I rolled over, I heard voices in an adjoining room. Heard them without spears of pain, I noted, and was even able to make out Arthur's and Alistair's voices, although they were keeping it down, doubtless for my sake. I was still groggy, but I could sit up. Only then did I notice that my mouth was packed full on the inside, my head entirely wrapped in a cloth containing an ice pack. The relief was so sudden, so complete, I began to weep.

"There he is!" It was Alistair and Arthur. "You're not still in pain?"

"Ahhm mgcch bbbttrr," I said and shook my head emphatically no to his question.

Arthur untied the head wrapping and touched my face, saying the swelling had already gone down a great deal. He looked inside, removed about a half ton of gauze he'd put in there, declared himself satisfied, and stuffed it all back in. He told me I'd slept three hours. "It's the morphine I gave you."

"Mrrffnn?"

"A strong derivative. That's all I had here. I don't as a rule use this office. Only in emergencies."

"Thhhnnks, Rrrthrrr." I managed to convey my gratitude.

He told me the wisdom tooth had moved faster than he'd dreamed it would, in effect pushing the back molar pretty far toward the jawbone. The shooting pains I'd felt were actual nerve tissue touching bone tissue. He'd removed the wisdom tooth and cauterized any nerve endings he'd seen. He told me I had a hole in my mouth big enough to put my thumb tip inside. I was to go to bed and stay in bed for the next three days.

"Mmmpssblll!" I declared. "Ssslcctvv ssrrvvsss mmmrra mmmng!"

"He's saying he's got to go down to the Selective Service tomorrow morning for his physical," Alistair explained. "He's got to go. They hunt you down if you don't make an appearance. It's when? Seventhirty?" he asked me.

"He's not in any condition to take a physical!" Arthur said. "Besides which, a blood test would show up all the morphine in his body. I'll write a note excusing him until he's better."

While Arthur was in his office, Alistair explained that if I wanted, he'd go to Rector Street with me the following morning, have someone look at Arthur's letter, and get me home again.

"There! I wrote it on my NYU stationery," Arthur said, handing me the letter. "I've got a position there! That should add a bit of prestige!"

I still couldn't focus, so he read it aloud. It said that I'd had major oral surgery and lost blood, and was still under medication. I should not be out of bed for the next few days. Arthur could be reached at any of three phone numbers to confirm this, although any dental surgeon looking into my mouth would see how badly off I was. He stressed at the beginning and ending of the letter that I was under his care and should at all times be treated like a patient recovering from surgery.

"Hand them this as you go in," Arthur instructed. "Find a seat and wait for them to give you another date."

I thanked Arthur again, even though I knew it meant putting off the Army physical to another time. Alistair led me to the car, and I snoozed all the way home. He had to half carry me into my apartment and put me to bed. The next morning at 7 A.M., to my amazement, Alistair was there again to get me dressed and to help me out of the apartment and down to Rector Street.

The way I figured it, we'd go in and be out again in a few minutes. A half hour at the latest.

I couldn't have been more wrong.

First, they wouldn't let Alistair past the front door. I suppose they'd had assaults or threats of demonstrations from activists: they only let in people holding "Greetings" slips in their hands.

Alistair carefully explained to the MP at the door that I'd had oral surgery and had a letter from my doctor. The MP moved his head in a manner that certainly indicated comprehension, but he didn't reply until Alistair again demanded entry, at which the MP said, "I'll take care of 'im!"

His way of taking care of me was to walk me in and promptly leave me alone. I found myself standing in a huge empty place with signs and arrows everywhere on the floors and walls. Among, I should add, scores of other young guys also holding "Greetings" slips—although without my added envelope—all of whom seemed as in the dark about what to do as I was.

In the distance, at one high, closed-in desk window, someone took hold of our "Greetings" slips, found our names, and handed us back manila envelopes to hold our medical files. We were told to go to Number One.

Speaking a bit better, despite the mass of gauze in my mouth, I said, "I've got a doctor's note."

"Show it at Number One," the soldier behind the high desk said.

Number One turned out to be merely secretarial: a desk where one could correct any incorrect data already written on one's folder.

"I've got a doctor's note," I said.

"Show it at Number Two," I was told.

Number Two was for those who questioned their current draft status.

"I've got a doctor's note," I said, showing the envelope.

"Show it at Number Three," I was told.

Number Three was in another section of the building, down a long corridor with arrows on the floor enclosing bold red threes and pointing ahead. A long line of guys waited ahead of me. I looked in vain for a chair.

When, at last, it was my turn, I saw that we were at the eye test. "I've got a doctor's note," I said, and thrust the envelope at the medical-looking person.

"What's it for?"

"Oral surgery. Last night. Here." I kept trying to give it to him, but he kept backing off. "Take it!" I insisted.

"Eye surgery?" he asked.

"Oral surgery!" I said, opening my mouth and showing it packed and bloody.

"This is for eyes. You have surgery on your eyes?"

"Of course not. In my mouth . . ."

"Then you can take the eye test."

Which I took.

"I'm supposed to be home, in bed. I just had surgery last night," I explained, as he marked my sight results on my file and handed it to me. "Where do I get this looked at?"

"Try Number Four."

Number Four, on the opposite side of the building, through another series of long, well-marked corridors, turned out to be hearing tests. Naturally, I found no chair, but another long line, and once again I was forced to stand and wait and take the test and from there was sent on to Number Five.

At about Number Seven, a floor up and halfway around the block, I finally arrived at blood tests. Once again I, my protests, and my envelope were completely ignored, as another medico took my blood pressure, then frowned.

"You got arrhythmia?"

"I had oral surgery last night. I'm supposed to be in bed," I tried explaining once again. "Here. It's in this doctor's note."

"How long have you had a heart condition?" he asked.

Once again I attempted to explain. But he merely untied the rubber from around one arm and put it around the other one, and tried testing again.

"You sure you don't know anything about a heart condition?"

"I had oral surgery last night," I explained. "I lost blood. Wouldn't that explain why your blood pressure test shows me close to death?"

He shrugged and marked down some numbers on my file.

At Number Eight, down in the basement, a city block away from Number Seven, I was supposed to give a half pint of blood. By now it was 11:30 A.M. I'd not eaten or drunk anything since yesterday morning's eighth of a cup of coffee. I'd been on my feet all morning without once sitting down. I'd been shunted around from one place to another, totaling about five miles. I was deeply fatigued, and there wasn't even a wall to lean against! I was waiting along with others on a long line defined by a waist-high, fragile-looking, wooden railing that twisted rectangularly around and around through a huge, otherwise bare room, when someone came up to me and asked me to roll up my other sleeve to get ready to have blood taken out.

"I can't," I explained. "I lost blood last night during my oral surgery." I attempted to thrust my letter at him. He too ignored it.

"Why can't you give blood?" he asked. "Religious reasons?"

"I just told you." I once more tried to hand over the letter.

"Then you don't refuse for religious reasons?"

"It doesn't matter," I said. "My blood is full of morphine."

"You're a morphine addict?" he asked.

I figured this might get me to a doctor who'd actually read my letter.

"My blood is full of morphine," I said.

"How long have you been a morphine addict?" he asked.

"Years," I said, still expecting to be taken somewhere. "Since birth."

He merely marked my file, gave it back, and moved on to the next person.

At the head of the line, I attempted once more to hand over my letter, and to explain. Again it did no good. When I resisted having any blood taken, two MPs were called over and they held me down while blood was taken out of my arm. I was so weak I offered only token resistance.

"There! That wasn't so scary, was it?" the doctor said, when he'd gotten his half pint of blood out of my arm. "You can get up now."

I sat up and felt distinctly odd.

"I don't know why you'd want to go around saying you're a morphine addict," he continued as I tried to get to my feet. "Anyway, that type of thing can be checked out, you know."

He covered my newest wound with a swab of alcohol and a lozenge of gauze. My elbow was bent back, my file was shoved under my other arm, and I was shoved out beyond the curtain, to walk the maze past those coming in to get their blood taken.

After six steps, the wooden railings seemed to lean in together, then move out again. I thought that a bit odd. After another few steps, I could see guys looking at me carefully, as though they knew me. Strange, I didn't know any of them. Another few steps and the walls seemed to angle in bizarrely and turn into yellow-and-black checkerboard patterns, which twisted around so curiously I began to lose my sense of balance. They crashed together, intermeshing, yellow into black. . . . I was still tightly gripping Arthur's letter, using it to prop me up . . . and a great cheer went up as I hit the floor and blacked out.

Alistair was there when I woke up. He was dressed in his best suit and tie and wearing horn-rimmed glasses, and he was talking in a tight little voice to a variety of military doctors who sat across from him looking red-faced and distinctly uncomfortable. Other men were coming and going rapidly from the room. I was lying on a cot, a rough wool blanket tightly wrapped around the mattress, a male nurse in uniform at my side.

". . . any long-term effects, naturally, we plan to seek considerable damages, both from those individuals involved, and the board itself . . . ," I heard Alistair saying, and I thought, He's got it well in hand whatever it is. I went to sleep again.

When I awakened, I heard someone protesting, "We can't possibly have an ambulance come to the doors."

"He'll not remain here for your malpractice another minute," Alistair said tightly. "I demand an ambulance."

Phone calls had to be made. Meanwhile he came over to the bed, smiled down at me, said everything would be all right, and explained that once I'd collapsed, Arthur's letter was found gripped in my hand, still unopened and unread, and the entire board staff panicked. They'd phoned Arthur, who'd phoned Alistair, as my next of kin.

After many more phone calls, one of which Alistair took, it was decided that no ambulance would be allowed, but a police van outfitted with a gurney would be waiting outside the side door of the SSS building, with a military nurse to attend me for a minimum of twenty-four hours. Alistair agreed, adding, "This is merely the least amount of humanitarian aid you could offer given the situation was entirely brought about by your medical incompetence. I want to stress that this in no way precludes any future lawsuit," at which the others all got huffy and irritated again.

My cot had wheels, and after a variety of papers were read and discussed and signed by Alistair and the others, I was quickly wheeled through corridors into a section of the building even I'd not been in before.

The minute the doors to the outside opened, I heard the chanting. We were in some sort of back loading area. Even so, I had to be lifted off the cot and into the gurney, which would then be slid into the police van. In the few minutes this required, I heard a familiar voice shout over a megaphone, "There he is! Another victim of the Selective Service's bureaucratic barbarism!" A chant from dozens of people rose, cries of "Stop the War Now!" and references to "Tricky Dicky." Two men with flash cameras jumped up to snap my photo, before MPs knocked them back down off the edge. I heard Cord Shay's voice once more: "You can't run! You can't hide the victims!" Then I was inside the van with the male nurse in uniform. The van doors were shut and locked, and it took off.

I couldn't believe my ears. I had to raise myself and look through the meshed window. Sure enough, there he was, Cord Shay, at the megaphone. And scores of demonstrators. All for little old me! I was touched, moved. It was so . . . But wait! How could they have all gotten here so quickly? Gotten so organized and . . . ?

Unless . . . Unless . . .

Oh, no!

"Now, don't get bent out of shape," Alistair was saying to me defensively a half hour later.

He was already there at my apartment when I was brought in. The nurse had gone into the living room and was on the phone, confirming his arrival.

"It was merely a matter of there being an opportunity," Alistair was saying. "It wasn't in the least bit personal. Anyway, this is bigger than you or me or any single one of us. An entire chain of these actions is occurring across the nation. So many at once are bound to cause a stink and to force change in the system. Do you understand?"

I understood, all right.

I also understood that Arthur should have operated last week and not waited. And that Cord Shay had not a shred of personal interest in me but had moved in and allowed me to . . . humiliate myself—he was probably not even gay—just to carry out their plan. Lastly, most devastatingly, I understood that Cord and Alistair had planned this weeks ago, and that it had been set into motion that night in his kitchen. I'd suffered intolerable pain and might have really been injured. But it made no difference to them. I was merely a pawn in their— No wonder I'd hallucinated chessboards!

"I understand everything," I told Alistair in the calmest voice I could summon. "Everything and all of its ramifications. I want you to leave. Now!"

"I'll check up on you," he said.

"Don't bother!"

I recovered, my mouth none the worse for it, after all.

The score of nationwide actions of which mine was merely a part were heavily reported in the media and had their intended effect: within months, the U.S. Congress had changed the law to approve a lottery for draftees, thus eliminating the worst abuses of the Selective Service.

Naturally I never sued them. But I did receive a new draft status: 4-F. "Cardiac Condition," it read. I laughed all day.

I never saw Arthur or Cord Shay again. By the time I was ready to forgive Alistair, he'd moved out of Manhattan and back to the Coast.

Book
Four

Chain of
Fools

1991 AND 1974

They didn't bring us to the nearest precinct house, but instead down-town, to the Tombs, which was both annoying and frightening. We did have an ACT UP legal counsel present, an anorectic-looking lesbian in a Bogart trench coat named Therry (short for Theresa) Villagro, who seemed to know her way around the system, and who arrived about ten minutes after we did, chain-smoking perfumed cigarettes, sipping coffee out of the largest Styrofoam cup I'd ever seen (a pint? a quart?), and yelling to no one in particular I could see that she was going to get everyone from the ACLU to the Helsinki Convention to come monitor what they were doing to us.

To us she said: "I didn't need this shit! I've already got a hemorrhoid flare-up and my roommate's cat just went into labor."

A half hour later, after we'd been duly fingerprinted and pho-tographed from two angles, Therry told us we'd be put in our own hold-ing cell, "in a somewhat nicer section of this hellhole."

Nicer and more isolated. It took the turnkey five minutes to locate it, another five to find the key to the corridor we were to be placed on, and once we did get inside, he looked around as though he'd never seen it before.

"Should I know who you guys are?" he asked.

"Just Your Everyday Urban Terrorist," Junior Obregon said. "Why?"

"This is our VIP lounge," the cop said, awed.

Not quite my idea of heaven, but the lounge was orderly and newish, with a not-too-battered sofa, coffee table, and TV, and in one corner, candy, cigarette, and coffee machines that, it turned out, actually worked. The three cells that opened onto the lounge looked comfortable, if not clean.

"Better than some motels I've stayed in," James Niebuhr summed it up, leaping up to the top bunk in the closest cell. "If I had to, I could hack this for a night."

"So could I," Junior said, and leapt up next to James. They began to make out while I fiddled with the TV, seeing if I could find a station. All I managed was voices, and most of those were cable. No remote control, wouldn't you know. Naturally there was nothing to read but some aging *People* magazines and one newish *Sports Illustrated* with a longish story on, but not a single underwear photo of, my favorite sports personality, quarterback Joe Montana. I kept fooling with the TV channels until I was bored, then I flattened out on the sofa and stared up at the stained tiles of the ceiling, trying not to be too anxious, and at the same time trying not to listen to the sounds of lust from the cell. Don't know how they could do it: sex was the last thing I needed to think about now.

We'd been there scarcely ten minutes when the door was unlocked and my attorney, Anatole Lamarr, entered. He was dressed in his idea of casual: a sea-green Ralph Lauren polo (with the collar kept up) under an overdecorated Italian soccer team sweatshirt, preppie tan slacks baggy enough for his thickish middle, penny loafers, no socks. With him, his attaché case.

Now my lawyer was no relation to Hedy, of course, except that the actress was indeed responsible for Anatole's last name. Seems as though Anatole's father emigrated to this country during the early thirties from some German-speaking enclave in *Mitteleuropa*, arriving with little baggage but an almost endlessly long and unpronounceable surname, which happened to begin with the letters *L-a-m*. Someone suggested he shorten and Americanize his name and handed him a copy of the *New York Telegraph*, where he found his future identification in the movie pages.

His scion, Anatole, now looked around the place we'd been put, waited till the cop on duty exited and until Junior and James stopped necking long enough to look up and see who he was, then dropped the attaché onto the coffee table and said, "Not bad! You been sucking off the deputy mayor?"

"We thought it was you!" I replied. "We were going to thank you."

"Not me." Anatole sat down. "Must have been your dyke counselor. Some of those ladies have real pull," he said admiringly. "As for you," sitting down next to me on the sofa and lightly slapping my face, "what's all this? You decide you've only got one life to live and you might as well do it as a revolutionary?"

Before I could answer, Anatole said, "Tucker saw you on 'The Eleven O'Clock News' and warned me I'd be hearing from you."

Tucker was Anatole's lover of the past few years: a sweet guy a few years younger, not even beautiful really but with the substantial attractions of a swimmer's body, big blue eyes, and pitted facial skin. Tucker came from Arkansas and still liked to pretend he was White Trash, an increasingly difficult pose now that Southern Discomfort—his soul food catering company—was edging into *Fortune* 500 territory.

Junior Obregon had dropped off the side of the bunk and come over to us. He was standing there staring as though Anatole were a celebrity.

I ignored Junior. "To answer your questions in their order of importance . . . First, the as yet unasked question," I said to Anatole. "The newscaster is cuter in person than on the tube. And shorter. And too butch to breathe."

"That's what Tucker thought," Anatole said. Then, to Junior, "You expecting an autograph?"

"No, I . . . we . . . You wouldn't happen to have a condom on you, would you? They took our wallets and we couldn't, you know, ask!"

Anatole looked from Junior to me with those hooded eyes of his and said, "Where do you *find* them? Do you *advertise*? Or *what*?"

I introduced them. James joined us and attempted to explain how he usually didn't get sodomized, but the excitement of the demonstration and the protest and the banner and the arrest and the handcuffs, what with the built-in fantasy potential of being in a jail cell and all . . . until Anatole put up a hand to stop him and promised he'd try to locate a condom if the two of them went away right now and stayed away while he and I talked . . . if they could manage to contain themselves that long.

"Now what *is* all this?" Anatole asked me. "You were arrested on criminal trespass. It remains open to question whether or not your statements on TV were slanderous. They're certainly not going to endear you to the municipal government. Or make it easier for me to get the charges dropped."

"Is criminal trespass a felony?"

"Misdemeanor."

"Find a judge who hates the mayor and get him to drop the charges."

"Perhaps," Anatole said, probably knowing full well that was exactly what he intended to do and already lining up potential candidates. "The real question is: What are you doing, Rog? This awning leaping isn't like you. It's behavior I'd expect from Wally. Not you. Where is Wally, anyway?"

"He was at the demonstration. I lost him. That's why I did this," I said and went on to explain what had happened.

Halfway through my explanation, I could see Anatole's eyes begin to glaze over. He'd already heard more than enough.

". . . so," I moved toward summation, "I joined them on the roof."

Anatole shook his head slowly. "Then I'm to take it this is an isolated incident and not early Alzheimer's or some manifestation of dementia?"

"Come on, Anny! It's politics! There was no self-aggrandizement in it."

"Maybe."

"We did it for all those poor queens dying out in the gutter. For all your yuppishness, that must mean something to you too."

"I said, maybe!" he said so strenuously he might as well have said no.

Now, I've known Anatole for close to a decade, and I know he can't be bullied. I also know that he carries some deep-seated resentment about being gay. Nothing personal or even psychological, mind you, and most of the time he'll deny it. It exists on a simple, practical level: Anatole believes that being gay has held him back, kept him from reaching his fullest social potential among the rich and powerful of this world. That, Anatole will be the first to admit, is all he ever really desired. He'll also admit that it's a silly, superficial desire, but desires being what they are, that makes no difference at all. Anatole's belief is,

of course, true: his gayness *has* held him back. What he hasn't recognized is that it's also protected him from getting too close to that great
source of American decadence and—worse—dullness: the upper crust.
To Anatole, however, it's all particularly irritating, in that he sees being gay as the only thing holding him back, when in fact being Jewish
with a made-up last name is at least as crucial a factor. However, as a result, at times—one can never predict exactly when—Anatole's resentment will suddenly settle in deeply and he'll take on some case, *pro
bono* or not, almost invariably against someone in power or position
who's been recently weakened. And Anatole will attack—with great
strength and accuracy and persistence, until his opponent is left evis-
cerated on the sidewalk. It was this very potential in Anatole I was now
counting on.

"Anyway," I asked, "when's the last time you had to bail me out?"

"You've made your point."

"You *can* bail me out, can't you?" I asked.

"It'll take an hour or two."

"Good. Because I've got to get out tonight."

Anatole looked suspicious.

"I'm not going back to the demonstration. Cross my scrotum and hope
to get crotch rot if I'm lying. What time is it?" I checked my $29.95 Radio
Shack black rubber special against Anatole's thousand-dollar diamond-
studded Tourneau Special. "After midnight. The demonstration'll be over
in a half hour."

"So what's the hurry?" Anatole asked.

"It's nothing."

"Ro-ger!" Anatole suddenly sounded like my Great Aunt Lillian.

"Okay, okay! It's my cousin, Alistair. You remember him?"

Anatole remembered. In fact the way he looked made me suddenly
wonder if I were on shaky ground. "Did you guys have a thing?" It was
unlikely that I'd not know about it. Or was it?

"Not a 'thing.' Anyway it was a century ago. What about Alistair?"

Now I really wondered. Should I tell Anatole? Maybe not. He was already pondering how flaky I'd become.

"It's his birthday tonight. A big party. I promised I'd go."

Anatole relaxed. "I'll see what I can do."

He stood up, tucked in his shirt, and picked up his attaché case. "What about them?" referring to James and Junior, still madly necking.

"They'll be okay."

As Anatole knocked on the door to be let out, Junior reminded him to get the condom.

They went back to their necking, and I went back to trying to get the TV to work, then settled for the sound from MTV, which I turned on low. The lights suddenly dimmed, although they didn't go out completely.

I lay back on the sofa and pondered: when did Anatole and Alistair have an affair? They did have one: that was obvious now. But it had to have been before Tucker arrived on the scene.

Let me think. It must have been . . . By 1976 I was back here in New York, working at the magazine. Could they have met that summer at the Pines? No, Alistair was still in Europe with Doriot. Yet it had to have been earlier than '79, because after then it was years before Alistair and I spoke again. When had I first met Anatole? Fall of '78! Up at the Cape! Of course! Alistair had left his wife in Italy and had visited there briefly at the time and . . .

"Bake, broil, or boil?" Patrick asked.

"Why ask me?" I asked, helping to chop the crudités.

"You're the seafood maven," Luis explained.

"Give me a break!" I said, and moved along the counter to reach for more ice cubes. Patrick's Bloody Marys were superb, but strong. We didn't have too far to drive to get home from here later tonight, but the night was still young, and Truro can get totally fogged in mid-September; I didn't trust the others behind the wheel trying to locate the place we'd rented.

"Lu said you were into biology," Patrick said.

"I know something about animals. Biology sounds . . . well, like paramecia and all that."

"Animals then. So you'd know which way kills the lobsters fastest. With the least pain and thus the least release of bad chemicals."

"Lobsters don't have brains," I explained. "They have four clumps of neural retia. Here, here and . . . along this axis." I illustrated with the knife point on the cutting board, then saw Patrick and Luis's nearly blank looks in response and tried again. "Have they been in the freezer?"

"Four hours."

"Boil 'em!"

"Don't they kick against the sides of the pot and scream in high-pitched voices?" Patrick asked.

"Sometimes. It may be a reflex. You did ask for the quickest way."

Patrick opened the freezer compartment and poked at the bags filled with several unmoving four-pound crustaceans. He chomped down hard on a carrot stick and did his best Bogie imitation: "You're gonna take the fall, angel!"

Luis pulled me halfway out of the huge kitchen, to where Patrick couldn't hear us. A little stairway rose from this side deck to the wraparound deck. Unlike up there, from here the sunset view was at best sketchy.

"Well? What do you think?" Luis asked.

"As I said before, freeze 'em and boil 'em!"

He slapped my face lightly. "Queen! I meant about Patrick!"

"He's divinity fudge."

"You're just saying that to be nice."

"Okay! He's Quasimodo in a Speedo. Happy now?"

"What do you really think?" Luis insisted.

"Luis, puss, I'm sunned out, I'm fucked out, I'm grassed out, I'm Bloody-Mary-ed out. Truth is, I'm far too fagged out to be able to evaluate anyone!" But since Luis was unhappy with this, I added, "I think he's handsome and nice and smart."

"That's all I wanted to hear."

"Sis-ters!" I moaned.

"Speaking of which," Luis said, "I just heard from our very own Sister of the Eternal Suntan. A long, detailed, and extremely dishy letter."

"From Miss Ritchie? No! I want to read it too."

"Later. It's all about getting down in the Jaguar Bookshop and Mike Muletta's weekend parties on the Embarcadero. Those West Coast girls are getting it together, you know."

"About time. The last time I was there—"

"Yes?" Luis interrupted me to speak in a semiprofessional tone of voice as he simultaneously moved aside to allow two guests to pass down the stairs and toward the kitchen. "Need a refill, kids?"

One held up his glass. "I'll marry whoever's making those Bloody Marys!"

"Too late, Roy-Jean," Luis beamed. "He's already taken! Tell you what, though, why not go back up to the deck and I'll try to convince him to make another pitcher."

Patrick was happy to oblige, and I was handed a freshly made pitcher-ful and appointed Aquarius.

The other guests were gathered on the main deck that opened off the cathedral-ceilinged second-story living room and went three-quarters around the house—perhaps the best and most extensive view of all among the scattered, expensive, jeu d'esprit houses in what we referred to as "Corn Hole (actually Corn Hill) Estates," one of the Upper Cape's posher neighborhoods. I looked for and located Matt on the side of the deck that gives a phenomenal vista of P-Town. He'd brought the token straight couple from Wellfleet there and was talking to them (leave it to him!) with that intensity of interest he sometimes had that made you feel you were the last human on earth.

Lest I embarrass him with my continued naked need for affection, I merely lifted the pitcher so they'd see it, then put it down on a table and turned in the other direction to watch the sun developing a fat red bottom as it descended into the enormous orange-speckled silver of Cape Cod Bay. Everything seemed to conspire to an absolute stillness and silence. Equally sudden a peroration of chatter from a local mockingbird broke the silence. I sighed for so much beauty.

"Shall we ever eat?" a voice next to me asked.

Alistair, leaning next to me over the terrace's little fence. He'd been at the beach all afternoon, long after Matt and I had left, somewhere out of sight, and, we'd assumed, up to no good. Now he looked splendidly healthy, with a casual splatter of fresh red-tan across forehead, cheeks, and nose, and pale streaks in his long dark-blond hair from where the sun had encountered his lemon-juice rinse.

"Crudités and aioli are coming," I announced, filling his glass.

"I've had crudités and aioli up to here!" He accepted the scarlet liquid, however, and sipped at it. "This is good! Well, what do you think?"

"Boiled. Even if they do scream!"

Alistair turned to me, puzzled. Then, "The lobsters! Of course they should be boiled!"

I leaned over the terrace and shouted down—"Luis! Patrick! It's settled! Boiled!"

"Only Brazilians know how to broil them properly," Alistair said.

"You are the cleverest thing. No matter how arcane I get, you still understand me."

"If after all this time I didn't, who the hell would? But no, dear, I didn't mean the lobsters. I meant what do you think about the manflesh upon the terrace here? Aside from your own totally scrumptious pussikins and the straight man who is off-limits and thus automatically intriguing, the question is: whom shall I have as an after-dinner mint?"

"I thought you got laid on the beach today," I said, not bothering to ask the even more obvious question.

"You know how it is: sometimes it just whets the appetite for more."

I turned with him to inspect the other six on the deck. "Domingo, the Cuban, has skin like silk, and he can't get fucked enough."

"Hmmmn!" Alistair purred. Then: "What do you know about the gaunt but athletic-looking one in the hot pink jams?"

"That's Nils Adlersson, the novelist. Brilliant but erratic writer. Don't know shit about his sex life."

"What do they say at the magazine?"

"Seems our much hated editor in chief is hopelessly in love with Nils, so not an iota of dish has been able to freely circulate. It's unnatural!"

"If the staff of New York's premier fag mag doesn't know about his sex life, he probably doesn't have one. But I'd bet that other one has a beer-can dick. Look at the way it bulges athwart the inseam in those shorts!"

"Which one?" I asked.

"The half-handsome, half-prissy one in the madras shirt and cream-colored shorts. He's a little stouter than I like as a rule . . ."

"He's a lawyer, Luis told me. From the city. Staying at P-Town with Ian and Phillip."

"He's got something swinging in there! Probably one of those big, fat, East-European . . ." Alistair all but hugged himself. "Just what the doctor ordered."

"Didn't know you were ailing, Miss Scarlett."

"Duh vapors, chile. Duh vapors. Nuthin' but a li'l horse meat won't cure! Let's get a little closer so I can better check out his basket. Mother really doesn't care to be unpleasantly surprised *ce soir.*"

Matt looked up from where he'd been intently speaking to Al and Muffy Weisberg and closed one glamorously lashed eye in a wink, provoking an immediate smile from me. I brushed his back surreptitiously as I walked past. Alistair's hand was down by his side, gesturing me closer to the little group where Luis was just finishing a description of Nils Adlersson's book by saying, "It's really fabulous!"

"Really?" Phillip asked. "As good as *The Persian Boy?*"

"Oh, honey! That book's trash," Ian quickly put in. "You'll have to forgive Lip," he explained to the attorney and Nils.

"What do you mean trash! I thought *The Persian Boy* was wonderful!" Phillip insisted. "I read it twice and cried both times!"

"He also thinks Belva Plain should get the Nobel Prize," Ian sneered. "Lip simply can't understand why all those Third World Wogs keep getting it."

Phillip was holding his ground. "What do you think, Anny?" he asked the attorney Alistair had expressed interest in.

"I never read novels. Fiction is . . . Well, it's not fact, is it?"

Nils's face set suddenly, but his mouth formed a crooked little smile.

Phillip and Luis looked to Nils for contradiction and, seeing they weren't going to get it, began to sputter—"Oh, Anatole, you're just saying that! You can't mean it."

"I do mean it! Lord knows I read plenty of nonfiction books. Perhaps twenty or thirty a year. Mostly history and biography. Then there's magazines. Aside from what I use for work, I've got subscriptions to [naming you can guess which eight of them] . . . You can't say I'm not up on everything. And after all, what's the point of reading fiction?"

"To discover other points of view!" Alistair spoke up, moving closer to Anatole. "To find out how other people live. What they experience. What they think about what they experience. How they feel about what they think they've experienced. I'd assume that richness of detail and roundedness of experience would be *invaluable* to an attorney."

Everyone had turned to Alistair.

Who concluded his eloquent yet seductively presented speech by adding to no one in particular, *"N'est-ce pas?"*

"I never thought of it that way," Anatole said, looking thoughtful.

"Perhaps you were exposed to the wrong novels as a young lad," Alistair explicated in that same seductive tone of voice, as he quietly sidled between Phillip and Nils so he was at Anatole's side. "Perhaps you'll tell me *exactly* what you did read as a lad and I could . . ."

The VIP lounge door loudly clanked open, shattering my reverie. Anatole stood arms akimbo, challenging me. The door clanked shut behind him.

"Wally says the party at Alistair's was over an hour ago! And he says you were both there earlier."

I sat up.

"Are you going to tell me what is going on?" Anatole demanded.

"Didn't Wally tell you? Is he out there?"

"He's out there. And no, he didn't *'tell me'*! 'Tell me' what?"

I looked at my options and compared them to what I knew or suspected I knew of Anatole's humanity or lack thereof.

"Alistair's sick." I let it out.

Anatole was about to ask sick how and stopped himself. "Go on."

"I thought in his condition, Alistair might be depressed being all alone after everyone left, so I said I'd return."

For a minute I wondered if Anatole was going to buy it, or if I was going to have to spill the beans.

"Not just diagnosed but sick," he clarified for himself. "How sick?" Exactly the right question.

"He's been hospitalized twice." Then, to punch it home: "He weighs about a hundred and twenty."

Anatole's comprehension and anger were immediate. His face darkened and reddened and clamped shut. "Doesn't he have anyone there?"

"Always. But you know how close we've been. Since we were nine."

Without losing a bit of his anger or ruddiness or clenched visage, Anatole relented.

"I'll do what I can to get you out tonight."

"Is Wally angry with me?"

Anatole shrugged.

"He is angry with me, I know. We fought earlier."

Anatole turned and began banging for the guard to come.

I went over to him. "Anny, how do I explain to Wally?"

"Explain what, about Alistair's illness?"

"No! He's asking all about Matt. What do I tell him, Anny?"

Anatole got suddenly flustered. "How should I know?" He banged even harder. Then he said in an oddly calm tone of voice, "You know, when I first saw Matt Loguidice I thought he wasn't real. I never thought anyone could be that beautiful."

"Even with his leg!" I added.

"Even so. He was so beautiful . . . I wondered how you dared to make love with him," Anatole said, his face reddening as he looked away to some stashed memory vision. "I thought anyone who would even *touch* . . . someone like him must end up . . . I don't know, struck down by a bolt from the heavens or . . ."

As he spoke, Anatole looked at me closely, as though assessing something in me he'd never considered before.

I had no idea at first how to answer him. Then the turnkey arrived, and Anatole grabbed my shoulder hard, wordlessly consoling me or urging me on or . . . something! before he turned to leave.

I found my voice. "Wasn't I struck by heaven, Anny? Weren't we *all*?"

Left alone, and even though I didn't want to, I was forced to remember Matt.

"I've got it!" Calvin said. "We'll recommend *Agnes von Hohenstaufen*."

"*Agnes von* who?" I asked. Where was that catalog? There it was! The little bugger! Under everything else. I grabbed it, opened it, began going through its pages. Slim pickings.

"You mean you've never heard of *Agnes von Hohenstaufen* by Gasparo Spontini?" Calvin asked, delighting in his one-upping me. I knew he was at his office, not ten blocks away, over on Sutter Street. Even so, our Bell West connection made him sound like he was in the Antipodes, or Oakland! It could be worse. Last week we didn't have phones two entire afternoons. Would they ever finish building BART and screwing around Market Street?

We were discussing the new opera production the director of the San Francisco Opera company was looking for. He'd come to us for suggestions, as we were the staff of the most knowledgeable magazine, local fan club, and general opera-going claque in town. Each of about a dozen of us was to come up with a suggestion for something different and wonderful and present it to him at a staff meeting in a few weeks. He promised to mount a production of one of our choices. I was only a part-time staff writer for the rag, but even so, through my friendship with Calvin Ritchie, its new editor and general factotum, I was as deeply involved in this selection as anyone else.

"Never heard of it," I was forced to admit.

"It was *only* Spontini's greatest success," Calvin emphasized. "You know Spontini's *La Vestale*, of course."

"Naturally," I said, half lying: I'd heard of it, not heard it.

"*Agnes* was the biggest hit of that year. Seventy performances! Bellini was said to have wept at the Parma premiere. The young Verdi, still a student, pawned his score of the *Missa Solemnis* to attend."

"Miss Ritchie!" I warned in my best schoolmarm voice. "If you're making this all up, you shall be se-ve-re-ly chas-tis-ed."

I slid over that catalog and went to the next. I was myself at work, at Pozzuoli's, San Francisco's most chi-chi bookstore and art gallery, cultural emporium really, located on two breathtakingly expensive and overdecorated floors of the primest real estate in downtown's newest hotel, with one entrance out on the Embarcadero, the other indoors, facing a sixty-foot rectangular bank of calla lilies growing inside the thirty-floor open lobby. It was late July 1974, and the *Chronicle*'s national headlines were all about Judge Sirica and Senator Sam Ervin, and the shit finally hitting the Nixon Administration fan. Even Patty Hearst and the SLA were second-sectioned for the new dirt. We'd already just bypassed two admitted Constitutional Crises, and now it all seemed to be in the hands of those Fates that rise out of the mist and soil in the prelude of *Götterdämmerung*—of which, by the way, everyone agreed there hadn't been a decent production in this town since the days of Schorr, Flagstad, and Karen Branzell.

Meanwhile, local news was spotlighting and thus busily pumping up the "Downtown Renaissance"—which is to say the construction mess from City Hall, the Opera House, and the rest of the so-called Civic Center building on lower Van Ness Avenue, and the subway extension along Market Street right to the Sausalito ferry—with an occasional editorial nod at the upcoming municipal election, sure to bring in an old Machine pol named Moscone as mayor, and our first gay city supervisor, some guy named Harvey no one really knew.

Directly across from my little open-air balcony office at Pozzuoli, I noted a pair of scrumptiously garbed Japanese women looking at Monika's little shelf of bibelots. Their dresses were cut modern—Chanel? Saint Laurent? it was *someone* French—but used native fabrics: great pink peonies on a field of ashy silver for one, white-and-gray storks flying against a midnight-blue sky for the other. Industrialists' wives. They moved with the small-step shuffling, semi-awkward grace of geisha hostesses.

"You'd love *Agnes*. So would Miss Thing over at the Opera," Calvin said. "It's simply spectacular! Set during the Hundred Years' War in Swabia, with scenes in the Alps and the Black Forest. There's an emasculated version, natch, but the original's in five acts, needs two, count 'em *two*, coloratura sopranos, each of whom has a great *scena*, and together a trio with the contralto. Oh, and there's also a light soprano trousers role. The male parts are equally juicy, with great arias and duets for—get this, Flora!—a pair each of tenors and bassos. And it has an all-baritone chorus in the . . . I think it's the third act."

"Is there a full score of this unknown masterpiece in existence?" I asked, sweeping that book catalog off my desk and onto a chair, and moving on to the next one—a few more titles, but Holly would have to look at it later. She knew more about art books than I would in a lifetime, despite my title.

"Not only a full score," Calvin said, "but, Divina Angel Cake, a recording!"

"Leontyne!" I gushed back. "One *is* impressed!"

Monika had arrived to help the Japanese women. They looked like serious buyers. Good. My reign at Pozzuoli's had already been marked by profits. It allowed me to get away with setting my own hours, my own style of management, and quite a bit else.

"In fact," Calvin went on, "I've heard a reel-to-reel tape!"

"No! I've just made jizz stains all over my chinos!"

"Wait'll you hear it! Pirated off a radio program by some ditzy French number: the ORTF direct from the Aix-en-Provence Festival. It was a Franco-Italo production, put together by the great impresario de Bailhac in 1936. And, Margery Daw, get this cast: Ebe Stignani and Germaine Cernay; Fedora Barbieri with Hina Spani in the role of the messenger; Lauri-Volpi *and* Georges Thill parted against Pinza *and* Marcel Journet! Have your feet left the ground yet?"

I had to admit, Calvin had me gasping. "Who conducted? God?"

"Close. De Sabata!"

"May a human person hear this recording?"

"If said human person promises to recommend it."

"Nice try, Dalmatia. I'd have to hear it first."

"You honky twat!"

"Watch your sass, Miss Ritchie! We're not in Oakland anymore."

"Okay, you can hear it." Calvin paused. "And what, if I may be so bold as to ask, was your choice?"

"Donizetti's *Emilia di Liverpool*."

"All I know of *Emilia* is the cavatina and rondo Sutherland sings."

"Sang!" I clarified. "She couldn't negotiate that cavatina today if her vocal chords were wearing ice skates."

"True enough, girl! Her coloratura is a shadow of its former glory."

"I was thinking of Caballé doing it."

"She's no slender child," Calvin said. "Never was. Odd that you should mention Monsterfat Cowbelly. Herself sang the title role of *Agnes* in Rome a few years ago. Muti conducted. Bruno Prevedi, Antonietta Stella, Sesto Bruscantini. Don't know who else was there."

"How do you know all this, Dorothy?" I asked.

"One has sources," Calvin replied enigmatically.

The Japanese women were buying the bibelots. Good idea. Monika

half turned and saw me and began to blush as she always did whenever
the amount of money involved was too high for her down-to-earth
Wisconsin Methodist morals. On the other side of me—on the far balcony, in the record department—Justin was standing talking to three
male foreigners—Swedes or Norwegians, given their clothing, especially the blocky sandals and socks they wore with pale-colored jackets.
He was playing what sounded like a two-piano piece by Mendelssohn
I'd never heard before, so I caught his attention and sketched a question mark in the air. He held up an album cover: Rimsky-Korsakov!
Imagine!

"There is a score for *Emilia*," I said, having looked it up. "But the
only recording I know of is duets sung by Delia de Martis and Aureliano
Pertile in the early thirties on the Italian Victor label and a baritone
scena by Apollo Granforte. Execrable sound and a ten-second dropout.
A Preiser LP."

"I'll ask around for more of it. If the girls here at *Opera Queen* don't
know of a full recording, it don't exist."

"Thanks, Cal." I finished marking and threw over the last two catalogs. My meeting with my boss was due in ten minutes. God only knew
how long that would drag on, Pierluigi pontificating about his expansion plans.

"If, however, *Emilia* is chosen," Calvin said, snickering, "the scenery
must show the 'mountains of Liverpool' in the background, exactly the
way the tenor aria puts it. So, meet you at Toad Hall as usual?" Cal
asked, mentioning our favorite hangout on Castro Street, the up-and-
coming gay area in town.

"Don't know when I'll be able to get out of here tonight."

"You work too hard. Or is it lust for *die Grossmägtige Italiener*?"

"Pierluigi? Grow up! Marian A! It's all I can do to keep from barfing
in his presence."

"Are you quite certain? One cannot help but note," Cal said, "that
since this particular woman of color has known you, you have not had a
single boyfriend—indeed not a man beyond a one-night stand—in what
is close to a full year! Which, for a lad considered not unattractive by
many, and indeed hot by several—although admittedly demented—
numbers, must be considered, at the least, vee-strange."

"While you have at least two boyfriends at any given time. I know, I know. Lots of men and little taste. Let's drop the subject, okay?"

"Okay. But I'll be at your favorite pool table," he tempted, knowing how much I enjoyed beating him at the game.

"I'll try to make it by seven. Oh, and Cal, *Agnes* sounds like an absolute winner. They'll love it!"

"Except where can one find two coloraturas with mezzo ranges?"

"Surely you jest! Of course you might have to search a bit for a second coloratura bass. Come on, honey! It would *fun* to cast! Miss Thing at the Opera would make all sorts of enemies over it."

"It would be fab, if they chose it," Calvin said, cheered again.

"See you at Toad Hall." I hung up on that high note.

And moaned.

Walking through the mezzanine-level art gallery of the store at least ten minutes early and coming at me across twenty-five feet of open air was my boss, Pierluigi Cigna. Flanking him was the smarmy art dealer Vincent Faunce and my cousin Alistair. The three looked as though they'd just hatched some plan, which meant I'd spend most of my meeting with Cigna having to explain exactly why and how it was absurd.

Yes, Alistair. I'd forgiven him for the Selective Service madness. Forgiven him, and moved to his elected city, where he'd returned himself early in '71 in an attempt to save his real estate business from his unscrupulous ex-lover. That had taken several years and many lawyers and lots of money, with this result: Alistair retained full partnership in the company, but what was left of the assets had been judicially frozen while the company completed its most recent project. Until the suit was settled, it could be thawed only long enough to pay off all creditors. Of course it wasn't that simple; I could go into more detail. Lord knew Alistair had, and sometimes still did whenever some new legal crinkle occurred. I'm just giving the basics he laid down when he applied for the art gallery job.

Actually, Pozzuoli's had been open almost a year by then; the bookstore, that is, with all the foreign language departments, the magazine section, the record department. All that remained was that lovely blank undecorated space upstairs which led up to the administrative offices. I'd arrived by then. I'd been hired in Manhattan and boosted quickly up the ladder at the main Pozzuoli's—around the corner from the Plaza and the Sherry—and when the Genoan Goose (*cigna* actually means "swan," but . . .) offered me the position of store manager of what was the largest and newest and most glam . . . So I moved to San Francisco last November, knowing absolutely no one in town but Alistair, whom I'd barely spoken to in years, and I sailed into this new shop in the middle of this incredible hotel lobby and I did what anyone with any sense and a still unspent building budget would do: I decorated.

Decorated like mad whatever was left to do in the store—the marble floors and ceilings were rose-red from Albania!—and when I was done there, on a somewhat smaller budget, I restored and decorated the bright, handsome, elderly four-room apartment I'd taken on Fell Street in the Haight (I know! I know!) within sight of the Panhandle, where the grass had sprung back from where it had been trampled into the greensward, the lawns were now occupied by neckers and occasional sunbathers and more frequently dog walkers, and the whole was completely bereft of flower children, although every once in a while a visiting drug dealer might be discovered standing on a curb looking around, stoned, evidently A Little Late and wondering Where Everyone Was (down in Laguna, in Venice, Key West, or Maui).

In the near year I'd been here, I'd learned to like the town a bit, learned to hate the psychotic changes in the weather a lot (forty degree drops in temperature in ten minutes is not fun, ever!). I'd hired and fired at the store until I had a staff more or less useful if hardly to my wishes. I'd publicized the place with author appearance parties, evidently a new idea here, although the venerable City Lights Bookstore over on Broadway still managed to throw together a reading every half decade for Allen Ginsberg or Paul Bowles, flown in special from Morocco.

Pozzuoli's own parties were more formal, more expensive, and infinitely more superficial. The books we feted were "written" by interior designers and flower columnists, by celebrity bridge players and experts on Calabrian majolica and Cretan faience. After much consultation, I'd fixed on a list and invited what was considered the city's "Arty Social Set." I stretched this group considerably with fakers, nouveaus, and snobs, stirred well with a handful of presentable gays, added a dash of media types, and guess what? It worked!

In ten years in New York, in twenty years in Rome, and in a half century in Florence, a Pozzuoli shop had never been discovered in the black. The shop had merely been a display for the company's huge publishing empire (mags, books, and newspapers); profit had seemed rather beside the point. Thus, everyone was vaguely astonished when my shop made money. Triplets of Italian men in expensive gray suits would suddenly arrive, badly jet lagged, at our offices and would remain upstairs with our accounts for two days before leaving suddenly, still shaking their heads. Usually, the Genoa Goose managed to get word of them and would himself fly in—or up from La Jolla, where he was hunting out a new spot for a store—and accompany them back as far as the Atlantic. Which was fine with me since my Italian was Paleozoic in vintage and the Italians' English virtually nonexistent.

It was after their penultimate visit that Cigna had okayed opening the art gallery. As the Manhattan shop did, it was to contain lithos, etchings, and drawings, most of them already framed and hung on the walls, along with some unframed ones in sets by the handful of chic contemporary artists like Dubuffet, Dali, and Hockney. Everything would be numbered, but only an occasional special set would be placed in the coffinlike glass display cases for sets smaller than ten. We sold no statuary or paintings, or anything famous, or old, or as expensive as the Fauves, certainly nothing controversial—the kind of thing a middle-level exec would get his wife for their anniversary: not a Major Investment.

Alistair had been at the "book" signing party where I'd made the formal announcement that the art gallery would be open by the next party. Afterward, he'd taken me to dinner in his neighborhood—Pacific Heights at Broadway—and pumped me so completely about the art gallery I'd finally said, "You sound as though you want the job."

"Want it? I'd kill for it!"

"You're kidding! Alistair Dodge work for a living?"

It wasn't the nicest thing to say. But his response was perfect.

"I'm not desperate, you understand. . . . The tax concept 'operating expenses' is a wide umbrella and covers a multitude of sins. But I have to admit, I have been burned by this past partnership and have given serious thought to other areas, other lines of interest."

"You'd be trained by the Bitch of Bari."

"I met Giuseppina," Alistair said. "She can't be that bad."

"If anyone can bring out her latent humanity, you surely can."

"As it turns out, I know a deal about contemporary art. Had to learn quickly when my stuff began going out to be sold."

"Poor Alistair!" I commiserated. "Why don't I buy dinner?"

"Make Pozzuoli pay. You worked overtime tonight."

"I work overtime every night."

"How can you have a life?"

"This *is* my life."

"How ghastly! What about . . ."—Alistair looked around—"boys?"

"I occasionally go to the tubs! The Ritch Street Baths," I clarified.

"Oh!"

"And an occasional bar. A few interesting ones opened south of Market."

"You mean . . . Aren't leather bars dangerous?" Alistair asked.

"Don't be silly! I used to go to Kellers and the Eagle in New York all the time. These places are no different."

"Really? Near Hamburger Mary's off Folsom Street? We drove past one last month and . . ."

"It's not what you think, Alistair."

"I blame myself for ruining you," he overdramatized.

"Grow up, gir—" I caught myself. "Grow up, Alistair. It's not all pain and stuff. It's mostly attitude and costume."

"You have a lovely apartment, a good job: you should have a lover."

"I don't want a lover."

"Surely you don't want to hang around street corners at three in the morning wearing dead cow and waiting for someone sleazy to come by and . . . do whatever you do?" He trailed off aimlessly.

"Why not? I used to do it down by the trucks in the Village."

But the way in which he was asking, his very manner of insisting, made me suddenly think, oh I know it was ridiculous, almost unforgivably absurd, but still . . . Could Alistair possibly be coming on to me? No! Impossible! Wait, it was possible! Stranger than strange, but possible. He was young and attractive. I was young and attractive. He was hardly a "sister," as Calvin had instantly become, despite the circumstance in which Cal and

I had met. And yes, there was enough distance and tension between Alistair and me to . . . I don't blush often. I blushed then.

"What *do* you do when you're picked up off street corners in Folsom?" he suddenly asked.

"Alistair!" I protested and blushed even more.

"It must be something . . . you're ashamed of."

"Drop! The! Sub! Ject!"

"Or is it some intensely recalled memory?"

"I'm getting up and leaving now, Alistair."

"It's dropped! Dropped!" he assured me.

We sat there a few minutes while my color faded, and I stuffed all thoughts of sex with Alistair deep into the file marked "To be looked at again—maybe never!"

"It's all my fault anyway," he suddenly said. "Well, it is! I'm the one who brought you out, and I'm the one who screwed it all up. Well, not I, exactly, but because of who it was who . . . I mean if it were virtually anyone on earth but . . ."

He couldn't bring himself to name Julian Gwynne, who, like Hendrix and Jim Morrison, Keith Moon and the astonishing Janis Joplin, hadn't managed to get into the new decade along with the rest of us. To his credit, my first boyfriend and first ex-boyfriend had at least been a bit original in his passing. He'd OD'd in transatlantic flight. Only when the cleaning attendants had broken down the jet's john door had he been found, beatifically smiling, an emptied needle trembling in a ravaged vein of each arm, with a third hypo shivering empty in his neck, barely an inch from his carotid pulse.

I'd read about his death in the papers. But I'd not gotten details until Gwynne's loyal chauffeur "retired" back to New Jersey months later thoughtfully called to tell me. Naturally, I'd not thought to phone Alistair for details. He'd returned to California by then anyway and was deep in his own woes.

Out of which I was elected to help him rise.

Was I being naive in considering him for the job? Foolishly indulgent? Sure, a little of both. Magnanimous too. But I thought practical too. I'd begun studying Taoist philosophy and using *I Ching* by then, and all the signs seemed to point clearly toward Alistair joining me. Besides which, I needed an ally at the shop, someone to watch my back should things get hairy.

So I hired him to run the art gallery.

And this was where we were six months later: Alistair in league with the Genoan Goose and Fatuous Faunce. Not against me, but not quite with me.

The three had stopped to confab on the step leading down from the gallery to the balcony opposite. The Asian women turned and looked at them, then quickly away, probably because of how good-looking two of the men were—not Faunce, he's a dog! Monika, meanwhile, had moved to the little table and begun wrapping the bibelots. I could see she'd phoned some credit card operator—doubtless American Express—for approval on the sale. She saw the three men and began to blush even more. I'd heard gossip around the shop to the effect that she'd at one time conceived the hots for our boss. In response to her blushing and sudden awkwardness, the two Japanese women snuck looks behind her, whispered behind big sleeves, and giggled, causing poor Monika even more consternation. On the other side of where the three men stood, Justin in the record department balcony changed the music from Rimsky to a guitar quintet by Boccherini—the Goose's theory was that the seriousness of the music was inversely proportionate to sales—and was writing up sales for the Scandinavian discophiles.

I gathered together the art book catalogs and paper-clipped a note to them reading, "Holly! Help!" She'd know what I meant.

I pulled on my jacket, straightened my tie, checked my shoes to make sure they looked vaguely polished, checked my face in the compact mirror the women kept in my desk drawer to check makeup, and strode off, headed toward the three conspirators by way of Monika and the Edo darlings.

Halfway across the walkway, I stopped to look down and inspect the first floor of the shop, most of it visible from here. I checked the front cashier and saw that no obvious disaster had befallen while I'd been at my balcony desk. I contented myself that no browsers looked like thieves, and that Thea and Katja had seen me and broken up their gossip fest. I didn't see Andre, but I intuited that he was among his beloved French books. I moved on.

And stopped again. There, below me, not twenty feet away, in the poetry section, holding a book in one large outstretched hand, while he
turned a page with the other was—I would have sworn it—the Archangel
Ariel himself, his wings folded up, hidden away somehow in a U.S. sailor's
eyebright middy and thirteen-button "broad-fall" flap-front trousers.

In an unexpected dimensional shift, his eyes moved to the other page,
tilting his head suddenly in another direction, and now I could see the single huge black curl falling across his Alcibiadean brow, the total roundness
of those large dark eyes, every tanned plane of that amazing head.

I felt a sudden burning in my breast and recalled that St. Theresa of
Avila had written of being struck in the heart by the blazing dart of Di-
vine Love, and the paradox of enduring such Sweet Agony. So shocked,
I had to lean against the walkway railing.

The sailor must have caught my sudden motion in his peripheral vision: he looked up suddenly, and dimensions shifted again. His direct
gaze was so intense it was as though someone had suddenly pulled the
blazing dart down through my torso and out of me again via my urethra.

My head spun, but I managed to get to the far wall, where I found a
seat and dropped my head between my knees, glimpsing Daliesque visions of his individual facial features as they fled and cavorted and
chased one another through a Palladian cathedral of pastel-hued clouds.

"You okay?" It was Monika.

I was able to look up without feeling total nausea, so I sent her back
to her customers.

"They're gone. We were done," she protested.

I still shooed her away. Alistair took her place.

"That time of month?"

"Go away. Fuck off. Die," I said with no emotion.

"You'd recover in a second if you knew what Fate just dropped onto
the floor of the shop. Down in poetry. The. Most. Beautiful. Young.
Man. A sailor . . . You've seen him!" Alistair suddenly said, intuiting
something. "In fact, if I'm not completely gaga . . ."

"You are! Completely gaga!"

". . . said lovely is the cause of this sudden attack."

"Lunch," I corrected. "A touch of food poisoning."

". . . said Héloïse to Abelard. If I were you—and to quote Tom Eyen:

'Who of us is not each other?'—I'd go after that sailor. Or I *will* go after that sailor."

"At your own risk," I threatened.

"All I know is that life would be too unfair if he managed to escape two perfectly good queers without being in some way molested," Alistair said.

"I have a meeting with Pierluigi."

"I'll stall him. C'mon!" Alistair urged. "Up and at the lad."

"What if he's not . . ."

"I'll tell Pierluigi you went to the boys' room." Alistair was pushing me toward the stairway. "Go! Will you!"

I managed to stumble down the stairs to the main floor, hid myself under the edge of the balcony, where Alistair had returned to Faunce and the Goose, fooled around straightening out a volume or two here and there among the gardening books and something new on bargello, and sort of wandered nearer the sailor, half circling him all the while, ready to flee at the slightest sign of disinterest.

From this close, he was taller than I'd expected. Six feet, almost six one. Big shoulders. Incredible deltoids, biceps, buttocks, and thighs outlined and simultaneously gripped by the tight cut of his sailor suit. I found myself thinking that the term "animal grace" had been coined just for him. He was still holding the book in his hands, reading it. I tried to make out the cover and thought it might be a recent anthology of poetry. He shifted his pose in place, and it was like continents gliding across the surface of the planet—and that Michelangelesque face!

Just as I was thinking I can't possibly do this, he peeked over the top of the book at me. Almost inhumanly silver-hued eyes set in a bed of black lashes.

"Hi," I said, held my breath, and moved to one side of him, adjusting various books on display that didn't at all need adjusting.

He half smiled. Surprisingly small teeth. Was about to say something.

"You're fine where you are," I said, about to pass by. Understatement of the century.

He put down the book. It *was* the anthology.

"I should probably buy this," he said in an even-toned baritone. "And not just stand here reading it all." No accent at all. Certainly not from the West or South. Yet not from the Bay Area.

"No problem," I said, trying to move away, yet magnetically held by his field of attraction. At that moment, I realized I would have said 'no problem' if he'd demanded to remain where he was and behead passing customers. Then, in a flash of unexpected poise, I added, regarding the book he'd been perusing, "It's supposed to be a good sampling."

"Is it?" he asked, so intensely naive and questioning I stopped about a tenth of my fidgeting.

"It's supposed to be better than the *Oxford Book of American Poetry*. Of course this one has English poets too."

"What about this Auden? He considered English or American?"

He held out the book, and I saw the lines "Lay your sleeping head, my love/Human on my faithless arm."

I must have blushed, because he said, "What?" and pulled back the book and read the page. And half snorted a laugh. "That one's pretty good. But I like this one better." He showed me "Fish in the unruffled lakes." "You?"

" 'Doom is dark and deeper than any sea-dingle . . .' " I quoted the title from memory.

" 'Upon what man it fall/In spring,' " he continued. "Yeah, I like that one too. You don't think it's strange?"

"I always thought that particular poem very strange. For example, here," nervously pointing, and now so close I felt sea-deep within his ambience, his smell like toasted wheat bread that's not yet cooled, "in the second stanza, where he writes about dreaming of going home and kissing his wife under a sheet, then instead he wakes and sees 'Bird-flock nameless to him; through doorway voices/Of new men making another love' . . ."

"Oh!" I suddenly said aloud. I'd for the first time realized what Auden must have meant with those phrases. "Oh, he must mean . . ." I stopped myself and began to blush. Gays, Auden must have meant, I thought but didn't say. "New men making another love." Opposed to a wife. What else could it mean?

"Mean what?" the sailor asked and read aloud. " '. . . new men making another love.' "

He looked up, those remarkable huge, pale, silver-gray eyes so extravagantly set in dark, long, curled lashes, and seeing me red-faced, he too must have suddenly realized the words' import, since he too began to color.

Which meant that against all expectations, all possibilities, all percentages, all fears of it not being so, the sailor *must* be gay too!

I couldn't believe it. I almost levitated off the imported Albanian rose-red marble floor.

In that moment I felt us connect. It was as if a double-sided grappling hook had suddenly been flung and caught under each of our sternums, grasping tight into bone, biting deep into vital organs.

I calmed down a bit. The rest of the conversation was carried on in bits and pieces, as I continued to more slowly orbit him, still straightening out displays and "point of purchase" areas.

He remained where he was, slowly revolving to face me, a rotating star to my ellipsis of erratic wandering. He closed the book and held it close to his side as he answered my questions, telling me he was on a sort of leave, staying in the Presidio while he visited San Francisco. He'd spent most of the past year in the South China Sea and around the Mekong Delta as a gunner's mate on board a destroyer, "assisting friendly fire further inland," he said enigmatically. He'd also seen some "land-based action," he said. (I trembled to think he might have been killed.) He'd had two "tours" of active duty, he said, but had only another few weeks left, and he wasn't sure whether he'd "re-up" or not. He'd sort of liked being in the Navy, as it gave him plenty of time to be alone and to think and to read and write poetry. He wrote poetry, he repeated twice, though he'd never revealed that to anyone else on board ship. He'd asked to come to the Bay Area to be demobilized, because he'd never been here before and thought maybe he might want to live here once he got out of the Navy—that is if he didn't re-up. He originally came from the East, he said. His folks lived in Westchester County, though he didn't say where exactly. He was an only child. His name was Matthew Loguidice, which he pronounced "Load-your-dice," which he said was a Sicilian name. He was half-Italian, half-Finnish.

Meanwhile I told him a few things about myself, including that I read—but didn't write—poetry and had studied it in college and would like to see his poems (he demurred) and that I got off work in about an hour and would be pleased to talk to him more if he'd join me for dinner; he could stay here or return, I said, nervously doing all kinds of semi-janitorial things within a six-foot radius of his gravitational pull, unwilling to move any farther away lest he vanish into thin air, unwilling to leave the spot until he'd agreed to everything I'd suggested, well, everything I'd suggested aloud at least. Then I suggested one more thing: he could take the poetry book and wait upstairs in the art gallery, where there were chairs, till I got off work—in a half hour.

Matthew said that sounded like a good idea, as he'd been on his feet all day and was a little worn out from sight-seeing in the city, which required a good deal of shoe leather. He thanked me, and our eyes connected very hard and my chest tightened suddenly. I had to force myself to look away.

As he went up one way, my boss, Faunce, and Alistair came down another.

"Don't you look like you were struck by a semi," Alistair commented.

"Do I? We have a dinner date. After my meeting with Pierluigi."

Alistair followed my eyes, following Matthew going upstairs.

"With Apollo himself? How could you?"

"But Alistair! You insisted."

"I never dreamed you'd actually do it."

"Well, I did."

"Or that he'd agree." Alistair bit his lip, looking up at the record department, where Matthew had stopped. "For a supposedly shy little thing, you certainly . . . I can't believe your nerve! How could you bring yourself to speak to him?"

"Sheer fucking terror!" And explained, "Terror he'd get away. Terror I'd never see him again."

"It seems to have paid off," Alistair admitted sourly. "Dinner?"

"Dinner," I replied.

"Who's paying?"

"We didn't discuss that. I assume it's Dutch treat."

"Don't assume too much with types like that." Alistair tapped the sentence out on my jacket lapel. "They're used to being treated."

"You'd know from your tons of experience with Trade," I sneered.

Alistair was about to say something else, then stopped himself just in time to half smile at our boss, who'd reached the main floor of the shop and was busily brushing off Faunce about something.

Pierluigi gazed around the store, giving it the once-over, then addressed me. "Mees-ter Sannns-arcc! We have a meeting."

"I'm ready when you are."

"My office!" he decreed and headed for the elevator. Alistair and Faunce said good-bye and left the store the other way, doubtless headed out to dinner with Mrs. Faunce, to hatch who knew what new conspiracies.

As Pierluigi and I ascended past the mezzanine art gallery, I briefly saw, through the little octagonal window, Matthew's head—as though in a cinquecento tondo—turned in profile as he stared at an Erté print.

I thought, God, if he's still here when I return, I'll never say a bad word again in my life. Never! I promise!

Pierluigi told me his expansion plans as though they were already solidified—which I suspected was pretty much the case.

I, however, still saw this talk as a chance to fry my own fish: especially one particular big-mouthed Vincent Faunce. I knew I had to tread gingerly. Though it was a part of the store and thus under my titular control, the art gallery was run by Faunce and Pierluigi as a separate demesne, and thus for all practical purposes out of my control.

"In these new shops, what are you going to use to fill up the new art galleries?" I asked, and rapidly answered myself. "Don't tell me. Faunce will supply all the art?"

"Not all," Pierluigi temporized.

"But most of it?"

"This you don't approve of?" He asked the obvious.

"I wouldn't mind. Except he does have a lot of crap."

The word seemed to offend Pierluigi. "Mees-trrrr Sans-arc!"

"Well, a lot of it definitely is *not* authenticated. And some of the things I've seen framed and hung in his apartment look as though he and his wife spent a morning and simply ripped them out of Skira books and hand-penciled the numbers."

He seemed genuinely intrigued. "You don't think?"

"I wouldn't put it past him. Or her!"

Pierluigi tsked. "Such a cynical view from one so young."

"Maybe," I admitted. I wasn't at all cynical; in fact I was prepared to be a complete naif, a ninny if needed, about my Adonis downstairs, who I hoped was still waiting for me. I wished the Goose would come to the point.

"Your Alistair, for example, seems to think we could get a good price if we purchased more from the Faunce."

The use of "for example" was one of Pierluigi's affectations. He seemed to use it whether it made sense or not.

The possessive my boss had used, on the other hand, was one of the few signs that Pierluigi was at all aware Alistair and I had known each other before the job. I wondered exactly how much he did know. I'd certainly not said anything, and I doubted that Alistair had allowed any glory to be reflected away from himself. There were thirty people on staff: something could have gotten out.

"If you want to attract more Mill Valley trade," I said, "you should up-scale the art. Get more expensive items. Send Alistair to private auctions."

"No, no, no, no, no," Pierluigi quickly said.

"Well, you asked."

"Why do you keep looking at your clock?"

My watch, he meant. "I'm meeting someone for dinner," I admitted.

"Go then!" He gestured imperiously with his hand.

I hated being dismissed like that. But I sure wanted out.

"I'll let you know before I decide." Pierluigi stood up to pull down his roller map of central coastal California.

I doubted that. As with most decisions, I'd hear about it after it had been implemented. As I left, he was searching for Palo Alto on the map. I rushed to the elevator and down to the art gallery, dreading that . . .

But Matthew was there.

We didn't get to dinner. Not that night. We left the shop and headed the few blocks toward Chinatown, considering various restaurants but evidently not considering seriously enough. Matthew was carrying a black grip with him and said it contained a change of clothing. I asked if he'd be more comfortable out of his Navy whites, and admitted I wouldn't mind changing out of my work clothes and into jeans and a flannel shirt. I thought we'd find some place to eat we both liked in my area, along Ashbury or Masonic streets. He agreed, and I began calculating how long it would take to get home with a change of busses, and how it would feel sitting next to Matthew all that way and not knowing if . . . At Montgomery and Market, I spotted an empty cab in front of a taxi company office. On impulse I got in.

Matthew joined me without a word. A fog had begun to roll in off the bay, straight up Market Street. Even with headlights and streetlights on, it provided sudden darkness. A touch of chilliness, and yes, privacy too.

I was surprised to feel Matthew's hand reach over and touch my knee. "You're shivering," he said.

I couldn't deny it. "I'll never get used to these sudden changes of weather," I said. His hand hadn't lifted off my knee. I covered it with my own. "Last week, I went to sleep with the window open and a light sheet on, and I woke up freezing." His hand slid under mine off my knee and ranged along my thigh. "Two quilts later I finally managed to warm up," I added, moving my hand onto his knee and from there onto his thigh.

Our hands slid and caressed and ultimately managed to get to almost every inch of the lower parts of each other's body during the cab trip to Fell Street. While I paid the fare and before we could get out, we had to arrange our erections in our trousers.

That didn't last long; once in the building's foyer, we found ourselves smashed against the wall, necking and groping each other. And inside the door, once I remembered to unlock it. And up the two flights of stairs. And inside my apartment door, even with the two locks to undo. And inside the flat, along walls and bookcases. And despite sudden obstacles like closet handles, until we finally made it to my bedroom, where we tore off each other's jacket and shirt and ripped off each other's belt and tore at each other's pants as though, like Nessus's cloak in the story of Hercules, they were soaked in flaming poison. Thus, mostly undressed, we fell upon each other like leopards exposed to fresh meat.

Something like two hours later, I called for a cigarette break. We lay amid the ruins of my bedclothes and our own clothing. Certain areas of my body ached from being grasped so hard, held so tightly, while others continued to sting, having been so well beard-burned. We lay athwart each other, his larger limbs more than half covering mine.

"That's better!" I made smoke rings Matt poked a finger through.

"Want some grass?" I offered. "You have to roll it."

"Think we need it?" We both giggled. Clearly we didn't.

Ten minutes later, we broke off that kiss and I said, "How hungry are you, really?"

"I don't know. How long do restaurants stay open?"

"Another hour or so."

Matt rolled onto me. "We'll never make it," he groaned.

"There's one right downstairs," I protested. "Five minutes from here to there if we got dressed now." Instead I let him take me away with him. When I came up for air, I said, "You're right. We'd never make it."

At our next break, I said, "There's food here. In the fridge."

"Sounds good," Matt admitted. Then we started in again, and he said, "We'll never make that either."

Sometime later I actually managed to escape Matt's unstoppable hands and probing tongue long enough to get up and put together melted cheese sandwiches with tomato slices. We sipped a single bottle of root beer through two straws.

"Yourrr foudssll nnyrrspnmnnts," I said, while being rolled over and having a pillow stuffed in my mouth.

"What?" Matt asked.

"Yourrr foudssll nnyrrspnmnnts."

"What?" he asked again, this time removing the pillow.

"Your foot's still in your pants!" I said. Pointing to where his sailor pants hung off one shoeless foot. "Might as well take it off."

"It's okay." Matt shrugged off the problem.

"Take it off. Especially if, as I hope, you're going to spend the night."

"I'll take it off later on," he said.

I heard something unexpectedly hard in his tone of voice. Maybe he didn't like commands. Maybe he didn't like contradictions.

"I give up!" Hands up in the air, I simpered. "Make love not war."

He laughed and grabbed me. "You dare to say that?" he demanded. "To me? A man who's seen action?"

I wrestled back. "You've probably seen more action in the last few hours than you did in the past two years."

"Oh yeah?"

"Yeah!"

An hour later, I said, "Dear Abby. I've met the most wonderful man. Except for one peculiar fetish he has. He insists upon keeping one pants leg on while we're in bed. Do you think it's a sign of noncommitment? In case he wants to make a quick getaway? What do you suggest? Signed, Half-panting."

Matt reached up and moved the lamp on the table. He threw my dress shirt over it so all was pale blue. Then he took the other pants leg off.

"Satisfied?"

"Am I ever?"

"I meant about my pants."

"Want me to get up and hang them so they won't wrinkle?"

Together we answered, "No! Never make it!"

We lay next to each other listening to the radio. It was playing low, but it was audible now that we weren't quite so distracted.

"That's pretty," Matt said.

"Saint-Saëns's Third Symphony. Second movement. Here comes the organ. It's sometimes called—"

"Don't tell me." Matt fluffed up his poor overused dick. "The *Organ Symphony*!"

After laughing, we listened awhile.

"I wish I knew music like that," Matt said.

"You hear enough of it, eventually you get to know it."

"The last time I spent any time in the missile room," Matt said, "this wild guy Jerry who we used to call Jerry the Axe was there playing this reel-to-reel tape he'd gotten from some guy or other in Bangkok. It was beautiful. Just beautiful. From Strauss. Richard Strauss," Matt explained, pronouncing the first name the American way. "And it was from some opera. I don't remember exactly. But Jerry explained the story. This woman's left stranded on this island and left to die. Only she's not alone. She's with this theater company. Strange, huh? I never completely got it. Only she sings about how much she wants to die. . . ."

Matt's voice fluttered slightly. "You know, because this man she loved has left her there and all."

"*Ariadne auf Naxos*," I said, not believing what he'd been describing.

"Yeah! That sounds right."

I went further. " '*Es gibt ein Reich!*' is the name of that aria."

"Do you have it?"

I got up and found the album and looked for the libretto, and there it was, close to the beginning of the third disc, "*Es gibt ein Reich, wo alles rein ist,*" Schwarzkopf's most effusive outpouring, her love-death paean. I began to play it and came back into the bedroom, where Matt sat on the edge of the bed, listening.

"Come," I said, pulling him and the quilts along with him, until we were out in the living room, plumped down in front of the couch.

"Play it again," he said, when the aria was over and Harlequin, Scaramuccio, and the other commedia dell'arte figures came out to sing. I put the libretto in his hand and showed Matt where we were in the translation, while the Vienna Philharmonic's strings and winds caressingly rose to the same fever pitch as Schwarzkopf, and he looked at me. "Don't you think it's beautiful?"

What could I say? As beautiful as he was.

"You were playing this on the ship?" I had trouble believing it. "While you were firing missiles?"

"Yeah, we were all three-quarters tanked on bennies, and we'd been eating opium for about a week. We were stuck in this sort of big, round turret, only it was completely electronic, deep inside the front deck of the ship. We'd been there an hour already, busily popping away, when Jerry the Axe pulled out this tape and switched it with our usual soul and blues tape. At first everyone complained. It was weird music. Long-hair. Beyond long-hair. He insisted on playing it. And this guy Jerry the Axe was like a lunatic, whenever he wanted something bad, you know. So we gave in. Then as we kept listening and following the blips on our screens telling us where to aim our shots deep upriver, in support of some platoon or other, we came to like it a lot. A lot. Jerry'd gotten the whole set of three reels. And we played 'em all. But mostly this middle one, and whenever we'd reach this part, we'd sniff Amyies and go nuts, mo-rassing them VC motha-fuckers!"

The image he'd presented was so . . . was it tragically funny, or absurdly sad? I'd be damned if I could tell.

"When was this?" I asked.

"Some months ago."

I wanted to ask, *Was that when you were wounded?* Since now I was sure that his lower left leg had scars on it. That was why he'd not taken off the pants leg or sock before, why he kept his leg wrapped in the quilt now, and probably why he was getting out of the Navy at last—because he might not have a choice anymore. Instead I said, "Sounds like you had some times there."

I guess I expected him to tell me more, to continue on in that same tone of voice. Instead he darkened up and said, "It's over now."

"The war?"

That's what we—my friends and I, the doves, the antiwar people—hoped. Not what they—the Nixonites, the hawks, the gung-hos—were admitting. At least not yet.

"The war too," he said. Then, "Let's not talk now, okay? Let's just listen to this."

"Rossini's *Torvaldo e Dorliska*! Would I make that up?" Calvin asked.

"Of course you would."

"Bitch!" he replied, without emotion. "However, I did not. That was Miss Smith's choice. Either that or Donizetti's *Imelda de' Lambertazzi*. Go on, say it."

"Say what?" I asked.

"That ain't real either."

"Who knows, girl! Donizetti wrote about a million operas. Besides the dozen or so we all know about, just this week I've heard of *Torquato Tasso*, *Il Duca d'Alba*, *Poliuto*, *Maria di Rohan*, and *Linda di Chamounix*! But, are you ready, Leontyne? 'Cause, lucky you, the dish-mobile has driven up to your door."

"What dish-mobile?" Calvin asked suspiciously.

"I actually talked with Estelle this morning and finagled her recommendation out of her."

Estelle Thunneman had been editor at the magazine before Calvin took over, and she remained the magazine's doyenne, still much beloved and respected among the staff. At least some of the staff. Calvin remained ambivalent.

"Well?" he asked.

I let it spin out: "Marschner's *Der Vampyr*."

"Whaaat!"

"Marschner's *Der Vampyr*," I repeated.

"Get real, Hildegarde. This is Big Girl Stuff."

"It is real. She's even got a recording of it."

"Honey, Miss Estelle's been smoking banana peels again."

"And furthermore, there's a soprano part in it with a tessitura that lies directly within Leonie Rysanek's range. It goes without saying that Miss Thing at the Opera will do *anything* to get Rysanek back. Anything! So, if she gets wind of *Der Vampyr* and wants to do it, you can believe it will get done. I don't care what else . . ."

"Nurse!" Calvin called out. "Oh, Nurse! Hurry, please! This one's gone off the deep end!"

"Just don't tell anyone what I said, Calvin honey, or you'll be eating fried chicken out of your ear like the Abominable Dr. Phibes. Understood?"

"You've done wonders with the local poultry, Vulnavia," he misquoted Vincent Price from the movie. "Understood," he grudgingly admitted. Then, "By the way, I played pool until my fingers got bent. Where in hell were you?"

It was the day after I'd met Matt. I was back up in my balcony office at Pozzuoli, allegedly on my lunch break, the *Chronicle* and the *New York Times* spread out in front of me: old habits die hard, and the latter did have the *only* crossword puzzle worthy of me.

"Didn't I tell you?" I asked.

"Tell me what?" Calvin asked. "And if this is going to be another story about seeing some boy who reminded you of that dead rock guitarist only six white people ever heard of . . ."

"Better than that. I met an angel and got laid."

"Laid?" he asked. "You ain't been laid in months!"

"It's not been that long. Yes, laid. Laid! Relaid! And parlaid!"

"Whooo-ooh!" Calvin's voice squealed into stratospheric tonal regions previously only approached by Mado Robin. "Tell me every-thing!"

I told him everything.

"If I were you, girl," Calvin said, when I'd come up for a temporary breather, "I would keep that angel away from every living faggot in town. And espexially away from that cousin of yours."

Calvin even uses the *x* when spelling out the word in notes.

"I know you don't particularly care for Alistair . . . ," I began.

"I don't particularly care for honkys who say 'Have a Nice Day' and girls with teased hair and dead-porcupine meat. Alistair, I plain *hate*!"

". . . but you don't think he'd seriously interfere, do you?"

"I do believe he'd not only seriously interfere, I also think he'd eat your eyes out! Without condiments," Calvin clarified.

"Well, the funny thing is, you know, when we were kids, everyone said how much Alistair and I looked alike. And, frankly, since then, we've both just assumed he was better looking than me. But yesterday Matt passed him twice and he didn't even *notice* Alistair!"

"Umm-hnnh!" Calvin said. "Your cousin is a Badly Burned Queen. And what does history, never mind opera, teach us about how Badly Burned Queens act? Honey, keep this angel to yourself. No kidding."

An employee, Andre, was standing at the end of my balcony, a step down, with a hangdog look on his face, defining him as suppliant. What now?

"Well, I can't simply lock Matt up. Look, Cal, gotta hang up. One of the peons is demanding another extension of largesse. We'll talk later."

"You seeing him tonight?" Calvin asked.

"Alistair? I see him every day. Why?"

"The Angel."

"He went up the coast for the day to Bolinas and Mount Tam. We're meeting at my place."

"I sure do hope he's the one," Calvin said.

I hung up—and inwardly I thanked Calvin for loving me so well.

"*Oui, M. Brun? Qu'est-ce que c'est alors?*"

Evidently Pierluigi had already made his decision in favor of the Faunce's further involvement with the art gallery, and done so without bothering to tell me—though I was store manager and he had, recall, promised.

Following Andre's doleful complaint in wildly inappropriate English translation, I headed toward the elevator, aimed for the stockroom, where, allegedly, an entire section of Andre's French language stock had been "molested and dematerialized" (exact translation of what he said) by an invasion of so-called art.

At the elevator, I rang and rang. I spotted the car coming and going up and down, but it was only when I rapped hard on the little window between and yelled at Faunce inside to stop and open it up that I began to get a full picture of what was really going on.

Faunce was deep amid cardboard- and brown-paper-wrapper-framed somethings or others (we shall not dignify it by calling it art). There was no room for me even to stand.

"As you can see," Faunce said, "we're full up."

"Then empty out," I replied. "As you well know, this elevator is the only means of conveyance between here and the offices and the stockroom, and I can't have it out of order."

"But . . . ," Faunce began.

I was already tossing things out of the elevator and onto the floor.

"Wait! You can't . . ."

It was only when he'd moved forward reaching for one of them that I saw my chance. He was half out the elevator doors, and I moved him a bit more, shut the doors, and descended to the stockroom.

The doors opened up to a mess of more wrapped, framed works scattered everywhere. In the distance, at the end of one row of metal shelving, I saw Alistair's back in the midst of what had once been French book inventory.

"Just leave them!" he said to me, without turning around. "It'll be another half hour till I can get to them."

I let the elevator close behind me, and approached.

"My French department is about to quit."

Alistair whirled. He'd taken off his jacket, and his shirt had underarm sweat stains—evidently from labor: a most unaccustomed sight on him.

"Alistair, I'm running an international bookstore for which I require a French department. I do not require an art gallery."

"Pierluigi said I could take some of this space."

"Some is not all."

"Well, as you can see, Faunce had more stuff than I'd anticipated."

"I need my French department. Where is it?"

"I've only moved these old leather binding things. Packed them up. They've been sitting here since Charlemagne croaked," Alistair said.

Actually, he wasn't too far off.

"Surely they can be put somewhere out of sight?" he asked.

"Maybe you're right, and maybe I can make amends to Andre, but you still don't have room for all . . . this junk!" I gestured.

Alistair sat down dejectedly, wiping his neck with his handkerchief. "That's for sure."

Oddly, I felt sorry for him. "Well, concentrate on trying to put away what you've got here, because no more's coming down. I can't have the elevator tied up all day."

Alistair sighed deeply. "He's got tons more."

"He'll have to bring it later."

"Tonight then!"

It was Faunce who said that. He'd found his way down the rickety staircase into the stockroom and stood there with two or three more framed thingamabobs under each of his arms.

"Tonight's no good," I said. "I'm leaving the minute I lock up."

"We'll do it while you count the money," Faunce said. "Don't you have to count out the money?" he asked.

"As you can see for yourself," I attempted to reason with him, "there is no room here for your stuff."

"We can find room by tonight," Faunce insisted.

"Tonight's no good," I repeated. "I have a date."

"Call and make it later," Faunce said.

"I'm meeting someone coming from out of town. No phones. No way to change it," I said, trying to remain calm despite my growing irritation with him.

Faunce persisted. "There's always a way to call and change a date."

The smug look, the whiteness of his pinched nose in the middle of that florid face, the particular slant of his porcine eyes—all of it, allied to the querulousness of his voice, decided me.

"If I'd had a little forewarning," I said, controlling myself with every ounce of effort, "perhaps I could have—"

"Why should you have to be told?" Faunce sniffed.

That did it.

"Faunce, this is *not* going to happen! Face it!"

His face looked as if I'd just slapped it.

"The world happens to not always move to our whims," I went on. "And my particular area of the world does not move to *your* whim. Is that clear?"

"Pierluigi will hear about this!" Faunce had the nerve to say. "And you'll hear from him!"

"It'll be the first I'm hearing about *any* of this shit! So I expect it will be accompanied by profuse apologies!" I said. "And you know how much Pierluigi likes to apologize," I added, letting that sink in. "Now, keep your so-called art off my elevator until tomorrow morning before we open. And do not," I turned to Alistair, "I repeat, do not harass any more staff. Or blood shall flow!"

Behind me, as I rang for the elevator, I heard muttering.

A few hours later, Alistair joined me up at my desk.

"Very impressive!"

"Don't start, Alistair."

"No, really! I'm impressed! Who would have dreamed that you of all people would pull such a Margo Channing?"

"It was hardly a Margo Channing."

"When you left, Faunce was chewing nails! Face it, kid, your princesshood is over." Alistair lit a Tareyton and inhaled deeply. "Full regnitude has descended upon your shoulders."

"Alistair, stop!" I said, but I suspected he was right about the scene I'd pulled.

"You've made an enemy, you know," Alistair said. Then in another voice, "So tell me. This date? Not Mr. Beautiful from last night?"

Calvin's talk had put me on guard.

"The same."

"We getting serious?" Alistair all but cooed.

"We are having a second date."

"We talking a September wedding?" Alistair asked.

"He's a sailor!" I said.

He shrugged. "Domesticity comes in all forms."

"I'll settle for a few more dates."

We talked a bit about Matt, Alistair eliciting a great deal more information about him than I really wanted to tell. But as we talked, it seemed that he was genuinely disinterested and genuinely glad for me—not at all bitchy or envious as Calvin had said he'd be.

"Maybe you should be looking around for a lover too," I suggested.

"I'm done with love!" Alistair said theatrically, and smashed out his cigarette on the desk ashtray so assiduously that little of it remained. "After what that son of a bitch did to me, I'll never let another man into my life."

I hadn't known he was so bitter. He'd hidden it well.

"That wasn't love, Alistair. That was business! *Bad* business!"

"Business," he said very primly, "is what I'm going to concentrate on from now on."

"Said like Roz Russell. You'll have to start wearing those pin-striped suits with wide lapels and little Robin Hood hats with enormous feathers."

"You're joking, Rog. I'm not. Why do you think I'm doing all this with Faunce?"

"I've been wondering."

"Building a nest egg. A solid one. We may even go into business together later on. But I'll have my attorney devise a breakout clause which leaves anyone who tries to screw me so high and dry Mount Everest will seem like the tropics!"

"Do you really think there's money in this?" I asked.

"Some. But Vincent and his wife, Elena, know all the right people here in town, oddly enough. That's what I really want them for. To connect me up right."

Odd was right. I would have thought Alistair far better connected than either of them.

"Are we talking new sources of capital here or rich husbands?"

"New capital! Silent partners! Rich husbands! Rich wives!"

"Wives? Come on."

Alistair defended himself. "I've had affairs with women."

"Judy What's-her-name a million years ago!"

"Since too," he said staunchly. "In Nob Hill circles, I'm a noted bisexual."

"Fine. I'll dance at your wedding," I said, then added, "Me and Mr. Beautiful."

"It's a deal! Meanwhile try to bear with Faunce, even though I'll do my utmost to keep him out of your way."

"That's a deal," I said, and we shook on it.

You see, Calvin, I told myself, *you're wrong about Alistair.*

"If I lived this close, I'd probably come here every day," Matt said. We were just leaving the Japanese Tea Garden, slowly walking along a loop of asphalt embedded in lawn, headed for the front of the de Young Museum. We'd been on our feet for several hours, and I was beginning to worry about his leg.

"I come here whenever I can," I admitted. "And did so more before I became gainfully, if tragically, employed."

Matt looked at me in that way that showed he appreciated that I was "using" language (i.e., doing something with it) to please him.

"I'm beat!" I added. "Let's stop."

It was a late Sunday afternoon, and quite solidly sunny and warm for San Francisco. Despite the day, a school bus was lined up in front of the museum. We'd been inside earlier, looking mostly at the Oriental Arts collection ("Shoji screens for weeks!" Calvin said of his one visit. "And enough fans for every Madama Butterfly that ever trod the boards!") but we'd not seen any kids. Maybe an older tour group was using the bus. Now I dropped my jacket onto the lawn and fell atop it. Matt looked hesitant. Until I reached up and pulled him down next to me.

"What's that?" he asked, just now spotting another building through the trees.

I told him it was the California Academy of Sciences, "which no living human has ever willingly entered."

Matt laughed. "You're funny."

He put his head next to mine, as we looked up at the few small, dappled clouds. San Francisco is generally lousy for cloud watching, unless you maybe go to Land's End just before a major storm arrives. For high whites, the East Coast is superior, and the Midwest best of all. So while he watched clouds, I watched Matt.

I still couldn't believe he was here with me, next to me. Still couldn't believe he'd been with me nearly a week, or that he was so astonishingly good-looking. In fact, every time I looked at him, I kept finding new aspects of his beauty. The creaminess of the skin on the high insides of his arms. The massive, almost tumorous, solidity of his biceps. The extraordinary soaring architecture of his shoulder blades seen from behind. The seemingly Chinese delicacy and porcelain hardness of his clavicle. The tornado swirls of dark-colored hair around his navel, and their vectors south into a hurricane of pubic bush, then north and thinner, reduced to a virtual pencil line pointing toward each perfect areola surrounding a nipple atop his breastbone. The auricular curlicues of modestly fuzzed cartilage that composed his ears. The slight dimple at the end of his nose that could only be noticed close up, and which made it seem so much more defined from farther away. The astonishing definition of his upper lip, almost a line, and its cherrylike coloring, as though someone had applied lipstick in embryo and it had never rubbed off. The near-agate mosaic of his eyes, corneas mostly a silver-gray, but speckled lighter, a star-burst pattern at the center in paler gray, ice green, turquoise, sienna, amethyst, even lemon yellow. From the tiny perfect knob under his knee that connected the two long muscles running beneath his thigh down into the one that ran below his calf, to the nearly feathered tiny V's of hair that made up his sideburns, I'd never before encountered such an idealization of form, or, more impressively, such a lavish extravagance of detail! As though once he'd been shaped, his Creator had been so surprised, so pleased with the result, He'd come back again and again, dotingly, to touch up his Work.

"You know what that little pagoda in the garden reminded me of?" Matthew asked, suddenly sitting up.

It was fruitless to guess. In the few days, I'd already learned he might say virtually anything after an intro like that.

"This *wat*—a Buddhist temple—in Danang," Matt continued. (See what I mean?) "The funniest thing happened when I went inside."

"Oh?" I encouraged him.

"Not funny, ha ha, but . . ." Matt looked at me. "You don't want to hear this."

I grabbed him around the neck. "Kill and eat!" I threatened.

"Well, okay, I'll tell you. But I warned you, it's really dumb . . . When we were stationed there, I used to go around Danang. You know, like a tourist, with a camera and all. I guess I shoulda been a little afraid. The VC were all over the city, as we found out once it was retaken. And there were incidents—delivery boys riding by on a bike who'd assassinate you, that sort of thing. But for some reason I never felt afraid in Danang. I'd leave the guys at a café or restaurant and go wandering on my own. I liked the place. It was more, you know, *Asian* to me than Saigon, which is sort of like Paris done up in neon and chopsticks.

"So this one late afternoon, I'm half-lost, wandering through the more isolated back alleys of the warehouse district of town, and I see this . . . It looked like a lion. A female lion. Not with a mane and all. But the biggest damn cat! Just walking around. I couldn't believe it. So I follow, like at a distance. And it walks on, sniffing here and there. No one in the alley. I turn a corner and it's gone. Then I see its tail just going in some doorway. Up some stone stairs. Very old-looking stairs, covered with, what do you call it? Verdigris! I'm thinking this must be a really old building! But it's hard to see it all, hidden among all these Danang-type wooden shacks and buildings mostly made of slabs of particleboard and aluminum. At any rate, I still can't believe a lion lives here, so I go up the stairs and into this dark doorway.

"I find myself inside the temple. Gongs are going off, and the place reeks with incense, and there are candles and statues everywhere, and it's huge and smoky and dark and empty. Takes me a while to see there's no lion anywhere.

"I'm about to go back out, when I spot this old guy in a yellow robe. We've seen these yellow robes all over the city, naturally, and since they're against us, we're never too happy to see them. This guy, however, is like really old! And skinny. Just a bunch of bones. He's just pulling up the yellow cloth around him when he spots me.

"He stands up and comes over, asking me something or other, walking with difficulty. I see he's like really arthritic; his arms and legs are bent and the joints are swollen. Very pathetic the way he looks, the way he moves. Yet he's smiling and happy, and his old eyes are like really bright.

"So I ask him if he saw the big cat. My Vietnamese is shit, but that much

I know how to say: 'Where's the big cat?' He laughs. I tell him I followed the big cat inside. He laughs more, covering his toothless mouth with his yellow cloth. I'm about to leave, when he says it's him. He's the cat!

"Obviously he's loony. But then so am I if I saw a lion wandering around the back alleys of Danang, right? So I say okay, and I give him a few piasters. And I say, '*Amida Buddha*,' and I keep smiling, and I back away until I'm about out of that room. I turn to leave, and suddenly, I don't know, I feel something behind me. I turn around and . . . I don't know, maybe it was power of suggestion or hypnotism or the smoke and darkness, but I swear to you, Rog, I saw that lion inside that temple room. I didn't see that old monk anywhere.

"I hightailed it the hell out of there! But for the next coupla weeks I couldn't stop wondering about it. These monks are supposed to, you know, gain powers. What if that rickety old man, who could barely move around inside that temple because of how ill and deformed he was, what if through the power of his mind, he became that lion, and in that powerful, healthy body, he walked the alleys of Danang? . . . You think I'm crazy, right?"

"I'm totally blown away," I said.

He looked at me from that other angle of his: wondering if I were serious or not.

"I think that's the best story anyone ever told me," I said.

He relaxed. "Well, it happened."

"It's great!" I said, meaning he was great, which I didn't feel ready to say to him. "It's beautiful," I said, meaning he was beautiful, which I also didn't feel ready to say to him.

"I told only one other person besides you," Matt said. "This Hawaiian guy I met in the VA down in San Diego." He looked suddenly stricken, although I did nothing to betray his lapse.

He quickly covered it up. "I went there for some tests when I got back from Nam. Anyway, we got to talking about weird shit, and I told him what happened to me. Know what he said? He said I'd been given a sign. What kind of a sign? I asked. He didn't know, but he was damned sure that seeing a monk in his animal form, and recognizing that's who it was, *had* to be a sign. He told me it was a power sign. He thought I must have a special task. He used a word . . . like Karma, but . . ."

"*Dharma*," I said

"Right!" Matt said. "Special work I have to accomplish in this life."

"That's wonderful."

Matt looked thoughtful. "Full of wonder, yes. But maybe not wonderful-good. What if I have to do something bad?"

"It must be your poetry."

"It could be like meeting and connecting people up."

" . . ."

"It could be, like, meeting you," Matt said.

I melted, as somewhere far-off a hundred guitars softly thrummed.

"It says it's a Seurat!" Holly declared. Her arms were akimbo. Two dots of red flamed above her thin red-brown eyebrows. I'd never seen her like this: "If that's a Seurat, I'm Aretha-fucking-Franklin!"

Tall, slender, with an almost pancake-white uncosmetized complexion, Holly Francis wasn't even close to resembling the Diva of Soul. She did, on the other hand, somewhat resemble another diva, La Sutherland herself, when she arises from her bed to woodenly sleepwalk in that second act *scena* of *La Sonnambula*. Holly's nostrils flared, her shoulders tightened, her small but shapely breasts fought to protrude through her argyle sweater. She was all woman! She was glorious! She was seriously pissed off!

I removed the small, offending, admittedly well-framed litho from the wall and tucked it under my arm.

"There! All gone," I said.

It was Wednesday of the following week, before lunch. We were on the main floor of the store, in what must have been its precise geographical center. Of course everyone was staring at us.

"I mean, if he's going to hang fakes," Holly continued, "he could at least do me—and the art department—the favor of making them plausible!"

"Holly . . ." I tried to dampen her.

"There's about sixteen damn Seurats in existence, for Chrissakes, and every one of them has been pored over and pawed over and monographed about a skillion times."

"Holly . . ."

"If he knew anything about art . . . But then why would an art dealer bother to fill his head with facts about art?"

"Holly. . . ."

"What is he trying to do? Make a laughingstock out of me and my department? Is that it?"

"Holly . . . ?"

"Is that what I've put a billion woman-hours into this department for? So this scumbag can mock me?"

I said the obvious. "Holly, you're becoming hysterical."

"You better believe I'm hysterical. Where is that fucker anyway? *Faunce!*" she screeched up toward the art gallery balcony. "*Faunce! Get your fat ass down here now!*"

Two beats passed as every employee in the store and a few customers who'd come in—unwittingly thinking to buy a book rather than to enjoy an impromptu floor show—all suddenly pretended to be not listening to her.

At length, Alistair appeared at the edge of the balcony and, dismissively waving a hand, shouted, "Can you girls keep it down? We're trying to do business up here!"

It took six of us to hold Holly. Luckily a lady physician was nearby—in Travel, looking askance at the Balearics—and she prepared a tranquilizer in a stun gun of a hypodermic she kept at the ready in her Balmain purse.

Several hours later, I was talking to Pierluigi on the phone in Manhattan. One of his spies—Andre or the Bitch of Bari—had told him of the outburst, but not what it was about. I was happy to expand on the problem. Especially since it was partly Pierluigi's doing, and especially since I'd warned him about it.

"If you don't put a stop to this soon," I said, "your Albanian rose-red marble will be blood-red!"

"You're the manager," he protested. "It's your job to keep order."

"You should have thought of that before you appointed so many employees to their independent little duchies, then asked them to play KGB for you," I replied coolly.

Dead silence greeted that. I'd done the unspeakable: I'd spoken the truth about Pierluigi's soi-disant "management principles," which resembled less Peter Drucker (whom he read on every jet trip) than Cardinal Richelieu. Criticized to his very marrow, I knew that Pierluigi would be deeply offended. So what? Fuck him, I thought. I can always get another job. Even so, I thought perhaps I ought to temper it.

"Can't you see they're revolting," I joked. "No one more than Faunce."

Pierluigi sighed so intensely that if he had been anywhere near my desk, he would have blown every paper off. "You see how I am driven when all I want to do is be right by everyone?"

I did my best to ignore the twisted logic of that grammatical nightmare and asked, "What if someone *buys* one of those things thinking it is a Seurat? And brings it back?"

A deep groan—centuries of Italic *miseria* within it—a moan, a sigh. "I will talk to him."

I doubted that. But we all had our little roles to play in this charade, and I was playing mine.

As though on cue, Alistair appeared at my desk just as I hung up.

"I need a favor bad. I need you for a double date this Saturday."

"Sorry. I'll be with Matt."

He looked surprised. "That's still going on?"

"Sure is."

"This is early evening. You'll be home by eleven at the latest."

"A true double date?" I asked. "This is 1974, isn't it?"

"Come on, Rog. I promised Doriot. Her cousin's in town."

"Doriot?" I stopped. "Who's Doriot? And who's her cousin?"

"You know Doriot," he said, as though I were obviously joshing. He went on to mention her family name, which, while not Hearst or Coit or Van Ness, was somewhere up there. "Her cousin's Joy Kirkham. She grew up here, but she's been away for years going to school in Florence and—"

"Girls?" I asked, disbelief I hoped clear in my voice. "You're talking about double dates . . . with . . . two girls? Girrlllls?! What are we supposed to do with them? Strip off their slips and make up like Mommy? Or steal their bras and go fly kites?"

Alistair was insulted. "You needn't be so *gay* about it."

"Alistair, the point is I am gay. Even if you've decided you're not.

And I'm dating someone. Someone special and nice and beautiful . . . Girls?" I couldn't help asking again.

"Well, I'm sure Paolo won't be insulted," Alistair said, and stalked off, muttering to himself.

Good work, Rog, I told myself. You've managed to deeply, and no doubt irrevocably, offend both your boss and your cousin in less than fifteen minutes. Without a single pause or even a cigarette break in between. That has to be some kind of record!

At dawn I awakened, needing to urinate. When I returned to the bedroom, the place looked like a battlefield of pillows and bed covers. The air was still and tight, cold too, with that non-humid-seeming yet all-pervading dampness of San Francisco mornings. Shivering, I closed the blinds more tightly—wanted no offending sun yet, despite its potential for heat. After last night, after any of these nights lately, I was so physically exhausted, I really needed sleep!

Matt's large, solid body lay in the middle of the bed, rolled onto his stomach, one arm out, his head turned so that most of his face was visible—that face!—and three fingers entangled in his front curls. As though aware of my admiration, even in his sleep, he shifted, one edge of quilt dropping demurely off his chuck of shoulder. I leaned over and kissed the perfect skin covering such bone, such muscle, and pulled the cover back up. His somnolent reaction was to twist half around—exposing his left ankle and leg.

The ankle! *The* leg!

I told myself I would cover it up and look away. But as though contradicting me, a beam of sharp sunlight popped through my jerry-rigged window shade onto the ankle and leg. So, of course, I felt compelled to look.

At first I saw nothing. Then I noticed what looked like a slight bump, not discolored, at a forty-five-degree angle to the verticality of natural skin wrinkles at his heel. As I moved my head, I could make out its other side, and now the marks of stitching were apparent, a wide, angled pattern of them. This had been a real bitch of a tear. I could imagine Matt's sudden pain, his fear of being hamstrung, unable to move forward, having to drag his leg like a dead thing behind. I kissed the scar.

That's when I saw the other scar. I'd missed it, because it was so much smaller, less obvious, higher up his leg, halfway along his calf. Like the first one, it wasn't discolored—as though the surgeons had worked hard to retain as much of Matt's physical perfection as possible—but its suddenness, cutting right across the back of his muscled calf, and its depth of cut and the lacework of broken little veins it held and the surprising doughiness of the skin and flesh around it all said it had been serious. Had been, might still be. I immediately wondered— Did it reach his sciatic nerve? And I drove the thought—and its potential for infinite physical mischief—out of my mind.

I stared at that scar until I began to really shiver. Then I covered it up—no kiss, it frightened me too much—with the quilt and got back under the blankets.

Matt rolled open a space for me and enclosed me within it.

"Why're you so cold?" he asked, nine-tenths asleep.

"Had to pee," I replied.

"Hmmmmm. Stay in bed."

"Okay, Lucia," Calvin said, "I've done a complete scan of the gang here at the magazine, and I'll tell you what I found out if you tell me what you've found out."

"I only talked to two people," I replied. "Estelle and Jeffrey. Listen, Calvin, I'm head over heels in love."

"We all know where your heels were last night, honey. What did Miss Madness recommend?" he asked, ignoring the second and for me only crucially important part of my answer.

Jeffrey Teller and Mrs. Estelle Lambert-Duchesne were the other most frequently appearing free-lance writers in the magazine. I should add that I wrote articles under the sobriquet "Henrici," the name of J. S. Bach's most often used librettist for cantatas and passions.

"Jeffrey's aiming for Paer or Mayr. Ever hear of them?"

"Of course," Calvin answered. "Early nineteenth-century—wrote Italian opera. Paer's *Leonora* is allegedly a forerunner of Beethoven's *Fidelio*."

Calvin had been raised from being her assistant to taking over from

Estelle at the magazine when she was fired for incompetence—read: alcoholism. Cherkin, his boss, who published six other trade magazines— mostly about ball bearings and fish packing and suchlike unglamorous stuff—sometimes treated Calvin like "the house darky" and sometimes as though he were H. L. Mencken. According to Calvin, it varied, and could not be predicted—which drove Calvin crazy, given the iffiness of his own self-esteem. Moreover, in Calvin's psychic life, his boss often became Calvin's father—and that invariably meant trouble.

"You're not listening," I said. "I just told you I'm in love. Any self-respecting homosexual would drop the topic, drop the dishes, drop the fucking Waterford crystal to discuss this."

"Well, this self-respecting homosexual has things to do. A magazine to get out. Trouble to make."

"Like hell!"

I suspected that his own love life—never very good—was particularly bad or, worse, nonexistent lately, which might explain his hesitancy now. So I resorted to my last weapon.

"If we don't talk about this now, Calvin, I will never, never, never, never listen to you when Harold or Bernard or Rastus or whomever the hell you are seeing does something terrible, awful, beyond words."

This I knew would be difficult for him to resist. Although Calvin had grown up in the black (and—let's face it, since it was Grosse Pointe— white) upper middle class and had gone to cream-puffy Berkeley, he'd fallen not for some nice white boy, not even for an Oreo like himself, but instead for a black heroin dealer in Oakland, a guy who'd swung both ways—when, that is, he wasn't swinging at Calvin. A year-long on-again, off-again relationship ensued, in which Calvin had lost some of his baby fat and all of his remaining innocence about—as he put it— "The Joys of Ghetto Negritude." He'd never become hooked on drugs or in any way involved with them, but Calvin had gotten emotionally hooked on butch African-American bisexuals whose beautifully mod-eled bodies were covered with knife scars, and whose large, vulnerable brown eyes lied without blinking, men who spent half their relationship in a jail cell and would as easily beat him unconscious for ten dollars as make love to him for hours at a time. All this I knew in the kind of detail only a best gay friend and Sistuh could know.

"Okay, Miss Borgia, you win." Calvin had thought over my ultimatum. "Tell me all about the eleven hundred and sixty-sixth alleged 'love of your life.' "

"I'll do even better. I will actually allow you to see and speak to this paragon of beauty—not to mention good taste—in person. Brunch tomorrow. Your choice of dive."

"Chile! This must be serious if you want Semiramide herself in all her gold lamé garments to meet, greet, and you know, pass judgment!"

"I have no fears," I replied grandly.

So he let me talk about Matt for about twenty minutes, then he got in a few horrible stories about how awful Cherkin had been to him at the magazine. We were saying good-bye for the tenth time when he finally said, "By the way. Did I tell you what Miss Thing at the Opera did? He called up yesterday using this all-too-recognizable voice, and he asked if I needed the name of an opera."

"Does bread need honey? Does . . . What did he recommend?" I asked.

"Guess," Calvin said. "Go on and guess."

"Don't tell me. Ummm . . . I know! *Dildo in Anus!*"

"Then it's true," Calvin marveled. "All small minds *do* think alike."

Calvin must have known the owner. Pleasant as the restaurant was, it had three tables in the picture window and we got the middle one. The view was reason enough for the place's existence: it looked north, straight down Divisadero to the Marina and the bay. The yacht club, the Presidio, the park, and of course the bridge dominated the view to the left. To the right were Russian and Telegraph hills, with Coit Tower just within view.

"This *is* something!" Matt enthused as a tall young woman seated us. I wanted to tell her to put her eyes back in her head. The place was crowded, but she remained at our table, fussing with our silverware and napery, trying to catch Matt's eye, until she was forced to break her cool with "Cocktails?"

Matt didn't even glance her way. "What do you say?" He put a big hand over mine and looked me directly in the eyes.

"Two Kirs!" I told her, feeling her die inside and need to get away instantly. "So! What do you want to know about Calvin?"

Matt shrugged. "Whatever you want to tell me."

"First, he's my dearest friend. He's from the Midwest. Michigan. His mother was black, from downtown Detroit, his father white, from the mansions. Calvin was the third child. His brother, Dante, was tall, light-skinned, and a three-letter athlete. His sister, Christina, was even prettier than her mother and lighter-skinned than her brother. Calvin came six years after her, unexpectedly. He was sickly, pampered, bright, a fat, dark-skinned little boy who developed instant behavior problems and was a complete sissy by the time he was ten. This," I added, "I have on good faith, not only from Calvin."

"Wow!" was all Matt said.

"We met a week after I arrived here, in the Ritch Street Baths. In a big room that looks like a gymnasium or something. Huge pillows all over the floor. I was resting when two guys came in. Ten minutes later we were in the middle of a three-way. Then some more guys came in and we were in the middle of an orgy."

Our drinks arrived, and I told the waitress we'd wait to order when the rest of our party came. The setting sun was low, out of view, casting a crepuscular scarlet over the Golden Gate Bridge, flecked with spots of hot orange and deep lilac. The sky behind it was a contrasting put-your-teeth-on-edge ultramarine.

"It was all pretty hot and heavy. I happened to look up and see this guy a few feet away, wrapped in a towel, staring. I thought he was, you know, a voyeur. When I really looked, he seemed so sad and out of it. So, I don't know, hungry! I gestured for him to come closer. He hesitated. I gestured again. When he was close enough to reach, I pulled him into the mass of bodies. He resisted. I became occupied myself, and when I came up for air, he was gone. I found him later, when I went up to the roof to sun on the decking there.

"He came over to me and thanked me for trying to involve him in the group. Then he told me he only liked black guys." I suddenly panicked. "It's okay that Calvin's black, isn't it? Well, half black."

Matt seemed surprised. "Okay with me. Why?"

Relief—what if my best friend and Matt didn't get along? "You never know. Especially among kids who grew up ethnic—Italian, for example."

"That wasn't the case with me," Matt said. "I didn't grow up in an Italian neighborhood, and my folks, well, my folks are real special people themselves. They made sure I grew up being tolerant of everyone, no matter who or what they are."

"That's great. They do sound special."

"Yeah," Matt said. "Well, they encountered their own share of prejudice. You know it wasn't the same back then as it is now."

I loved how serious he'd become. This was the first time he'd spoken of his family, and it confirmed that Matt's convictions ran deep. And he was right: inter-ethnic and inter-religious marriages *had been* a big deal a generation ago. I was glad that Mrs. and Mr. Loguidice had done it. Just look at what their unique gene mixing had made: fjord-white skin, coal-black hair!

"My Grandpa Loguidice's a little old-fashioned," Matt said and laughed. "I've heard him call black people *melanzane*. You know, eggplant. But I never heard him say it in a disparaging way, only descriptive."

"So to get back to our meeting," I continued, "Calvin thanked me and we said a few more words, then I pulled out my radio headphones and put them on my head. I suddenly felt tapping on my chest. It was Calvin, he wanted to hear. So I let him listen. And he was . . . ecstatic! I don't know how else to say it. Ecstatic!"

"Schwarzkopf singing *Ariadne*?" Matt asked.

"Close. Sutherland singing *Norma*. Well, it turned out he was as crazy about opera as I was, and he worked for this opera magazine, and we talked until the sun went down, and when we left, it was to go to his apartment—he lives near Mission Dolores—to talk more and to listen to more opera. After that, we never stopped talking and listening to opera. Now, of course, we go together. He gets free and cheap tickets through the magazine. We speak twice a day every day. And I guess by now we know absolutely everything about each other."

For example, I knew that Calvin was not happy at work or in his love life; not happy with his body, which remained chubby no matter how much he dieted and exercised; not happy with his face, mostly because his color was too café au lait and his features insufficiently Negroid—or

Caucasoid—although I thought he was both cute and unusual-looking, combining some of the best features of both races; not happy with his position in the opera/music world of the Bay Area, where he was always "token nigger" and yet so obviously gay that he was also "treated like one of the girls," and thus he often didn't feel he stood out enough.

"That taxi took forever!" Obviously Calvin had arrived. He was brushing off his suede jacket. "The fare cost the same as the gross national product of a medium-sized East African nation, and on top of that, the seats were filthy!"

"You must be What's-his-name," Calvin added, slapping Matt's shoulder coquettishly with a fawn kid glove. "This one's such a pathological liar, I'm sure you've heard nothing but awful things about me."

He sat himself down, endlessly unwrapped a long scarf, which went around his neck several times—July being the closest thing to winter in San Francisco—checked the angle of his tam in a pocket mirror, sighed, and shouted, "*Hel-lo!*"

The tall dancer serving us knew him. She arrived smiling.

"You kids need more." Calvin glanced around him. "I think I'll have a sidecar. Yes, a sidecar. And bring menus. We're starved. Despite ocular evidence to the contrary."

When she was gone, he said to Matt, "We *only* have cocktails from thirties and forties films. If Bette or Joan didn't order it, we won't dare. Thanks! You and the bartender are total dears!" The waitress dithered. "Hmmmmm!" he added. "Have him make up one more. He has?" Calvin reacted to her. "A bona fide angel that Luis!" He made smoochy-lips at her, and she laughed and left. "Now! *Le repas!* The Chicken Pot Pie, with peas and French fries, believe it or not, will cause convulsions of *plaisir*! What do you think of the view, Matt? Look at the colors in the fog swirling about the bridge. One should simply bring Armani here and point them out—there! there! and that one, dear! In a nice houndstooth! The Alaskan king crab is flown in fresh. If you don't mind having to suck something out of a long, hard, tubular object, that is. We are not, I repeat, *not* going to discuss opera or the magazine or the shop once tonight! Deal? Matthew, is that your name? So biblical! You're to be referee and slap our hands, faces, or fannies—your choice!—if we do. Now . . . what is it? Have you lost all capacity for conversing? Speak!"

"Give me a crowbar, and I'll try!"

By the time our appetizers arrived—"Oh, I'll just *bet* you kids need a dozen oysters each!"—Calvin had completely charmed and befuddled Matt. As usual, I was amused. By the time our entrées came—two pot pies; we didn't *dare* go near those crab legs!—Calvin was talking about his live-in lover, his family and foibles.

"Antria—true name, kids," he turned to Matt, "she's my husband's wife. Is that too confusing? Antria calls the other day. She says she's looking for Bernard. Needs his social security number for the Welfare Department. I told her he's sleeping. Call back. She tells me to go look in his wallet. I say, 'Girl, I don't go looking in his wallet!' And she tells me back, 'Girl, if you don't go looking in his wallet, why's he there in the first place!' "

By the time we were picking over three different desserts placed in the middle of the table, Calvin was flirting shamelessly with Matt.

"Oh, that's what all you *men* say. But then you go and do something bad. Are you bad, Matt? No, I can see you're not."

"I am," Matt protested. "Very bad."

"Shee-it! I mean 'bad-motha-fucka-bad'! You're not bad like that."

"I have been."

"You're too white to be 'bad motha-fucka bad.' You're not half a looker, either," Calvin said, dismissively, leaning against one of Matt's Michelangelesque shoulders, "but you're just too fucking white! I want my men to be dark as tar and have done at least a nickel's experience in the joint. No shee-it!" He enjoyed Matt's reaction to that, then said, "Now, why don't you go to the men's room or make a telephone call or something so we can talk about you behind your back?"

"I really should call in to the base," Matt said.

"What's keeping you?!" Calvin pushed him out of the chair. "Oh, don't be disgusting," he said, as I reached for Matt's hand to touch before he left the room. "He's not going to Zanzibar!"

"Well?" I said, when Matt was gone. "What do you think?"

"Rog, pussikins. You're obviously in love with the man. Why ask? If you were just meeting him or just breaking up with him, I'd be bone-crunchingly honest."

"Meanwhile . . . ?" I prodded.

Calvin shook his head. "Miss What's-Her-Name-in-the-Sky sure can get it together every once in a while for the looks department."

"Next time bring Bernard."

"They wouldn't let him through that door. And *I* wouldn't blame them."

"You and Antria becoming sisters?"

"She'd like exactly that, but . . ."

Calvin stopped and stared ahead. "Well, you weren't pulling your old Aunt Calvina's tail after all."

I turned to follow his gaze—to Alistair, with a tall, slender, really quite lovely young woman. She had that long, straight, five-alternating-shades-of-natural-blond English hair that just drops in sheets, and a perfect oval face with huge blue eyes, button nose, and pouty mouth. Her clothing was so very simple you might almost have believed it hadn't cost a fortune. They were shown to a table across the largish room. He sat, and she excused herself to go powder her nose.

"Doriot Spearington," I said.

"My dear! Your cousin doesn't fool around when he decides to become a breeder, does he? But then he never did fool around, did he?"

"What are you talking about?"

"He's spotted us. He's coming over."

"Calvin, what do you know about Alistair?"

Alistair arrived at that minute, ending any possible explanation. I had to admit he dressed the part. He was wearing gray slacks with knife-edged creases, penny loafers, tan socks, a blue blazer with fawn leather buttons, and to my utter astonishment, a pale-blue mock turtleneck. One could only wonder—had he all that preppy drag in his closets at home, or did he rush out to Bashford and buy it especially for the occasion?

"I might have known you two would not only know about this place but know it so well you get the best table," Alistair said, genially. "May I?" he asked, seating himself in Matt's chair. "Now, *this* is the advertised view!"

"Baseball! Beer in a can! Pussy!" Calvin said in his gruffest voice.

I wanted to slap him.

Alistair ignored him. "Too bad you didn't join the three of us last night. We ended up taking the Spearingtons' sailboat out from the yacht club." He pointed to it as though we didn't know where it was.

"All the way out under the bridge. Turns out all of us are pretty good sailors. We sailed all evening in the most tremendous easterly."

"RBI's. ERA's. Vaginal douche!" Calvin went on.

Just then Matt arrived back at the table. There was a bit of awkwardness as Alistair noticed him arrive, got up, and shook hands. "I believe we've met."

Matt made me love him even more: "Sorry, I don't recall."

Matt sat down and Alistair stayed up.

"White Sox! Chicago Bears! Muff diving!" Calvin said.

"The Bears are a football team!" Alistair corrected. "Keep away from the cocktails here," he warned me and Matt, "or you'll all end up babbling like him. Come meet Doriot," he said, pulling me up by the shoulder.

As we crossed the room, he said, "Your new friend sort of reminds me of my mother's gardener. Remember him?"

"Matt does? Really?"

"Same color eyes!" Alistair said. "Same . . . Ah, she's back. Doriot Spearington! My second cousin and childhood friend Roger Sansarc! Sit a second." He offered me his chair and searched out another.

Doriot had a model's face, also a kind and intelligent face.

"Sorry you couldn't come last night. We had a great time on the boat."

"I'm not a great sailor," I said. "The mind says yes, the tummy no."

"Well, maybe it's better," she said. "It was a bit rough."

"Roger manages Pozzuoli!" Alistair told her, then explained, "Except for the gallery. Doriot's agreed to help us put together the little do for Wunderlich! Don't tell me Pierluigi didn't tell you about our coup! Wunderlich has agreed to let us do his first exhibit outside Europe. You're coming, of course," he said to me. "Bring Matt, if he's still around. Calvin, too. In fact, why not let me have his work address? I'd like his employer to come."

As he spoke, I found myself alternately watching him and Doriot and trying to put my finger on something that seemed the tiniest bit off-kilter. She watched him and reacted as fully and intently to what he was saying as any young woman interested in a man: looking surprised, making a moue, all of it completely natural. And he played to her—and a bit to me. No surprise, really. I'd never really gotten over how in love with him Judy had been, how much he'd counted on that love, and what a price in integrity Judy had paid for it at that charade of a trial.

It was something Alistair was doing—No!—saying.

His speech was a little less colorful than usual, but not by much. He'd never been as openly queenie as, say, Calvin could be, or for that matter, as I myself could be talking back to Calvin. Camp had never been Alistair's métier: he'd gone in for a higher-handed wit spiced with irony, and based on sarcasm. But it was more than cleverness. Alistair had always possessed a uniquely slanted view of life and, more important, a well-justified view of himself as someone so beyond normal conventions that he couldn't help but let that come through in his conversation. In recent years, however, he'd come more to control his speech, relentlessly eliminating the wild arrogations and pretensions of his youth. At first, I'd thought that a sign of his maturity. But that business with the Selective Service several years before had taught me otherwise. No, Alistair remained as egotistical and arrogant as ever: he'd just learned to hide it better. In the months since I'd re-encountered him here in California, he'd become noticeably more reserved in his speech, almost taciturn. As though if he did let go and begin to say what he really meant, he'd unloose some demonic, unstoppable logorrhea. Yet here he was, with me and Doriot, being what I'd never dreamed he could be—a little ironic, a bit funny, desirous of pleasing, wanting to push his little projects but not that much, unwilling to offend. In short, just like anyone else!

With this realization, a dull horror gripped me, although I smiled and half laughed, and made all the appropriate responses.

By the time I finally felt free to get away, Calvin had dragged Matt over to the bar to meet the bartender, and I sat alone at our table, staring out at the *l'heure bleue* view, sipping tepid coffee, and wondering how someone as remarkable as Alistair could have become so drearily normal. Or was I being oversensitive?

"Well! It's official!" Calvin said, as he returned. He was attempting to enfold his sweatered pulchritude within Matt's longer, leaner expanse. "You're dumped and we're the item!"

I was checking out Matt's eyes, which I thought I knew pretty well by now. They didn't at all resemble the gardener's. Those had been gray with darker streaks in them, almost green. Flatter. These . . .

"Bad joke, huh?" Calvin said, noticing my distraction and misinterpreting it. He quickly sat down. "C'mon! It wasn't *that* bad."

"It's not the joke, Calvin. Why does Alistair hate you?"

"He doesn't. I hate him."

"Why? What did he do to you?"

"Nothing to me. To a friend. A once dear friend. But this is hardly the time or place for that discussion."

"We're going to have it *some*time."

"Nag. Nag. You're worse than Bernard's wife," Calvin said. "This is on me," he said, reaching for the check. "I insist. Expecially as I get a substantial discount. Drinks free. I think that bartender is interested. He's a bit paleface. But sweet. Named Luis. Reads the mag cover to cover. Knows the libretti to all of Mozart's operas, including *L'Oca del Cairo*! You know, of course, the game being played in every gay bar in town?" Calvin looked at me.

"How old's your Kotex?"

"How vee rude!"

"Hepatitis A or B? Which do I have?" I tried.

"Aren't we being Mr. Mean-Jeans tonight? Give up? Which Nixon asshole would you do it with? You know, Ehrlichman, Haldeman, et cetera."

"And I thought Polish jokes were bad."

"Brownie's honor." Calvin did something with his fingers supposedly indicative of swearing. "You know what Bernard said when I asked him? Charles Colson! Isn't it perfect?"

"Isn't he in jail?" Matt asked.

"Didn't he find Jesus?" I asked.

"I don't see where either would automatically disqualify him," Calvin said. "Well, come on. You choose."

"Does Sam Ervin count?" Matt asked.

"The rules are clear: only those under indictment or about to be. By the way, you are one sick bunny. Sam Ervin!"

"How about Stu Erwin?" Matt tried.

"They're all so slimy," I protested. "Obviously the gung-ho break-in guys are out. Haldeman is the one with the square head and crew cut, right? Oh, I don't know! John Dean? But it would have to be S and M. With me as master and him dressed like Ronnie Spector. You know, that quilted black leather skirt she wore with a slit up to her waist."

"Bangle earrings the size of coffee cups!" Calvin put in.

"And boots made for walking that'll walk all over you!" Matt added.

"Perfect!" we agreed.

"For makeup ... Mary Quant white lipstick and enormous fake lashes," Calvin suggested.

"With his hair grown out, swept up, and shellacked into a Lynda Bird special," I put in.

"Crotchless lace panties," Matt said. "From Frederick's."

"Where did you ever see those?" Calvin asked.

"In a catalog." Matt began to blush. "One of the guys on board had it."

"Bernard chose Colson?" I asked. "Doesn't this say something to you?"

"No more than John Dean in a bouffant and crotchless undies does."

"I take it back," I said. "I'm sticking with Haldeman. From a sexual point. I heard that he was . . ."

". . . one hundred percent prick!" Calvin joined me.

"Oh, why?" He turned to Matt and slid a cupped hand under his chin. "Why couldn't your ancestors have come from Benin instead of Bari?"

"Remember what we were talking about at dinner?" Matt asked.

"Doing it with Haldeman?"

"No! I meant when I told Calvin that I'd been bad. I *have* been bad."

We were in bed—naturally! Virtually all our conversations in the two weeks since we'd met had either been precoital or postcoital.

"I'm glad you and Calvin liked each other," I said. "You did like him, didn't you?"

Matt was busily playing the left-hand part of the Rachmaninoff Second Sonata on my chest.

"Didn't you?" I tried again.

"Of course I did. Are you going to address my statement or avoid it?"

"Avoid it," I admitted weakly, stopping his hand. "I don't want to know anything bad about you."

"You know that telephone call I made today to the base?" Matt seemed to be changing the subject. "I have to go away a few days. Maybe longer."

I sat up. "Don't punish me. I'll listen to the bad things."

"I'm not punishing you! I really do have to go away."

"Where?" I demanded, hearing—and hating!—the pout in my voice.

"To San Diego. The base," and when he noticed my eyes widening, he added, "the VA hospital. It'll be all right. Just tests on some bugs I picked up there."

I knew he was lying, shielding me from the truth. Part of me said it was his leg, that's why he was going. But another part of me said, *No, it's far worse: cancer, leukemia—he'll be dead in a year.*

"C'mon, Rog. Don't be like that."

"Like what?" I asked. "Horrified?"

"I told you it'll be all right."

I grasped at him as though he were being pulled out of my grip by a fierce wind. "You're coming back, right? Staying here with me?"

"Of course I'm coming back," he said. "As for staying here . . . well, that's up to them. The brass. Not me."

I thought: I'm going to lose him. And there's not a thing I can do.

"You're fantasizing it all out of proportion!" Matt said.

"Am I?"

"Are you going to let me tell you about the bad things I've done?"

"It's not some atrocity, is it? I don't want to hear atrocities."

"Lie down and listen," Matt said.

I did as he said. He'd not let go of me, and that made me feel calmer. His voice did the rest.

"This happened in Saigon. I'd been there on leave a few times, but I never went crazy like the other guys did. And it's not what you're thinking."

"What am I thinking?" I asked.

"You know, about being with guys instead of girls."

"Was there any of that there?"

"You kidding?" Matt laughed. "Plenty! Not that I did much. Really, I didn't! But there are places you could go. Certain hotels, where you could buy a six-pack or a bottle of Scotch, maybe some opium or grass, and party. They call them homesteads. Don't know why. Then there are the guys who double up with a chick. They pay her and send her away. Not too many guys go after native boys. If they like Asians, they usually wait till they can swing a longer leave and a plane ride to Bangkok. The boys are cleaner and prettier and more experienced there.

"There are some gay bars in Saigon. There used to be one that had a back room just like some of the bars here. For servicemen only! No gooks! Sorry, but that's how you say it. I went there a few times, but I only looked in the back. Most of these gay bars are just like ordinary servicemen bars except without girls. If you came in off the street without knowing, you might never know.

"It was in one of these bars that I came to meet this fly-by. That's what the gays in Nam call Air Force jet pilots, 'fly-bys,' because that's what they usually do the next time you see them, fly right by you without even saying hello."

"This fly-by's name was Todd Griffes, and he was an army brat. Family originally came from the Panhandle of Florida, but he'd grown up on bases all over the world, mostly in the East, as his father had been a marine. Well, Todd took me to a homestead and we did it a few times, which was okay, though nothing special. But he never flew by me. He always stopped and would try to get me in the sack again. Which was sort of nice.

"What wasn't nice about him was that he was always broke. Never had enough money, was always cadging. One time I was in a USO just hanging around, trying to make some free trunk calls home to my Grandpa Loguidice, and I see Todd Griffes coming my way. I figure he's going to hit me up. Instead he offers to buy me a drink. He's been on a four-day leave and he's returning to Manila the next morning. I keep waiting for him to hit me up, and when he doesn't, I finally ask why not.

"It turns out that while he was in Saigon, Todd earned money. A lot. Doing what? Dancing. Actually, doing a striptease in this gay gook place called Bubbles Dao's. Todd tells me all about it. You dance up on this circular platform in the middle of the room, and all these gooks lean over the fence surrounding you and try to get at you. Meanwhile, not only do you dance, but you also jerk off. For which Bubbles Dao pays a hundred dollars a minute!"

"You're kidding," I interrupted.

"I thought for sure Todd was kidding. Putting me on for, you know, turning him down. So I asked him how to get to the place and how to contact the owner and if I could go earn money there and all. I was really just waiting for Todd to admit he'd been jerking my chain. But he was consistent. He even offered to show me the place and to introduce me to Bubbles Dao.

"It was getting late, and I thought maybe it'd be nice to spend the night with Todd. He wasn't great sex or anything, but at least I knew what to expect. So I make the offer. And Todd turns me down. No offense, he says, but he's going to spray his next load all over a bunch of gooks at Bubbles Dao's and collect thirteen, fourteen hundred bucks for the pleasure. If I wanted, I could tag along.

"I went with him. The place had been built as a gambling casino in the forties. It was off the main street, with a good-sized main room, octagonal, with booths around some of the sides and bars around the other ones. In the big middle room was a dance floor, with colored lights and a few gook couples doing the fox-trot. Most of them were in suits, a few in uniform, and the uniforms we spotted half-hidden in the dark booths were pretty high-up ARVN! Very few Yanks, so the minute we walk in, everyone checks us out. Todd takes me to the central bar, where this real nelly guy in semi-drag—you know, makeup, hairdo, and blouse, but he's a guy!—is introduced as Bubbles Dao.

" 'You bring me a new boy!' is the first thing he says when he sees me. Todd says no. But that we're pals and he wanted to show me the place. Bubbles Dao wants me to do the show. 'So handsome. Like Tony Curtis!' he keeps saying."

"You don't look anything like Tony Curtis!" I protested.

"I know. Anyway, when I turn around, Todd is gone. Five minutes later, he appears on the circular platform, which is slowly rising through a hole in the floor into the middle of the dance floor. The fence goes up too. Just in time. Because it seems like every gook in the place charges it. The lights darken, then spots come on Todd. Theatrical lights. The music suddenly changes to Elton John's 'Candle in the Wind.' Todd's wearing some kind of field dress—fatigues, equipment, everything but a loaded rifle. He begins to gyrate and strip. When he takes his shirt off, he's got a sweaty grunt A-shirt on underneath, and every gook in the place moans. When he opens his pants, they sigh. When he pulls them down and grabs his dick, they groan and cheer. By the time the third Elton John song comes on—'Bennie and the Jets'—he's naked except for his boots and a cap, and he begins to masturbate. Mind you, the little platform is slowly revolving, and mind you, even with the fence, they're all reaching out their hands, so that at certain times, depending upon the angle, they're stroking his legs, the boots, sometimes even his ass, which Todd sometimes sticks out for them to reach—just barely.

"I told you Todd was boring sex. Well, in Bubbles Dao's place, he's Marilyn Monroe and Paul Newman and Sally Rand and Elvis all rolled into one. I've never seen such a hot act. I'm immediately and totally hard watching him. And I hardly notice that Bubbles Dao touches my thing as he keeps talking about Todd's act and how I should do it too, how he'll fix me up with an outfit and the right music and all.

"When Todd comes, he yells like some guy at a rodeo, and all the gooks yell right along with him, and he does what he said, he sprays them with his jizz, and they reach out for it. It's like completely animal-istic and the all-time hottest thing I've ever in my life seen. The gooks are still begging for more as the platform begins to descend, with Todd dropped down on it with his knees spread out, sitting on his haunches, like a rock guitarist who's just played the wildest set, only Todd's hold-ing his dick instead of a bass guitar.

"Well, I found him down in his dressing room, and I was so hot, I just screwed Todd right there, even though I'm sure Bubbles Dao and some other guys were watching through the poorly constructed bam-boo walls.

"When we left, Bubbles Dao told me to come again, anytime, and work for him. He already had an act in mind for me."

"Did you go back?" I asked, already knowing the answer.

"Not only did I go back, I became Bubbles Dao's star," Matt said. "On every leave, I'd do two, sometimes three shows a day. I did soldier and cowboy acts and construction worker and surfer boy acts, and I packed 'em in. He had to pay me two hundred dollars a minute. And sometimes I did it for special groups, smaller groups, including women, for three hundred a minute, people who would stay there after I sprayed them, as I kept milking it, and who'd stand there as I sprayed piss all over them."

"You must have liked it," I said, not sure how he'd respond.

"Sometimes . . . I liked the money. I liked the attention. Being in the spotlight. I didn't care much for the smaller, special shows, even though I was paid more. What I liked was dancing, stripping, jerking off for all those guys, seeing their hands and their faces and their mouths, and watching sometimes a hundred or more, five or six rows deep, become one person, one sexual partner I could play on like an instrument."

"But you stopped?"

"Soon as I had twenty thousand dollars."

"Twenty thousand dollars! That's a year's pay for me."

"More'n the Navy pays me!" he admitted. "No, I lied, I did one more show. With Todd. Back to back and side by side with him on that tiny platform. My farewell performance."

"Hot?"

"Outrageous!" he said. "They tore the fence down to get at us. But you know, the guys who broke through didn't do anything. They just knelt all around us. Row after row of them kneeling and looking up at us. Funny, huh? You think Americans would have done that?"

"They would have torn you limb from limb."

"That's what Todd said."

"Like the very first poet, Orpheus, torn limb from limb . . . Twenty thousand dollars!" I repeated. "You can take the next year off and . . . *become* a poet!"

Matt smiled. "That's what I thought too."

"Then why say it was bad?" I argued.

"Sex for money is immoral and illegal."

"That's complete bullshit!" I protested. But something else interested me more. "They were all Vietnamese? And they all fantasized about Americans?"

"Bubbles never admitted it, but I'm certain some high-up VC came to those special shows I did. At *those* shows, I was *always* in complete gyrene duds," Matt said. "And once outside Bubbles Dao's I was outranked by most of the ARVN that I came all over inside."

"What a crazy, fucked-up war."

"What? What's so funny?"

I'd begun laughing. "I was just thinking. What a great thing to write up in your memoirs! You know, when you're eighty-five and this distin-

guished old poet, all grandfatherly and sage, and you write this. People'll
scream!"

We laughed until I demanded he dance for me.

He did, briefly, on top of the bed, badly, to the last ten minutes of
Strauss's *Salome*. Until neither of us could stop laughing.

"Have you listened to it?" Calvin asked.

"I listened."

"Well, what did you think?" he added when I didn't answer immediately. "Didn't you think Journet and Pinza were fabulous?"

"What I could *hear* of them. They sounded like they were at the
end of a tunnel a mile long. And the condition of the tape itself isn't all
that great. There were more snaps, crackles, and pops than in a Rice
Crispies box."

"Miss Smith claims to have located another pirate of *Agnes*," he said,
soberly. "More modern. Fifty-four. Franco Corelli, Ludmilla Udovic,
Maria Colzani, but only one bass. Giangiacomo Guelfi's baritone isn't
really low enough. It's live but heavily cut. The Maggio Musicale in
Florence, with Vittorio Gui conducting. Want to hear it?"

"When's the decision going down?" I asked.

"The final decision is next Wednesday. We're meeting at your hotel
and then coming straight over to the Wunderlich party. The whole
group of us."

"Including Miss Thing at the Opera?"

"To see and be seen. The Pozzuoli Gallery will be the place to be
next Wednesday. Have to hand it to that white girl your cousin's boffing. She sure knows how to get publicity. Did you see what's-his-face's
column today?"

"And yesterday and two days ago! The *Chronicle* in debt to Doriot's
daddy or what? Look, Cal, I don't have to listen to the Gui tape. I'll vote
for *Agnes* on the first round." I wanted to tell him I might be the only
one besides himself who would be voting for it. People I'd talked to
were less than amused by Calvin's strenuous campaigning. I wanted to
try to ease him for a disappointment to come. But how?

"You are the sweetest! Ready for your weekly Donizetti update?"

"Why not? I have no other reason to live."

"Don't despair, child!" Calvin said. "That big hunk of honky boy'll be back soon, and then you'll be complaining about him being underfoot."

"He jests at scars that never felt a wound," I said.

"Never felt a wound, my café au lait ass!" Calvin declared. "Now, shut up and listen. In the classical history category, *Belisario* and *Poliuto* . . ."

"I've heard of *Poliuto.*"

"Hush till I'm done! And *Il diluvio universale.* Noah's Flood to you."

"Every watersports queen in town will come for the stage effects!"

"Tell me, gee. Now, in the who's-certain-which-era category, we have *Pia de' Tolomei, Gemma di Vergy, Parisina d'Este, Imelda de' Lambertazzi,* and *Alina* among the women, and *Marino Faliero, Gianni di Parigi, Betly,* and *Il Duca d'Alba* among the men. Then—"

"Are these all real? I'm sure you've told me more than sixty titles in the last month!"

"Know who else wants to come to the party? Are you holding your ovaries, Despina? Mr. and Mrs. Bernard."

"Antria? You're kidding."

"Scout's honor. Antria wants to socialize. If they do come, I plan on keeping as far away as possible. I mean Bernard is my honey, Dorabella, but we are talking here about colorful, dress-up Negroes from South Chicago."

I could picture her arriving in a sequined red strapless and stiletto heels. It would be terrific. Alistair would commit hara-kiri.

"You've got to help dress her!" I said.

"Nnn-nnnh!"

"Calvin! We're talking about a possibly unmitigated disaster."

"Mmm-hhhmm! We'll see," he trilled, "the mood I happen to be in."

I decided to change the topic. "I went out last night. You know, in and out of bars on Polk Gulch. Hated every moment."

"I thought you were talking to Matt every day?"

"I couldn't reach him all day yesterday or the day before. When someone did finally pick up the phone last night, it was his hospital roommate, who said Matt was sleeping and had been pretty groggy when he'd come back from . . . He wouldn't say or didn't know where from. I'm sure he's had surgery, Calvin. I called the front desk at the VA this morning and lied through my teeth. Said I was his brother to get information. They wouldn't tell me shit!"

Over the phone lines, I could hear Calvin's sudden intake of breath. "Want to spend the night at my place?"

"What if Matt wakes up and phones? No, I've got to be here. Cal, I'm worried about him!"

"I'll light a candle."

"Thanks."

I admit it, I was *not* in the best mood circa lunchtime, as I went through the main floor of the shop, checking everything, which was my job.

As the record department was within my view from my balcony office, I generally kept away. Now I was drawn to it by a sudden lack of music. By the time I'd gotten there from magazines, however, music was on again, a concerto for two oboes by Albinoni. Even so it was a bit loud.

Where was Justin, my record department salesman? Not there, although the department was filled with shoppers. That was strange. If Justin were alone and he had to leave or needed help, he'd ask Monika or Barbara to spot for him. Not leave the department alone with six customers while he hunted down some recalcitrant LP downstairs in the stockroom.

I turned to the customers. "Can I help anyone?"

It turned out I could help *all* of them. Fifteen minutes later, I'd answered a dozen questions, recommended a *Traviata*, sold a *Messiah*, two discs of the Albinoni concerti, and a new Nana Mouskouri, and still not laid eyes on Justin. I was in the middle of a slow burn, about to phone Monika to come take over, when he appeared, putting on his sports jacket, arranging his tie. Had he been ill?

"You okay?"

"Sorry. I didn't think he'd have me away for so long," Justin apologized. And when I still didn't understand, he said the magic name: "Faunce."

He said more too, but I didn't hear another word. I was already marching into the art gallery, where Faunce was talking to a tall gray-haired couple—hapless tourists—giving them some line about the third-rate Simbari aquarelles he'd spread out on the display case.

I stood there fuming until I was noticed. The gallery is not a small room; even so, I'm certain the waves of fury emanating off me finally became too much for the three of them. They turned and looked, and I crooked a finger at Faunce. He continued talking to the tourists, until finally he or they or all of them lost their concentration, and he shambled over to me. His "bohemian" jacket looked as though it hadn't been to a dry cleaners in a decade.

"Where's Alistair?" I asked in a soft-toned voice.

"Having lunch with Wunderlich's rep. She got into town yest—"

"Tonia?"—Alistair's assistant.

"At my place going over some things with my wife. She was there when Wunderlich's rep called and—"

"Pozzuoli store employees are not your personal servants. Not Tonia, not Justin. Not any of them."

"It was just a minute. I needed help with this folder of aqua—"

"You're a liar in addition to perpetrating fraud! I worked the records twenty minutes!"

"It was just this once."

"Not just once. Every day it's something. If you ever—I mean ever—take one of my employees away from their post for any reason, I will ensure that you never set foot in the shop again. Is that clear?"

"It was only—"

"Furthermore, you do not work here. You are merely a supplier. Please leave the gallery now. I'll help these people, until the gallery staff returns from doing your little errands."

"But you know nothing of—"

"As much, I'm certain, as you do."

"But—"

"There's nothing I'd like better than to throw you off this balcony. You're trespassing. Don't give me the opportunity I'm itching for."

Before he could say another word, I walked past him to the couple and introduced myself as the store manager. The couple was, as I'd guessed, Midwestern, and they were pleased and a little flattered to meet me. Since I'd kept my voice quiet while talking to the creep, they had no idea I'd just kicked him out and threatened his life.

"We just have to tell you," she gushed. "This is the most beautiful store! We've got nothing even close to it back home in Davenport, Iowa. Do we, Vern? And the people," looking at Faunce, who'd remained where I left him, "are the nicest . . . !"

"Thank you, ma'am. How long have you been collectors?" I asked.

One hour before the party was to begin, Holly came up to me on the balcony. She was acting starnge. If I hadn't known she was psychically incapable of it, I'd even have said she was acting sheepish.

"Yes?" I rearranged the sales accounts protectively in front of me.

I was distracted. I'd just gotten a phone call from Matt, who'd been about to board a plane down in San Diego to fly up to San Francisco, and who continued to refuse to answer any question I happened to throw his way—and they were considerable in number and complexity. He was planning to arrive at the party, and so I would either have some immediate answers or—more likely—have to wait hours more, until we were finally alone again, to find out what had happened down there. Distracted, and more than a bit pissed off.

"I'm about to go change for the party," Holly declared.

"Have you notified WKUV-FM and the State Department?"

She ignored that. "I thought I should tell you. I can't find Alistair."

So? "Isn't he in the gallery?"

"Tonia hasn't seen him all afternoon."

"You wouldn't happen to know the reason for his disappearance?" I asked, sensing somehow she did.

"Well . . . I did hear him and Doriot arguing this morning."

I knew that women—even seemingly heartless women like Holly— loved this sort of shit even more than seemingly heartless queers like myself.

"Yessssss?"

"He stalked off. She threw something at him."

I slammed shut the accounts containing last month's sales broken down into sixteen different categories—now insufficient protection.

I didn't know how to tell her how absurd I found any heterosexual lovers' quarrel involving my cousin. "He'll be back in time for the party."

"Well, see, here's the thing . . ." Holly was sounding curiously ambivalent. "Maybe he shouldn't . . . I sort of did . . . something!"

"Clarify please. 'Something' on the order of—what exactly, Holly? Canceling the canapés? Or wiring the store with *plastique* to go off at the height of the party?"

"Somewhere in between." Holly was definitely looking sheepish now. "You know how upset I was about Faunce and all. Well, one of my friends came into the gallery and bought one of his fake Vuillards."

I began to intuit what was next. I clutched the account books.

"Of course I told her it was a fake, and she and I went down to the local precinct and she swore out charges. Fraud!"

"'I see we might be hearing from WKUV-FM."

"I thought, well, I thought they'd just go after Faunce. But it turns out there's more than one subpoena. As art gallery director, Alistair will be served one. And . . . ," here her voice got very small, "so will the store manager . . ."

She was telling all this to me, the store manager.

"I was just trying to stop Faunce."

"I know, Holly, and thanks for the warning. I'll remember it when people begin calling asking job references for you."

"You're firing me?" She had the crust to be upset.

"Not I. And I won't tell either. But Italians tend to be a little hotheaded, not to say vengeful. Or weren't you aware? Once it comes out who filed the complaint, Signor Cigna certainly will—"

The phone rang, interrupting me—the devil himself! Pierluigi had just arrived from New York and was at his suite at the Drake. I spoke a few minutes, then covered over the receiver to say, "Find Alistair for me. Now!"

Alistair was found in the coffee shop one level down from the hotel's main lobby, but he would not be budged.

When I arrived, he was drowning his sorrow in weak coffee and gooey pineapple pie.

"If you don't come back to the art gallery with me, I'll murder you on the spot," I said. This was language Alistair understood. "I don't care how many witnesses there are."

"If you insist," he said dispiritedly.

That having been easier than I'd feared, I went on to warn him about the subpoena: he was not to admit to his name—not the easiest thing to do in a party of this sort, when one is meeting new people, I had to admit, but still . . . This news didn't seem to in any way alter his already Tenebraen gloom.

"Come on, Alistair, I can't believe you're moping over some . . . skirt!" I deliberately used the obsolescent slang to get a rise out of him.

"I asked Doriot to marry me," he said.

"You are sick sick sick!"

"She refused."

"Thankfully you both don't have rocks in your head."

"I've never wanted anything more in my life, Rog."

"Maybe after the exhibit's open, you should take a vacation. You know? Laguna Beach, Fire Island, P-Town. Maybe a tour of all three. With Key West thrown in for—"

"I never get anything I want, Rog."

I couldn't believe he was sulking over this.

"You'll meet some cute boys. Take lots of recreational drugs. Go shopping. Try drag—you know, high heels and makeup . . ."

He gripped my arm hard. "I've never gotten anything I've ever wanted, Rog. Never!"

He'd talked himself into this. How could I talk him out of it?

"You've always gotten *exactly* what you wanted, Alistair. What about Dario? What about Judy? What about . . . ?"

"I mean *really* wanted! I really want this, Rog!"

I'd just noticed that Dario and Doriot sounded very much alike. Could that have anything to do with . . . ?

"What do you want? Are you that in love with Doriot? Or is it, pardon me for being so vulgar but others will ask the same, her family? Her connections? Her social set? Her money?"

"I love everything about her! You know how I am, Rog. I don't separate it out."

Sure.

"But she doesn't love you?"

"Madly! Wildly! It's just . . . well, she's only twenty-two. Her family did expect something different for . . . her first marriage."

I could hear them saying that to Alistair: exactly that, in that feebly disappointed tone of voice rich parents use with suitors they don't want hanging around.

"Look, Alistair. Doriot is lovely. And the lifestyle she presents is a charming one, but ... perhaps this isn't quite for you. Have you thought of that possibility?"

"I really care for her. Maybe not the way most guys care for their girls, but ... It's not that. Oh, Rog, I'm so *tired* of always being on the outside looking in. Of being deprived of all the good things in life!"

I couldn't believe what I was hearing. Alistair deprived? Alistair?

Suddenly there was an idea all too apparent on his face.

"Rog, what if ... ? They see me as being rootless. Parents divorced. Mom remarried twice. Me living alone so long. I never thought of it before, but *you're* my family."

Uh-oh! I began backing off the stool.

"I've known you forever."

"Hardly for—"

"Years! You'll speak for me. Tell them what I'm really like."

He was kidding, of course.

"They'll be here tonight. At the show. Say you will, Rog? I know that coming from you, it'll make all the difference in the world."

"I'm not so sure."

"I am! Really! You're so ... stable, so settled. Please, Rog. Say you'll meet them? Say you'll talk to them?"

He all but went down on his hands and knees in front of what passed for the six-thirty "tea crowd" at the Hotel Coffee and Cake Shop.

"Would I abase myself like this if I weren't desperate?" Alistair asked. "Would I?"

I had to admit he had a point. The Alistair Dodge I knew wouldn't dream of begging me for anything. Of course he'd asked for the art gallery job, but in his usual manner: as though doing me and Pozzuoli a favor.

So I had no choice but to say I'd talk to Doriot's folks, bootless as I thought it would all turn out.

"What about ... after?" I asked. "If you do marry. The gallery? Faunce?"

"I'll quit," Alistair said. "We've already talked about opening up our own gallery when we get back from the honeymoon. Without Faunce."

We were now ascending in the teardrop elevator to the mezzanine, one level above the immense open lobby, giving direct entry to the art gallery. People were already gathering at the substantial Pozzuoli lobby entry: we could see black suits and evening gowns with wraps dominating. It was going to be quite an affair! Was that Pierluigi? I'd been with Alistair twenty minutes. It seemed like forever.

"You'd better go through here and get changed," I instructed. I'd barely waved him in through the mezzanine-level door, when I heard my name called and looked down to see Calvin amid the Opera crowd. All of them were there, doubtless fresh from their meeting in some chic executive suite at the hotel: Calvin's boss, his wife, the rest of the staff, then the administration of the S.F. Opera itself, including its most recent, most junior conductor, present with his wife *and* his boyfriend . . . But it hadn't been Calvin who'd called. It had been Miss Thing at the Opera himself!

I waved back. "Doors'll be open in a sec," I said.

Inside, I gestured wildly down to Andre who, while all dressed up, was standing around counting flies. After getting my message past the considerable obstruction that his mind constituted, I watched Andre open up, the guests enter, the party begin.

I swept down the front staircase, just in time to snatch Calvin away from the others.

"You look fabulous in that tux," I said. He did. "You really ought to dress up more, Cal. I mean it."

He looked at me and his lips quivered. Uh-oh. This was not going to be a Fiordiligi and Dorabella talk but instead a Norma and Adalgisa one. Then I understood why he was shattered. The meeting had just ended. They must have turned down *Agnes von Hohenstaufen*.

"The word 'asshole,' " I began, "was created expecially to describe that person!"

Calvin's lips continued to quiver. His face contorted with passion.

" 'Flaming asshole'!" I corrected, and hugged his substantial and expensively clad body to mine. "Holly *should* have wired this place with *plastique*! Kill about a hundred assholes at once!"

After a minute, Calvin pulled away. He'd regained control. "They chose . . ." He'd regained control only with some effort. "They chose a twentieth-century opera by some Czech no one's ever heard of."

"Janáček?" I asked and immediately regretted it. "I was reading something and—"

"*Jenůfa.*" Calvin could barely pronounce the title and ignored my oral betrayal. "It's neo-realism. And you were right! Rysanek has agreed to return and sing it."

"No? Damn!"

"I quit the magazine," Calvin said. Suddenly he resembled Verrett on the cover of her recording of *Orfeo:* noble, determined, tragic.

"You *what?*"

"Cherkin accepted my resignation."

"The bastard! How could he?"

"He'd been looking forward to exactly this. I see now, he engineered the whole thing!" Calvin went on. If an Afro-American could do Callas in those moments after she's killed Scarpia and she spits out the words "And before him all Rome trembled!" Calvin was La Divina now, filled with fire and spite: "An utter conspiracy! Fool that I was, I gave him the very opportunity he wanted."

I was so enthralled I kept waiting for the ensuing cabaletta.

"Mees-ter Sannsss-arrrrcc!" The near basso tones of the Genoan Goose could be heard coming closer. "When-ev-er you are rea-dy! Your clo-thinggg!"

"*Momentino!*" I warbled in reply. But Pierluigi would not be waved off. "Cal, we're going to have to discuss this in exhaustive detail later."

Vincent Faunce and his wife chose that moment to enter the shop arm in arm, and I was filled with homicidal thoughts, until I recalled that he would have his comeuppance by the end of the evening. Now all I had to do was figure out who was the process server. And change my clothes. And talk Doriot's parents into allowing their darling daughter to marry my crazed homosexual second cousin. And straighten out Calvin's career. And avoid getting a subpoena myself. And . . . anything else? Matt! Who knew what with Matt. Convince him to trust me and love me and stay with me forever.

Light stuff.

"Now, go up and join the party, Calvin. And when Matt arrives, grab him. Okay? And Cal, remain calm! Nothing is final except death. And even that's up for grabs. Remember. And . . . I really do love you in that tux," I said as I pushed him into the throng and myself fled down to the men's room.

Naturally, the fly button on my tux trousers flew off the first time I went to use it and had to be sewed back on. After wrestling with it as though I were Laocoön, I gave up altogether on the cummerbund. I looked at myself in the small employee-john mirror and thought: You're not half bad-looking, you know, kid. Aging well. Matt might go for you after all. The fooo-ooool! Obviously I was becoming completely un-hinged by all the pressure.

I was still laughing to (or at?) myself as I ascended into the main floor of the shop. People were still coming in, being greeted by Andre, who'd been joined by the marginally more human Holly, who directed the guests up the second set of stairs to the gallery.

"Someone was here looking for you," Andre said.

"Oh?" I looked at Holly, who averted her gaze. "Who was it?"

Andre did that elaborate Gallic shrug that involves every bone in the upper body. Holly was inspecting the wooden dowel on the staircase with the intensity of an archaeologist with a shard.

I went up to the record department—Vivaldi's Two Mandolin Con-certo was playing: Heaven!—where people unknown to me held flutes of bubbly and chatted. Then I headed around the corner and up two steps into the art gallery.

"Therrre you arrre, finalllllllly!" The Genoan Goose had staked out his position and all too loudly announced my arrival, which, given the circumstances, I'd hoped to keep a bit quieter.

I was surprised to see he was in a good mood. He held a glass but wasn't drinking. He was talking to various people with more gar-rulity than usual. "Someone was looking for you beforrrre, Meees-ter Sannns-arrrc!"

No doubt. Even the most cursory glance showed me the crowd did look awfully grand. The party seemed pretty damn spiffy altogether.

"Mr. Sansarc?" a voice behind me asked. "Roger?"

I turned, about to flee, about to deny my name, about to— The man looked familiar. Past middle-age, a bit portly, curly hair framing his puffy face—it was . . . it was . . .

"Budd Cherkin! We've only met once before. Associated Publishing."

Calvin's boss. Here was my chance to—

"Cal's leaving will be a loss to the magazine," Cherkin said, his pert features turned into solemnity: had he been reading my mind? "But I'd like to move *Opera Quarterly* into a new direction, and this seems like the perfect time to do so. Especially since we'll need a new editor in chief. I understand you have substantial writing and editorial experience."

Me?

"Not really. I worked for a book publisher back in New York. But that was history books. Textbooks."

"Three years. And only a year here and one can see how well you've managed to do with it. Here's my game plan, Roger. I want to expand the magazine. Make it a monthly. Cut it down from book length to about sixty, seventy pages. Flatten it out and make it a newsstand size. Photos. News. Illustrations. Glossy cover. Trenchant articles on the state of opera in the country, hell, in the world! I'm prepared to recapitalize it considerably. And I'm prepared to pay you thirty-five a year to start. What do you say?"

I could see my hand reaching out to hold onto something solid. Instead, Cherkin grabbed it.

"Great!" he said, interpreting my grasping for a handshake. "We'll discuss details tomorrow. Give me a call and set up a meeting."

"Wait? I . . ."

He'd already turned around and begun to speak to some crony.

"Smmmille, Mees-ster Sannns-arrrcc! It's a success. Everyone who counts in San Francisco is here. Go. Go socializze!" Pierluigi pushed me into the crowd.

I landed between two women in their sixties with nearly identical hairdos. I smiled with the least falseness I could muster, then skittered away. Wait! Wasn't that Doriot?

"You're exactly who I'm looking for," she said.

"Where's Alistair?" I asked.

"I was going to ask you the same thing. He vanished the minute I got here."

"I'm going to strangle him."

"What's wrong with him?" she asked.

"If anyone should know, it's you. He's been impossible lately. He's acting like a complete jerk."

"Why?" Her baby blues were very big and very azure tonight.

"Why? Because of you! I never dreamed I'd be saying this about Alistair, but it seems that he's heartbroken."

The baby blues grew larger; the eyelashes fluttered dangerously fast.

"Heartbroken over you, Doriot. Because he can't marry you."

"Marry me?" she gasped.

"Of course! Something awful went down between Alistair and your parents over it and—"

"He asked my parents for my hand in marriage?"

"And they turned him down. Now he's a complete lunatic."

"Of course they'd turn him down! They'd turn down God if He asked. But I didn't think he was that serious."

"He's made my life impossible here."

"Roger," she put a hand on my tux'ed arm. "You've known Alistair for years and years. Since you were little boys. What's he like? I mean really like? This is important."

I knew I was supposed to lie to her for Alistair's sake, and . . . I couldn't bring myself to do it.

"He's usually honest. And he's always smart. And he doesn't pull arms off babies, but he can be a real shit! He's arrogant and demanding and self-serving but seldom violent. Cross him and you're dead. But those he loves he protects and cares for like a lion with her cubs."

She half snorted. "That's pretty much what I figured. Thanks!"

"Then what your parents think isn't important?"

"*I've* got to live with Alistair. They don't. Thanks again." She turned to leave.

"Try the stockroom," I suggested. "Two down on the elevator. Or the coffee shop outside," pointing, "one level down."

I watched her thread her way through the crowd, toward the elevator. Almost there, she stopped and spoke to a middle-aged couple who I immediately guessed from the woman's out-of-date-by-a-few-years gown and his well-worn tux must be Doriot's skillionaire parents. She turned them toward me, so we all glanced at one another. Even from this distance, I could tell that Doriot had won the genetic lottery, getting her mother's eyes, her father's cheeks, her mother's lips, her father's hair—i.e., all their best features. We all smiled politely. Alistair's future in-laws. I dawdled up to them, pushed the elevator button again for Doriot, and shook their hands.

"We know nothing about art," Doriot's mother said in a voice with a slight wobble to it, as though she'd been singing Wagner all day. "Thad's uncle collected whatever we have around. That was when you had to go to Europe to get it."

"And it didn't cost an arm and a leg," Doriot's father put in.

I pictured Renoirs, Matisses, and the odd William Merritt Chase wrapped in heavy gilt frames, hung virtually out of view, high upon dark walls.

"Your uncle's taste must skip a generation," I said to him. "Your daughter has a terrific eye. Really professional."

"Like insanity," her father said. "That skips a generation too, although we've never openly acknowledged it in our family."

"Or tone deafness," I softened it. I decided I liked these people's modesty and irony.

"Thank God we're not tone-deaf," his wife quickly said. "In fact, we support the symphony and the opera."

"Sometimes I think we support them single-handedly," her husband added. "But then, we go a lot too. So I guess we get our money's worth."

I wondered whether to tell them I'd just been offered a job with the local opera magazine. One of them must read it. I was just formulating how to say it when I felt a tap on my shoulder. Justin from the record department.

"Someone's looking for you."

Uh-oh! I glanced around, not recognizing anyone who looked familiar, or too obviously like a process server, quickly excused myself from the Spearingtons, and moved in the direction opposite where Justin said I had someone waiting, still checking around myself for trouble.

And right into Calvin's arms.

Who said, "You missed him!"

"Missed who?" I asked, blushing out of guilt that I'd even considered thinking about taking the job he'd just quit.

"Your hunk of white boy. He was here and now . . ." Calvin grabbed my arm and pulled me away. "You'll never guess what?" He was no longer down in the mouth. He was wearing a mischievous grin. "Greg Herkimer is leaving."

Who? What?

"Greg Herkimer? Miss Thing at the Opera's assistant!" Calvin explained. "He's leaving next month. And . . . well . . . I've been offered the job."

I'd been sipping. I nearly choked. "When?"

"Ten minutes ago. Miss Thing found out I'd quit the rag and hired me on the spot."

We held each other by the shoulders and screamed silently into each other's face with joy.

"Now I can tell you!" I said. "Your boss offered me your job. Of course, I'm not taking it."

Calvin gasped. "Take it! I'd have been stilettoed and dropped into a canal if I'd allowed him to cheapen and tart it up. But he's right. It's totally moribund and it really needs a thorough overhauling. You'll do wonders for it."

"Calvin, I couldn't!"

"You will. But just think of it, Gilda," he whispered fiercely into my ear. "I'll be helping choose the programs for the next . . . five . . . fuck . . . ing . . . years!"

"And we'll have a bona fide reason to talk to each other on the phone all day," I said.

Once again, we screamed silently at each other.

"Meees-ter Sannnsss-arccc!" The Genoan Goose loomed behind Calvin, who looked at Pierluigi, made funny eyes at me, and scooted away.

"I'd hoped, Mees-ter Sannns-arcc, that you would socialize with our guests in the manner of store manager a little more."

"I'm doing what I can."

"Hmmm! I suppose that includes insulting Mr. Faunce on a regular basis."

"Faunce," I said, "is a total scumbag!"

"No. No. I'm afraid this is not the right attitude," the Goose said.

"I'd better go socialize." I began to move away. And felt grabbed at the shoulder. The Goose's large, square face pushed close to mine. He was not smiling. He was, however, pushing me into a corner, out of sight of the crowd.

"I had hoped, Mees-ter Sanns-arrcc, that we wouldn't have to have this conversation."

I looked not at him, but at his hand grasping the tux's fabric.

"When I make far-reaching decisions for the store, I expect my staff to implement them. One such decision I made was about Mr. Faunce. Ever since, I've heard nothing but complaints about his mistreatment at your hands."

"Faunce is a liar, a thief, a cheat, and probably beats his wife too!"

"What Mr. Faunce may happen to be is none of your concern. I expect you to work with him with complete respect and regard."

"I won't. My own self-respect won't allow it."

He looked surprised at that. So surprised he pulled back momentarily.

I pulled out of his grip and put some distance between us.

He stared at me, calculating. In a less threatening tone of voice, he went on. "All very good, but as long as you are working here . . ."

"Then I suppose I shouldn't be working here. I quit!"

"I expect you to follow my orders," he went on, not even hearing me. So I repeated myself.

He threw his head back and assumed full stature. "Oh, come now, Mees-ter Sannnnss-arcccc!"

But having said it, I now felt strangely elated.

"In fact, having quit, I think I'll go home now. I'm tired and I'm bored!"

He blocked my way.

"You can't quit."

"Thank Faunce for me," I said, and slid under Cigna's arm and out into the gallery and the crowd, feeling slightly light-headed. Now, where was everyone?

"Excuse me. You the store manager?"

I looked at the guy: dark suit; about thirty-four; heavyset. He had "Process Server" written all over him.

"I don't work here anymore. Maybe you'd like to see that fellow. The tall one over there." I pushed him in the direction of my ex-boss.

Budd Cherkin passed by, introduced me to his wife, and said, "We'll throw a party like this when we launch the new magazine."

"Budd, I—"

"Thirty-eight's my last offer," he said.

"I'll call you in the morning."

He and his wife introduced themselves to people who before this evening had never dreamed a person could be named Cherkin—or Cherkinovich, for that matter.

"You did it!"

Alistair, suddenly, was all over me.

"I knew you'd come through. And to think, all these years, how stinting I've been in praising you."

I put a hand over his mouth. I'd seen Alistair in a great many moods. Never quite so elated as this. I guess it was contagious.

"I did nothing but tell the truth," I said. "Now, go be happy."

He hugged me. Alistair actually hugged me in front of hundreds of people, including his future in-laws and the city's most important socialites.

"I'll never forget you doing this for me," he said.

I watched as he found Doriot and hand in hand they moved more deeply into the crowd. I wondered, naturally, how and when reality would reassert itself. Then I wondered if maybe it wouldn't. Hell, we all had our destinies. Look at Cal's changing jobs so fast tonight, or for that matter, my own changing jobs so unexpectedly tonight. Perhaps Alistair was right: his gay life had been the exception rather than the rule. Perhaps he could get back on that track he'd fallen off sometime after *l'affaire Dario*, and go on to be conventional and straight and rich and Republican and—

"Roger. Someone's looking for you."

Holly was saying it this time.

"He found me." I pointed to where Pierluigi was staring down at the subpoena just handed to him.

"Not him. Some dreamy big guy in a naval uniform."

Matt!

"Where?"

"I left him downstairs about ten minutes ago. Make that fifteen. He said he wanted to look at books."

I charged down the steps onto the main floor of the store, now dimmed yet not yet completely dark, lighted on one side by the bright streetlamps outside and on the other side by the general illumination of the hotel lobby.

Even more eerie was how quiet it was down here, how chatter and music and laughter and the clink of glasses from the art gallery party above filtered down, trying to but still unable to utterly fill the space.

Where was Matt?

The children's section had a little leather sofa built into one corner, with a curved indirect lamp mounted above it. That's where Matt sat, reading *Babar & Celeste*.

I checked his leg. Nothing special—no cast, no apparent bandages— showed through his trousers. He was wearing Navy dress blues. He looked very big filling up that little sofa.

I wondered how long I might watch him before he noticed me, and in those minutes, I tried to gauge if I really loved him. I would have to love him a great deal, I guessed, enough to put up with a great deal from him, with him, because of him. It wasn't just that I thought him hand- some as a god. It wasn't just that he was the best sex I'd ever had. Nor was it that he'd been wounded physically and psychically by the war and so was utterly vulnerable. Not even that he might need substantial help from me in the future. It wasn't that he'd opened up so completely about his Vietnam experiences to me. Or that he was a poet who'd de- cided not yet to open up his poetry to me.

Yes, it was. It was all that.

It was also that he could sit here quietly, while near chaos whirled above his head, sit here and unself-consciously read a children's book with total concentration, utter absorption in the present.

He looked up. Saw me, began to put the book aside and stand up.

I went to him and kept him from rising. I knelt at his feet and looked up at him. His face was a little drawn. He'd lost some weight. His eyes glowed like polished agates, like those marbles I'd owned and valued so much as a kid and which I'd lost without a jot of regret in a game where honor had been at stake.

"Tell me a story," I begged.

"This story?" He held the book.

"No . . . this story." I touched his right leg.

He wasn't lame. He was all right. And he was back. I was expecting him to be able to talk about it now. To tell me something good about it.

"It began about six, seven months ago," he began.

I let a beat go by, then asked, "Was that when you were wounded?"

He looked at me suddenly with a momentary flare composed equally of fear and exposure. I thought for a second he would stand up, push past me, and walk out of my life.

He remained where he was and took a deep breath.

"I was bored. I volunteered. It's my own fault. I was tired of being so protected, in the middle of a tin can, firing missiles at people so far away only electronics could see them. I heard of this mission from a few Seals on board I used to smoke weed with. Just a search and recon on shore. It was supposed to be a really minor mission. I pushed for it. They let me go. But it was fucked from the second we pulled out of the water. Frag got me," he said. "Frag from a whirly mine. I was the lucky one. The two guys ahead of me blocked the blast. They ate it whole. There wasn't enough left of them to scoop back into the raft. . . . We all got decorated!

"It wasn't too bad," Matt said in a curiously even tone. "You know, for me. The pain and all. Except for this one." He guided my hand back to the lightly bandaged deep scar. "The frag there cut my sciatic nerve. That's the nerve that goes up to the spine. They've tried reconnecting it two times now. That's why I was down in the VA in San Diego this time. But it didn't take. I don't have a whole lot of feeling in this foot. I've got to be careful, banging it around and all. No trouble walking because my muscles and bones aren't affected. Yet. But it can get infected easily and I might not know it. Get gangrene. Have to come off. That's what will probably happen to it. Sooner or later.

"Don't do that," Matt said, his arms reaching down to surround me.

"I don't mind it too much! Really I don't! I'm sort of happy not to be so ... you know, perfect, anymore. Really I am. It's better this way if I'm going to be a poet. Come on, Rog, you shouldn't ... Think of how it coulda been worse. . . . How it coulda been so much worse! Hey! I've got an idea. I wrote this poem at the hospital while I was on morphine. I'll show it to you. Right now. Okay?"

Book
Five

Dancing with
the Mirror

1991 AND 1979

"*Guilty?*" I couldn't believe my ears.

"Bu'chy'are, Blanche! Y'are guilty!" Anatole said in the worst Bette Davis imitation I'd ever heard.

"I know that. But it's the principle of the thing!"

"Give the rhetoric a rest, if you don't mind," Therry Villagro, the ACT UP attorney, said.

"We're on your side," Anatole agreed.

Perhaps I was jumpy because we were sitting in one of the sleaziest offices I'd ever seen. It appeared to belong to some minor functionary connected to the public defender's office, and was reachable only by long, dim, badly painted corridors. Anatole assured me that it was attached to one of the numerous small night courts connected to the Tombs. Although, after the night's activities, I wasn't the cleanest person myself—I'd climbed the side of a building, slid across its filthy roof, been thrown to the ground and frisked—this place disgusted me with its years-old layer of untouched grime, its odor like that of old hamburgers and uncleaned cat boxes, its audible rustle in the wainscoting of what had to be hummingbird-sized roaches—or worse! Anatole sat on newspaper he'd carefully spread on the slatted wooden chair he'd selected. Therry had turned her chair and sat astride it, leaning over the back.

She didn't seem to notice the sanitation problem at all. I wondered, not for the first time tonight, exactly how nearsighted she was.

"Here's the deal," Therry spelled out. "You plead guilty to trespassing, which is a misdemeanor, and you pay the hundred-dollar bond as a fine. The judge drops criminal mischief and endangerment charges and lets you off with time served. Case closed. No one in the city can ever go after you again on this."

"This judge a close personal friend of a sister's ex-boyfriend's mother?" I asked Anatole.

"Better. He's queer."

"And closeted!" Therry said.

"So far!" Anatole said in the man's defense.

"What about the kids?" I nodded toward somewhere within the building. "Junior and James?"

"Same deal for all of you," Therry said.

And when I still demurred, Anatole said, "You can't get better!"

He suddenly sounded as his father must have sounded fifty years ago, selling bolts of material on Orchard Street. I loved him for that.

"What's the problem?" Therry asked.

"Wally! My lover." I explained further: "Lenin in denims."

"It's okay with Wally. We discussed it with him."

"It is?" I was surprised. "Where is he anyway?"

"Sitting in the last row of night court soaking up atmosphere," Anatole said.

"Soaking up years of future indignation is more like it," I said. Indignation that I knew would be expressed at me in weeks to come.

But Wally wasn't in the courtroom when we entered fifteen minutes later. And the judge turned out to be not only queer and closeted but also someone I knew. In fact, over the past twenty years, I'd come across him sooner or later in most if not all the less savory gay male haunts the city had to offer. Not a bad-looking guy, though a little careless of his appearance, he had a face composed of two similar if slightly ill-fitted halves; I'd more than once speculated that his face had been frozen, cracked, and too hastily put back together when he was a boy. One late summer night in 1981, out of a combo of ennui and let's-get-it-over-with-itis, I'd let him suck me off. This had taken place alfresco, between two pizza delivery vans in that little V-shaped parking lot across Hudson Street from a trashy bar named J's, when it was closed and still known by its former appellation: Hell. Ever since that blow job, in those increasingly few times whenever our paths crossed, he and I would silently acknowledge each other, and since it had been a pretty good blow job, I would always wonder whether or not to approach him. Now, on the bench, he looked at me without any sign of recognition. I noted that with age and a general softening of his features, one side of his face had sagged a bit and at last looked even with the other. His fine, longish brown hair was photogenically tinged with gray. His blue eyes—his strongest feature—gazed impassively, judicially, at me. I wondered how much he remembered of me—and how fondly.

Over the next few minutes, while I was before him, we continued to glance at each other in rapid sideways flashes, reminding me of nineteenth-century Spanish women flirting behind black lace fans. Since attorneys between us were doing all the talking, the judge had no reason to address me directly.

Therry had warned that due to the publicity of the case—i.e., my being on TV and what I'd said—the judge might feel the need to make a more public statement than usual about the arrest. I thought not, if he were as closeted as she said he was. And it turned out that if he did have anything to say, he kept it to himself. At the end of arguments, he provided exactly the terms of the deal I'd earlier reluctantly agreed to. Therry said what had to be said, and it was over—I was being moved to another area of the court, a desk where a paper was handed to Therry, then outside to a smaller office, where Anatole stepped forward to present a bail-bond check and clap me on the shoulder.

"Unless you decide to get into the slate business, try to stay off politicians' roofs, okay? Say something for me to Alistair!"

Anatole left before I could ask what exactly I was supposed to say to Alistair. I had to stick around longer to initial papers reassigning the already posted bond, and to hear the D.A.'s assistant whining at Therry Villagro, who seemed to enjoy thoroughly how upset the other woman was.

I was watching the two snipe at each other, when I felt Wally behind me: I knew he was standing there without having to look.

I suspected that a great deal lay in exactly how I acted and reacted during the next minute or so, but knowing that Wally was angry with me—if not exactly why—I wasn't sure exactly how to act or react. If I were too contrite, he'd guess I was faking it and probably blow up. On the other hand, if I were completely uncontrite, he'd have no trouble finding that reason enough to do anything—from making my life miserable in little ways for months to come, to denying me sex, to breaking off our relationship: none of which I particularly wanted. What I needed was to find the perfect balance: an impossible, a Grail-like, search at the best of times in our relationship.

So, without turning around, I reached back a hand and groped his crotch. Not hard—in a friendly, in an almost exploratory, manner.

He didn't jump, he didn't take my hand away, until it became clear even to me that several people in the room had both noticed and were shocked. A clerical person handed me my finished papers, and I grabbed Wally's belt and used my grip on it to pivot myself around and face him.

Looking him in the eyes, I declared, "Free. Free at last! Free at last!" sassily quoting Martin Luther King, Jr., in hopes of amusing Wally.

At the same time, I became aware that every single person in the little side chamber had stopped talking and was now looking at the two of us.

Wally couldn't help but become aware too. He did what he does best: he made a scene. He kissed me squarely on the mouth; he hugged me close.

I tried to respond with passion. But he was having none of that. This wasn't romance, this was a needed public spectacle, to be ended the moment it had achieved its intended effect.

"We'd better go now," Wally said in what Victorian novelists used to call "measured tones." Holding me by the shoulder, he guided me out of the room, past Therry, the openmouthed assistant D.A., past the desk, past everyone.

Out in the corridor, I began to say something, but luckily for me, since it was something stupid anyway, Wally put his hand over my mouth.

We remained silent as we threaded our way through various hallways to an elevator, silent as we waited there, as we descended, as we walked out of a side lobby of the building, silent as we walked out onto the street.

It was quite cool. Behind us, Foley Square with its attendant court buildings was desolate. Only the most perfunctory of night lighting still gilded the lower floors and huge porte cochere of the enormous Municipal Building and the more stately Georgian lines of the Surrogate Courthouse. Peeking out between them, chunks of the Brooklyn Bridge glistened icily in the night. I checked my watch against a building clock hung over the sidewalk: both read 3:37 A.M.

"Now!" Wally suddenly let me go. "We find a taxi to Alistair's."

I wanted exactly that, but first there was Wally and me to deal with.

"Are you sure you don't have something to say first?" I asked.

Meaning, why he was so angry. Now that we were alone, it was even clearer from his regal indifference that Wally was stupendously pissed off.

"Whatever I may or may not have to say, first we do what we agreed to earlier," Wally insisted, with a tight little smile.

This was getting us nowhere fast.

"Wally, do you remember how we met?"

He turned and began to stride into the middle of Lafayette Street: empty, cabless. For that matter, carless.

"It was in the Pines Pantry," I said, following him. "As I was checking out my groceries, I happened to look up and I noticed the two dimples on your naked lower back."

"Either we walk to Canal Street and see what's coming from the East Side off the Williamsburg Bridge," Wally calculated our taxicab chances aloud, totally ignoring what I was saying, "or we go down to Park Row and try the traffic coming off the Brooklyn Bridge."

"You were wearing nothing but a forest-green Speedo with a white side panel," I went on. "The embryo of a ponytail draped your neckline."

"Canal Street! It's closer!" Wally decided, and headed uptown, walking in the middle of the empty street.

"I had a huge bag of groceries, because I was a guest and I'd decided to pay my way by filling my host's refrigerator," I continued my story. "Even so, I followed you out of the Pantry and around the harbor and along Fire Island Boulevard, although it was in the direction opposite to where I was staying. I walked barefoot on that sidewalk and boardwalk, which in the late-August afternoon must have been a hundred and ten degrees Fahrenheit."

Wally speeded up and impulsively threw out a hitchhiker's thumb at a passing carful of what looked like Guatemalan laborers, already so tightly packed inside the pastel-green Plymouth of barely postwar vintage that you couldn't have wedged in one of those near-naked, half-starving, fly-blown infants with huge brown eyes, from those guilt-inducing magazine ads that said, "For just two dollars a day, you can save her life."

"I didn't for a second dream of getting ahead of you on the board-walk," I continued. "I was in a trance, following those dimples in your lower back, the Wagnerian rippling of your back muscles, the Apol-lonian heft of your astonishing buttocks, barely contained in your Speedo."

The sedan blew its horn at Wally to get out of the way, and the driver swerved extravagantly to avoid hitting him and sped on. We were ap-proaching Canal Street. Chinatown. Food. I was suddenly starving for Hunan Eggplant with Lake Tung Ting Shrimp. Nothing could be— nothing was—open this late.

"I was entranced by those dimples on your lower back. No, more, completely mesmerized by them. I couldn't think of, couldn't even see, anything else. I wanted to put the tip of my tongue inside each one si-multaneously, physically impossible though that was. I knew they would taste like pistachio ice cream and turkey sandwiches and caviar from the Caspian Sea all at once. Someone I knew tried to stop me along the boardwalk, tried to talk to me, but I walked past him. He was offended for months afterward."

Wally and I had arrived at Canal Street now, and it was as dark and desolate as Foley Square had been. Wally turned to the East River, searching for signs of oncoming taxis. There wasn't an unparked car on the street.

"It was a bright, cloudless August day, Wally. Remember? Secretary birds perched in mimosa trees chattering. Gloria Gaynor's version of 'How High the Moon'—one of my absolute favorite songs—played in a house we passed, and queens there danced, sniffed poppers, and loudly carried on. Still I trudged on after you, hypnotically drawn by your dim-ples. All the way to Coast Guard Walk, then left, off the boardwalk and all the way to where you finally turned into your house, unable to pull my eyes away from those dimples in your lower back, the play of your lower back muscles, the totally edible ice-cream scoops of your ass, the perfect chamois tan of your skin, the wet, drying streaks of cinnamon in your hair."

A car went by headed for Broadway and honked its horn at us to get out of the middle of the street. We ignored it.

Wally spun around and began walking along Canal Street muttering, "Maybe the Bowery . . . ?"

"I stood entranced even when you went inside the house where you were staying. I remained on the boardwalk for I don't know how long— twenty minutes? a half hour?—never having seen your face—or the front of your body. Entranced. Unable to move. Until you sent a house-mate to ask what I wanted."

"I thought this was the city that never sleeps," Wally said irritatedly. "Where are all the cabs? It's only three A.M. for Chrissakes!"

"Remember what I told your housemate when he came out?"

"There's always cabs on the Bowery," Wally said to himself.

"I told him I didn't know what I wanted exactly. But that I couldn't live another minute without your lower back dimples. Remember, Wally, and you had to come out of the house and talk to me? Remember?"

"I remember!" he shouted back at me. "I remember that my room-mates were convinced you were a fuckin' psychotic. Martin Gernsen wanted to call the Pines cops and have you taken to Islip State Hospital for observation."

"But you didn't. You came out. Came out and talked to me."

"I should have checked into Islip State myself."

I followed him along Canal Street to the Bowery. Not a car.

"I must have like the worst taxicab Karma of any person in modern history," Wally mused. "In a past life I must have constantly cheated fares, beaten up, even murdered hackney coachmen, for all the bad cab luck I have. I must have been a Jack the Ripper to hansom drivers in nineteenth-century London."

"That's how we met, Wally. You walking away from me."

That stopped him. He spun around, his face, his entire posture gathering together for some total utterance. But he stopped himself, turned, and walked toward Grand Street.

"Walking away from me." I said the obvious, and followed.

He allowed me to catch up

"Are we going to talk?" I asked.

"We're going to Alistair's. We're doing what you said you wanted to do before we went to Gracie Mansion and all this . . . went down . . ." He gestured vaguely, then figured he'd said enough to explain. "That is if you still think saving Alistair's life tonight is important."

"Of course it's important."

"Given your earlier antics tonight, I naturally wondered."

"What's that mean?" I demanded.

Wally held out a quarter. "You want to call him? If Alistair hasn't swallowed all sixty-four pills yet, we might help."

"What if the White Woman doesn't believe us and hangs up?"

"Why wouldn't he believe us?" Wally asked. "Oh, you mean, Alistair's talked about offing himself before?"

"You know how melodramatic he can be."

"How will our actually being there be different?" he reasoned.

"I don't know! It just will!"

"I have no intention of going there and—"

"We'll see for ourselves if Alistair's okay. We'll demand to see him," I said. "And if he is, we'll leave."

"You really think Dorky will let us in this late without a reason?"

"I'll give him a reason. I'll threaten to call the police if he doesn't let us in! Do you think we should call and say we're coming?"

Wally looked at me with a combination of amazement and incomprehension, then turned and trudged up the street.

The Bowery was, if anything, even bleaker, less peopled and less trafficked than Canal Street. I followed as Wally reached Delancey and faced the hollow yellow glitter of the Williamsburg Bridge, searching for a taxi.

"Not even a gypsy cab! Fuck! We'll get a subway!"

"At three-fifty-two A.M.?"

"There must be a subway station around. What line do we need?"

"A West Side line."

We found a station for the F train on Delancey off Essex. Perhaps the worst sixty square feet in Lower Manhattan for crime. Tonight, it was completely dead. And no wonder. All six exits—on four corners—were locked up.

"What is this, London?" Wally asked from the still taxiless island in the middle of Delancey.

We trudged back the way we'd come until finally, at Grand and Broadway, we located an open IRT station with three gated stairways and one open one. Downstairs, on a level above that along which the trains ran, the entire area was relict but for a lone, heavily defended token booth. Within, through double panes of well-scratched bulletproof glass, we made out a token seller, a heavyset black woman wearing an enormous headdress of apparent Nigerian manufacture, influenced in colors and style by the Classic Dogon period. She was reading a celeb-rag, too immersed to hear us. After we'd determined that one closed panel was supposed to be an open grille, after we'd knocked for her attention, she threw down the paper in disgust and opened a completely different panel on another side of the booth.

"Must be pretty interesting!" I said as I shoved money in.

"Whaaaaa?" she asked.

"Must be an interesting story!" I shouted.

To my surprise, she actually brought the paper over and held it up so I could make out the headline. So it was that I learned the indispensable news that Dolly Parton's tits would never droop—though she lived to two hundred—as they were made of interstellar non-sag material, payment to the country singer-actress for a series of unborn fetuses she'd regularly delivered, for experimental mating and surgery, to bug-eyed aliens from an unnamed star in Galactic Cluster NGC-235.

Our tokens managed to jam in three of the four token machines.

As we dropped down to the platform, the smell of industrial-strength ammonia nearly knocked us over.

The station's waiting area across the tracks was being hosed down by workers in yellow rubber suits and helmet-hoods with plastic eye windows—outfits designed for walks in outer space and dioxin spill cleanups. Our side was already hosed down. I could tell from how sudsy water dripped off the platform edge, ate into grouting, puddled in small depressions in the plastic sheets covering opaque pods of the homeless sleeping on subway benches.

Wally turned to me and screamed silently, looking for a second like Nebuchadnezzar in that William Blake print at the Tate.

Then, to our complete astonishment, a train pulled into the station.

More astonishing, it stopped and the doors remained open long enough for us to get in.

The train was empty.

I went to a graffiti-covered glass panel behind which I made out most of a Transit Authority map. The train lurched twice and took off.

"We can get off at Fourteenth Street and take the L over to the Seventh or Eighth Avenue line." I scanned on. "But the L's slow as shit at night. Let's go to Grand Central and grab the shuttle."

By now, the train was shaking so hard we could barely stay on our feet, even holding onto the metal bars hung from the ceiling. We finally relaxed and allowed our bodies to be whirled into seats. The train's sign read "Local," but it sprang past Spring, screeched past Bleecker, and we were gasping as Astor Place slashed by the windows. It did stop at Fourteenth Street, but barely and with an enormous amount of noise. I wondered whether we should get off while we had a chance. The doors shut—too late! The train seemed to switch to the express track, where it belonged in the first place. This allowed the driver to pick up speed. The train streaked past blurs of the Twenty-third, Twenty-eighth, and Thirty-third Street stations.

"How fast do you think we're going?" I had to shout to be heard above the intense clanking every loose bolt in the car made as we charged on.

Wally shrugged. "Eighty? Ninety per hour?"

Faster, I thought.

And I panicked as the train shot into, through, and out of Grand Central Station without a hint of slowing down.

"That was *our* stop!"

"I know!"

"*All* trains stop at Grand Central."

"I know, I know!"

I was thinking of that song from the sixties about some guy who got stuck on the Boston subway system just as it was completed and turned into an infinite Möbius strip, riding forever and never returning. Neither would we!

The train speeded up and shot like a bullet past Fifty-first, Fifty-ninth, Sixty-eighth . . .

"Where's the next express stop?" Wally held onto his seat with both hands just to stay in place, it was rocking so much.

"On this planet? Eighty-sixth, I think."

The train slammed to a stop, and the doors opened with a shudder—at Seventy-seventh Street of all places! Without bothering to wonder how that was possible if we were on the express track, I jumped up and held the doors open until Wally could get out. They were pushy, edgy, greedy steel jaws. They almost caught me as I let them go. The train sped off, bound for who knew where, probably some "Twilight Zone" episode.

Upstairs on Lexington Avenue, I said, "From now on, we walk!"

"Through Central Park?" Wally asked. "At . . . checking my watch, four-thirteen in the morning?"

"You going to find us a taxi?" I asked.

A brief look around confirmed that Lexington and Seventy-seventh Street was as desolate as downtown. We began walking toward the park. Taking advantage of the lack of passersby, I moved alongside Wally and put an arm over his shoulder. He shrugged it off.

"C'mon, Wally! Don't be like that!" I said, still trying to get near him. But no matter what I did, he continued to elude my attempts at closeness. So I fell back on that old standby in relationships: I began to argue.

"You still haven't explained that crack you made downtown. The one about whether I still thought saving Alistair's life was important."

"What's to explain?" Wally said in that airy way that reminded me of my older sister when she was a teenager, and which had always made me want to wring her neck.

"What's to explain is some reference to my . . . What was the word exactly? Antics?"

"Most people would call thumping about on the roof of Gracie Mansion antics."

"Except, of course, if you had been one of the people doing it."

"And especially since I know very well *why* you did it," Wally said.

"Really? Care to let the rest of the world in on the secret?"

"For the same reason you did that 'Eleven O'Clock News' spot."

"What are you talking about?"

"You really think I'm too naive to see that was planned?"

"Planned? Planned? That business with the TV reporter was a complete surprise. Totally spontaneous. You were there. You saw how it happened!"

"I saw your old childhood buddy arrange it all. First with you, then with the reporter. That's what I saw."

"Ronny Taskin? You're crazy!"

"I know what I saw," Wally insisted. "One minute he was talking to you, the next he was meeting with the reporter, and not long after, the reporter shoved a microphone in front of you and the video camera was going."

I'd suspected that Ronny was a Very Efficient Queen, but *that* efficient?

"I had nothing to do with it, Wally. I didn't! Honest!"

"And the proof of that statement is how completely tongue-tied you were once you were in front of the camera."

"Are you saying I knew what I was going to say? That I practiced it?"

"Or were fed it all by your palsy-walsy."

"That's a lie. It just . . . came out."

"With every comma, every period, just right," Wally sneered.

"Well, I'm a public speaker. I'm used to it, you know." There are few things I hate more than having to defend myself for abilities. "And I do sometimes teach. I'm used to standing up in front of . . . Anyway, if you're right about the interview being set up in advance . . . how could that possibly fit in with being caught and arrested? That couldn't possibly help the image I was supposedly projecting."

"You know, Rog, just because I'm half your age doesn't mean I was born fucking yesterday!"

"Meaning?"

"Meaning, you know damn well that *saying* something and *doing* something are two different things. No one remembers what you say. But I'd lay money down that when we get home there's going to be a dozen messages on the phone machine left by newspaper editors and magazine reporters and radio and TV news program producers. All because of your shenanigans atop Gracie Mansion tonight."

Wally was right. I'd not thought about it; the media would descend like locusts. Then what? I knew: I'd lock myself in. Not say a word.

We'd reached Fifth Avenue, across which the chest-high brick wall surrounding Central Park was illuminated by those sulphur-yellow streetlights they put up a few years ago that supposedly give off an "Old New York" glow, but instead make everyone look as though they've got the first stages of hepatitis. I grabbed Wally by the shoulders.

"Maybe that's true, Wally. Maybe everything you said is true, and maybe unconsciously or subconsciously or without being completely aware of it, I did act like a heel, like a louse, like someone bent on exploiting the situation. But openly, consciously, at the time I believed I was doing it because I thought you wanted me to."

You could have knocked Wally down with an unwrapped condom.

"Me?!"

"That's what James and Junior and that guy Paul told me. That you'd put together the whole thing with the banner and—"

"I knew nothing about it!"

Now it was my turn to be skeptical.

"Come on. They said you were the brains behind it! They told me how disappointed you'd be if it weren't hung on Gracie Mansion. That's why I did it. To make up to you. To do something you'd be proud of . . . happy about . . . for once."

Wally was shaking his head. "I never knew anything abou— Are you trying to tell me that they . . . ?"

"Conned me into doing it," I shouted, realizing the fact. "They were *counting* on being caught and arrested. Especially on *me* being caught!"

I thought it through in a flash: how the subject of the banner hadn't come up till they were certain Wally had left the demonstration and gone home; how they'd played on my stupid pride in my past history of activism—they probably *had* set it up with Ronny Taskin so I'd be interviewed; how Paul had managed to get away at the end; how calm Junior and James had been about being jailed; how, more than likely, they'd tried to get away earlier with that phony stuff about Junior being acrophobic. What a fool I'd been. I moaned.

"You know, Wally, I'd accept all that if it weren't that the bastards managed to drive a wedge between us."

When I looked up, Wally was somber, his handsome face motionless, in thought.

"They did keep avoiding me," he was thinking aloud in a quiet voice. "It took me forever to find them when we first got there."

"Then you *do* believe me."

"I don't know. It's possible." He sounded half-convinced.

We crossed the empty street and began walking the uneven stones alongside the Central Park wall. I began to tell him exactly what had happened from the moment they approached me, playing up those aspects that I was now certain confirmed the conspiracy theory.

"Am I forgiven?" I asked, laying a tentative hand on his shoulder.

"I still want to talk to them. Or . . . maybe not. Maybe I don't ever want to talk to them!"

"They were just being good revolutionaries. Using whatever was at their disposal for the greatest effect."

"All I know is tomorrow afternoon's 'European Film Auteurs' class is going to be pret-ty awkward."

"If they're there. After a night in jail, they might not be."

Wally seemed to be coming around to seeing the situation from my point of view. The way he held me around the waist as we half stumbled over the cobblestone sidewalk seemed to prove it.

We'd reached the Seventy-eighth Street entrance to Central Park. It looked no different now than it would look at any time after dark, except, of course, for how quiet and unpopulated the entire area was.

I knew from many daytime walks that this entrance went clear through the park, letting us out north, at Eighty-first and Central Park West. I'd sometimes use the route from my periodontist's office to East Side museums—the Whitney, the Gug, the Met—treating myself with late-afternoon art for having heroically undergone periodic assaults upon my gums.

In fact, this path went through the park *too* directly. It descended and thinned to single-person width along the two-lane road cut into the earth to speed automotive traffic through Manhattan. It would make escape difficult if not impossible if one were being chased or attacked. As a rule, and despite yellow journalism headlines about attacks in the park, I didn't feel especially unsafe here. But I had Wally to think of. Even so, and despite the darkness and contorted paths, I preferred an indirect route: a chain of paved and dirt walkways I knew semicircled the boathouse and lake would take us through the paved terrace and up its stairs, straight along the road at Seventy-second Street a ways. Then, where it curved, we'd turn off, threading small meadows and softball fields, crossing one north-south road, bypassing the Carousel, until we exited in the low seventies, not far from Tavern on the Green.

I suppose I was expecting Wally to contest my route. But he didn't, and I made sure we remained pretty well within areas illuminated by overhead lights. I'd expected to see many homeless people sleeping in the park, or at least wandering its paths, disheveled and madly nattering, but it might have been too chilly; we didn't encounter a soul. Once we were a hundred yards in, the sighing of wind through the trees was louder, clearer. Paradoxically, the night was colder, yet less breezy.

Naturally such peace couldn't last. We were both too nervous, too het up from earlier in the evening. And since there was no one else to irritate or scare us, we'd have to do it ourselves. Afraid of once more being the victim, I attacked first, hiding it under miles of goo.

"Wals," I began all lovey-dovey, "remember what you said before?"

I felt his body stiffen, despite my constant caressing ministrations as we walked.

"Mnnnn. I forget," he said. Meaning "Drop it if you know what's good for you."

"You know, Wals," I went on in that half-cajoling, half-whining way lovers use when undecided how much they're succeeding in irking their partners. "About whether I still thought saving Alistair's life was important or not? . . . Why did you say that?"

His back stiffened more. "I wondered," he now allowed himself to say. "You have to admit, you *have been* of at least two minds about it all tonight. Before that phone call, you were ready to rush to Alistair. Afterward . . ."

"Wals, you reminded me I had plenty of time before Alistair's party was over."

Which was only half-true.

"Maybe so. But I wasn't aware at the time you'd end up getting yourself arrested. What if you'd never got out tonight?"

"But I did get out."

"It's reasonable to assume that you might not have."

"I don't see why you say that. I . . ."

"And, since it's reasonable, it's equally reasonable to ask why you'd even take the chance, why you'd allow the possibility of not getting back to Alistair tonight. Unless you had no intention of returning."

"Are you saying I got arrested on purpose?"

"No. But since we were talking about the unconscious before . . ."

"Then you're saying that by getting arrested, I was setting myself up so I wouldn't be able to keep Alistair from taking the pills?"

"That still may be the case," Wally pointed out. "Which is why we're going there now. And why we're having this conversation."

"Let me get this straight, you mean I hate Alistair so much—"

"I mean you found whatever was handy to support your earlier decision. Which, as you recall, was to assist, to abet, indeed to *make possible* his suicide tonight."

"No, you're saying I hate Alistair."

"Which you do. At times. As at times you love him."

I couldn't deny it. We walked on, no longer arm in arm, but still holding hands, if at a bit of a distance. We were coming up on that section of terrace that stuck out into the lake by the Bethesda Fountain. It was empty now, as glamorously romantic as it appeared in print ads for perfumes and in TV commercials featuring mannequins trailing yards of tulle; as romantic as it must have looked when Olmsted first built it a century ago. I recalled summer Sunday afternoons here in the late sixties and early seventies when people gathered in wonderful, innocent masses to fly kites, to brunch at the restaurant laid out in parasoled tables, while under the overhanging bridge competing groups of madrigalists sang Gabrieli and Monteverdi motets.

"But you don't know the entire story," I defended myself. "I mean of Alistair and me."

"I'm sure I don't," Wally said with enormous sangfroid.

I'd been heading toward the steps. He pulled me away toward the lake. The moon was out again, pale and, yes, full. It glittered on the water. For a moment I thought he wanted to waltz. Instead, he held me by the waist.

"How can you be so sure?" I asked.

"Because I've heard plenty already and there are obvious gaps."

"Gaps?"

"Obvious, substantial gaps. One gap in particular."

We were beginning to tread on dangerous territory. I disengaged myself and sat on a low granite wall. Wally joined me.

"Until tonight," he went on, unswayed by the beauty of the scene, "I was never certain how substantial that gap was. Now I see it's crucial."

I wasn't about to admit a thing. Especially in light of how Wally had acted earlier in the evening at the mere mention of Matt's name. I wished I knew how to change the subject. I wanted nothing more than to be kissed by him here, now. Then to make love, partly here, partly at home, in our own apartment, our own bed. The very last thing I wanted tonight was to have to deal with Alistair and/or the White Woman again.

"Of course I'd picked up bits and pieces of it earlier," Wally continued, "but something Dorky said earlier confirmed it."

I was afraid to ask what he'd said. I was aware that our intertwined fingers had become strangely dry and hot. I lifted his hand to my mouth and kissed. *Let it go, Wals,* I silently pleaded.

"I admit," Wally continued, his telepathy dimmer than usual, "I made a mistake in how I reacted when it came up. That was my fault, Rog. I was still feeling vulnerable, still afffected by what Dorky had said."

I was biting my tongue. I couldn't stand it. I knew if I asked, it would end all possibility of romance here, now, tonight. At the same time, I knew we had to face it or it would always fester.

"What did Dorky say tonight?"

"What he said, or rather what he let slip, earlier this evening was a particular phrase. And while I don't for a second remember the context, the phrase was, and I quote 'You know, that gorgeous poet who was the Love of Roger's Life.' "

I heard the capitals in how he said it: Damn the White Woman! Damn!

"That's exactly how he was described," Wally continued. "I have to assume that's how Alistair described him. I have to assume that's how you'd describe him."

"Poor Wally."

"Don't patronize me." He tried to pull his hand away.

"It's a terrible thing for you to have heard."

Wally was motionless. I became aware of a shudder running over and through him.

"You mean you're not going to deny it?" His voice was tremulous, incredulous.

"How can I?"

Wally stood up. I grabbed at his jacket, but he fought free.

"So, you can understand," he said in a somewhat changed tone of voice, "the awkwardness of my position at the demonstration, when the man who is supposed to be my lover gets up and publicly names—the Love of His Life!"

"You had every right to be upset. To run away. To move out. To never speak to me again. Every right in the world."

For the first time ever, I heard what sounded like begging in his voice. "You're not going to even . . ."

"Even what?"

"I don't know . . . ameliorate it? Question it?"

"No. I'm not. Matt Loguidice was the great love of my life. The lover fated for me. No question of it. No amelioration possible."

I swore, despite the bad light, that tears formed in the corners of his eyes.

"I never . . . I never dreamed you'd be so cruel to me!"

So he *was* capable of melodrama! Wonderful!!

"Oh, Wally, I'm not being cruel. I'm just telling the truth!"

I managed to pull him down next to me.

"I'm not saying Matt was the only lover in my life or the best lover, or even the lover I liked most! You're that, Wally. You're sweet and funny and too smart for either of our good. You're mysterious as the Loch Ness monster and at the same time as comfortable as an old sweatshirt, and you're pretty much everything in between. If I'm not a complete jackass and if you can put up with me, I'd like it if we remained lovers till one of us dies.

"But Matt Loguidice . . . Someone, some*thing* like Matt happens only once in a lifetime. Everyone within a certain radius is affected. Like an H-bomb dropping. Some people, most people in fact, never experience it. Shakespeare did. The Dark Lady of the Sonnets he writes about, that's what Matt Loguidice was. A quirk of destiny, a force of nature. You're going along living your life and the Dark Lady arrives—male or female, good or bad, young or old—and you're forever changed. I was. Alistair was. All in our circle were. It almost had little to do with Matt himself after a while. Especially after he began to be photographed, and appeared in all those magazines: Mr. Macho. Mr. Leatherman. Mr. Whatever-Your-Dream-Is-I'm-Better-By-Far.

"You see, Wally, it's not a matter of competing. You *couldn't* compete with Matt. No one could. He was of another ilk. Of another era. Some people claimed even back then that he *was* that era. I wouldn't *want* you to compete. You're too . . . too much Wally for that. Whereas Matt . . . I sometimes wonder what Matt was. And I'm the one who knew him best, who was with him at his most human, at his weakest, his most vulnerable!"

You could have driven a truck through the silence that ensued. Hell, you could have driven the entire Indy 500 through it!

I wondered whether I'd made a Major Error. I'd known since earlier in the evening that Wally and I would have to have it out sometime. Had I been wise in laying out my entire hand now? Too late for second-guessing.

I waited for Wally. Behind him I heard a soft hooting sound: an owl. I'd read that the Parks Department had been stocking owls to keep down the wild mice and rat population attracted by human debris. It sounded again, distant and cold and very wild: untamed, untamable. The wind rose and riffled the lake in shirred patterns. Matt would have turned it into a poem. But Matt was dead.

"Well . . . I asked." Wally's voice sounded hurt.

"Don't take it like that." I was trying to pull him down next to me. "It's ancient history. It's over a decade since Matt and I broke up. What were you doing in 1979? Studying social studies in the fifth grade? Playing with the Donkey Kong computer games? Think, Wals. Think how far away it is. How much has happened since then."

"And you did break up."

Better. Sometimes the tooth had to be pulled lest it forever rot.

"A complete divorce."

"Incompatibility?" Wally asked.

"It's a long story."

"Involving Alistair?"

"Involving a lot of people," I said, too glibly. "Involving Alistair," I admitted.

"Dorky said you two didn't talk to each other for years after."

"Six!" I admitted. Reminded of Alistair, I stood up and pulled Wally with me. "It's getting late. We'd better go."

As we were climbing the steps out of the fountain plaza, Wally said, "If you're willing to let Alistair die, it's because of what happened then, isn't it? With Matt? In 1979?"

"I don't know. I think I forgave Alistair. I told him I did."

"Because he stole Matt from you?"

"Oh, Wally! It should only be that simple!"

"Well! Tell me!"

We were walking in the middle of the road that led off Seventy-second Street on the East Side, headed west.

"You'd have to know the entire situation! All the shit going on between me and Sydelle and Harte at *Manifest*. What was going on between Patrick and Luis, our housemates at Withering Heights that summer. The way all of us—"

"Withering Heights?"

"That's what our house was called. Partly because while it wasn't much to look at, it was high on a hill. Partly because of us in the house. Matt, of course, was Heathcliff. I was usually Cathy Earnshaw. Marcy and Luis took turns being Nelly, the maid."

I explained further:

"All the houses at the Pines had names in those days. Sometimes the name referred to the building's style—the Kodak Pavilion, because it was shaped like the one at the '64 World's Fair. Or the Ramada Inn, which looked like a motel. Or Lincoln Center. Or the A-House. Sometimes they were named after their owners or whoever lived in them: the

House Bananas Built, owned by a Central American fruit millionaire, Camp Tommy, Wrangler Ranch, Bus-house. Sometimes people put up their own names—the Ogre, Seven Beauties, Tea and Bigamy, Fire Island School of Design, Surfside Six. Sometimes the house was named despite what the owners wanted. It was a small, homogeneous community. Everyone knew or knew about one another. People received nicknames. Mrs. B. was Trude Heller's girlfriend, sometimes called Isadora for how she'd run naked along the surf trailing a gauze scarf. Or Spare Parts. Or Eisenhower or—"

"*Manifest* was the magazine you worked for?" Wally asked.

"Actually it was MAN-i-fest, until Sydelle arrived. With an accent on 'Man.' You've seen copies. Remember? I took them out when Martin Landesberger was here from upper Michigan."

Wally recalled. "Did I see *him*?"

Meaning Matt.

"You couldn't help but see him then. He was the model for the most popular commercial popper, and Mr. Leather as well as Mr. Gay Northeast and Mr. Gay America several years in a row. His photos were everywhere."

"The clone hunk, right? With the black leather vest and curly black hair and beard!"

"That was Matt."

"I didn't think he was real. I thought he was like a composite or something."

"He was real all right."

Wally was silent for a while. Then he said, "Then you broke up?"

"Finally," I corrected. "We met in July of 1974. There were plenty of trial breakups before that."

"Over other guys?"

"No. Over . . . I don't know over what. Over Matt being Matt and me being me. I wasn't always like I am now, Wals. I wasn't always cool and laid back and thoughtful and grown-up. I used to be . . . temperamental . . . something of a bitch."

"Used to be?" Then before I could punch his arm, he said, "Tell me about it. Tell me all about it."

"You sure?"

"I want to know everything that happened that summer. Everything!"

"In-suf-fic-i-ent Re-sponse from Con-tes-tant Num-berrr Thu-ree!" Patrick said in a most mechanical tone of voice.

"Hold your horses!" I replied. "I'm looking."

"For what?" Luis asked. "The Lindbergh Baby?"

"For something to discard," I said. There wasn't much of anything in my hand. I'd been dealt garbage this time around, which would probably be the final hand in the game. And so far I'd been unable to pick up anything in the least bit interesting. I was so badly off, I was working on a low club run!

"Playing the game of 500 Rummy does *not* require a genius IQ!" Marcy needled me in a put-on snooty tone of voice. "It does, however, require the rudiments of a memory."

"Oh, pul-eeze! I left the rudiments of my memory on the sidewalk in front of Les Mouches in '76, sometime during my four hundredth tab of acid! . . . I hate my hand," I concluded, throwing down a five of hearts.

Naturally Luis picked up the card, shoving it into his hand and speaking as though continuing a conversation, which he had not in fact been having. "So I says to her, so I says, Ceil, Ceil honey, I know you love your husband. I happen to love a good cigar. But I sometimes take it out!" He laid out a low heart flush, four cards long, in front of himself on the table and discarded a club jack. "Knocking!"

"I'm going to knock you," Patrick declared. But I noticed that he quickly enough snapped up the discarded jack.

"So when am I going to see the Incredible Hulk?" Marcy asked. She'd lifted one leg up high and was inspecting her mosquito bites. Her leg was shapely, her skin very pale, but the scratched bites were not a pretty sight.

"You've met him, haven't you?" I asked, using the question to turn the topic back over to Marcy, and thus away from myself temporarily. The last thing I wanted today, the last thing I wanted among these three sharpies, was to give a hint of my currently more than usually addled feelings about my lover.

"Never met him," Marcy said.

"Where *is* that husband of yours, Rog?" Patrick asked. "It's what? Seven-thirty? Tea Dance *must* be over! Especially in this weather!"

"You know how Matt is at Tea," I said, hiding my irritation under an overacted moan. "And afterward!"

"Hanging out at Hard-Wear," Luis said, "unable to tear himself away from his large, admiring public."

"More like upstairs at the Crow's Nest trying to get Ralph to slash prices," I said.

"Up there, trying on body-fitting T's." Patrick shivered at the image. "Allowing himself to be ogled by the hoi polloi."

"Well, he'd better manage to find his way to the Pantry," Luis said, "and buy some food. You guys promised to make dinner tonight."

"I know. I know."

It had been raining since dawn that Saturday—which was why, instead of getting dressed, getting a little high, and going to Tea Dance along with Matt and four hundred other queers at the Pines, as we usually did, Luis Narvaez, Patrick Norwood, and I decided to remain at Withering Heights for the afternoon and early evening, watching the varieties of rainfall and hoping it would stop.

Once Marcy Lorimer arrived at the house—she'd been staying at Davis Park and had come over by water taxi—it became another thing altogether: an afternoon party! We'd all laughed and kissed and put mint julep facial masks on one another. We'd twisted on various *shmattes* as kerchiefs until—with those pale green faces!—we looked like characters out of a Kabuki play.

We'd sat around the dining room catching up and listening to tapes Ray Yeates had put together for Halston's most recent fashion show. We drank beer and old-fashioneds (Patrick made them). We went through our own and each other's wardrobes, picking out ensembles to wear that night: one for the Ice Palace if the rain ever let up, a completely other outfit for the Sandpiper if it didn't let up and we remained here in the Pines instead of trekking over to Cherry Grove for the night. We snacked on Nacho Chips and Entenmann's coffee rings. And we played cards.

"Patricia, are you ever going to discard?" I asked. "We all know you have those jacks lined up ready to march."

"I do not!" Patrick protested. "And as you well know, my drag name is Isadora. Not Patricia." He then laid out three jacks on the table and dropped an ace on the discard deck.

"I'll take that, thank you!" Marcy said, sitting up very straight. She proceeded to lay out three aces and a club flush, queen to ace, very businesslike indeed. "Eat that!" she said to me with mock sweetness.

"Fla-ming twat!" I mock-cursed her in return. But in fact I liked the queen she'd discarded and picked it up, dropping the now useless four of hearts.

"God, this looks awful!" After that flurry of card-playing activity, Marcy had gone back to inspecting her calves.

"You said it. Not me."

"And I spent hours yesterday on my legs," she moaned, "foolishly thinking there might be a hint of sun to tan them this weekend."

"Did you hear about that Bowery bum they found?" Luis asked. "He said he'd drunk everything with any alcoholic content at all. Including Nair."

"Ooooooh! Disgusting!" Marcy squirmed.

"Reminds me of that Gene Wilder sketch in Woody Allen's *Everything You Always Wanted to Know About Sex*," Patrick said. "You know, the one—'What is Bestiality?'—where Gene falls for this sheep who throws him over for some other guy. Gene ends up on skid row. But when the camera does a close-up on him, we see the bottle is marked 'Woolite'!"

"I loved that movie. Remember the gay commercial? The guys in the locker room making out like crazy while the voice-over tells you to buy the hair product?"

"So, you were out west," Marcy said to me. "For the magazine?"

"An article on homosexual writers. Most of them in their senility."

"I thought all the gay writers are young?" Marcy asked.

"You're talking about Andrew Holleran, Edmund White, and that gang? Well, yes, they're all in their thirties. But everyone's writing about them. I thought I'd write about some of their forebears," I said. "You know, the less famous gay writers."

"*Forebears* is such a strange word," Marcy mused. "The bears that came before us?"

"Patrick love, go already!" Luis urged. Patrick took his sweet time.

"Like who?" Marcy asked.

"John Rechy was the youngest. Although it's obviously all relative. He was sweet really. He's got these wall-sized photos of James Dean and Marilyn Monroe in his dining room. Very, very H-Wood, if you ask me. He was so nervous at first he was stammering. I thought, you know, maybe he wanted . . ."

"A piece of your prize ass!" Luis said.

"In short!" I admitted. "I mean, after all, the man does teach at the university there. It may be L.A., but that does presuppose *some* basic poise in front of strangers."

"He was probably putting you on!" Patrick said. "Didn't you say he still hustles Santa Monica Boulevard?"

"Marce, you wouldn't believe it! Ten at night, I'm driving around West Hollywood looking for this place where the local queens do country-western dancing, you know do-si-do and all that shit, and I almost dropped my teeth. There was Rechy on a street corner near this porno theater, wearing boots, tight jeans, no shirt, dark glasses. Upper torso naked, but all oiled up. He was standing indirectly under this streetlight so you couldn't see his face."

"But he was sweet," Marcy said.

"They were *all* sweet. You know, big gay New York mag sends its editor out there to interview them in depth. What's not to be sweet about?"

Finally Patrick discarded. We applauded.

"That's not the card I wanted, darlinggggg!" Luis trilled, pretending to backhand Patrick. He picked up a card and discarded. "Still knocking."

"Suck my six-inch wedgies!" Patrick said, then turned to me and Marcy. "So, now, how is it again that you two kids know each other?"

"Kindergarten Brownie troop," Luis said.

"We used to work in the same office in the late sixties," Marcy said, distracted enough to drop another queen on the deck.

"As textbook editors," I said. "*Quel* dreary place! We didn't really know each other then," I added. "Marcy was much above me in position."

Quietly, I picked up the queen. That meant three of them.

"Banana oil!" Marcy declared. "But it's true we didn't know each other. Rog hung around with the smart set. He was straight then."

"Our little Rogina? Straight? Hush your mouf, girl," Luis joshed. He picked up, looked at the card, and discarded, filled with ennui. "Better yet, wash it out!"

"With Nair!" Patrick added, taking his turn, which left a six of clubs, which I was sure Marcy needed. Would she notice?

"Well, he was always with these two very hot girls," Marcy defended herself, "so naturally *I* thought he was straight. Everyone thought so!"

"Including himself," I admitted. She hadn't taken the six, too bad for her. "Marce, whatever happened to my supervisor there?" I asked, partly to keep her distracted. "What was his name? Kovacs?"

Marcy almost dropped her cards. "You mean you don't know?" Her lovely, guileless brown eyes were huge now. "You're going to die!" she said, her voice rising. "Just die, when you hear!"

"Spit it out, girl!" Luis demanded. "Don't hesitate!" He'd picked up, looked, and discarded in one movement, almost automatically.

Marcy looked like the teenager she'd once been as she began to dish. "Kovacs was slipped LSD at some weekend party or other in I think '71, and he went completely gaga. I don't mean he freaked out. In fact, he didn't. He returned to work, and then little by little people began to notice changes. Tom McQuill, remember him? Well, Tom *swore* he walked into the men's john one day and caught Kovacs in—I love it!—pink silk undies."

"Whooo-whoo!" Luis and Patrick intoned together.

"Then we began to notice him wearing makeup. First it was only a touch of rouge. Then eyeliner. Well, he went on vacation, and when he returned, he wasn't Frank anymore, he was—"

"Fran-cine!" we all shouted.

Her face fell. "You knew?"

"Guessed," I said. "And?"

Marcy was no longer so forthcoming. She was studying her cards.

She'd noticed the six she'd failed to pick up before. I saw her lips make the word "Shit!" as she began to shift around the cards in her hand.

"And? Did he go all the way? Get the operation? Snip-snip!"

"I guess. I left to go work at the Book Club and lost track of him." She looked in front of her. "Whose turn is it?"

"Yours!" we all said at once.

"It's spectacular dish," I declared, tapping her wrist with my folded-up hand. "Simply spectacular!"

Marcy looked at me slyly, then winked. Then she picked up a card from the deck that she could use, and cheerfully dropped another three-card straight on the table. "Were you alone out west? Or did you take Matt?"

"Matt took him!" Luis said.

"It's true," I admitted. "*Drummer* flew him out for a shoot: cover, full spread inside with a fold-out centerfold. I just tagged along. Then I managed to get Harte to agree to the interviews with the writers, so I'd be able to pay a few bills and not feel like a complete hooker."

"Matt's the one who earns all the money," Patrick said.

"Matt's the one who gets all the attention," Luis said.

"No!" loyal Marcy protested.

"It's true, Marce. I could commit murder in a crowd standing next to Matt, and there wouldn't be a single witness. That's how little they see me."

"Poor Roger!" she cooed. "*I* think you're handsome. Don't you guys?"

"Too old for me," Luis said, sneering.

"Too young for me," Patrick said, scowling.

"He's just right for me!" Marcy laughed and half hugged me. "But I thought Matt was a poet. A serious poet."

"Well, he's that too!" I admitted, with a groan. "And therein lies . . . the nub of it, my dear!" I affected a British accent so as to avoid having to discuss anything else concerning Matt, who had chosen for the past month to stay out at the Pines during the week, while I returned to town.

Marcy took my hint. She usually did. "Who else did you meet out west?"

"He did *not* meet Patricia Nell Warren!" Patrick said and sulked.

"Patrick may be pretty," Luis said to Marcy, "but he has the literary taste of a housewife. I've tried to learn him. Lord knows, I've tried!"

"Samuel Steward in San Francisco," I said. "He was interesting."

"Who?"

"Phil Andros! Well, that's the name he wrote under. Before that, in the thirties and forties he was palsy with Gertrude Stein and Alice B. in Paris, when he was a mere youth. He's going to write about them."

"Speaking of dykes, Marcy," Patrick said, "did Rog tell you about the new dyke who's come to work for the magazine?"

"Marcy knows her," I warned.

"Marcy recommended her to Harte," Marcy said, "and God help Marcy if she doesn't work out."

"She seems okay," I said, noncommittally. After all, Sydelle Auslander had been at the magazine only a few weeks. And in that time she'd made an "interesting" impression: thin, nervous, elegant, attractive in that gaunt way that modern dancers have; aware that she was new and even that she was out of place, yet determined not to let that deter her; all too conscious but ironical about it too, which was sort of endearing.

"I don't get it." Patrick had to, as usual, say the obvious. "What's a lezzie doing at a men's magazine?"

"The idea," I said, "is that Harte would like it if *Manifest* weren't only a men's magazine, but a magazine for *all* gays and lesbians."

"You're kidding, right? With all that male flesh in it?"

"I'm just repeating what Harte told me."

"You mean you're repeating what Mr. Millions told Harte," Patrick said, using his and Luis's pet satirical name for the money man behind our publisher, known by other names in the city, including "cheapest faggot breathing."

"Luis?" I said, reminding him. "Go! Will you!"

"It's *your* turn!" Luis said.

"Really?" I'd gotten lost in the conversation. What did my hand need? Rather, what *didn't* my hand need!

"Wake up!" Patrick tapped my forehead with the flyswatter.

"Try to use that on the flying variety of pests!" Marcy directed him.

"Sorry!" I apologized and went to the deck and picked up another queen. That would go onto the straight. And the three queens. And the three sixes. And the king would fit on Patrick's flush and . . . Gee, I might be developing something. Cautiously I dropped a low three. Luis didn't seem interested in picking it up. Hmmn! How amusing!

"I also met Isherwood. He was the nicest."

"Tell her about Phil Andros's tattoo," Patrick said.

"I will not! You know, Marce, Isherwood is about seventy-five these days, and ill."

"She *does* know who he is?" Patrick asked.

"Christ, Pat! She's editor in chief of a university press!"

"Sor-ry!"

"I've got to do it!" Luis suddenly declared with utter Cuban passion, apropos of what, none of us could guess.

"He's picking up all the cards!" Patrick shouted with the intuition of a lover.

"If I don't, I'll die of boredom!" Luis said and picked up all but two we'd discarded. "I hate waiting around." He promptly set to work arranging the cards as a hand.

"Don Bachardy is Isherwood's lover," I continued to Marcy. "A fine artist. Well, he phoned and said he'd drive and pick me up because I might not be able to find my way to their house. They live in Pacific Palisades. Which is way down by the ocean."

"And *not*," Luis said, "to be confused with Pacific Heights in San Fancisco."

"Pronounce the *r*, Luis," Patrick nudged.

"He never did pronounce it, even when he was living there," I said, which necessitated explaining to Marcy that that was how Luis and I knew each other. "He was a bartender. A friend of my friend Calvin Ritchie. Did I ever tell you about Calvin?"

"Miss Ritchie the Mad?" Luis tried the name on her.

"This was before you opened the catering firm?" Marcy asked.

"We opened it there and I moved it here," Luis said, still arranging his many cards. "When I broke up with my partner."

Marcy turned to me. "Wasn't that when you met Matt, Rog?"

She knew something was up and, like a trained hunting dog, she was going to flush it out no matter what.

"When and where," I admitted.

"Romance! Romance! Must be something in the air out there," she mused.

"Either that or it might be that one is easily blinded by the fog," Patrick said. "God knows, Luis was certainly befogged by his partner."

"What was I talking about before?" I quickly asked, in case the question came up of whether I myself had been befogged in San Francisco.

"You were talking about Isherwood!" Patrick reminded me.

"Right! So Bachardy arrives in this like basic gray Ford sedan. And as I'm getting into the front seat, I hear someone say hello from the back. And there's Isherwood, all laid out on some sort of foam cushion, with pillows galore. With that childlike little head and face and that short-cropped hair. Can you picture it, Marce? He looked like a little boy with a cold who'd managed to talk his parents into going along for the ride."

"Was he a good interview?"

"Not bad. But the best part was off the record. Although he did say he was planning to write about it someday. Seems that in the late thirties, he was an interpreter and something of a go-between for the bosses of several Hollywood studios and the German émigré writers who'd escaped Hitler. All of them Jewish, mind you, but as different as they could be from each other, Isherwood said. The writers were highly educated. Cultured. Snobby. Very European. And except for Thomas Mann, who had this huge international reputation, they were broke. The film producers and studio heads, on the other hand, were first- and second-generation immigrants from dirt-poor families. Even the Yiddish they spoke was lower class. . . ."

"So, Marcy," Patrick said, obviously bored and unsubtly changing the subject, "you going to be at the Pines for the big party?"

"Well, I don't know . . ." She looked at me.

"It's going to be fabulous!" Patrick said. "We're all doing thirties and forties movie stars. The party will be in a place designed like the Mocambo nightclub. And guess what it's called?"

"She'll never guess," Luis said.

" 'Jungle Red'!" Patrick said.

"Like the nail polish from *The Women*?" Marcy asked.

"You see, Mr. Smarty Pants!" Patrick said. "She knows what's important!"

"What *is* important?" Luis asked rhetorically.

"Shoes! Hair! And skin care!" the rest of us shouted.

"I'm not going to have skin if these mosquitoes don't stop," Marcy declared.

"I still want to know what this dykelet is going to be doing at *Manifest*," Luis said.

"She's not that young," I said. "Maybe . . . thirty?"

"At least," Marcy admitted. "And she's been around a bit, doing all kinds of different work. She was a law clerk. And a social worker. Worked for local newspapers in White Plains, Scarsdale, Albany."

"And danced?" I asked.

"Still does. Like many of us, she wanted to be a real dancer."

" 'Everything is beautiful at the ballet.' "

At that moment, I picked up the fourth queen in the deck and proceeded to lay out three sixes, a queen high run in diamonds, my queen trio, and a low flush. I turned over the last card. "Rummy!" I said, casually, showing my empty hand.

"*No!*" Luis screamed. He was still holding about a dozen cards. "You can't *do* that. You didn't knock."

"I can and I am. I don't have to knock."

"Nurse! Oh, nurse!" Patrick called out, pretending to faint. "A Reg-is-ter-ed Nurse is re-quir-ed im-med-iate-ly!"

"Marce, add seventy-five points to my score," I said, enjoying their pain. "I believe I win."

"I'm stuck with hundreds of minus points," Luis groaned. "I'm doomed! Doomed, I tell you!"

Patrick was already counting how much he'd have to subtract.

"Good thing I melded those aces," Marcy said, nearly inaudible amid all the breast beating. The rest of her cards were low points.

Naturally, Matt chose that very moment to come home.

"Well, look what the cat dragged in," he said, shaking the big umbrella outside the back screen door and folding it up.

"We hope," Luis said, "the cat remembered something to eat!"

"I did, I did." Matt produced a brown paper bag and set it on the counter. "C'mon in," he urged someone.

Because of the dark, I couldn't make out who was behind Matt until they'd both stepped into the light. I was paying more attention to

Matt, whose voice sounded a lot cheerier than it had when he'd gone out earlier in the day. But then, that was the reason he'd gone out in the first place: to get away from me, which lately equaled his being cheered up.

"Who is it?" Patrick asked. Then, "Is that . . . ? It is! Look, kids! It's Alistair Dodge!"

The rain abated by nightfall. It was merely a loud, irregular dripping off the edges of the blue-and-white canvas protecting the outdoor dining area of the Blue Whale. The candles in their squat, white-netted, carmine glasses upon the oversized wooden table suddenly burned higher and brighter in that way they do just before they gutter into darkness. Around us, the decking steamed gently, as though we were in the middle of the third act of some singspiel where mystical enchantments are about to be unveiled. Beyond the fogged glare emanating from beneath the sodden canopy, beyond the definiteness of the thin white railing, a mist had rapidly gathered to float atop the black and silky boat-slip waters. Transforming the topmast lamps of the yachts and yawls and ketches parked opposite into a carnival dazzle. Curiously filtering the outdoor lights of the sprawling house behind through screw pine saplings and monkey puzzle trees. Metamorphosing what had been a simple walkway into a half-shut sideshow.

"On nights like this, I wouldn't trade the Pines for Saint-Tropez," I said, trying to be ironic, tacky, and sincere all at once.

"It's all rather Glam," Alistair agreed. His face, newly highlighted by the illumination, seemed, I found myself thinking, even worse than I'd thought when he'd come in the door of our house earlier that evening with Matt. Not so much older (although that was certainly true) as more set: a pinched, an almost disappointed, attitude.

And his clothing! Alistair hadn't been a fashion plate since adolescence, but with his height and shoulders and perfect size forty, he'd always managed to look casual, even elegant. The polo shirt he now wore was an oddly orange shade of pink with something remarkably like a Peter Pan collar from the late fifties. French or . . . His slacks, too, were foreign-made, cut too flat and too wide, stranding his narrow hips in excess cloth, while the legs were almost pedal-pusher tight. Docksiders were docksiders, even these slate-blue ones with cream trim, but the matching belt made them appear to be a Statement—a mistaken one. And that windbreaker! Composed of material resembling solidified napalm, it had been cut on biases not seen since Iceland in the twelfth century. I was dying to ask Alistair what circumstances had caused him to be forced to leave his own clothing behind in a hurry and borrow all this gear from some deckhand, but I was afraid he'd tell me that wasn't the case at all: that, instead, all this had been "chosen."

Oblivious to my silent devastation of his outfit, Alistair now squashed a Sobranie filter-tip into the Creole Rice he hadn't touched on his plate, and poured himself the last of the Saint-Emilion '74. "That handsome fellow behind the bar?" He motioned with the tip of his glass.

"Mar-tan. Swiss. Enormous cock. Only likes slender twenty-year-old boys," I reported.

"Cuz is invaluable," Alistair said, regarding Matt with a steady eye— Matt, who was peering inside the restaurant all the while. "I was saying how invaluable my cousin was. He knows everyone here and everything about them. Hel-lo?" he trilled.

"Sorry." Matt came to. "I wanted to see if Thad was free yet."

"Thad's the tall, handsome, thin blond," I explained. "Our maître d'."

"The one who pinched your right nipple as we arrived?" Alistair asked.

"The same."

"He lost his lover a few weeks ago," Matt went on. "He said he was depressed and needed to talk."

"You a close friend?"

"Well . . . You know how it is when you need someone to talk to."

"Why, Matthew! You're a regular altruist!" Alistair said.

"It's now or never!" Matt stood up, excused himself, and went inside.

"You remember that big model, Jed Billingsly? With that great head of corn-silk hair?" I asked Alistair. "He was Thad's lover. Freaked out on angel dust and jumped out a thirteen-story window."

I'd meant to shock Alistair. I succeeded.

"You meant he . . . *lost* his lover," Alistair said, as he tried milking the near-empty wine bottle. "Not merely misplaced him somewhere . . . but really lost . . . Not that hooch is any better. Except, of course, with liquor, by the time the real paranoia kicks in, one is far too gone to be able to wreak much violence upon oneself."

"Spoken like someone who knows," I half probed.

"Spoken like someone who's seen it enough," Alistair corrected. "Most recently on Ibiza. Lovely older man. Charming. One of those *echt*-European types. Bastard son of some famous duke or other from the Austrian Empire. Was left a pish of loot. But even so, he'd gone through it. Connected? My dear, he could compare three coronations he'd attended from frontish rows! Useless, of course, except to drink and talk. Utterly useless!"

"Don't think we don't have them here too," I said. "If you stick around long enough, you'll see one in particular. About fifty by now, still in great shape. You can see through the ravages how stellar he must have been. Wears shorts to show off those legs. Smokes a small pipe. Totally blitzed! Day, noon, or night."

"He was in Mykonos in April. Hasn't been seen unstoned in a decade." Alistair evidently knew the man. "One of the great gay courtesans of the century. The king of Belgium settled on him. Baudouin, was it?"

I nodded. Silence descended. Alistair sipped. I smoked. The rain dripped.

After a while, I was feeling uncomfortable enough to say, "You know, Stairs, for all the drugs I've taken, I've never gotten into angel dust. Some people swear by it. This guy—"

"Matt's looking good." Alistair changed the subject without, I was certain, being totally aware of what he was doing. "Well, better than good, really. He's . . . One forgets," he began and seemed to rethink what it was he had to say. ". . . One forgets over there how absolutely beautiful American men are! Of course there too one will chance upon something breathtaking—a young Alain Delon look-alike about to commit a felony, or an Alpine Adonis fit to burst his lederhosen. But here! Here they're everywhere you turn! We'd not been docked more than a few hours, and already I'd seen one more splendid than the other. Tea Dance was . . ." Words escaped him. "And you, Cuz, you're looking especially . . . ," he searched for the word and settled upon: "fit! As though all this agrees with you."

I wished I could say the same about him. But my silence spoke enough.

"I, of course," Alistair pretended to pull out a compact, open it, check his image in the mirror, and then flinch, "I look like month-old *merde*. But what can one expect after a week at sea?"

He proceeded to tell in some detail about the trip across the Bermuda Triangle from the Turks and Caicos in a sixty-foot yacht. Evidently they'd encountered all sorts of weather—not to mention various odd people—upon the bounding main. Alistair ticked them off: "The Bahamian Coast Guard. One great strapping black fellow kept stroking himself with a hawser just like in those old American Guild photos I used to keep under my bed in a shoe box. I could have come right there! Then there was a pirate boat with a mixed and not very attractive crew. Evidently we were too small for them to bother with. Then those Nicaraguan spongers who'd somehow gone adrift. Poor dears, we set them straight . . . well, only after being very queer to them. Then that trio of big-bellied blond Aussie sport fishermen out searching for bluefin but willing enough to, and I quote, 'sod around a bit with a boat full of poufs!' which was to say Tom and Juerg and myself." Alistair chuckled and turned to search through the fogged-up restaurant windows for Matt. "He'll be all right?"

"Matt? Sure!" I asked, "A walk?"

I got up, caught our waiter's eye, and mimicked signing the check. Paolo pointed at Matt and Thad at the bar. One or the other of them had taken care of it.

Not knowing how tanked he might be, but knowing quite well how treacherous wet decking could be, I held Alistair's arm going down the steps of the deck and aimed us toward the inner curve of the little Pines harbor. Up several wide steps and behind glass walls, the half dozen office- and storefronts we passed glowed a dim orange, as though preserved in amber.

Alistair kept on talking about the trip. He'd still not told me what he was doing in the Caicos with Tom and Juerg—middle-aged lovers and owners of the yacht now parked in the last "guest slip" at the tip of the harbor. This evening, while he'd been with us, they'd dined at a friend's house on Holly Walk: someone older and European whom I didn't know.

We passed the Sandpiper, rainwater pouring out of spouts from the upper deck. Peering into the thrown-open windows, I could see dinner was officially over; the staff was removing chairs and tables from the low-ceilinged central area that would become in a few hours a busy, exciting dance floor.

I thought, well, Alistair may be badly dressed and he may look like shit and he's definitely been drinking too much, but at least he's not a pod-person, as I'd been convinced he was about to become when I'd left San Francisco. Instead, he was almost his old self again: funny and cynical and uninhibited in that peculiar way of his. But where was Doriot?

At the ferry landing dock, where the Pines' only streetlamp splattered enough illumination to show every lath of decking soaked through with rain, the harbor mist had gathered together to bob upon the surrounding black water like meringue upon an incompletely gelled chocolate pudding pie. Already, above and beyond the shredding mist, we could make out the black curtain of night, speckled with hints of constellations.

Alistair took off his windbreaker and spread it over the bench that had been built into the landing area. We sat. Behind us, pine trees dripped and dripped.

"That house?" Alistair began. "It's yours?"

"I wish! We rent. Matt and I and Luis and Patrick."

"But it's an official address, no? If I wanted something mailed, I could use your address here?"

"I guess. But they don't deliver the mail. You have to go pick it up at the little P.O. Why?"

"Do you mind if I have something sent to me in your name?"

"Mail delivery's sporadic. Tuesday, Thursday, Saturday. Why?"

"That's okay. I plan to stay here a short while. With Tom and Juerg."

Since he wasn't about to tell me why, I said, "Sure, send it in care of me, 420 Sky Walk."

"Sky!" Alistair mused. He pulled out a cigarette and lit it. "But you don't call it that?"

"We call it Withering Heights. The name sort of developed among the Ozone Beach Club last summer. It's supposed to be clever."

I found I had to explain that the Ozone Beach Club wasn't anything formal but merely our pals from the area—along the walks from Tarpon to Shell—who entered the beach at and generally remained near Ozone Walk and who sometimes played at the volleyball net someone had set up there.

"You make it all sound like a boys' camp," Alistair said.

"One with drug overdoses and fist-fucking."

"Well then, a very *naughty* boys' camp!" Alistair laughed. "The only interesting kind, really. The address," he explained without missing a beat or changing his tone of voice, "is so I can receive the final divorce papers."

I was about to say "Excuse me?" and ask him to repeat himself, but I found that I'd very well heard what he'd said.

"I am sorry, Stairs."

"Not as sorry as I am."

None of it was completely unexpected. Yet it was. I had a moment of horror, wondering if he was about to break down on me, here, in the most public twenty square feet of the Pines.

Behind us, the trees dripped loudly. Before us, the mist was being slowly sucked backward out of the harbor. The orange lights on the second floor of the Botel were clarifying, as though cleaning people the size of Tinker Bell were wiping the lenses of my eyeballs.

I knew their marriage had not been an easy one. They'd honeymooned endlessly in Europe and returned to the Bay Area just as I was spending more and more time out of San Francisco. They'd opened their art gallery on Sutter Street there, and I'd attended the first few openings. By then I'd moved back to the East Coast, and I saw them on their frequent trips: they stayed at the Sherry and hit all of the choicest clubs night after night—Régine's, Le Jardin, you name it! Then they were gone back to Frisco to the gallery. I heard that they'd stuck with it for a year, then ditched it and moved to Europe, traveling from here to there, living in places—Saint-Malo, Rimini, the Balearics—I didn't know and couldn't afford, associating with people far too rich for my blood. I'd assumed that whatever problems I'd envisioned in Alistair and Doriot's relationship were subsumed under scads of money and the distractions of European high life.

Not quite. A few years passed, then Alistair suddenly resurfaced in America. He and Doriot were on a trial separation, which he was treating like an extended solo vacation and fuckfest. He'd come to spend a few days with Matt and me at the funky little house we rented in Truro on the Cape. We'd seen little of Alistair after that first afternoon, and even then he'd been intent on having sex with every halfway decent male who cruised him back. He'd returned to France, to Doriot, and, I'd assumed, to a continuation of their married life.

Now I remembered a late-night phone conversation I'd had not eight months ago with Doriot. We'd not spoken or met in several years, and I'd been astonished that it was she on the other end, calling from the château they'd been living in somewhere outside of Paris.

"You know Alistair better than anyone," she'd begun, sounding tight-voiced and thus barely in control. "You've got to tell me what I must do to . . . keep him . . . *human* here with me. He's become . . . a monster."

If she hadn't sounded so desperate, I might have bullshitted her. But I knew Alistair well, and I recalled how he'd swept Anatole Lamarr off that Cape Cod roof deck before the lobsters were ready to eat, and how they'd reappeared later from some spare room in the tall house, looking flushed but by no means sated, and how Alistair had driven off to P-Town with Anatole for the rest of his stay on the Cape.

"Send him to Paris for the weekend. Send him to the baths."

Her answer was slow in coming. "Aren't . . . I enough?"

"Wrong thinking. It has nothing to do with you. Do what I say and let him get it out of his system. He'll be okay for months!"

"I can't do that," she said and changed the topic immediately, talking about inconsequential matters. Before I hung up, I'd said again, "Send him to Paris for the weekend."

She hadn't. Hadn't been able to bring herself to. And now they were divorcing. I wondered if there had been some lurid discovery: Alistair and the groundskeeper, say—he had always gone in for the staff.

"Doriot was everything I'd ever wanted," Alistair said now in a tragic voice. "Ever since I was a little boy."

I recalled him in our suburban Long Island living room late at night watching old black-and-white movies, surreptitiously smoking a ciga-rette. I remembered his declaration about how he wanted to live in a Manhattan penthouse and be with clever and sophisticated grown-ups. He'd achieved that wish early on. Evidently he harbored other, even more ambitious, dreams I'd not heard of.

"I'll never get over this failure! Never!" Alistair moaned.

"Come on, Stairs. You got over the breakup with what was his name? Michael? This is hard, I know, but it'll pass too."

"Speaking of him, the day I left Sainte-Anne-en-Haute, I found out Michael had died. Went down in that Cessna he bought with my money, somewhere over Santa Catalina Island. And guess what? I get back the property we co-owned on the Coast."

"So you won't be destitute?"

"Hardly. Also Doriot's family lawyers have worked out a substantial settlement. In fact, I'll probably be better off than I've ever been. Ironic, no? I didn't want it. Her *father* insisted. Turns out he *liked* me! The crazy bastard! He insists I stay in touch."

"Well! You see? Already it seems—"

He gripped my arm. "What's the difference how much it is or who likes me, Stodge? My life continues to be a series of unending failures! Disasters! I've still never succeeded at one single thing I set my mind to doing. The L.A. development? A shambles! The Santa Cruz property? In litigation for a decade. Well, now I get it back and I know well enough to let it run itself and to stay away from it. The gallery? A loss of money and a complete failure! My affairs? Catastrophes each and every one. Culminating in my marriage! Oh, Stodge, there was so much promise! So much fuck-ing prom-ise! What happened?"

Even in the half darkness, I could see his eyes brimming.

I began talking quietly to him, saying all kinds of stupid, irrelevant, unanswering things which I'd hoped would distract him.

Finally he said, "Okay! Okay! Enough! Stop, stop!"

And when I did stop, Alistair said, "You make the worst Pollyanna! I swear! You simply don't have the knack."

People had begun to gather slowly in the Pines' "downtown": four waiters just off work confabbing; a man and a woman walking their dogs (the animals approached each other and were sniffing); a trio of "numbers" who had stowed their bags under the back deck roof of the Sandpiper and began to strike poses—apparently the last ferry was due any moment now.

Alistair and I stood up, and he threw an arm over my shoulder and, to my astonishment, scratched his cheek against mine.

"Thanks for listening to me. I swear I won't subject you to too much more Sturm und Drang in the future, although I'm afraid there will be some."

"Whenever," I said.

We edged past the waiters along the harbor walk. Alistair said, "I'm drunk and I want to go to bed. Walk me home?"

I did, past the Blue Whale, the Pines Pantry, the row of parked boats, to the end, where Tom and Juerg had berthed.

As I helped him onto the boat, Alistair did suddenly seem especially awkward in the way only alcohol can make one.

"Years from now, when you talk about this," he began, quoting Deborah Kerr in *Tea and Sympathy*. "And you *will* . . ."

"I *will*! And when I do," I interrupted, "I'll say that all the while we were wearing red rubber dildos on our heads."

Alistair half collapsed with laughter but made it below deck.

I walked out to the final spit of walkway built into the Great South Bay. I knew it well. Seaplanes took off and landed from this little deck during daylight hours, bobbing upon the water like slightly larger and more elaborate versions of the balsa models I'd constructed as a child. I'd arrived at the Pines via this very spot yesterday at noon, and I'd be here again in less than twenty-four hours, awaiting a plane back to Manhattan. At the inner facing of the dock had been erected one of the harbor's two parallel safety lights, flashing yellow to define the narrow entrance at night, or in fog. Here too was one of the best viewing places in the Pines for sunsets, especially later on in the summer, in September and October. Matt and I used to come here often the first years we estivated on the Island, bundled up in high-collared sweaters against sudden chills, watching the sun descend into the bay waters like a huge time-release tablet of manifold tinges that slowly, inexorably dyed sea and sky in ever-changing, slightly mismatched colors. We'd speak in a hush for minutes afterward whenever we'd manage to espy that rare and wondrous spectacle—the green flash!

We were seldom alone. Tonight, however, I was. Alone, in the rapidly drying air, watching the mist blow off the island and retreat to its hidden lairs within the water. Alone, left to consider what Alistair had said about failure, about promise.

The truth was, I'd never been as goal-oriented or as ambitious or even as determined as my cousin had been almost from the first. With me, life's promises had been vague, gleaming with all sorts of wonderful possibilities, but always somewhere over the horizon. My way of getting there had not been the straight line Alistair had forged, with its sharp successes and equally sharp setbacks, but a more indirect approach, encouraged on the one hand by my slowly increasing belief in myself as I got older and saw what I was capable of, yet always tempered by an equal fear and lack of confidence and even more by a deep-seated distrust, not of myself so much as of my own destiny. If pressed to the wall suddenly with a gun held to my head and asked if I thought I would *be* someone, *do* something, I wouldn't have known *how* to answer, really.

And still didn't. Sure, I'd had some excellent jobs. College textbook editor, manager of Pozzuoli's in Manhattan, then in San Francisco, editor of *Opera Monthly*, and now of *Manifest*, the fastest growing and most influential gay magazine in the country. Doubtless, I'd done far more with my B.A. in English (from a college by no means highly rated) than most of my coevals. Not to mention the sheer amount of writing I'd had published, not only in the magazines I'd worked for, but in others too, and in some gay newspapers. It was hardly the big time, hardly what my shy new friend Andrew Holleran (who wrote reviews for our mag) called "Big Girl Stuff"—not *Time*, not *The Atlantic*—but lately, whenever people of importance in the gay world were mentioned, my name always seemed to come up. By my position alone, I'd managed to become a sort of central switchboard for gay life in the country in all kinds of odd areas, from poetry to resorts to sex toys to fads and the latest party places. "Queen Control," Luis and Patrick and I laughingly called it—disparagingly. But at times—when a desperate person needed someone to talk them out of suicide, when someone had a sudden illness, an accident—what I knew, whom I knew, could prove awfully effective in mobilizing real help.

None of us in the media, none of us in the so-called gay community that had developed in the decade since the Stonewall Riot, seemed to have any real program for what we were doing. Naturally we had a public agenda: sodomy laws were to be repealed, discrimination was to be ended, all that. But in other, less defined, more ordinary, more social areas, we were experimenting with different things. This entire "gay" business was still so new, so unprecedented, how could we know what we were doing? We were just trying to do things right. Which meant *not* as heterosexuals did them, or perhaps not as our parents and teachers did them, and that sometimes meant being outrageous and sometimes meant being merely true to ourselves.

That, of course, brought on a new fear, innate in the former one: that I'd already far exceeded my promise, already shot beyond the tiny bit my destiny had laid out for me, and was now dangling—unknowingly— over the precipice, with only a ragged shoelace to keep me from dropping into the abyss.

Thus was I mentally torturing myself, when from behind, I felt the air close up to the exact height and girth and depth of . . . and at the same time I sniffed that peculiar yet specific combination of hints of body odor and leather and incompletely worn-off shaving lotion that could only be from . . . and in that very instant I felt slide up over my back and simultaneously across my left pectoral the insinuating yet proprietary caress of . . .

". . . dark and deeper than any sea-dingle/Upon what man it fall . . . ," Matt quoted incompletely, if appropriately given where we stood, slipping his hand between my short-sleeved arm and polo shirt to emerge at my right nipple, which he held and gently kneaded. He'd pulled up so close behind me he completely blocked the lightly rippling wind from the west bay I only now realized had been a slight, unceasing annoyance.

"Done with Thaddeus, already?" I asked.

"Hardly," Matt said with a hint of a chuckle. Then, "For tonight."

Meaning who knew what, exactly. I didn't. And didn't want to know.

In the semi-distance we heard the speakers from the Sandpiper go on, as the DJ began trying out his equipment for the night, using the instrumental version of "Fly Robin Fly." I remembered that Howard Merritt would be playing, with his cute lover Jorge—John Iozia's eponymous "My Favorite Cuban"—on the light board.

From his greater height behind, Matt nuzzled into my hair.

"Hark, my lord," he said in a stagier voice. "A galleon nears!"

Against a storm-tossed night sky, the last ferry to the Pines emerged from the mist and presented itself, theatrically defined by its black silhouette and many tiny yellow lighted windows. It was surprisingly close.

"I put him to bed," I said, meaning Alistair. "He's going to be here for a few days. So will you, right? I know you don't care for him. But try not to let him see it."

Matt was making little popping noises, his lips against my left ear.

"Matt?"

"Umm-hunn," he murmured. "You don't think he'll like . . . foist himself on me, do you?"

"Alistair's hardly the foisting kind. He's here with friends."

Matt was at my ear again.

"What's with you?" I asked.

I'd assumed Matt was seeing Thad during the week. Could their relationship be—of all things—platonic?

"Matt, you're . . . you're acting like a horny teenager."

He snuggled even closer, binding me by the upper arms.

"Matt?"

"Fucka fucka fucka," he chugged into my ear as he dry-humped me.

"Stop! You're tickling! Stop!"

"Fucka fucka fucka." He continued chugging and humping.

I tried to squirm away. Tried being mean: "Go say fucka fucka to one of your little numbers."

"Nnnh-nnnm. You're the official lover. You gotta do it when I want."

"Who says?"

"It's the rules," he insisted. "You get the perks. Gotta put out."

"What perks?" I laughingly demanded to know.

"Endless perks. Social standing. The jealousy of a thousand queens a day. Endless perks and endless delight! Like in Handel."

"In your dreams!" I scoffed, but as usual, his holding me, caressing me, bussing my ear, my nape, hell, even his voice were, after all these years and after all his efforts, still perfectly tuned erotic instruments to me. As I spoke, I heard, with only a bit of diffidence, my voice softening, felt, with only a hint of betrayal, my body begin to yield.

It was at that moment of half-involuntary surrender that I noticed the lights do something from below deck on the yacht where Alistair was staying: go on or go out, I couldn't be sure which really, but change somehow; signaling to me that he was not asleep as I'd thought, not fallen unstripped into his bunk in a semi-alcoholic stupor, but awake, even alert, watching us, wanting us to know he was watching.

"Lezz go, hnnh?" Matt insisted.

"It's a long, long way to Sky Walk," I teased.

But it wasn't after all that very long a walk, and we'd already had a few summers' practice in this sort of thing, so it just encouraged us in finding new ways to play with and taunt and sex-tease each other at every other crossing boardwalk all the way there, and even before we'd gotten to the branch-off to our house, we'd stripped off our shirts and belts, and by the time we'd made it inside the house, neither hurricane nor the End of the World itself could have stopped us.

Some time into it in our bedroom, I lifted up Matt's head from just below my clavicle, where he seemed to be methodically love-biting an entire necklace of hickeys. "Wait! Shh! Do you hear something?"

"It's the Pines! Remember! The house is twelve feet off the ground, swaying on wooden stilts," Matt replied, "I'll bet they can hear us in here too."

"No, it's not that. The front door maybe."

"Patrick and Luis. Going out dancin'," Matt said and went back to work on my love bites.

I heard the sound again. Of course, Matt might have been right. One heard every kind of noise with these houses. Maybe it was just Marcy, getting up to go to the bathroom.

"What if it's a thief?" I asked. Matt seemed oblivious in his lovemaking.

"We don't have anything worth taking."

"What if it's a rapist?"

"Too bad for him," Matt said. "I've got first dibs."

"So I see. What is it with you tonight anyway?" I asked.

"Hold on a sec," Matt said, and came a second time.

He kissed me gently, lifted his body off me, and lay next to me, his long, well-muscled body all but purring, lightly vibrating the entire mattress.

"Now, what was your exact question?" he asked. "Are you telling me that I've got to make up excuses for screwing the man of my dreams?"

"Well, you are here on the Island all week. I'd just assumed . . ."

"Assumed what? That I'm fucking everyone all day long."

"Something like that, sure."

"Well, I'm not. I've got standards, you know. A reputation."

"Said," I said, "in the exact tone of Little Lulu."

"Which is?" he asked.

"Snooty, yet unable to completely pull it off."

"Oh? Little Lulu from the comics," Matt said, ignoring the rest of my explanation and going off to ask, "Do you remember Mr. Myxtplqztrx?"

"Sure. From the sixth dimension. Weird, little weasely guy in *Superman*."

"He wasn't that weasely!" Matt said.

"Sure was! Cross-eyed. Hair went off in all directions . . ."

"I sort of liked Mr. Myxtplqztrx's bowtie. And his little suit."

"That's not how his name was pronounced," I said.

"The point was, I thought, that his name was unpronounceable," Matt corrected me. "At any rate if Mr. Myxtplqztrx were out here in the Pines, that's who I'd screw around with!"

"And here I've been, fool enough to think you loved me for my body."

Matt groaned heavily. "Aaaah! I'm bushed!"

Unsurprisingly. By the clock, we'd been fucking for an hour and a half.

"I guess I won't go out either tonight," I said. "Harte's in L.A., so I have a break. I know what! I'll get up early and make a big breakfast for my honey and for my feminist guest. I'll rush down to the harbor for the Sunday *Times* and fresh scones. It'll all be ter-rib-ly civilized. Ter-rib-ly *Architectural Digest*."

Matt hoisted himself into a sitting position. And sighed. "Piss."

"No, thanks, I'm full."

He was too exhausted even to laugh. He got off the bed slowly and stood up, swayed left slightly, caught himself on the door joist, went into the john, and urinated loudly.

When he came out again, he held a razor and a fresh emery board and tossed them onto my lap. "C'mon boy, get up and work. That's all you're here for, you know! That, and because you're a fair piece of *poontang*!"

He lay down again heavily and began to push his denims off his legs. I crawled to the far edge of the bed and pulled them completely off. I removed his boots, the one regular one and, far more gingerly, the other one, with its built-in plastic construction. The socks. And the special nylon stockings over *the* foot. It looked swollen tonight, and while I knew it didn't—couldn't—hurt deeply, I knew he felt the skin, and so I was extra careful pulling down the nylon. I lightly shaved the area so no hairs could treacherously turn inward and fester, used the emery to rub off dead skin, and covered the foot with antibiotic talcum all over. I moved to his other foot and felt at the clipped-back-to-skin toenails and filed them back even more, so he wouldn't scratch himself in his sleep and unknowingly infect himself. I reached down and did the same to the nails on my own toes, so that I wouldn't, in my sleep, next to him, be the agent of harm. I gently massaged his foot—*the* foot—trying not to let any feelings show through my touch, at the missing toes, at the unhealthy plump softness and potentially fetid flesh. Just to be fair, I massaged his other foot too. And finished by pulling the sheet up his legs.

"Matt?"

"Thanks, babe. Come up here, yeah?"

"Okay. But first . . . about Thaddeus. . . . You're not . . ."

Matt was sleepy but still strong enough to pull me up next to him.

"I'm not what? . . . I told you I wasn't screwing with Thad."

"You're not . . . you're not falling in love with him, are you?"

His head had rolled over on the pillow. It swerved back to stare.

"Why are you doing this?" he asked—accused, really. "We were having such a good night and you—"

"I have the right to know if you are," I said, feeling myself on shaky ground.

"You know, the next time I want to make love," he mumbled into his pillow, "I'll call your assistant and set up an appointment."

"Exploitative bastard!"

Even turned away, even from in back, he was still strong enough to grab me and pull me close to his face. "Get serious, will you! Who but you would do all this shit for me?" he asked, gesturing at the edge of the bed, referring to our ritual that kept crippling incapacity at bay a few more days.

"They all would!" I said. "Thad! Any one of them!"

"You are Mr. Myxtplqztrx! Sixth-dimensional jerk!"

"All I ask is give me advance warning when you . . . split. . . ."

"Idiot!" he moaned, letting me go and turning away.

". . . So I don't end up looking a complete fool," I finished.

"Anything! Anything you want!" He covered his head with the pillow.

I got in bed next to him, still irritated, and in the dim light I picked up and began to read the novel I kept on the bed table.

Fifteen minutes later, he was lightly snoring and I was involved in the book, but my eyes were beginning to smear the words on the page. When I shut off the light and slid down the mattress, Matt moved next to me in the dark and we assumed our sleep position: me on my back, flat and motionless as a corpse in its coffin, he on one side facing me, one arm thrown over my midsection, one leg thrown over my lower body, effectively trapping me, his other hand lightly gripping my dick.

"Mr. Myxtplqztrx!" he murmured once in his sleep.

Four phones were ringing at once. And all of them were for me.

The Grunt fielded them one after another, writing down messages, then he looked up and pointed to the phone, held up a finger so I'd pick up line one, and picked up his own receiver. Not six feet away, at her own desk, also on the phone, Sydelle Auslander had crossed her long legs, as she was rifling through a folder while on hold. This, I thought, is my staff. God help me.

"Boss wants you!" the Grunt said. "I don't know. He didn't say," he quickly added, cutting me off at the pass.

"Sit on it, Bernard," I said casually, "and rotate! Who were the others?"

I could see him go through the messages. "No one important. No one important. And your dance buddy."

"Jeffrey? I wanted to talk to him! Did you tell him I've been trying to reach him?"

"I did. He said he's been living at the tubs. He met Mr. Wrong from—are you ready?—Cincinnati there and hasn't been home for two days."

"Is he home now?"

"He gave me three phone numbers. Aren't you going in?"

"In . . . a . . . minute!"

"Do *you* know what it's about?" the Grunt said.

I didn't. I thought a bit. Maybe . . . No, I didn't have a clue. But I did know that whenever Harte called me into his office on the afternoon that the magazine was going to bed, it was bound to be trouble—real trouble!

I hung up the receiver. Stood up. Turned toward the door to our publisher's office. And strode instead directly into the art director's studio next door.

Newell Rose was seated on the floor in full lotus position. The darks of his overlarge pale-blue eyes were hidden somewhere deep in their sockets. Around me, the studio looked unusually spotless, even for such a complete anal-retentive type like Newell. His light board was clear, pristine, shut off. His desk was clean. Rolls of tape and wrapped bunches of rubber bands and stickums were arrayed by size and color to one side. Upon the walls around us, in precise, perfect double-page boards was the entire current issue of the magazine, all neat and clean and finished. Ready to be picked up by our printer in about an hour. Or so I hoped—against hope.

I thought, Newell knows trouble's looming. Or at least he guesses that it's on its way! Otherwise he wouldn't be so intent on centering himself like this. But I couldn't be certain.

"I'm not even dreaming of interrupting," I said. "But Harte just called me into his office. So . . ."

"Shit! Fuck! Piss! Nigger! Kike! Wop!" Newell chanted his mantra aloud without even moving his lips.

". . . I just thought I'd warn you," I said and quickly ducked back out of his office.

If Harte wanted to see me, that meant changes would have to be made at the last minute, and any changes to be made at the last minute meant Newell would have to stick around and make them on the boards—painfully make them, since by this stage in the magazine's production, he'd already formed a complete universe of order and beauty and perfection centering around what? The finished issue, of course! Which Harte—with me as his agent—was about to suddenly, mindlessly, demonically destroy.

Back out in the oversized, big-windowed pressroom I could see the Grunt on the phone again. He spotted me, raised the receiver above his head, and shook it from side to side. In the odd if somewhat primitive semiology of Bernard Gunzenhausen's body language as my assistant at *Manifest*, holding the phone up in the air and shaking it like that meant crucial, meant desperate, meant one of only two persons could possibly be on the other end of the line—the President of the United States, whom the Grunt respected for his power yet personally despised, or Matt Loguidice, whom he adored unstintingly and for whose sake he would willingly die the most humiliating and painful death.

I went to an abandoned advertising person's desk with the nearest empty phone and picked up line four. It wasn't Matt. It was:

"Hi, Cuz. Hope I'm not getting you at a bad time."

"Alistair? Where are you?"

"Actually I'm at the Pines Harbor public telephone. Reason I'm calling is that something has come up and . . . Tom and Juerg have decided to continue on to Bar Harbor in the boat and my . . . the . . . you know, papers haven't come through yet."

"You checked the post office?"

"Again! I can't really do anything until all this is settled. I was wondering . . . You have a spare room. Could I possibly stay at your place out here until . . ."

Gevalt! Matt would have kittens if I called and asked him.

"You know, it's okay with me," I said. "But I'd have to check with the others. Luis and Patrick and . . ."

"Matt called them already and they agreed," Alistair amazed me by saying.

"He did?" My Matt did that for Alistair?

"I explained to him that it won't be for long," Alistair said. "Just until I get the papers and the cash draft comes through from our Parisian bank to the little Chemical office out here."

I was still astonished Matt had agreed. He was so finicky about his privacy. Unless . . . Could he have done it for my sake? To be good to me because he was feeling guilty about spending so much time with Thaddeus? (I knew how much time exactly; I had my acquaintances, my

friends, my spies, in and around the harbor and at the Botel.) Whichever it was, I'd have to call Matt later and promise to do something extra
nice for him when I flew out. . . . If I even managed to get out there this
weekend.

"Well, if it's okay with Matt and the others . . ."

"He couldn't have been more gracious about it, " Alistair assured me.

". . . I guess it's okay with me."

"That'll be a big help! Thanks. We'll see you tonight, right?"

"Depends upon what happens here."

"The reason I ask is that we decided to cook dinner tonight."

Matt cook? He burned boiled eggs! But Alistair surely must have
learned to cook in his years as a French château co-owner and house-
husband. I told him not to bother. Or at least to wait an hour. "I'll call
Matt and tell him my plans for tonight when I know them."

"Thanks again, Cuz. You're a lifesaver."

"Sweet with a hole in my head," I responded, but he'd already hung up.

"I thought you'd want to take that call," the Grunt said. He'd quite
shamelessly eavesdropped, leaning on the desk adjacent to where I'd
perched.

He was just oozing questions: Who was Alistair really? What was his
place, his function, his precise importance in my life?

That's one of the down sides to having a really good, a truly involved,
assistant: they give themselves over completely to your life. They adore
whom you like. Despise and abhor whom you dislike. Go out of their
way to do things you might do for some in your life if you only had the
time to do them. Go out of their way to ruin and undo those you'd make
trouble for if you only had the time. In short, they help you live your life
a bit better, fuller, and more satisfyingly. Yet at the same time they de-
tract from it by always being there and always letting you know that you
wouldn't enjoy, say, the latest Broadway hit if they hadn't moved heaven
and earth to get you the best seats in the house, or you wouldn't have
gotten so spectacularly laid by that cute and terribly grateful number if
they hadn't arranged the job interview for him that you'd promised un-
thinkingly that night, when the head of your dick was running your
brain, even though you were meaning actually to follow through and

somehow never managed to get around to it. For this, and for his as-suming control over things, whether or not I wanted, the Grunt, like all such good assistants, had to be kept in place, even knocked down, rea-sonably often.

"What is *wrong* with your pants cuffs?" I suddenly asked the Grunt, having just noticed them and seeing an easy way to get back at him. "Is this some sort of play for sympathy so I ask Harte for another raise for you?"

He stood up and smiled his crooked smile, which was the only time the Grunt even remotely approached human standards for cuteness. He knew we'd begun to play the Game; he'd half expected it, even if he'd not known precisely how I'd introduce it this time. Before his basic submissiveness asserted itself, he said, "Frayed denim cuffs is the cur-rent style."

"In Bora Bora, perhaps! In Lvov, certainly! Or Ouagadougou!"

"What would a Pines Queen know about style!" he said, lisping saliva all over himself. He grandly spun away and waddled off to his desk, where he sat down primly and picked up the ringing phone. I could read his still-quivering-with-anger lips form the words "Hello, Beverly Hills Hotel, Front Desk!"

At her desk nearby, Sydelle pretended to be too engrossed in search-ing for something in her purse to notice the Grunt's irritation.

I now dared enter the lion's den.

Harte was on the telephone—naturally. He saw me right away and gestured me into the office with that youthful eagerness that convinced me that I—or the magazine—was facing a real problem.

"You're right you're right you're right," Harte was saying into the phone to someone, his surprisingly deep baritone voice sounding totally insincere, at least from this end.

His pale, wildly curling caterpillar eyebrows trembled as he shook his head from side to side, mimicking something silly, the head of a jack-in-the-box perhaps.

"Tell me everything! Every single word!" Harte said, sounding even more insincere to me, but evidently not to whomever he was speaking, who began to tell him just that—everything. Harte now aped a suddenly deflated balloon and almost vanished behind his desk in his airlessness.

I took the time to look around at the office. Despite the fact that it was located not ten feet from my desk, I seldom came in here. Harte's involved approach to *Manifest* meant he was often at my desk or at the ad manager's desk or in Newell's inner sanctum. Even so, the place had its idiosyncrasies—some constant, others changing—by which one might gauge our publisher's mood.

Among these, "Jersey Joe," Harte's nearly life-sized stuffed panda, was the most mutable and thus more or less the most emblematic. Joe partly derived his name from the sweater he'd arrived wearing: a basic pullover in the colors of Harte's alma mater, Swarthmore. The other part of his name came from his face—surely the most pugilistic of any teddy bear, never mind panda, ever manufactured: not evil, simply aggressive. Over the years since Jersey Joe had taken up residence in the office, he'd moved from the desk to the floor to a lamp table to the wing chair. His clothing changed too: sweaters exchanged for antique rayon Hawaiian shirts (with matching Ray-Bans, natch), and then onto argyle vests, to Greek boat-neck shirts, to formal shirtfront and black bow tie—all with appropriate accessorization. Today, I couldn't help but notice, Jersey Joe was hung from a wall peg some eight feet off the ground, by the straps of his studded black leather S/M harness. Hung facing the wall! Each of his stuffed arms and legs had been bound with leather thongs, heavily knotted, pulled up behind his back! His motorcyclist's cap had been knocked forward, shoved down over his always inscrutable button eyes! Uh-oh!

"Blithering idiot!" I heard Jersey Joe's master utter, and I spun around to see the phone already hung up. Harte picked up the receiver again and punched his assistant's line. "If you let him get through to me once more, An-Tho-Nee, I will personally feed you ground glass! Do you understand?"

Then to me he said, "What's all that on your neck?"

I looked down at myself. "I guess they're hickeys!"

Annoyance vanished, and Harte's childlike face lit up with glee. "Dirt!" he shouted. He jumped up, ran to the door, opened it a few inches, and screamed out, "Dirt! Dirt! At last! I've got dirt on Roger!"

"Calm down, Forrest." One of his many affectations was to be called by his middle name. "My lover did it."

His infantine mouth opened all the way. He slammed the office door shut and turned to me. In his preppy chinos and loafers, his pale-blue oxford shirt and school tie, Stephen Forrest Harte resembled an eleven-year-old trying to look adult. His prematurely gray hair, almost platinum in color but purposely kept long enough for Shirley Temple-esque curls, didn't help change that impression. Nor did his bambino features: the pudgy cheeks, the playing marble-blue eyes, and pug nose. With all that so prominent, his sketchy mustache and five o'clock shadow virtually vanished.

"Your lover? Your lover of five years? Matthew the gorge-o?"

"The same."

"How perfectly gro-tesque!" He returned to his desk chair and sat himself down wearily. "Roger Roger Roger, when will you ever learn? To have actual, consensual, physical intercourse with one's lover of five years, even a lover as admittedly spectacular as Mr. Longudick, is barely comprehensible. To have that intercourse in such a manner that one perforce bears upon one's very person the unambiguous and ambulatory proof! . . . Even if one's lover *is* half-Italian *and* given to strange bursts of inappropriately spousal passion . . . This, in the eyes of Nature, not to mention Art, and it goes without saying all Civilized Tenets of Behavior, is gro-tes-quely unacceptable!"

"You mean you and Twining don't play 'Hide the Salami'?"

"Heaven forfend! Twining and I have a *mariage blanc*. It's one reason why we're invited to the best homes in East Hampton, you know."

Mmmmn, I thought, I can live very well without invitations to East Hampton, and you may eat your heart out, little fellow. "You wanted to see me?"

"I did?" Harte asked, looking like a preteener caught inspecting a condom for rips.

"The Grunt said . . ."

He suddenly remembered. "Oh right! It's this!" He held up a photocopy of the second spot feature article from the issue that in about nine minutes was to leave the art director's studio and go to press. My heart sank. I'd guessed it would be bad. Now I steeled myself and peered more closely at Sydelle's article, an exposé titled "Jocks in the Powder

Room," with my subline "When it comes to sex, some dykes in the sports world are real wolves!"

"What's the problem?" I asked, trying not to sound too concerned.

"Her!" He pointed to a picture of an all-too-well-known athlete. "If we're going to print that she laps cunt juice, we need proof."

"We've got proof! Two girls said . . ." I hunted for the place.

"Three! We need three!" he insisted.

"Oh, come on!"

"Three!"

"What is this, *The Daily Planet* or something?"

"Three or the dirt on her goes!"

"It's the linchpin of the entire article!" I argued.

"Three!"

"Well, then take the article out. . . . I don't care! You were the one who wanted her to do a feature," I said wearily.

"I still want it!"

"I'll tell her the feature's gone," I said, about to leave the room.

"You're not listening, Rog. I *want* the feature! *You* get the third piece of evidence!" Harte said.

"You want Brenda Starr?" I asked. "I take size ten fuck-me pumps."

"We've got to have more than one journalist involved. In case we're sued. And it'll help that you're a male. With only a woman giving the evidence, they could say it's sour grapes or something."

"And how exactly am I supposed to get evidence between now and the time the issue goes to bed?"

"Wasn't Sydelle working up something? Some maid at the motel?"

"Fell through. She wouldn't talk without money. Up front! U.S. Post Office money order!"

"You've got to get her on the line and pressure her."

"*You* pressure her."

"You're the editor."

"Ex-editor! The hell with you and her out there and all the dykes in sports," I said. "Because I just quit."

"You quit every month." Harte said the obvious.

"I'm so relieved!" I ignored him, addressing Jersey Joe's back in an exaggeratedly relieved tone of voice. "Now I can spend some time with my macho lover at our lovely summer house. Instead of being treated like dirt in this hellhole."

"Please, Roger?" Harte suddenly fell on his knees and grabbed at my pants and begged with his little-boy face and voice. "Please, please, please? You know it will be great. You know everyone will be talking about the article. You know that you'll scoop 'em all."

He went on and on like that, in his usual totally bogus self-humbling act, dragging in my so-called personal pride in the magazine, throwing back at me things that I'd previously said in completely different contexts—in short, irritating and infuriating, yet also daring, me.

When his whining had reached a certain decibel level, I said, "I'll try. No promises!"

"I know you can . . ."

"I'd just as soon see the article out, her working for *Ms.*, and you fucking your lover!"

Harte drew himself up to his complete five feet, three inches and said with the greatest of dignity, "Now *that* last was unnecessary *and* scurrilous!"

I was already out the office door, wishing I had a dozen daggers to toss at the cause of all this *ágita*.

"Bernard! Mizz Auslander!" I called them to my desk. "Newell! Betty Jean! Nurses of all sizes and shapes! Help! Disaster looms!"

Only the first two that I'd called actually arrived at my desk. I held out the offending paragraph, but before I could get out a word, the Grunt said, "He wants a third attribution, right?" He turned to Sydelle. "I said you'd never get away with two!" he added, having long ago mastered the art of making someone feel like shit.

For her part, Sydelle looked one part nauseated, one part secretly pleased she'd managed to make trouble for me, and one part actually frightened. I found myself torn between wanting to comfort her and wanting to pitch her out the window and watch her land directly atop her chic Mako slantcut.

"Mizz Auslander! Get the motel maid on the phone," I instructed. "Bernard! Once she's reached her, you take over!"

"What are you going to do?" Sydelle asked.

"Soften her up! Bernard, you know what to do! Promise her anything. David Bowie's genitalia on toast points if you have to. Then, scare her. Not too much. Do Mr. Sinister. When she's ready, transfer her to me. I'll be waiting."

"Wait a minute. I don't understand . . . ," Sydelle began.

The Grunt had scurried to his desk. He was hunched over the phone, a great hairy spider, cracking his knuckles and chuckling to himself with glee.

Sydelle's eyes began to widen. "What are you . . . ?"

"Mizz Auslander! *Ne* say a word *pas*! Just dial!"

It took fifteen minutes for Sydelle to reach the hapless motel maid, ten minutes more for the Grunt to turn her into trembling aspic, another fifteen minutes for me to take down a statement while two other people in the office—including Harte, *lui-même*—listened in.

Two hours later, when the new piece had been typeset and laid into the article, and Newell Rose's artistic ego had been stroked and Harte's publisher's ego caressed, and the printer's messenger had left the room with the corrected boards, I looked into Harte's office and said, "If you're smart, you won't expect me in on Monday."

And slammed his door before he could explode.

"They're holding the last seaplane of the evening for you," the Grunt told me as he handed over my weekend bag. "There's a cab waiting downstairs."

"Bernard, you're an angel," I said, folding my Dunhill sport jacket over my arm as I turned and rushed to the door. "When I return," I shouted behind myself, "I'll give you anything you want. Anything!"

"The head of Sydelle Auslander," he shouted, following me out into the hallway, where I'd just pressed the elevator button. "In a Peck & Peck hat box!" he remembered to add, as my car arrived and I stepped in.

"Hello? Anyone home?"

I dropped the weekend bag onto the floor, unrolled my pants cuffs, which hadn't gotten wet, and aimed myself toward the kitchen, looking for something to drink and munch on and smoke.

The seaplane trip had been madness. The company pilots were obviously hired only after they'd completely failed any mental exam designed: they ran the gamut from the merely irresponsible to the totally schizophrenic. Today's sky jock had thought it amusing to "dive-bomb" any staidly flying smaller aircraft within visual range. We three passengers had given up trying to convince him to cease these antics after he'd responded to our first try by declaring, "My wife left me this morning and took my only son! *I* have no reason to live!" So we three quietly shared a handful of Valium 10s, thinking that, at the least, fewer bones would break in the crash if we weren't Quite-So-Tense!

Despite my calls, no one answered: I had the house to myself. I located, put together, and sipped a gin and tonic, found a lengthy roach of Matt's best Michoacán grass in an ashtray and lighted up, stripped to my briefs, and stepped out onto the little deck on the side off the kitchen.

As a house, Withering Heights wasn't much: an early sixties cottage on stilts with a living room, dining room, kitchen, and master bedroom suite. Sometime later, another wing with two more bedrooms and bath had been added on the other side of the living room. This separation made it almost perfect for two "married" couples like ourselves to rent together. Even so, the rooms weren't large, nor were they well laid out, nor were they even particularly attractive. The walls were thin, storage space was barely adequate, kitchen and bathroom fixtures nothing to write home about, and those touches of "individuality" that had existed originally—artwork, throw pillows, curtains—were in such ghastly taste that after one exchanged look of horror, we instantly consigned them to a chest under the house uttering a collective sigh of relief.

On the other hand, the location was perfection. The three-quarter wraparound deck provided a front view of the ocean, with intervening houses giving what the rental agent called "foreground definition." No matter, we saw enough of the ocean, and heard it clearly, constantly. The much wider side deck was hidden from neighbors, and from the boardwalk, behind fast-growing, unruly beach plum; away from the wind, it was ideal for sunning and eating. The narrow strip of back deck facing north was the real prize: it lofted so high above its surroundings that we had a truly spectacular 180-degree view—the entire community all the way east to the harbor, all the way west beyond the Burma Road.

Included was a vast seascape of the Great South Bay, from the little beach at the end of our walk scarcely big enough to launch a few skiffs from, but six miles deep on the horizon to where Sayville glimmered during the day and glittered yellow and white at night.

Back there, facing what promised to be a divinely multitonal sunset, I sat, nine-tenths naked, the crack of my ass athwart a railing some fifty feet above a sheer drop down to sand and a wind-twisted pine, puffing a joint and sipping my gin, wondering where the hell everyone was.

A thumping sounded along Sky Walk: two people had just turned off the main walkway, Fire Island Boulevard, and had begun climbing the hill toward our house, though I couldn't from this angle make out who. Matt's steps were familiar to me, naturally: I'd often lain in bed editing copy or reading and listened to his approach. No. Not him. This must be . . .

"*Carajo*! Just what I needed today! A nail in my foot!"

. . . Luis and Patrick! Out of their hands, two brown bags full of grocery shopping dropped onto Sky Walk, while Luis hopped around swearing and Patrick dashed in, tall and tan and distraught. "I need the first aid kit!"

"Fuck that!" Luis shouted. "Get a hammer!"

I found the tool, and Patrick dropped the first aid kit on the outdoor table and mimicked someone about to tear out his hair by the roots. Luis proceeded to hammer the nail so deep into the wood one couldn't see it.

"The foot, Thor!" I said when he hobbled onto the deck. And when he'd lifted it onto the chair, I added, "What a baby! That's not bad. I'll fix it in a jiff."

"Oh, honey," Luis sighed. "The day I've had you wouldn't believe!"

"Have a joint!" I said. "Have a Valium! Have three!"

"You're not even surprised to see me here?" Luis asked, as I disinfected and lightly wrapped his bruised toe. "Let me tell you why I'm not in the city. This guy, Sternmetz or whatever his name is, we're doing the humongous party for tonight? He comes by the place this morning and he asks to see everything. Then he says, 'You're not going to be there overseeing, are you?' And I said, 'Sure, why not?' Then he says he don't want no spics around. He calls me a spic! *Me!* I tell him I'm no

spic, I'm a Cubano! My grandfather born in Spain, a *hidalgo* from Ex-
tremadura! You think he cares? If Tommy and Eloise hadn't been there,
he would have walked out with a carving knife in his chest! Then . . .
Thanks, hon, you're an— Wait a minute! Don't I get a lime wedge?
That's better."

When I could get a word in edgewise, I told Luis about my day. We
all commiserated, and they went in to change for Tea Dance, leaving
me on the side deck in a deck chair, by now, with grass on top of gin on
top of those Valium, feeling little even recognizable as tension, never
mind pain.

The sky was doing something wispy and purply—what a display!—
when Matt and Alistair arrived home.

They were singing "My Girl," what sounded like the Rolling Stones'
rendition, and they were carrying a half dozen shopping bags between
them.

"You made it!" Matt seemed surprised. He slid onto the deck chair
and tried to nuzzle up to me. He had tequila on his breath and stared at
the marks he'd made on my neck with apparent satisfaction.

"Guess where we were!" Alistair asked, dropping the bags.

"Harry Belafonte's Casa Calypso?" I ventured.

"No, silly!"

"At a fund-raiser for Tom Hayden given by Jane Fonda in complete
Barbarella drag?" I tried.

"Tea! And before Tea, shopping! Come! I'll show you what we
bought."

We trooped into the guest bedroom, where Alistair dumped the bags
onto the double bed and began to display, explain, and try on each item. I
noticed that they were well chosen, expensive as one could manage, and in
the exactly correct colors and shades for his by-now-two-week-old tan.

"*You* could wear this!" Alistair put the cotton sweater against my
chest. "See, Matt! How good it looks. We have the same coloring. I'll
bet you didn't know that when we were children, Rog and I were almost
identical. I swear!"

Luis and Patrick joined us long enough to ooh and ah sufficiently,
then headed off to Tea, Luis complaining. "Not so fast. My poor toe."

"Of course, I have better bones," Alistair said at the mirror.

"More of them, certainly!" I added. "Especially in your head!"

"Cunt!"

That led to a pillow fight, which Matt was forced to break up by threatening spankings—"Yes! Spank me. Or better yet have the head-master spank me!" Alistair shouted. I was dragged out of the room and told to change for Tea. Alistair threw a new sweater into my bedroom. "It's yours, Cuz."

Fifteen minutes later, cleaned up, dressed, separated by Matt in the middle with an arm over each of our shoulders, yet not at all sobered up, we ascended the three steps to the Blue Whale, where Gloria Gaynor's cover of "Reach Out, I'll Be There" was tearing the place apart.

Seeing us come up the stairs, Luis turned on his heel and said in an overly loud and desperate tone of voice, "Stop!"

". . . in the name of love!" we all three sang back, totally unprompted, complete with the extended halt gesture the Supremes had used.

A round of applause greeted this arrival on the deck. Luis put a hand to his chest and said, "I've haven't been so moved at Tea since I heard that Spanish Anna walked into the surf wearing a nine-hundred-dollar Halston with a drink in each hand and was never seen again."

Patrick guided us to the back bar, where Carlton Fuller, once and eternally the "Marlboro Man," though he never smoked a cigarette in his life, was just putting together one of the blue liquidities which were a specialty of the *maison*. He winked at Matt: we'd arrived!

It had been a while since I'd been at Tea, never mind been there with Matt, who, on the other hand, did go fairly often. So I was somewhat surprised by how he'd managed to work out a way of dancing without moving that one foot at all. Evidently, Alistair was oblivious to the prob-lem. I must have looked puzzled as I moved around my lover, because he suddenly caught me around the waist, lifted and dipped me, leaving me off balance and thus vulnerable.

In those seconds before he hefted me back onto both of my feet, *something* passed between Matt's eyes and mine, although I wasn't cer-tain then or afterward what exactly it signified.

Jeffrey Roth, my dance buddy, appeared at that moment, as though

out of thin air, and pulled me away from the others with his terpsi-
chorean skill and sheer *joi de danse*. We continued dancing for several
more cuts, long and short, even though I noticed the others leave the
floor to go out onto the open deck. I had to beg Jeffrey to stop.

As always in the ten minutes before Tea ended on a good-
weather weekend eve, the place was completely jammed. Jeffrey
pulled me over to the metal steps leading up to the Botel's upper
floors, and we leaned and looked.

"Congratulate me! I'm in lust!" he said.

"You're always in lust," I said.

"His name is Lawrence. Not Larry, Lawrence! He's an investment
banker from Shaker Heights. He's got a washboard stomach, eyes the
color of the Pacific in July, and the Dick of Death!"

"So you're tinting your hair blond, having your tubes tied, and buying a new wardrobe from Bendel's before you move to Ohio."

"You're just jealous! Who's the number dancing with your lover?"

I stood up and peered in.

"That's no number. That's my cousin Alistair."

"*That* is a number, no matter who you claim he is. Look at his buns in
those white ducks," Jeffrey said. "Like two babies fighting under a blanket. Not to mention the sublimity of his long, sun-streaked ash-blond
hair falling over his sun-splashed cheeks and aristocratic nose."

I looked again. All I saw was Alistair. "You're making that up."

"Ex-*cuse* me!" Jeffrey grabbed a lad—Owen, known for giving blow
jobs while humming Rossini's "Largo al Factotum"—and said, "Owen,
see that one? Tallish, slender, blond with the ass and legs?"

"Dancing with Matthew Loguidice?" Owen asked. (Everybody
knew Matt.)

"The same. Would you do it with him?"

Owen pursed his lips and went "Mnmmm."

"Get closer if you need to," Jeffrey suggested.

Owen left the staircase and went inside. When he emerged, he
gave a thumbs-up sign, stuck his tongue out the side of his
mouth, and rolled his eyes.

"What'd I tell you! Your cousin's a bona fide number!"

"Pul-eeze! Owen would go down on a flagpole."

"I'd watch your little country cousin," Jeffrey said. "Those types seem so innocent, until they get their claws into your man. Then . . ."

I laughed. "You're way off. Alistair Dodge couldn't be more sophisticated. Or uninterested. He's nursing a broken heart from his divorce with one of the Bay Area's wealthiest heiresses."

"In the immortal words of Maria Montez in *Cobra Woman*, 'I haff spo-ken!' " Jeffrey declared. "Are we on for tomorrow at the Ice Palace? Say no and I'll have both your legs broken. Wait up, Owen. I've got to dance to this song or I'll scre-eam!"

No one was answering the phone. So I did.

I dragged my body out of bed and into the living room. Astonishment: it wasn't three in the morning. It was too bright for that, too sunny, too . . . What did the clock read? Ten? No! Impossible!

"You sound three-quarters asleep," Marcy said on the other end.

"I'm *completely* asleep. Where are you?"

"In town. And I'm Nile green with envy. Is it as beautiful out there as I suspect it is?" she asked.

"Scrumptious," I said, trying to focus on the deck.

"Make that forest green with envy. Russian green. Crocodile gree—"

"Hold on, will you? I'll move to the kitchen. Got to get coffee."

"I'll call back when you're awake," Marcy said and hung up.

I made an enormous Chemex of it, drank an entire mugful, and was carrying a second mug outside along the side deck, trying to shake myself into semiconsciousness, when I heard a voice from out of the guest bedroom.

"That coffee I smell?"

Alistair: awake.

"Tons of it."

"I don't think I can move. I danced so hard last night. You wouldn't bring in your cup so I could have a sip?"

He sounded so pathetic I did as he asked. The bedroom appeared pretty much a-tumble. But while sleepy-looking, and with his hair swept up in six different directions at once, Alistair—nude but for a pair of pale-yellow briefs—certainly didn't look as terrible as he sounded. In fact, I was thinking, this divorce seemed to be doing at least his body some good. The last time I'd seen him this unclothed he'd been a bit zaftig.

I perched on the edge of the mattress.

"Now, don't tell me I should have been a good little boy like you last night," Alistair began.

"Because I plotzed at dinner before even dessert?"

"Because you stayed home and got beauty sleep. I do admire your stamina. Work your butt off all week, then out all weekend boogying. This coffee's good. I promise I'll get my own."

"You better. You've almost finished this."

To my surprise, he threw an arm around my shoulder, drew me close, and rubbed his cheek against mine.

I moved away, embarrassed, suspicious, and covered it by saying, "Please! Beard burn! What'll people say?"

"I know what Matthew will say," Alistair said and leaned back on the pillow. "You know, I had no idea. Sim-ply had no i-dea!"

I waited.

"That Matthew was such a wonderful man!" Alistair explained. "I mean, I do have eyes, so I could *see* he was gorgeous. But . . . so bright and smart and sensitive . . . as though he reads your mind and then does exactly the right . . ." Alistair shook a finger at me. "You should have told me when I arrived that what I was wearing was . . . And Matthew's taste! You must trust him in everything! Simply everything!"

"Almost everything," I demurred. "You stayed here last night? At the Sandpiper?"

"No one goes to the Grove on a Friday night! We didn't get home till I don't know. Sunrise. God, this place is scrumptious! You're so lucky."

"Tell me."

"I mean really lucky. I envy you."

"If we were in China, now I'd have to disfigure myself so as to ward off evil spirits," I said.

The phone rang again. Marcy: "We've got to talk seriously. Whatever did you do to Sydelle?"

"Do?" I asked.

"She said . . . It took me a half hour to get it out of her, she was so upset. I couldn't believe . . . She said . . . Well, really, Rog, I didn't expect this from you!"

"Expect what?"

"She said you humiliated her."

"I saved her fucking article! Which was about to be thrown out."

"Sydelle said your publisher told her *you* wanted it thrown out."

Little two-timing creep—I'd stuff him inside his panda!

"Marcy, listen . . ." I then explained the whole business.

"I don't know," Marcy said. "I could understand Sydelle being upset about the way you two treated that hotel maid."

"We were scum!" I admitted. "Journalists can be scum! She'd better get used to that if she's working with us."

"Don't take it out on me," Marcy defended herself.

Just then I heard a noise. Someone at my end picking up or putting back the receiver. Wait a minute! Not here, but there! Sydelle herself. She'd been there all the while. Listening in. Hearing what I had to say. That . . . !

"You tell Mizz Auslander if she can't dish it out with the big boys, she's got no business in the kitchen," I shouted and hung up.

A few minutes later, the phone began to ring again. I ignored it, still fuming from the last call, and took a fresh mug of coffee out to the front deck. Luis appeared in the doorway, holding the phone. He was wearing only white jockeys and had a piss hard-on. The rest of his body looked extra hard, dehydrated from a night out, his taut skin an edible cinnamon tan. Once again I thought what great-looking guys I had as pals and roommates.

"Well?" he asked about the phone call.

"Under no circumstances." I shook my head, and Luis shrugged, said something into the phone, hung up, and toddled off, no doubt to the john.

Sometime after Luis, Alistair, Patrick, and I had breakfasted, Matt deigned to awaken. I'd just made a fresh round of French toast and eggs for him when Marcy phoned a third time. She sounded upset. She said if I hung up again, our friendship was over. It took almost an hour to calm her down, by which time the others had all eaten, showered, and taken off for the beach.

Even Matt had gone, and he seldom went near the sand. Not that he didn't want to show off his body—he did—but because it was so difficult hiding his foot on the beach, and because of the many possible injuries he might sustain if he went barefoot. At the beginning of each season, he'd go out there with me wearing sneakers and socks. Later on, when those were too hot to wear or seemed too silly or obvious, Matt stayed away. In vain did I attempt to explain that not a single one of the dozen numbers who hung around our beach towels as pesky as blackflies in August gave a thought to his foot, for Chrissake! About the lowest their eyes ever traveled was Matt's crotch. Now, however, it seemed that Alistair and he had worked out a better solution: a tightly wrapped bandage over the top of Matt's foot covered his missing toes and allowed him to be otherwise barefoot while sitting down. He'd use a pair of loose-fitting loafers to walk in. It looked natural and required little explanation.

Neither did the way in which Ivan—the Australian bathing suit model—suddenly got up from our beach blanket when he saw me coming down the stairs onto the beach at Ozone Walk. Alistair had joined Luis and Patrick in the surf. Matt was alone at the towels. I saw Ivan say something final to Matt, then take off. He swerved gracefully around the volleyball players and jogged off down the beach. I dropped my beach bag next to where Matt sat, took out my towel, paperback, and sun block.

"I know, I know," Matt said before I uttered a syllable. "He gave crabs to John Neary last month."

"Well, he did!" I handed him the Tropic Tan. "Smear some of this on my back!" I commanded, putting myself in his hands.

"This stuff's really thick! What is it?" Matt asked.

"Solidified semen. Read the label."

"You read; my hands are covered. This stuff reminds me: did I tell you? Last weekend I was in Gunther's house on Coast Guard Walk and found some great cucumber-avocado dip in the fridge. I was poking into it with some pita when his housemate sees me and screams 'Stop! You're eating my face mask.' "

"Dieter? The skinny one?" I asked. "His complexion's so bad he needs Plaster of Paris as a face mask! That feels good. Thanks for going out last night with my cousin. In fact, thanks altogether for everything with him."

"It's okay. I like him," Matt said. And finger-wrote R-O-G inside a heart on my back.

"Well, he told me he thought you were the cat's pajamas. You've got a regular mutual admiration society going."

"Don't be bitchy," Matt said. "It makes those lines around the edge of your mouth that you hate."

"Now who's being bitchy!" I said. We wrestled until the others emerged from the ocean and shook cold water on us, making me jump up.

Soon enough we were holding court for the entire Ozone Walk Beach Club, not to mention passing acquaintances. Even that other great-looking and "Socially Significant" Pines couple—Nick Rock and Enno Poersch, who'd been together a year less than Matt and me—felt compelled to stop by and schmooze.

After a while, Alistair pulled me up and dragged me into the surf. After some body surfing, I noticed that Ivan had returned to our beach towels. And even though Matt was ignoring him as I'd asked him to, I was afraid I'd be unable to hide my nastiness toward the model if I went back while he was still there, so I remained standing around the strand, lounging in a tide pool, watching two guys madly necking in the surf à la *From Here to Eternity*, while a few feet away, two oblivious little boys with beach pails and shovels were busily conferring about the sand edifice they were building, and a black retriever was enjoying the hell out of rolling himself back and forth in the wet sand.

Alistair hooked his arm into mine. "Got the divorce papers," he said.

"Oh, Stairs, I'm sorry!"

"It's okay, Stodge. In a way, I'm glad. I rented a house here."

"You what?"

"For the rest of the season. You can see it from your back deck. It's on Floral Walk between Fire Island Boulevard and Bay. Not very big. No great views like your place, of course. Too flat for that. But it has a garden. Big deck. Pool."

I must have looked surprised.

"I figured I'd be able to lick my wounds and recover here as well as anywhere," Alistair explained. "Especially surrounded by such good, helpful friends. Back on the Coast," he began haltingly, "when we were working together . . . remember? Even though it was San Francisco and even though we had it good, I thought I'd have to . . . you know, be like everyone else."

I wasn't sure I knew what he meant.

"Funny, isn't it? I came out years before you. But once you came out, you were *out*! I never suspected there could be a life like this. A place like this where I'd fit in, and not ever have to make excuses or give explanations for what I said and thought and felt and did . . . I don't mean everyone so beautiful and so free to be themselves and of course to be gay. Well, yes, I guess that's exactly what I do mean! Am I babbling?"

He was, but I was glad he was.

Three great-looking numbers—one corn-silk blond, one darker blond, and one redhead—with three different but absolutely stunning bodies, in three similarly paneled Speedos, were walking toward us, smiling.

"CYT's ahead," I announced.

The Cute Young Things split apart to let Alistair and me through, then immediately turned around as they passed, to see us turning around to look them over. All five of us laughed, then continued on our opposite ways.

"Get you!" Alistair scolded. "With Matthew Loguidice not a hundred yards down the beach."

"You're right! Absolutely right!" I admitted, in a tone of mock shame. "But they are cute!" I allowed myself a dramatic sigh. "God, I love men!"

Alistair whooped and began to do cartwheels on the sand.

I don't know if Roy Thode actually had a name for the sequence, although I wouldn't be at all surprised. He'd been playing it more or less intact for the past several weekends at the Ice Palace, around 4 A.M. Sunday morning, when the place was at its most crowded and dancingest. Jeffrey Roth, my dance buddy, had recognized the sequence first and called it "Good Times," because it usually included the Chic song of that name, the biggest hit of the summer, which Roy himself claimed to have been the first DJ to "break," earlier that year at Twelve West's White Party. The next four or five numbers varied but generally included "Party of the First Part," Gloria Gaynor's "Casanova Brown," and Carly Simon and James Taylor's very danceable remake of Inez and Charlie Foxx's sixties tune "Mockingbird." Whatever other cuts were included, the sequence generally climaxed with the Trammps' sizzling "Disco Inferno," and when one thought it couldn't go any further, Thelma Houston's unstoppable "Don't Leave Me This Way," which had—in its short history—already become known as the Gay National Anthem. After that, three loud, clanging chords slammed in, followed by a much lighter instrumental mix, say Abba's "Dancing Queen" or Gaynor's "Searchin'."

Patrick and, especially, Luis swore that behind the anodized gold and brushed aluminum dual turntables, Roy Thode used the sequence to end his "uptrip" of the night and to launch his "downtrip."

One cloudy afternoon a month before, while I was shopping in the Grove, hanging around with Barbara, an attractive transvestite I knew from the city, who worked at a clothes shop just off the dock, I'd almost casually encountered the DJ himself and had gotten to flirting with him. One thing led to another—Barbara's offer of a Quaalude apiece (Rorer 412, the best) hadn't hurt—and Roy and I had ended up at the place he rented off Doctors' Walk. After sex, I asked him to confirm or deny the Luis Narvaez theory of the "climactic sequence." I soon discovered that while Roy was sweet and possessed a stiff, long wiener, drugs had—as we were wont to say—already significantly T.T.T.—i.e., Taken Their Toll—on the lad, particularly upon his memory circuits. He seemed unaware of what he had played the previous weekend, and had no idea what I was talking about, which to Jeffrey, the Jungian Supreme, proved absolutely nothing.

Tonight, Roy had begun the sequence more subtly: A Taste of Honey's "Boogie Oogie Oogie," Anita Ward's new hit "Ring My Bell," then Shirley and Company's naughty "Shame, Shame, Shame" leading into the key "Good Times."

Me and Jeffrey were "dates" for the night, as we'd been for the past two summers. Matt's infirmity pretty much limited his dancing to begin with, and as he had become progressively more lionized as a model, he'd also become more leatherized—"Naugahydized," Jeff said in mockery—with a public stance that put down disco dancing as "Twinkie Stuff." Tonight, however, Matt had come along with us to the Grove as companion to Alistair, who also hadn't planned a full night of drugs and dancing.

Alistair had watched and listened earlier as I explained what our usual "contoured" drug trip for the night consisted of: a hit each of windowpane acid, softened with a few joints of good grass before we left the house and on the way to the Pines harbor, where we would catch one of the small water taxis to flit us across the black bay waters. Upon disembarking at Cherry Grove, we'd cosmetically inhale a hit of coke for that "Entrance Buzz" into the Ice Palace, a sort of last-minute blush-on. During the remainder of the night, we'd pick ourselves up with poppers whenever appropriate. As a rule, we eschewed angel dust and ethyl chloride, two quite popular "enchancers" among our set. But we always carried a light hypnotic—Quaalude or Dormidina—to ease our way off the acid, which could at times become speedy and teeth-clenching.

The trick to taking one's down was to do so at the exact point when one was about to be physically and mentally exhausted, yet before one actually was, so if an emergency came up—e.g., one had to trek the mile home along the beach from "Downtown" in the Grove to Sky Walk—one didn't collapse along the way. Those who didn't contour their drugs, who took too many ups or downs, or took them too early, were "pigs." Tales of extreme piggishness were gossiped about—"She was found facedown on the edge in the Grove Meat Rack, out like a light! Not even the deer would fuck him!"—and laughed at all the following week. One group of buddies so looked down on this behavior that they handed out an annual Luis Henriquez Award (named after a famous downhead) for the year's most spectacular example of a public passing-out.

Jeffrey and I had already been on the Ice Palace dance floor since after midnight; the most recently past hour without once stopping. Our drugs had peaked with the expected machine-milled perfection. Our smooth, tanned, muscled, shirtless torsos had effortlessly and rhythmically bumped and grinded and slid along six hundred other smooth, tanned, muscled, shirtless torsos from one end of the long, wall-and-ceiling-mirrored dance floor to the other, and we were back where we'd begun, near Roy in his elevated DJ booth.

To our left, Patrick and Luis were dancing together, and when I looked at them long enough to read their lips, I could tell Patrick was demanding the downs they'd brought, and Luis was shaking his head, saying no, it was too early for their downtrip. On the other side of us were Hal Seidman and Paul Popham with his cute new lover. Alongside Nick and Enno was Wes Weidener, not with his lover, tall John, but with two of the three Michaels who were their roommates that summer. Nearby was Frank Diaz with the incredible Rainer. Off to one side, against the wall, stood George Stavrinos, next to and saying something to Rick Wellikoff, the two of them laughing uproariously. Bart, in from L.A. for his annual vacation, was dancing with his pal Ray Ford, tall and lordly and blond no matter how wild he became. Near them, darkly handsome Jack Feiner was getting down with someone whom he'd flown in from Miami, while behind them Val Cavaliere was dancing with two doctors named Larry, next to big, rangy Texan Steve Lawrence and his ex, the always adorable Zeb Freedman, the two of them criss-crossing with Jimmy Peters and his boss, Mel Fante, owner of the Pines' tiny boutique.

Gloria wanted to tell us about that jive time, and everyone shouted, knowing we were in for a good long boogie. Next to me, someone—Mark Mutchnik or John Iozia—began to shake a counter rhythm on a tambourine.

We were surrounded by acquaintances, previous tricks and lovers and friends—close, old, to come, but friends, people I knew and loved and trusted and enjoyed being among.

Twice so far that evening I'd arrived at that specific and desirable point in a night of hard dancing which I named "stepping into the box." This was how Jeffrey and I had come to express that almost magical, seemingly impossible moment we'd both experienced and in search of which we drove ourselves onto the dance floor week after week. In laymen's physics, it was that precisely perfect output of physical energy required to sustain a high degree of complex rhythm and motion without any apparent effort. In more Zen terms, it was the attaining of a certain point of mental and emotional abstraction and physical enervation in which our bodies ego-lessly, will-lessly, danced by themselves! Were danced! The effects were exhilarating, the intricate cross rhythms virtually levitating our bodies off the dance floor for periods of nine or ten seconds at a time. A friend had once filmed from the sidelines while we were in "stepping into the box," and he reported that our feet did touch the dance floor, but only once for every six or seven times anyone else around us touched down.

There, I was totally relaxed, completely fulfilled . . .

I closed my eyes and spun around, and when I'd completed my spin, I opened my eyes. The hundred ceiling and side mirrors from which the Ice Palace got its name were completely fogged over, dripping with the condensation of hundreds of male bodies' perspiration. The air itself in the huge space seemed to have condensed and begun raining down in a fine, pervasive mist.

Suddenly it was no longer fever-hot inside that modernistic mirrored hogan filled with twirling limbs and thumping feet, but cool—cold, frigid, frozen, ice itself. Every chord emerging from the hundreds of suspended tweeters clanged weirdly, transformed into the clashing of vast glaciers calving massively against each other, titanic ice floes ripping themselves asunder in herculean dissonances.

As I turned in amazement, seeking confirmation in the faces of those around me, I was astonished to see all of them paralyzed, their features crystallized into finite attitudes of excruciating ecstasy or intense rictuses of agonized release, their perfectly modeled shoulders rimed blue-white, their expensively styled out-swirled hair solidified to stalactites, every worked-out limb stilled within its own glaring, gelid, unreflective light, every well-exercised torso almost transparent, encased, hollow, organs replaced by glassed drifts of icicles, every single so-familiar eye frosted by inexorable chill, blinded from final sight.

Wonder stopped me.

Terror gripped my heart.

Panic shoved me away . . . away . . . away . . .

Away from it all and out! Out! *Out!* the glass side doors into fresh air, into the night, onto the upper deck surrounding the pool. When I turned and looked back in through the sweat-frosted glass, everything, everybody was normal, in motion again.

I staggered against the railing. Behind me I heard voices. I recognized one but couldn't move yet, my chest hurt so with the devastation I'd witnessed.

A hallucination, of course. I knew that. Why that hallucination? Why so terrifying? Why now? And worst of all, why hadn't it gone away?

"Rog?"

Matt had me by one shoulder. At the other, I recognized through the recurring flashes of that arctic vision, Alistair, asking, "What's wrong, Cuz?"

"Put that shirt over his shoulders. His T's soaked through," Matt said, doing it for me. "Rog? You okay?"

"Is it . . . your drugs?" Alistair asked.

Safe, I accepted their ministrations and distractedly, slowly began to narrate what I'd seen; tried to explain how awful it had been, how alone I'd been, how horrified and alone amid images of those I knew. How cold and alone.

They listened. It was important I convince them of what I'd seen, what I was saying—Matt especially. But I could see I wasn't convincing him. He was only half-there, thinking of something else. Or someone else. Thaddeus?

That only saddened me more.

They got me to the other side of the deck. Matt wangled hot coffee from the big dyke in a WAC uniform who tended the inside bar, and that helped. I began to feel warm again, though I continued to shiver. I wanted Matt to hold me, but I was afraid to ask. I was surprised really that he didn't see what I needed. He always had before.

The big sequence ended. People poured out the glass doors onto the deck. Jeffrey and Luis and Patrick found us. Naturally they asked what had happened.

"Roger had some sort of . . . scare," Matt said.

It sounded so unserious the way he said it.

Not to Jeffrey, though, who was all concern. "What kind of scare?"

Matt attempted to piece together what I'd said, but evidently it hadn't made much of an impression on him. Jesus! I found myself thinking, what if all that I'd just experienced were nothing more than, like, some sort of correlative to our relationship, showing how Matt was, I don't know, freezing me out for Thad or something?

Jeffrey, however, took visions seriously. He asked for a description complete with details, which he helped pull out of me. I half resented this, and was half relieved that Jeffrey kept me so busy at it that I couldn't meanwhile concentrate on Matt—or he on me.

Before I was done, Luis interrupted, "Remember at the Flamingo Black Party?" he asked. "You had another vision. Remember, Rog? I found you against the wall shaking, and you told me you'd seen the entire floor drop out and all of us falling? Not just the story-and-a-half into the bank below, but far deeper, into an abyss. Remember?"

I remembered. In that earlier vision, I and a few others around the edge of the dance floor had been left standing, untouched, while all the others had plunged. But the sense of panic, of fear, had been identical.

"Time to change your medicine!" Alistair tried levity.

I was already utterly sobered up. I let the others go on talking, let them forget about me. What was Matt thinking? I couldn't tell. He seemed so far away, so not there.

Patrick emerged from the john excited. At the urinals, he'd just encountered the first guy to suck his cock. "Way back in Beloit! In college!" He'd been staggered to see the guy.

"Did he recognize you?" Alistair asked.

"No, he didn't!" Patrick sounded nonplussed. "And when I told him, he looked at me with this dead eye and said, 'Honey, I sucked more dick in college than you have hairs on your head.' For me it was a first! It was a big deal!"

That led to a discussion of first-time blow jobs and who'd given them. Everyone seemed to have a story.

After a while, Matt asked me quietly, "You okay? The last water taxi leaves soon. We're going to catch it."

Meaning he and Alistair would. Somehow the way he said it automatically and totally excluded me.

Jeffrey was still hopping around, all wired up; I supposed that I should stay and dance. He'd be annoyed and I'd regret it if I didn't. So I said, "Yeah, I'll be okay."

"I'd stay," Matt offered. "But it's such a trek home."

Meaning it would be one with his bad foot.

"Go!" I insisted. "I'll be fine!"

But I wasn't fine. I was unhappy when a few minutes later they did leave. Luis and Patrick had stepped into the Ice Palace to dance, and I heard Jeffrey say out of the side of his mouth, "Guess who's cruising you? For the third weekend in a row?"

"Who?" I asked. But I wasn't able to work myself up into even the pretense of caring.

"Wake up! Telephone."

Someone in our darkened bedroom.

"Alistair?" I asked.

"Shh! You'll wake Matthew!" he whispered. "Telephone! Your boss at work!"

"Forget it!" I said, turning over in bed. "I told him I wasn't coming in today."

"He said it's an emergency," Alistair insisted. "A fire."

"At the office?" I asked, turning back over. I could picture the next three months' worth of features in my files up in smoke. That's all I needed.

"No. The baths."

"What?"

"The baths!" Alistair said. Then, annoyed: "You talk to him!"

"What did I do to deserve this?" I moaned rhetorically.

"Keep it down! You're going to wake Matthew!"

Matt, naturally, continued sleeping like a two-year-old.

Out in the living room, it was barely dawn. I picked up the phone. If this was some dumb stunt of Harte's . . .

"There you are, finally!" Harte said. He sounded excited. "Get on the next seaplane back to town! I'll have a cab waiting for you at the East Side Heliport!"

"What the hell's going on, Forrest?"

"Really bad news! There was a fire at the tubs earlier this morning."

That was a shock. "St. Mark's? The Club?"

"The baths at Twenty-eighth Street. Do you understand what that means?"

"The absolute worst bathhouse for a fire to happen at. The others are all modernized, with sprinklers and—"

"I see you understand."

"What happened?"

"We don't know yet. We don't really know anything. Neither the fire department nor the police are even admitting it happened. I found out from someone who lives across the street."

"I don't get it. Why . . . ?"

"For years rumor said that place is owned by cops," Harte said. "Think of the scandal if people don't get out and that fact becomes known?"

"But everyone got out, didn't they?" I asked.

"C'mon on, Rog. That doesn't seem very likely, does it? Think about all the guys who go there on Sunday night and sleep over and go straight to work from there on Monday morning."

Now it began to sink in. I could picture dozens of stoned gays in those tiny, fire-loving, wooden-walled cubicles, those narrow corridors. People making out or talking after sex or sleeping. Then the lights suddenly go out. The narrow corridors fill with smoke. People begin to yell. To try to get out. In seconds, it's a complete horror show. Who did I know who'd be there on a Sunday night? Armando? Billy Bressow? Jeremy? Any of them was possible.

"How many didn't get out, Forrest?"

"I don't know yet how many, if any! But I do know we've got to get someone officially gay inside there, Rog. You understand that, don't you? So collusion doesn't take place between the owners and the cops who are on the scene and the fire department. And so if there *are* any dead, we find out about it. And who they are. And how many. Otherwise skeletons are literally going to be swept under the carpet. That's why you've got to come back here."

"You want *me* to go in there and do it?" I didn't believe it.

"The fire isn't out yet, Rog. They won't start looking for another hour. I want you on the site when they go in."

"Why me? Why not some bona fide reporter? Get, I don't know, Joe Nicholson from the *Post!*"

"You, Roger, because someone high up in the fire department owes me a favor. I'll supply you with the press pass."

"Even so, Forrest. Won't the cops stop me before I—"

"They won't stop you, because, Rog, your cousin told me he knew someone high up in the administration. His name and my connections should walk you right into the smoking ruins of that place."

I stared at Alistair, who was drinking grapefruit juice straight out of the carton. "Who do you know in the administration?" I asked him, dubious.

"He stayed at the château last year. I'll get him on the phone as soon as you've rung off."

"Will he come through for you?"

"He's in the closet. But he'll help."

Now I was impressed.

Harte hung up and I went to change. Matt slept through it all. Amazing how much I wanted to awaken him and hear him say something, I don't know what, maybe give me his blessing, or tell me I was doing good, or . . . I didn't, however. In the twenty-eight hours since he'd left me at the Ice Palace to take the water taxi, we'd barely spoken a word—certainly not one unnecessary word—as though something important, something crucial, had occurred between us, when in fact nothing had. Or had it?

When I emerged from the bedroom dressed and with some semblance of my weekend bag packed, Alistair pulled on a shirt and loafers.

"I talked to my friend. This is his name." He handed me a piece of paper. "Everything's jake. Nobody'll dare stop you from going in. C'mon," he urged, "I'll walk you to the plane."

"You don't have to come with—"

"I can't go back to sleep anyway."

The seaplane was just turning around in the bay to take on passengers when I got there. I squeezed into the third seat and watched Alistair waving. Then we were out in the mainstream, speeding along on pontoons, rising, the sun hot on the back of my neck and hair through the rear window.

Naturally, I couldn't help but think about what I was about to face. One thing was certain: I probably knew the layout in the bathhouse better than any fireman going inside.

Not that I'd been there much recently—in fact, only once in recent years. Not long after it was refurbished, someone Matt worked for—modeling semi-nude for calendars and greeting cards—had begun a new line and had thrown a large and actually quite lavish party at the remodeled bathhouse, complete with catered food. A true toga party! Everybody in the gay media had been there. People had talked about it for weeks, comparing it to other great "in-town" parties—Jean-Paul Rossel's 1978 New Year's "Rainbow Room Bash"; the '76 Flamingo Black Party, complete with a carny sideshow including over-the-hill female strippers, male fire-fuckers, S/M acts, and a six-thousand-pound hog; and the 1977 Valentine's Day "Broken Hearts Aquacade" party thrown atop an East Side co-op, with its fifty-story-high glass-enclosed Olympic-sized pool and three hundred nude guests.

As a rule, however, this particular bathhouse, allegedly the second oldest extant in the city—the St. Nicholas Tubs up in Harlem were first—was definitely not known for being stylish.

I'd first gone in 1969, some weeks after the debacle at the Selective Service Office and following my own, somewhat quieter, decision to look more deeply into being gay. I'd heard the place mentioned by someone at one of Alistair's penthouse parties and thought it might be just enough off the beaten path so I'd be able to investigate my homosexuality in some depth, and experiment with various aspects of it, in a more or less free space, somewhere I could be fairly anonymous. We're talking about a few years before bathhouses became popular and contained nightclubs and cabaret acts and such froufrou.

This one was without froufrou, definitely no-frills. Seedy. Sleazy, even. Someone once calculated that every disease germ known to man had collected in its undusted, unwashed corners over the years. Not to mention its un-Ajaxed tile floors. (I'd thought the cloth slippers they handed one at the door were silly until I looked closely at that floor.) When I'd first gotten a look at the "bathing" pool in the basement, I was reminded of a slime- and fungus-encrusted sacrificial cistern attached to a Mayan temple in some Grade B horror flick, out of which every night emerged creatures dripping with gore, gurgling eldritch monstrosities.

Despite these unsanitary conditions, the place did have a reputation for housing the hottest sex on the East Coast. Which was why I was there, aged twenty-four, barely touching the scuzzy mattress of the cot I was perched upon in my nasty little cubicle, its pressboard walls so thin I could hear every whisper and grunt in the dozen booths on either side and across the corridor.

Nervous? I was petrified! Surely only the most hard-boiled of homosexuals with nothing left to lose came here: those who'd do anything with anyone. Several of them had already scowled at me as I'd entered and found my way to this room. One was heavily muscled with a buffalo mat of hair on his chest and arms and a milky eye in a crushed socket. Another was bald and much tattooed, but wiry like an over-the-hill prizefighter. The third was simply fat, grossly fat, rolling with . . .

Well, they couldn't get at me if I stayed locked in my cubicle, smoking a joint of grass followed by one cigarette then another, could they? Neither, of course, could anyone else, assuming anyone presentable was out there. Perhaps I'd been too hasty coming here? Perhaps I wasn't ready yet?

Just then I began to hear grunting and groaning from the cubicle adjoining mine on the right. Grunting and groaning, then the sounds of a mattress, a cot, rising and falling, rising and falling: the unmistakable aural proof of sodomy only inches away! On and on the cot creaked rhythmically, until soon even those noises were covered over by voices, men's voices dragged up from deep within their larynxes: grunts and groans, sounds unthinking, primitive, primeval as the first enzyme sludge in Precambrian seas.

I leapt up from my perch. Should I leave? I couldn't possibly stay. Not with them . . . reaching such an audible climax, going "Oh, oh, oh" and "Uh, uh, uh" until I thought I'd burst with embarrassment at their now triply shared passion.

When it was clear they would not stop, one of them uttered something in a deep baritone voice. Uttered it twice, which was a good thing, since I had not been precisely certain the first time he'd said it. This time I distinctly heard him say the words "Uh! uh! uh! Pinch my tits and call me Alice!"

I never stuck around to hear if his bedmate had in fact called him Alice. I was out of my cubicle, down the stairs, outside a shower one floor below, collapsing with laughter.

The ice broken, that first visit to the baths had ended with me meeting someone young and cute and the two of us having a terrific time. I'd returned time and again, until I moved to San Francisco. But no matter whom I met or what we did, or what attitudes were posed, I could never take that place seriously again, without hearing that deep voice moaning, "Pinch my tits and call me Alice."

Now, in a single phone call, that was changed forever.

The seaplane alighted on its pontoons in the East River. I searched through the window for the familiar dumpy figure of the Grunt, who was supposed to be meeting me there. No Grunt. But I did see a gypsy cab from the usual company our cheapskate editor always hired whenever a car was needed. And there, walking toward the dock to meet me, was, of all people, Sydelle Auslander.

"Where's Bernard?" I asked, letting her take my bag. She shrugged and handed me an envelope. I opened it and took out an official-looking press pass. We'd barely gotten into the cab when it took off.

With all the fire engines, Twenty-eighth Street would be impossible. But not Sixth Avenue, and I stopped our driver there, leapt out, and began threading my way through the dozen or so fire trucks. There were three companies represented, including those from the West Village, always the cutest firemen in Manhattan—a few of centerfold quality.

"No press past dis here spot!" a detective in a streaked trench coat said and held me back. The fire had evidently been put out. I had to hurry.

"I have to get in. I know someone who was in there."

He looked me straight in the eye and said, "No one was in there. That's an abandoned building."

"Like hell it is!" I said. I spotted a guy wearing a heavy poncho over what looked like a fire department uniform.

"Captain," I called out, getting his attention, "I've got a press pass and this flatfoot isn't letting me through."

A good-looking heavyset guy in his fifties, clearly in his element and not happy with the police, the captain came over to us and took a look at my pass. He reminded me of someone, a young Cap'n Kangaroo or . . . I don't know.

"Pass looks good to me," he told the cop.

"No press on the premises. I've got orders."

I mentioned the magic name Alistair had given me. "He thinks the press should be on the premises. At least he did when I spoke to him about this, a half hour ago," I told the cop. "You want to call his office and explain to him why you're not letting me through? Or should I call myself from the pay phone and give him your badge number while I'm at it?"

He glared at me. "You stay here," the cop said, suddenly very nervous.

I saw him talk to someone in civilian clothes, evidently his superior. As I waited, the fire department captain looked me over.

"You've got some fancy friends, Mr. . . ."

"Sansarc. Roger."

"Fahey. John Anthony," he offered his name but no hand to be shaken. "I take it there's a reason your fancy friend wants you inside?"

"He wants me to see if there are any bodies. To I.D. them. To count them. He's afraid the count might be incorrect at Arson Division."

Captain Fahey bit his lower lip. "What bodies? That's an abandoned building."

"That's the official lie. The unofficial truth is that it's a well-known and heavily attended homosexual bathhouse," I said, "and it was operating when the fire broke out. I take it that the employees split at the first whiff of smoke, and I assume the management is at this moment booking long vacations in the Bahamas. But I'm going inside!"

Trench coat returned. "We don't know nothing," he said. I noticed that he'd covered over his badge with a wrapped hanky and that the guy he'd been speaking to had vanished. "But we don't want any trouble."

So I pushed my way through the wooden horses, ignoring his faint attempt at a protest, and addressed myself to Captain Fahey.

"You going to help me?"

"It's going to be . . . No one knows where to look."

I looked directly at one merry pale-blue eye and said, "I know the layout of the place pretty well."

Without flinching, he asked back, "Upstairs and down?"

"The whole place. I've been inside several times."

"You're full of surprises, aren't you? How easily do you throw up?"

"Doesn't matter. I've still got to go in."

"Okay, tough guy, let's see how big your chops really are," he said, handing me a hard fire hat and an axe, and taking one up himself, along with a long, deadly-looking flashlight.

The space directly behind the entrance booth had been knocked completely in. The ground floor of the bathhouse looked strangely open and gutted. It smelled really awful. It was still pretty dark and smoky and almost comfortingly warm.

"Downstairs!" I pointed. "The showers and the pool."

"Whoever was down there got out." He pointed up the half-burned-away stairs. "Same here. All the staff. So did the people on the next floor. If there's a problem, it's up top."

There were plenty of firemen chopping away at the remnants of the thin walls as we ascended. The captain borrowed an oxygen unit from one, and he and I both took sips from it.

The stairs to the top floor were gone. We had to be hoisted up there by rope. The air was better: no wonder—the roof had come down in sections and the place was open to the gray morning.

Fahey held a building plan in his hands. I glanced at it.

"Forget it! The place was remodeled a few years ago!"

I remembered that dozens of new, low-ceilinged booths had been installed up here in the remodeling. Some had been around a corner. It took me a while to locate them: they were through another doorway. Here, the walls were still warm, the cubicle walls still standing. It was darker too: the ceiling had held here, although it could be heard dropping in places behind us. Surely this was the least affected area of the place. It must be vacant.

As we advanced, I held up the axe protectively as Fahey instructed. Our flashlights provided only dull gleams of light. Even so, as we kicked our way into booth after booth, I ended up seeing far more than I wanted to.

Three bodies. All of them alone. Given the way his body was twisted and the contortions of his facial features, only one man had come to consciousness during the fire. It seemed to have been a momentary awareness, a rising out of sleep perhaps, though much too late for him to do anything but claw his way out the cubicle door, then retreat back inside from the smoke, and lie huddled down, and choke to death. The others both appeared to have been overcome by fumes in their sleep. Possibly drugged sleep, I thought. Doubtless exhausted-after-sexual-climax-sleep. I'd seen two of the men before. Even knew the name of one. Ironically, it turned out that a cardboard pane had been installed instead of a window on the other side of the pressboard wall in one cubicle. Had he known it and awakened, he might have punched a hole, crawled onto the ledge—and lived.

I remained outside the line of cubicles while the captain left and returned with a Homicide photographer and Forensic detectives, both of whose names I took down. I witnessed them opening the wallets and I.D.-ing each victim. Then I went with another firefighter looking for any more hidden rooms.

We didn't find any. Only the three on the top floor.

That's what I corroborated with Captain Fahey and a lieutenant from Arson Division once we were down on the street again. I saw a few reporters from the daily city desks of big papers, and I told them. My job was now done; once they moved in with their sharklike instincts for news, I could leave.

"Can I have that back?" Fahey asked.

I looked down at the fire axe I was still gripping.

Only then did I realize I'd also been clenching my teeth for maybe the past hour.

Fahey made a big show of shaking my hand.

"You were right," I said. "I wanted to barf a half dozen times."

"But you didn't," Fahey said, still holding my hand. "I've got ten-year men wouldn't have poked around like you did, looking for what you didn't want to find."

"You don't get it! I could have been one of those guys."

And when he didn't respond, I tried again.

"Those three? They're . . . We're like . . . brothers!"

"Ah!" he said quickly, darkly, with a look of agony. So he did understand.

"By the way, you happen to count the ceiling sprinklers?" I asked.

He looked at me as though I were crazy and began laughing. I could still hear him guffawing as I threaded my way through the hook-and-ladders down the block.

Sydelle Auslander jumped up from a doorway where she'd been sitting doing the *Times* crossword puzzle. "Forrest said to call him right away. There's a pay phone in there!"

A Greek luncheonette. She was smart enough to have taken the receiver off the hook so no one else could use it, to have found us a booth, and to have ordered me coffee and a bear claw for when I was done telling our editor everything I knew. I gobbled up the pastry in seconds.

"You were awfully brave," Sydelle started to say.

I thought, Come on, Harriet! Certain she was putting me on with all the bullshit about how she could never go into the building like I had.

"We were afraid of a cover-up. Interdepartmental collusion," I quickly said, watching her closely. "You know, no bodies—no fire!" She picked at her corn muffin.

I kept thinking, Okay, she doesn't smoke cigarettes. . . . She's drinking juice, not black coffee. . . . Her fingernails aren't bitten halfway down the digits. . . . Her makeup isn't off a sixteenth of an inch. . . . Why then does she seem to be a complete nervous wreck?

I ordered more food. When the waitress was gone, Sydelle said, "I *asked* to come here, today. Instead of Bernard."

That was news. I'd assumed Harte was up to something, throwing us together, hoping we'd act human toward each other. I'd meant to ask him during the call, but forgot in the barrage of his questions about the fire.

"The reason I asked," she went on, "was I wanted to be alone with you when I asked why it is that you act like . . . well, not like Marcy Lorimer says she knows you to be."

I could have acted surprised, but on some level I'd been expecting this question for a month.

"You're not Marcy," I said by way of explanation. "You're an employee. Not an old friend."

"What I mean is, why are you acting like by my being here I'm taking something from you?"

She said it with intensity, and immediately pulled away from her question, as though dissociating herself from it, or allowing it to stand on its own and do its own work.

Was I really acting like that?

"You are, you know," she answered my unspoken question, which only half fazed me: I like to think my basic honesty shows up on my face, in my attitude. "And you shouldn't," she said. "You *have* everything you could want!"

Her assurance amused me. "Oh, I do, do I?"

"You have a great job that pays well and has the potential for shaping and influencing gays all over the country. You've got terrific connections in the arts and media. You get tickets to everything. I hear you've got a nice apartment, rent-stabilized. You take a big house with great views in the Pines. You have interesting and talented friends. You're good-looking, with a nice body. You're healthy and relatively well-off. You have a handsome, famous lover, whom every gay in the city envies you for . . . despite the rumors."

I'd been listening to her, rapt, wondering exactly how much longer she intended buttering me up, and where exactly she was heading, until she'd arrived at that last, intriguing, problematic phrase.

"What rumors are those? That we're breaking up?"

She began to waffle until I gave her my own brand of "deadeye."

"Well . . . he is reportedly seen out with other guys."

"Thad Harbison is the only other guy! I know all about it. Completely platonic! Not that all of Matt's—or my own—affairs, for that matter, have been without sex. We're liberated. We've been together a few years. We have an open marriage."

"The rumors I meant weren't about Thad but . . ."

But what? She was holding firm. And of course, simultaneously withdrawing into objectivity.

". . . about Matt's background," she said.

His background? Did she mean the war?

"Matt was a gunner on a Navy destroyer and served in Southeast Asia," I said. "He received a medical discharge after two tours. Medal of

Honor. He's not particularly proud of it. Neither will he deny it. Matt was a kid when he joined up. Satisfied?"

"I didn't know he was in Nam or wounded. I was talking about something else in his background . . . his family."

"What about his family?"

"Loguidice Carting in Rye is the largest private sanitation contractor in three counties."

"What's that have to do with Matt?"

"Don't you know? I mean, he's your lover for how many years and you don't even know your lover is a major Mafia princeling!"

"He's *what*?" I began to laugh. "Wait a minute here, Mizz Auslander! The reason I know little about Matt's family is that he has virtually nothing to do with them! He talks to his folks maybe once a month on the phone. Sees them maybe once a year. He's hardly Al Capone's heir. . . . *If* what you're saying about Loguidice Carting being connected to the mob is even true . . ."

"It's true. When I was a reporter in White Plains, I found out all about private sanitation contractors upstate."

". . . And even if they are crooked, it's Matt's grandfather who owns it, for Chrissakes! Not Matt. Even his dad has nothing to do with it."

"What kind of work does his father do?" she asked.

I'd never heard that Matt's father ever held a job. "He doesn't. He has some sort of medical history. . . ." I left it vague, since that was all I really knew. "The old man, Matt's Grandpa Loguidice, pretty much takes care of the family. Which," I was fast to add, "doesn't mean he's Mafia. I've met the old man maybe twice in all these years. He wasn't even close to being Mr. Monster. Any other rumors?"

None evidently, since she was silent. My breakfast arrived and I attacked it. After being withdrawn with her juice for a while, she said, "Okay, maybe I'm out of line with all those rumors."

"Matt would probably be tickled to hear them. I, however, am offended for him. And for his ethnicity."

"I said I apologize! Let's get back to the magazine. What I'm saying is I just want a chance there."

"The *cri de coeur* of every assistant editor hired! Look, it's nothing personal," I said. "I just happen to think it's an especially stupid idea having women's stuff in *Manifest*. It'll be patronizing to the few women readers we have and ignored by the many men readers. Harte knows where I stand. I told him he ought to start another, different magazine and have you write for it."

"I see," she said quietly.

"That's where I stand."

"But right now you're stuck . . . with me," she said.

So it seemed.

"Why not make the best of it?" she asked. And before I could say something snide: "I'll keep the *Manifest* attitude in all my articles. Brash, irreverent!"

"Evidently, you've given this some thought."

"I've worked up some ideas. Articles on women that gay male readers will enjoy. For example, the meanest women in movies. Complete with photos. Crawford. Davis. Stanwyck."

" 'Golden Bitches of the Flicks!' " I said.

"Or motorcycle girl clubs on the West Coast. 'Dykes on Bikes!' Maybe a full-page color photo of one tough chick on the inside back cover . . . ?"

"No! That's prime advertising territory. Inside front cover and back cover, inside and out. But anywhere else inside the book's possible. As long as it doesn't get in the way of the male centerfold."

"It won't."

"What else?" I asked.

I listened for the next half hour to suggestions. I guessed she'd already run them by Harte, and even talked to Newell Rose, since she gave visual touches with his undeniable stamp.

The result was that I opened myself up to possibilities, and she felt she'd cracked the door open. I knew Harte was going to be breathing down my back about her work, so I might as well get the best I could. More important, I wanted her to take a load off me. Copyediting articles and stories, captioning, and fact checking were tiresome and time-consuming. If I kept her happy, allowed her to think we were a team, she'd take on more work, help me and the Grunt.

I finished my third cup of coffee and said, "Put together three trial articles. Use anyone in the office except the Grunt. Bernard," I explained. "Can you be ready in a week?"

"Can I ever."

When we got outside, Newell had arrived with his ancient Hasselblad camera and was making the usual nuisance of himself with firemen and cops. I left Sydelle with him, hoping they'd keep each other from getting into too much trouble.

"I'm glad we had this talk," she said, following me as I got into a taxi down to the magazine's office. She sounded sincere.

"Mafia princeling!" I scoffed when the taxi took off.

"What's that?" the cabbie asked.

Even so, I wondered: How much did I know about Matt's family? I'd never met his parents, though they lived an hour away by car. I'd spoken to his mother on the phone, true, but just to exchange one-liners, to say, "Matt isn't here. I'll say you called," or "Sure, I'll get him." She'd never made conversation with me while waiting, not even about the weather, for which I'd been grateful. As for Grandpa Loguidice, as I'd told Sydelle, I'd met him twice, each time in a different expensive midtown restaurant, where he'd treated Matt to dinner.

A heavyset, almost round, man in his late seventies, the senior Loguidice resembled his grandson in size—he was almost six feet tall—in the vibrant black of what little hair remained on the sides of his head, and in the entire lower half of his face—perfect Calabrian lips, astonishing dimples on either side of his mouth, a cleft chin!

He'd been warm, welcoming, intelligent. His large, dark eyes—Matt's gray beauties came from his mother—were clever and curious. I'd been impressed by how at ease old Loguidice had been (Caravelle is *way* out of our range) even though he'd admitted he seldom "dined out. Only now a little since your Grandma passed on, God rest her soul!"

Both times, Grandpa Loguidice mentioned that he'd had a playmate named Roger he'd lost track of years before. There was no doubt at all that the old man ruled his family; yet with respect and with love. Doubtless, his money paid for many of their needs and all their luxuries. But he enjoyed independence in them—"Your cousin Sylvia, sixteen, tells me to go to hell. She says she'll pay for college and go wherever she wants!"

I never had a hint that he was dictatorial. The proof was how many family members—two sons, a daughter-in-law, and two grandchildren—worked for his company.

I did get the sense he adored Matt: the way his eyes followed him doing anything—calling the waiter, say, or pouring the wine. He was proud of Matt's Navy service. He was even proud that he wrote poetry—"Can you imagine? A Loguidice a literary man with literary friends like yourself! Back in the Old Country, you know, only the *nobilità* read and wrote! Not *gabons* like us. A wonderful place, this America!"

From what I'd been able to gather over the years about the Loguidice family, Matt's father was the youngest of four brothers. Sickly from youth, he'd been pampered and protected, first by his parents then by his siblings. Because of his sporadic long hospitalizations as a youth, he'd never finished school or held a job long, but he'd married early—"My parents are one of the great romances," Matt had once told me. "They married against everyone's wishes and expectations and haven't been apart a day since." Matt had been born a year later, their only child. And while Grandpa Loguidice had plenty of grandchildren by his other sons—"I could field a football team with 'em!" he'd said over dinner—Matt, son of his favorite son, had become his favorite grandchild from the moment that the old man called his "miraculous birth!"

During those two meetings, I couldn't get any sense of whether or not old Loguidice knew Matt was gay and that we lived together. I definitely had the impression that Grandpa Loguidice had gotten around in his day. He possessed that quiet acceptance of things and people that suggests a widely lived past. The one time I'd pressed Matt on the subject, he'd irritatedly answered, "I could be sleeping with Rodan for all he cares!" Though I'd gone around the next week swooshing through the apartment as though on long, leathery wings, making what I thought were properly pterodactyl roars, Matt never said anything more. And his parents? They must know, I thought. "Who do they think I am?" I demanded. "The butler?" Matt had been vague about that too.

He saw them only for Thanksgiving. His father's birthday was close to the holiday, which coincided with their wedding anniversary and other family birthdays. So Matt would take a train up to his grandfather's big house in Rye, where the entire Loguidice clan gathered, and he'd generally be away anywhere from a day to an entire weekend. He'd invited me twice. But it had seemed so much a family affair, I'd passed it up, and he'd never mentioned it again. When I'd asked what he did there, Matt answered, "Talk, eat, play cards, eat, play touch football, eat, rake leaves, eat, watch the game on TV, eat!"

Christmas we spent together. Seasonal cards from his relatives were addressed to Matt, except those from his parents, who addressed both of us on the outside envelope and on the inside of the card itself. Lucille always signed the card in her neat elementary school penmanship, "Love, Dad and Mom."

That was better than what we got from my parents, who seemed determined to remain blind to the true nature of our relationship, even though on their invitation, Matt and I spent nights in the guestroom at their new house in Oyster Bay twice a year, and we always pushed the twin beds together. Once we'd been in the shower loudly screwing when my mom opened the bathroom door a slit to ask if we minded her washing the underwear we'd dropped on the floor. Twice, when my dad decided to discuss investments and insurance and other monetary things with me, I'd insisted Matt be present since "Our bank accounts, all our resources, are combined!" All to no avail.

I now thought that despite how much more time we actually spent in their company—both in town when they came in, and out on Long Island—and despite their chatting with us on the phone, my own family must have seemed as mysterious and unknowable to Matt as his did to me. But wasn't that one point about our new gay lifestyle? That we'd formed our own family? Not based on blood, children, or ownership, but on shared tastes and pleasures, on the love of another?

Even so, it would give me a *louche* sort of pleasure to be able to go around saying, "You know my lover, Matt Loguidice? The Mafia princeling!"

I'd hoped to get back out to the Pines early that weekend to compensate for having come into the city early. But what with the magazine's accountants flying in from wherever the hell they hung out, then having to entertain both personal and magazine-related guests from out of town, I wasn't able to free myself until the middle of Saturday afternoon, when I hopped on a seaplane.

"We've laid eyes on him maybe twice," Luis said when I asked where Matt was, "and we've been here all week."

"You have?" I asked. I didn't hide my surprise. I'd arrived at Withering Heights ten minutes before, dropped my bag, ripped off my Lacoste, and thrown myself—still sneakered and rugby-shorted—upon a chaise longue in the welcome sun on the side deck, where my housemates had set themselves up for the afternoon—complete with portable tape deck, magazines, telephone, drinks, and prerolled joints.

"We were *all* going to take off vacation time this week," Patrick said.

"Not only us, but you too. Remember?" Luis asked.

"Vaguely," I said. Of course, I remembered it now. We'd planned to all be together the entire first week in July and the third week of August. Thanks to the fucking magazine, I'd managed to miss both weeks.

But I was more concerned with what Luis had just revealed about my lover, which seemed to confirm what I'd silently gnawed on all week. Matt had stayed out here, of course, not come into town at all. We'd talked by phone twice, each time brief as telegrams.

"What you're trying to tell me," I said, "is that Matt's been with Thad all week?"

"Tha-a-ad?" Patrick hooted. "Honey, you're so totally out of it, you're weeks behind the dish on your own husband."

"Don't insult me! Just bring me up to date!"

"Thad resigned as maître d' a week ago."

"What?"

"From what we heard, he went back home. Elkville, Illinois. Can there be such a town?" Luis shuddered.

"I guess." I was still calculating. "But if that's true, and I'm not really too surprised, since I thought it was less of a 'thing' than what all the gossip said, then why didn't Matt come into town?" Before either of them could answer, I did. "Of course! To be with you two!"

Luis and Patrick exchanged looks I couldn't interpret.

"But," I quickly corrected myself, "you just said you've only seen him twice this week."

"The girl's a whiz!" Patrick said. "We saw him twice—fast!"

"Then where . . . ?"

"So are we going to put together our costumes for 'Jungle Red' or what?" Luis asked, deliberately changing the subject. "That was one of the things we were supposed to be doing this week, you maybe recall?"

I recalled all right. And it could wait. "Where *has* Matt been, if not here with you guys?"

"When we asked, Matt said . . ." Patrick stopped and looked at Luis, as though checking his story before turning to me. "He's been at your cousin Alistair's all the time."

Now I remembered. During one of those brief phone calls we'd had, Matt told me that Alistair had moved into the house he'd rented for the final month of the season. Next walk over, Tarpon Walk. Matt had helped him.

"Oh, well. I guess that's okay then," I said.

"It's *okay then*?" both of them said, not hiding their disbelief.

"Well, sure. It's not like it's some stranger."

"You trust Alistair?" Luis asked. "I mean, I know I'm supposed to be a hysterical Cubano queen and all, but do you actually trust him?"

"Matt's there *all the time*!" Patrick added.

Now they were getting to me. "He sleeps here though, right?"

"We don't exactly check up on where he sleeps," Patrick said.

"He's usually sleeping here," Luis says. "But that doesn't mean much."

It wasn't that I couldn't for the life of me see Alistair going after Matt, using weapons no more subtle than a harpoon. The problem was I couldn't for the life of me see what attraction Alistair could possibly offer Matt.

And said so.

"Novelty!" Patrick suggested. "Pines boredom sets in. Someone new arrives. Someone with as much if not more money than Matt himself, for a change. Not to mention the novelty of Alistair's traveling and living abroad. His widespread social contacts and—"

"Well, maybe you're both right." I wavered. In fact, I could picture it all far too clearly. I'd seen Alistair charm people whose language he didn't speak, for no more reason than he was looking for a little diver-

sion. Remember poor Dario, deported back to Sicily . . . The only problem was if they were right, which was still only half credible, the last
thing I could do with someone of Matt's temperament would be to face-
off on it. First thing he'd do was throw it back at me, say how I'd made
this summer's plans, how I'd then stayed away from the Island even
more than I'd said I would, leaving him alone. How it was therefore all
my fault. Which it would be, naturally.

Having failed to find an answer, I decided to change the topic. Cleverly, I chose one I knew would totally involve them. "By the way, I think
I've found my costume for the Jungle Red party."

"Oh no you don't." Luis jumped for it. "*We* are dressing you."

Patrick just shook his head at me. I knew he was still thinking about
Matt and Alistair. And was aware of what I was doing. But then, what
else could I do?

"I'm not doing drag," I said. "I'm just not the type."

"You're just afraid you'll like it so much," Luis said. "You'll end up
being a TV!"

"I mean, look at my build. I should be thin and . . ."

"Oh, pul-eeze, Marie," Luis charged back. "You've got the exact
same build as I do. Not to mention half the people out here! You've got
to try it once."

"Maybe," I temporized. Then I peeled myself off the longue, went in
to shower and slap my face into some semblance of humanity. I emerged
fifteen minutes later with a dyed cantaloupe A-shirt dangling out the
side panel of my forest-green-and-cream-colored Speedo.

"Sure you're not overdressed?" Luis asked.

"Every time you say something bitchy, Luis, Miss God makes those lines
around your mouth deeper. . . . I thought I'd pay a visit on my dear cousin.
Isn't it down the walk and on the other side of Fire Island Boulevard?"

"Yes, but we heard . . . ," Patrick began. Then he mimed buttoning
his lip.

"Heard what?" I asked.

"Nothing!" Luis said for the both of them.

I shrugged. "It's summer. The Pines! Even the shirt's *de trop*!"

Halfway down Sky Walk, I realized that I was surrounded by

monarch butterflies, some the size of my hand. One perched on the cream side panel of my Speedo, a very lifelike brooch, and would not be shaken or shooed off.

The number they'd given me was one house left from the Bay, beyond a fence too high to see through. The front door lay immediately beyond the open gate and was also unlocked.

As I stepped in, the house seemed empty. The red floor tiles were large and cool against my bare feet. The furnishings in the living and dining room looked one stage more costly and thought-out than what I'd call Pines-Beach-House-Rental-Generic: lots of white rattan furniture but with better-than-average upholstery and coverings; the expected woven sisal rugs, but these were thick and looked handmade. The giant stands of indoor elephant-ear plants appeared healthy, stuffed in hip-high hand-thrown ceramic pots. All of it was lighted by narrow, ceiling-high windows.

In that second, and for no reason I could fathom, lines of poetry flew into my mind: "Come, gentle night; come, loving, black-brow'd night/ Give me my Romeo: and . . ."

And . . . and what? I couldn't for the life of me remember the rest of it. Did we have Shakespeare at the house? Between *Hints from Heloise* and *Leatherman's Handbook*? Not likely. Some more literary queen in the Pines might. . . . La Kramer? . . . Maybe.

I became slowly aware that I was hearing a rhythmical sound, or rather several rhythmical sounds meshing. The sounds came from the left, where a wide doorway opened onto what looked to be a bedroom wing . . . all of the doors ajar.

My thinking went like this: people are fucking here. Since it's his rental, it must be Alistair and someone else. I'd better leave and come back another time. But what about Matt? Where's he?

Before I could take the next step and put two and two together, I realized I was hearing Alistair's laughter. Not from the left—ergo not from the bedroom—but from the right, which meant outside!

Relieved, I walked toward the wall of glass, opened the doors, and found myself in a good-sized yard. Unpainted pine decking dropped to a large sundeck, and beyond it, the pool, not Olympic-sized but big enough, and beyond that, under a canvas marquee, a semi-enclosed screened dining room, set up for lunch. Six of the eight deeply curved rattan chairs were occupied by Alistair, Matt, and four men I didn't know.

"No room! No room!" Alistair shouted loudly as he saw me. In his sudden effort to rise and greet me, he knocked over a glass on the table that had been holding a mimosa. Clearing himself from the table where some version of a Mad Tea Party did indeed seem to be in progress, Alistair swooped out of the screened veranda to meet me by the pool with much exaggerated near-kisses, the way women greet each other in middle period Fellini movies.

"Finally!" he exaggerated, sweeping an arm around my shoulder and half pushing me under the marquee.

Where I noticed most of them but Matt were older—mid and late forties—and all of them clad—very un-Pines-like—in shirts and slacks or shorts and even shoes.

"Come for a swim?" one gray-haired fellow with a good-sized, heavily pedigreed nose asked in a thick accent. "How nice of you, Alistair [Al-ees-stare!] to provide us with boys frolicking à la Esther Williams!"

I placed the speaker as a Pines resident, scion of a European noble family. Alistair pulled me to the table.

"This bit of business, gents, is my very own dear second cousin, the estimable Roger Sansarc. And although some of you may take his cuteness as pure, physically unadulterated fluff, he's an important magazine editor."

"We *are* impressed," a jolly, handsome, thick-bodied Asian man said. "Angling for interviews, are you?"

"Barry Wu," Alistair introduced us, "the *real* last dowager empress of China."

"Charmed!" I heard from closer up. The large serpentine hand that insinuated its way into my grip belonged to a equally slender, long person, virtually colorless in skin, eye hue, or distinguishing feature, wearing what appeared to be a complete safari outfit sans only the hat.

"Timothy Childs-Shillito," Alistair introduced him, "*not,*" he clarified, "of the Middlesex Shillitos!"—as though that made a big difference, or as though I'd even know what the difference signified.

"Heavens, no!" the named one declared. "*You* may call me Aunt Tim," he declared, "and you may park your substantially filled bathing costume directly—that's it!—*directly* athwart Aunt Tim's suddenly pulsing lap."

I smiled and demurred.

"You already met the Count of No-Account," Alistair said, adding the long French name in hushed tones. Then louder, "No matter how pushy he gets, we never tire of reminding him that he's not duke until his brother croaks!"

"Your name sounds awfully familiar," I told the Count candidly, looking to make trouble. "Old family?"

"So old, our family crowned Charlemagne," he replied huffily.

"Oh my! Was that a good idea?"

The others laughed. Even the Count cracked a smile. "Perhaps . . . on reflection . . . not!"

"And this fellow," Alistair pointed me to someone who looked much younger and handsomer than any of the others, and also somewhat familiar, "is Horace Brecker the Third . . . my ex-cousin-in-law! Brecker's in town from the Coast, shopping for real estate. He's obviously a fish out of water in this company. But he's pretending not to be—noblesse oblige!"

Now that I thought of it, Brecker did resemble Doriot: the same heavy, multishaded blond hair dropping straight off his head like a helmet, his cropped closer, the same startling, eaglelike, probing eyes (his green) that pulled into focus a face otherwise almost Norman Rockwellish, WASP American.

"And of course, the beauteous Matthew!" Aunt Tim said, his hand raised in a flourish. The others all looked Matt's way, giving tacit homage.

"We know each other," Matt said, quietly. He was looking, I thought, completely different today than I'd ever seen him, his thick dark hair uncharacteristically parted in the middle, curling to either side. He wore small octagonal green-paned glasses, which imparted a bookish air. His costume consisted of a loose, scooped-neck muslin shirt, delicate mustard-colored knee-length Bermudas, and well-worn moccasins; he might have been a Bengali day student.

So this was what Luis and Patrick had meant about how I was dressed!

"Do we detect some mut-u-al his-to-ry in the way that was said?"

Barry Wu asked, looking back and forth from Matt to me. "Dare we hope . . . scan-dal?"

"The very worst!" Alistair assured them. "Close your ears, Brecker," he warned, then explained to me, "Brecker's only here on spec. He isn't at all sure what he thinks about men who like other men."

"Do too! I think it's their own business," Brecker said forthrightly, in that flat, accentless tone of voice I'd come to associate with Bay Area natives of a certain class when I'd lived out there. "I've always thought so and said so!"

I was about to have to decide whether or not I was going to attack Brecker—who, after all, wasn't half bad-looking—as "bigot of the week," when he suddenly continued.

"I feel compelled to add," he said in a somewhat less certain tone of voice, "that until I arrived out here, I'd never been exposed to so many of these fellows, nearly jay naked all day long! In the bank, and the grocery store, on the beach naturally, but also cutting hedges, and delivering propane tanks and manning the fire truck, testing its gear as I saw earlier, or just ambling along the walkways, and well, really anywhere I might happen to be. And all of them in such healthy physical condition! Like Matt and our new arrival. Until now, I have to admit I'd never seen much point to this male-male business," Brecker finished off, red-faced, out of embarrassment at having spoken so long or at suddenly realizing what he'd ended up saying, it wasn't clear which.

I wondered who could possibly gloss that statement. Alistair?

No, it turned out: Barry Wu. "You do understand, don't you, Horace, that the 'fellows' here feel that since they 'have *it*,' they might as well 'flaunt *it*!' " Barry's last word dissolved into glissandos of giggles.

"There are two more guests," Alistair pointed to the empty chairs.

"I heard them," I explained, "as I was coming in."

". . . We've forgotten who they are," he concluded.

A mimosa was poured for me, and a sweet and crumbly French confection put between my lips. I chewed, sipped, and observed.

Observed Alistair among his "old" friends—"Who knew *cher* Hervelois would be here?" he said to me of the Count, "or that Brecker would arrive?" Observed Alistair being comfortably, thoughtfully social again—"Stiletto here plays the total naïf, but you've never met a wickeder puss!" Observed, reminding myself that it had been more than a decade since the enormous curry-dinner-and-LSD galas at Alistair's Chelsea penthouse.

I also observed Matt, who accompanied his unexpected new costume with a new intellectual, offbeat persona—"Ah, but that's not what Chuang-tzu said," I heard erupt out of his mouth at one point.

To which Barry Wu made some complex, alternately sweet-tempered and irritated reply, before demanding and receiving a tangerine and a small knife.

"This is the only thing I recall of my childhood on the outskirts of the court of the Yellow Emperor," he announced to us, taking the fruit in one hand and applying the sharp tip of the knife to it so lightly and cutting so quickly I was certain he was going to end up with an elaborately bloodied palm. Finished, he dropped the knife and held up the hand with the fruit. Lightly gripping one tip of orange skin between two fingers, he pulled, and the sliced peel spun, flavoring the air, as a single unbroken length of inner skin. When he dropped it on a napkin nearby, it formed a perfect shell of tangerine. The fruit itself had been evenly divided: it fell open, shameless as a gardenia, ready to be eaten.

Applause, whistles, foot stamping.

"That," Barry concluded with more chimes of laughter, "in a nutshell—or should I say a mandarin peel?—is the result of five thousand years of culture!"

A ringing phone pulled Alistair indoors, where he insisted I attend him. It turned out to be a brief, hilarious, and to me completely enigmatic call. Afterward he dropped onto the sofa, weak with laughter, and gesturing around him, said, "It'll do, don'cha think?"

"It's fine."

"It's only a few more weeks. But I feel better with my own place."

"Only natural."

"Not that all of you weren't superb about me as a guest!"

"Brilliant and superb."

"Except for you, who are never there. Bad you," he added, playfully slapping me. "Leaving poor Matthew to his own devices. You're just lucky I happened along and rescued him from that ghastly, bloodsucking, dependency addict! What's his name?"

"Roger Something or other?"

"No, stupid! Thaddeus! About to sink her claws bone-deep . . . ," Alistair said. "Imagine, all these years! You never told me what a prince he was," gesturing outside.

"You expected maybe chopped liver?" I asked. "Anyway, you're the one who picked him out. Remember? The day he came into Pozzuoli?"

"Yes, of course. But he was some hulking country bumpkin! You've taken him in hand. You've done things. Rounded the edges! Polished the surfaces!"

"You make me sound like some Vegbian potter."

"What kind of potter?" Alistair asked. He looked wonderful, I thought. Hadn't looked this good in years. Relaxed. Happy.

"Vegbian! Vegetarian Lesbian! That's what we call the Lorraines and Elaines who move to rural lanes with their lovers and who eschew males and machinery and who don't shave their underarms and who wear enormous overalls and get very fat and very strong and who raise other people's children and lots of animals using only breast-feeding and who only eat vegetables and who suffer in silence when some male has an orgasm sixty miles away."

Alistair looked at me in wonder. "You were never so smart! How did you get so fucking clever?"

"Oh, please!" I groaned—partly because most of the company had come into the house and overheard not only Alistair's last words but also part of my description, which I'd unashamedly spun out for them.

"No, really!" he insisted. "You were the densest . . . He was!" he said for them all, now settling around us. "The very *dullest* of boys! He played in dirt! He pitched softballs! And he had this golden retriever of a boyfriend who adored the very earth he trod on."

"Who?" I demanded to know. Then: "You remember August?"

"Ghas-tly child, I always thought," Alistair admitted. "Which is hardly the point. What *is* the point is that even back then you had one lad or another trained to kiss your pink little behind."

"Don't believe a word he's saying!" I addressed the others, Matt especially. He'd come in last and now slouched at the open door.

"It's perfectly true," Alistair said. "They literally fought over his favors. I marveled. I envied. To no avail. They'd regularly come to fisticuffs over which one of them dear Cuz would sit next to in the mud. For years I sought the secret."

"He could have cared less," I explained, remembering how cold-blooded about my pals he'd really been.

"Matthew would know the secret!" the Count said, confirming that his nose wasn't so far in the air as to not have noticed that we went together.

"He would?" Brecker asked. "Oh, hell! You're not going to, like, suddenly reveal that you guys've been secretly . . . are you?"

"It's hardly a secret," Barry said.

"I should've suspected something like this!" Brecker said. It wasn't clear whether he was titillated or disappointed.

"Well, Matthew?" Shillito asked.

"Yes! Tell us Roger's secret, Matthew!" Alistair insisted.

Matt had been frowning, not liking the sudden attention, never mind the pressure. Now he smiled and said, "Damned if I know."

"Hypnosis," I said, to distract them and to fend off how much his words had hurt me. "You are falling asleeee. . . ."

"Sure it isn't drugs?" the Count asked.

"Speaking of drugs . . . ," Barry Wu began, "weren't we offered some killer Maui-Wowie?"

"Yeah! Where is that Maui?"

"I left it outside," Alistair said, and rose. We followed in a group.

As I passed last through the doorway, Matt stopped me. He kissed me hard, but I kept my mouth closed. He didn't let go of my arm. I couldn't tell if he knew how much he'd hurt me by what he'd said a few moments before.

"Surprised to see you here," I said.

"I'm surprised you made it to the Island at all," he accused.

"I understand you had to be rescued from a mere trick," I sniped back. "Losing the magic touch, are we?"

"Maybe my emotional needs are growing," he said. "Not that you'd notice."

We stood there, our faces inches away from each other, out of sound if not out of sight of the others, and I thought he'd never looked so completely appealing as at that moment, wearing those dopey grass-green octagonal glasses with that inane Reggie-from-*Archie*-comics hairstyle, and how totally and stupendously I loved him, so why couldn't I just give in? Just give half an inch and once and for all bridge that narrow yet continent-wide gap, that seemingly gelatinous yet after all adamantine gap between us? What would I lose really? My manhood? My sense of self? My independence? My self-respect? Some or all of them? So what? What did they mean in the long run? At the end of the race? In the cold, black silence of neverending night?

"Not that you'd deign to notice if I did care," I said back.

Matt smiled sourly: I'd proven something, or he'd won himself a bet.

I started to go, but he held me back: "You think you're so smart, because your vision came true!"

"What vision?" I asked.

Just then I heard, "Maree-whore-anna." Alistair gyrated in front of us like a cobra, holding out a joint. "Dee killer droag!"

The two other guests, Bebe and Enrico—at least that's what I thought their names were—emerged from their bedroom, looking neither exhausted nor sheepish. They were treated exactly as though they had come back from attempting, and failing, to obtain for us a not very good dinner of Chinese takeout.

Matt went to sit where he'd been before. Only now he was closer to Alistair, who, I now noticed, seemed, without ever once making a point of it, to turn half his body and about two-thirds of his attention to Matt.

At first I thought it was me—me being a bitch for failing once again to break through to Matt, me overnoticing Alistair.

But as the time passed, I began actually to count how many times Alistair would gloss something someone else at the table had just spoken about and add something like "You know, Matthew, Stiletto is right! Ireland in April is the most magnificent green! Pool tables can't compare. You should see it." Or: "Now, she's someone Matthew would like! Don't you think, Bebe? She's followed poetry since—who was that Spanish writer? Alberti! She translated him. She's so droll. Ugly as a staircase, of course. You'd love each other!" Or: "Vevey! And not just because Nabokov lives there! Personally the man is a complete cipher! But the town! The little château! Remember, Princess Wu, when we took the rooms there? The frog concert all night? The stable boys in their

union suits hunting mice with maces taken off the walls? Would Matthew love it? You would! Take my word for it!"

After a while, I thought, no, he's not just being kind, not just being
solicitous, not just being enthusiastic. What he's doing is, he's telling
Matt, *Get wise and ditch this second-rate cousin of mine and come to Europe
with me. See the world. Be. Meet. Do. Fulfill yourself!*

Look at him! And look at Matt lap it up! Encourage him. Bastard!

"... creaking sofa," I heard or thought I heard someone say, and I
immediately thought back to when I'd come into the house. I'd heard
someone—Bebe and Enrico, it turned out—fucking, and for one horrible moment I'd thought that it was—yes, I could admit now, given all
the time I'd heard they spent together, and given Luis and Patrick's
meaningfully shared looks—I'd thought it had been Alistair and Matt in
that bed. And I'd been fool enough to be relieved when I found out it
wasn't them! When all the while they'd been doing this! Not staying
discreetly hidden in some room, but out in public for everyone to see,
out among all Alistair's friends, passing mimosas and joints and artfully
knifed-open tangerines and ...

It nauseated me. I got up to leave.

"Going so soon? Oh, is it Tea time now?" Alistair asked. Explaining
to Brecker, "You'll see plenty of other healthy and nearly jay naked men
at Tea. We'll go. We'll *all* go! Is this the best time, Cuz? Cuz knows the
exact times to make one's appearance anywhere out here. It's all very
exact, you know. The times. The places. I suppose because it's otherwise so unstructured. Tell them Herve— Wait up, Cuz! It can't be that
exact, can it? Don't we have to change outfits? Are we all right, dressed
like this?"

Tea Dance with Alistair's group might have been amusing—if I'd been
more stoned. At first, I attempted to make the most of my undressed
condition by placing myself where I'd overexcite poor Horace Brecker,
whom I guessed from his earlier outburst to be confused and probably
just horny. About the same time that my tasteless act was getting fairly
old—Jeffrey Roth, my dance buddy, passed by and loudly asked, "Pos-

ing for animal crackers?"—several attractive females came out of the
Blue Whale and Horace excused himself to head toward them. Seconds
later, I found my own salvation with the appearance on the dance floor
of Pensacola Rick and his pals.

That wasn't his real name, but it pretty much described him. Rick
was one of those loose, wiry Southern ash-blonds whose faces are far
too pretty for any living male and thus have to be covered over with
scars from drunken fights outside of backwoods bars by the time they
are sixteen, a lad with velvet skin still not ruined despite years of solar
abuse and bad weather, whose luxuriant dark lashes and bruised-looking
cheeks held an houri's almond-shaped eyes of the palest, the most hypnotic, green.

Obviously one of my physical types, I'd encountered variations of
Pensacola Rick over the past decade, at times in the oddest places (the
last had been a Con Ed worker right outside our building; I still trea-
sured the plastic yellow helmet he'd given me), and I'd always been impressed by his sweetness, oversized genitals, omnivorous appetite for
drink and drugs of all colors and effects, as well as his propensity for doing just about anything in bed, if it "feels good and don't cost neither
money nor blood."

I'd come upon this latest avatar a month previous at Sunday Tea:
we'd flirted at the urinal before his pals had dragged him away.

I should note here that Sunday Tea at the Pines had become the most
"mixed" dance of the weekend, having for some unknown reason come
to attract not only couples from the other, allegedly straighter Fire Island communities of Water Island, Davis Park, and as far away as Ocean
Beach, who arrived via water taxi beginning at four in the afternoon, but
also pulling in less tony types from towns across the Great South Bay—
Sayville, Patchogue, and Islip—who ferried over, partied till sunset,
then ferried back.

That first brush with Pensacola Rick hadn't been lost on Matt. He'd
noticed me gawking at the boy dancing—wildly, naturally, two girls for
the four boys—and with some sixth sense, Matt had remained annoyingly at my side until they'd all left.

This however was a Saturday Tea, and Matt was disarmed, unalert, busily being literary with Shillito and Barry Wu and company, so I was free to throw myself onto the dance floor and with the appropriate rhythm and energy manage to land within the orb of Pensacola Rick's little coterie in minutes. He remembered me instantly, sweet lad that he was, and introduced his cohort Bobby (whom I recalled from the first time) and their date, DeeDee, a woman closer to my age (mid-thirties) than to theirs (early twenties).

My poppers were a big hit with them and the music was good, and the place was crowded enough that we could remain hidden from those I'd come with, who seemed content to remain out on the deck anyway. During a break we all took to get fresh drinks at the inside bar, Pensacola Rick made a very public announcement that he had to take a leak. I followed him into the john, fought my way to the urinal next to his, and played with his dick while he pissed—pretending nothing at all was going on.

We found Bobby and DeeDee dancing, and rejoined them. Ten minutes later, I recognized from Tommy DJ's selections that Tea was about to end, and I managed to make this fact understood over the music and disco whistles and tambourines, asking Rick if he and his pals were going back on the next ferry.

"We're on a boat," he said, nodding back to where they must have parked it. When I told him this party was over, he asked, "Want to come with us?"

Did I? By now I was completely taken with Rick, more than a little excited by Bobby, who, though jet-haired and blue-eyed, was about ninety-eight percent as cute, and I was even intrigued by DeeDee, who struck me as both attractive and extremely cool about my edging in on her boys. From my college days, I knew that girls with sleepy eyes like hers were capable of all sorts of surprises and indulgences. So I wangled all four of us out the side exit of the Blue Whale seconds before Tea officially ended, without attracting the attention of Matt, or any of Alistair's gang who might alert him.

As promised, on the little sailboat with its spartanly furnished bunk, we found a mostly filled bottle of Black Label, several joints, and a well-stocked eight-track deck. After some body dancing in the cramped space, Bobby and DeeDee began necking on the bed. She took off her bathing suit, and suddenly all three of us guys were on the bed, kneeling naked around her, while she stroked and sucked us. Bobby began going down on her, so I decided there was no time like the present. Remaining poised over her mouth, I pulled Rick around and began to blow him. Ten minutes later, DeeDee and I were side by side on the bed, face-to-face, kissing, with Bobby fucking her and Rick fucking me. "This is fun!" Bobby allowed. He and Rick climaxed, and Rick suggested they switch places. Whenever one of them came, they both would whoop like cowboys in a rodeo.

As DeeDee and I had dared to hope, given enough grass and poppers and dirty talk and sexual byplay, the lads were virtually indefatigable. After a while, out of boredom with the missionary position, she and I decided to add some spice by turning ourselves around and making it orally with each other while the unceasing needles of the two lads' automatic Singers continued to sew away at us from opposite sides—a pleasant change.

"What say, Bob? Is this real perverted?" Rick suddenly asked his buddy. He'd just moved away from helping DeeDee tongue my genitals and now lifted Bobby's mouth away from where he'd been tonguing away at DeeDee's clitoris.

"Yeah, real perverted!" Bobby agreed, rolling his eyes. At which, Pensacola Rick amazed Bobby by grabbing and soundly French-kissing him. Bobby pulled away suddenly, red-faced, and said, "Hey! Stop! That's queer!" At which all of us laughed.

Around eleven-thirty, the two of them finally ran out of vinegar. I extricated myself from the other twelve limbs to go urinate. When I returned, they'd formed a sort of knot and were all snoring away. I covered them with a blanket, dressed, and staggered all the way home to Sky Walk.

Our house was quiet; only a single bulb over the kitchen sink was still on. I knew that after their week-long vacation, Luis and Patrick were napping, preparatory to a long, late Saturday-night party at the Ice Palace.

Not a clue to where Matt might be. I vaguely recalled Alistair and his group attempting to make dinner plans before I'd been driven to distraction by the appearance of Pensacola Rick. Maybe I should call and let them know I hadn't drowned. On second thought, maybe not. In truth, I had barely enough energy left to eat a blueberry yogurt, brush my teeth, and fling my abused body upon the mattress.

Which I did.

I slept twelve hours. Awakened, I was still groggy after two cups of French roast coffee at one-thirty Sunday afternoon, when Luis and Patrick sat me down to an enormous brunch. Present also were Matt, who'd awakened next to me, and Alistair, who'd arrived ten minutes before, looking as though he'd been up and personally written, edited, printed, and thrown together the three thick Sunday newspapers he proceeded to toss onto the deck table for our perusal.

"We're not going to even *ask* what happened to my dear cousin yesterday evening!" Alistair began, speaking across me—and plates of the most enormous blackberry-speckled buckwheat pancakes I'd ever seen, freshly concocted by Luis and Patrick.

I was barely awake. I'd not thought I'd have to jump into the fray quite so early. So I filled my mouth with pancake, washed it down with coffee, and stuffed it again with pancake.

"Your dear cousin spent yesterday evening in the company of White Trash," Matt told Alistair, casually leafing through the *Times* Travel Section. So he had seen Pensacola Rick—or me leaving with him—after all! "I hope you've de-loused?" he addressed me.

"Zeese nnnccaakes rrr gdd!" I enthused at Luis, and gobbled more.

"Roger won't even consider drag for Jungle Red," Luis pouted.

"I don't know why not," Alistair said.

"It's not as if he can claim having a single shred of ethics left," Matt added darkly.

"Mrr ccffeee!" I held out my cup to Patrick, who'd arrived with a fresh Chemex-full.

"Well, that's too bad," Alistair said, "because I've had Bebe pick out *the* most exquisite gowns at the Astoria Studios." He turned to me. "You know, that place in Long Island City where all those films were made in the twenties and thirties? Bebe's got entrée to the costume rooms there."

"I'd kill for one of those," Patrick said in a tight voice.

Now I spoke up. "I don't hear anyone insisting Matt wear drag."

"You ever hear of a smart little bolero in a size-sixty shoulder?"

"Not to mention the shape of the high heels I'd need," Matt added. They had a point.

"Bebe's got a summer tux Johnny Weissmuller wore to the '37 Oscars for you, Matt," Alistair said. "Adrian made it for him out of Italian silk. The color allegedly matched Weissmuller's semen."

"Stop or I'll faint!" Luis warned.

"For me," Alistair went on, "a gown made for Norma Shearer. Eleven hundred rhinestones sewn on a field of samite! And for you, Cuz, one made for Stanwyck. Chinese watered silk in Breton blue with embroidered pearls!"

"It's not that I don't appreciate it . . . ," I began.

"What is it, then?" Alistair asked.

"He's afraid of being called a girl," Luis said.

"No! That's not it. But isn't men wearing drag demeaning to women?"

"Look who's talking," Patrick said. "Mr. Abuse My Female Help!"

"Sydelle and I see eye to eye. Lately," I defended myself.

Alistair ignored that. "If one's making fun of women, then yes, I suppose it *is* demeaning. Not if one's honoring them. It is a great queer tradition, you know."

"Acceptable even among the most macho of today's gays!" Matt said.

"How many high-heels parties were there this summer here at the Pines at which body builders with mustaches showed?" Patrick asked.

"It still seems . . . what do the French say?" I asked. "*Travesti!*"

"*En travesti!*" Alistair corrected. "Anyway, what we're doing is not just throwing on a dress and going to some party, Cuz. Not you and I. No, we shall begin by going into Manhattan and spending Friday afternoon with full treatments at Georgette Klinger's, where I've already made appointments. From mud baths to facials to shampoo and cut. Falls will be woven into our hair, all of it tinted and styled. Then we'll cab over to Bebe's place, where he'll lightly cosmetize us and give us tips on how to emphasize our best facial points. We'll then put on a complete undergarment foundation from Enrico's own collection, bought over the years from Bendel's lingerie counters. We'll be stockinged, shod, and dressed in women's casual wear, sweaters, and slacks. Dressed thus, we'll enplane back out here the afternoon of the party. We'll not only dress, but also walk, talk, act, and think like women equal to wear those gowns. That night, Bebe and Enrico will fly out with our outfits, make us up, dress us, and only when they are satisfied that we are masterpieces will they send us off to the party. Others at Jungle Red will be drags, Cuz, but you and I will be goddesses; others will be fit only to be our servants, ladies in waiting. Matt, of course, will be our escort, our very own Apollo."

"I can't stand it!" Luis promptly fell over in his chair.

"Say no to that!" Patrick said. "If you dare!"

I sighed deeply. Outvoted, I looked to see what Matt wanted.

"And you?" I asked.

"I'll go in that Weissmuller tux," he said, throwing down the Travel and beginning to look through the Book Review.

He meant with me or without me. He meant without me but with Alistair. Alistair done up as a movie star—beautifully, tastefully done up. No way I'd allow that after having Thad out of the way so recently!

"I guess I can be a sport!" I said.

Alistair hooted. Luis applauded. Patrick oohed and aahed. Matt sort of quietly looked at me, slightly surprised.

For the next ten minutes, they wouldn't let me alone. Luis said he'd get four-inch wedgies to my apartment for me to wear at home and get used to. They were so full of it all I almost changed my mind and said no again. What made me clamp my lips tight was that at one point while the others were all busily gabbing inside, Matt quietly said, "See if you can't find some of that Mitsuoko perfume. . . . The one woman I ever made it with was wearing it."

I almost forgave Matt everything in that moment. But it passed, and we went out to the beach and the day continued and it was just like the day before: Alistair seducing, Matt accepting—all very public.

I couldn't stand it. At the same time, I knew I wouldn't make a scene. All that counted in the world's eye was that Matt and I ended up in the same bedroom at night. I concentrated upon that, even though there

were moments I would have gleefully speared my cousin on a shish ke-
bab skewer.

I didn't because I knew that in less than one week's time I was going
to be new and exciting to Matt: female yet male, familiar yet different;
an entire intriguing package wrapped in watered silk, liberally doused
with Mitsuoko.

Alistair wouldn't have a chance!

"It's me," Alistair identified himself when I picked up the phone. "Is
Matt there?"

"He's at the Botel gym."

"Good! I'll be right over. I've got something to show you."

"Can't it wait? I'm getting ready to leave."

"Taking a seaplane?"

"It'll be at the harbor in a half hour. I wanted to stop at the bank and
at the Pantry deli to get a nosh and—"

"I'll go with you. Don't leave without me." Alistair hung up.

It was nearly noon, Monday. I was alone in the house, more or less
dressed and packed. Without Matt and Luis and Patrick, Withering
Heights looked and felt empty. It was better outside, sitting at the little
table overlooking the view of the Great South Bay. Except that now
streaks of long, thin clouds had begun to scrim in from Sayville. I prayed
they wouldn't thicken and cover the Bay until my plane had already
taken off. Seaplane pilots didn't fly in mist, and the last thing I was prepared for today was the alternative—a three-hour ferry, cab, Long Island Rail Road train, and subway ride home.

I was wondering whether or not to leave a note for Matt. We'd still
hardly spoken, although we'd ended up making love early in the morning. Nothing conclusive in that, of course, nothing even indicative: it
had become clear by now that Matt's and my physical contact led a life
virtually independent of anything else in our relationship. We would
not talk for a week and still screw like mad every night. A note saying
what? What could a note say Matt wasn't already aware of?

"You waited!" Alistair was huffing; he must have dashed up Sky

Walk's steep hill to make certain not to miss me. "Here! Look at these!" He thrust a handful of typewritten pages into my hand.

I glanced at the top one: the uncapitalized title, "solstice," and two lines down, margin left, the continuation. "nightcall" was the title on the next page. The third one didn't have a title, but began directly with:

first
i unlace the shoes, then i take off my watch.
unbutton the pants. the shirt comes out.
the tongue comes out

and then the air.
i take the teabag of my brain out
leaving the cup of blood to grow cold.

i'm beyond glass now. i am hard on
one side of the wind, on the voice you raise
from lungs i gave you. now i
give them up like a bird and rise.

if absence casts no shadows
then i am the sun
whose only shadow is your skin.

"This one must be new," I said. "Haven't seen it before."

Alistair stared, openmouthed. "You know about them?"

"Sure, I know. Matt's showed me about thirty over the years."

"You know about them?" Alistair repeated. "And you've done nothing about them?"

"I've admired them. In earlier days, I'd make suggestions here and there. These," shaking the other sheets, "used to have conjunctions until I suggested they be taken out and everything tightened up."

"That's all?" Alistair insisted.

"I've told him to send them out. I've given him addresses, names. . . ."

I didn't like feeling put on the spot in this way. I stood up, pulled my weekender onto my shoulder, and threw my lace-tied Stan Smiths across the bag.

"Alistair, I will not be late! I'm walking along the surf."

"I'll go with you," he said.

When we reached the Ozone Walk entrance to the beach, I said, "I don't want to seem blasé, and I know how exciting it can be when you discover that someone you like is a good poet. But . . . he just *won't* get them out where they can be read. Afraid of rejection, of not being understood. I don't know what all else is involved."

"Whatever's involved? Don't you feel a responsibility to him?"

The tide was ebbing but still strong. The sand looked roughed-up from the previous night: where the ocean had eaten into the shoreline, a four-foot cliff rose, twisting and turning as far as I could see in either direction. We could either walk along its crumbly top edge or down below, upon wetter, harder-packed sand. I opted for the upper level, Alistair for the lower.

"Responsible? No. They're Matt's work," I said, attempting to keep my balance.

"I don't believe this!" Alistair insisted.

"Well! As Dorothy Parker said, 'You can lead a whore to culture, but you can't make her think'!"

"Very clever! Always finding the clever, the easy, way out!"

"What do you want me to do with the damn poems?"

"Publish them! You are a magazine editor!"

"In *Manifest*?"

"Why not?"

"Between 'Tips from Mr. Leather Master' and the centerfold? A nineteen-year-old model/actor/waiter from Cedar Rapids who loves 'Dynasty' and wants to be president of his 4-H club?"

"Why not?"

"It's too lowbrow for Matt's work."

"Then make it higher-brow. Commission artwork. Photos, maybe. What's the name of that guy who did those great photos last month? Maplejuice?"

"Mapplethorpe."

"Use some of his photos! Make a photo-poetry essay! Four pages long."

"You really think so?" I asked.

"Don't you think you owe it to Matt?" Alistair asked.

Who knew anymore what I owed Matt? Or he me? I decided it was far safer to change the subject.

"Did I gather from various hints yesterday that Horace Brecker's going to be staying with you?" I asked.

"Ought to raise the fun potential a bit. Don'cha think he's cute? Actually, he is totally straight."

"Perhaps. But you know my definition of straight: a man who doesn't suck cock *regularly*. Anyway, after a few weeks here at the Pines, he'll either give way somewhat or rape the first female he can lay hands on. What's the story with him?"

"Had a woman friend for some years. But now he's career-building. They were kaput months ago. Stayed with us in France, and it was obvious they were waiting for someone to send them a telegram to confirm the fact."

"I was surprised how much like Doriot he looks," I said, suspecting I was treading on dangerous ground. "By the way, you never actually told me what happened to lead to your splitting up."

"Nothing actually 'happened.' She simply failed to grow in sophistication as I'd hoped."

"In other words, she wouldn't let you screw the gardener?"

"Actually I thought women were far more, you know, flexible, about these matters. Not old Doriot."

We were at the co-ops, almost in the middle of the Pines now, starting toward the harbor, when I suddenly heard the loud rotor of a helicopter. It hovered over Ocean Walk, which separates the beachfront houses from the next line in, then it edged onto the beach, coming our way, descending fast.

There weren't many people on the sand, but everyone cleared out as the police helicopter slowly revolved and dropped. When it landed, it blew sand a hundred feet in all directions. What was going on?

Julio, one of the Pines' two-man police squad, could be seen now standing on the long walkway extending from Nick and Enno's house out to the beach. He was signaling to someone inside the chopper.

A man in a white uniform popped out of the copter's side door and ran up the stairs into the house. Another man in white stepped out, half carrying, half hauling a metal contraption. Once he got it up the stairs, he and Red, the other Pines cop, kicked it open—turning it into a gurney on wheels—and rolled it across the deck to the sliding glass doors. They went inside too.

In seconds they were out again, carrying someone on the gurney, one of them holding what looked to be a breathing apparatus.

What the . . . ?

Enno came out of the house, talking fast to Rick Wellikoff. Enno had to bend his tall body to follow the gurney into the helicopter. The chopper rose with another blast of sand, hovered, spun around, then headed away over the co-ops to the Bay.

I ran to the walkway where Rick stood with the policemen.

"What happened?" I asked Rick.

"They took Nick to Babylon State Hospital. Pneumonia! Spiking fever!"

"Jesus! I hope he's going to be okay."

"Phone here later and check in," Rick suggested. Then Julio and Red pulled him inside the house before I could get any details.

"Pneumonia?" Alistair was as startled as I was when I reported it. "They haven't been doing ethyl chloride? I hear it freezes the lungs."

"Unlikely. Nick and Enno are health nuts. Bee pollen. Vitamins. You name it. They don't even use sugar."

By the time we'd gotten to the little Pines harbor, the chopper was invisible. Alistair nodded toward all the wagons chained up in rows: the only way to move groceries or large objects in a community without roads or cars.

"They look funny, don't they?" he said.

"I came across on a ferry one afternoon earlier this summer with an insurance claims adjustor," I said. "Cute young guy. We got to talking. He'd come to check out the house on Black Duck and Bay that burned down. I told him all he'd find was a few charred sticks of foundation left in sand. He'd never been to the Island before. When we landed and saw all the wagons, he asked if there were many children here."

Alistair laughed. "What did you say?"

"I told him this was the Isle of Lost Boys."

"From *Pinocchio!*"

"*Peter Pan* . . . Give me the poems, Alistair. I'll publish them."

"You're a doll! Now, don't forget! Friday afternoon at three on the dot, we meet at Klinger's!"

"I know I'm going to regret it," I moaned.

"I don't believe this is happening!" I turned to the Grunt in panic. "Say it's not! Say something!"

Bernard looked me as straight in the eye as he could, given his squint. "It's happening. I could have predicted it. It's your own fault."

"*My* fault?"

"Your fault!" he insisted.

"Because I tried to cooperate with Harte? Because I tried to accept and accommodate her?"

"Because you didn't kill her and scatter her body in ash cans around the city when you had the chance," the Grunt said.

I stared at Jersey Joe, spread-eagled by thongs and pushpins on the wall above our publisher's desk. Joe wore a silver bathing cap. A black racing suit wrapped his lower torso. Six fake Olympic medals were splayed upon his considerable, stuffed chest. His button eyes were inscrutable behind solarized water goggles.

Mad and amusing as this was iconographically, it could in no way compensate for the past ten minutes of my life. I'd sailed into our monthly update meeting, at which editorial staff and publisher laid out and discussed a rough "book" of the next issue. This meeting had been attended by myself and the Grunt as well as by Sydelle Auslander and our art director, whose increasing interest in Eastern mysticism had led us to refer to him as "Swami Powell" or, more simply, the Swami.

For a while, the meeting had gone well. Harte found Sydelle's feature on "Biker Dykes" a strong follow-up to my lead story on the fire at the baths. Those were followed by my interview with Isherwood—third of my "Homo Authors of the Past." The two commissioned pieces—the one a report on gay resorts in the Pacific, the other a humorous essay on how to be openly gay on your college campus and still have fun—for this, our "Back to School" issue, were deemed okay. The centerfold was a recent also-ran for *Playgirl* and of high quality, though his rep in Waikiki was pure diva. Our news items—what was "hot and breaking" concerned the Greenwich Village protests over the filming of the movie *Cruising* with its sure-to-be-negative gay images, the recent success of the movie *Alien*, which forever changed how one thought of tummy aches, and Tennessee Williams's revision of his *Summer and Smoke*, called *The Eccentricities of a Nightingale*, starring Blythe Danner and Frank Langella, just aired on public television. Then we'd come to the four-page layout the Swami, the Grunt, and I had put together last night using some Mapplethorpe photos in our files and six of Matt's poems.

I thought the Grunt's choice of typefaces excellent. I thought the Swami's layout equally classy. Alistair was right: the poems and photos looked so good the entire issue now edged a bit toward the higher-browed.

"Gee," Stephen Forrest Harte, our publisher, said, looking at the layout, the most childish of looks upon his already childlike face. "What's this?"

"Surprise!" I said.

"Poetry?"

"Good poetry," the Grunt—Matt's biggest fan—said.

"Gay poetry," I added. "*Mandate*'s already run poetry by—"

"Saw it! Nice photos! Do we own them?" Harte asked Swami.

"Pub rights only. He keeps all originals."

Harte had gone back and forth, back and forth, page after page, reading the poems. He'd finally looked up and had been about to say, "Fine, next!" when Sydelle Auslander spoke up.

"I realize it isn't my place to be concerned with the image of the magazine," she began.

"Of course it is," Harte responded, falling into the trap. "It's all of our place. That's why we all attend these meetings."

"Well, then . . . I personally think that publishing those poems will open up the magazine to attack. Especially our editorial policy."

I couldn't believe what I was hearing.

"Why is that, Ms. Auslander?" Harte asked.

"It would be different if we published poetry on a regular basis. But we don't. To have these suddenly appear, so lavishly produced, with everyone knowing the nepotism involved . . ."

I'd nurtured this viper at my breast, encouraged her. . . .

"We've got to start publishing poetry with someone's work, no?" Harte took the role of devil's advocate. "Loguidice's seem as good as any."

"They're fine. But everyone will know they've been published because his lover's the editor," she said.

It was at that moment that our harassed advertising director barged into the meeting with a major crisis he had concerning a large client of the magazine, who hated the latest placement of an ad by our art director. Swami and Harte rushed out to confront the advertiser; and, sensibly, Sydelle excused herself before I could leap up from my chair and tear out her throat.

"What do you suggest we do?" I finally asked the Grunt.

"I could have forgiven her anything else," he said darkly.

"Bernard?" I asked. His voice sounded so odd.

The Grunt looked up. "For all my talk, I could have, would have, really forgiven her anything else. But to do this . . . to Matt!"

His tone of voice reminded me of those women in British telly movies, at the moment they slip a fatal convulsant into the kiddies' marzipan.

"We'll get over it, Bernard! Matt doesn't know I wanted to use the poems. He needn't *ever* know."

"It's actually better this way," the Grunt went on in that same I'm-fine-it's-all-of-you-who're-bonkers tone of voice, "because now I see it all writ large and what I merely suspected about her is all too clear. She is Evil incarnate and must be destroyed."

"Now, Bernard, slow down. I'll handle this. You must do nothing."

"I must!" he insisted.

Before either of us could do anything, however, Harte and the Swami returned to the office. The disaster of losing a major advertiser had been narrowly averted, and the triumph in this achievement made it all the sweeter, even for someone as allegedly "egoless" as our art director prided himself on being of late. To my surprise, Sydelle did not slip back in their wake. But then, why expose herself so needlessly? She'd done the damage already. That was soon evident.

"Okay, so we're close to a frozen September issue," Harte said.

Neither the Grunt nor I wanted to ask what that meant in terms of Matt's work. Which left the Swami to ask, "And these pages of poetry and poems?"

Harte looked up. "Sorry." To Powell: "What else do you have for here?"

Naturally Powell had what I'd shoved aside, which Harte eagerly approved. And our meeting was over.

Two hours later, Harte called me into his office.

"Roger! I'm worried about you. About us?"

"It's Friday," I said. "I didn't lunch. I leave in five minutes."

"You didn't scream. You didn't throw a fit. You didn't remind me of all you've done beyond the call of duty for the magazine. You didn't even threaten to quit, which you do whenever your wishes are thwarted," Harte said. Then corrected that to "Hell! Which you do monthly, whether your wishes are thwarted or not! I'm worried, Roger. Should I be worried?"

"In fifteen minutes," I said, "I shall be meeting my cousin at Georgette Klinger's, where we'll begin preparations for *the* society event of the summer, *the* most lavish and most publicized party in the history of Fire Island Pines. Compared to which, Forrest, your magazine, your decisions, your staff, and yourself are as though grains of sand in a sunless sea." I mimed the casting of sand upon the office floor and washing the grit off my hands.

"It's a matter of professional ethics, Roger. You know that?"

I pivoted a perfect one hundred and eighty degrees on a single heel—having practiced in four-inch wedgies all week—and threw open the door to exit.

"I had no choice!" he wailed.

"However," I spoke over my shoulder, à la Betty Grable in the famous World War II pinup, "should you wish to have *any* editorial staff come next week, I strongly suggest you obtain the services of two very large and experienced bodyguards. One to lock in the Grunt. The other to watch over Mizz Auslander."

"What do you mean *any* staff?" I heard his voice rise. "Roger! Roger! Don't do this to me! Ro-ger!"

"Five minutes, Miss Stanwyck!"

Alistair was knocking on the door of my "dressing room," the larger guest bedroom in his house on Tarpon.

"Can I look?" I asked Bebe, who was still fooling with my hair.

"Momentino!" He held my head in place. "I still think you should have the full wig. But . . . !" He pulled back to look at me, even—I swear—put his thumb up as Lautrec might have done, and sighed. "Okay!"

He spun me to face the vanity's mirror.

I don't know what I expected to see: some ghastly, some wonderful transformation; a revelation, I suppose. That's what Luis and Alistair had insisted I'd see. Instead, I saw myself. Cosmetized to the nines and dressed expensively, and more feminine than I could ever have imagined looking. Still it was me, Roger Sansarc, no matter how cleverly Bebe had frosted and combed my hair for a swept-up-off-the-neck effect: me!

"You did wonders with my hair."

"Up!" he commanded.

I stood. I was wearing a slinky pale-blue silk evening gown with Japanese lotus flowers on it, the bodice recut by Enrico so it exposed the natural cleavage between my own pushed together, worked-up pecs. My biggish shoulders were artfully downplayed by the bias on the sleeve. They'd aimed for a Classical Late Thirties look: long lines, flat sides. All the past week, I'd practiced walking in those damn wedgies at night, nearly spraining my metatarsi whenever I'd gone over in them, but these pumps were softer and lower and fit better. I swiveled my hips, and the gown below my knees swung in place!

"Perfection! I'd say Kate Hepburn rather than Babs S.," Bebe concluded.

"I can check Alistair now?"

"Go ahead."

When Bebe left, I reached for the little sequined purse, took out a silver cigarette box, slipped out a cigarette, checked my manicured, painted nails, put the Benson & Hedges Filter between my Cold Carmine–painted lips, and lit it—all the while carefully observing myself in the mirrors.

I didn't look unnatural or forced. But it was me—not a woman. I saw a little bit of my sister Jenny when she'd been a teenager, eternally stopping at one mirror or another in the house to check her lipstick, and maybe too a bit of my mother getting ready for church. I copied her tone of voice whenever she'd say warningly, "Rog-gerrr!"

I could admit now that I'd been afraid it would *not* be me; afraid that, like Frank Cioffi the year before at Flamingo's Halloween party, I'd turn out to look, sound, and behave totally different. Frank, a sweet, handsome, timid male, had in drag become a pushy, oversexed harridan.

But I'd always been me, no matter the circumstances: totally stoned out of my mind on acid, checking in the mirror to see who or what was really behind those eyes, or pulling myself out of my sickbed during the least restful week of sleep in my life, when I had hepatitis, to stare at my eyes, through taxicab-yellow whites.

Now I went out of my way trying to act girly; I openly posed at myself. Oddly, the only attitudes that seemed natural, despite yards of silk and the softly glowing pearls at my ears, wrist, and throat, were the ambivalent ones—the "gun moll," the "wisecracking girlfriend," the "career-woman," the "tomboy."

Another theory thoroughly shot to hell: queers weren't women in men's bodies. I'd always known that, of course. Now it was proven.

Another test passed. That's what it was for me: another ritual, another competition. Like my first orgasm. And my first major broken bone. My first orgasm with penetration. My first fistfight. My first orgasm on an LSD trip. The first time I'd realized I might die. My first orgasm with a man. My first bout with V.D. My first orgasm in public (where I might be caught and arrested). My first case of crabs. Each a step, a test, a ritual of manhood, sometimes long approached and worried about, often achieved unexpectedly or without much effort. Yes, even contrarily, this one of dressing as, being for a night, a woman. Because I'd done it on a dare, determined to fulfill that dare. And now I was content I need have no fear of ever losing my essential self or of questioning its gender, no matter what I did, how I dressed.

A knock on the door. "Showtime!" It was Alistair.

"C'mon in." I'd decided on my usual voice, moderately pitched: I'd softened pronunciation.

Alistair looked terrific. With his high cheekbones, his longer, blonder hair, his more strongly colored and eye-poppingly cut gown, he looked a great deal more female.

We did a Fellini "big-hats kiss" at each other's vicinity. Then stood and looked each other over. Bebe and Enrico pushed into the room, looking us over, primping us.

"You look so natural," Alistair said.

"You're a knockout!"

"Let's see," he insisted. "Turn around." When we faced each other again: "Amazing!"

"You picked it! It feels okay. But with all this silk sliding around, my nipples are always erect." Pecker too, I might have added, only it was held down, not very comfortably. "Turn around."

Bebe and Enrico hugged each other with pleasure. When they left, Alistair sat down on the vanity seat and pulled me near.

"I've only done this once before. Always wanted to. Ever since I was seven or so."

"Not me," I said. "Give me sneakers and jeans and I'm happy. Good thing this outfit's simple."

"Had to be. By the thirties, girls wanted to get out of them fast." Alistair laughed. "Real stockings in this era were silk, you know, not nylon, and held up by garter belts."

He'd brought in a drink. He was posing in the mirror. "We *do* have fun together, Cuz, don't we?"

"Do we ever!"

It was only natural, given all that shared stuff, that I decided to tell him what had happened with Matt's poems at the magazine.

"Of course," I concluded, "Harte's running scared that this time I'll really go. And I will. Soon enough. As for Sydelle, well, she acted no different than I'd expected. It's like this clothing in a way. It's all so prepared and yet at the same time so indirect. Poor women, taught all their lives to bend to men even when the men are stupid or wrong. Taught not to be direct or forward or openly angry . . . No wonder they become backstabbers. I'm ranting, aren't I?"

"It's okay. It's just that . . . Well, the same day I gave them to you, I airmailed the poems to a pal at this magazine in Europe—you might have heard of it, *Paris/Transatlantic*—and he phoned today to say he'd take them and whatever else Matt has. In a way I'm glad. . . ."

Paris/Transatlantic was only the toniest quarterly in literature. Even if I had gotten them into *Manifest*, Matt would have preferred the poems in the *P/T*. And, of course, Alistair just happened to know the editor, just happened to undercut me. I could have spit fire.

"You didn't think I'd even try?" I said.

"Of course I did, darling. I was just so . . . What's the line from Yeats? 'I had a fire in my head.' That's all. I had to see them in print!"

I fooled with my face. *I'd like to set fire to his head. Between the fake falls and the tint and hairspray, it would go up like a torch.*

"Does Matt know about this stroke of fortune?" I asked.

"He will tonight, when he comes to escort me—us. I thought tonight we'd celebrate."

Why not hire the Rockettes while he was at it?

"Clever Brecker," Alistair went on, "he's gotten someone to take us in a yacht." He pretended not to notice the smoke steaming out of my nostrils.

As though on cue, Brecker knocked on the door and opened it—to Alistair's relief.

"Well, Jesus H. Christ! Aren't you two remarkable!"

"Our boat?" Alistair leapt to his pump soles and held out perfumed gloved fingers, which, to my astonishment, the overbred Horace bent to lightly kiss, evidently before he realized what he was doing.

"Any moment now," Brecker said. "Matthew's arrived."

"He'll be so pleased!"

Brecker allowed Alistair to spurt out the door (and thus escape my wrath). I nervously lit a cigarette.

Through the smoke I could see Brecker was dressed in an old-fashioned black tux. It fit superbly, and it was obvious that Horace—who at six-one looked good in most clothing—possessed those precise genetic Anglo-Saxon qualities that made him a paradigm in body and stance for the black classic designed for his forebears—from the reflective tips of his patent leather shoes, up his calves and thighs (looking well-muscled through the silky cloth), crisscrossing his crotch and leaping a flash of creamy cummerbund, up the snowy field of frilled shirt-front sealed at his throat by a white, almost avian, bow tie, up his blankly good-looking, tanned rectangle of face, with its vee at the chin, to his one defining softness: a wave of honey-colored hair.

"I wasn't certain about tonight," he stammered from the doorway.

"I've never done this before."

"You should! You look . . ." He calmed himself to say, "Swell!"

At this very moment, Alistair and Matt were meeting in the living room. I couldn't be out there, even though I knew that Matt was just now hearing exactly how well placed his poems actually were, how "made" his career as a poet probably was, all in one fell swoop, thanks to Alistair. Probably Matt was hugging Alistair in gratitude, even kissing him. I couldn't stay here while that happened. Nor, on the other hand, could I witness it!

I turned around, stubbed out my suddenly sour cigarette in the vanity ashtray, and caught a glimpse of myself. Dressed like that, with that betrayed look on my face, I thought, I don't believe it! I've seen an actress look exactly like this!

Suddenly Brecker was behind me in the mirror. Even with my pumps on he was taller. In my little blue slinky, I was frail next to his tuxedoed bulk.

"You feeling okay?" One meaty hand reached toward me, patted my shoulder, unsure. "You seem . . . Fresh air? . . . The garden?"

We went out through the bedroom's glass doors. The night was moonless, glassily clear. A jillion stars shamelessly conspired against me.

"Your cousin says this'll be quite a party," Brecker made conversation. "You don't mind my coming?"

"No. You do look perfect," I said, truthfully. We'd neared the living room, but I couldn't spot them. Then I did. Matt was pouring drinks. They were close. He'd gotten his good news. He was happy. They appeared to be together. Matt looked a mile wide at the shoulders in Weissmuller's spermatic jacket, his face quite tan because of the contrasting light-colored silk, his hair blacker and more thickly curled than usual. I thought he looked more ethnic than since he'd worn sailor whites; a bit gangsterish. Because of what Sydelle had said?

Brecker blocked my view. "I don't know what plans you made, exactly, and naturally I'll understand if you say no, but I'd very much appreciate it if you'd let me be your escort tonight."

I began to snicker, and then stopped myself. Obviously, he'd been put up to it. It was *all* put up: the poems, the party, the outfits, all of it! And now I'd be worse than a fool, I'd be a spoilsport, not to go along.

"Sweet of you." I took his arm. "I'll try to tell you who everyone is."

"Okay." I thought he sounded breathy.

We went inside. Compliments, congratulations, drinks—Bebe and Enrico took bows for their work. A foghorn tooted. Alistair and Brecker went to find our boat. I lit another cigarette, put it out, and lit a joint from my silver case. Despite how I was feeling, I had to keep in mind that Alistair and I had each taken MDA, which would kick in less than a half hour from now. It was still new stuff, who knew how powerful. It made sense to ease into it via pot.

"Can I have some?"

Matt joined me at the glass doors. As I handed him the joint, he sniffed the air.

"You wore it." He meant the Mitsuoko. I had, although it had meant the poor Grunt chasing it down through the aisles of Bloomies yesterday during his lunch hour. Wasted effort now.

As Matt handed back the grass, he said, "Harte called. He was upset. Said something about an argument you two *didn't* have . . ."

I took the joint. "I'm through there," I said quietly.

"What?"

"I'm leaving the magazine," I repeated.

"Just like that?" Matthew asked, in an accusing tone of voice.

"I've had it there!" I said hard, too tired to go into detail.

"Why?"

I shrugged.

"Did you argue about the story? Bernie said you were having a conference today . . ."

Did the Grunt know Matt called him Bernie? Once, feeling mean, I'd brought a pair of Matt's nastiest underwear into the office for the Grunt, wrapped in paper with ribbon. He'd received it as though it were the crown jewels. For the next two weeks, he'd come to work looking like hell, as if he'd been up jerking off all night. Imagine loving so selflessly, content with so little in return: mere recognition, some used underwear?

"Was the argument you and Harte had about the fire you went to cover?" Matt asked. "You know, the fire in your vision!"

The question surprised me. I thought I'd explained. "I saw *ice* in my vision! Everything frozen! Not on fire."

"Fire. Ice. Same thing!"

I thought of the man in his tiny cubicle knowing he was choking to death. He'd been pathetic, not mind-sweepingly catastrophic.

"It's *not* the same! The scale is completely off . . . the absolute horror of the *scale* of what I saw . . . both times . . . and the sense of isolation . . . of being utterly alone!"

"What do you mean, alone?"

"Alone! Alone! I was the only one not affected at the Ice Palace. The time at Flamingo, there were a few others left. Four, five, out of thousands. The fire at the baths affected only three guys. . . ."

"If you're alone," Matt suddenly asked, "where am I?"

I scanned the images seared into my memory. Where was Matt? I couldn't see him, couldn't find him.

"Did I fall?" Matt asked. "Was I frozen, like the others?"

I couldn't for the life of me find Matt. Why not?

"Well?" he asked with that tone of voice that assumed he had the right to ask. "Exactly where *am I* in your visions, Roger?"

I found I couldn't answer.

He grabbed me by an arm. "Are you saying I'm not even there?"

"I don't know!"

" 'Cause if you are, I'm not surprised. *You* haven't been *here* for a while. Not with me. Not at the magazine!"

Grabbing me, he'd knocked the joint out of my fingers. As I became aware of it, I also became aware that Alistair and Brecker were in the foyer.

"It *was* our boat," Alistair reported with false gaiety. "We'll get ready." They left.

I bent to pick up the lit joint but was stopped by the tight gown. I'd forgotten I was wearing it.

Matt stomped out the joint. He was angrier than I'd ever seen him. It scared me. He turned away.

I reached out to stop him, feeling—in that dress, in those shoes—unreal, as though I were saying pre-scripted lines. "What's wrong?"

He looked at me disbelievingly, shook off my hand.

"Wrong? Jesus! You could at least . . . let me know it's over! Send me a telegram. . . . Something!"

"Over?"

"Isn't that what it means, when you can't even *see* me in your future? Lousy as that future may be!"

"That's not what it means!" I argued.

"Isn't it?"

I didn't know what to say. Matt sounded so convinced.

Just then Brecker came back. Oblivious of what was going on, he told Matt jovially, "I'm escorting the lovely lady in blue. You don't mind?"

"She's all yours!"

Matt couldn't get away fast enough.

The MDA hit as we were stepping off the yacht's gangplank.

"Whoopsie!" I heard Alistair say ahead of us. I thought, What amazing drug timing! The entire scene in front of us shattered in my vision— I too was off!

Brecker had my arm quite solidly, however, and he wasn't letting go. In fact, ever since we'd left the house, he'd taken a proprietary view of me, keeping me to himself, intent on amusing me, distracting me from the others, which—whether or not he knew exactly what he was doing—I particularly appreciated tonight. The boat ride had been short, ten minutes along the bay from Tarpon to just beyond Beach Hill, where the party was being held.

We were stepping onto a little dock. I'd half given in to the drug's primary sweep over me, and I'd half held back, trying to gauge how strongly and on exactly what sensory levels those effects would manifest.

Only somewhat visual, it turned out. By the time we were on solid ground, everything was "itself" again: somewhat outlined, it was true, and a bit over-three-dimensionalized, yet not morphologically distorted. I suspected that if, on the other hand, I closed my eyes . . . I'd experienced hallucinations of incredible cartoon likeness before on MDA! Meanwhile, in line with the "classic MDA high," sounds were intense, odors—even the bland local foliage—resonant, and touch far more sensitive and diverse—the silk of my gown felt astonishingly different from the sleeve of Brecker's tuxedo.

By now, Horace was gliding me up to one of the two gateways into the party, this entry for those arriving in boats and via Bay Walk and thus more private, although by no means entirely vacant of the spectators and hangers-on who always dangled at the edges of the bigger Pines fêtes. While most of these gawkers appeared to be in ordinary Pines garb, others had clearly been placed by the party organizers; dressed in thirties high-school-girl drag, complete with pigtails and notebooks with fat pencils, they'd rush up to arriving guests and loudly, whiningly, plead for autographs.

It was as I was signing "Kate" that two huge, slowly revolving klieg lights nearby happened to cross in midair, suddenly illuminating the scene and making it appear exactly like some gigantic Hollywood premiere from a former age or a made-for-TV film. I shuddered lightly. Horace's lips brushed against my earlobe as he whispered with a hint of amusement, "What name do I sign?"

"Joel McCrea," I said, because in that minute that's who he most resembled: the stunning young bare-shouldered god in Hurrell's photos.

Matt—ahead with Alistair—had our tickets. They'd just signed autographs themselves—doubtless as Weissmuller and Crawford—and handed the tickets to two gigantico lugs in rented tuxes who then checked our names against their lists and ushered us in.

"Did you see!" one queenlet in painted freckles loudly gushed to her cohorts in the crowd. "Kate Hepburn's dating Joel McCrea!"

Her fat buddy in green-yellow pigtails screeched, "I could just die!"

The rest of the crowd applauded, and we were through the gate.

Two large pieces of property on the bay side of the Pines had been temporarily donated for the party. The larger belonged to the Count, Alistair's large-nosed friend, the slighter to a designer pal and former inamorato: doubtless an enormous tax write-off, as it was a charity do for the Pines Conservation Committee. Even so, major work had been done: fences, bushes, even small clumps of trees between the adjoining properties had been pulled down, and fresh planking connected them, quadrupling the decks along the designer's long lanai and the Count's already amply decked, Olympic-sized dual swimming pools.

One of those remained unaltered: we'd been promised a musicale involving synchronized swimmers later on. The other pool was decked over with a dance floor. From its ten-foot diving board hung a DJ's booth.

In front of and surrounding both pools was the "Mocambo Nightclub," architectural motif of the night. This consisted of dozens of thirty-foot palm trees set in vast terra-cotta tubs, interspersed with deco-style café tables and chairs (and booths) on several levels, parts of it covered by the flimsiest thatching: all of it as genuinely "exotic" as Trader Vic's.

Before we could even reach the tables, we had to thread a flagstone path down through foliage and the "receiving line"—i.e., the hosts, the party's producers, the property owners and/or their representatives, and several women of a certain age, all attended by the inevitable Eddie Rosenberg, a.k.a. Rosatic, Doorperson Supreme of all gay parties in the city, garbed tonight in a shiny snake-green tuxedo with silver edging, and spats, his thinning hair slicked down and his upper lip sporting a small, obviously fake mustache—his intention to resemble Bugsy Siegel or some similarly ruthless Hebraic gangster being undermined from the start by Eddie's puppylike delight in parties, costumes, and pretty people.

Horace and I had been greeted along the line, the Count had just recognized my disguise (and told me I looked "Ravishing! Worthy of being ravished in or out of a dress!"), his designer had just assured me I might "Freshen up later on. Several rooms have been put aside in both houses," when I heard Eddie's low, insistent voice to one side explaining, "Loguidice. *The* current model, indeed icon, indeed *God* of the Manhattan gay scene. And with him one . . . Alistair Dodge," to which his female companion appended, "I know *him*. Recently divorced from one of the San Francisco Spearingtons!"

"Is that you, Rog?" Eddie asked. "Who would have guessed? You should dress up more often." He introduced me to one of the two women of a certain age (her hair was "champagne" blond despite the thirties gown), evidently a reporter; her name was familiar. "I know you," she warned Horace, and then explained to Eddie, "Horace Brecker the Third! Also of San Francisco."

We'd just made it past them, down a few flagstones, when I heard Eddie excuse himself and rush up to me. "That's ——— ——— herself! from the *Times* Society Pages. Thanks to you and Matt and your tony escorts, she's absolutely convinced the party's a hit. It's sure to get a full page in Sunday's edition."

I was just about to remonstrate with Eddie when I heard "Look here please!" and we all turned to flashing light bulbs from a photographer.

"Stop them!" I told Eddie. "Horace isn't even—"

"Photos are okay," Horace interrupted. "I've seen those old biddies before," he added, nodding toward the receiving line. "They make this party bona fide."

I thanked him and turned to find Alistair to tell him how wonderful Horace was being, but neither Matt nor Alistair was anywhere in sight.

Brecker had gotten us away from the pesky photographer and was brushing against my ear again, asking what kind of drink I wanted.

The bar—an imitation of the one in the Hollywood nightclub—had been constructed against one side of the designer's house. It was a huge, semicircular affair, the back screen woven through with birds of paradise and monkey faces on coconut shells. Brecker settled me in a high-backed fan-palm stool and ordered drinks from one of the three cute young bodybuilder barkeeps, who wore Samoan sarongs and garlands of fresh flowers around their heads.

When the drinks arrived, Brecker moved up his bar stool so he half surrounded me, and murmured into my ear, "Now I want to hear who everyone is. You promised, remember?"

His voice seemed awfully vibrato. I wondered if I was hearing that because of the music, half baffled by trees, or the MDA, or what?

At first I didn't recognize anyone. Then, as I concentrated and as people left the dance floor and wandered closer, I began to. Unsurprisingly, Horace had only heard of a few of the most famous Pines denizens, so I was forced to explain who everyone was. "That's La Putassa, a famous transvestite. She models for Bendel's. I once visited her apartment. A railroad flat, very long, narrow rooms, all with mirrored closets. Each closet *filled* with expensive women's clothing. That's Bill Whitehead and his lover, Tony. Bill's an editor at Dutton. Edited Edmund White's latest book. Those three are Jerry Rosenbaum, Stan Redfern, and Al Cavuoto. They rent the Shakespeare House, that place on Crown Walk that looks like the Globe Theater, where the *Star Wars* party was thrown last summer. Jerry's a stockbroker, Stan's in publishing—isn't he handsome? Al's a doll too. He's an actor. Modeled for *Playgirl*. There's Mel Cheren—co-owner and A&R man of West End Records, one of the hottest disco producers in town—with his partner in Paradise Garage, Michael Brodsky. That's Dr. Downs—Larry Downs to be precise—with his current fling, Michael Fesco, owner and operator of Flamingo, the gay hot spot in town during the winter. Besides being extremely hot and sexy, Dr. Downs has recently developed a new treatment for amoebiasis. There's his partner, Larry Lavorgna. Haven't seen his ultra-cute ex-lover Scott Façon yet. There's mucho gossip that Scott is to be seen walking his black Great Dane nude on the beach early mornings with a certain gay novelist. Speaking of writers, there's George Whitmore—great profile, no? And his pal, playwright Victor Bumbalo. Near them 'Max' Ferro and 'Mickey' Grumley, lovers for decades: supposedly they discovered Atlantis somewhere in the Caribbean and wrote it up. Ed White and his beau Chris Cox should be near. That group always hangs out together. Those guys with the muscles are Jack Brusca, the artist, and his lover, the exquisite Rafael. Jack's been in Brazil to do an enormous monument for a government complex. With them in the housedress, scarlet wedgies, and cinnamon fright wig is Jack's housemate, Frank Diaz. Does that black eagle in flight on Frank's bicep look familiar? Mapplethorpe photographed it. Besides being the hottest Puerto Rican in the city and the most desirable of lovers, Frank's the number-two person in the New York State Council for the Arts, after Kitty Carlisle Hart. There's John Curry, the Olympic gold medal winner for figure skating, and Bob Currie, the designer who recently redid the entire Takashimaya department store in Tokyo, and those two we call the dancing professors, George Stambolian and Dennis Spinninger—they could go on all night. . . ."

And so on. As I spoke, I stopped to watch and figure out who others were. Some were a cinch. My dance buddy, Jeffrey Roth, and his pal Josh Gonzalez had done themselves up not as movie stars but as soda-fountain waitresses right out of a Garland–Rooney "Hey-kids-let's-put-on-a-musical" movie: pastel-yellow tunics with bubble-gum-pink piping and contrasting pink swirly skirts with canary trim; prewar wigs with high rolls in front and extra-long pageboys in back, topped by hamburger-take-out-box hats; half-falling white socks; embroidered names over their falsies ("Madge" and "Gabby"); faces cosmetized with five-and-dime eyelashes and lipstick so scarlet it resembled dried blood. Not to be outdone by any potential rivals, Josh and Jeff had found white lace-up roller skates, and they skidded and chased each other across the decks, sending into mad angles yet never quite tipping over the period Coke trays, with glued-on plastic fudge sundaes, they carried.

As stylish, if more recognizable, were my own housemates, Luis and

Patrick, the former a sliding, sequined Dolores Del Rio, the latter stressing rather than hiding his height and rawboned thinness to be Marjorie Main as Ma Kettle. Alistair's pals had also arrived. Bebe's girth had been turned into Mary Boland's Countess from *The Women*, complete with tiara, "diamond" choker, too-tight black satin evening gown, and white fur; while Enrico had opted for the Paulette Goddard role, in a Nevada divorce-ranch outfit complete with pony-skin boots, vest, and porkpie hat.

Other characters from the quasi-eponymous film were present: from Virginia Grey's perfume salesgirl, to the upstairs maid, to the big-mouthed blond manicurist, to the aging downstairs cook—even the ghastly sentimental little girl. There were Shearers, Crawfords, Fontaines, Roz Russells, plus Joan Bennetts, Lana Turners, Ruby Keelers, Olivia de Havillands, Vivien Leighs, Bette Davises, Fay Wrays, and Mary Astors galore, naturally. My favorites were the character roles: the gawky queens who made stabs at being child stars like Shirley Temple or Jane Withers, even the young Liz Taylor from *National Velvet*, and the far from attractive guys who dressed as Judy Canova, in farm girl overalls, with half-dollar freckles smeared on their faces. I enjoyed the ethnics too: Cubanos who'd gone out for Lupe Velez or Anna May Wong or even leopard-skinned Jane out of the Tarzan movies. Horace and I *adored* the four guys from one house (the Ogre, wouldn't you know!) who'd come dressed in sensible suits, fox-headed fur stoles, and wild hats, as Hedda Hopper, Louella Parsons, and Perle Mesta, followed by a moaning, diaphanous Bridey Murphy. I kept wishing our Frisco buddy Calvin Ritchie were there doing his Butterfly McQueen act. But Alistair's pal Shillito almost compensated: he was a knock-kneed Lady Archaeologist, complete with water canteen, rock pick, and magnifying glass, accompanied by an unknown companion, a raggedy, altogether convincing mummy, who, when pinched, giggled in such glassy glissandos it could only be that tangerine-carving demon Barry Wu.

"This sounds familiar," Horace said of the music, disco till then. "A rhumba? I'll dance that."

We stood up—a little shakily in my case—to rhumba. Naturally so did every queen in the place wearing anything even halfway Latin. At one point, I counted three Carmen Mirandas on the dance floor. "Fake fruit everywhere!" Horace yelled into my ear, and I thought, Not as fake as you think! But Richie Rivera had taken over in the DJ's booth, and he'd decided to give us a complete étude on Latin-Afro blends.

It was an hour before I managed to pull a semi-stunned Brecker off the dance floor and back to the big bar, by this time absolutely packed. There was no doubt now that the party was a hit. Everyone who was anyone was there. Even the Broadway celebrities and movie stars had arrived and appeared to enjoy mixing in almost seamlessly with so many other "stars."

The more he'd danced, the more Horace had loosened up. His bow tie had come unclipped and lay dangling from one edge of his shirt, now open several buttons down. His cummerbund had come undone, and been hastily tucked in at the ends. His perfect hair had been whirled into a mess of honey curls. His face was flushed, riant, unembarrassed, young.

Perhaps it was the MDA I was on, perhaps merely the night itself and the excitement of the party, perhaps it was everything together, but the way that Horace's hands began to rove over the pale-blue shot-silk of my shoulders and back as he handed me my drink suddenly felt awfully erotic to me. I slid out of his reach as prudently as I could. A few minutes later, when the sky lit up above us, as the giant kliegs crossed high in the air to pick out of the night three parachutists clad in silver lamé, floating down onto the rapidly clearing dance floor, Horace's hands seemed to roam even more insistently. I looked at him and was surprised to note there that slightly deflated look men's faces always seem to get when their penises are erect. I looked down. Sure enough!

I thought, Naw! *Can't* be! He's so excited he forgot who he's with.

I excused myself to freshen up.

"Aww!" Horace playfully refused to let me go. When I pulled away, he pleaded, "Remember you're supposed to take care of me tonight."

Meaning what, exactly? I wondered, making my getaway.

"If you were thinking at all of trying to get into the johns here, forget it!" Mark Glasgow said.

I'd just entered the designer's house. Despite his deadpan Thelma Ritter delivery, Mark was done up glamorously, à la Roz Russell in *His Girl Friday*—or was it Celeste Holm in *All About Eve?*—in a svelte forest-green dinner suit with ecru suede trim and patches, a close-fitting

Robin Hood hat sporting the most astonishing feathers, and over half his face a jet veil loosely woven to resemble a spider's web.

"Crowded?" I asked.

"Honey, there's more crinoline in this building than there was at the Goldwyn Studios in '37 and '38 together!" He made a moue, which spotlighted a natural mole on his cheek, and before I could comment, he bitchily added, "I did just see your loverboy and some Shanghai Lily stepping inside Froggie's *maison*. Why not try there?"

"Hope you don't get too much insect life caught in that veil!"

"Twat!" he spat out as he spun around to leave. I couldn't help but notice that Mark's perfect buns had been silkily enclosed, amazingly highlighted by his outfit as he swung off sexily toward the bar.

A few minutes later, I was inside the Count's house, entering a bedroom set up for heavily costumed guests. A slim Jean Harlow and a high-shouldered Crawford with eyebrows like caterpillars were checking each other's hemlines against a line of floor-to-ceiling mirrors, while at the vanity, a hairy-chested, dark-skinned guy with full mustache in some sort of Toulouse-Lautrec danseuse getup was liberally applying pancake makeup. "Whadda ya think?" he asked me.

Not all the concealer in America, I thought. "Divine! The can?"

"Occupied!" he said, then back to the mirror. "Hell! Another damn imperfection! I give up!" He arranged the dangerously tilting *croquembouche* upon his short dark hair, then reached into his matching satin drawstring purse for a vial of coke, which he sniffed deeply and offered around. "Hey, Myrtle!" He slapped the lav door. "We got a lady in a hurry out here!" He stood up as the two others left the room, then he suddenly bent down to peer even more closely at his big, sweating face in the mirror. "They'll never believe me when I tell them I was beautiful."

"You can't be certain." I pretended to commiserate.

He exited. The lav door opened, revealing Alistair: the next to the last person in the universe I wanted to see.

"Cuzzikins!" he cooed. "I'm having the *be-est* time!"

I dashed past him, lifting the skirt and just managing to get my dick out of those black silk panties to whizz what felt like the Deluge. Outside I could hear Alistair ask, "How's Horace treating you?"

"In a sec," I shouted. Pissed out at last, I rearranged the illusion back together again and exited. Alistair and I were alone in the big bedroom. He, at the vanity, made space for me on the bench in front of the triple mirrors.

"I hate these. My profile's so vulpine," I said.

"Nonsense! We all need a touch-up," Alistair said. Then, "Well?"

"Actually Horace is a bit more demonstrative than—" A thought suddenly struck me. "Is he *on* something?"

Alistair shrugged. "How should I know?"

"Has he used MDA before?"

"Why? He's not being difficult, is he?"

I stared at our images in the mirror. Whoever had thought up this party would have been completely fulfilled at this moment—we might have come straight out of the movie.

"Because," Alistair went on primly, "if he is being difficult, you tell me!"

His tone suggested that Alistair had planned for Horace to be stoned on MDA and out of control. With me forced to handle him. Why? I decided to take the long way 'round that question. "Honey," I cooed, "has Horace slept with a guy?"

"One would think not. I honestly don't know." Alistair carefully picked at his mascara, convincing me that he did know, and the answer was definitely no. "Still, given how he leaped at this party, and his excitement seeing us dressed, how he cajoled you into being his date tonight . . . Let me do that, dear." Alistair took away my lipstick. "You'll never learn to put on lipstick if you live to be eighty. . . . It all does rather add up, doesn't it?"

"Surely, you don't expect me to deflower him just so you have future blackmail material."

"Stop fidgeting, will you! As you very well know, Cuz, I never blackmail. I do however believe that a well-placed 'anecdote' can be as effective as a sword thrust. And neater. However, you seem to have a far bigger problem tonight than dear Horace. Stay still, will you? I'm referring, of course, to the contretemps he and I happened to walk in on tonight. Not that I'm in the least surprised. See, Cuz, you literally paint the outline of the lip then fill it in. Just like with crayons and coloring books . . . You remember a short while ago, when I said what a wonderful job I thought you'd done with Matthew? Of course you do, and I'll not take back a jot: I still think so. Only . . . I didn't know then what

I know now. Now the upper lip! We both know I'm speaking of
Matthew's marvelous gift. He knows and I know and we all know how
ghastly you feel about not being able to help him as much as you'd like
to. But it's not only his talent I'm talking about, it's this whole American
gay image business you've trapped him into—"

"*I* trapped him into?"

. "Close your mouth or I'll get it on your teeth. Not you directly, of
course. But you helped certainly. Being so successful! What choice did
poor Matt have but to try to emulate you in the only way he knew how?"

"That's not the way it happened!"

"Of course, *you* don't see it. You're so tied up with your magazine and
all. And it *is* important. I'm not putting it down, Cuz. It's just that what's
good for you, growth potential for you, is where Matthew can't expand,
can't grow. Face it, Rog, you've done all you can for Matthew. You're
holding him back. It's not anyone's fault that he has more potential than
any of us dreamed. It simply is. You know it. I know it. He knows it!"

I did know it, of course. I had known it increasingly of late, known it
earlier this evening as one of the unspoken truths that lay behind our
confrontation. Now, speeding and blinking on MDA, I knew it again,
this time with an emotional certainty, a finality that . . . Now Alistair
was confirming it.

"Let's see." Alistair held my face, then turned it to the mirror. "So
natural! So! What do you think?"

"About what?"

"You see how well he fits in with even the most scattered remnants of
my little entourage, peripheral as they are. I think, well, to be brutally
frank, dear, I think Matthew's reached the stage where all he needs is a
final polish."

For a second our eyes found each other in those three mirrors, mine
dark, nearly black with fear and drugs, his lighter, clearer, so much more
lucid, and I wondered if our gaze seemed so ambiguous, so incomplete,
because the mirrors were so new, so unused to reflecting back.

". . . the final polish that living abroad almost naturally gives one,"
Alistair completed his thought.

So that was why he'd saddled me with Horace tonight. To keep me occupied while he put the final make on Matt. "It's not my decision. Talk to—"

"I have. Not in so many words. I merely suggested abroad. Doriot's abandoning our place in France. A month or two in Paris. A few side trips to meet editors, to slip Matthew into the right salons . . ."

Hearing that made me suddenly cold.

So even before tonight, it had all been decided between them, and my part, my decision, was merely ornamental—or to make them feel they'd done the right thing.

But wait! What if Alistair were wrong? What if I'd not harmed Matt but helped him? What if he'd not been trapped because of me and my career, but because of his own needs and desires, his own decisions?

Despite being so high, I was cogitating, formulating some way to offer all these arguments, when a quartet of Scarletts and Jezebels entered the room, giggling and chatting. I began to rise from the vanity stool, but as though intuiting my change of mind, Alistair held me down.

"You mustn't fail Matthew now, Rog. He needs you more than ever now to do what you know in your heart is right for him."

Staring at my own suddenly estranged and conflicted face in those three mirrors, I barely heard his whispered words through the chatter and the loud rustling of silk and taffeta around me.

"I know he can count on you," Alistair sighed. He stood up to leave.

I *had* to stop him. Stop him and stop Matt from leaving!

"Wait just one minute!" I said.

"You girls done in here?" one queen in pink crinoline asked petulantly.

"We're *not* done," I said, irked by his tone of voice. "And if you want to go back to the party with any hair left on your skull, you'd better get out right now. Alistair, stay right where you are!"

"But, Cuz . . ."

"All of you!" I shouted, knocking aside the leg of one queen who'd dropped into full lolling upon the bed. "That means you too, Melanie."

"Pushy bitch!" he said, getting up.

"Overweight! Overdressed!" I retorted, shoving her out the door. And turned to Alistair.

"I might be having trouble with my lover, and I might be stoned on MDA, but believe me, I see exactly what you're up to."

His lipsticked mouth puckered in surprise.

"... And what you've been up to since the minute you arrived at the Island with Hugger and Mugger in that beat-up old tug."

"Exactly what do you me—"

"What I mean is that for all the money from your settlement and all the fancy and titled friends you've collected and all your many many experiences in world travel, the minute you got here, you saw what your poor little cousin had and you turned fucking forest-green with envy. *You're* the one who insisted on marrying a woman even though you knew it was going to be nearly impossible to pull off. And now that it's failed, as it had to, you have the nerve to come here and try to break up *my* marriage."

"If it's solid," Alistair sneered, "I couldn't even try to break—"

"Who in hell gave you the right to make that decision? *I* never did. *I* never heard Matt do it. From the moment you got here and saw us together, you were bent on breaking us up."

"You can't bear that Matt would come with me, can you?" Alistair asked. And just then, someone stepped into the doorway dressed as Judy Garland from *Meet Me in St. Louis*. Without a glance, Alistair shoved him out the door.

"I've got to pee," the lad protested.

"Use the sink!" Alistair yelled and slammed the door shut.

"I can bear it!" I said. "Let Matt go to Europe with you. I'm not afraid. Let him go to Patagonia with you! To the planet Saturn, for that matter! It doesn't *mean* anything! It doesn't mean he'll ever *sleep* with you."

"Oh, please!" Alistair scoffed. "You're becoming infantile."

"And even if he *should* happen to sleep with you, it still won't *mean* anything. And even if, after years and years, it happens to come to mean something, it will still never mean what Matt and I mean to each other, even when we haven't seen each other for days, even when we're fighting each other tooth and nail."

"You admit your relationship is crumbling?"

"I admit nothing. The truth, Alistair, is that no matter what you do, you'll still never know the intimacy we've had, even in our worst moments."

"It's crumbling! This is your final pathetic attempt to hold onto shreds of dignity!"

"The truly surprising thing, Alistair, is that with your IQ and after all these years, you don't have a clue to what really counts in life, do you?"

"Pathetic and not even worth comment if it weren't for— I *said* stay out!" Alistair slammed the door shut again.

"But that's not what bothers you, Alistair. What bothers you is that you realize that it's all over for you. You already attained what puny little peak was destined to be your acme *years* ago! At twenty-four? At sixteen? And it's all been downhill since, hasn't it?"

"We'll see what my acme is when Matthew is a world-famous poet at my side!"

"Maybe even earlier. At nine, when you still had a complexion! When exactly did you pitch a perfect no-hitter softball game? 1954?"

"I'll show you!" Alistair shouted.

"Not the face! Anything but the face!" I shouted back, still in character. But I watched him pick up and throw a heavy bronze box straight at me. Not only that, but the fucker managed to slip out of the room while I was busy cowering from the missile he'd launched. Meanwhile it smashed into the wall with enough force to leave a good-sized dent and to break a hinge. Luckily it missed the triple mirrors, or I might have been picking glass out of my flesh for weeks.

By the time I was congratulating myself on emerging unscathed, more costumed party guests, including the previous Southern belles and some seriously post-teen "fans," had pushed into the bedroom and headed for the mirrors, the vanity, and the loo, all of them commenting on how rudely Alistair had behaved.

"The worst is," one said, "I couldn't tell whether that deranged queen was supposed to be Carole Lombard in *My Man Godfrey* or Veronica Lake in *I Married a Witch*."

"More like Irene Dunne in *The Awful Truth*! And I *do* mean awful!"

I, however, managed to calm myself down. As I exited the bedroom and sailed into the living room, I heard two acquaintances:

"He looks good, doesn't he?" Scott Jacobsen said behind my back.

"As I've always said, my dear," Bob Brasswell replied, "beauty is all a matter of lighting and distance."

"But he was only inches away! And the lighting here is fatal!"

I was still laughing over that exchange when a few minutes later I emerged from the house and found Horace Brecker III awaiting me.

He seemed breathless, eager: evidently lighting and distance were all in my favor as he looked up and saw me. I knew then that the MDA, "the love drug," he'd taken had achieved its eponymous effect on him: Horace was smitten with me—me and no one else but me.

I now faced a choice: I could ease him off, try to dance him into the ground, leave him exhausted and good for nothing but a full day of sleep—or I could give Horace exactly what he thought he wanted and let him worry about what he'd done.

I was still unsure whether or not Alistair wanted Horace seduced. Would it provide some arcane revenge on Doriot? Or would it thoroughly piss off Alistair that I'd gotten to this "straight" man when he clearly hadn't? Pissing off Alistair was my only aim now.

"I thought you'd left," Horace said, and the way that he said it— half-pathetically, half-challengingly—instantly, irrevocably, decided my course.

"That's what I wanted you to think," I teased.

"Don't be mean," he pleaded, taking me by the arm.

"You're so strong! So determined!"

"I am determined."

As we moved away from the door, Horace suddenly flattened me against the wall of the house. He covered me with his body as he nibbled and kissed my neck and ear and nose and lips, breathing into my ear.

He was so far gone he didn't care about making a public spectacle.

"I paid the boat's captain to ship off soon as we're aboard," he said.

This was getting intriguing. Should I turn him into a public love-slave and throw that into Alistair and Matt's faces?

Without waiting for a response, Horace began tongue-kissing me with such fervor and in such depth, I thought I'd pass out from lack of oxygen. When, after some time, he finally retracted his prehensile tongue from thoroughly exploring and simultaneously ravishing every square inch of my glottal insides, he said, "Promise you won't say no!"

"But, Horace," I managed to moan through the continuing palpable steam of his coruscating passion.

"Oh . . . Babe," he protested back, as his hands seemed to double

then triple in number and at the same time slide in through every possible entry and exit, front and back, of my borrowed blue shot-silk dress,
". . . you've . . . got me . . . so . . ."

"But, Horace!" I continued in that same tone of voice, which anyone
over nine years old and not MDA'ed to the kazoo would instantly have
recognized as being as fake as Mother's rhinestones, "are you sure you
want to do this?"

Another ten fingers emerged from nowhere to slip into my panties
and fondle me.

"Oh . . . Babe, I have to have you tonight. I won't be stopped by anything. By anybody."

"So you spent the night with Horace," Wally said. "And I suppose
you're proud of that."

"Not really," I quickly said.

That was untrue, naturally, but in the months we'd been together I'd
discovered that Wally (like so many of his generation) possessed an
ethical system astonishingly more rigid than my own (or that of my
flower children generation); a system wherein a deed like screwing with
a straight boy was not only not the turn-on, subversion, and giggle I
considered it, but also somewhat suspect. Suspect of, if not "internalized
homophobia," then at least a Serious Lack of Seriousness.

Wally and I had exited Central Park, crossed CPW, and walked a
block and a half. We were a few doors from Alistair's building.

"So what happened to Alistair and Matt?"

"We're here!" I announced, aiming myself at the building foyer.

Wally held me back. "Tell me!"

"Later. Why don't we deal with this mess now?"

"One answer! No, two!" Wally corrected.

"Okay!" Wally had now opened himself up to being annoyed on my
terms. "Horace Brecker III turned out to be a terrific lay. Partly, I suspect,
out of a month or so of horniness, partly out of drug-induced passion. We
made love for hours while the yacht circled eastern Long Island, and when

the MDA wore off, we passed out completely. We didn't return to the Pines for over thirty-six hours, and when we did, Horace packed up and jetted to San Francisco the next day. There, after a scandalously short time, he proposed to that woman he'd been seeing for years. And she accepted. No, he and I never saw each other again, although he did send me a note thanking me, saying not only that he never once regretted what we'd done, but that the night had been exactly the kick he needed to convince him to settle down once and for all."

"Jes-us!" Wally said. "Heterosexuals are crazy."

I let that pass: to me gays had always seemed at least equally gaga.

"And Matt?" Wally insisted.

"They went to Europe, just as Alistair said they would. Both were gone by the time Horace and I returned. Without even leaving a note. Of course I thought I'd hear from one or the other soon enough. But it was two months before, one day at work, the Grunt rather sheepishly asked for the keys to my apartment. Matt had empowered him to collect his things, to pack and ship overseas."

"So you *didn't* quit the magazine as you threatened?"

"Did too!" I defended myself. "Right after the holidays, when I had what I considered enough savings plus a bonus. It was another half year before I even had to think of money again."

"Did Alistair make Matt a literary lion in Europe as he said he would?"

"For a while . . . after a fashion. . . . Matt was published in a few quarterlies in Paris and London. He did a poem suite in *Paris Vogue* with photographs by Helmut Newton, which wasn't too shabby. He appeared with an interpreter on 'Apostrophes,' the Frogs' so-called intellectual TV show. But that was about it! The poetry didn't cross to the States until some time after I'd left *Manifest*, when Harte finally published Matt's poems.

"I never found out what happened, whether Alistair and Matt disagreed on the next step in Matt's career, or whether they developed personal disagreements, or if Matt suddenly felt that he'd sold out. After a year or so, even those few mentions and photos of him in foreign magazines stopped. I knew from friends that Alistair and Matt were no longer seen in each other's company. No surprise, given how hardheaded both of them were.

"Alistair returned here, then to L.A. Matt stayed in Europe and moved to Italy, modeling for Armani in Milan for a while. There was talk of him dating another model, some Brit who people said resembled me. But I never confirmed the rumor—or checked out the model. However, over the next year or so I'd never open *Esquire* or *GQ* and come upon Matt's photo without having one emotion or another. Usually when I came upon his photo, I'd simply be irritated the rest of the day, but one time—you're going to laugh—I didn't even recognize Matt in the picture at first, given the way he was dressed and posed, but I got a hard-on, a real diamond-cutter!"

Wally didn't laugh. Neither, however, did he seem upset. "And that was it?" he asked. "You never saw Matt again?"

"Once, at the Pines. It was a late Sunday afternoon, and I'd been visiting someone who parked his ketch there. I was opposite the restaurant and shops and disco. Across the water, I saw these three guys come out of Bay Walk next to the Pines Pantry. Two of them looked European. Older. It took a minute for me to recognize Matt as the third. His hair was long, past his shoulders. He'd shaved off all facial hair. He was wearing a loose turtleneck top and baggy linen trousers. His face looked, I don't know, harder, more adult somehow. Maybe because, as predicted, he'd lost his foot."

"You mean he . . . ?"

". . . wore a prosthetic. I couldn't see it clearly, but he was walking with a cane. It was from how he walked and leaned on it that I could tell."

As I spoke, I remembered how stunned I'd been when I'd seen Matt that day at the Pines. How I'd been so elated to see him I'd lifted one hand and opened my mouth to shout across the harbor slip for his attention. Then Matt had moved, walked maybe three steps, and I'd seen and instantly known his foot had been taken off. My shout died in my mouth, an expanding blue balloon fizzling.

"Did he confirm it?" Wally asked.

"I . . . I couldn't talk to him," I admitted.

"Because he wasn't perfect anymore?"

"Because I knew if we'd stayed together, he'd still have had his foot."

"That's medically ridiculous!"

"I know."

"And *that* was the last you saw him? Then you'd heard that he died?"

"Well . . . ," I hedged. Hoping to change the subject, I went on. "I did see Alistair again, when he moved back to the city. Wally? Can we go up now?"

That distracted him.

"What exactly are you going to do up there? What do you want me to do?"

"I'm not sure, Wals. Support me with the White Woman."

"A cinch!"

And then, before he let me go, Wally said in a different tone of voice, "Thanks for telling me all about you and Matt."

"Do you feel better about him now?"

"This may sound weirdso, but I feel like we would have gotten along if we'd ever met."

"Right," I said. Perhaps it was my own ego-generated shortsightedness, but I had this terrible feeling that each of them was so self-involved, they would have totally ignored each other, or at the most, brushed each other off.

"Gird your loins," I cheer-led. "We've got Dorky to deal with!"

"Where are loins exactly?" Wally asked. "And what precisely does it mean to gird them? To use a girdle, or . . . ? What are you muttering, Rog?"

Book
Six

Don't Leave Me
This Way

1985 AND 1991

The outer glass door was locked. We had to stand there and knock and gesticulate and make stupid faces to get the attention of the nighttime lobby attendant. And when he did finally deign to tear himself away from his magazine long enough to peer at us, he turned out to be some-one I didn't know.

"Oh great! A stranger!"

The magazine dangling from one large, hairy, pale hand was *Health and Fitness*, a Spandex-clad couple—overoiled and overmuscled—prominent on the cover, throwing "show" poses at each other among cutouts of giant oranges and lemons, doubtless in citric reverence of Florida. The lobby attendant was white, young, with a square head, big shoulders, and that specific kind of thick neck only found on obvious fans of bodybuilding. I assumed he was an incessant masturbator. His first response to us was that universal shrug denoting "What's up?"

I gestured for him to unlock one or more of the several glass doors separating us. When he'd disappeared and appeared again with a me-dieval chatelaine's set of variously sized keys, managed to get a few doors open, and was flat against the final glass separating us, he shouted, "What do you want?"

"To get in and see someone!"

413

"At . . . ?" checking his watch, "four-fifty A.M.?"

"That *is* what you're here for, isn't it?" I shouted back. "To let people in."

"Who you seein'?" He was looking us over, Wally and me, sizing us up but not giving away his evaluation. Were we dangerous? I couldn't tell what he'd concluded, until he suddenly opened up and let us into the outer foyer.

I said my cousin. It was something of an emergency.

Exactly the wrong move: he grew instantly suspicious. "What kind of emergency?"

I'd been phoning and not been able to reach my cousin all night.

"They had a party. Till late," he explained. "Might have had the phone off the hook."

"We were *at* the party," I explained back. "Left early."

"It's over." He shrugged. "You got a key to the apartment?"

"Not with me."

"You sure they're expecting you?" he interrogated.

"Yes," I lied.

"No!" Wally told the truth.

"You expect me to wake them up?"

That was exactly what I expected.

"You're living in a fantasy!"

"Something's wrong. I know it. My cousin and I grew up together. I know whenever something's wrong with him."

That bullshit unnerved him a bit.

"What's wrong?"

"He's sick. Even in a coma."

"Not a fire?" he asked.

"A fire?" I stupidly said, "No! No fire!"

To his relief. "If you and your cousin are so close, how come I never saw you before?"

"I don't usually visit at five A.M. Call upstairs! I promise to take any flack. In fact, I'll take the phone as soon as you—"

"I thought he's in a coma?"

"I'll talk to his roommate!"

"Oh." He lifted the phone, still hesitating. "If you were here before, how come you left?"

Who did he think he was? Hercule Poirot?

"We had to be somewhere!" I tried to hide my growing irritation.

"Where?"

"What's the difference?"

Wally said, "Across town. To demonstrate at Gracie Mansion!"

A minute of incomprehension from the attendant, then: "Oh yeah! I saw it on the news. That makes sense, you being gay and all," he added for his own benefit. Then, still testing us: "You see what some of them put on the roof?"

"He did it." Wally tapped my shoulder. "He was one of the guys who put the banner up on the roof."

"No kidding!" The lobby attendant smiled, and the smile humanized him. I could picture his mother showing around a photo of him, a few years younger, wearing that smile, proud of her son. "You got some fuckin' balls!" he added with a chuckle. "You're lucky they didn't catch you."

"They did catch me. I was in the Tombs most of the night."

"No shit!" That information seemed to do the trick—out of sympathy or something else, he began to dial upstairs, as he asked what the jail was like.

It took a while for anyone to answer. In fact, he was about to say "See!" and hang up, and I to interfere and try to take the receiver from him, when . . .

"Sorry to bother you, sir. It's Stanley downstairs. Someone to see you. Mr. Dodge, really. Says he's his cousin . . ." To me: "Name?" I gave it, and he reported it into the receiver and hung up. "You can go up."

"We can?"

Before I could say anything else stupid, Wally took me by the shoulders and guided me toward the elevators.

"So far, so good."

In this harsh light, I thought Wally looked pale. I hoped he wasn't coming down with a cold or . . . I suddenly trembled with the thought. . . . How many times in the past decade had some gay man thought exactly that—that he was coming down with a cold or flu—only to find himself in a hospital bed surrounded by tubes and machines from which only death released him, months later?

"Hel-lo?" Wally chimed to get my attention.

The elevator arrived. We got in. He punched the floor number. The door closed and we began to rise.

"Cold feet?" Wally asked.

"I was just . . . It's been, you know, a while since I've thought of so many of the people from the Island, from the late seventies, I told you about tonight. . . . I still can't believe that I'll never see them again. I keep expecting to turn a corner and have Ray Ford grab me from behind and spin me around and bear-hug me till my ribs threaten to crack, and I never go to any gathering without expecting to see Dick Dunne or George Stavrinos or Vito. . . .

"I don't get it! Nature is usually so tightfisted with what it provides. So very prudent how it husbands its resources. Why would Nature go to the trouble to create so much luxuriance in what after all was a group of nonreproductive creatures? Why create such an extraordinary generation of beautiful, talented, quirkily intelligent men, and then why let them all die so rapidly, one after the other? It doesn't make the least bit of sense. It's not natural. It's not the way Nature behaves.

"It's certainly not comprehensible in a society filled with such mediocrity. And, Wally, before you begin to argue, I do consider your generation of gays to be filled with mediocrity! What made my group stand apart was not only our attractiveness, our social cohesion, but that by the time we appeared at the Pines in 1975 or so, we were already achieved individuals, architects and composers, authors and designers, illustrators and filmmakers, choreographers and playwrights and directors and set designers and . . .

"Not perfect, God knows, not anything like perfect! Troubled. Hassled certainly. And why not? We'd been the first generation of gays to force ourselves or to be forced out of the closet. We had to experience the traumas of coming out, and of making the gay movement happen, not to mention the more general trauma of just getting through the roller coaster of the late sixties. . . . But despite that, we were almost godlike in our creative power. Face it, we pretty much created the seventies! Its music, its way of socializing, its sexual behavior, its clubs, clothing, its entire sense of style and design, its resorts, its celebrities, its language! We were always creating, always doing something! To what end? . . . It seems such an astonishing waste!

"And worse, it seems to never end. Tonight it's Alistair. Tomorrow it'll be . . . Who's left? How few of us? Why bother to leave any of us? Why not just wipe the slate clean and admit it was a mistake? A mistake to have striven for once to create something so . . . I don't know, creative and individual and wonderful, really. Perfect for everything but reproduction."

"Golden lads," Wally said quietly. "That's what Housman called the huge promising generation of young Brits mowed down in the First World War."

The elevator door opened. I teetered on the edge of another Act.

"You ready?" Wally asked.

"I don't know. I'm depressed. I'm enraged."

"Sounds right. Let's go!"

The White Woman might have been hovering at the apartment door, he answered so instantly. Strangely, given how long he'd taken to answer the lobby clerk, he didn't look in the least bit sleepy. As he ushered us in, I couldn't help but note that he was wearing the oddest pajamas. The bottoms were Bermuda shorts length, lightly ribbed, of some sheer material. They showed off his blondly downed thighs, his big square knees, thickly muscled calves, and strong-boned bare feet. The pajama top was equally sheer, a loose-fitting buttonless chemise with elbow-length sleeves, meant to be belted closed, but worn open now, exposing his fillet-of-sole skin hue and well-proportioned chest, with its flat pectorals and chessboard stomach muscles. In all the time (perhaps two years) I'd seen him with Alistair, I'd never thought of him having a body, never mind one so gymnased. I should have guessed. Aside from the occasional "sleazy number," all Alistair's mates had been strongly physical, even his wife, Doriot.

"I was just making hot chocolate," he said as he led us through the big hall past the study and living room into the kitchen. "Couldn't sleep. Guess it was the excitement from the party and all the people tonight."

I tried to peer down the hall toward Alistair's room, but the White Woman at the kitchen door blocked my view, instead guiding Wally and me into the warm, brightly lighted room. I thought I made out the closed door to Alistair's bedroom. Signifying what? I couldn't say.

"I'll bet you guys want hot chocolate." He followed us into the room, blocking our retreat.

Although the big prewar apartment was laid out lengthwise along an axis of hallway, the centrally sited kitchen and bathroom occupied their own architectural anomaly. With its high, tin-patterned ceiling and twenties built-in cabinets above the refrigerator, sinks, and stove on both sides, the kitchen jutted out from the building at a distinct right angle, forming an unexpected space large enough to hold a table and four chairs hemmed in by tall casements of narrow, mullioned windows.

By day, and in the best of circumstances (strong sunlight, a recent Windexing), one could barely make out one slab of the building and the blank wall across the airshaft, with a tempting sliver of street toward the Hudson River. Tonight all was darkness as we sat down, Wally and I, removing our jackets and placing them over the back of the fourth chair as we always did. Unsure how to proceed now that we were in the apartment, so close . . .

At the stove, the White Woman chatted about the party, adding milk to the pan he was heating, reaching for more cups.

"None for me," I said. This night was definitely not over; I'd need all my wits about me. "In fact, if you'd reheat the coffee . . ."

"Sure. Meanwhile . . ." He handed us mugs, the sugar bowl, a blazing carmine cardboard box of Dutch cocoa. "Why don't you mix it?"

Wally looked up at me for help, and I saw his eyes slide left—indicating Alistair's room.

Our host saw the signal. "What?"

"You can do it, Wals," I teased, explaining, "He's a little spastic." I watched Wally bite his upper lip as he mixed the cocoa and sugar and milk. I hadn't been completely lying, although he wasn't spastic so much as awkward: he reminded me of a five-year-old mixing finger paints.

"You want me to reveal what I know?" our host asked.

Wally and I almost fell out of our chairs.

"Well," he tried a conspiratorial smile, "we did see it all on 'The One O'clock News.' "

"The demonstration?"

"Don't be modest. Know what Alistair said when he saw it? He said 'There goes Cuz again! Doing umbrella steps on me.' "

"Umbrella steps?" Wally asked.

I didn't know what he meant either. "Those ready?" he asked Wally. " 'Cause here comes the milk."

He brought the pan over and expertly mixed the hot chocolate.

"Seems that when Rog here was a kid growing up on Long Island, they used to play a street game called 'May I?' " he went on, explaining to Wally, looking to me for confirmation. "Alistair said that in the game one person was 'it.' The other kids stood some distance off at a line and had to advance to tag him. To advance, they could take baby steps or giant steps or scissor steps or umbrella steps, just as long as they said how many they wanted to take, and—crucially—if they also asked, 'May I?' "

"Scissor steps," I explained to Wally, "meant jumping with your legs out, then sharply in. Umbrella steps meant twirling around as though you were going around the edge of an umbrella you held by the handle."

"Evidently Rog here always won 'May I?' using umbrella steps." The White Woman poured my reheated coffee. "Because they were variable, Alistair said he could never judge how many steps to allow Rog. Rog would take advantage of this to embellish his umbrella steps wildly. According to Alistair, he would fascinate any watcher, until zoom! he'd suddenly sail past the line and Alistair would find himself tagged."

"So . . ." Wally was puzzled. "Tonight . . .?"

"So tonight, by not only appearing on the news but by hanging the banner on Gracie Mansion and then by being arrested on camera, Rog once again threw smoke in everyone's eyes and jumped ahead. At least that's what Alistair said. He seemed to think you did it especially for him. As a sign. Or for his birthday."

"What do you mean? What did he say?"

"Just that you'd taken umbrella steps again! But the way he said it signified that over the past few years you'd done it a lot, kept fooling him, kept shooting ahead." He concluded by looking on me fondly.

That nearly blank face almost undid me.

"Listen, I've got to . . ." I stopped myself. "Is Alistair asleep?"

"That's almost all he ever does anymore."

"He doesn't need anything?" Wally probed.

Orkney scoffed. "Hardly!"

I was still trying to do this without letting him know anything. So I continued to probe. "Alistair didn't say anything else . . . about me? For you to tell me?"

"No. Why? He expect you back tonight?"

"I guess not."

"Why did you come back?"

"Didn't you have to use the john, Rog?" Wally interrupted.

"You *did* get off legally tonight, didn't you?"

"Don't worry. I'm not taking sanctuary." I rose. "I *will* use the john."

All the night's earlier coffee flushed out. Then I quietly tried Alistair's door. Locked. Sure sign he'd taken the Tueys. That did it, no?

As I sat back down at the table, Orkney was telling Wally about whatever Asian body discipline he was involved in, which somewhat explained the pajamas. Wally was trying to be interested, but his eyes shot over to mine, screaming questions I not only couldn't answer, but couldn't even respond to.

I waited until there was a gap in their talk, then casually said, "I tried looking in but . . . That bedroom door stick?"

"Not that I know of."

"I couldn't get it open," I said.

He looked at first me, then Wally. "What's going on?"

When it instantly became apparent from our embarrassed silence that we knew very well what was going on and weren't about to answer, a sudden gust of cold air filled the space above the table, as is said to happen when a ghost enters a room. He never took his eyes off us as he slowly got up and pushed past me out of the kitchen. We followed and found him outside Alistair's bedroom, thumping against the door, pulling at the handle.

"It's locked!" he said, hysteria an undertone in his voice. "He never locks it! What's going on? Something's going on! Why did you two come back?"

I decided to brass it out. As I moved toward the door, I said, "I wasn't certain he'd do it."

"Do what?" His voice began to rise. "What's going on? What do you know? Why are you here? What did you plan behind my back tonight?"

"It's probably for the best." I attempted to calm him down.

"What's for the best?"

"Alistair and I discussed it in great detail long before tonight," I said. "For months. It was always a viable option. You must have known that too."

"Nooooooo!" he suddenly wailed in full comprehension of what we were talking about. He turned around to begin kicking and thumping at the door with his bare feet and bare hands.

"You'll hurt yourself!" Wally shouted.

"Alistair! Boopsy! Open up! Wake up and open the door!" He kept hitting the door. He spun on us, his eyes wild. "I'll find the key!"

"Why not leave him? Why act like this when . . . ?" I tried.

He was having none of it. "Murderers!" he shouted and began making what looked like karate chops at us, trying to get us out of his way.

"But Alistair wanted it!" I cried. Wally and I were backing up, less out of fear of his karate than out of embarrassment at his antics. "You know Alistair would never do anything he didn't absolutely want to do."

"You connived behind my back! The three of you!"

"Count me out!" Wally said.

"Then you two."

"Don't you understand? Alistair's not going to get better. He *can't* get better. He's going to get horribly worse and die horribly."

"We'll make it! We made it through the other illnesses!"

"It gets worse! Believe me! His body'll go to pieces. His fingernails will drop out, and where they were, his fingers will ooze. Old wounds will open up and bleed. His hair will fall out and his skin fester. I've seen it. I've been through it before."

"Nooooooo!" he kept wailing. His crazed gesticulations had moved us to the kitchen doorway, which he more or less got us into before he made good his escape into the living room.

"That queen is completely possessed!"

"Did you expect any different?" Wally asked.

"I guess not. What now?"

"Are we sure Alistair took the Tueys?" Wally asked. He was terrifically upset but determined to remain calm.

"Why else would he lock the door?"

Wally looked despairingly at me. I knew what his next words were going to be, so I said them for him. "Look, Wals. I know I've gone back and forth about this all night long."

"*I'll* say!"

"But after all, it's a person's life here. Not a carpet color. No matter what one thinks of the person. This is for keeps. And I'll be totally up front with you. I really haven't known *what* to do here. Actually, I've sort of counted on you to let me know."

"*Me?!!*"

"Sure. The more you said it was wrong, the more I thought it was right. It was when you began to waver that I did too. No matter what any of us does tonight, Alistair's going to be out of the picture in a short while. It's us I'm concerned about. You and me. Tonight . . . tonight we've gone through a lot and I know it's not over yet. But I really feel that this is the test. This now. Do you understand what I'm saying?"

"Yeah." He looked about five years old. "I think so."

I had to take a chance now, just in case he didn't understand fully: "I failed once, Wally. With Matt Loguidice." There. I'd said it. "I loved Matt. I really did. You were completely right about that. And I failed with him as a lover. I failed because I was egotistical and selfish and, oh, who knows, just generally fucked up, like most of us. And for some reason I'll never understand, when Matt was dying, I was given a second chance to prove myself to him. Maybe it was his doing. I don't know. It was close, though. It was almost too late. I don't want that to happen with you. I want you to tell me what to do."

Wally's face showed amazement at what he was hearing. Although there was no doubt in either of our minds that he'd been harrying me about exactly this all night long, now that I'd brought it up, he was surprised.

"A deal!" Wally said. And raised his hand to slap palms. Instead, I kissed him. "A deal. Now what? You tell me."

"We've got a choice. Let Dorky run wild and maybe end up saving Alistair's life or . . ." Wally showed me his fist.

"Just what we both need. An assault charge."

"It's one or the other."

We located the White Woman as he was charging out of the living room into the hall, something—the key?—in his right hand.

The next few minutes would prove if Wally and I really were a team.

"You up," I whispered. "Me down."

I threw myself at Orkney's groin, butting him and pushing him over onto his back. As he fell over, Wally wangled the key out of his hand.

We backed off and stood over him. I began to explain in what I hoped were supremely rational words what we were doing and why.

The White Woman was fit, however. Despite having the air knocked out of him, he managed to get to a half-kneeling position.

"So you see," I was saying, "nothing you can do will— Oof!"

He leapt into the air, pantherlike. Taking us unaware, he threw us into the wall behind. He and Wally were down on their knees scrabbling around the edges of the hallway carpet for the key.

"Rog! Grab him! He's— Ah! The fucker *bit* me!"

The White Woman stumbled back, grabbed the key from the floor, and fled down the hall. By the time I'd reached his back and was pummeling him, he'd managed to get the key into the lock. We both fell into Alistair's bedroom as the door opened inward.

I don't know what I expected to see. It was just Alistair in bed. On his back, faceup, his hands on either side of him, the sheet and light cotton blanket pulled to his chin.

The two—then as Wally came in, three—of us became still, oddly respectful.

Orkney crawled to Alistair and took his hand. Evidently it was pretty cold. I couldn't see any indication of breathing. Orkney lowered his ear over Alistair's half-open mouth.

"He's still alive," he whispered. He jumped up to his feet and began to pull Alistair off the bed, along the bedroom floor.

"What the hell are you doing?" I cried out.

"Have to get him breathing!" he explained. He'd dragged Alistair along the floor halfway out the room before we could stop him. Alistair's T-shirt had been pulled back to his armpits, revealing his skeletal torso spotted with dark lesions.

Seeing his poor, disease-ravaged body, I panicked. "Stop! Stop!" I pried Orkney's hands off Alistair.

"Have to get him moving," he kept repeating mechanically.

"You'll just kill him faster!"

"Nine-one-one. I'll call nine—" The White Woman dropped Alistair's arm, which hit the wooden floor with a thud. He turned toward the phone on the bed table. But I'd foreseen that move, stumbled to my feet, and got there first. As he reached for it, I ripped the cord out of the phone, then out of the wall.

"Call nine-one-one!" he continued to mutter. Moving back from me, he half tripped over Alistair in his haste to get out of the room.

"Wally, stop hi—" The White Woman managed to dash out the door. He slammed it shut on Wally, catching him on the nose.

"Son of a bitch!" Wally was jumping around.

I was seriously irate now. I got past Wally and Alistair's body on the floor, opened the door, and charged down the hall to the living room. The White Woman was there, holding the phone, dialing, and he wasn't sufficiently prepared for my anger. I flung myself directly at the receiver, ripped it out of his hands, threw it on the floor, pulled the cord out, pulled the other cord out of the wall, and began hammering the receiver against the metal edge of the TV set. Orkney scuttled off, still muttering, and I ran for the kitchen, getting there a fraction of a second ahead of him, in time to rip that receiver too out of the wall unit and tear it too apart.

"Here! Fucker! Use this!" I threw it at him.

He looked at it. "Murderer!" he shouted. Tears streaked his cheeks. He suddenly looked like an old woman: an old peasant woman fending off Cossacks.

He fled—I assumed to the building hallway, possibly to awaken the neighbors and try to use one of their phones. I also ran to the apartment door, intending to block his way. He was there all right, and we wrestled hard for control of the apartment door. Meanwhile, at the other end of the corridor, I could see Wally bending over Alistair's body, checking his breathing, straightening out his T-shirt. The apartment looked like a war zone. How could this be happening?

It finally seemed that the White Woman was running out of steam. After he was unable to dislodge me with a particularly vicious rabbit punch, he moaned loudly and fell onto his hands and knees upon the hall carpet. Holding his head in his hands, he kept moaning and repeating, "I can't let you!" over and over.

Suddenly he was up again, rushing into the living room. I tried to guess where he was headed next, what he was planning to do next. I knew I shouldn't move away from the front door. Then, he was out of sight, aimed for the kitchen. Probably planning to shout out the window and wake up the neighborhood.

"Wals! Grab him before he gets us arrested, will you?"

As Wally entered the kitchen, the White Woman leapt out past him, across the hall into the study; and from the study into the living room, back and forth across the hall, totally lunatic.

Suddenly there was silence—no motion, no sound. I edged away from the apartment door, listening, slowly headed for the living room. The White Woman suddenly dashed out, followed by Wally, and I ran back to the front door.

Just as he'd planned. He feinted for the door, then, as I fell against it with my entire body, he instead dashed for the wall phone to the front desk, a few feet away, but just beyond my reach. Before Wally or I could say or do a thing, he shouted into the receiver, "Stanley. This is Sixteen-J. Get EMS. Do you hear? It's an emergency. We need an EMS upstairs! Now!"

Wally was so outraged by this trick, all the Taurus in him suddenly emerged: he began to paw at the hallway parquet with his black Patrick-shod feet the way a bull paws at the earth just before charging, inching forward all the while, his head lowered, his face so screwed up with fury I expected steam to start pouring out of his nose and ears.

The White Woman was still shouting instructions into the receiver when Wally hauled off and socked him. I could see the surprise on Wally's face at how much the punch hurt his own knuckles as he connected on a superb uppercut to Orkney's big, solid jaw. The punch made a sort of *clunncck!*—oddly metallic for bones, I thought. But it sure worked. The White Woman's head snapped back, his eyes fluttered wildly, and when Wally reactively withdrew his bruised fist, the White Woman's head snapped forward and his entire body collapsed under it, a marionette instantly cut from its strings.

I moved into line to catch him. He might be a complete turd, but I didn't want him damaging his head. All that dead weight falling on me brought me into a kneeling position on the hallway floor. In this pietà pose, I began to check through the disarray of flopping limbs and Jap pajamas in my arms for pulse, breathing, and blood pressure. Everything seemed okay. Except, of course, he was out cold.

"My hero!" I overdramatized to Wally.

He was still shaking his fist as though he'd burned it. "Jeez! Nobody ever said it would *hurt* so much!" Then re the White Woman: "He all right? I didn't mean to . . ."

"You'd better get some iodine and a bandage on your hand."

"I thought he'd never stop," Wally said.

"He'll be okay." I got up and began drawing the unconscious body by the shoulders into the study, toward the divan.

"He wouldn't stop," Wally was complaining.

"It's o-kay! Wals! You did what you had to."

"He was like fucking *Alien!*"

"Fix your hand. I'll try to get him comfortable."

I sort of heaped the body onto the divan. Alistair sure knew how to choose 'em. Who ever thought the White Woman would be this loyal? Who dreamed he would even dirty his hands to protect Alistair? Not me, I had to admit.

Suddenly I had a seven-year-old's desire to lift up the PJs and look at his dick.

"Tales . . . calculated," I began aloud, remembering a magazine title from a time only shortly after I'd actually been seven years old, "to drive you Maddddddddd!"

I left the study door slightly ajar so we could hear when he woke up. And there, where we'd left him on the floor of the bedroom, was Alistair.

Wally had wrapped his hand with toilet paper when I pulled him out of the john to help me. We were just bending over Alistair's body, our arms out, our knees bent, our bodies poised to lift him as gingerly as possible so as to avoid any further marks of damage and yet still get him back onto the bed; I was suddenly flashing on how much in doing this the three of us resembled a line drawing by John Flaxman, an illustration he'd done for the *Iliad* late in the eighteenth century, titled, I believe, "Sleep and Death bear off the corpse of Ajax," which I'd first seen and been impressed by as a teenager . . . when the apartment door burst open.

Stanley, the downstairs lobby clerk, wielding his enormous set of keys. Behind him, two heavyset guys in V-necked pink shirts and loose-fitting pants, a variety of utensils at their necks. Despite my amazement at their sudden appearance, I knew them instantly: EMS.

We almost dropped Alistair.

"Jeez! You were right!" Stanley shouted. "You called just in time. Their truck was just passing by. He still alive?"

Wally and I were swept off Alistair's body by the two. I stumbled over one leg of the bed table and reached to keep it from falling: four Tuinals and an empty glass of water right there!

The Latino medic dropped to a knee over Alistair, feeling for a pulse. The shorter guy—balding, with a tiara of Clarabelle-orange hair—glommed onto the Tueys about a second after I did.

"Pink and blues!" he said in a staccato voice. "Self-inflicted."

These two looked very professional. I had to do something to delay them.

"He threatened suicide before!" I said. "He has AIDS!" I added, for maximum shock effect.

It sure worked on Stanley, who had stepped forward out of natural human curiosity and who now fell back against the hallway wall as though someone had sprayed the deadly virus into the air. It worked on the EMS guys only for a second. The one kneeling down pulled on a pair of rubber gloves before he shoved two fingers into Alistair's mouth.

"He's breathin'. But shallow. Pulse's a butterfly. I figure hour. Two."

"Bad news!" Clarabelle replied. "Gotta get a tube in an' pump 'im!"

"That may not be a good idea," I said. "He had candidiasis of the esophagus a few months back. He sustained damage. You might rupture it if you put a tube in."

The Latino looked up. "If we can keep 'im breathin' till ER . . ."

He was out of the apartment. A minute later, he was shoving past Stanley, carrying a metal contraption he shook open into a gurney.

I exchanged glances with Wally: desperation.

"You seem to know a lot about his health," Clarabelle said.

"I'm his cousin."

"Next of kin?"

"Yes. He's been hospitalized. He's been close to death . . . several times already," I said in a tight voice. "Obviously . . . tonight he meant to . . . We'd talked about this and . . . What I'm saying is I don't know how extreme the methods you use should be. . . ." I clammed up, feeling guilty as shit under his cold, unwavering, judgmental gaze.

"I hear you. But the fact is, whenever we get a call for service like this, by law there's stuff we have to do. Heart. Lungs. You got a problem with him breathing better?"

What the hell could I answer?

"Once he's at Roosevelt, you can tell 'em whether you want extraordinary methods or not," he added in a less accusatory tone.

"Fine. I'm coming with you." I'd make certain nothing extraordinary was done to "save" him.

They opened the gurney and lifted Alistair onto it, surprised by how lightweight he was. The Latino rubbed Vaseline on Alistair's lips, then managed gently to insert a ribbed tube into Alistair's mouth. He attached it to a small hand-driven pump. The tube suddenly swelled, thick, opaque, like the shaft of an Alien's cock.

We moved down the hallway.

"You hear it?" Clarabelle asked as we passed the study door.

The White Woman moaning, evidently coming to.

"The dog." I shut the door all the way. "You'll take care of Dorky while we're gone, Wals? Won't you?"

Stanley was in the building corridor, holding the elevator door. At the sight of Alistair in better light, he was shocked and disgusted. The gurney fit into the lift by a thirty-second of an inch.

Wally grabbed the keys out of the apartment door and locked it. All of us crammed inside the elevator and it dropped. I kept my fingers crossed, expecting at any minute for the doorman to remember that someone else lived up there. He didn't.

In the lobby, the EMS guys wheeled Alistair out to the van.

Wally grabbed me by the arm. "What are you going to do?"

"Who knows? What a nightmare this has turned out to be! You?"

"I'd better stay here. Go back upstairs. As soon as the Dork's better, we'll come over to Roosevelt. I'll bring your jacket."

"He took them, Wals. He took fifty-six fucking Tuinals tonight! He really wanted to die. He expected to die! What if he doesn't die tonight, Wals? What then?"

"Be strong. Do whatever you can." Wally hugged me.

"You comin' or what?" Clarabelle shouted at me.

"I'll be right there," I yelled back. "What do I say if he wakes up?"

"Tell him we tried . . . !"

We tried. That's what Wally said. Seeing Alistair like that, he'd come to accept his decision, and to support me in my decision. Despite this agony of frustration, I'd never felt so close to him.

One door was open to the back of the EMS van. As I began to climb in, Clarabelle shouted, "Wait a min' huh?"

He and the Latino were at Alistair's head. The gurney had been fixed to the floor and walls. The Alien-cock tube was now attached to a fixture on one interior wall. Something was happening: the two of them were grunting messages at each other in a verbal shorthand. It was only when I twisted my neck and peered deep into the far corner of the van that I got a hint—the other end of the tube in Alistair's mouth entered a compression chamber. The two of them were drawing a gauze bandage around Alistair's head and tying it to the tube to keep it in place, further taping down the tube's winglike flaps to Alistair's chin. I guessed what had happened and asked anyway.

"He stopped breathing," the Latino said. "He'll be okay once we get him to ER."

"You better drive, Nestor," Clarabelle said. "I'll stay back here."

Nestor got out and I got in. Clarabelle had a little pull-out seat attached to the front interior wall of the van. My own seat pulled out of the back door once it was shut. I knew he didn't trust me: that's why he was staying here instead of driving.

The van was filled with machines. The oxygen compressor seemed to be the only one on, and it was making a lot of noise. Its loud rhythms reminded me of Darth Vader. As I sat down, a little square window slid open in the front wall. I could see half of Nestor's face, his expressive brown eyes, before he moved away.

"We all ready?" he asked. Given the phony sound, he must have been using a connecting mike.

"All ready!" Clarabelle spoke through the window, then hammered on the connecting wall.

The van took off, headed west. The siren began, despite the early-morning hour and the probably thin traffic. I calculated our route: we'd turn left at Columbus Avenue, zip into Broadway at 68th Street, then down Ninth Avenue and into the Roosevelt emergency room at 58th. It would take ten, maybe twelve minutes.

And so it seemed, at first, though I couldn't see where we were going, with Clarabelle's big head blocking the tiny window view. The van turned left sharply, picked up speed on the avenue, swerved a bit left to right, obviously getting out of the way of slowpoke drivers, slowed down for cross traffic—some idiot not quite awake—sailed past the complex of lights where Broadway entered, sped on—and came to a screeching halt.

At the same time, I heard what sounded like two skyscrapers collapsing against each other. One—or both—hit the ground with a tremendous, an explosive, a scarifying thud, not far in front of the van.

"*Jesús! María! Y su amor Her-man!*"

Nestor wasn't through with his imprecation when we heard another thud.

Clarabelle got up and began shouting through the window, asking what the hell was going on. Just then the van was battered on the left side, then even more soundly battered on the right.

"Nestor! What the hell is going on?"

"Oh, my God! The crane fell down. What a disaster!" Nestor was shouting through the microphone. "The whole thing tipped over! Sixty, seventy feet!"

"Can't you get around it?"

"It's blocking Ninth Avenue."

"Back up. Back up!"

"I can't. There's cars everywhere."

"Put on the siren and back up!"

Nestor did as he was told. We felt the van move a few feet back before it hit something. In a second, Clarabelle was past me, to fling open the door.

We were some twenty feet in from the corners where Columbus became Ninth Avenue and crossed Broadway. I could make out most of Avery Fisher Hall to our left in the paling darkness. Behind us was a sea of headlights—not only directly behind us and at odd angles to us and to one another, but farther behind, lined up all the way back for a mile.

Clarabelle jumped off the back of the van and began going to the cars, shouting, trying to direct them to back off. But the crane, in falling upon some cars ahead of us, had evidently led to an immovable three-lane pileup all around, with minor accidents. One middle-aged man got out of his car, holding his head, and almost collapsed onto the hood of the Caprice next to him. Nobody was paying attention to the EMS van, our siren, or Clarabelle's shouting.

A minute later, the siren slewed to silence. Nestor emerged.

"He okay?" he asked about Alistair, shoving me deeper inside as he hunted through the inside fender lockers.

"I guess."

"You stay with him. Watch that monitor. You see? If anything happens to his breathing, turn it up. You see there? If anything happens to the machine, hit the red button. It restarts the motor. Got it?"

"Where . . . ?"

He'd already pulled out a thick blanket; now he grabbed a metal valise, then another, which he thrust out of the van's back door.

"We got two men hurt at the crane," he shouted, explaining to both me and Clarabelle. "It's bad. I phoned them into ER. They'll get us out of here."

And they were gone.

I stepped out of the van door, edged along the back bumper to the side, surrounded by a knee-high blanket of headlights. People were yelling, horns blowing. Not thirty feet ahead in the dark blue morning, I could make out the shadow of a giant openwork metal structure fallen at what looked like a sickeningly wrong angle. What a mess!

After a few minutes, I was chilled by the morning air and got back into the van. When I closed the door, it damped the noise considerably. I shivered upon the front pull-out seat, where I could stare down directly on Alistair's face—that terrible tube!

"Well, Cuz!" I said aloud, hearing trembling in my voice. "I wouldn't have guessed it possible. But we seem to be alone. Now what?"

I looked at the compressor. Clearly, if something were to be done, that was where it would have to be initiated. Where? How?

Alistair's lips were bruised where the tube had been pushed in, and I could make out yellow-and-black marks on his neck where we—the White Woman or Wally and I—had manhandled him tonight. I couldn't stop myself from crying.

To stop, I checked the connections and located what seemed to be a simple electrical plug. Once that came out, the compressor would simply stop.

Aloud I said, "I should have suspected you'd have this much clout with the Powers That Be!"

What I was thinking was, It's your decision now: his life or his death. It's in your hands, yours alone, now.

"Why is this happening again? Didn't I do it right the first time?"

"I've had just about enough of this shit! We've *all* had enough of this shit!" Sal said.

The others assented, shifting their poses for more menace.

"Good. Good," Blaise quietly urged them on.

"This is *our* bar! *Our* space!" Sal half pleaded. Then, harder, "You've no business being here. Ever heard of the Constitution?"

"Ever hear of this, faggot?" Sherman pushed his nightstick into Sal's abdomen, just under where his falsies would jut out. "Suck on this, fairy!" he added, poking harder. He turned to Andy and Big Janet. "Okay, men, let's round up these swishes. What are we waiting for?"

As they moved to surround the others, grabbing at them with open handcuffs, Sal stood very stiffly where he was. He clicked together his high heels. Then whirled his large purse at Sherman's head, catching him a good cuff, surprising even Sherman, who was poised for it.

Everyone froze, then the other three clicked their heels together, turned, and slapped Andy and Big Janet upside their heads. Even readier than Sherman, they also fell to the stage.

"What have we done?" Eric imitated Bambi's hoarse voice.

"What we're doing," Sal said, beating at the now stumbling Sherman again and again with his purse, "is getting ours, finally!"

The melee worsened. David M. jumped over the bar and deftly mimicked karate kicking the rising Andy back down to the floor. Big Janet crawled downstage to the left, then aped opening and closing a door. Again everyone froze, this time longer.

"One of the cops made it to the men's room," Carolyn began, as she moved in front of the *tableau vivant*, "where he radioed for help. Another cruiser in the area responded, but its occupants were pulled inside the bar and stomped. The cop in the john called for backup, saying he had four men down. By then, a crowd had gathered outside, and some of the drag warriors were leading an assault on the parked cop cars, breaking windows, turning the cars over, as the sirens of more cruisers screamed closer. The event that would change the world for lesbians and gays forever had begun at the Stonewall Inn."

"And . . . curtain!" Blaise Bergenfeld announced, standing.

Those onstage relaxed. Blaise turned to me. "Naturally, Cynthia's sound effects will be top-notch."

"Naturally."

"You have a problem?" And when I didn't answer: "You don't like something? I know! The speech at the end is too long."

I was afraid to say a word. Fear gripped my trachea, stomach, tongue.

"We'll cut it a little," Blaise agreed. "But it's okay."

"Blaise," I managed to spit out, "it's not the scene. It's the whole thing. It's . . . awful!"

Those onstage caught my words.

"Not you guys!" I quickly shouted. "You were fine." Dropping my voice, "But, Blaise, the whole play, it's going to be a disaster!"

"What could possibly be a disaster?" Blaise lighted one of those overly sweet Egyptian cigarettes. "I know. My staging?"

"Your staging's fine." I used an old program to fan off the stench. "I wish you'd smoke tana leaves somewhere else. It's not your direction, not the acting, Blaise. It's the writing."

"*You* wrote it!" Blaise reminded me, unnecessarily.

"I wrote it and it stinks! I said it would when you first asked me to do the adaptation. Stinks worse than the mummy rags you smoke."

Blaise raised an eyebrow and a shoulder. "You're just depressed. You'll get over it." He spun around. "Okay, kids, take ten. We reassemble for the Casement trial scene. Sal, you were divine and we think it's sheer perfection that a solidly built hetero like yourself wants to act in drag for the company, but try to control your enthusiasm. You clobbered Sherm!"

"I'm sorry. Really I am," Sal said. "I apologized twice."

"You're certain unconscious homophobia isn't emerging?"

"Jeez, I hope not." Sal raised his hands like an Italian matron witnessing a statue of the Madonna suddenly bleed. "I'll bring it up with my therapist next session."

As he exited, Blaise said in a voice only I could hear, "One would give a goodly sum of one's teeny paycheck to be a fly on the wallpaper at one of those therapy sessions. To hear how it came about that doctor and patient have managed to arrange it so that ladies' man supreme, Sal Torelli, of Bay Ridge, Brooklyn, is not only working for the only openly homo theater company in town, but plans to wear full drag in a major role in the gayest theater spectacle of the decade." He sighed. "Rog! Go home!"

"You really intend to continue this torture?" I asked in a panic.

"You've been here all day. The theater wasn't meant for authors to sit inside of all day. Go home to your desk and write or jerk off or something!"

"Why can't you admit it's tacky and melodramatic and it's going to be a disaster?" I was desperate now. "Is that so difficult to admit?"

"The play's fine. You'll see. The scene's okay. Listen, the last play I directed . . . we put in this absolutely stupid, if somewhat funny, line a week before opening. During the play's run, no matter what else happened night after night in the audience, that one tacky funny line got a laugh. Moral: never underestimate the audience's intelligence. What may seem tacky and melodramatic to you is 'moving' to them. Take my word for it." Blaise turned around completely, as though modeling the cigarette-ash-dusted blouson and loose black pants he affected—designed to hide his waistline, I suspected, but actually making him look like a Japanese art student living in Paris. "Thanks, Cyn. Those new blues work just as you said they would. Go home, Rog. Sleep. Get laid. Don't come back until you're in a better mood."

He pushed me up the aisle of the tiny theater, past the curtain into the minuscule lobby.

The sudden brightness reminded me that it must still be afternoon. I checked the clock over the ratty sofa. Only 3 P.M.? Couldn't be. I felt I'd been inside the theater for days, weeks!

Someone stepped down and out of the hole in the wall off the lobby that held lighting controls. A statuesque black man dressed in what looked like a hippie version of buskins. Very statuesque, indeed, with—I saw as he turned toward me—the face of a Xhosa prince. Next out of the booth came the broadly pink-corduroyed bottom of Cynthia Lomax, coming out of her demesne, the control room. She jumped to the floor, grabbed Mr. Africa by his wide shoulders, and her cloud of carrot hair shook as she said, "Deal?"

"It's a deal," he agreed in a honeyed basso.

They rubbed noses.

Cynthia approached me and perched on a sofa arm. "Blasé's right, you know," she said, using the entire company's joke name instead of the real, if pretentious, one our director sported. She spoke in an eternally surprising little-girl voice. "Authors always get jitters." Her almost featureless face looked as though it had been hastily copied off a Raggedy Ann doll: button eyes dragonfly blue, mere pinch of a nose, cartoon-tiny mouth, apple-tinted cheeks. "This *is* your first play?"

"And my last! I should never have listened to him when he came to me with that outline. I should have shut the door."

"Blasé would have gotten it on the stage one way or another. He's had his heart set on turning your book into theater since the day he read it. If you hadn't agreed, he would have stolen the material and written it himself. *Then* we'd have had a real disaster."

"You've stage-managed a lot of shows?"

"My share."

"And you *don't* think this one's going to go under?"

"Nah! It's fun!" Cynthia said, merrily. "It's always interesting. The next scene they're rehearsing? . . . The trial scene . . . I knew nothing about Casement before, and now . . . well, I adore it! I tell everyone about the show. My girlfriend even read the script."

I didn't know Cynthia had a girlfriend. The way she seemed to be constantly surrounded by a pickup-truckful of handsome little lesbians clad in overalls, with tool kits on their belts, certainly showed how popular she was. I wondered which baby dyke was her inamorata.

"I wish I had your faith," I said, but I felt a bit better. Cynthia had that effect on everyone, everything she came into contact with.

"You'll see," she insisted. "We'll run way past the showcase period, and then Blasé will have to worry about Equity making us pay real salaries and run ads and all that."

She hugged me so fast I didn't have a chance to push her away. As Cynthia passed through the curtain into the theater, I couldn't help but notice that the guy she'd kissed before was still lingering inside the lobby. He looked as if he would say something to me, spun as though leaving, then turned back.

"Don't tell me," I said. "You were watching the scene from the control room and you agree it stinks."

"I was mostly talking with Cynthia. But what I paid attention to in the show seemed fine." Then, "You're Roger Sansarc. The writer."

"Guilty as charged."

"Reason I axe is, I think we had a mutual friend? Back a few years in the Bay Area. My name is Bernard. Bernard G. Dixon. The friend's name is . . ."

His name had turned a key in a door into 1974. I was on a balcony overlooking Pozzuoli's main floor, looking down at people entering for a vernissage, talking about Donizetti's *Linda di Chamounix* with . . .

"Calvin Ritchie!" We both said the name at the same time.

"I don't remember any friend of Calvin's named Bernard. I met all Calvin's friends. Most of them were white. Only his boyfriends were . . . Oh, my God!" I suddenly got it. "You're Bernard!"

"I just said that."

"Of Bernard and Antria?"

"When I wasn't going with Calvin, I . . ."

This vision of Kenyan pulchritude was Calvin's Bernard? No wonder Calvin had gone through such shit.

"I'm afraid I have bad news about our friend," Bernard said.

"There's no bad news left," I said, feeling the familiar bitterness sweep over me instantly again. "I was on the Coast last week when he died."

"You was?" Bernard said. "I was in a show. Couldn't get away. We talked up until a few weeks before . . . until he couldn't speak anymore on the phone. I should ask how it was."

"Don't! I don't want to remember the details." But of course I did remember them. "Whatever happened to you and Antria the night of that big party at the bookstore? You know, the night we all quit our jobs and the others got subpoenaed?" I asked.

Bernard didn't recall.

"So, you're what now? Living on the East Coast?"

"East Side. Alphabet City."

"And you know Cynthia?"

"From productions. I'm an actor. And dancer. I've worked pretty steadily since I got here. I live with someone. A guy from El Salvador. He's an orphan. Lost his family in right-wing shoot-ups. Came here not knowing anyone or even English. I help him along. You know, Calvin taught me a lot about myself. It took a while to sink in," Bernard admitted. "And it wasn't until recently that I found out who I really am . . ."

Imagine Calvin's Bernard being sensitive—sensitive, nurturing, with teak-colored thighs like tree trunks and that face . . . ! No wonder Miss Ritchie had upped and died. Why bother going on? I couldn't help but recall those last few sessions at the hospice, Twin Peaks and its TV-transmitting antennae filling the view through the window, that perfect white California light, Calvin's face shrunken into that of a hundred-year-old—"Miss Jane Pittman as drawn by the artists of *Tales from the Crypt*," as Calvin accurately, cruelly, described it to my horrified amusement. No lies between us, not ever. His bony, sore-cracked knuckles grasping my hand, his stertorous breathing—even with the tube.

". . . compared to the one out there. Even so," Bernard was saying, "it turns out that Calvin had many friends and even family now in the tri-state area. So, it's tonight. At six."

"A memorial service?"

"Just across town." Bernard handed me the invitation.

The card was dove-gray, with brown ink: classy.

"It'd be really nice if you came. Bein' how close you were and all," Bernard said. Before I could answer, he was out the door.

I stared at the invitation, remembering how Calvin's eyes had grown to the size of fucking Crenshaw melons just before . . .

"You still here?" Blaise charged through the curtain, headed for the control booth. He climbed up and began doing things with lights, followed by Cynthia, who climbed in behind him.

A memorial service for Calvin—how many did that make this month?

Heads peered out of the booth. Together they said, "Roger! Go home!"

The address on the invitation must be wrong. Could that be the chapel behind the low, wavy fieldstone wall? That tiny building (given what must be prohibitively expensive midtown East Side real estate) shaped like something Le Corbu might have designed late in his senility and curiously sited within the looming shadow of the United Nations' Secretariat Building?

Must be . . . Inside, what I could make out of the chapel continued the motif of subliminal grotesquerie: more low, wavy walls in dark tulipwood and "comforting" warm tones. Only a hint of the externally overused fieldstone surrounded what I guessed to be the altar area (little else hinted at it) and around one capriciously rhomboid window that peered into the heart of a stand of ginkgo trees, devoid of leaves this early spring evening. Above was a matching rhomboid skylight. Slabs of yet more tulipwood and teak formed the sides and backs of pews, softly angled, more or less concentric, already filled.

I signed in and located a seat not too far from center. I squirmed on the cushion, then became aware of piped-in music: the adagio to Bruckner's Eighth Symphony, appropriately dirgelike, if by no means one of Calvin's favorites (Calvin's absolute fave, Bernstein's *Candide* Overture, was undoubtedly too bubbly for the occasion).

I concentrated on the program, although I was far more interested in who all the people around me might be. From the cursory glances I had made, they seemed of mixed skin color, age, and gender but on the whole white, professional, thirtyish, and female. Strange. However did they know Calvin Ritchie? From his work with the San Francisco and Santa Fe operas? From the two or three TV programs of those productions? From Calvin's few articles over the years since he'd quit the magazine? From his one small book, *Singing—and Acting—Donizetti's "Four Queens"*? Unlikely: that densely reasoned monograph (almost doubled in size by footnotes and quirky discography) had been published by a university press somewhere in the Australian outback, released in an edition of no more than a thousand copies, by now unquestionably out of print.

Perhaps the program might give a clue to the group by indicating how Calvin was to be acknowledged tonight? The copies carefully laid out upon the pews exactly mimed the expensive style of the invitation—who'd paid for it all? On the front cover, along with Calvin's dates, was a photo taken maybe two years ago, in which he looked wonderful—chubby and balding and happy, his mouth open as though about to make some devastating quip about Gruberova's *"Caro Nome."*

Instead of explanation, however, the program seemed to be a cryptic sketch of who would be taking part in the memorial. The only name I recognized was "Signor Dane Bryden-Howard," the pseudonym of a young male countertenor whose career Calvin had pushed at one time. Bryden-Howard was to be one of two "artistes": he was to sing the coloratura aria, "Let the Bright Seraphim" from Handel's *Samson*, an aria Joan Sutherland had debuted with in the Laserless Dark Ages. Cheeky lad. But Calvin would have loved it, Calvin the greatest Opera Queen on two coasts. Calvin who'd called me many things but most often "My vanilla Malibran," after the nineteenth-century diva and whom I had called back "Leontyne!" or on an especially good day simply "Miss Norman."

The other "artiste" on the program was listed as "Mademoiselle Francine—'Francie'—Faeces," who would be reading a poem: author, title, and subject unlisted. The rest on the program were Sarah-Anne Schenk, "Miss Upper Peninsula, 1975–1978," and three men: Leonard Barber, Andrew Reese, Jr., and Darius Miller. The host would be the Reverend Mr. Foot, from the Jersey City Ethiopian Church.

But if none of this program calmed my already serious misgivings, seeing how precisely the Bruckner movement's tempo had been described in the program—*"Freierlich langsam: doch nicht schleppend"*—relaxed me a bit. I might not know a soul here, but in that listing I sensed the unmistakable hand of a Very Efficient Queen.

I looked up in time to spot Bernard Dixon entering with a smaller, lighter-skinned man, when there was a general murmuring from those in the pews. Near the altar, a very tall, very bald, wildly mustachioed young African-American had stepped out of some heretofore hidden inner sanctum (the good Reverend Foot?), followed by a pretty, stunningly built young brunette (Ms. Schenk?), whose attempts to "dress down" in a black mourning suit had clashed with her physical prepossessiveness, resulting in an outfit monklike yet form-fitting, her breasts so prominent you expected her to constantly try to flatten them down with her hands. Behind her, an overcosmetized woman dressed as a child, in a too wide and too-short-for-her pale-blue frock, with frizzy Crayola-yellow hair pastelly beribboned into double up-in-the-air pigtails, carrying a dazed-looking teddy bear (Miss Faeces?). Behind her marched three slim and very grim-looking black gentlemen garbed in what looked like ninja assassination outfits, save for spots of red and green color here and there (Messrs. Barber, Reese, and Miller, I assumed), each carrying a differently shaped smallish object, like a fetish or juju I couldn't quite make out, they seemed to be so rapidly, surreptitiously, hidden within the capacious dark folds of their uniforms.

The five personages quickly sat down in one of the pews nearest the lectern, kept reserved until now, where they were joined by Bernard Dixon and pal. As they too sat down, Bernard's blocky companion turned around, checking me out. He had to be the boyfriend from Central America I had heard about: his facial features so perfectly Mayan he might have been any of a hundred sacrificial victims pictographed on ruined temples vine-encrusted for centuries within the miasmas of the Yucatán.

In the pew behind me, I heard someone pushing his way into the already crowded row with a lot of "excuse me"s. The voice seemed awfully familiar.

Before I could turn to look or indeed do anything more than note the words or the voice, the reverend faced the congregation. In a velvety deep voice, he murmured, "Our brother and friend, Calvin Coper-nicus Ritchie, 1946 to 1985. The Lord giveth and the Lord taketh away."

"Copernicus?!" that same voice behind me asked, dreadfully familiar now and awfully close to my left ear. "*I* thought the name was Albert!"

Despite my instincts, which said, *Don't*, I now could no longer hide from myself the fact that I did recognize that all-too-familiar voice. Instinct also said that above all I ought to avoid turning around to be certain. Then I felt a hand on my shoulder from behind, confirming that indeed it must be, of all people, my second cousin, the dreaded Alistair Dodge.

"What's this Copernicus business?" Alistair asked.

"What are *you* doing here?" I whispered furiously.

"Same as you, sweetheart," he whispered back. Leaning closer: "Albert! I'm sure of it."

"How would you know?" I asked. After all, Calvin and Alistair had only spoken in my company, around me as it were, and usually in very pointed phrases that revealed what they thought of each other.

Immediately from somewhere behind me came the sound of a plucked instrument, in obvious prelude, its sketchy theme filled out by a high, blaring trumpet, then by a disembodied, bright, genderless voice: the Handel aria.

People turned to look at the singer, but all they saw was the blank fieldstone wall. Somewhere nearby was an obscure chamber that opened slyly and acoustically, if not visually, into the chapel.

It was a *coup de théâtre* Calvin would have adored, I found myself thinking, still puzzling over that name Reverend Foot had said: whoever suspected Cal's middle name was Copernicus? Co*per*-nicus?!

Bryden-Howard moved into the area's echo section, trading stratospheric phrases back and forth with the trumpeter, until they united amid trills, the vocalist's decorated, the instrumentalist's barely negotiated. The keyboardist then began to noodle in the slow middle section and was joined by the singer, whose plummier tones were now evident. They were joined by the brass, and the duettists once more rose again in tandem, gaining speed as they circled each other, until first the trumpet then Bryden-Howard hit their final phrase and high note, the instrument a teeny bit flat, the singer dead on pitch.

It was glorious! Astonishing! I hadn't listened to his *Art of the Prima Donna* LP—nor for that matter the CD that had replaced old OS 25232—in months, but Bryden-Howard seemed perfectly to mime the Australian diva in her palmiest early days. Could singers channel the living? That pianist in Europe a few years back claimed she was playing Liszt's Second—until then totally unknown—Sonata (as well as a few allegedly undiscovered "*Nuages*"). But Bryden-Howard's technique! His tessitura! It was uncanny! No wonder Calvin had been intrigued.

Even so . . . what was one supposed to do now?

"At the least, it calls for a bravo," Alistair said, leaning over onto my shoulder. "Or a bouquet of roses thrown onstage. Instead all we can do is sit here, unfairly excited."

Maybe if I ignored him. . . .

What sounded suspiciously like a scuffle in the front, reserved row of seats of the chapel suddenly arrested everyone's attention. The Reverend Foot stood up straighter, and behind him first Miss Upper Peninsula then Mlle. Faeces appeared—could it be?—pushing for position. The Beauty Queen won. The reverend noted the fact and said, "We're here to memorialize our brother and dear friend, Calvin Coper-nicus Ritchie. As you may know, he grew up in a suburb of the state of Michigan."

"Revisionist history!" Alistair loudly said from behind me. "He came from Grosse Pointe, not some slum!"

The Reverend Foot was only stopped momentarily.

"Sarah-Anne, that is Ms. Schenk, was a close friend, also from Michigan, and in fact if you've looked at your program, you will have read that for three years running she was Miss Upper Peninsula, which any man with eyesight will confirm." As a murmur began in the audience, he quickly added, "Miss Schenk will speak next."

Sarah-Anne strode to the stage and took the microphone.

"She looks like Ann-Margret in the role of a hopeless spinster in that English feature a few years back," Alistair said. I found myself giggling at how precise the description was.

"Hi," Sarah-Anne said. "My title is not, as several people already expressed to me earlier here, some joke! It's a quite real title and I am quite proud of representing, not as some have suggested, environmentally damaging industries such as zinc mining and whole-forest logging, but the natural beauties of the lovely lake country that just happens to lie in the very geographical center of our continent."

The minute she opened her mouth, I felt unable to stifle a long, deep yawn. She nattered on about how and when she'd come to know Calvin, but some near fatal combination of tone and rhythm in her speech induced somnolence faster and more surely than the second act of *Siegfried*. I had to pinch myself awake, only to look around at people sitting very stiffly, very still, themselves no doubt also locked in the throes of her absolute verbal torpor. Vainly I fought it, until finally with no misgivings at all, I succumbed, and only came to again when Alistair leaned over from the pew behind.

"What say we have dinner after the show?"

"Show?" I tried to wake up enough to sputter outrage.

"My treat?!" Alistair's eyebrows danced with unspoken promise.

". . . and after that humorous incident," the beauty queen was at last concluding, "we were friends for life!" If she expected some reaction, she would have to go around and awaken more listeners. "How close a friend was Cal?" she asked, I hoped rhetorically. "This close: Calvin picked out my entire last winter makeup. *That's* close."

"In the words of Debbie Reynolds," Alistair said, "ask any girl!"

Smugly Sarah-Anne curtsied, and couldn't help but let out a single long-repressed giggle before flouncing from the lectern.

Behind him, Alistair clearly enunciated to his neighbor, "... One case where the lobotomy seems to have taken beautifully!"

But the Reverend Foot was on his feet again, booming out in marmoreal tones, "Next to speak will be Calvin Coper-nicus Ritchie's colleague in theatrical productions, Mizz Francine Faces."

"No! Feee-ceees!" She made a moue and, grasping her teddy bear and substantial handbag, approached the lectern.

"Oh, brother!" Alistair said. "Is she going to spell it?"

"Hoooii!" She placed the stuffed animal over the lectern, so its head drooped over the edge. "I know," she responded to someone invisible. "The dust'll all rush to his head. But you know, he likes it. Likes it? He's addicted to it. I mean, what else does a teddy bear have to get him high? Okay, some people—some nameless people—do use stuffed an-i-mals for lewd and lascivious purposes, and I guess there's that ..."

All the while rummaging through her enormous bag.

At last she located a small pad. "His name, by the way, is Sully. But I call him Silly. What I'm going to read in memory of Calvin is a poem I mentioned to him a lot which I learned in preschool and which Calvin said he also learned in preesk." She found the page, squinted, declared, "Glasses," and began rummaging in her bag again. The glasses were large and red plastic, with lenses shaped like '59 Buick headlights. She let her head fall to the shoulder, first one way then the other—obviously an acting method she'd learned to loosen up—and in her totally Bronx accent began: "An-i-mal crackers. And cocoa to drink. These, I think, are my fav-o-rite things, to eat. To eat. To eat and drink." She paused and smiled at the audience and sailed into verse two: "An-i-mal crackers. With lions and pandas. Giraffes and ..."

"What *is* this *shit*!" asked a male voice from the front row.

Behind me, I heard Alistair loudly, incompletely hold in a guffaw.

"... horsies and birds with wings," Mlle. Faeces continued.

"Birds with *what*!?" The interrupter from the front row couldn't hold in his outrage: "All damn birds got *wings*!"

Alistair's guffaw spilled out through his hands.

Undaunted, Miss Faeces continued: "I like them all. Like them all. To eat."

"You probably like to eat sum'in else, Miss Frenchy," the heckler intimated. Then, annoyed at someone's comment unheard by me, he loudly responded, "What do you mean, hush?" Turning around: "I'm here too. I'm not outside the building. And I know shit when I hear it."

"Let her finish!" someone shouted.

"Why?" he wanted to know.

"Let's get it over with. Or we'll be here all night."

But there was no chance of that. Deeply offended by the criticism, Mlle. Faeces closed her pad with an audible slap upon the lectern, thrust it into her capacious bag, grabbed poor Sully out of his semirecumbent posture, and stomped away from the lectern, indeed right out of the chapel.

Alistair was enmeshed in mirth, half rolling onto his pew neighbor. She, rotund and primly dressed as an office manager, seemed to countenance my cousin's excessive demonstration with her own giggles.

Again a scuffle, as Reverend Foot stood up at the same time as the ninjas and Bernard Dixon. Bernard pushed his way to the lectern, immediately revealing that his had been the voice we'd just heard interrupting.

"I don't know who-all you are out there. The reverend and all says you was Calvin's friends, even though I don't recognize any of you— okay, yeah, I see *you*, Malcolm!"

"Cuz-a-rooni! Look!" Alistair whispered so loudly that everyone in four rows had to have heard it. "Didn't he used to beat up and rob Calvin every weekend for drug money back in San Francisco?"

"He used to be bad," a sedate woman in her sixties agreed, "but he's found Jesus!"

"Jesus better keep a tight grip on his wallet!"

"That's uncharitable."

"No one is uncharitable around Bernard," Alistair assured her. "Voluntarily or not!"

That scandalized her, and drew protests and calls of "hush" from around us, as Bernard continued.

"I just want say one thing that's kind gotten out of the way so far here today with all this Handel-in' and Environmental-in' and Animal Cracker-in', and that's my man Calvin was a faggot, in case you didn't know, although how you couldn't if you really were his friend I can't say. An honest-to-god, sometimes fucked-up faggot, and who should know better than Calvin but myself? You know, cocksucker, take-it-up-the-ass faggot, which is how he got sick and died in the first place. And proud to be a faggot. No one's spoke about that. So I wanted to say it," Bernard added a bit lamely now that his anger was spewed. He seemed chastened at his own impulsiveness in standing up, or more probably at the blank expressions he now faced. "Thank you," he ended contritely and sat down.

Prodded by the reverend, evidently afraid of further spontaneous interruptions, the three ninjas stood up and pulled out of their shirts what turned out to be two smallish drums and a set of sticks.

"As you probably know, Calvin was into opera an' all, but he supported Pan-African arts too, and he got our group a grant to appear in junior-highs across New England. We recite and sing and play instruments and, well, you'll see."

Leonard dropped back and grasped his drum close to his lower torso. Andrew Reese stepped forward and clacked the sticks together, ceremonially announcing, "The Story of Prince Calvin!"

The rest was in patois. Or maybe in Swahili. It wasn't English, although it was undoubtedly exciting, both the narration—accompanied by sticks and drums—and those spots of solos—instrumental riffs and combos, as well as songs. It sounded wonderful, but it was so incomprehensible, so out there, it might as well have been Venusian.

Finally, the Reverend Mr. Foot said it was time for anyone among the congregation who wished to speak a few words in memory of the deceased.

Alistair pushed me. "Now's your chance."

"Stop!"

"Anyone?" Mr. Foot asked.

The reverend himself broke the silence by haltingly beginning to half mumble a eulogy which he'd evidently that moment just received, obviously written quite small on three-by-five index cards.

The brief eulogy over, Reverend Foot announced, "We will now sing a psalm from the Holy Scriptures. If you look in the pocket of the pew in front of you, you'll find . . ."

"That's my cue. I'm out of here!" Alistair said. "C'mon, Cuz, my reservation at Demetrio's is for eight. Mustn't be late."

For the twentieth time in my life, again completely embarrassed by Alistair, I also stood up, and as my pewmates scrabbled through their Psalters looking for the right page, I stumbled over them to get out.

Unfazed, Alistair didn't stop talking for instant. "The lobster gnocchi with black angel-hair pasta tastes like a twelve-year-old's scrotum. . . . And the waiters!"

Out in the fresh night air, I stopped and looked around. It had turned to night while I was inside, and now across the street the buildings of the United Nations Plaza were lit in three shades of yellow, framed by a polarizing cobalt sky featuring the ghost of a crescent moon.

It's beautiful, I thought. Then I considered: it's beautiful, yet it looks like a photo off one of those dollar postcards of New York you buy in Times Square.

"Fabulous view!" I heard behind me: Alistair, with an edge to his voice I couldn't quite make out. It was clear now that Alistair wasn't about simply to vanish as I would have preferred. He was going to hang on until he'd gotten what he wanted—which meant I would have to have dinner with him. It could have been worse.

"What was it Noël Coward said about the terrible potency of cheap music?" Alistair asked, rhetorically I was certain. "He should have included postcard views."

"I was just thinking the same thing."

"Terrifying, isn't it?" Alistair said.

More terrifying than he'd ever know, I wanted to say.

"Of course, nothing surprises me anymore," Alistair said. "Although I must say that memorial service came close."

"It *was* odd," I admitted.

"If we were any closer to Broadway, you could have sold tickets. Can you see the playbill? Miss Faeces and her addicted teddy! The Eddie Murphy Trio singing the adventures of Prince Calvin in Zulu!"

"You forgot Miss Upper Michigan Peninsula speechifying on the Wonders of Ecology."

"I wish I *could* forget America's cure for insomnia."

"The Handel aria wasn't bad."

"Sound the trumpets!" Alistair hummed and laughed. "Can you imagine how Bridey Murphy's card must read?"

"The diva of your choice . . . " I began.

" . . . alive or dead!" we finished it together.

Well, maybe, I allowed himself to think, this dinner might not be so unpleasant after all. One thing Alistair wasn't was stupid: he'd be aware of how little he could presume upon me. And it *had* been a long time since we'd even seen each other—six, seven years? It might prove amusing.

"If we're going to do a full critique," I heard the Alistair-like brittleness in my own voice, "we might as well begin with the reverend."

"You mean his Paul Robeson imitation?" Alistair said, his own voice dropping an octave. "Or his Stalinist revision of Calvin's history? I *thought* you'd pick up on that. And where did he dig up that phony middle name?"

"I *was* right! What *was* Calvin's middle name? Edward or . . . ?"

"Albert was the name *I* read when I went through his wallet one day while he was in the kitchen making tea."

"You didn't."

"Just checking his age," Alistair said with complete aplomb. "You'd be astonished how many lie about it."

Six years supposedly allowed every cell in your body to die and be replaced. But not Alistair's. He seemed unchanged.

"And what about 'An-i-mal crackers and cocoa to drink,' " Alistair chanted in a Bronx accent, then cut in with "What is this shit!"

We laughed again.

"But the truth is, Cuz, I could have taken anything in there but that spectacle of spectacles, Bernard Dixon Reformed . . . looking like some dowdy statuary in Hyde Park. . . . That is where this runner stumbled."

"Did you know him in San Francisco?"

"Before. In L.A. He was hustling some of the fancier Beverly Hills gyms as a so-called 'athletic trainer.' "

"So you knew what he looked like?"

Alistair slid a hand through my arm and nodded toward where others who'd been in the chapel were now beginning to creep out. No explanation was needed. Together Alistair and I began to walk, Alistair aiming south.

"Cuz, when I first laid eyes on Bernard, he was like that six-foot solid-candy bunny made especially for Lilac Chocolates on Christopher Street every Easter. . . . You could have feasted for a month without hitting a single inedible inch."

The old, exaggerating Alistair.

"How much did he get from you?"

Alistair was offended. "Surely, you know no one steals from me and lives to tell the tale! . . . It was a friend he lifted from. And it was a Porsche! The friend got it back. Paid to get it back, actually. Had to go pick it up somewhere in Altadena." Alistair had to laugh. Serious again: "Very traumatic for him, of course." More laughter.

"He's an actor now. And a dancer. . . . He may have reformed."

"Makes no difference," Alistair assured me. "Big Bad Bernard has been felled by the mightiest of foes. Way beyond the reforming skills of any mere Jesus." And when I didn't understand: "Bernard's been grasped in the unforgiving talons of that archenemy of mankind, Eros—in the form of Miss San Salvador 1986."

"I notice."

"Did you notice how Bernard leaned forward every two seconds? He's in thrall. He's a footstool!" Alistair exulted. Adding: "I'm phoning my friend and telling him we already have the revenge we wanted. Here we are!"

He'd stopped in front of a chic Italian restaurant.

"It looks pricey!" I peered in the window at the menu, which seemed to be one of those sheepskins with thin lettering and barely readable prices.

"My treat!" Alistair insisted, as I knew he would. "I did invite you. I come here all the time."

For one of the waiters rather more than the others, it turned out.

"Demetrio," Alistair whispered, as we entered the white-tablecloth-and-dried-flower-arrangement ambience and were greeted by an old oak bar, several facing booths in oxblood leather, and beyond, a room of tables sparsely settled at this predinner hour. Half-standing, half-leaning over the bar, talking to the barkeep, were three slender, attractive, olive-skinned young men in dazzling white shirts and tuxedo slacks. One, handsomer and more whiplash than the others, glanced at us and smiled a knife-cut of lips and teeth, a glitter of mica-gray eyes. "Demetrio,"

Alistair repeated as, graciousness itself, Demetrio met us, guided us to a booth, snapped it free of demons with a napkin, and bid us be seated, all the time flirting back at Alistair.

When the waiter had left—with a sincerely taken vow to mix our negronis himself—Alistair looked across at me from the steeple of his folded hands upon the tabletop and sighed. "To think, those buttocks, and that secret place they close upon, have never ever felt the total onslaught of a ravaging tongue. It makes one sad, Cuz! Sad! But," he recovered quickly, "I content myself with believing that with a name like his, there must be prevalent Grecophilia in his lineage, and who knows but also an inbred openness to that glorious civilization's sexual preferences!"

The negronis arrived perfect. Alistair was coy as a schoolgirl as Demetrio hovered about him, explaining the night's specials and hinting at how he would personally improve them, concluding with a demonstration in mime of the Caesar salad he would toss at the table.

When he was gone, Alistair sighed theatrically, and I said, "I must admit your taste is consistent over the years."

"I never dated anyone who in the least resembled him."

"What about Dario? The Sicilian gardener you got deported!"

Alistair dismissed the idea. "Superficial similarities! Totally different gestalt!"

I toyed with saying it, then decided to go ahead: "I visited him in jail the night before they flew him out of the country."

"Dario? Why?"

"He asked for his things. Your mother's second—or was it third?—husband brought them, and he made me take them inside to Dario."

Alistair could have cared less, so I went on.

"I didn't understand it until years later."

"You weren't that dense, dear. You knew we were screwing."

"I knew that. I saw you. What I meant was, I didn't understand until much later why it was he made me do it."

"Take the stuff in to Dario?"

"No. Show him my ass."

"My mother's second husband asked you to show him your ass?"

"Dario asked me."

"Right there in the jail-house visiting room?"

"Some room in the courthouse area. We were alone."

"You are full of surprises, Cuz."

"You see what that meant," I went on. "It wasn't you specifically he was obsessed by. It was . . . He could barely bring himself to ask me."

"And . . . ?" Alistair asked.

"What it meant was that he didn't blame you for what happened." I spelled it out. "He blamed it on his taste; his misfortune, he called it."

In response, Alistair shrugged and went on to butter lightly what seemed to be a homemade breadstick. I found myself wondering how much Alistair actually did remember of the past. I didn't remember everything, naturally, but what I did recall I recalled vividly, in fullest detail. From discussions over the years, I knew others' memories were less vivid. But surely not Alistair's. Not with a bear-trap mind like that.

"Forget old beaux, Cuz! Tell me about yourself. Not that I'm totally ignorant of your doings, even from afar. For example, I know that you've been teaching at one of the local universities . . . and that you wrote and published a book! In fact, lately, I can't go anywhere without people asking if I'm related to you. It's terribly ego-deflating."

"Very funny," I commented. But just to keep the subject going a bit longer, I added, "The book did get around a bit. And I've actually allowed myself to be talked into writing a play based on it. In fact, I came here, to the memorial, directly from rehearsal." Having gone that far and watched Alistair's eyes widen and perhaps also harden a tiny bit in envy, I immediately qualified what I'd said. "A small gay company, naturally. The tiniest theater. Stage is so small, we've had to write in a part for the assistant stage manager so people won't be too disturbed when he changes the scenery."

As I'd thought, Alistair hadn't lost an iota of teenage stagestruckness. "Cuz, you really never do cease to amaze!"

"Off-off-off-off Broadway," I said. "In the far West Twenties. Virtually in the Hudson River!"

"An author of a critically acclaimed book now to be a hit play and soon after to be a motion picture! I'm green with envy. Nile green, I believe, is the exact shade." He pretended to check his arm. "Or is it Russian green?"

"Motion picture, my ass! Starring who? Rock Hudson and Liberace?"

"Both bankable," Alistair chided. "However, one hears," Alistair leaned over the table to confide, "that poor Roy has but days, at most weeks, to live!"

"Roy who? Rogers?"

"Hudson! That's his real name."

The same pretentious Alistair. I enjoyed the bitter sweetness of the Campari, the chill of ice against my front teeth. Why didn't I order negronis more often? Probably for the same reason that I was liking Alistair tonight, but wouldn't dream of looking him up.

"Is it too late to ask if the play is cast?"

"We're in rehearsal, Alistair. We open in two weeks!"

"Ah, well! But if your male ingenue has an unfortunate accident . . . Who is your male ingenue, anyway?" He mimed writing down the name on his shirt cuff. "But seriously, Cuz, it's too exciting. I'll come, of course! I'll come opening night. I'll bring and send everyone I know!"

"Given the size of the theater, if you send half of who you know, we'll run a year."

Our gladiator namesake from Ravenna reappeared, with giant wooden bowl, dishes, cruets, utensils, and comestibles, and before our eyes turned mime into reality—and into Caesar salad. My cousin watched so closely, it gave me a chance to inspect Alistair. He didn't look bad, despite what he'd always said about blonds falling apart after thirty. His skin was taut, with the shadow of a winter vacation tan. His hair was thinner on top, and rising atop the brow so his widow's peak was more pronounced. The streaks of color were perhaps artificial. A mole on Alistair's neck I remembered him complaining about and demanding to have cosmetically covered for the Jungle Red party was gone, doubtless surgically removed, and possibly some light surgery had been done under his eyes, where sagging had threatened for years.

The salad made, Alistair tasted; I tasted; we approved. Demetrio served, bowed, and vanished.

"He looks exactly like Dario," I insisted. "I'll bet you already know the size and shape of his dick."

"I wish! But as you've no doubt correctly guessed, I am single again, and very much in the market. And yourself? You're not getting into the greasepaint by any chance?"

"There are a few guys in the cast. . . . But I've been single pretty much ever since . . ." Rather than continue and have to say since Matt and I broke up, which was pretty much true but would implicate Alistair and thus seem to be critical and open a can of worms we'd tacitly agreed to keep unopened, I decided instead to be grown-up. ". . . for a few years." I added, "By choice! Anyway, with people dying like flies around us, it's not exactly the best time to be diving headlong into romance."

"All the more reason to keep some glimmer of romance alive."

"Speaking of mothers' husbands," I changed the subject as Alistair might have, "how is your mother?"

"Fine. Boring. Married again. In fact, I've come to believe she knows how boring she is, that's why she marries more and more interesting husbands. This one's a Danish Jew. Handsome in a throwaway way. A bit zaftig for my taste. But he likes me. And he's easy to get along with. He's in Fine Stones, by which I do not mean granite and mica." Alistair displayed his right hand, upon which a double helix of gold was linked by a setting holding yellow diamonds. "Daniel Henriques is husband number six. I think six. That's right, she's taken to saying she's one husband and fifty pounds behind Liz Taylor. She doesn't mention the few million she's also behind. Your parents?"

"Retired. Bought a sixty-foot ketch. They dock in Key Largo, motor and sail around the Caribbean. My father's taken up snorkeling, believe it or not, at the age of sixty-six, and my mother has become the Fisher Queen of the Gulf of Mexico. They're perpetually tan and fit."

"How disconcerting!"

"It gets worse. I flew down for Christmas. They picked me up at Mallory Pier and we cruised around. One morning, my dad takes me out swimming to some nearby atoll. Once there, he begins talking. Serious talk. At first I thought it was about my book being so gay and me being so publicly out with the MLA and all."

Alistair acted as though he were hanging on every word.

"Instead, well, I swear he was trying to tell me about some gay affair in his own past."

"No!"

"I just managed to stop him."

"You're sure?"

"I'm not sure. But that's where it all seemed headed. Some affair he'd had in college or in the service. Before he met Mother. Believe me, I did not want to know."

"They've been supportive?" Alistair asked.

"You know Mother: practical in all! My father never threw the expected fit. He said he was proud the book was reviewed in the *Times*."

"My father threw a fit," Alistair said.

"Your real father?"

"He had to bail me out of jail. A jail, I might add, located in a suburb of Detroit, to quote the Reverend Foot. And I don't mean Gross Paint."

"Buying or selling?" I couldn't help but ask the old joke.

"Neither, I thought. Which turned out to be the problem. A knife was drawn, and Cuz, you know how paranoid I get around knives. So the number ended up at the emergency room and myself in stir. He wasn't hurt badly. Good thing he realized that and checked himself out," Alistair said primly. "Meanwhile, however, they'd contacted Mr. Dodge senior, who came down on me like a collapsed parachute. Called me a godless pervert, if you can credit it. *Moi?* Blamed Mother, natch. Said I was worse than godless, because I should know that I was leading my a-hem inferiors into crime and perversion."

If he only knew half of what Alistair had gotten into, I mused. "Sounds like he's born again."

"He can manage to offend several races and religions in one pithy phrase. But he was pissed. For the first time I saw the word 'livid' illustrated. He was white and yet purplish at the same time. Like a dead tuna."

"When was this?"

"Few years ago. After I got back from Europe. His fault really. Only reason I was in that dump was some scam connected with a dummy corporation he'd set up. Four times a year I go there to sign their manufactured lies."

It had been cleverly done, I had to admit, this little reminder of how dysfunctional Alistair's family was, how screwed up, and by extension how little he should be blamed for all the wrong he'd done.

"The entrées!" Alistair announced. Then to the waiter, "I hope you did terribly personal things to mine as you were bringing it out of the kitchen."

In reply, Demetrio displayed a flicker of his very pointed tongue.

We played "catch-up" for the next half hour. Alistair seemed to edit far less than he'd been given to in the past. Because he no longer had pretensions to be anything other than gay? Because he no longer had anything left to hide? Or was it even more subtle? To let me *think* he no longer had anything left to hide? Whatever the reason, the précis of his recent past was virtually seamless: events he'd attended (mostly "charity do's") thumbnail, totally Alisterine sketches of new people he thought might intrigue or charm me; unsuspected connections among acquaintances we knew. Demetrio would sail past and be snagged by the silk running up one trouser leg as Alistair made yet another slightly unreasonable yet easily accomplished demand upon him.

"Tell me," I suddenly said, "whatever did you do to Calvin Ritchie that he hated you so much?"

"Calvin hate me?" Alistair vamped.

"Alistair," I warned.

"Actually, it wasn't anything really bad at all, considering. Remember Tony Bishop with the scrumptious body, enormous nipples, and not terribly big wee-wee for a person of the colored persuasion? No? Well, he was a sweet and pretty lad, and I was in my Third-World Phase, so when we began screwing, he invited me up to Russian River to share in his share in a group house there. Calvin was the only other *homme nègre* there, and I thought by far the most intelligent among the eight. But it turned out he had a tiny little thing for Miss Bishop, who anyway wasn't his type at all, since his taste ran to fantasies in which he'd put on an old A-shirt and old jockeys and pretend he was a plantation-slave house beauty who gets her clothing ripped off before being soundly sodomized by the white Mastuh of the Big House. Well, anyway, sometime between the third and fourth weekend we shared at Guerneville, Calvin cottons on to our scene and becomes quite bitchy. The way he did this was by insisting that everyone do his share of work around the cottage."

Alistair paused.

"Not precisely my style. And anyway I was paying for both Tony and myself. So he'd do the dishes or the food shopping or whatever for both of us. Miss Ritchie began commenting on this, and commenting and commenting, and commenting. Anyone else might have become embarrassed."

Alistair giggled.

"This went on for several weeks, then Tony's grandmother back in Winston-Salem died and he went to North Carolina for the funeral. I went up to the Russian River house alone. All weekend Calvin needled me about doing my share around the house, feeling he'd got me now. I put it off and put it off and finally said I'd do the last, Sunday evening dinner dishes. Well, Sunday evening dinner arrives, is eaten, and the dishes placed in the sink. I vanish up to my room, change, and descend just as my ride arrives outside the deck, blowing the horn. The others are all sitting around. As I rush out with my weekend bag, Miss Ritchie is furious and screams, 'What about the dishes? You're supposed to do the dishes!' "

"What did you do?" I asked Alistair.

"I stopped, looked abashed, said, 'Silly me. I forgot. Why not just send them to me via Federal Express!' "

"He should have," I said, when I was done laughing.

"*You* would have," Alistair agreed, standing up suddenly. "Which reminds me, I have to call my friend in L.A. and tell him about Bernard Dixon."

"Everything good?" Demetrio stopped by the table to ask once I was alone. A nice touch, I thought, since he must know Alistair was tipping.

He'd no sooner gone than someone else hove into view: a rather large, all but bald man in a stylish linen suit, who'd entered the place not five minutes before in trio with two slender women, all of them obviously very "Design and Decoration."

"Jerry Barstow," he now said, approaching the table rather shyly yet intently. "I used to see you in the Pines."

He had seemed somewhat familiar. I wondered whether to stand up, invite him to sit, or what. His hesitation was understood.

"I've got to get back to my table," Barstow explained. "Clients." (So he *was* a decorator!) "I really just wanted to ask about his condition."

Complete confusion—for a second I thought Barstow meant Alistair—when Barstow said, "Matt Loguidice, I mean. Scott Rubin told me— Oh God! I've said something wrong, haven't I?"

I was aware that I'd automatically begun to stand up. Then all strength left my legs and I had to hold onto the table.

"I thought you knew," Barstow defended himself. "I thought if anyone knew . . ."

"We've been out of touch," my mouth said. "What hospital?"

Barstow named a local hospital. "Look, I'm sorry." He backed away. Was back at the table with his clients.

I tried to push out the single image that leapt into my mind: Matt's face pasted over Calvin's, in those last awful moments at the hospice.

Alistair was back at the table, sitting down, saying something. ". . . left a detailed message on his machine. You would have been proud of it. You okay, Cuz?"

Matt's dying and Alistair doesn't know, I thought. Matt's dying. I can't let Alistair find out. He can't already know or he'd have told me! Or would he, like Barstow, assume I already knew? It was all too complex.

I panicked.

"It must be the play and all . . . , " I muttered. Standing up, I felt steadier. Alistair was staring at me.

"Why not wait a sec. I'll pay and see you ho—"

Alistair didn't know. Or he did know and was specifically not telling me. Perhaps the entire dinner had been designed to hide the single, awful fact.

"*No!* No," I said. "I'll get a cab. I'll be okay."

"Why not wait a sec. I'll pay and step out with you."

Why? Did he now realize that I knew? Had he seen Barstow at the table? Did he suspect Barstow had told me? Would he deny knowing it or . . . ? It was all too complex and difficult. And Alistair was complicating it more.

I just want out of here, I thought. Away from this!

"I'll be okay. Really."

As I reached the door, I wasn't so lost in thought that I didn't hear Alistair say, "I'll call you tomorrow."

"That's a pretty sick-looking boycott!" I moaned. Either this play was going to kill me or I was going to kill it.

Onstage, Eric, David M., Sherman, Big Janet, Sal, and David B. marched in a tight oval, necessarily even tighter because of the narrow stage. All of them wore Ray-Ban sunglasses and were carrying picket signs. Three of the men were clad in light-hued polyester suits, cut close at the chest and shoulders, with narrow lapels. Sal alone sported a pale purple turtleneck and a glen-plaid jacket. His olive slacks were more peg-legged than the others', aspiring to pedal-pushers. Socks were visible through his open-toed leather shoes. David B. and Big Janet had pale pastel kerchiefs wrapped around their heads with Helen Gurley Brown "working girl" A-line skirts and "sensible" shoes. All six carried protest signs with tame sentiments like "End Official Persecution of Homosexuals!" and "First Amendment Rights—No More Postal Discrimination!"

"I don't know, Blasé! It's so lame!"

"That's *exactly* how many protesters were photographed!" Blaise defended. "Cynthia! Do you have those shots of Mattachine at the Postal Service?"

Anthony and David J. entered stage left, David a cop, Anthony (anachronistically—it was the fifties) a black newspaper photographer. They said their lines. The picketers marched their oval.

"I hate this play!" I groaned. "Hate. Hate. Hate."

"Cyn-thee . . . Ah! Look, Rog. Six people in these photos. Five in this one."

"I knew you were right. Anyway we have no more cast."

"There's always Henry," Cynthia half joked.

Henry was her assistant, who when the play opened would already be onstage a good deal of the time, moving around those objects that constituted what little set they possessed.

"Hen-ry!" Cynthia and Blaise called.

The compact lad was pushed onstage as an "onlooker."

"Maybe he should carry an anti-gay sign?" Cynthia suggested.

"This was the first ever protest by a gay group! An onlooker would be more astonished than anything," I said.

"Look astonished, Henry!" Blaise directed. "Move closer to Anthony and David J. Frightened Hets snuggling together."

"I still think it's too scrawny!" I said.

"If you'd seen the original Battle of Bunker Hill, you would have thought *that* was too scrawny."

"Let me try something with the lights," Cynthia suggested. Back at her booth, she dimmed the stage and lighted an inner oval so that the demonstrators had no shadow, while the few others had towering shadows: more menacing.

"Fab-u-lous! I have an idea. Take five!" Blaise instructed the actors, who gratefully fell out. He ran up the aisle to confab with Cynthia. The actors shook themselves limber, lighted cigarettes, sat in front-row seats chatting, ate yogurt, went to take a leak. David B. and Eric faced off, pushed each other, kissed: love in bloom.

I couldn't *staaaaaand* another minute of it.

The problem wasn't the scene, which sucked. It wasn't even the play, which completely sucked. I'd realized that already. It would be a complete fiasco, and there was nothing but to see it through to the end. No matter that the producer, Ivan "Bob" Jeffries, was an alcoholic sleazebag and could care less about the production, despite having declared that the play must succeed or it was curtains for the entire company. No, I would see it through for Blaise and Cynthia, bless them, who still had creative ideas; or Sal, who thought his portrayals of Harry Hay and Roger Casement were worth an Obie; or for Big Janet and Henry and the three Davids.

A day-and-a-half had passed since Barstow's news about Matt, and in that day-and-a-half I'd been virtually paralyzed. Morally paralyzed, for sure. Once I was in the taxi fleeing Alistair, I'd broken down, wept, thought, I'd better get tested again! I realized with some internal Delphic certainty that I wasn't infected: it had swept like a raging fire over the plain, had taken light everywhere around me, on every branch and every twig and blade of grass, and for some unknown reason, not on me: I would never sicken like the others, never die of this. My doom was of another kind. Perhaps survival was to be my doom. With the knowledge that the dying alone seem to comprehend, of how things truly were, Calvin had all but said it. With his intuition, Matt would also know. Maybe that was why, after I saw the taxi shoot past K-Y Plaza into the hospital's neighborhood, I'd shouted for the driver to change destinations. Yet once the cab arrived at the hospital, I'd changed again and had the cabby drive me home, to Chelsea. Perhaps that was why, although I'd spent the better part of two nights awake thinking of nothing but Matt sick and hospitalized, I'd done nothing about it. Not one single thing.

"That your *Post*?" David J. stood in the aisle.

"It's Blaise's. Go ahead, read it!"

"Just want to see my horoscope," the young actor riffled to page six to check gossip, then farther inside the paper. "Mnnmm . . . Umnh! . . . Ah!"

Was he flirting? Who could tell anymore? All the actors were respectful around me. Too respectful, really, for my taste.

"She seems on today!" David commented. "What's yours?"

I pointed to the appropriate sign.

David read: " 'Constant improvement in beautifying . . .' "

"Too late for that!"

" ' . . . important projects'!" David continued. "That sounds right. And . . . 'Someone from your past is more wonderful than you thought possible.' "

"You're kidding?"

David offered the paper. "I told you she was on today!"

Matt. This meant Matt. I couldn't put off visiting Matt any longer. Matt couldn't be as bad as I feared. He couldn't.

"Phone call for you, Mr. Sansarc," Sherman shouted from behind a panel that led backstage. He left the pay phone receiver hanging.

"Doesn't anyone answer the phone there? I've been ringing all morning," Alistair all but chirruped from the other end.

"We shut off the bell during rehearsal."

"I assumed that whatever it was that sent you fleeing from me the other night is *not* contagious and has quite passed?"

"How did you find me?" was all I could think to ask.

"I called an old pal at *Variety*. They know everything about every show in rehearsal. And lucky for the two of us, your little theater is only footsteps away from my favorite Chelsea restaurant. So mark in your penis-length *Day at a Glance* 'Lunch. Tomorrow. Noon.' "

"I can't."

"Then tomorrow at one! Don't say no. You're not escaping, Cuz. I've found you and I'll haunt you until you buy lunch at Claire and let me sit in on a rehearsal."

"I don't think that's such a good idea, Alistair."

"Of course it's a good idea! If I know your young actors—and I must say I *have* known my share of young actors—they'll simply gloat on having an audience, no matter how small, if they think it's someone important. And you'll tell them I am. Well, you needn't even do that. They'll *see* I am. And don't tell me the show isn't ready to be seen. How can you expect me to go around trumpeting your play if I've not seen one rehearsal? Tomorrow. One."

"You done?" Big Janet pointed to the receiver dangling from my hand. " 'Cause if you are, I need to use it."

"Check this!" Blaise enthused when I returned. "On your marks, kids! Lights!"

It was unclear at first what Cynthia and Blaise had concocted: the scene looked the same. But it did feel more alive. The protesters seemed more highlighted, more isolated; the three in the back seemed even more a crowd, even more menacing. Why?

"It's audiotape. A crowd scene. Car traffic? Is it subliminal?"

"Audible but low," Blaise confirmed. "Cynthia! From the top."

The scene seemed a smidgen less awful. The others seemed pleased. Blaise repeated it, then called a longer break.

The small theater emptied as actors rushed out to local delis and take-out stands to replenish their strength. Blaise hit the backstage phone to continue the ongoing argument with his boyfriend that was about all they still had left of a relationship. In back, Cynthia and a woman in the control booth had their arms wrapped around each other.

A silence developed.

"It's moments like these . . . that . . . I'd prefer . . . a Pall Mall!" I heard myself dopily utter the fifties commercial to no one.

I jumped out of the seat, up the aisle, and into the little lobby. I knew. I'd *phone* Matt! Phone and get an idea of how Matt sounded about whether I was welcome or not. What was the room number I'd gotten yesterday from Patient Information?

In the theater lobby, I waited as Matt's phone went unanswered.

"He may be out of the room," the hospital operator suggested.

I made her try once more. Cynthia was emerging from the control booth and with her the more spiffily dressed other woman. They turned in profile to me. I almost dropped the phone. Wasn't that . . . ?

"Rog, meet Second Why," Cynthia said, proud as the young Liz Taylor with Pie in *National Velvet*.

"Second Why?" But the silly nickname made instant, horrible sense. For the sportily dressed woman, lightly but securely gripping Cynthia by her jumper strap, was none other than Sydelle Auslander. And she was beautiful. Well, as beautiful as Sydelle would ever be. Full, sleek, voluptuous. Not thin and haggard. But somehow the Emily Dickinson word "ample" came to mind. Her skin clear and creamy, her eyes dark and lazy, her posture regal, calm.

"We . . . ," I stuttered.

"Roger and I worked together," Sydelle said smoothly, without a hint that she'd once spoken only with nail-biting anxiety. "Briefly."

"You look great!" I managed to get out without choking. "Being with Cyn seems to agree with you."

"Second Why is the Wonder Lesbian!" Sydelle gazed fondly at her. Without a hint of irony, she added, "Super Dyke."

It crossed my mind that Sydelle was from my past, and while not precisely "wonderful," then at least part of something miraculous. But then, so was Alistair. Why bother? When had a newspaper horoscope ever been right?

We kept talking, and Sydelle seemed so relaxed, so off the hook-and-ladder, so altered really, that I found myself not trusting her, not trusting any of it. It was a fabrication, yes, a veneer, and beneath it was the same creature, broken-clawed, hungrier than ever.

Wait! There was no reason to believe that. I was being paranoid. I'd been paranoid with Alistair, paranoid just now, distrusting the hospital phone operator, thinking she was ringing someone else's room. Why? I was losing my mind, that's why. It had finally happened. I'd snapped. I smiled and chatted and thought, What's next? Do I start hearing voices? I had to get out of here or they'd begin to notice, so I made a not too awkward parting, said the expected things to pass on to Blaise, and managed actually to get out of the theater and onto the street with only a bit of cold sweat. Then, although walking fast and not sure where I was headed, I knew at least I'd escaped before they'd seen what everyone coming at me must for certain notice. Thank goodness they were all strangers. Or were they?

By the time I reached Fifth Avenue, I realized that no one was bothering to notice me. Meaning, I wasn't acting loony, no matter how I'd felt for a moment there. I'd try another block, walk along Broadway. I did, and again no one especially stared. So I walked on, occasionally

checking faces for odd looks. Gramercy Park was visible down one avenue, and then I was there, at the hospital's front door, so I might as
well go in, no?

Three people were at the desk. I gave the room number and was
given a large red plastic visitor's pass you'd lose only if you were legally
blind, and I waited with other visitors at the elevators. They all seemed
to be carrying flowers and shopping bags filled with cards and gifts and
fruit baskets. I carried nothing. I couldn't believe I was here.

The walls on Matt's floor were covered with children's drawings and
pleasant reproductions, everything modern and cheery, although as I
passed the open doorways, the patients inside looked pretty bad. Anything
in the least out of the way or resistant would stop me, I suspected—
anything at all. But nothing did. I continued to follow the numbers past
the nurses' station. No one there more than half glanced my way.

As I neared the corner of the floor where I supposed I was headed, I
heard music: *The Magic Flute*, the middle of Act I. I knew this part. Pa-
pageno and Tamino and the Three Ladies. The Queen of the Night
had just sung the first of her two big numbers. The three women now
introduced a new theme, telling the men, *"Drei Knaben, jung, schoen, hold
und weise umschweben euch auf euer Reise: sie werden euer Fuehren sein,
Folgt ihrem Rate ganz allein."*

The tenor and baritone (Wunderlich surely, and wasn't that Walter
Berry?) repeated the first two lines, then all five moved apart to sing the
separate lines leading into a glorious little *fughetta* on *auf Wiedersehen*.
Who but Mozart was so prodigal with melodies? Who else would have
bothered to turn a mere "Goodbye" into such a delicious moment?

I wished I could hear it again, but the orchestra had moved on . . .
No! Wait! The music stopped. Was the tape being rewound. Yes. As I
located the doorway of the double room I was looking for, the little
quintet started up over again. I stepped in: the bed nearest the door was
empty. Just past an undrawn internal curtain, the room's walls were
tinted red by a luscious sunset filling the entire sky over New Jersey and
pinkly staining the leaves of a small forest of plants and flowers set upon
the double windowsill. Stacks of books and magazines tottered against
one wall. A few gifts recently opened lay *en déshabillé*. Two chairs, a mobile bed table on which the cassette player was hidden by tissues, water

pitcher and glass, vials of unguents, all dominated by an oversized post-card depicting someone's quattrocento *Expulsion from Paradise*, featuring a spherical Earth rolled like a hoop by a cherub-lofted deity, while an archangel poked two slender youths of unclear gender past what looked like a stand of fully fruited peach trees. Headphones stretching behind the postcard connected to the cassette player: the quintet was once more singing the beautiful good-bye.

Upon the bed, as though just resting a second on a chaise longue, listening, his eyes closed, clad in almost diaphanous pale-green hospital pajamas, slightly frowning in concentration on the music coming through the earphones, was Matt Loguidice—beautiful as ever. No, more beautiful—his face not much thinner, not drawn and Auschwitz-skeletal as Calvin's and so many others' had been, but clarified, ennobled. Matt's hair was still rich and thick, not chemo-dry and dying, but full and curly, spattered with diamonds of gray, and one striking four-inch lock over his left brow had gone completely white. The large, easily grasped, muscular flesh of Matt's body as I had known it was gone, of course, replaced by a new spareness, but it looked taut, with very little looseness of skin visible through the open vees of his pajama neck and the unbuttoned top at his waist. Matt's legs were visible through a tangle of sheets, the false one made of expensive "fleshlike" plastic, covered with a skin-colored net fabric, so it bent and even wrinkled a little like skin. Doubtless from the VA.

My relief was so extreme, my pleasure at seeing Matt not ghastly and dying, as I'd feared, was so heartfelt, so complete, that when the pale gray eyes finally did open a second later, Matt's own surprise was genuine.

"Mr. Myxtplqztrx!" He smiled as he greeted me as of old. He removed the headphones and adjusted the bed to lift his torso.

For a second I was afraid I wouldn't be able to speak.

"My hero!" I responded, aiming toward the night table to shut off the cassette player.

Matt misinterpreted that movement as a kiss, so I shut off the machine and let myself be pulled down to buss Matt's cool dry forehead. Those eyes I'd known so well looked up, curious, expectant, slightly unclear.

When I pulled back, I said, "I'm obviously the last to visit."

"People have been great!" Was Matt's voice a little hoarse? "Some came from out of town."

"I thought I'd have to wait in line."

"Most come after work. A few at lunchtime. This is in-between."

"I'm not tiring you? If I am, I'll go."

"I've just been lying here listening to music. Take a seat, Mr. Myxtplqztrx! See that wooden thing? The chess set? Would you set it up here?" Matt pulled the bed table over in front of himself. "That's fine," he said and began setting up first the black then the white chessmen.

"Planning to be a grand master?" I faced the board and Matt. As ever, I couldn't get over how beautiful Matt was.

"My way to check for dementia. You're white. You go first."

"It's been years. I don't remember any but the most basic Capablanca convention." Even so, I made an opening move.

Matt moved a pawn. The sun streaked the wall behind him orange-red, edged with hot green. It reflected on one side of Matt's face. It must be pretty colorless to have done that.

"It's like swimming or driving a car," Matt was saying. "You have to think a bit, but you never forget the basic moves."

As we played chess, we talked slowly, and I found myself thinking that too was like playing the game, still knowing the basic moves but just a bit rusty on procedure. Matt was more serene than I had ever known him to be. In the past, there'd always been an edge—at times imperceptible, then later on all too evident. Now it wasn't there. Something else was changed: in the past, Matt always favored the bad leg and foot; sometimes touching it too much, at other times leaning toward it. That was gone. He had a new leg: fake or not, it served, it filled the need.

"Can I do that?" I asked once, uncertain about a ploy.

"Sure. Bernard was here," Matt reported. "Said he saw you."

"Bernard?!" For the first time since I'd arrived inside the room, I almost panicked. Bernard the Grunt was dead. Died last year. Set aflame by the same enormous brushfire that swiped Calvin and so many others. Ironic to think the Grunt had developed even the tiny sex life needed to get caught.

"Bernard Dixon," Matt explained. "He said you have a play opening."

Meanwhile, Matt had been using his queen, one bishop, and a knight to mercilessly raid my pawns. In turn, I put up a defense, used my queen, a rook, and two knights to set up my own aggression against Matt's side of the board. In the past and despite Matt's experience—he'd learned the game as a child and for years had played against his grandfather—we'd always been pretty evenly matched.

"Speaking of Bernard and people from the past," I said, "you'll never guess who showed up today. Acting like she's been on a vacation at the Betty Ford Clinic. Sydelle Auslander."

I wanted to tell Matt how unsure I was of her, but Matt merely commented, "I've seen and heard many people from the past since I'm here."

Stung a little, I said, "Like me."

"You?" Matt touched my arm. "You're different. I knew you'd come. You belong here. I don't have to pretend or watch myself with you. Stay as long as you want."

It was the closest thing to a declaration of love Matt had ever made. Touched, I asked, "Is it okay if I come at this time, after rehearsal? Five or so? I'll call and check first."

"You don't have to call. Five's fine. Others don't arrive for another hour. This way I'm occupied yet rested. You don't have to come every day. Whenever you want."

"We'll play chess. And what else? I'll bring you stuff."

"Maybe you'll read to me. My eyes aren't . . . "

"A book? Magazines?"

"You sure about that?"

"Of course I'm sure!" I protested, then I saw what Matt was talking about. I'd not noticed that my king was cornered. Good thing I'd kept one rook in the back row. I "castled" the king and tried to concentrate. "But I am sure. They're all dying to have me out of the theater while they rehearse." I immediately regretted using the word, but Matt seemed not to notice.

Even with my concentration, in a few more moves Matt had me in check and, after some desperate moves, checkmated.

"I'll call before I come tomorrow, to see if you need anything." I moved the bed table aside and kissed Matt's forehead. It was warmer now and a little moister. Was that normal?

Walking across town, I caught my image in a shop window. I looked as though . . . something wonderful had happened.

What precisely had my horoscope said? Someone from my past will be more wonderful than I thought possible. It hadn't mentioned that it would be someone I had never gotten over. Someone I had never stopped missing. Wouldn't it be terrific if when Matt got out of the hospital, this all continued? As friends. Who knew, maybe even again as lovers? It would be different, of course. We'd have to be very careful to safeguard Matt's health. But with no great claims on Matt's attention from other admirers, with me myself now finally adult enough to know when and where and how to compromise, it could be terrific.

No wonder I look happy, I thought. I am. To hell with the play. Matt is back!

Spring finally arrived in Manhattan. The cold that had held the city in an unrelenting grasp to the last bleak, snowless yet sunless day of March was broken by gentle rain the first of April. Every tree seemed to bud simultaneously, hell for those with allergies, but picture-card loveliness to everyone else. Crocus and magnolia blossoms pinkly and yellowly threaded every breeze that now wafted, softly, from across the Hudson through the streets of Chelsea.

Inside the little theater, rehearsals were no longer accompanied by the incessant racket of the house furnace. Actors no longer had to shout themselves hoarse to be heard over stage heaters. Nor upon arriving and before warming up did they have to unwrap themselves from Isadora Duncan–length scarves, dig their way out of Siberian anoraks and floor-length coats. The take-out food in the lobby and dressing rooms—based around the constellation of hot coffee, hot tea, and hot soup—became tepid: apple juice and yogurt prevailed. Cigarette breaks were no longer half in and half out the front lobby, a door braced open an inch. Smokers could go outside, and if the wind were down and the sun hot enough, they could sit on a brownstone stoop dotting the long block, thespians begging Sol for the flattery of an early tan.

The play had reached that point in rehearsal where all major areas were completely limned, only minor points of character delineation or refinements of action still needed to be gone over—often again and again. David J. couldn't for the life of him say a particular line as I'd written it. He'd get it wrong every time, despite the fact that it consisted of ordinary phrases and no long words. Blaise finally turned to me. "He'll go up on it when we open. Better rewrite it."

I did. Without complaint. In fact, now that I'd more or less accepted that the show would quietly die, I found a few scenes weren't so bad, were even—was it possible?—okay. For example, the day I'd finally met with Alistair for lunch at nearby Claire restaurant, after putting it off several days: On Alistair's insistence, we'd returned to the theater and walked in on the Casement Trial scene. Unexpectedly, almost embarrassingly, I had found myself riveted: the acting, the staging, the drama itself—it all came together. A fluke, I told myself. Or worse, the writer's ego, hypnotized by something it had written it couldn't get enough of—for a day, a week at most. It happened all the time!

No, no, Alistair insisted, with a tiny hint of awe in his voice. The scene was good. Alistair remained in his seat the rest of the afternoon, as Blaise and the cast moved on to two more scenes from the second act. When he'd gotten up to leave, Alistair hadn't been his usual effervescent self, but low-key. Before I could comment, he'd quickly said, "What I've seen so far has really left me thinking, Cuz. You know how much I pooh-pooh all these gay politicos and all. Yet, what I've seen today, even though it may not be refined yet, was really moving. Thought-provoking. What if Hay and those folks hadn't forced the court to overthrow the ban on *One*? What if Stonewall hadn't happened? Would we all be zipping around and hiding like those poor fifties queens? Daring our jobs, our lives, to be ourselves, to even protest? Yes, definitely thought-provoking," he declared, walking out of the theater.

Cynthia agreed. She'd worked on many shows, and when they reached the crucial weeks before opening any real flaws, any deeply ingrained problems became all too evident. Here, all the problems were being solved as they arose; all the disparate elements were coming together, knitting into a whole.

I would have liked to believe her. Everyone else believed anything and everything Cynthia said. Unfortunately for me, she had something even more difficult for me to believe: a mission, and that mission's main point was Sydelle Auslander.

Following that first surprising reencounter outside the control room,

I'd often seen Sydelle at the theater. Almost every day. No problem. We'd sometimes sit outside together, Sydelle stealing puffs of forbidden cigarette smoke (she was still trying to quit) and, in a desultory fashion, talking. So we too had more or less caught up with each other's lives. Sydelle hadn't remained at the magazine after I left as editor. She hadn't stayed anywhere very long until she'd met Second Why (i.e., Cynthia), she admitted. Furthermore, she admitted she'd often left magazines and newspapers after having made trouble and either forced someone else out—as she had with me—or left such a shambles the publication had collapsed. I was forced to admire her honesty if nothing else as she told me point-blank that she herself was incapable of being editor or even as- sistant editor at most of these places. She knew that. She also knew she didn't do any of it consciously. Well, not most of it. She half blamed as- trology for it: "I'm a triple Scorpio," she once said. "Sun, moon, rising sign all square Pluto. I renovate wherever I go. Can't help it."

If Sydelle presented herself as being the unwilling instrument of extraterrestrial forces, Cynthia, in her long discussions with me about her lover, presented Sydelle as the twisted result of a typical patriarchal upbringing in a hypocritical society. She laid out Sydelle's past like a quilt for the two of us to inspect, critique, deconstruct. Her food bing- ing, her anorexia, her smoking and drinking, her failures in relationships (until now), her sick and guilt-ridden relationships with her father, her mother, her brother, her excessive sensitivity and vulnerability, her . . . Didn't I think Sydelle should try acting? Cynthia did. Sydelle, of course, had so very little self-esteem, Cynthia told me, it had taken weeks to get her even to enroll in HB Studio, where, of course, she'd been brilliant, had Sydelle told me about that? No, Cynthia guessed she wouldn't. But Sydelle was good. In fact, if it weren't for her and my past difficulties, Blaise would have let her be an understudy in the show. They only had one understudy. That was news to me, who was unaware we had any. As was the news that Bernard Dixon was that one understudy, although that explained somewhat why he was often found in a lower row of the theater, eating sandwiches and doing the crossword puzzle various af- ternoons. They really could use a second understudy, Cynthia insisted. Especially a non-Equity one. What did I think? If I approached Blaise about Second Why, wouldn't that be proof I'd buried the hatchet?

It would, I agreed. So I said sure, okay, why not? I could afford to be philosophical: my life no longer centered around the play; it was wider now, beyond the shabby little theater.

Walking across town every afternoon to the hospital, I found myself stopping to sit a few minutes at whatever part of Union Square wasn't at that hour being ripped up by jackhammers or steam shovels in its endless ongoing redesign. The shops of the upper teens at Fifth Avenue and Broadway also seemed to beckon more. I could always tell myself that if I did spend hours at Barnes & Noble or China Books or the big discount mart, it was to pick up a book or cassette or sundry Matt would like.

Every day, I found myself leaving the theater earlier, spending time in the open air, and arriving at the hospital earlier. One time I'd arrived so early, lunch trays still hadn't been collected and Matt was in the bathroom, audibly brushing his teeth and gargling. I left without being noticed, and walked around Gramercy Park before coming back as though I'd not been there already, afraid, although I couldn't quite explain it, of seeming too eager, like some young suitor. Another time I'd arrived just as lunch trays were being collected, only to find Matt already asleep. I wondered whether I ought to leave, but Matt awoke slightly and, seeing me, smiled wanly, took my hand, and said, "Today's not a good day." But when I said, "I'll come back later," Matt quickly replied, "Don't go!" Then explained, "I like knowing you're here," before slipping back into slumber for another hour. What had he meant? That this way he would know where I was? That he felt protected with me there?

Following the early afternoon bustle serving lunch, was a quiet time in the hospital. Trays were removed by orderlies. Nurses came to check temperature and blood pressure. Patients read or slept.

Increasingly, I couldn't help but notice, Matt too slept. He slept after lunch, and sometimes again after our daily game of chess before dinner and night visitor hours. At first, our chess games had been true tiny battles, tests of skill, plots and counterplots, long sallies and retreats, reveilles and sudden defeats, that had taken up most of my afternoon visit, interrupted though they might be by nurses or the arrival of an unexpected snack, accompanied as they often were by conversation and phone calls. But more often now, our chess games were brief, enigmatic: an unconventional opening, a few skirmishes, pounce, I'd be checkmated!

The shorter the games became, the more concentrated and arcane was Matt's technique shown to be, as though decades of play and thought about the game were being explosively revealed. Traps and mysteries abounded. I would make four moves and discover myself completely enclosed, way out of my league, unable to mount anything approximating a challenge, at times unable even to understand Matt's explanations of how he'd done it. The game would be over, or Matt would charitably say, "to be continued," though they seldom were continued, and I would try to figure out what had happened.

Equally brief, concentrated, and arcane was the poem of Matt's I'd stumbled across, carefully written on a hospital pad and dated a few days earlier, found under the bed while I was hunting one of Matt's slippers. When Matt sleepily acknowledged the poem to be his, I asked if I could copy it. "If you want," Matt said, unconcerned. But when I asked if he'd written any more, and were they too on hospital pads somewhere around the room, behind the curtains, in the shower stall, under the bed, Matt put a sweating palm up to my mouth, stopping my questions, saying, "Don't worry about it." Then he turned over in bed and went to sleep.

The poem was titled "nightcall":

> *the whirr of leather*
>
> *over the river of your voice*
> *the pause & clatter the*
> *telephone brings   i am skating again*
>
> *as fast as i go*
> *you flow beneath me   white*
> *white   our lives coming down*
>
> *to these two small blades*

What was it about? I felt, I couldn't say how or why, that it was about us. Matt and me. Years ago. At the Pines. And now.

As my question about the poem went unanswered, as our chess games shortened, our reading sessions got longer, with Matt farther back on the bed, looking out the window at the afternoon light (looking for his future, it sometimes seemed) while I read aloud from gossip columns, news items, and reviews in the *Times* or *Post* or one of the magazines left by a visitor the previous night. Yet if I should stop reading for a minute, Matt would invariably, gently protest, "I love the sound of your voice! It's so soothing!" And I would go on reading, soothing with my voice, until Matt would fall asleep, and I would get up and check that the little oxygen tube Matt now kept close by or right in his lips was loose enough and wouldn't inadvertently shut off. I'd brush Matt's forehead with my lips for fever, button or unbutton his pajama tops, lightly sponge him with alcohol if he seemed too hot. If Matt happened to be attached that day to a metal hat rack of IV tubes inserted into his wrist, giving anti-virals or nutriments, I would make sure they were all open and dripping. Then I'd sit and do my own reading. I sat close, as Matt had taken to reaching out suddenly in his sleep to grasp my thigh or hand, sometimes gripping so hard, during a dream or while mumbling in his sleep, that I would wince in pained surprise.

That was rare. Less rare, if equally inexplicable, were those times Matt would suddenly wake up while I was reading—in the salons or streets of Paris, in the grand hotel dining rooms and on the beach at Balbec in 1885—and suddenly say, "There's a favor I have to ask of you." To which I would reply, "Sure. What?" To which Matt would enigmatically respond, "In time. All in good time. But it's very important. No one else can do it." And I would—even the fifth or sixth time this occurred—say, "Anything! Anything at all."

Seconds later Matt would be snoring, and I would be utterly at sea, unable to discern whether Matt had been truly awake or just seeming to be awake but really talking in his sleep, his question not real, the favor he expected of me not so much a real one, but some kind of reassurance he required, that would allow him to more comfortably sleep.

If those sudden events of reaching out or asking for a totally mysterious favor were strange adjuncts, they were worth having to put up with, worth the equally inexplicable contentment I seemed to experience—and which I'd never dare admit—sitting and reading the new translation of Proust on a spring afternoon that smelled of fresh flowers, while Matt slept so close by.

Not only was Matt sleeping more, but so was his roommate, one Joe Veselka, a man barely thirty, who'd been very ill indeed, suffering a variety of minor ills and irritations beyond the pneumocystis that had kept him in intensive care a week. Joe's sessions with a nurse, overheard through closed curtains, to help alleviate some awful skin condition, could get so loud and disturbing I usually managed to get Matt out of the room, over to the little lobby near the elevator.

Out in the hospital's twelfth-floor lobby, Matt and I would play chess or read, and in a small way hold court among visitors and other patients, occasionally even an intern or two. All the staff adored Matt, naturally, and would come by, stop to ask how he was. And I never failed to remark how gracious Matt was to them all, how distinctively beautiful with his single lock of white hair, his posture so erect, even though he was undoubtedly thinner now, his attitude modest despite his regal looks.

How proud I was that Matt wanted me near him, how proud he would tell anyone who would bother to ask that, yes, we'd been lovers, still were, really, in another, higher sense. Matt's courtesy was so easy. He'd never deflect questions, no matter how pointed. Not even when another patient on the floor—a middle-aged harridan with a Dutch-boy haircut of obviously dyed yellow—said to him, "Donch'a feel weird going around with a hole in your chest?" She was referring to the infusolator surgically embedded in Matt's upper left pectoral, a medical device called a Hickman catheter, through which he was receiving far more directly than was otherwise possible a potent new drug to fight off the cytomegalovirus that had begun to cloud his eyesight and infect his throat. "It's not open all the time," Matt replied, opening his pajama top to bare himself—an alabaster torso from a Gothic crucifix—to her. "See! It's got a lid!" At other times, he'd tell visitors, "I'm the lucky one. Poor Joe and poor Raimundo in the next room. They're suffering so much. I'm just a little tired."

And afterward, when I, leaving for the day, stopped at the nurse's station, one of the staff there would invariably say hello, stop me, ask if Matt needed anything, and if, as increasingly happened lately, I asked them to bring Matt a sleeping pill (he complained of awakening in the middle of the night and not being able to get back to sleep), they'd say, "Oh, sure! Right away!" Then they'd confide, "He's no trouble. Never complains. Never asks for anything. If his room light goes on here, it's always for his roommate." And I would feel even prouder of Matt, more certain of him, and I'd make sure that even with a full night's schedule, say concert and dinner, I'd find time to phone Matt before lights out.

Once, I was at dinner with Alistair and a woman named Toni Kauffer, whom Alistair had somehow talked into doing free publicity for the show, when I excused myself to go make that phone call to Matt. When I returned to the table, Alistair took Toni's bare arm and mewed, "Look at him, Toni! *L'amour! L'amour!* As Mary Boland said! Don't deny it, Cuz! You're, as they say of the newly engaged and the freshly pregnant, 'simply radiant.' "

From the minute I arrived at the theater that morning, I sensed something wasn't as it ought to be, but I couldn't put my finger on what.

Up onstage, all seemed usual enough: Blaise was working with virtually the entire cast, trying to put together more smoothly the complex series of spoken lines and carefully choreographed action that would constitute the "fight" for the Stonewall Inn. They mostly seemed to be working on details, and they seemed awfully intent, so I paid more attention to the newspapers I'd bought that morning: *Times, Post,* and the *New York Native* with its scary "11,234 and Still Counting" headline. Meanwhile, around one end of the stage momentarily cleared of actors, Henry and Bernard Dixon were up on ladders, moving ceiling stage lights, replacing bulbs, etc., to Cynthia's direction from the control booth.

Sipping coffee, I moved on to the *Times* crossword puzzle.

"That your *Post?*"

David J. Temporarily not needed onstage. He didn't even wait for me to say yes, but immediately turned to the middle of the paper, found the Horoscope section, and read. His shoulders slumped a little more, and a sound like "hummmph" emerged from somewhere deep inside him.

"Bad news?"

David J. looked as if he wanted to say something, but instead shrugged and went back up onstage.

I took the discarded paper and checked my own horoscope for the day: "Disasters abound. Unpleasant news in the A.M. is followed by a P.M. disappointment. Later tonight, it's all you can do to keep body and soul together. No matter what happens, keep a cool head, and something will be salvaged."

Wow! I thought these things were always Pollyanna-positive. This one was a complete downer.

I scanned the other horoscopes, and several looked equally bad. As I read mine again, I felt a tiny twist inside my guts, as though something were alive in there. I recognized the sensation. I'd last felt it a few years back, swimming back to the Pines, suddenly discovering myself having to fight against a tide that seemed intent upon drawing me out to sea: fear, the beginning of unreasoning, unceasing fear.

Was it my imagination? Or did everyone in the theater suddenly look as though they'd been suffering from food poisoning all last night? Slightly dazed, sour looks on all their faces. Even the love-struck Bernard and the normally giggly Henry looked dour.

I watched them more closely for confirmation. Trudged up the aisle to the last rows to check Cynthia. She too looked subdued. The final proof.

I knocked on the window to get her attention, then gestured that I was coming into the booth.

"We've *got* to have a *few* more blue gels," Cynthia was saying through the microphone, into the headphones Henry and Bernard were wearing. Her voice had a querulous edge I'd never heard before. She remained at the board, barely acknowledging my presence. "Then try those two greens. Double them if you have to!" she insisted. She still hadn't turned to where I had perched on a stool. "I guess that'll have to do."

From here, distant, yet within it all, I *knew* something was wrong. I waited another few minutes, then quietly said, "Tell me."

When she did turn, it was clear she was trying to keep her Raggedy Ann face from squinching up, to keep her cornflower-blue eyes from tearing up. "Jeffries filed Chapter Eleven this morning."

It hit like a punch to the solar plexus.

"What . . . are you talking about?"

"He's going bankrupt. The rent on the theater hasn't been paid yet this month. The company's going under."

"And . . . ," I was afraid to ask, ". . . the play?"

Tears were freely coming down her cheeks. She shook her frizzy red head slowly left to right.

"Why are they still rehearsing? Why are you still doing lights?"

"Blasé said to keep working. Until we *have* to stop."

"Everyone else knows?" I asked, already knowing the answer. Of course they knew: what else would explain the strange quiet? "Why are they still rehearsing?" I had to ask again.

"Final paychecks arrive tomorrow afternoon. We're professionals. We work as long as we were hired to work."

Unpleasant news in the A.M. *Unpleasant?* This was a . . . *Disaster* was the only word for it.

"My play's not going to open?" I asked suddenly, and I distinctly heard the childlike quaver in my voice.

"I'm sorry!" Cynthia smothered me in an arms-and-tits embrace.

This couldn't happen. Not to me. It couldn't.

I let her comfort me awhile, then pulled away.

"I won't accept it. I *don't* accept it. If we keep our heads," I quoted the horoscope, "we can still salvage something. Get Blasé in here!"

Five minutes later, the actors had been given a break. I, Blaise, and Cynthia were in the lobby, Blaise on his third cigarette.

"The play opens Friday! That's just three days from now. This is ridiculous!" I expostulated. "How much money do we need to open?"

"What's the difference?" Blaise moaned.

"How much?" I insisted.

"The rent on the theater is the big cost." Cynthia quoted the amount. "A month past due. Worry about electric and phone bills when they're overdue."

"Or, when Con Ed threatens to turn us off," Blaise said. "Okay, add to that a week's payment of salaries."

"Defer mine," Cynthia said. "I don't need it."

"Defer mine too," Blaise said. "Just the cast."

"Henry will do without," she suggested.

"What else?" I asked. "Advertisements? Flyers? Anything else?"

The total came to three thousand two hundred dollars.

"That much went up Jeffries's nose today!" Blaise was bitter.

"Tell the landlord I'll have a check tomorrow," I said.

"Since when does a teacher have that kind of money?" Cynthia asked.

"I'll borrow on my credit cards."

"You'll be in debt for years!"

"The show must go on," I said, thinking with a sinking feeling of the interest I'd have to pay for the next few years.

"I'm going to tell the cast you're personally going into debt to float the show," Cynthia said.

"Don't bother!" I said. "How much for the entire run?"

We calculated it would cost another ten thousand dollars to keep the play running the initial six weeks planned, less whatever box-office was collected, of course.

That toned down the bit of excitement we'd managed to generate.

"We'll figure out something," I said. "We're not licked!"

"At least it'll open!" Blaise said what we were all thinking. "I'll tell the kids. We continue rehearsal. Open Friday. Play the weekend."

As we were leaving, Cynthia said, "I thought you hated it?"

"I hate more having something dangled in front of me and then having it suddenly pulled back."

"You must like it a little."

"A little," I admitted. Then I told Cynthia the truth. "This has little to do with the show. It's just another skirmish in a long battle between me and . . . Fate."

When I returned to the theater, the sounds from inside were almost boisterous. I didn't see Cynthia in the control booth, but inside the house the actors were standing around the stage, talking and laughing. As I appeared at the top of the aisle, David J. announced, "Our savior!" and began salaaming.

The other actors joined in bowing to me.

"Save it for opening night!" I was surrounded and being patted on the back and kissed on the cheek from all sides. "I'm not kidding! So far we've only got the place for the weekend."

"No *problema*!" David M. insisted. "We'll sell out next week."

"The next two weeks!" Sherman agreed.

"Hell! The entire run!" Big Janet took up the cry.

I let them gather around and all work at cheering me and one another up. Unsurprisingly, Sal, the only admitted heterosexual in the cast, took me aside with a well-muscled arm over my shoulder to say, "I'll never forget this! When I make it big . . . which no doubt I will do, if not during this run then soon after . . . I'll make sure that everyone knows of your commitment and personal sacrifice."

"It's my play, Sal." I said the obvious.

"I know. I know. But you don't need it, man! You've got a career. You've already got a rep. We need it. Me, I need it! In this part, you know I'm going to be noticed. You knew I'd be right to play the key roles. And I know you had a hand in that."

"Blasé and I agreed, Sal. Even Cynthia had a—"

"But it was you! I know it was you, man," Sal insisted. "Even though you've been like completely ethical and aboveboard about it—which, believe me, not every person of your persuasion, in your position, faced with the temptation I myself offer, would be—so I just want to let you know I appreciate it and someday I'm going to pay you back."

I wasn't sure whether Sal had in those words just thanked me for not couch-casting him, blamed me for not couch-casting him, or made a covert invitation to couch-cast him after the fact. That, and the surprising weight of Sal's muscled arm on my shoulder, suggested discretion: "Just do well opening night, okay?"

"You're a fucking saint, man!" A close hug, and a fuller whiff of the cologne—Drakkar Noir?—Sal used to complement his own virile odor.

A short time later, rehearsal had started up again and Blaise leaned over. "You two planning to post banns next Sunday?"

"I'm a fucking saint, man!" I used Sal's "Bay Ridge" tone.

"How about the money?"

"In my checking account, thanks to Miss Mastercard and Lady Visa."

"The landlord's number. He's expecting to hear from you."

"Didn't you tell him I'd have a certified check for him?"

"He wants to hear it from your own pearly lips. Seems he *trusts* college teachers' words. He won't even take a theater person's check."

"He must have had a positive experience with higher education," I said and loped up the aisle to the lobby.

Jaime from the Pearl Theater Company up the street was shouting in Spanish into the receiver. When he spotted me, he toned down and said, "Ours is broken. You mind?"

After a few minutes of Jaime's alternate wheedling and swearing into the receiver, I decided I would not stick around but instead use the other phone. Back through the house, past the stage, where some piece of action was being rehearsed, with Blaise, Cynthia, Bernard, and Henry all watching from different rows, behind the curtain.

The theater's wall telephone was in use, its line wound into the smaller of the two dressing rooms, the door ajar. I didn't intend to overhear, but simply meant to look in and ask whoever was on the phone—who could it be? the entire cast was out front—if he or she would be long.

Thus it happened that as I moved toward the slightly open door, I heard the words, even before I understood them or realized who was speaking:

". . . a ridiculous farrago supposedly linking various allegedly important moments of homosexual history of the past century. Period. Next paragraph. The playwright, comma, a history professor, comma, and author of the book upon which this absurd assemblage of purported theater is based, comma, hasn't a clue how to build drama throughout a single scene, comma, never mind an act, comma, never mind the evening. Period. An unqualified failure. Period. New paragraph. The cast is surprisingly adequate, comma, given the dearth of material they have. Period. But surely the author must have had a hand in ensuring that the strongest and most sensitive roles in his dramatic abortion are trounced by one Salvator Torelli, comma, a mesomorph of superficial attractions, comma, straight out of the Neanderthal school of masculinity and the early Tony Curtis school of acting. Period. Doubtless, there is more than meets the eye to Mr. Torelli, comma, although he manages to arrange his crotch often enough during the play to suggest exactly what that is. Period. And doubtless, comma, our author best knows precisely what that is. Period. Next paragraph. The direction by Blaise Bergenfeld is good, comma, the sets and lighting by Cynthia Lomax are exceptional. Colon. The only exceptional thing in this god-awful production. Period. Next paragraph . . . "

From even this narrow a slit, I could see Sydelle Auslander alternately making flourishes with and puffing on a (forbidden) cigarette, while wildly swinging one crossed leg, and that she gave other kinds of physical evidence that she was thoroughly enjoying her dictation: smiling, chortling, fixing her hair in the mirror. Obviously that's what this was: a pre-review for the one magazine where she'd not managed to alienate every single member of the staff. And while the review wouldn't run for a week, still, it was a stunningly bad review—a hurtfully bad review.

I felt a sort of hot knot in the pit of my stomach. Not the fear I'd experienced before, but some primal tearing apart from within. I tried to keep myself calm, tried to tell myself that no one of any importance read the magazine, or for that matter, read Sydelle Auslander, and that it couldn't affect the play's run, really. But even so, the knot began to unravel and with it a rage that had lain hidden for years.

I had to get away from that voice, that smugly swinging leg . . .

I turned to leave and faced Cynthia Lomax.

She was holding onto a scrim lath, staring at me—no, beyond me, at the open doorway, through which both of us could clearly hear Sydelle dictating ". . . comma, suggest Bob Jeffries stick to the Mike Todd Room, comma, where he's far better known lately than in the theater, comma, and where his money is wasted to no better effect. Period."

I didn't know what to make of the look on Cynthia's little-girl face; it was so very very blank.

Unsure what to say, what to do, I stood there, might have stood there a good deal longer, but I heard a tiny gurgling sound in Cynthia's throat. And this, I told myself, is the sound of the rest of the body recognizing the fact that its heart has just been broken.

I could have, possibly should have, raced past her, stumbling and catching myself on a lintel as I charged out of the backstage area and into the house, half falling across the stage steps and barreling up the aisle and out of the theater, unable to think anything—but I'd been illused already today, and I moved slowly.

Cynthia sketched the air in peroration with one embarrassed hand. As I reached the curtain I heard Sydelle step out of the little room. Two beats followed, then I heard her say, "So you've *both* been spying on me."

It was time to see Matt. Matt would listen, comprehend all the terror and beauty—and calm me down. He always did.

The room was unoccupied. Joe Veselka had gone back into Intensive Care a few days before, and Raimundo had come in for a few days, then, surprisingly, had been released. The bed nearest the hallway was un-made, sheetless, coverless, the curtain tied back, the entire area ready for a new patient. But Matt wasn't in his bed either, although his section of the room was more evidently lived in, so brightly lighted the dirty gray afternoon didn't have a chance of creeping in over the plants atop the windowsill. A little disappointed, I sat down, straightening out the bed sheets. As I did, one of them seemed wet. I touched it. Sopping! I looked through the lower shelf of the bedside table and found clean sheets. I stripped the bed, as well as the pillowcase, feeling little stabs of anxiety. This was, after all, a strong indicator of night sweats, which were by no means a good sign. I wasn't aware that Matt had been get-ting night sweats here. It made me wonder even more where Matt had gone to. Or had he been taken somewhere?

Before I could become crazy with worry, I sat down. That was when I noticed the bathroom door shut. I heard sounds behind the door. Odd sounds. So odd that . . .

Matt was shirtless, barely standing up, in fact supporting himself on the bathroom sink. His head was bent over, his face contorted, throat visibly moving up and down, his skin both wet and dry: marbleized.

"Didn't hear you come . . ."

He dribbled liquid, turned, spasmodically retched into the basin.

I held him by a shoulder, the skin burning, the fleshless joint almost pure anatomy. In the toilet were Matt's previous attempts.

"Lunch?" I asked.

"Could . . . n't eat . . . lunch."

It must have been breakfast. The tall, unsteady body lurched against me, until I held it still. "You done?"

" 'Kay."

Terror scrimmaged across the skin on my face and hands. Matt was so out of control. In *my* hands now. "Let's get you to bed."

And once his body had been managed into the room near the bed and flung against the new sheets: "Thanks." Matt took a few seconds, then touched the sheets, realized they were fresh. "Thanks."

"Forget it!" I said wise-guy to hide my total, extreme fear now of dealing with a suddenly very sick Matt. I'd never seen Matt, never seen anyone, like this. I had to find a nurse, a doctor—someone who knew what to do. "You're burning up! What's your temperature? Has anyone been here recently?"

"It's high. They're all busy."

"I don't care if they're busy. You're too hot. I'm going to find a resident."

"No, wait! Don't go!" Matt held me in a surprisingly tight grip. After a minute, he again said, "Thanks."

"Okay, I'll stay a minute. But only if you use a thermometer and if . . ." I managed to extract four cubes from the pitcher of ice water, knotted them loosely in a cloth napkin to go on Matt's forehead. I got out four more and began rubbing Matt's face and neck and chest with them. "When's the last time anyone saw you today?"

"Before lunch. That's nice. They've been busy . . . emergencies and . . ." Matt half sat up, and his neck and face twitched spasmodically in his attempt to vomit. Despite the wad of tissues I instantly held up to his mouth, nothing came out. Not even a dribble. "Everyone . . . had an emergency today," Matt managed to continue.

"You're not so great yourself. Don't talk. As soon as we cool you down . . ."

The ice cubes against Matt's skin melted as though against an August sidewalk. I reached for more.

"Where's your little oxygen tube? There it is."

His temperature was 103.4.

"It's been a hundred three all day," Matt confirmed.

"That's not good. We've got to get you cooled down. An ice pack and some kind of antibiotic." I looked around for an IV rack, for a nurse passing by—for anyone, anything! And as Matt tugged at me: "Don't worry. I'll stay and cool you down. I said I would!"

A few minutes later, that ice was gone too. I switched to an alcohol rub. That seemed to work a bit, as Matt began to cool down and his body to relax, until it almost seemed as though he would fall asleep again. Was that good or not? I wasn't sure. The body did need rest. What if he began to sweat again? I needed to find someone to tell me what to do.

An orderly blundered a few feet into the room with a wheeled gurney. Saw his error, withdrew.

"Wait!" I was up instantly. "My friend has fever. He needs a nurse."

Just then the hospital paged, "Dr. Heart. Dr. Heart. Fourth floor!" I knew the code—someone was having a heart attack.

The orderly looked up at the source of the voice. "All day, man! No nurses anywhere!".

"Can you help me? Find an ice pack? A blanket with coolant inside?"

It took a few more sentences to explain, but the guy seemed to understand and took off.

Matt's eyes were closed.

I'd take the chance. Unfortunately, both Matt and the orderly had been right. The nurses station was empty. Not a doctor, not a nurse.

The ice cubes on Matt's head were melting now. Matt's arms were reaching out for me. I eluded them, then easily held them down at Matt's side, rubbing more alcohol over his entire body.

When that was gone and Matt was still not much cooler or relaxed into sleep, I hit the hallway again. Still no one at the nurses station. Where the hell did they keep ice packs? I began throwing open closet doors, anything not locked. A woman went past using a walker, almost incurious. Where was the orderly? I looked back in the room. Matt had turned on one side, knocking off the ice pack. I charged back to the nurses station. Someone was there: that young resident, shuffling through papers.

"Hi. Dr. . . ." I couldn't see her name plate. "Room 1265. He's running a terrific fever. I've used ice. Alcohol rub. Everything. He needs—"

"Veselka?" she asked, baffled.

"Loguidice. Matt."

"Soon as I can! We're up to our ears today. Keep him cool. Don't let him sleep."

"Can't you give him anything to fight it?"

"To fight what?" she asked.

"Whatever's giving him the fever. An antibiotic?"

"It's . . . The virus itself is giving him the fever," she said as though explaining what should have been so evident. "When it's this late . . . he's got no immune system left. There's nothing that'll work anymore. Look, keep him cool. I'll be there as soon as . . . Promise!"

There at the door to the room was the orderly. But that wasn't an ice blanket. It was merely a rubber foot-wash tub filled with ice.

"No ice blanket." The orderly shrugged. "This is plenty ice."

"What'll we do with it?"

As the orderly set it down, he motioned with his hands: "Tub."

He meant put the ice in the half bathtub, and put Matt in the tub.

That took the two of us a good ten minutes, as Matt was now burning up again and raving and flailing about. We did get him sitting down in the square little tub/shower and got it filled with ice up to his chest. His head kept falling to one side, and I had to sit on the widest side of the tub and hold Matt's head. Soaking wet with sweat, it stained my pants, my shirt, soaked right through to my skin, to my thudding heart.

"Nice. . . . Thanks," Matt would occasionally utter, but I heard as though from a distance and said, "Forget it" from an equally great distance. All I could hear clearly, hear with a chill colder than any ice bath, were the resident's words: *The virus is giving him the fever. This late he's got no immune system left. There's nothing that'll work anymore.*

Nothing'll work anymore this late. Disasters abound. Nothing'll work anymore this late. Disasters . . .

"Lis . . . nn . . . Roger. Lis . . . nn."

"I'm listening."

"Lis . . . nn. Fav . . . or. You said . . . fav . . . or."

"I remember. I said I'd do you a favor. Anything, Matt! Why not ask me a little later, okay? Do you need it now? Can't it wait?"

"Can't . . . wait! Now . . . favor."

"Okay."

"Parents . . . bring . . . here."

"Your parents? Bring them to the hospital?"

Matt slumped a bit and his eyes closed in fatigue, but he could exert enough tension with his fingers on the palm of my hand to communicate yes.

"They've not been here yet, right?" Matt signaled no. "They know you're here?" Yes and no. "Meaning yes, but not what for? Do I have to explain . . . what? How you got sick? That you're gay? How much do I tell them, Matt?"

"Explain. . . . sim . . . ple . . . peo . . . ple . . . But they'll un . . . der . . . stand. 'Xplain . . . I . . . die!"

"I can't do that. I won't tell them that."

Matt signaled yes.

"How?"

No answer to that. But after a while, Matt spoke again, "Add . . . ress!" He gestured toward the other room.

"I'll find it. And as soon as this fever is gone, I'll get them. Tomorrow?"

Matt signaled yes.

"Tomorrow then," I said, begging for him to stop, change the subject. "Let's take your temperature."

A half hour later, when his temperature had dropped to ninety-nine degrees, Matt began to shiver. I lifted him awkwardly, wrapped the shivering body in a towel, half pulled, half carried him back to bed. He'd just gotten there when the resident arrived. She was looking as harried as before.

I sat back in the visitors chair, aware of how gingerly I was touching every single object around myself now, as she took Matt's temperature again and asked questions and took his blood pressure.

"He always says no to the machine," she reported.

"Machine?" I asked.

"No iron . . . lung!" Matt said.

"That's our only recourse if he goes out during fever . . ."

"No . . . lung!" Matt repeated

"If he says no, then no breathing machine!" I said from close up, so Matt could see and hear clearly. "Don't worry, I won't let them put you on a breathing machine," I assured Matt, even though the resident shook her head. Already Matt's skin was less clammy, warming up. She'd brought more alcohol, and together we rubbed him down. I tried to catch the resident's eye, but she never looked up. As we reached Matt's legs, she stopped at the false one.

"Vietnam. Medal of Honor," I explained.

She shook her head, her lips quivered as though about to say something. Then, regaining her composure, "If he gets too hot, find an orderly and put him back in the ice. 'Bye, Matt."

He did get too hot, a half hour later, and I did find an orderly, and we got Matt back into the tub, with more ice. But after a while, the ice was insufficient, and the orderly went for more, and when he didn't come back in a while, I reluctantly left Matt and went for more myself, heading for the seventh-floor cafeteria kitchen.

I cajoled it out of a caf worker who needed someone to be nice to her, and I returned with a big bag. The orderly had come back already and was there at the bathtub with Matt, filling it up with ice.

Wait. That wasn't the orderly. It was Alistair.

"What are *you* doing here?" I asked.

"I always come here at . . . What time is it exactly? . . . Six-thirty. Every night. Don't I, Matt, darling?" Then back to me: "Are you going to just dangle that ice temptingly or can we have it here for his poor hot head!"

And when I began taking the ice out, Alistair said, "I've been expecting something like this. You know it may go on for hours! Days!"

"I'm staying," I said.

"Of course you're staying. And so am I," Alistair said.

"Nice . . . thanks . . . ," Matt murmured, totally out of it.

The bouts of fever and chills alternated closer and closer in time, until finally, around seven o'clock, even the night resident looking in as he took his watch recognized the seriousness of Matt's condition, and after my pleas and Alistair's only slightly veiled threats, the resident managed to get Matt onto a gurney and down into Intensive Care. Alistair carried his jacket and I the few items in the empty plastic ice tub, alongside the gurney, helping to push and steadying the hat rack of intravenous fluid lines the young medico had inserted into Matt's wrist: "Septra. It's potent enough, although who knows what good it'll do now. And sugar solutions to keep his electrolytes balanced."

Whatever combo it was, it worked. Within an hour, Matt—now attached to a heart machine and an electroencephalograph (though without any breathing apparatus other than his little wall-to-mouth oxygen tube)—showed signs of fever abatement. Within three more hours, the resident came by the two chairs dumped at one end of the Intensive Care Unit hallway, which served as a lounge, and told us, "Aggressive treatment sometimes pays off. Fever's gone. He's stabilized. We'll keep him here all night. And if there's no return of fever, we'll return him to his room tomorrow morning."

We could leave, the resident said. But, of course, we couldn't leave, wouldn't for hours more, not until we were thrown out, except for a quick hop to the seventh-floor cafeteria, about to close for the night, then back to the ICU hallway to wait. To say the least, I was astonished Alistair was staying so long.

"Don't you have some heterosexual to deflower?" I asked.

"That is so beneath you, Cuz," he said, looking up from his copy of *The Amway News*, "I won't even reply."

I chose not to point out that he already had replied. Instead I hunkered down, prepared for a long wait.

"You could go home and go to sleep, you know," Alistair said. "I promise I'll never tell a soul."

"I'd rather have sharpened bamboo hammered under my fingernails," I replied.

"That could be arranged. Just kidding. But you don't—and I am *not* being snide—don't look your usual fabulous self, Cuz."

"I've had a bit of a day," I admitted. "In fact, I came here to relax."

"Wrong move," Alistair said.

He listened to my tale of theatrical woes and betrayal, listened with more interest and niceness than he'd expressed in any matter in my life in a long time—so much so, my distrust grew and I finished off recounting the horrible day by asking, "So you've been seeing Matt since when?"

He could have easily—and correctly—accused me of bitchery. Instead he said, "The beginning. Eleven months ago."

"Eleven months ago."

"When he was first hospitalized with pneumocystis."

I realized that I'd not asked Matt anything about his illness. I knew nothing really about his recent life. What a jerk I'd been. "Here?" I asked.

"Another hospital. Second bout was eight months ago. Then, three months ago, the CMV began. Then this time. And, of course, all the time in between. Luckily I retired just after the first hospital stay and decided to become a stock market whiz kid, although some have suggested I'm already approaching my sunset years. So I had time to keep an eye on him."

I had no idea how to ask it, so I just blurted it out: "You two lived together?"

"Not since Europe. Matt's been house-sitting Count Ugo's *pied-à-terre* in the U.N. Plaza. But naturally, whenever he wasn't well, I spent time with him."

"Weren't you ever going to let me know?"

"I knew you'd find out soon enough. That night at Casa Mercadente, after the atrocious memorial? That was when you first found out, wasn't it? No wonder you fled like Cinderella at midnight. But you do understand why I personally couldn't say a word?"

"Because Matt wouldn't let you?"

"Darling! Wake up and kiss the carnations! Because I felt so fucking guilty about Matt being sick!"

"How's that your fault?"

"Well . . . I don't know that it *is* my fault. I only thought if I'd not . . . you know, interfered with your relationship at the Pines when I did . . ."

"There's no proof of that, Alistair. I'm now hearing the incubation period may be seven, ten, twelve years. A hepatitis test was done in '76. Four hundred gay men in New York and San Francisco. They've just tested the frozen blood for HIV. Twenty percent of the samples showed it present. Back then! Anyway, you saw how guys threw themselves at Matt. He couldn't beat them off with a stick. It could have happened anytime."

"I still feel somewhat guilty."

"Well, good! Keep feeling guilty."

"Which is why I want to know more about Bob Jeffries's bankruptcy."

"I don't follow."

"Not for nothing, Puss, but all those junk bonds I've been buying and having my stockbroker sell—by the way, he's a simply ghastly human being. Cute as shit. But *perverted*! You don't know the half of it! And of course, he thinks like a machine. And naturally in return for all of his money-making for me, I've occasionally forced myself to submit to his less outré fetishistic whims. But anyway, as a result of all that, I've simply tons of cash! So why don't I just buy the theater company and fund the show for its run?"

"I can't ask you to do that. Besides, there's no guarantee you'll make money. Or even break even."

"Roger, Roger, Roger! I just told you I've simply oceans of cash. I don't need to make money. On the other hand, I could use a good investment loss."

"Really?"

"Cross what's left of my heart. Do you know I'm still wet," he added. "That child's hair does absorb sweat!"

"Aren't junk bonds terrible risks?" I asked.

"The worst. They're virtually nonexistent. Paper written against paper. Which is why the take is so high. Until someone pops the balloon, but Guy—that's the name of my darling little shoe-licking fiend of a broker—insists we've got maybe a year or two before the shit hits the fan. So say yes, Roger, let me buy the theater company."

"On one condition."

"A condition! I don't believe this! Here I am, saving your ass, not to mention your entire theatrical career and . . ."

"That you don't fire the male ingenue and take his role until two weeks into the play's run."

"When all the reviews are in." Alistair picked it up instantly. "Max, you sly puss! Okay. Deal! I'll have them come re-review it for me."

"One other thing . . . not a condition! There's this supposedly straight man in the cast. . . ."

"You're not going to make me promise to keep my hands off?"

"Would I subject you to such temptation? Not at all. I just want you to make a videotape when you get him."

"Well . . . videotapes are awkward. Would audio do?"

Another silence developed. And again, although sitting right next to each other, we fell instantly into our own worlds of thought—his, I thought, probably, like mine, about Matt Loguidice. When we did speak again, several times Alistair seemed to begin a sentence, or he'd lead up to a place where the inevitable next topic would have to be the past that still stood between us: a past in which, for all intents and purposes, Alistair had stolen Matt away from me. Stolen him away, and then not even been able to keep him—which made it seem all the more a gratuitous act, an act of perfidy, of pure destruction. The six years since that had occurred, although a long time, still wasn't enough to have healed it, or for scar tissue to have formed. So each time it seemed that Alistair might broach the topic and even hint at asking forgiveness, I was prepared simply to get up and walk away. Because I knew I couldn't forgive him. Not with Matt the way he was. Even though I could forgive whatever poor schmuck it was who'd infected Matt. He'd probably suffered, or would suffer, enough himself, might even be dead already by now.

At nearly three in the morning, Matt was deemed awake enough to say hello to us, and although it was supposed to be only one of us at a time, of course we went in together.

Matt looked completely exhausted. "I was hallucinating like crazy," he managed to speak hoarsely through the chipped ice in his mouth. "It was stronger than acid!" He tried a thick, chapped-lip smile. "Look at you two!"

"Garbo's back!" Alistair threw his upper torso at me so suddenly I was forced to catch him. "And Redford's got her!" he finished the line, pursing his lips at me.

"Together again," I mocked. "Through thick and mostly thin." I pushed him aside and went closer to the bed. "You feeling any better? I'm sorry you had to suffer like that."

"Depends on what you call suffering," Matt replied. Despite his voice, his eyes were clear, bright, almost mischievous. He was himself for the first time all day. But he began to blink again, as though sleep were overtaking him.

That was when Matt repeated that I'd promised to go get his parents and bring them to him. And with Alistair standing right there, what else could I possibly say but of course I would?

Not long after that, Matt stretched, yawned, and was asleep in an instant.

"Larchmont, next stop," the conductor called out.

Larchmont, Mamaroneck, Rye, Port Chester, then into Connecticut— I knew the stops from the years I'd taught part-time in a New Haven prep school. On occasion and without any explanation at all, the late morning train I regularly took four days a week would transform itself from express into local until it reached the state line. This afternoon, I wouldn't get that far, I wouldn't even reach Rye. I'd be getting off at Mamaroneck and from there finding a taxi or wandering around until I found 172 Foothill Drive, home of Mr. and Mrs. Loguidice. I would be returning with them, helping them onto the 4:24 to Manhattan, taking them directly from Grand Central Station to the hospital, to Matt.

Would they agree to come with me? Would they grasp how this

could happen to their son? How it was happening all over the city? the country? the world?

Matt said they would. "They've heard me speak of you so often, for so long. . . . They trust you," he'd argued this morning when the resident returned him to his room and bed without all the monitoring devices attached (though there they were, lurking under the plants, replacing one chair, still in the room). "You've got to tell them what's happening," Matt said.

"You tell them!" I flared up. "I'm not telling them anything."

Exasperated, Matt sighed. "I've already told them. I'm not sure they believe me. You've got to explain or they won't come! They hate hospitals. They're afraid of doctors. They've had bad experiences. If Grandpa were alive . . . I'm depending upon you, Rog! Go! Bring them! Once they see . . ."

At last I agreed. It was too late to argue. Matt was so close now. Why give the Other Side an edge against him? Why not make it as easy as possible for him? Help him however . . . maybe he'd stay a bit longer.

I couldn't believe I'd agreed to do this.

No, that I could believe. After all, Matt had asked. How could I deny Matt anything? No, what I couldn't believe was that there was a need for it, that even I had to admit there was a *need* for it. Some twenty-six hours ago, I would have scoffed at the necessity. But then that was before yesterday.

"Mamaroneck! Mamaroneck Station! All those departing, please check your seats and the nearby floor for any belongings. Have a good afternoooooooon!"

Matt said the house was five minutes away. Once past a few blocks of small shops, it was a delicious, early spring walk—forsythia, magnolia, trees all in bloom, the sky pale blue, with the lightest whisper of clouds. It reminded me of a little town on the south shore of Long Island. I might have been a teenager, walking home from high school again, coming from a pal's house where we'd done homework together. The large houses—Colonial, mock-Tudor, French gray brick, sprinkled with a few huge old Victorians—were just like the ones where I'd grown up. The air fresh with new growth. I might have been sixteen again, visiting my brand-new friend Matthew for the first time. Excited at seeing him at home. Scared at meeting his parents. Afraid they might not like the way I looked or dressed or behaved, and would say no, after all, Matthew couldn't come out with me this afternoon, so sorry. And probably not tomorrow either. Or, yes, he'll be right down. Have some cookies, milk, or soda pop. Sit right here. And then Matt would have bounced in, holding a football, looking amazing at sixteen, not filled out yet. Maybe not as perfect as he'd become, but still a bit awkward, slightly flawed, say his ears sticking out a little, his already tight-fitting chinos . . . and Matt and I wouldn't have had merely our few short years, but more, twenty-four years together: a whole life.

Here was Foothill Drive. That fourth house, the pale-yellow ranch with white trim and a pale slate-gray roof surrounded by birch trees, the front entry amid rhododendron in bud, was number 172. I stood a minute, suddenly reminded of a movie I'd seen—had it been a Hitchcock movie?—set in a small town somewhere in New England, where a stranger suddenly arrived one bright day, a professor who turned out to be a gestapo spy or informer or fifth columnist, preparing the area for a future Nazi takeover. That's exactly how I felt carrying my terrible news, bringing the horrors of last night in Matt's hospital room to this quiet, sunny town, the knowledge itself a virus, once contracted never to be gotten rid of again, and I the bearer, the infecting agent.

Before I could change my mind, I ascended the thick slab of fieldstone set in concrete and rang.

The tall, dark-haired, heavyset man who opened the front door wore a heavy gray vest over a striped shirt. It only took a second to recognize the thick movement and slow eyes and round face and distinctive mouth of a person with Down's syndrome.

"Hi! I'm looking for Loguidice?"

"You Roger?" the thick-tongued voice asked.

"That's right. Are Mr. and Mrs. Log—"

The screen door was flung open, and I was half lifted in a bear hug over the lintel into the hallway.

A brother, cousin, friend of the family Matt hadn't mentioned?

"Mama!" the voice called out, still not letting go of me. "Mama. It's Roger. Matt's friend." Then more quietly: "You look just like in the pictures." Louder and off to one side: "Mama!"

No brother: Matt was an only child.

Seeing my expression, the man let me go. "I'm bein' a bad host. C'mon in. Sit down. Did you have a good trip on the train?"

He guided me into a bright living room. Everywhere around us, on every table, desk, pyramid of tiny shelves built into wall corners, were photos of Matt. In his Navy uniform. On board a destroyer in his Navy work togs. In a tuxedo, with and without a pretty girl (high school prom?). In a graduation gown. On the lawn of the big Rye house, standing hugely next to his small grandmother. Playing on the lawn outside this house with a big sheepdog. On a bicycle with two other youths on their bikes. With me at Fire Island Pines, wearing nothing but tiny scarlet Speedos and carmine-tinted translucent visors, at the Red Party. With this very man and a similar-looking woman, standing next to a shining Ford Escort, a ribbon across its hood, evidently Matt's first car. With the same two again, outside an ivied building, Colgate, where Matt had gone to school before he joined the Navy. With them again somewhere out in the country.

"You see?" The man pushed another framed photo toward me. It was of me and Matt hugging, outside my apartment in the Haight. "That's when you first met. That's how I recognized you." Then louder, "Mama!"

She stepped into the room, recognizable from the photos, her hair Europeanly braided in an oval flat behind her head, lustrously blond. Her pale-gray eyes were Matt's eyes, even though most of her facial features were more similar to those of her husband, the unmistakable features of a woman with Down's syndrome. Shyly she smiled at me, then allowed her delighted big puppy of a husband to pull her into the room, where I stood up to shake her hand and was surprised to have her place a breath of a kiss on one cheek.

"Are you thirsty?" she asked. "There's coffee."

"It's good coffee," her husband assured me. "Matt got us that professional machine that measures it out and everything."

"It's easy to use," she agreed.

"Sure, fine," I said. In the few years Matt and I had lived together, I'd never met and seldom spoken to Matt's parents. A phone call: "Hello, I'll get Matt." Or a word about the weather. It had always been Grandpa Loguidice, the still-active-at-eighty-eight-years-old patriarch of the family, who'd visited, who'd taken Matt and me for dinner at some crony's place on Mott Street or to a Yankee game when he was in town. I was still absorbing what Matt had and had not told me about his parents. . . . What had he always said? They were special. . . . Theirs was a love match no one had expected to succeed. . . . They'd flown in the face of all convention. . . . Yes, but the one thing Matt had never said was what that convention was.

"This was outside the VA hospital." Matt's father was pointing out more photos. The room was lovely, beautifully furnished and upholstered. Light poured in through many windows. The coffee must have already been made, because Matt's mother was carrying out a lacquered black tray containing a celadon tea service and silver flatware, with a larger celadon plate holding various cookies—all of it probably a gift from Matt's tour in the Pacific. "And this"—another snapshot, of a smiling strawberry-blond retriever—"is Lucky, Matt's dog. Matt never got another dog after Lucky."

The tray was set upon the coffee table, and they sat and drank coffee, and I was asked to try various cookies. "Those reddish ones are made with wine." Matt's father pointed to the biscuits. "Don't take one if you're on the wagon. They're from upstate . . ."

"Syracuse," his wife said.

"Syracuse! My cousin sends them. Can't get them around here anymore."

"Still some Italian neighborhoods in Syracuse," she agreed.

"Matt used to buy them in San Francisco. Ghirardelli Square. That how you say it?"

As they sipped and chewed and talked, my despair deepened. How was I going to *do* this? How could I possibly tell these people what Matt wanted me to tell them? It was clear the two of them lived and breathed for their son—his accomplishments, his beauty, how smart he was, how talented he'd been in school, his successful military career, even with that terrible wound, how he'd become a poet ("Imagine! My boy!" Mr. Loguidice beamed with pride) and been published. They had the two stylish European magazines and a copy of the limited edition Alistair had arranged. ("Course, we're not good at understanding what he wrote. Are we, Mama?") How could I even hint at what Matt had sent me to do?

For the briefest of seconds I thought, This is punishment. Matt is getting back at me. That's why he sent me here. Then I reconsidered. No, Matt sent me because it was so hard, too hard for anyone else to do, and because that's what you did for someone you loved.

"No, thank you. I'm fine," I replied to another offer of coffee. Then feeling very awkward, "Do you think . . . I mean . . . will you? . . . Matt said . . . The next train's in fifteen minutes and if . . . ?"

I was rewarded with a complete lack of comprehension.

I tried again. "Matt thought the four-twenty-four train to Manhattan . . ."

"Mama?" Matt's father now looked nervous. "If I helped you clear up?"

"Yes, of course," she said blandly, rising.

It was agreed upon then. I almost sighed with relief. They'd discussed all this, and all I had to do was bring them and not—

"But, Roger," she stood there, "why do we have to go to the city to see Matt? Why can't you bring him here?"

They didn't know! Didn't understand.

I looked to Mr. Loguidice, who also seemed to await an answer.

"Didn't Matt . . . ?" I began, then I bit the bullet. "Matt's too sick to come. I was with him all day and all night. He was throwing up. He can't eat. He's lost a lot of weight. He runs high fevers. Very high fevers. The doctors said the next time he'll go into a coma and . . ."

The two of them looked at me: not a glimmer.

"Papa talked to Matt," she argued. "Didn't you, Papa?"

"I talked to him. He said he was very sick and we had to come now."

It seemed forever for that to sink in.

"I don't like the city," she suddenly switched to another area of complaint. "It scares me."

"I'll be with you every moment," I assured her.

"I don't like hospitals," she went on. "Remember what they tried to do?" she asked her husband.

"No one will hurt you at the hospital," I vowed.

"Why can't we wait until Matt's better?" she asked. "Then you bring him here. That'll be nice. Papa?"

She looked at her husband, who looked at me.

I stared at the floor. Why must I say this? "He's . . . not . . . going . . . to . . . *get* . . . better!"

I couldn't face them. "He's . . . going . . . to . . . die. Your son has a fatal illness. AIDS! Have you heard of it?"

They had. They murmured.

"People with AIDS don't *get* better! They get sicker. They die."

Having forced myself, I couldn't stop now. "Matt has been sick. Now he's going to die." I couldn't believe I was saying it.

They were frozen in position, that same look on their faces!

"Matt will *never* come back home alive! And if you don't see him today, you may *never* see him again." Couldn't they understand? "He's dying! Dying!"

From out of nowhere a wail began. She lifted her apron to her mouth and lurched into her husband. He caught and held her, looking so hurt.

I came out of whatever horrible place I'd been driven to, aware that I'd gotten my point across. "I'm . . . sorry," I mumbled.

She was alternately wailing and muttering cries. It was pathetic, like a child wounded in a playground. I couldn't stand it. I backed out of the sight of her, and of her poor oversized husband uselessly trying to comfort her, backed away from the damage I'd wreaked, at last located a door, and lurched out of the house altogether, onto the flagstones. From here I could still hear her, but they must have moved into the kitchen, because now she sounded muffled.

Would she never stop?

I'm the cruelest bastard that ever walked the earth, I thought, dropping in exhaustion to sit on a concrete step. But if I am, then I curse the God that forced me to be so cruel to these two brave and loving people, whose impossible lives I've just now destroyed!

Behind me, the house was silent.

Before me, ants were carrying chips of leaf across the rock slab from one side of the garden to another. They walked on cement, avoiding the slate. I wondered if the stone were too smooth, too slippery for the ants, if the cement had tiny imperfections, enough for their legs to get better purchase. What were they doing with these leaves? Where were they going? Why bother? Why shouldn't I just crush them all? Now? Totally obliterate them? Keep them from more suffering?

After a while, the door opened. Mr. Loguidice. I began to rise. He leaned on my shoulder to keep me down and sat heavily next to me. He took out a package of cigarettes and matches, shook out a few. When I looked surprised, he said, "In the photos . . ."

I had stopped smoking, but took one. Matt's father deftly lighted two off the same match.

Deep drag. No coughing. Instant high.

"Mama's getting dressed. She'll be ready soon. Then we'll go with you," Mr. Loguidice said.

We smoked.

"She's a woman. They get emotional," he explained.

I didn't know what to say. "I'm sorry. I shouldn't have . . ."

"Matt told me on the phone. . . . I told Mama. . . . We thought . . . you know . . . maybe there was a chance he was wrong. Until we heard it from you . . . You wouldn't lie to us. Not Matt's friend Roger. That's why Mama's upset. . . . She'll be fine. She's getting ready."

We smoked and watched the ants carrying leaf parts across the flagstones. At one point, Matt's father put an arm across my shoulder and it felt like a truce.

"She'll thank you."

I panicked. "Thank me?"

"For going to the city with us. For staying with us at the hospital."

"Matt said you don't like hospitals."

"Did he tell you why?" Mr. Loguidice asked. A big kid, I thought. He's like a big kid. He doesn't really understand. How could he?

"He didn't tell you," Mr. Loguidice said. Then slowly: "It's because it was at the hospital that they tried to take Matt away. When he was born. They saw he wasn't . . . you know, like us. They tried to take him away from us and give him to other people. But Mama held onto Matt's leg. She wouldn't let go of his leg. I held on too. We wouldn't let go. When my papa saw us holding onto Matt's leg and not letting them take Matt away, my papa said, 'Okay, you can keep Matt. But you've got to do right by him. You can't let him lack for anything!' "

Matt's mother called from somewhere indoors for her husband.

"It was the same leg that got shot," Mr. Loguidice said. "The leg he lost. You saw his bad leg?"

"I saw it."

"I read this story once . . . ," Mr. Loguidice began. "It was Matt's book. *The Golden Book of Greek Myths*. He loved that book when he was a kid! I read a story in it he marked. That meant he especially liked it. I don't remember all the names, but it was about a war hero. When this hero's mother and father got married, someone was against it. She sent them a bad gift, an apple that caused a fight at the wedding. And she put a curse on the baby. So when the baby was born, his mother and father dipped him to take away the curse. I guess like baptizing. They had to hold him tight by one leg and not let go."

"Papa?" Mrs. Loguidice called from a bit nearer.

Matt's father stood up, groaning a little, revealing his age for the first time. (How old was he? Sixty? More? Did people like him live much longer?)

"A minute, Mama. I'm talking now." Then to me, "This baby in the book? He grew up to be the smartest and handsomest and bravest hero ever. Do you know that story?"

"I know the story."

"And he had a friend he loved more than anyone."

"Patroclus . . ."

"This hero," Mr. Loguidice went on, "he was shot in the leg where he was held. . . . He died young too."

I hadn't expected that. I couldn't know how far Matt's father had thought all this through; how far he could think it through, never mind come to this conclusion. I stood up.

"Matt's not dying because you wouldn't let him go when he was a baby."

Mr. Loguidice looked away.

"He's not."

A bird began calling out, twittering, chirping, a long roulade of sound. A secretary bird, Matt used to call them, at the Pines. A gray jay, I had called them. This one had a great deal to say. It went on and on.

"I don't know, Roger. Someone didn't want Mama and me to marry."

"It's not your fault!" I insisted.

"It was worse when Matt was born. A lot said we shouldn't have him."

"It's not your fault, believe me! It's not anyone's fault."

"Well . . . maybe not." Mr. Loguidice interrupted the birdsong reluctantly. Then, "But you know something, Roger? If it was my fault . . . if

I knew Matt would die now, I *still* wouldn't have let go of his leg. . . . Do you know what I'm saying?"

To save his marriage, to prove that he and his wife were capable, despite everything: to save their lives.

"I know what you're saying."

"I wouldn't have let go of his leg for anything! Not for anything!"

He crushed his cigarette against the wall.

"I'd better go see what Mama needs."

I finished my cigarette, suddenly tasting all the tar and crap. I crushed mine against the wall too. I didn't think I'd ever forget Matt's father's big kid's face as it had looked admitting what he'd admitted just now: sick with knowledge, sick and enraged with understanding.

A few minutes later Mr. and Mrs. Loguidice emerged, dressed for the city, smiling, calmly bland again as though nothing had happened. They locked the house and joined arms with me, and then the three of us walked, arm in arm, through the lovely spring afternoon, through the lovely neighborhood, to the picturesque train station.

"Final dress rehearsals are supposed to be disasters!" Alistair assured me. "It's an old theater tradition. The worse the final dress rehearsal, the better opening night."

"Then tomorrow will outdo *My Fair Lady*!" I moaned. I finished my margarita and spun around on the bar stool. "Bartender. Another of these confections. Who *are* all these people, anyway?"

"They are Claire's Thursday evening nine o'clock crowd," Alistair explained. Then, checking his watch: "Correction! Nine-fifteen dinner crowd! Are you certain you should? That's three on an empty stomach."

"It's curtains one way or the other!" I insisted. When the drink had been slid into place and the empty whisked away, I said, "To . . . Who have we toasted so far tonight? The muse of comedy, the muse of tragedy . . . ?"

"The God Apollo, leader of the muses."

"We'll add Dionysus, God of Final Dress Rehearsal Disasters!"

"I don't think . . ."

"No? Then we'll toast Matt Dillon, who just went past into the other room. Barkeep. Send a drink to Matt Dillon. On Mr. Dodge."

"That *wasn't* Matt Dillon." Alistair followed with his eyes.

"Sure it was, and he was cute!"

"As cute as Stanley Kowalski in our production?" Alistair asked. "Sal Torelli to you. Now, Sal *is* the straight one you were talking about?"

"The very one."

"Mr. Torelli's not bad. And he is butch."

"A butch Harry Hay in Two Act. And a butch drag at the Stonewall," I said, and moaned, thinking of all there was that could still go wrong tonight. The first act had been bad beyond belief. The most embarrassing moment had come early, in the Thoreau, Emerson, and Stranger scene. Big Janet had actually just stood there, stood there, looking stupidly at what there was in the way of an audience (little more than half a house, even though it was totally papered), having forgotten the fact that she had an exit line, perhaps having even forgotten she had a part in the play. Not one of the others had managed to save her. Not David M., who had the next line, or Sherman, or . . . until Cynthia dipped the stage lights twice, activating Henry, who had not been paying that much attention himself but who—always game—jumped onstage shouting, "Back to the raft again, Huck honey. I got a hungerin' for you," before tackling Big Janet and wrestling her offstage so the play could continue.

Worse perhaps was the end of the act: Bernard Dixon in the Casement Trial with its split stage action: front stage action accompanying the words of the Irishman's notorious private diaries, being read to the jury in back. Bernard mimed the prosecutor's lubricious words by rubbing so hard against Sal's customs inspector uniform that Torelli had a job to keep his trousers from being ripped off. Bernard's own frailer costume came off completely, revealing not only his un-Brazilian-slave-like two-toned cranberry-and-mouse-hued Calvin Klein underwear, but also a substantial hard-on. At which, his boyfriend, who'd been sitting in the third row of the audience, stood up and shouted, "*Bicho! Puta!* I cut it off. You wait!"

Add to that the uncountable times in less than an hour when the cast went up on their lines, missed their cues, forgot their stage spots, miscrossed stage lines, and knocked over the scenery, which thumped loudly in protest. The middling, mostly middle-aged guys, mostly sitting alone, that constituted the audience had applauded at the curtain.

But since they'd reacted to nothing but the wrong things, they'd doubtless return after intermission expecting Act II to be more knock-down-
the-scenery-and-show-dick farce—which, Lord help me, it probably
would end up being.

Alistair called over to the bar one of the less prepossessing back room
waiters, Chip—earlier he'd patiently explained that he was a "professional food services person," which was to say *not* a model, not an actor,
not a roman-fleuve novelist, not even a slumming tepid-fusion physi-
cist—and Alistair was now grilling Chip in detail about the foursome
he'd just seated. I finished my margarita and, with foam still on my lips,
asked, "Why not invite Dillon and his friends to the play?"

"Tonight?" Alistair asked.

"It probably won't run after tonight," I reasoned.

"It *would* be an excuse. . . ." Alistair mused. "C'mere, Chip"—who
listened to what was whispered in his ear and vanished.

I began to order another margarita. "I'm not paying," Alistair said
succinctly. I replied, "I'm tanked enough. How about we get back?"

"*Momentino!* You were right! It is Matt Dillon."

"Course, I was right."

"And he's coming . . . Stand up straight!"

Dillon came right at us, his large extended hand suddenly coming at
my midsection. I fumbled for it, let it pump my hand.

"You'll never believe it, but I write plays too!"

Nice, deep, manly voice. Close up, he looked like a tall version of
some kid I had played softball with—what was the kid's name?—except,
of course, for the million-dollar silk jacket and eleven-thousand-dollar
lizard-eyelid shirt. Lots of eyelashes. And the complexion.

"So, congratulatons! Thanks." He took a flyer from Alistair. "I'll try
to make it while I'm in Manhattan."

I felt compelled to ask Dillon, "Is it true? The worse the dress rehearsal, the better opening night is?"

His serious brown eyes were half-amused, half-sorry for me. "That's
the tradition."

"I'm the producer, Alistair Dodge. My phone number is on the flyer.
Call me for comps." A second later, Alistair said, "Did you smell him?
Cuz? Pure pheromones. Come on, let's get out of here. And did you

check out that peaches-and-cream skin? I know women who'd give away their firstborn for that skin."

The second act had already begun when we got back into the theater. Our entry came during a sort of hush. The by now three-quarters full (where did *they* come from?) audience seemed not to be laughing. And in fact, onstage, everything seemed to be going pretty well. Across the aisle in the opposite row, Blaise Bergenfeld wasn't sitting with his hands half covering his eyes, but leaning over to the seat in front, gazing, making little hand gestures at the actors, who couldn't possibly see them.

The extra direction wasn't needed; the scene went off without a hitch. As did the following one, the relatively complicated Harry Hay scene in which Sal Torelli suddenly revealed depths of languor and feyness until this moment unsuspected. Revealed them not with a nod and wink as though to say, "See, guys, I'm straight but I'm playing this fag," but by finding his character and adding depth to the role, not to mention emotion to the scene, in which the police move in to bust up the picketing. Sal was so effective, the audience began to verbally murmur discontent at the cops.

I caught Blaise's eye. The director mouthed, "I don't get it."

"What does it mean, Alistair, when the dress rehearsal is half-bad and half-good?" I asked.

"Shhhh!" Someone turned around.

Alistair too remained rapt. Especially when Sal Torelli emerged in the final scene dressed as Miss Matches, a fictional drag denizen of the famous bar on the famous night, and revealed yet another level of female impersonation: flirting, teasing, fixing her nylons, checking her purse like a lady before transforming herself into the outraged spitfire who turned the fighting words "I've had just about enough of this shit! We've *all* had enough of this shit!" into something out of Victor Hugo, out of Thomas Paine, out of the Declaration of Independence.

Everyone froze, then the other three drag queens—Bernard Dixon among them, done up to the eyeballs—clicked their heels together, turned, and began to attack Andy and Big Janet. Like the recently felled Sherman, they too fell to the ground.

"What have we done?" Eric cried out as one drag, imitating the hoarseness of Bambi's voice.

"What we're doing," Sal shouted in triumph, beating at the now stumbling Sherman again and again with his purse, "is getting ours back finally!"

His words were greeted by whistles from the audience, calls of "You bet!" and "Yea, Sister!" and applause. The melee continued onstage.

I couldn't believe it. For a minute it looked as if the audience were going to leap onstage and assist the actors in drag beating up the actors in uniform. The scene played on, now accompanied by continued shouts and calls for further action from various rows in the theater, until at last Carolyn, in fifties male drag as a reporter, came onstage, stepped in front of the action, freezing the scene into a *tableau vivant*, and uttered the historical commentary ending the play. The audience erupted into applause, gave the cast—especially Sal, and a beaming Bernard—an ovation, and left the theater buzzing.

Alistair and Blaise went out with them, but the director returned a few minutes later, with his mouth pursed, rubbing his hands. "We still have opening night, but I think it's going to be a—" He slapped his hand over his mouth.

Alistair arrived arm and arm with Cynthia.

"What say we give Sydelle the acting chance she's been begging for?" Cynthia suggested slyly, revealing a sense of humor too. "Onstage tomorrow night as one of the cops. *And* we let the audience at her," she added.

"Did you believe them?" I asked.

"I did! I saw and heard them."

"Who knew we'd end up being so politically correct?" Blaise asked. "Well, I mean a show that gives a gay audience a chance to relive Stonewall close up every night is a . . ." He didn't finish his sentence.

"Well, there goes my capital investment loss!" Alistair moaned, with a television-dumb look on his face. "Don't just sit there, Cuz! We're a hit!"

Phone ringing. I sat up in bed. Five thirty-nine. Phone ringing in the middle of the night and wouldn't stop. Why me? I was so tired. Tired when I got to bed at three tonight. Dead tired now.

It wouldn't stop ringing. I got up, still sleeping, barely able even with the night-light to locate and—*Ring, ring, ring!*—slide on my moose-hide slippers, find and pull on—*Ring, ring, ring!*—a robe, step into the other room—why hadn't the machine gone on?—*Ring, ring, ring!*—and pick up the receiver, still sleeping.

A woman's voice. "Roger Sansarc?"

"Hmmmmnnn."

"We have you listed as next of kin."

What?

"Hmmmmn. Next of . . . ?"

"To Mr. Log-u-deechee. It says here . . ."

What? . . . ? Could she mean Matt?

"Load-your-dice. It's Matthew Load-your-dice. What's wrong?"

"Mr. Load-your-dice," she pronounced it correctly, "expired at four thirty A.M. Since you are listed as next of kin . . . you'll have to come identify at the Medical Examiner's Office. Do you know where that is? I'll give you the address. Do you have a pen? It's . . ."

I hunted around for one and copied the address.

"What's this about?"

"I just told you. Mr. Load-your-dice expired an hour ago."

"Expired?" Like a credit card?

"Died," she explained. "Your name is down as next of kin for his family. You have to come identify his body."

"Not my Matt Loguidice? He was okay today! I was there at, I don't know, eleven at night? He was better than he'd been all week."

"I'm sorry. I don't know anything about it. I'm just an administrator here. I've been told to contact next of kin."

"There's a mistake. Has to be."

"You *have* been asked to go to the Coroner's Office."

It made no sense. "Only a few hours ago . . ."

"I'm sure they'll tell you there, sir. You have the address?"

"Yes. I still don't unders—" The receiver buzzed.

I looked around at the apartment. It seemed strange at this unfamiliar hour, in this light. And I was so tired! The last few days . . . ! I had to get some sleep. I'd call and straighten it out in the morning.

Lights out. Back to bed. Slippers off, robe off, sheets still warm. I slid in. Ahhh!

I was just there a few hours ago, I thought. He was eating, smiling. He kissed me . . .

It had to be a clerical error. I'd call and clear it up later.

"This is it!" the cabby said.

The building he'd pulled up to was the smallest, whitest, squarest edifice of the ten-block series along Second Avenue in the East Twenties, in what over the past few years I and my acquaintances had come to call—familiarly if without pleasure—Hospital Row. There, right on the outside wall, was a sign that read "Medical Examiner's Office." Plain to see. Why hadn't I ever put it together before? Probably because I hadn't had to.

"I'd say, Have a good day . . ." The cabby turned, taking the fare.

When he pulled away from the curb, I saw what he meant. It was a flawless late spring day: not a cloud in the postcard sky, and that particular quality of light that redefined and beautified every tree, every bird, every blade of grass, even automobile fenders, even the huge white bricks of the building I now entered.

Deep within the overhang, a large glass-enclosed lobby. Inside, a Latino couple sat in the plush rec-room sofa arrangement, each sipping coffee out of a Styrofoam cup, each reading a section of the *Post*. A receptionist sat before an S-curved white brick wall. A young woman, barely out of her teens, her pretty face hidden behind too much eyeshadow and lipstick. She too was sipping coffee, reading what looked from upside down like *Seventeen*.

I gave my name. She checked a list.

"Relation to the deceased?" Her accent was Bridge and Tunnel.

"Friend. Lovers. We were lovers."

Unfazed, she said, "Because you have a different last name, I'll need two pieces of ID."

I handed them over. She copied down some numbers, then slid them back and asked me to have a seat. She lifted the peach-colored phone and called someone, speaking softly into the receiver.

"I still . . ." I remained at the desk. "I still don't understand why I'm here. Why I have to do this."

"Whenever the cause of death is unclear, the city requires that a coroner determine actual cause of death and that someone identify the body."

"When I called the hospital an hour ago, they told me the cause of death was 'cardiopulmonary.' "

She was leafing through the file. "That's pretty much always the cause of death. . . . Ah, here!" She looked up. "It seems there were discrepancies. Extraordinary traces of . . . ," she had difficulty pronouncing the medical terms, "in his bloodstream. That's why they sent the body here." She looked kindly at me with her overcosmetized eyes.

"Could that have been something he was taking? He had AIDS. He'd been running high fevers. He was on heart machines a few nights before. At first, when I heard he'd died, I didn't believe it, but then . . ."

She shrugged, increasing the mystery.

I sat at the huge square coffee table opposite the young couple, opened the *Times*, and began to look through the third section. Someone in the cast had told me a reviewer had come to the show last night. Neither Henry, at the box office, nor Cynthia—who knew most of the second-string reviewers—could verify the rumor. If it was true, the review hadn't run yet. The *News* had sent a reviewer and the *Voice*. The reviews had been great. The second and third nights were sold out.

"Betancourt!" the receptionist called. The young couple put down their newspaper, looked at each other, and got up. I couldn't help but think they were there because of a violent incident, a knifing, a shooting. Was I being prejudiced?

When they'd gone through the double glass door built into the curved wall, the receptionist picked up the phone and motioned me over.

"My friend." She nodded back, evidently into the building. "He says this 'iolate' stuff I mentioned in the report is from sleeping pills."

No surprise. Matt had taken sleeping pills to get through the long nights. Was this showing up because so little else in the way of an actual determining factor was showing up? Because they had no other cause? With Calvin, the listed cause had been herpes! That was like saying he died of hangnails.

After another endless period of time—really only ten minutes—the receptionist said, "Loguidice."

Through the double glass door, the corridor rose and curved. A small

Asian woman in a green medical smock appeared and guided me into a square room. Three chairs fronted what looked like a huge, partly curved shop window, blanked out by curtains. I sat and waited, thinking this was like a private show of Saint Laurent's fall line.

The woman left the room, and a minute later the curtains opened. She was standing next to a body on a sort of cloth-rippled plinth. She made a single, delicate motion, arranging the sheet on the torso.

They'd left Matt's eyes open.

Unable to do otherwise, I stood and went right up to the window. Matt's eyes were open, and as though imprinted on them forever were emotions I couldn't help but recognize: surprise mostly, relief, curiosity. At what? Death, as it arrived?

The body was so wasted, the flesh so burnt away from within, Matt looked like art: a sort of Roman funerary piece.

"It's him. It's Matthew Loguidice." I was surprised at how steady and strong my voice was. Could she hear me?

Evidently she could. She stepped forward to close the curtains.

"Wait!"

She looked up.

"His eyes? Why are his eyes open? Can't you close his eyes?"

She closed the curtain and a minute later joined me.

"The eyes," she spoke precisely, "had to remain open until identification."

She led me out of the room, into an office, where she made me sign three copies of the death certificate and checked with me that Matt's body was to go to the funeral home in Mamaroneck the Loguidices had already approved.

"Can't you shut his eyes?" I asked.

"Will there be an open coffin?" she asked.

"I hope not. Is it too late to close his eyes?"

"I will see," she said. "Sometimes a little snipping of the muscle . . ." She illustrated with a gesture. "I'll make sure of it. You now go to the hospital administration office to pick up his things? Items left in the room?"

I'd forgotten all about that. "Yes. Of course." I was checking over the certificate for cause of death. "They said . . . sleeping pills."

She shrugged. "Contributory. He was very sick."

Her soft, sane words partly managed to efface the startling vision of Matt laid out on that slab, sheets draped about him as if he were some poet of ancient Rome about to be covered in treasure and set afire, eyes open.

I got lost returning to the lobby. At the receptionist's desk, wearing a light-colored checked jacket, was Alistair. He turned, saw me, and quickly joined me.

"Do you want to sit down? You look . . . Well, I don't know exactly how you look. . . . Did you see him?"

"Don't go in there, Alistair. They didn't close his eyes. They said they had to keep them open for identification. Don't go."

"I won't! I won't! Are you done here?"

"Have to go get his stuff. Hospital administration office. They said they brought him here because of discrepancies. They found, I don't know, contributory factors . . . sleeping pills."

The unsurprised response from my cousin made me grab Alistair's arm. "Did he say he was going to . . . ? You *knew* he was going to take sleeping pills, didn't you?"

"I guessed as much when I saw him collecting them."

"Collecting them?" Now I remembered going out past the nurses' station every night and asking them to bring a sleeping pill to Matt. He'd not taken them. He'd collected them. "Stupid me," I moaned. "I *helped* him collect them."

"We *all* helped him collect them, Cuz! What else did he have to look forward to? More of what he went through these few past days? Come on, let's get out of here." Alistair guided me out of the building and into the astonishing glare of daylight. "Seeing him . . . was it horrible?"

"Oh, Alistair, it was as though I could actually see what he was thinking when it happened—the moment he died, I mean. God, I'll never forget it if I live forever."

"You poor, brave thing! Are you sure you want to do this business with Matt's stuff now?"

"Yeah, might as well. We'll do it fast."

The administrator's office was on the first floor of the hospital, and what there was of Matt's clothing had been packed in a big cardboard box.

"Send it to his folks?" Alistair suggested.

"They said to give it to charity. Could you do that?" I asked the assistant, who said she could. That had been another remarkable thing about that day, that train ride with the Loguidices into the city: how calmly and how thoroughly we three had discussed what was to be done once Matt was no more.

The assistant handed me a large Jiffy envelope. "This was his."

Matt's Sports Walkman. A handful of cassettes. When I put on the headset and turned it on, Mozart emerged: Sarastro singing *"In diesen heil'gen Hallen."* I would never listen to *Magic Flute* again without thinking of Matt.

Also in the envelope was the oversized postcard Matt had kept within sight, upon his bed table: the very medievally designed *Expulsion from Paradise*, with its depiction of the Earth as a rocky, mountainous, inhospitable, lava-threaded desert, deep within rings of multicolored hoops. I turned it over and read, "Giovanni di Paolo (1403–1483), The Robert Lehmann Collection."

"It's from the Met Museum. Imagine," I mused.

"Look how long di Paolo lived. In the fifteenth century, eighty years was at least three lives long," Alistair commented. "What else is in that Jiffy?" He pulled out the yellow foolscap pad Matt had written messages—and that poem—on. Half-hidden inside were sheets of paper folded in three. "Look, Cuz, it's addressed to you!"

When I cut the tape, it opened to two poems, the one I'd already read, and a second:

> *beach, north truro, 1985*
>
> *the sun rolls out and covers you,*
> *arranging the letters of your body into one*
> *beautiful and dark word.*
>
> *the waves repeat it,*
> *like counting, reassurance in each one*
> *finding you*
>
> *there, among the sweet cousins of the grass.*

"Wonderful," Alistair said.

"But the year's wrong. It was . . . what, '75 that we were up at the Cape?"

"He wrote it last week," Alistair said. "Between the fevers."

"But it's all about us. Our first years together. I remember him saying something like this at the time. . . ."

"I watched him write it," Alistair said. "The night before he got so sick. He wanted to give it to you."

"I don't understand. How . . . ?"

"How? Because the time in between vanished, Cuz, when Matt fell in love with you all over again. That's how he could write the poem, even though a decade had passed."

"But . . . I fell in love with Matt again too!"

"Then it's all fixed," Alistair said. "You see, after all, I did manage to fix it. I suspected as much when he showed me those two poems he'd written for you. He told me you'd found the other and wouldn't leave him alone about it."

"What do you mean? What's fixed?"

"What I broke," Alistair said. "You and Matt. Truthfully, Cuz, it's the only thing I've ever done I've regretted."

I could only stare at Alistair.

"Will you be taking these?" the assistant interrupted.

"Yes, of course." Alistair quickly gathered everything up, as though pleased to break out of this moment of reconciliation. He placed it all back into the Jiffy bag and asked, "Will that be all?"

Out on Second Avenue, Alistair hailed a taxi.

"And now, to get this ghastly taste of hospitals and morgues out of our system, I've arranged lunch at Tavern on the Green. Don't say no. You have no choice. I'm kidnapping you. I've gotten my old table back. The one without intervening terrace. Afterwards we'll go look at this apartment I'm thinking of buying. It's nearby, right off Broadway. An old building, really, and quite spacious, two bedrooms, high ceilings, allegedly cute breakfast nook, otherwise nothing special. It's not the Ansonia or San Remo or anyplace even halfway famous. But an old acquaintance has to sell due to poor speculation and a divorce bankrupting him, and thanks to your play being a hit, I'm suddenly forced to find another way to lose money, so I might as well invest it in an apartment and get credit on my income tax, no? Aren't any of these passing taxis vacant? Where are they all going so full at this hour? By the way,

Sal Torelli is going to be a tiny bit more of a project than I'd at first thought. Not that he isn't interested. He's intensely interested. It's just that there's a great deal of family and home influence to be gotten past, but if you, Cuz, can so easily make a perfectly straight creature like my cousin by marriage—What was his name? Doriot's cousin? You know, with the thunder thighs and rippling stomach?—then I can certainly convert Mr. Torelli into jelly. There's a cab. Grab it! Don't let that old biddy slip in before us. Those old tarts look so fragile, but they'll break your leg to get a cab. Ah! Air-conditioned too. Driver! Central Park West! Tavern on the Green! Now, where was I? The show! Blaise and I have already discussed moving somewhere larger and off-Broadway. So that we're in competition for Obies, natch. And no, that isn't merely part of my ploy to get Torelli on his belly, though that wouldn't be a bad side benefit. We thought the Lortel, but it's booked for months. Too bad, because that's the perfect venue for this show, right on Christopher Street, only blocks away from . . . Maybe the Perry Street Theater? Of course we'll advertise weeks in advance. Cynthia thought that billboard in Sheridan Square, you know, over the roof of Village Tobacco. By the way, did I tell you I met this divine man from Montpelier or someplace Way up North in New England and, let me tell you, butcher than Connie Stevens. So even if Mr. Torelli doesn't fall under my spell . . . Speaking of which, there's this new waiter at Tavern on the Green you've got to lay eyes on. One of those corn-silk blonds with those pale ice-blue eyes you usually only find on Akitas and Norwegian elkhounds that can absolutely hypnotize you. Makes me all but quiver. . . ."

And now Alistair was gone too.

I'd unplugged the machine, silenced the terrible breathing apparatus. All had grown silent inside the EMS van.

I held his hand till the fluttering pulse died to nothing. I touched his carotid artery till I was sure blood had stopped flowing through it. Alistair's face seemed to relax suddenly, as though freed from the astonishing effort of having to respire, and I thought for a second I saw his lips ever so slightly curl into a smile, or a word, or . . .

When I was certain all possibility of breathing had ended, I counted slowly to one hundred and twenty and then turned on the oxygen again. It hissed against his unmoving, now blue lips—unable any longer to alter anything. And listening to that inutile hissing, I found myself unexpectedly recalling a moment several years ago I'd completely forgotten.

It had been winter, mid-February, deeply packed in months of ice. I was driving home to Manhattan after visiting friends in Connecticut and was so stymied by the rush-hour traffic I'd gotten off the highway I usually took somewhere in the Bronx and began to drive along side streets, headed I hoped south. I was sure that as a long-time New Yorker, I'd somehow intuit the location of some avenue familiar to me by name or reputation that would be direct and empty and that would speed me into Manhattan. Instead, endless streets of empty tenements surrounded me. Then I spotted what I took to be the pillars of a road I knew, Bruckner Boulevard or the Cross-Bronx Expressway, I wasn't certain which, but it would be a way out, I knew, if I could only find my way onto it.

The street that seemed to lead to the main road was even worse than what I'd been driving through. It went through a wasteland of abandoned buildings, row upon row of them, looking in the infrequent, hard, unflattering yellow streetlamp illumination like Hiroshima after the Bomb, and interspersed with them were lots of razed and semi-razed buildings, some cut off at odd angles, like cakes cut into wrong, filled with the remnants of domiciles—plumbing lines snaking out into nowhere, toilets facing emptiness, a built-in cabinet that now opened onto an abyss.

After driving another ten minutes through this devastation, I saw that the street did indeed finally swerve ahead up to a ramp that led to the raised highway. I had found my way and would be safe. At that very moment, I felt a total, intense need to pass water. It would be half an hour at the earliest before I'd make it home, even with this shortcut, so I stopped the car, left the motor running, and stepped out. I walked into the devastated lots, to a heap of rubble in what had once been the first-floor shop of some old delicatessen—metal stamped signs advertising Nehi and Yoo-hoo Soda—and I began to urinate.

Complete and utter relief! At the same time, I thought I heard a noise, the clanking of pipes and a sudden *sssss*. I spun around, spraying piss all over the rubble at my feet, knowing myself alone and surrounded by what must have been three-quarters-of-a-mile square of nothing but devastated tenements as I searched for the source of the sound.

There, not two yards away, placed against what had once been a piece of patterned pressed-tin wall, stood an old steam radiator. Nothing special, an object common to buildings in New York City for decades, its paint mostly peeled off, but I could tell it had last been cream-colored. It was still attached at one end to a pipe that dove into the floorboards, down into rubble. A pipe that somehow, unaccountably, remained attached to a boiler somewhere below, which itself somehow, unaccountably, remained connected to a gas line, which somehow, unaccountably, remained still turned on.

I stood in the freezing darkness and desolation, and that radiator chugged and rattled and spouted, and its whistle hissed out steam so noisily and with such intensity of purpose that I slowly—amazing myself—became certain it really *did* have a purpose: to carry on as long as it had the power to do so, and while it remained active, to do what it did best—even if that meant attempting to warm up the entire immense, vitrescent, frigid, indifferent night.